NOT ALL FLOWERS FACE THE SUN

Mark Zanzibar Boyde

First published in the United Kingdom in
March 2021 by Mark Zanzibar Boyde.

A CIP Catalogue record for this book is available from the British Library.

Publisher: Independent Publishing Network.
Publication date: 8th March, 2021
ISBN: barcode: 9781800492820
Author: Mark Zanzibar Boyde
Email: markboyde@aol.com
Address: 6/16 Mitchell Street,
Edinburgh, EH6 7BD
Website: www.markzanzibarboyde.com
Please direct all enquiries to the author.

For my children, Charlotte, Jameson and Craig. My guiding lights.
And for Linda, who always tried to keep me safe.

Dedicated to the memory of Ian Melville, the only father I ever knew,
and to Debbie, the sister I'd love to have known.

Acknowledgments and Foreword

I have people to thank who helped me to start and finish this book. Vicky Gumley, who joined me in Nepal and climbed to Everest Base Camp by my side, who summited Ben Nevis with me on an ice cold winter's day and walked with me on the last 120kms of the Camino de Santiago. She also climbed Ben Lomond with me on my 56th birthday and surprised me with a cake at the top. Hers is a friendship I thank the Universe for. I remember you asking me where I wanted to be in five years' time, while sitting in your garden going through my own personal hell, I answered, 'to be gone from this world.' Instead, I took your advice. 'Keep walking, you told me.' I did. It kept me alive and sane enough to write this book. Three years on and I'm still here. You'll never know how much you helped me.

To Louise Shardlow (Lulu), who walked across northern Spain with me on that same Camino journey, then shared her home in Geraldton, Australia, where this book was partly written, thanks for all the feedback and advice. You were influential in helping me develop this story. To Sylkie, the feral crab-hunter, and Ella, who loves to chase ball, thank you for all the walks along the beaches. To my old friend, Howard Begg, thanks for the coronavirus flop last summer, East Linton was a delightful rest period after my round the world tour. It gave me time to write another significant part of this story.

To Ruth Robinson and Mark Rae, the other two souls in my Camino family, who walked with me, listening to me going on about the book I would write at the end of our amazing trek - my friends, what a time we had. Our journey was beyond incredible and changed each of our lives. I hope I do it justice here. To all of you who recognise yourselves, here, thank you for being part of the story. I also owe a nod to Emilio Estevez and Martin Sheen, their film, *The Way*, started all of this. It was my inspiration. I got exactly the story you told in the film. I'd say coincidence, but the Universe knows better.

To my long suffering test readers, Janell Cannon, Lulu, Marion (Merron) Sommerville, Dionne Callaghan, John Brogan, Ruth Robinson and Catherine Thompson, thanks for being so patient. If this ever becomes a movie you guys have red carpet invitations. To my friend, Stuart Gristwood, whose proof reading skills were invaluable, you have helped me no end in getting this project over the finish-line. And to Paul Palmer-Edwards, for the typesetting, as well as for having the patience of a saint with me, a massive thank you.

"Flowers" has been a personal journey for me. It is, in the main, the story of my life. It is part fiction, mostly fact, and brutally honest. All of the places across the world in which the book is set, I have been fortunate enough to have been. The adventures Sean undertakes (Everest Base Camp, summiting Ben Nevis and trekking the Camino de Santiago) were my adventures. What happens in the book happened to me in reality. I almost died, twice, doing them. The darker elements of the book, too, are mine, the descriptions sadly accurate, the scenes of child abuse are real. The pain and guilt Sean Jameson carries throughout his journey is also mine. He failed his family as I failed mine. His losses are my losses. His regrets are my regrets. Those experiences, however sad and brutal, have guided the paintbrush on this literary canvas.

For all the silent sufferers of PTSD, I know your pain. I have lived it all my life and live it still. You are not alone, despite I know how much you sometimes feel you are. There are angels out there, you simply have to let them in. This book is for you as much as anyone else.

It is especially for my brothers, Stephen and Peter, who shared the pain and carry the same scars.

You cannot call for death and demand she come, no matter how you might suffer. You may ask only to be considered, and hope she will, if that is what you truly desire. But once you have called for her you cannot undo that call. It is out there, echoing through the Universe, and you will have piqued her interest. So be warned. Think carefully on what you ask. Death will never come at the right time. She will come like a thief in the night. At a time of her own choosing.

SEAN

1

Sean woke with a start, aware, first, of the blinding light, and then the bitter taste of last night's whisky in his mouth. He became acutely aware, too, of the smell of his own body. He cared little that he had sunk so far. It was deserved. Consciousness came in rough waves, but his first feeling, as it was each morning, now, was of unbearable loss. He rubbed his eyes and gazed across the bay beyond the high bluff he'd slept upon, huddled into a grassy scoop in the ground. He knew full well *where* he was, he just had no idea how in hell he'd ended up there. But then he remembered, and the guilt and shame returned.

A sweep of sandy shoreline curved away from him, disappearing into a roll of lingering sea-fog like a fading lifeline. *Like my own lifeline*, thought Sean. But then he was still alive.

Life! My penance!

The thought bothered him almost as much as the screams from the gulls overhead, balancing in the air like wobbly, paper kites, mocking those still standing on the beach watching the receding tide for whatever might be left behind to fight over. The sky rats littered the wet sand like cocaine granules on a smoked glass tabletop. The image took him back to the previous night's debauchery. Different birds. The same inane squawking. Another pathetic interval in his daily schedule of hopelessness and self-loathing.

A small, orange crab scuttled by and stopped to stare at him, its eyestalks swivelling oddly in its head. Unimpressed, it moved away, as if disgusted by what it saw.

'Screw you! Get back in your hole and let me get back into mine.'

Sean meant it metaphorically, not literally, but the irony wasn't totally lost on him.

He sat up and brushed away the sand clinging to one side of his face, fumbling in the pockets of his *seen-better-days* black leather jacket. A wave of relief flowed through him as a crumpled pack of Marlboro revealed two remaining cigarettes, one up-ended for luck. He almost laughed. The cigarettes were crushed and bent, but somehow *they* weren't broken.

The first draw tasted like hell, the smoke making him cough like a forty-years-in coal miner, reminding him of his father, whose cigarettes had turned to coffin nails. The image of a gravestone he would never visit slipped into his mind. A cold, grey stele stood in a cold, grey graveyard in his childhood home of Fort William. A nothing and nowhere, coastal raintown set in the mountainous west highlands of Scotland. Dour and dreich, filled with fishermen and fools. At least, it had always seemed that way to Sean. The second drag was more familiar.

On the beach, a hundred feet below, early risers trudged the rippled sand close to the water's edge, throwing an assortment of things for their dogs to chase. Some of the dogs ran headlong into the sea without breaking stride, caring nothing for the bone cold water. Others, the ones with more sense, stopped at the waterline, unwilling to enter, barking at the waves as if that might somehow draw the floating prizes to them, ignoring their owners encouragements to *go fetch.*

'Get into the fucking water yourself.'

Sean's words were directed at a blonde-haired woman, wrapped up against the September chill in an olive-green jacket, scarf and knee-high boots. She was waving her arms at her canine charge, a nondescript, brown terrier with stubby legs and a busy tail, urging the dog into the sea after a stick she'd thrown. She was too far away to hear him, but the dog was looking at her as if to say, *why don't you listen to that waste of space sitting up there in the sand dunes.*

Why he was so angry with the woman, Sean couldn't say. But then he lied to himself, every day, about almost everything. It made it so much easier to cope. Of course he knew why he was angry. He knew damned well.

She reminded him of Linz!

The thought of her was like a full-blooded punch to the face, delivered by someone who really knew how to deliver a punch to the face. A smoke breath caught in his lungs and his hands began to shake. He stared down at them, confused. It felt like they weren't his hands. As if he wasn't really sitting there but could see what was happening to him. Suddenly, he felt very afraid. And very sad. And very lonely. Tears began to form at the corners of his eyes.

Don't let him see you. Don't let him have that satisfaction.

Sean listened to himself and fought them back. That, he knew how to do. But he still felt frightened.

Another drag on his cigarette, now more crumbling ash than tobacco, didn't help. He flicked the glowing butt away on the breeze, watching it disappear into the "bendy-grass" growing in clumps among the sand dunes.

'Take me with you,' he called after it. 'Don't leave me here.' But it was gone. Like everything else. He felt his chest tighten and his vision began to blur. *It's happening again.* He had to fight it. He was holding it together. But only just. 'Help me. I need you.' He pinched the silver crucifix hanging around his neck between his thumb and forefinger and gazed up into a moody sky that threatened rain, praying he would be heard. But the only answer that came was his own. 'Same as it ever was. You never came when I called.'

'Hello.'

The voice startled Sean.

A couple of children, a blond-haired boy and an equally blonde-haired girl were standing beside him. He hadn't seen or heard them approach. They were no more than five or six years of age, with bob haircuts that made them look all cute and innocent. They looked like twins. Brother and sister, at least. The sight of them smiling at him and the memory it invoked nudged him closer to his edge. He felt the anger coming back. Building up inside him. Until it vented.

'I'm not someone you should be fucking smiling at!' He'd shouted louder than he'd meant to, shocking himself, as well as them. But he needed them to go away. They were tearing him apart. 'Leave me alone! Leave me alone! Leave me alone! Leave me alone!'

The screams sent the kids scampering up the sandy beach-path, to the car park, just above the dunes, where worried parents would no doubt comfort them then come to see the strange "shouty-man" sitting in the sand dunes.

Sean carried on screaming. Aware he was doing it, not understanding why. The screams weren't words. At least, not words that were legible, just six months of over-stretched emotions forming their own strange shouty-language. A cry for help at the breaking point. He knew he should stop, but he couldn't.

He was more afraid of that, than anything else.

He began to rock, back and forth, his chin resting on his drawn-up knees, arms wrapped around his shins, clinging to the only thing in the world he had left to cling to. A world he had never truly felt part of. A world he had always wanted to be part of and, for a time, believed he was. But it had been a lie. He should have known. He wasn't good enough for that sort of life.

He'd been told often enough.

After a few minutes, the screams subsided, sliding down the *totally-fucking-lost-it* scale towards aching moans of gut-deep pain. How long he'd been sitting there, lost in his world of hurt, Sean had no clue. But it had been long enough for the police to have arrived. Alerted, no doubt, by the parents of the children he'd frightened.

Above him, two uniformed officers plodded down the sandy path, moving cautiously, as if on some sort of urban, terrorist alert, rather than dealing with a shouty-man sitting in the sand dunes on a quiet country beach. They stopped in front of him, standing just far enough away from him for them to feel safe. Doing their first visual assessment. Sean knew they were looking at him. He didn't make eye contact. He just kept rocking. Moaning and keening like a wild thing caught in the steely jaws of a hunter's trap.

The officers spoke *at* Sean, at first, taking turns, using firm, commanding voices designed to control the situation. Not that they knew what the situation was, but it was how they'd been trained. Seeing the approach was having no effect, acknowledging he *could* be a person with mental health issues, they softened their tone. They had to ensure they were protecting his human rights. Sean knew what they were doing. He'd had that training. As if he gave a shit about any rights he might deserve to have.

He screamed at the officers, using the shouty-language.

'I have no fucking right to be here! They should be here! Not me!'

The officers looked at each other then back to Sean. Confused, but needing to take charge, the boy officer tried for first contact.

'Sir! Is everything all right?'

Sean brushed the fingers of his right hand over a clump of bendy-grass, stroking the pointy, wheat-coloured tips, absentmindedly, before grabbing the grass stalks further down and pulling his hand sharply away, wondering, as it cut him, why there was no pain, only blood. He licked his palm. It tasted of copper. Pulling another memory he didn't want. He looked skyward as it tortured him.

'Why didn't you come?'

'Sir! What are you trying to tell us? We can't understand what you're saying.'

The girl officer, as she spoke, took a tentative step towards him. The boy officer put a protective hand on her forearm.

'Careful, Rosie. I'm not sure about this one.'

Sean noticed his concern.

'Good lad. Keep her away from me. I kill people!'

As if understanding Sean's meaning, if not his words, the boy officer took over.

'We can't understand what you're saying, sir. You need to calm down and talk to us properly if we're going to be able to help you.'

Sean heard someone laughing. It came from somewhere deep inside him. Somewhere far away.

'He thinks he can help you.'

The voice shocked him. He hadn't heard it in a very long time. He wanted it to go away.

'Go away!'

The voice ignored him and spoke again.

'You need me, Sean. You always did.'

Sean dropped his head into his hands, hiding his face.

'Leave me alone! I don't need you anymore!'

'You're lying to yourself, Sean. You know you do. It's safe here.'

Sean looked up at the girl officer.

'Please. I don't want to go there. I promised.'

She held his gaze for a moment then looked away. She hadn't had *that* sort of training.

Sean knew he was scaring her and hated himself just a little bit more. He didn't want her to be afraid of him. That's not who he was. *Brave girl*, he thought, as she looked back at him. He smiled at her, trying to show her he wasn't anyone to be afraid of.

As if understanding, she reached.

'Can you tell me your name, sir?'

Her voice was soft and kind.

She sounded just like . . . *Linz!*

The thought of her cut into Sean's mind like a brain surgeon gone amok, slicing away the pieces he needed to keep the "bad things" away. Forcing him to remember.

'Don't think of them, Sean.'

The "faraway voice" came too late to save him.

Linz! Alice! Toby!

They arrived in his mind like a runaway train slamming into an end platform at full speed. Carnage!

Salty tears began to fall onto the sand between Sean's feet, blooming like ink drops on wet blotting paper. He wasn't sure whose they were. They couldn't be his. He never cried. He'd made that promise to himself a long time ago. The day the faraway voice had first come back.

The day of the mackeral and marmalade.

From somewhere else, the "empty place", where the bad things were kept hidden away, he heard another voice. Not the faraway voice, but a voice he'd banished long ago. A voice he'd never wanted to hear again. A voice that was impossible for him to be hearing now.

'Cry, you little bastard. Cry!'

Sean looked around him, expecting to see the owner of the voice. Terrified he would.

'You're dead! You can't hurt me anymore. Don't hurt me. Please. Don't hurt me.'

The boy officer could see Sean was becoming more agitated. His cries were getting louder but still making no sense. There was pain and fear in his voice, he could see that, despite he could not understand it.

'What's wrong, sir? What are you afraid of?'

Sean didn't reply. Even if he could, why would he? Nobody had ever listened before when he'd tried to tell them what was happening to him. Why would they listen now?

The girl officer with the soft voice took her turn.

'Please, sir. Talk to me. I *want* to help you.'

She was smiling at him. Sean knew she was trying to reach him. He felt sorry for her. He wanted to give her something to keep her smiling. *Perhaps someone would finally listen.* He looked up at her.

'Don't let him hurt me anymore.'

The girl officer could see Sean was reaching back. She instinctively moved closer to him, softening her voice and warming her smile a little more. Connecting! Her eyes were all green and kind and sparkly.

'I can see you're frightened, sir. But I can't understand what you're saying. Is something wrong?'

Sean looked away, severing the connect. Her question was a stupid one. He knew what was wrong. Why didn't she?

'I don't want to fucking be here.'

His scream was angrier than before. The words still unintelligible to anyone but himself.

Startled, the girl officer stepped back.

Frustrated and angry, Sean stood and faced the officers. His eyes were abnormally wide, his expression blank and distant. They backed away and shared a knowing glance. They'd both seen that kind of look before in other drug users.

But Sean wasn't looking *at* them. He was looking *past* them. Out over the open ocean. The mist has cleared. Not *his* mist, only the early morning sea mist. He hadn't notice it go. Now, he could see across the bay to the ancient Kingdom of Fife. Vague memories of being there played out in his head like the flickering images of an old black-and-white newsreel. There had been happy days spent there. He couldn't remember exactly where or when. But he knew there had been.

All gone now. Everything.

'Everyone always leaves you in the end, Sean. You know that,' the faraway voice whispered.

'Shut up! Shut up! Shut up!' Sean screamed, wanting it to go away.

Seeing the rage in his face and fearing something had shifted, the boy officer drew his baton; a telescopic bar of black steel. A modern-day sword being brandished by a modern-day white knight.

The balance of care had shifted!

Sean saw the baton and the change in the boy officer's attitude. He knew what was coming, if he wanted it. He took another step forward and saw the tip of the baton lift. Barely an inch, but enough to tell Sean they boy's grip on the baton had tightened.

'He's getting ready.' The faraway voice warned. 'I'm here for you, Sean. I'm here to keep you safe. I always took care of you, didn't I?'

Sean knew he had to make it go away. He wasn't supposed to listen to it. He'd promised.

'I don't need you anymore! Why are you here again? Why?'

'Because you *do* need me, Sean,' whispered the faraway voice, all sticky sweet and marmalade soft. 'Who else is there . . . now?'

Sean knew what it meant and hated it for saying it that way.

'Don't say that! Go away! Go away! Go away!'

Resolved she could not reach him, concerned at his increasingly louder screams and disoriented state, the girl officer drew her own baton, a new steel in her eyes as well as her hand.

'Stay back, sir! I'm warning you! We *will* use force if required!'

Her voice wasn't soft anymore. Her eyes no longer green and sparkly.

'We *will* use force,' the boy officer parroted, keen to stay in charge.

His voice was louder than hers, but his words just as pointless.

Sean looked down at the beach, where the dogs and dog walkers stood motionless, watching the drama being played out above them among the sand dunes and the bendy-grass, phones snapping and streaming. *Life in real time*, he thought, wishing he had a rewind button of his own to press. *Back to happy.* He looked back at the officers, flicking his gaze between them like a dog with two bowls of food to choose from. Unsure which one to eat first.

His expression concerned them further.

Sean's meaning was not what they were thinking. He had no desire to hurt them. Although he could, if he wanted to. But there had been too much hurt already. His meaning was the opposite. At least the pain would ground him. It was what he knew. What he understood. Pain was the only thing that could help him now. It was what he needed to become . . . *Closed! Hidden! Safe!*

He could see Linz. She was in his head. Smiling at him the same way she always had. He was in there with her. That confused him, the Sean in there and the Sean out here. He spoke to her anyway.

'There you are, my love.'

'Here I am.'

Suddenly, she wasn't in his head anymore. Neither was he.

'I don't want to be here, Linz. I want to be with you.'

'I know that, hun,' Linz whispered back.

Sean felt her breath on the back of his neck. She smelled of strawberries and chocolate. He liked it when she called him *hun*. She always called him that when she knew he needed to feel especially safe and loved. When he was frightened. He knew why she'd said it. He knew *she* knew what he was thinking.

'Linz, I . . .'

'I know what you're thinking, hun. Don't do it.'

Ignoring her, he took a shuffle-step toward the officers, now, backed by a few concerned members of the public come to see what had washed up on their perfect-picture seafront. Things like this just didn't happen in the sleepy, upmarket village of Gullane. Sean wondered who they were and why they were there. There were too many faces. None that he knew. It made him feel scared and lonely.

He spoke to Linz to make it feel better.

'I can't bear it, Linz. I don't want to be here without you.'

'But I am here, hun. You don't have to be afraid. You don't have to go anywhere.'

Her voice made him feel safe and loved. As he remembered it always doing. Right from the very start. On the mountain.

'I miss you, my love.'

'Are you're thinking about the mountain, hun?'

'Yes.'

Sean felt his heart breaking as the pictures played. Linz broke it just a little more.

'Which one?'

He understood what she meant and his guilt reached a whole new level. He so badly wanted to turn around and look at her, but was too afraid to see what he'd done. He couldn't see that. Not again.

'I'm sorry, Linz.'

Fresh tears pricked at the corners of his eyes. Itching like sand grains. It made him think about *another* beach. A beach they'd all been on, together, on the day of the birthday party. And of the song.

Linz knew what he was thinking.

'Are you thinking about the party, hun?'

'Yes, my love.'

'And the song?'

'Yes!'

'Me too,' said Linz. 'You know how much I love to sing.'

Sean knew she was going to sing. He couldn't bear to hear it. He didn't want to remember.

'Please Linz. Don't.'

Linz sang anyway.

'The first step is the one you believe in, the second one might be profound. I'll follow you down, through the eye of the storm, but don't worry I'll keep you warm. I'll follow you down…'

Sean's despair deepened to the point he could stand no more. The song, *Follow You*, by the rock band, Shinedown, was *their* song. He didn't want to hear her sing the next line. He knew it was a lie.

'We never got to dance, Linz. You can't make that happen. Not now. Not ever.'

'Never is a long time,' said Linz, moving up to stand beside him. 'But it's not forever. Not if you don't want it to be.'

'I don't understand, my love.'

'Yes, you do.'

More of Sean began to fall apart. He could feel it happening, bit by bit, inside his head, like a sandcastle being washed away by an oncoming tide, the base crumbling into water until the whole thing collapsed. He turned his head and looked at Linz. She was so beautiful. Surrounded by golden light, all glittery and sparkly. Her pale blue, summer dress and long, blonde hair were just as he remembered. She looked as she always had, not as he thought she would have.

It made him even sadder.

'I miss you, my love. So much.'

'I know, hun.'

Knowing what he was going to do, Linz walked away, past the police officers and into the sand dunes, leaving a line of shallow footprints in the bone dry sand. And then she was gone. Disappeared into the hazy place between the sea and the sky, the bit where you don't quite know what's what and where's where.

Sean crumbled into the waves.

Linz! My love! I miss you, I miss you, I miss you, I miss you, I . . .'

The sudden silence scared the officers even more than Sean's unintelligible cries. The look of anguish on his face not helping. They were frightened and confused. Unable to gain control of a situation they were struggling to begin to understand.

'They're ready.'

The faraway voice told Sean what he already knew.

'Follow me down then, Linz,' he whispered, using *almost-words*.

He took another shuffle-step towards the police officers, entering their safe space. Assuring the outcome he wanted. The one he so badly needed. The pain was brief before the darkness came, taking him to the place where he was . . . *Closed! Hidden! Safe!*

2

The light from a low but bright morning sun streamed in through a line of tall, arched windows, laying angles of muted gold upon the polished oak floorboards, the newly blossomed leaves on the chestnut trees lining the pebble driveway, beyond, cast as shadow-dancers on the once well-trodden dancefloor of Dunvegan Castle.

Like a lone grey sentinel perched on a jagged spit of rock on the Isle of Skye's remote Duirinish peninsula, the old fortress seemed to scrutinise the churning ocean out past the entrance to the sea-loch, ever watchful for the shadows of Viking longboats, filled with ghostly warriors, come to claim the island's glittering prizes.

A wooden rowboat, a solitary occupant sat at its centre, made its way across the loch below the castle windows. Looking down, Sean recognised the rower as Fergus, the estate ghillie, no doubt heading to the boathouse on the other side to prepare fishing gear for some new group of well-heeled guests staying at the castle later that week. He would be gone by then, thankfully.

He turned his gaze to the north end of the loch, to the abandoned crofting village of Caltragill, where the dew-soaked, rusted-tin roofs of the crumbling ruins sparkled like wetted seashells. Out past the ruins, where the loch met the open Atlantic Ocean, the water turned from copper-brown to sapphire-blue. The demarcation was stark and spectacular. Far-travelled waves broke over a protruding rocky shelf, casting great sprays of seawater into a freshening wind, exploding like splinters of shattered diamond against a cloudless, blue sky.

Sean glanced at his watch, a Breitling Bentley, given to him on his forty-third birthday, two years before. The sunlight reflecting off the solid gold, crisscrossed bezel laid an amber ghost on the ceiling, one of many that haunted the castle. He thumbed the crocodile-leather strap, enjoying the blood-warm feel of it, remembering, in the touch, those who had given it to him and the loss he forced himself to bear in the wearing of it. Their names adorned the underside, engraved in time for all of time. He forced the memory back to the place he kept such things.

Trampling the leafy dancers underfoot, Sean crossed the oak-paneled room and opened the door. He looked down the deserted hallway and shook his head. It was every American's imagining of what an ancient Scottish castle hallway should be; low and narrow with green tartan carpets and oak-lined walls strewn with swords, shields and an assortment of pointy, metal things the clans of old had regularly used to kill each other with. The weapons were interspersed with oil-paintings of sombre-faced ancestors from who knew when and who knew where.

'Dammit! Where the hell are you, Judith? You called the bloody meeting!'

He closed the door with more force than he meant. The sound of it slamming shut echoed down the hallway like a blast of ancient cannon fire.

Back in the stateroom, Sean stepped up to a gilt-framed mirror and gazed dispassionately at himself, pulling on the lapels of his Harris Tweed jacket to straighten its sit. A white, twill shirt, the top two buttons undone, revealed an ornate, silver crucifix hung around his neck. He reached up to touch it then stayed his hand. It was a pointless gesture. A habit he'd almost learned to break. The tan beneath the cross matched the colour of his face, but could not disguise the bags under his eyes or the glazed stare of a man who had barely slept in three days.

'Those cornflower blue eyes of yours are a bit more storm-grey this morning, Mr Jameson.' Sean said to himself. 'And little bloody wonder.' He ran a hand through his thick but immaculately groomed mop of hair that was growing more salt-and-pepper by the day. 'What a difference a year makes,' he joked.

No one laughed.

Turning his back on the mirror and the stranger staring back at him, Sean crossed back to the centre window and set his gaze upon the coastal settlement of Claigan, directly across the loch from Caltragill. The art gallery in the old village had always been one his favourite places. He would never visit it again.

At the limit of his vision, he spied a flock of puffins skimming the water. Their wings beat frantically as they headed home to the breeding grounds on the tiny island of Canna, a spew of bleak rock twenty miles south of Skye. Their crops and beaks would be filled to the brim with sand-eels for their greedy chicks to gorge upon.

'Damned good parents those little birds,' said Sean, despising himself just a little more.

He tried to force the thought away. It was the only way to keep himself together. He recalled the advice he'd been given in previous counselling sessions.

'When the panic attacks come, Sean, put your mind elsewhere. Picture yourself in a train station, standing on the platform looking up at an old railway clock. Watch the seconds hand moving around the clockface, ticking down. Match your breathing to it, and with each passing second any anxiety you feel will begin to disappear.'

'Put my mind elsewhere, Professor?' Sean's voice echoed around the empty room. 'How in hell's name can anyone normal even do that? And I'm the one with mental health issues.' He almost laughed. Instead, he visualized the clock face and breathed, as he'd been taught. It brought him back, although this time more slowly than it had done before. He still felt edgy. 'Dammit, I need a drink!'

'Come and have one.'

Sean looked over at the stinkwood drinks cabinet. It was watching him from the corner of the room, its impish, ruddy face set in a sly, wooden smile, beckoning him over. He knew it was locked. He'd found that out the first time he'd been left alone in the room. He crossed to the cabinet and tried the handle anyway. It was still locked. The cabinet smirked but said nothing.

'Fuck you! I suppose you think that's funny?'

Sean was angry. Not so much with the cabinet, although he hated it for teasing him, but more that Judith was late. He was bone-tired from a weekend he should have been ashamed of, but wasn't, and wanted to go back to bed. More than anything, he wanted to get the bloody day over with. It had taken long enough to come.

Come on Judith, for fuck sake.

Judith Sutherland was the senior lawyer employed by Sean's company, QuantumCloud Communications. They had been friends and colleagues for over ten years. She had recruited and managed the team of defence lawyers at his trial the previous September, after he'd been charged with the manslaughter of his wife and two young children in a horrifying car crash in the Scottish mountains in late May that same year. The trial had taken place at the Edinburgh High Court, close to Edinburgh Castle and opposite St Mary's Cathedral, where murderers had once been hanged before a baying, bloodthirsty public.

From the outset, the judge had made clear his concerns about Sean's actions on that fateful night, not least his disappearance from the scene of the accident. Sean's doctor, under oath, had insisted he'd suffered severe concussion and, in his confusion, walked away, having no knowledge of where he was or where he was going. His lawyer, too, had made an impassioned case for his client's innocence.

'Who in their right mind would walk out onto a remote, mist-covered mountainside, where at any moment they might fall to their death? Certainly not someone suffering from a dislocated shoulder and bleeding from a scalp laceration that had required twenty stitches to close. Not someone who had just lost his wife and two children. For the police to suggest that Sean Jameson, a decorated ex-soldier and now respected businessman, had callously abandoned them, fleeing the scene by walking into further danger, is not only utterly ludicrous, but crass, distasteful and heartless.'

The jury, many in tears, having viewed harrowing photographs of the deceased, taken at the crash site, had agreed. Sean had walked from the court a free man. But his troubles had been far from over.

The day after his acquittal, after a night spent devoted at Edinburgh's more colourful nightclubs, Sean had attacked two police officers in the seaside village of Gullane, south of Edinburgh. He had returned to the same Law Courts less than forty-eight hours after walking out of them, charged with breach of the peace. The presiding Sheriff had released him on compassionate grounds, under the strict proviso that he immediately undertook professional counselling to help him overcome the tremendous mental stress he was clearly still under after losing his family in such a shocking manner.

QuantumCloud's response had been as swift and decisive. Judith had read Sean the board of directors decision, the following day.

'Despite great sympathy for his loss, Sean, as a major shareholder of QuantumCloud plc, a leading telecommunications company with a global customer base, has certain responsibilities. In line with the court order, the board insists he take proper time to heal. That being so, a return to his role as Chief Executive Officer will be delayed until after a period of restitution and successful treatment.'

'Spoken like the shower of spineless bastards they are,' Sean had informed her.

But the decision had been made. Like it or not, he had four months of treatment to undergo which could not be avoided.

Judith had at least been able to ensure the treatment had been private, not, as Sean had put it, in some public-funded, psycho-ward smelling of piss and full of life's losers. Albeit reluctantly, he had chosen to come to Dunvegan Castle, on the island of Skye, a place he knew well and had always loved. It was remote, beautiful and private. If he had to be a patient somewhere, he wanted no company, especially not a shower of mental cases. The recovery program would be built for him, around him, and delivered to him alone. QuantumCloud were footing the bill, so cost was not a consideration.

To say Sean had not fully committed to the program would be to grossly overstate. He had simply endured what had to be endured. The only upside was that his recovery program was delivered by an extremely attractive lesbian, Sean figured she had to be as she'd failed to respond to his advances, who knew nothing about him or what he'd been through. But she was easy to manipulate, so, perfect for Sean's enforced holiday, as he saw his time at Dunvegan Castle to be.

Professor Emily McGregor, *the lesbian,* had been persuaded by QuantumCloud to take Sean on as her sole client at a truly exorbitant rate. The saving grace was that, every Friday, the sessions ended at lunchtime, allowing her to head home to Edinburgh by way of the privately contracted seaplane Judith had agreed upon to ensure she took Sean as a client in the first place.

What Emily and the board did not know was that, on these long weekends, instead of climbing the mountains he had used as the excuse to base himself on Skye, Sean chartered a private helicopter to fly him to Glasgow International Airport, where he would board a private jet, owned by a business colleague, Yuri Abramovich, and by dinnertime that same day would be aboard Yuri's yacht in Ibiza harbour. The party would begin on board then continue in Ibiza town, at some hedonistic club that satisfied their specific needs; Grey Goose vodka, Cuban cigars and cocaine, as well as, in Yuri's case, young, attractive women. Sean had no desire for a woman, preferring to lose himself in those vices that numbed him to the point of oblivion. If he couldn't think, he couldn't feel, and if he couldn't feel, he couldn't hurt. It was a more effective treatment than any doctor could offer.

He'd spent the first weekend on Skye alone, hiking up to the spectacular Fairy Pools, in Glenbrittle, under the looming shadows of the Black Cuillin Mountains. It was one of the special places he, Linz and the kids had loved to visit. But the memories of those happier days had been too hard to handle. He had not returned after that first visit. Instead, with a carefully cultivated plan involving the help of a local fisherman and one of the weekend staff at Dunvegan Castle, he created a lie to live in, leaving, each Friday, as normal, on the pretence of spending the weekend climbing. The weekly subterfuge had worked perfectly over the past months, however, getting back in time for his first therapy session, every Monday, was an exhausting routine.

Sean paid only lip service to Emily and her recovery program. He engaged with her in the sessions, practiced the mental exercises designed to help control his panic attacks and said what she expected him to, at times, becoming angry or emotional, acting as he felt she expected him to do. He cared little how he got through the sessions, only that he did.

All that mattered, now, was that it would soon all be over. That very morning, in fact, after his final session, provided Emily signed off on the program. Why she could not have done it the prevous Friday, who knew? It didn't matter. She would sign off on it, today, no matter what hoops she held up for him to jump through. Then, Judith, Emily, the board at QuantumCloud and everyone else who had helped put him here could go to hell. And if those bastards on the board of QuantumCloud thought he was going to come straight back into the fold, to help them complete the merger, they had another thing coming. He would return to *his* company in *his* own good time and under *his* terms and conditions.

3

The door opened, slowly, creaking on its hinges, and a wispy shadow slid in over the floorboards, stopping half-in half-out of the room, waiting for its owner to allow it to fully enter. Sean, although he could not see her, knew it was Judith, her rounded, Edinburgh accent, polished and refined at Kilgraston Girls School, in Perthshire, giving her away. She was talking to Emily, the lesbian, who was clearly hanging around the hallway with the painted ghosts and the wall-mounted weapons, their edges a damned sight less sharp than her tongue. The shadow fully entered the room. Judith closed the door as she followed.

'Where the hell have you been, Jude?'

Sean's expression was as cold as he could make it. He made a show of glancing at his watch.

'And a very good morning to you too, Mr Jameson. Squished any spiders this morning?'

Judith's voice was bright and cheerful, annoying him all the more.

'Very funny, Jude.'

She offered Sean a smile that he remembered only too well; a perfect row of ivory white teeth set behind full, rose-pink lips. It was natural and infectious. He returned it before he could check himself.

Judith crossed the room, the leafy dancers gathering around her feet like laughing children, and leaned in towards him, lifting her face to allow him to greet her. Her eyes were bright and clear with good living, flawless, blue mosaics framed by peach perfect skin that was clear of blemishes. As usual, she wore no make-up, save for a light brush of Milani blusher on her high-set cheekbones. The pale-cream, Stella McCartney, silk suit she was wearing, cut to accentuate her perfect ten figure, was matched with a pair of pale blue, Christian Louboutin ankle-boots that had red-leather soles and a chunky, patent-leather heel covered in silver spikes.

Just so Jude, thought Sean, *stylish and a little bit edgy.* She radiated the health he was here to achieve, which pissed him off, given how he felt after his weekend of debauchery.

'How are you, Sean? It's been almost a month.'

'That long? I really hadn't noticed,' Sean lied, looking down at Judith's upturned face.

He held her by the shoulders and kissed her on both cheeks in the French style greeting known as *La Bise*. The greeting was Roman in origin, not French, as most people thought it.

'You look good.'

'Don't be a bloody lawyer all the time, Jude.'

Judith smiled but said nothing. She had already noticed the tell-tale signs. The immaculately cut suit, polished brogues and crisp, white shirt couldn't hide the nicotine stains on Sean's fingers or the dark lines chiselled around his eyes. A touch too much aftershave and the faint linger of mouthwash, too, was a clear reflection of his dedication to the recovery program.

Sean hugged her, pulling her close and enjoying the press of her breasts against him. He could almost taste the summery aroma of her perfume and the clean, healthy smell of her shoulder-length auburn hair. He ran his fingers down the her arms, a purposeful, lingering touch, before sliding his palms in to hold her at the waist. Feeling no resistance, he followed the contours of her hips, reaching around to cup the cheeks of her bottom. Aroused, he leaned in to kiss her properly.

'Sean! Please don't.'

Judith's voice was breathless and husky. She pressed her palms against his chest and stepped back. He'd taken her by surprise, but she was annoyed that she'd almost responded to him.

'You weren't always so backward in coming forward, Jude,' said Sean, his mouth deciding a scowl was more apt than the thin smile it had opted for when she'd first entered the room.

The sexual innuendo was not lost on her.

'That was in another time, Sean. I wish I could change that. Erase what I did. What *we* did. You should, too.'

'Believe me, Jude, I do.'

He bored into her with uncaring, hooded eyes. Seeing the verbal thorn had pricked and drawn blood, he allowed the smile back onto his face. It settled and stayed like a crow on a cradle.

Freeing herself from his wasted gaze, Judith crossed to the oak dining-table that dominated the centre of room, attempting to escape the frisson that had smothered her. She set her Louis Vuitton handbag on the table-top, taking more time to open and peer into it than she required, giving her time to regain her composure. The *Petite-Boite Chapeau*, luxury bag, had been a gift from Sean, given to her while they had been on a business trip, eighteen months previously, only a few weeks before the accident that had claimed the lives of his family. She felt an overwhelming sadness as the memory of the time they had shared invaded her thoughts.

In Rome, in early springtime, she and Sean had walked hand-in-hand, heady with the glow of newfound love, down the world-famous Spanish Steps, then sauntered along the fashionable Via dei Condotti, where they had found the luxurious Louis Vuitton store. Sean had insisted she have the handbag to remind her of their days together. At the time, she had been thrilled to receive such a beautiful gift, a symbol of their love for each other, or so she had allowed herself to think. That their liaison had been as fleeting as a mayfly courtship on a summer's day was of little comfort.

Judith wished she could erase the memory that had once seemed so beautiful. She had betrayed Linz, her friend, which was bad enough in itself, but the true cost of that betrayal had been higher than she'd ever expected it to be. Paid for in shame and guilt. Linz had always been fiercely loyal and trustworthy, something Judith had admired her for and thought they had in common. The handbag was a constant reminder of her own failing in that regard. She turned back to face Sean, trying to hide the sadness she felt at damage the affair had ultimately caused.

'Why are you being so cruel?'

Sean, if he had noticed Judith's discomfort, ignored it.

'You used to want me to touch you like that, Jude. Anyway, what have I got to feel guilty about? I'm single now. I thought that's what you always wanted?'

His mock laugh and the careless shrug of his shoulders were empty gestures. Judith shook her head, dismayed by the crass and cruel words.

'Don't say that, Sean.'

'Well it's true, Jude, isn't it?'

A look of anguish clouded his face but was brusquely swept aside, as if something inside him had blocked a memory that threatened to overwhelm him.

In that brief moment, Judith noticed, Sean's entire demeanour changed. His features softened and his eyes grew wide, as if the little boy that still lived inside him had peeked out at her, seeking kindness and love. But the change was as fleeting as Peter Pan himself. She moved towards him, her smile and her eyes telling him she was there for him and wanted to help.

'Sean, why don't you . . .'

As if realising he'd been caught, knowing that Judith had really seen him and being ashamed of showing the part of him he had always known it safer to keep hidden, Sean took control. As quickly as he had appeared, the little boy was gone.

Closed! Hidden! Safe!

He turned away from her and walked across the room to the furthest away window, overlooking the loch, and spoke to the glass.

'So, Jude, are you here to review my end of term report card, or have you been sent to welcome me back into the QuantumCloud fold? Broussard's been in my chair long enough. It's time for the old broom to sweep his black ass back down to the lower half of the boardroom table.'

'Both, I suppose,' said Judith, ignoring the racist stab at Hublot Broussard, QuantumCloud's talented Operations Director and, in Sean's absence, acting Chief Executive Officer. Sean and Hublot had become close friends over the past ten years, after Sean had poached him from a business competitor while on a business trip to Hublot's hometown of New Orleans. Later, it was at Sean's personal recommendation that Hublot join the QuantumCloud board. He'd done a fine job in Sean's absence. It was that, she guessed, which had prompted the uncharacteristic outburst. But it made what she'd come to tell him all the harder. She took a deep breath. There was no sugar-coating this one. 'They don't want you back.'

Her voice sounded somewhat higher in her head than the cool, professional tone she'd aimed for. Sean turned to face her. His face was an eruption of indignant anger.

'They what?'

'They don't want you back.'

Sean could hardly believe what he was hearing. The fact that he didn't want to go back, at least, not right away, was irrelevant. He'd built the damned company, after resigning his commission in the British Army, growing it from a single mobile phone shop in Edinburgh to an international company with offices in London, Paris and Rome.

'They don't want me back! What the fuck are you talking about, Jude? I'm still a company director and the major shareholder. They don't have a fucking choice.'

Judith said nothing, knowing there was nothing she could say that would hold back the tsunami of anger being directed at her. She turned back to the her bag and removed a sealed, white envelope, then walked over to the window and handed it to Sean.

'The minutes from the extraordinary board meeting,' she said, quietly, 'called last night. And a private letter from the board members.'

'Extraordinary board meeting? On a Sunday night?'

Sean's confusion dissipated his anger and his voice returned to almost normal volume. He tore open the letter and removed the few stapled pages, turning away from Judith as he skimmed the communication.

'Last night, yes. It's why I was late getting here.'

'Which you, no doubt, attended, Jude?'

Sean stared at her with accusation in his eyes.

'No, Sean, I didn't. I only found out after the fact.'

Sean shook the letter in front of her, a warning flag for what was coming. Judith avoided his gaze.

'Have you read this?'

Judith shook her head.

'It's marked confidential. All I know is that they don't feel it's in the company's interests, or yours, for you to return. At least, not right now. What else does it say?'

Judith knew exactly what it said, having read it, word for word, that morning, on her way up from Edinburgh.

'It's irrelevant! Sean snapped. 'Some tosh about the confusion my return would create at a critical time in the current merger talks with YsangCom. The board feel, and I quote, that it would be unfair of them to expect me to return to such a demanding environment so soon after my treatment.'

'They may have a point,' said Judith, wondering why she was bothering to try to soothe the storm, 'given what you've been through over the past year. Perhaps you *do* need more time. This round of therapy was just the start of your recovery.'

Sean screwed the letter up and threw it onto the floor, kicking it away from him, under the table.

'My recovery, Jude, really? I'm sick and tired of hearing about my fucking recovery,' The venom in Sean's voice matched the anger contorting his face. 'You make me sound like a needle-jabbing junkie. I'm Sean fucking Jameson, for Christ's sake. It's my fucking company.'

'Technically it's their company, too,' said Judith, trying to reintroduce a modicum of calm. 'The board of directors are also shareholders. They have a legal duty to act in its best interests, which is what they feel they are doing.'

'That's bullshit, Jude!'

'It's not, Sean. They're trying to protect you, even if you can't or won't see it for yourself. Look at you. You're clearly not ready to come back yet.'

'I've done the fucking therapy, Jude. I've spent over months here doing everything that's been asked of me. I'm as recovered as I'm ever going to be.'

Judith gave a snort of derision and shook her head.

'Really? Everything? Tell me, how was the climbing this weekend?'

Sean opened his mouth to reply then paused, thrown off guard by the look on Judith's face. *Did she know about the clandestine weekend trips*? He decided she was fishing. She'd seen how rough he looked and put two and two together.

'I've told you before, Jude, don't be too fucking clever for your own good. I might have screwed you a few times, but that doesn't give you the right to get smart with me. If you've something to say then spit it out of that pretty mouth of yours. Remember, I've seen it painted like a whore's mouth more than once. And from personal experience, I know you like to get as down and as dirty as it can get!'

Judith's cheeks flushed with a rush of angry blood and her eyes blazed at Sean's cruel and inappropriate outburst. She moved towards him and pushed him, with both hands, in the center of his chest, sending him stumbling back a step.

'Screw you, you self-centered, arrogant, lying bastard. I know you've lost Linz and the kids. I know your life has fallen apart and you hate yourself and everyone else. But talk to me like that again, Sean Jameson, ever, and you'll lose this friend for good. And there's not exactly a long line of them waiting to take my place.'

The look on Sean's face, combined with a rush of adrenaline, sapped Judith's energy. Her rage evaporated as quickly as it had arrived. She looked up at him, standing, open-mouthed, looking for all the world like *Scuttle the Seagull*, one of the characters from the Walt Disney movie, *The Little Mermaid*. She'd watched it with his children, many times. Alice had loved the film, the seagull in particular. She brought her fingers to her lips and laughed. Sean, shocked at the uncharacteristic outburst, began laughing himself.

'Jude! Who would have thought you were such a foul-mouthed little minx? Did they teach you that language at your fine, all-girls boarding-school?'

'Oh, Sean.'

Judith started to cry, the tears coming despite her attempt to stop them. They came for the loss of Linz and the children, for her guilt at having been Sean's lover and letting down her friend, and for the desperate sadness she could see in him now. Sean took her in his arms, mistaking the intention behind her saying his name.

'Jude. My beautiful Jude.'

Judith looked up at him with wet, doe eyes. He could already taste the kiss.

'Seriously, Sean,' she whispered, 'are you really so far gone that you think I don't know about your weekly trips to Ibiza?'

Sean broke away from her as if he'd touched an electric fence. The kiss he had been certain was coming had turned to a savage bite.

'I see.' His voice quiet and flat. 'Well, that, as they say, is that.'

'It is, Sean, but it's not the end of things with QuantumCloud. They want you back, but they know you're not ready. I suspect you know that yourself. They feel that another six months of rehabilitation, taking time away from things, skiing, climbing, doing *whatever* helps you to reconnect with the world, would be the best way forward for you.'

'I thought you hadn't read the letter, Jude?'

'I lied. I'm still your lawyer, Sean. As well as your friend. I need to protect your interests.'

She gave him a hopeful smile that wasn't returned.

'Well, you can protect them now, Jude. As my friend *and* my lawyer.'

He spoke quietly and had a pensive look on his face. Judith had seen it many times before. It wasn't a good sign.

'What do you mean?'

The smile that Sean gave her was thin and cruel, like the kill stroke from a butcher's knife.

'QuantumCloud don't want me back! Well here's my response. And, believe me, it's going to be in my best interests. I want you to call Murray, at Caledonian Asset Management. Instruct him to place my shares in QuantumCloud on the open market. Sell them at best and sell them immediately. Have him transfer the proceeds to my personal bank account in Gibraltar.'

'Sean! No!'

Judith's face was decidedly less peachy than it had been when she'd first entered the room. Sean hoped it would have the same effect on the QuantumCloud board. But he wasn't finished.

'While you're at it, Jude, draft my resignation. I'm cutting all ties with QuantumCloud, effective immediately. I have a six-month notice period in my contract so they can still damn well pay me that. Finally, get hold of that news reporter from Business Insider Magazine, you know the one, Susannah, something or other. The porn star, you called her, remember? All blonde hair, tits and glasses. Utterly brainless but beautiful. She's been bugging me for an in-depth interview for years. I'll give her a one-to-one she won't forget, in so many ways! Neither will QuantumCloud. Remember, Jude, I know where the skeletons are buried. Mainly, because I buried them.'

Judith's surprise was reflected in her expression.

'Sean! You can't do that. That many shares dumped on the market will have a terrible effect on the share price, not to mention the news of your resignation and dishing the dirt on QuantumCloud. It could scupper the merger. The board of directors don't deserve that.'

Sean shrugged his shoulders, nonchalantly.

'Fuck them! They want a game, that's fine with me. They served. Consider this my return. On the volley with juice and backspin. You play tennis, Jude, explain it to the old farts on the board who don't.'

Judith shook her head, appalled at what he'd asked her to do.

'You're being vindictive and petty. You might destroy the board, but you'll also destroy the reputation of the company at the same time. The company you built. And you'll destroy part of yourself in the process.'

'I don't give a damn,' Sean growled.

'Well you should, Sean, you bloody-well should,' cried Judith, desperately trying to reason with him 'Hublot's one of your closest friends. All of the board members are your friends. People you've worked with and trusted for years. They're practically family to you, no matter what you think about their decision.'

'Trust! Don't make me laugh, Jude. They put me here. They've clearly been spying on me, waiting to use whatever they found out against me. That's no family I want to be part of. They're nothing to me. Not any longer. You're my lawyer, Jude. I've told you what to do. Just do it.'

Judith knew nothing she could say would change Sean's mind. He was too far gone, lost in his grief and running for his life inside a vicious circle of self-destruction.

'I will, Sean, if that's what you really want. But you're acting out of anger, not using your head. And that's not the Sean I know.'

'I won't ask you again, Jude,' said Sean, his voice as hard as cold steel. 'Get it done.'

Despite realising it was pointless to appeal to him, Judith tried.

'The Sean I knew always protected his family and friends. Even total strangers who were in need. The Sean I knew would always strive to do the right thing by those he loved. Where is that Sean?'

'The Sean you fell in love with?'

Sean dropped his voice, running out of steam for the fight.

Judith took his hand in hers and looked into his eyes, desperately trying to reconnect with him. Her words seemed to have hit home.

'The Sean I fell in love with. Yes.'

The sadness on Judith's face was hard for Sean to see, but he could not bend. He could not say what he wanted to say to her. He already carried too much sadness of his own. Adding hers would break him. He pulled his hand free of hers and looked out over the loch, unable to meet her gaze, hating the distance that had opened up between them. A distance, he realised, that should have remained between them when they had simply been friends and colleagues, but that, as Judith had already said, was in another time. He had no choice. He had to keep pushing her away.

'You're angry with yourself, Jude, not me. Why don't you take that razor-sharp mind of yours and point it at yourself. You feel guilty for what happened between us in Rome.'

Judith stared down at the polished wood floor. The leafy dancers had disappeared, gathered in the corners of the room, perhaps not wanting to hear what was being said.

Your right, Sean. I am. I despise myself for what I did to . . .'

She covered her mouth with her hand, unable to finish the sentence. Sean shook his head and gave a derisive laugh.

'If you're really determined to play the penitent, Jude, at least have the good grace to say her name.'

Judith's voice dropped to a whisper, as if too ashamed at herself to say the words.

'Damn you, Sean, alright! I despise myself for what I did to Linz. She was my friend and I betrayed her. We both betrayed her, God forgive us.'

'Don't bring Him into it, Jude, he doesn't give a shit about any of us.'

'Sean! Don't say that.'

Judith looked at him in despair. He had lost his faith. She prayed he would find it again. It was the only thing that might help him climb out of the hell in which he was living. But she knew it was pointless to tell him that.

'And what betrayal are you referring to, Jude, exactly?'

'The worst betrayal of all, Sean,' whispered Judith, giving him the saddest of smiles, 'we fell in love.'

She brushed away tears she had thought long since cried.

'If it makes it any easier for you, Jude. You weren't the only one I was screwing.'

Judith looked at him with such despair etched into her face.

'I see.'

Sean almost apologised, but a different response escaped his lips. He stared out of the window, too ashamed at what he was about to say to say it to her face.

'And just so you know, I was never in love with you.' Judith opened her mouth to reply but checked the response. Keeping his gaze fixed on the glass, Sean added injury to the insult. 'No witty or comeback? 'I thought lawyers were like comedians, always ready to destroy their hecklers.'

Judith put a hand on his forearm. The touch was meant to be reassuring, but the words she spoke were as bleak as death.

'Why would I try to destroy you, Sean. When you're doing such a good job of destroying yourself.'

Sean turned to look at her.

'You think so, Jude? You really think that's what I'm trying to do?'

Now it was Judith's turn to stare out of the window. She couldn't meet his eyes. It would make it too hard to say what she still needed to say.

'You're full of pain, Sean, and it's turned to bitterness and anger. I guess it makes it easier to bear if you can find someone to blame for your loss. You're pushing everyone away, that's obvious, but you're only running away from yourself.'

'I didn't know you knew me so well.'

Judith could tell from the sound of his voice that she'd wounded him. She was saddened that she had.

'Don't ever think I don't know you, Sean Jameson. I know you well enough, whoever you choose to be on any given day. And I will always love you, on any given day. But you need to learn to love yourself again, if you ever truly did.'

Sean looked back out across the loch, determined to show her words had not reached him. His breath misted the glass. Without thinking, he reached out and drew a smiley face on it, then just as quickly rubbed it away. Beyond the glass, the sky darkened, as a vast bank of storm clouds moved in from the Atlantic, smothering the sun.

'You've been listening to the lesbian, too much, Jude.'

'Perhaps, Sean,' said Jude, her voice a whisper, 'but so have you. Have you really learned so little from her?'

They stood in silence, neither of them knowing what more to say, both wondering how they had reached the barren ground on which they now stood, so far from the Trevi Fountain, where they had once tossed coins into the water and wished for more such moments to come.

'Do me a favour, Jude,' said Sean, his voice as empty as the moment, 'send Emily in on your way out. I doubt I'll be seeing you again. Not after today. Take care of yourself. We had fun, didn't we?'

Judith sighed and tried to smile.

'I suppose we did, Sean. But at what cost?'

Sean kept his gaze firmly fixed on the glass, wondering why the smiley face had reappeared, mocking him, it seemed.

'Probably best you go now, Jude'

It was finally over. Judith recognised the moment and wondered if Sean had.

As she walked towards the door, she stopped and looked back, willing him to look at her, hoping he would say one final farewell. But he didn't turn. She shook her head, sad that it had come to such an empty end. But even the greatest of loves sometimes did.

'Where will you go? Home, to Merrick?'

'I have no home, Jude. Not anymore. Merrick is a coffin. One I will not climb into.'

'So, to where?'

Sean whispered his answer so quietly that Judith did not hear him.

'I know exactly where I'm going.'

He heard the door click and Judith's footsteps echoing down the hallway, until there was no sound. Like everyone else, she was gone.

Don't get close, he reminded himself, *you only get hurt.*

Everything he had ever loved was gone. His family, his business, and now his friends. He looked up the room to the window directly across from the door Judith had just exited. Linz looked back at him and smiled. She knew what he was thinking. She always did. Sean smiled back at her.

'Be with you soon, my love.'

4

At thirty-one years of age, Professor Emily MacGregor was a leading practitioners in her field. With a double first in Psychology and Sociology and a PHD in Cognitive Science from the prestigious St Andrews University, her career was a shining example of overachievement. Her recent paper on Post-traumatic stress disorder in adults who had suffered child related abuse had been ground-breaking. She had been widely recommended to QuantumCloud as the best fit for Sean's specific issues, as well as for being female. He would only have butted heads with a male psychiatrist, so they had gone out of their way to get their woman.

'How's our patient today?' Emily asked, as Judith approached her from down the hallway. 'You were quicker than I thought you were going to be.'

She gave Judith a hug. They'd become close friends over the past six months and Emily sympathised with her difficult position. It couldn't be easy being the jam in the Sean and QuantumCloud board sandwich.

'Well,' said Judith, 'if I were to describe him in cartoon characters, he's somewhere between *Donald Duck* and *Taz the Tasmanian Devil*, with just a smattering of David Banner's *Incredible Hulk* alter-ego thrown in for good measure. You know, from the box-set I made you watch with me last Christmas, when you were ill?'

'I remember,' said Emily, 'the one with the sad piano music.'

'The very one.'

Emily laughed at the image Judith had painted of Sean.

'Honestly, Judith, you and your nineteen-seventies television series obsession. I could analyse that for you if you ever want to understand it?'

'Blame my Dad for that, Ems, it was his era. He was obsessed with Disney and Marvel. I'm afraid he passed that obsession onto me. Thanks, but I'll skip the analysis for now.'

'Okay, but the offer's open.'

'I'll maybe take you up on it at some point.'

Judith gave her a thin smile that did little to hide what had obviously been a rough meeting with Sean.

'I assume,' said Emily, 'he knows about the board of directors decision to postpone his return to the fold?'

'It was your suggestion Ems. We did as you advised.'

'It's for his own good, Judith. But I take it he isn't happy?'

'Happy is not a word I would choose to describe him. He's dumping his entire QuantumCloud shareholding on the market and resigning for good measure. It's going to hurt the company, if we allow it.'

'If you allow it? What do you mean, Judith, if you allow it?

Judith hesitated, glancing back up the hallway in case Sean had followed her out. She ushered Emily across the open landing to make sure she wasn't overheard.

'I spoke to Hublot a few minutes ago, from the ladies toilets. Honestly, I was so paranoid Sean might overhear me. He'd have lost it if he'd overheard what we were talking about. He's pretty angry, Ems. Angrier than I've seen him in a long time.'

'Isn't he always! So what did Hublot say?'

'Well, he wasn't entirely shocked at Sean's reaction. He's more worried about his mental health, which says a lot about Hublot, given how he's worked to keep the merger with YsangCom on track. It was Sean's deal, but he's worked tirelessly to keep it alive after all that's happened. He's damned if he's going to see it fall apart now.'

'But how can he do that, Judith, if Sean wants his shares sold? I might not be a high-powered business lawyer, but aren't you legally bound to do what he's asked. They're his shares after all.'

'Well, they are... and they're not.'

'Expand,' said Emily, tilting her head and nodding encouragingly. Slipping into her counselling role, thought Judith, a little ahead of her coming session with Sean. She explained anyway.

'Well, there's a clause in QuantumCloud's articles of association that allows the board to veto any sale of shares held by a director of the company. If the director is in any way mentally incapacitated.'

Emily took hold of the little silver and lime-green fish symbol she wore on a silver chain around her neck, rubbing it between her thumb and forefinger. It was something she did, Judith knew, when she was thinking. Sean had the very same mannerism with his own silver crucifix.

'I see,' replied Emily, tersely. 'So, what you're saying is that QuantumCloud will argue Sean is mentally unfit to make the decision to sell his own shares? Because, if you are, Judith, you need me to sign off on that, and I won't. Sean is ill, that's for sure, suffering from a trauma-based disorder. But he's mentally stable enough to make his own decisions.'

Judith gave Emily a wry but not unwarm smile.

'Don't worry, Ems, we won't be asking that of you. That's not what I meant to imply. If that's how it came across, I'm sorry.'

Emily was visibly relieved.

'That's good. I've already found my new offices in George Street. Uptown Edinburgh, no less. And now I've found them, I don't intend on giving them up. And the QuantumCloud funding I've been promised is absolutely crucial.'

'George Street!' Judith couldn't hide her surprise. 'Why there? It's so damned busy and the parking's awful. You'd be better off in the New Town. Down in Stockbridge, for instance. It's a cool and trendy, as well as being filled with the kind of people we both want to meet.'

'Good-looking guys, you mean?'

Emily gave Judith a wry smile.

'I don't know what you mean,' said Judith, shooting Emily a cheeky grin.

Emily shook her head.

'Nope! George Street is where I want to be. Right in the heart of the city. Anyway, it's a done deal. The decorators are, as we speak, creating a haven of peace and tranquility for me and my patients. QuantumCloud's funding is going a long way in helping adults dealing with early life adversity. The rates of depression, suicidality and anxiety disorders in those who experience childhood maltreatment are heartbreaking.'

Judith held up her palms in mock attrition.

'You don't have to convince me, Ems. The funding for your project's already been passed. It's not something we would go back on. In fact, it's something everyone at QuantumCloud is proud to be a part of, irrespective of how it might have come about, though Sean's misfortune.'

'Sorry, I don't mean to preach. It's just so damned important to me.'

'I know, Ems. Judith gave her a supportive hug.

'Okay! Enough chat. I'll go and face the Hulk. I'll call you after the session. It might be the last one, but it's going to be a rough one. Especially for Sean.'

'Rough?'

Emily wasn't surprised at the look of concern on Judith's face. She knew there was history between her and Sean. Not that Judith had spoken about it in any detail, but she suspected she'd been deeply in love with him. Perhaps still was.

'It might be, Judith. It might have to be.'

Judith nodded, realising she couldn't push for more. Emily was ethically bound to keep the sessions with Sean, even if QuantumCloud was footing the bill.

'Are you going to show him the . . .'

'It's in my bag,' said Emily, looking sombre for a moment. 'Thanks for getting hold of it for me. It must have been emotional for you.'

'It was, Ems, more than I thought it was going to be. It brought back memories I didn't want to have. God knows what it will do to Sean. How do you think he'll react when he sees it?

'It might be difficult for him, Judith. To say the least.'

'Oh, Ems. I think it's really going to hurt him.'

Seeing Judith was upset at the thought of Sean suffering in any way, Emily tried to reassure her.

'Look, what say we go for a drink tonight when we're back in Edinburgh? We can pop into the Tigerlily Bar. Monday nights are always quiet. I'll tell you as much as I can about the session and where Sean goes from here.'

'Okay, Ems. I'd like that.'

She gave Emily a thin smile.

'I might even tell you about the new man in my life,' added Emily, 'he works there, sort of.'

The look of sadness on Judith's face turned upside down.

'New man! Don't let Sean hear you say that. He's still convinced you're a lesbian.'

'Only in his fantasies.'

They both laughed and the mood shifted.

'Right, Ems, tell me when, tell me how, and tell me how long? And I do mean that last question in every sense.'

'Later, you brazen hussy.'

Emily playfully slapped Judith on the back of the wrist then turned and walked down the hallway.

'Well at least now I know why your new offices are in George Street,' Judith called after her.

'*Fateri nihil sum*,' said Emily, without looking back.

The denial of culpability echoed down the hallway, leaving Judith wondering how, as well as being the most intellectually brilliant young woman she'd ever met, Emily spoke Latin.

5

Sean took a seat on one of the two white-leather swivel-chairs Emily had insisted be purchased and installed in the state-room of the west wing of Dunvegan Castle, the "interrogation chamber", as he liked to refer to it. A modern aluminium and glass coffee table, set between the chairs, had the latest copies of Focus and GQ upon it. The magazines were pristine and un-thumbed, as much a finishing aesthetic as anything else.

The chairs were positioned by the north-most window, affording marvellous views over the loch and swathes of woodland bordering the water. Despite being at architectural odds with the other antique furniture, the modern touches did not upset the overall balance of the room. It remained a study in *Feng Shui*, which was no doubt what Emily had aimed for.

Sean picked up the copy of GQ. Its cover featured a dramatic monochrome image of the ever-increasingly cool Keanu Reeves dressed in a dark blue suit and wearing sunglasses with yellow lenses that made his eyes appear black. A strapline referring to the actor, which said, *Enters his Icon Era*, made Sean shake his head in despair.

'Magazines are so full of shit.'

From what little he knew of him, the Hollywood actor was a genuinely good guy who had overcome both adversity and loss in his life. Doing so with dignity. Refusing to shout to the world about how unjust it was and how sad he felt. He simply got on with things. Sean recognised the irony and tossed the magazine back onto the table, trying to avoid the message in Keanu's silent stare. *Just get on with it, man!*

'I wish I could, Keanu. I wish I bloody could.'

'Talking to yourself again, Sean?'

'Professor!'

Sean hadn't heard Emily enter the room. At least, it looked like Emily, just not Emily the lesbian whom he considered he'd come to know pretty well over the past months they'd spent together. He stood to greet her. She crossed the floor and stood in front of him with her hand outstretched. Her grip was delicate and cool.

'How are we this morning?' Emily asked, looking Sean up and down.

Her voice was gentle, but carried a tone that belied a strength of character easily missed by those who didn't really know her. If she was concerned about how he appeared, she didn't show it. He wondered if *she* knew about his trips to Ibiza, but guessed she didn't. He was certain she would have already baled if she did. She flicked a thick mane of wavy, red hair back over her left shoulder with a confident toss of her head.

No! Sean mused. *Definitely not a lesbian today.*

Emily wasn't beautiful in the classical way that Judith was. She was pretty, Sean had decided, with plain but finely-honed features, sky-blue eyes and a button nose. Normally, she wore flat shoes and a nondescript knee-length dress under a standard white doctor's lab-coat, an outfit that befitted her profession but did nothing for her figure. Today, she wore a pair of faded jeans, that were tight in all the right places, tucked into a pair of black cowboy-boots, with a Harley Davidson, biker jacket worn over a white t-shirt that did nothing to hide her small but pert breasts. Her naturally pale, Celtic skin was ruddy from a weekend spent outdoors, and across her cheeks and the bridge of her nose lay a smattering of light brown freckles. At just over five-feet four inches, she would never be considered tall, but her body was lithe and toned from days spent at the beach, kite-surfing, her second obsession after her work.

'I was talking to Keanu, if you must know.'

Sean directed his gaze to the magazine on the table. He reached down and flipped it over.

'Great guy, I'm led to believe,' said Emily, showing no more than polite interest.

Sean smiled. *Perhaps still a lesbian then. All the girls love Keanu.*

'Does that make me totally mad then, Professor?

Emily smiled and shook her head, She dropped her rucksack by her usual seat and took off her jacket, hanging it over the edge of the chair, and turned back to Sean to answer his question.

'Talking to one's self is actually considered pretty normal, depending on the circumstances. Everyone does it, whether they talk out loud or use their own internal voice. So, no, you're not totally mad.'

'That's something, I suppose,' muttered Sean.

'Then again,' said Emily, sending him a cheeky grin, 'talking to a picture of a guy on the cover of a magazine? I'd say that does make you a little crazy.'

'Yeah, yeah, Professor. I'll bear that in mind. No more talking to pictures of people.'

Emily sat down and nodded her head towards the empty chair, indicating Sean should do the same. He sat down and looked across at her, a silent challenge poorly hidden in his stare. She returned his gaze with a blank look most poker players would have been proud to be able to achieve.

'You're doing it again,' said Sean, swivelling his chair from side to side.

'Doing what?' Emily asked, innocently.

Her expression was still blank, but a Mona Lisa smile found its way onto her lips. It looked, thought Sean, like a bear-trap concealed beneath autumn leaves.

'Saying nothing. Waiting for me to speak first.'

'Am I? said Emily, wondering how best to play things.

He's still angry after his meeting with Judith. I need him more relaxed before we start moving towards…

'You damn well know you are,' replied Sean, cutting in on her thoughts. 'But I've decided, just for today, you can talk first. It's our last session, so we don't have to talk at all. We can just say goodbye and good riddance. I promise I won't tell the leeches at QuantumCloud if you won't.'

Emily shot him a smile that told him she wasn't even going to consider that.

'I don't mind the first option, Sean. But we're already here. It seems a shame to waste our time. Let's just chat for a while and see what falls out along the way. No boundaries and no limits to the subject. Is that fine with you?'

Emily leaned forward, challenging Sean's attempt to take control. She maintained eye contact with him but her gaze was bright and friendly.

Sean found he was enjoying the sexy, new and easy-going Emily more than the one he'd come to know. She'd obviously had a personality change over the weekend. Or maybe she'd just got laid?

'Sounds good to me, Professor. So, what will we talk about?'

Emily looked up into nowhere, fiddling with her silver and lime-green pendant as if mulling over what topic to choose. She was thinking about how Judith had described Sean's mood.

'Anything?'

'Anything,' replied Sean, leaning back in his chair.

'Okay, tell me this. Did you watch much television when you were a kid?'

'Of course,' said Sean, bemused, 'didn't everyone?'

Emily leaned back, mirroring Sean's pose. She felt he was beginning to relax, so baited the trap she was setting.

'And what about *Donald Duck*?'

'Disney's *Donald Duck*?'

Sean looked bemused.

'Is there another?'

'Not that I know of,' said Emily.

'Yes Sean, that *Donald Duck*.'

Sean smiled at the memory playing out in his head.

'We watched all the Disney stuff. *Goofy* was my favourite. That dog was such an idiot. He always made me laugh.'

Emily smiled at him and tilted her head, sending a warning to Sean that perhaps the conversation would be something quite different to what he'd imagined it would be.

'Well, let's talk about *Donald Duck*.'

'Go ahead then, Doc!'

'Touché,' replied Emily, acknowledging the *Bugs Bunny* reference.

'Donald,' she began, 'what a strange and highly amusing little duck. A classic study in dichotomy. On one hand, he's incredibly generous and kind, and there's a constant struggle within him to do the right thing, no matter how hard that might be. He's as caring as only a duck can be. On the other hand, he gets so wound up and can fly into a rage over the slightest of things. He swings from one extreme to the other, wreaking havoc on his life and on everyone around him.'

'So you're likening me to him? Is this a standard line of counselling or are we just winging it?'

'Very good, Sean, very funny. But bear with me for a moment.'

'It's your story, Professor. Tell it how you want.'

'You'll also have seen the *Taz the Tasmanian Devil* cartoons?'

'I loved him,' confirmed Sean, smiling at the memory of not only watching *Taz* but acting him out in the fields behind his home in Fort William, chasing his younger brother and sister like a crazed whirling dervish.

'Good,' said Emily, feeling she had created some real engagement between them. 'Well, as you know, this ferocious little devil is notorious for his lack of patience and even shorter fuse. He's always spinning out of control, is highly destructive, and rarely communicates. No one really knows why he's so angry. In fact, *Taz* sets the bar high in illustrating how anger can be a destructive force of nature.'

'Again, I get it. Seriously, where's this going?'

Sean gave her a condescending smile. Emily, seeing his patience was waning, pleaded for time.

'One more character and I promise I'll get to the point of this memory lane re-run.'

'All good, Professor. I can barely wait to find out who's next.'

'Well this is one of our most interesting characters. One who goes through a major incident and whose life changes because of it, in the most dramatic of ways. Someone who has anger at the very core of his existence, but, interestingly, someone who shows us that not all anger is bad. In fact, in his case, anger can be shown to be a catapult for good. Any idea who I'm talking about?'

'No idea,' replied Sean, 'but I'm enjoying the session. Normally you bore me senseless.'

Emily suppressed the reply that almost escaped her lips.

Sean was afraid of losing control. She understood that. Attack was his defence when that happened. But this last session was the key to the success of the entire program. She had to keep him on track. There was a mental door he had to open and walk through. Her job was to guide him to that door, knowing full well that, when he opened it, what he found on the other side could be devastating for him.

'Well, it's the *Hulk*,' said Emily, cheerfully, 'the one with the bodybuilder, Lou Ferrigno, who played the part of the not-so-savage green monster. And Bill Bixby, who played the . . .'

Sean preempted her.

'The scientist, David Banner! The mild-mannered genius who develops the machine that creates the monster in the first place. It was the best Hulk series ever made. It had a great soundtrack too. Every episode was bittersweet. Banner always ended up by himself, walking away but going nowhere. He never found any real peace.'

Sean's face reflected the sadness he felt remembering the image of the lonely and isolated David Banner. Emily noticed and quickly moved on. She couldn't allow him to slip out of the interaction and into a melancholy state.

'Well, if you think about it, Sean, the Hulk is a great example of how anger can transform us into something unbecoming. David Banner's hurtful past was instrumental in making him into the angry force that changed him from being someone kind and caring into someone who lashed out at everyone around him. To give him credit, he often verbalised a warning to his victims before he got past the point of no return. If only they'd listened to him when he'd told them . . .'

'Don't make me angry,' said Sean, once more finishing Emily's sentence, 'you wouldn't like me when I'm angry.'

Emily nodded, glad to see he had re-engaged.

'Yes, Sean, exactly right. But the one thing that stands out about him is that he tries not to hurt anyone, even though he knows he can, and will, if he loses his temper. He shows us how the beast within us can sometimes be tamed.'

'I hear what you're saying,' said Sean. Sometimes I get angry. People can deal with it or just leave me the hell alone. Frankly, I don't give a shit.'

Emily sensed the barriers she had begun to lower, rising. She had to keep them down, bringing them to the point where what she was about to do would allow Sean to open up to her as never before. He was suffering from PTSD, attributable, in the main, to the accident that had killed his wife and children, but, as she had discovered since taking him on as a patient, there was more than one layer of trauma he had to deal with. It would take years of therapy to get to the root of all of them. All she could do for now was, to a degree, psychological triage.

'Anger is normal, Sean, you're right, but uncontrolled anger is so destructive. Anger is, at its base, an energy that expresses itself in and through the body. We've talked about your anger management strategies; learning to recognise the signs you're becoming upset and taking action to calm down, dealing with the situation in a productive way, like visualising the clock-face in the train station when you feel a panic attack coming on.'

'I know all this,' snapped Sean, 'you've told me a hundred bloody times, Professor. Anger management isn't about keeping me from feeling angry or encouraging me to hold it in. It's about confronting it. I get it. Look, I'm getting bored. Are we almost done?'

Sean could feel his chest tightening just talking about his panic attacks. They'd been coming, recently, with increased frequency, and one was on its way right now. He wanted to get up and walk out, but needed Emily to sign off on his treatment. He took a deep breath and let it out slowly. Emily watched him, pleased to see him using one of the techniques she'd taught him. She gave him a moment before continuing.

'One last thing, Sean. Remember I'll always be there if you need me. You have my mobile and home number, but I'll give you my new office number as well.'

She lifted her black leather rucksack onto her knees and reached into it, pulling out a matching business card case. She opened it and handed Sean one of her newly printed cards. Sean glanced at it, briefly, before putting it into the breast pocket of his jacket. He'd taken it more out of politeness than anything else. Emily reached back into her rucksack and glanced across at him. An odd look, Sean thought, as if she was hiding something from him. It piqued his interest. Exactly as Emily had known it would.

'Got a going away present for me, Professor?'

'In a way, Sean, yes. Two, actually. I brought them with me, especially for today. We can talk about one of them, or both, if you want to. Then you'll be happy to hear our sessions are over.'

'Show me then,' said Sean, not bothering to hide the irritation in his voice, 'you've got a plane to catch.'

'Okay.'

Time to open the door, thought Emily, and took deep breath.

She hadn't known if she would use either of the props she'd carried into the room, hidden in her rucksack. Sean had to come to terms with what had happened to his family, that was crucial, but he also had to confront another deeply traumatic incident from his past. Something so horrific she still struggled to believe it had happened to him. There were others, too, but they would be for another time.

'Come on, Professor, don't keep me in suspense.'

Sean smiled at her, unware Emily was about to wipe his smile away in the most brutal of ways.

Emily steeled herself. *I have to do this. Forgive me, Sean.*

She removed the two items from her rucksack, one at a time, placing them onto the glass table-top. She watched Sean's reaction, awaiting an eruption of anger or for him to get up and leave. She hoped neither would happen. It was a gamble, she realised, but she had to force him to face his fears instead of burying them in his subconscious mind, where they would fester like an infected wound, the mental pus corrupting every aspect of his life. This was a journey he had to take. One he had hidden from since it had happened. What she was showing him would hopefully begin that journey.

Emily's hand moved in slow motion, it seemed, to Sean. His breath checked and his hands began to tremble. His sight tunnelled to the point where he could see nothing, save for the two objects sitting on the table. He began to rock back and forth in his seat like an autistic child. A voice inside him screamed at him to look away. The voice that had always been there, protecting him from the bad things. The faraway voice was calling him to the empty place.

'Closed! Hidden! Safe! Closed! Hidden! Safe! Closed! Hidden! Safe!'

From somewhere else, another voice called to him.

'Sean! Can you hear me? Sean!'

He tried to listen to it, but the faraway voice was still screaming.

'Closed! Hidden! Safe! Closed! Hidden! Safe! Closed! Hidden! Safe!'

'Breathe, Sean. Breathe.'

He heard the other voice and his focus shifted. It was close to him. A gentle, loving voice that made him check the urge to follow the faraway voice to the empty place.

'Linz?'

'Breathe, Sean. Breathe.'

She answered him and he felt his heart begin to beat again.

'Linz,' he whispered, and drew a breath. 'Linz.' He said her name again and the faraway voice began to recede. 'Linz.' He said her name once more and the faraway voice was gone.

'Breathe, Sean. Breathe.'

'Linz! My love!'

She was with him. Just as she'd been with him on Gullane Beach, the day after the trial, when he'd almost followed the faraway voice to the empty place. As she'd been, earlier that morning, standing by the window after Judith had left. As she'd been, each night, recently, in his bedroom, watching over him. Making sure he was safe. Making him feel loved. As she had always done.

'Breathe, Sean. Breathe,' repeated Emily, watching him struggle with the enormity of what he was being forced to face.

The look of fear on his face was raw and palpable.

Emily had come face-to-face with the deep, mental anguish that only human beings can suffer. That indelible, invisible scarring of the heart and soul that remains from unresolved trauma. Living below the surface of the psyche like a burrowing tick, feeding on the host at will, at times, manifesting into physical form. The manifestation she was seeing now was shocking. It was a sight she knew she would not forget.

Sean's vision had blurred in the mist of blindness that can come with sudden shock or high anxiety, but, slowly, as he listened to Linz's voice and breathed, it began to return. He looked around, frantically, seeking sight of her. But she wasn't there.

'Linz?'

He looked across at Emily, as if she had some answer that he might understand.

'I'm here, Sean. You're okay. Just breathe.' She pointed at the table. 'Look at them,' she said, gently but firmly.

Sean looked down at what Emily had placed in front of him. One was a small, pale-pink, teddy bear, the other, a wire coat hanger, the kind you get back when you take your clothes to a dry-cleaning shop. The hanger had been crushed and twisted around itself to form a single, thicker strand, the hook part crudely folded around its centre.

'Take *that* away,' he whispered, pointing at the hanger, 'please, Emily, take it away.'

Emily returned the twisted wire to her rucksack, relieved they did not have to talk about it, at least, not today. She wasn't ready for that session. Nor was Sean. She hadn't realised how savage the memory it would invoke would be. With the coat hanger back in her rucksack, she reached out and took the teddy bear in her hand, offering it to Sean. He reacted as if she had held out a writhing, black-mamba snake, instead of a harmless child's toy.

'You know this little bear, don't you, Sean?' Sean nodded, although his face was a mask of despair. Emily pressed on. 'Take it.'

'No!' Sean whispered. 'Please.'

Whimpering like a frightened child, he pulled his legs up against his abdomen and wrapped his arms around his shins, then put his forehead on his knees, hiding his face.

It was, Emily knew, an instinctual reaction to extreme stress or trauma, when the brain was no longer able to cope with the surrounding environment and, in essence, could shut down temporarily. She had to stop him from reaching that point. She raised her voice and firmed her tone.

'Sean! Look at me!'

Sean lifted his head off his knees and met her eyes.

'Please! Don't make me.'

'Take the bear, Sean,' Emily demanded. She reached further across the table, shaking it from side to side in front of him, her voice louder and more insistent. 'Take it! Right now! Talk to me, Sean! Tell me about that day!'

Sean kept his eyes on hers, not wanting to look at the bear.

'Emily. Please.'

The look of pain in his eyes and the childlike regression almost broke Emily's resolve. But she was unyielding.

'You were in Applecross, on holiday, with Linz and Toby and Alice. Weren't you?'

Emily saw his eyes flick to the bear and the pain that look had brought him. Her heart ached for him. She was breaking him open, she could see that, but he had to be broken if he was to be mended. If mending him was even possible.

'Take it!' Emily raised her voice again and saw him start. 'Now!'

Sean reached out and touched the bear. Its fur was warm and soft, as it had been when he had last touched it. He took it in his hand and draw it to him, holding it against his chest before resting it on his knees. He looked down at its face. And remembered.

'Pookie.' Sean spoke so softly Emily wasn't sure he had. 'His name is Pookie.'

And the tears finally came.

Sean's body shook as his whimpers became sobs. Raking sobs that brought tears to Emily's own eyes, but then, slowly, ever so slowly, the emotional door he had held so tightly closed, for so long, swung open, and Sean stepped though.

'Tell me about him, Sean,' whispered Emily, matching his quietness, 'tell me about Pookie.'

Sean began to talk, his knees still drawn up, clutching the raggedy, pink bear, the memories flooding his mind becoming words, the words forming tumbling sentences, his voice a trembling whisper in the storm of emotions engulfing him.

'Applecross, and the sea was so blue that morning . . .'

6

Applecross, and the sea was so blue that morning it seemed as if a little part of the Indian ocean had lost its way, caught in a gulf-stream that had carried it to that idyllic little bay on the west coast of Scotland. The shallow waters shimmered in the early afternoon sun, and wavy ripples of golden sand lay like sleeping water-snakes below the surface. Despite being late May and this part of the Scottish Highlands famed for its temperamental weather, the midday sun was doing its best to match the Seychelles-like bay water. The temperature was a glorious twenty-two degrees and the sea was flat and calm, the earlier breeze having disappeared like a wistful highland stag.

'Faster Daddy, faster,' cried Alice, urging Sean to drive their tandem kayak through the water at Olympian speeds, 'Mummy and Toby are winning.'

'Going as fast as I can, Princess.'

Sean spluttered as the mistimed stroke of his daughter's paddle-blade sent another explosion of salty sparkles into the air behind her, showering him. He laughed at her efforts but was proud of her desire to be first. It was a trait they shared. Off to his right, Linz and Toby were paddling in almost perfect unison, pushing their kayak through the water with ease. They had drawn slightly ahead, on the same course, angling out into the centre of the bay.

He turned his gaze south, looking over the whitewashed cottages of Applecross village, to a faded rise of rounded mountains behind them.

'Look, Princess, aren't they beautiful? We'll be crossing them again, later today.'

Alice swivelled around in her cockpit to look directly at her father, her paddle waving around like a mad conductor's baton.

'They are, Daddy. 'Maybe I'll see a fairy, this time?'

Sean had, earlier that week, told Alice that the high road over the mountains was a magical pass, alive with fairies that came out each night and danced through until dawn the next day. She'd had been annoyed that, after being woken so early, that morning, to get to Applecross from their hotel on Skye, the road had been shrouded in mist, foiling any chance of spotting a real, live fairy.

'I think we might, Princess.'

Sean's answer, by the look on Alice's face, was the correct one.

He lost his heart in her smile, wondering for the millionth time how he'd had a hand in creating something so perfect. Her skin was smooth as an alabaster bust, but a natural olive-brown, something she'd inherited from her mother, who could go nut-brown just by opening an exotic travel magazine, and her eyes shone like sapphires. Sean felt his chest swell with the love that only a father who has been blessed with a daughter could ever really understand.

'Daddy. Can we go on a fairy hunt, tomorrow?'

'Whatever you want, Princess. It's your birthday we're here for.'

He heard his mother's voice in his head. *That little madam has you wrapped around her little finger.*

'I'm seven today, Daddy. Can you believe I'm so old?'

'No, Princess, I can't,' replied Sean, fighting the choke in his voice.

He was happy to receive another soaking from Alice's wayward paddle, which hid the tears forming at the corners of his eyes. He wiped them away on the back of his hand wondering when he'd become so sentimental. *The day you first held her*, he told himself.

Alice, sensing she had his undivided attention, spoke again, the race against her mother and brother seemingly forgotten.

'Are you alright, Daddy?'

'Fine and dandy, Princess. Just some seawater in my eyes.'

Alice opened her eyes even wider and tilted her head, looking up at him from under long, curling eyelashes.

'Daddy. Do you think I'm old enough to have a mobile phone? My best friend at school, Lori Klien, has one. Her daddy bought her one for her birthday. She's seven, just like me. I think he likes to talk to her when he's away on business. Just like you are a lot of the time.'

Sean's surprise was momentary, but he suddenly realised what was happening. *Damn it if she's not playing me! That's her mother's look and subtle reasoning. For the love of God, how early do they learn? He* considered his reply, trying to remain as serious as his daughter obviously was.

'Has she now, Princess? Well, I suppose if Lori Klien has one then so should, just in case you *do* need to call me when I'm away.'

'Good idea, Daddy.'

Alice gave him a butter wouldn't melt smile and turned back to focus on a race that was all but over, the victory she had sought firmly won.

'But I think you should ask mum, don't you?'

Sean saw his daughter's shoulders stiffen. Asking her mother was clearly not something Alice had wanted to do. She swivelled back around and gave Sean a smile an angel would have envied,

'Perhaps, Daddy, you should ask Mummy. You're the boss of the house, aren't you?'

Sean barely stifled his laugh. It was over. Alice had won. A mobile phone was now firmly on the birthday presents list.

'Absolutely, Princess, I'm the boss. Now, let's catch Mum and Toby up before they win the race.'

Alice looked at him with pity in her eyes.

'It's not a real race, Daddy, you big silly.'

Sean reached up and touched the silver crucifix hung his neck, a present from Linz, given to him the day they had been married. *Dear God, help me out? I'm not sure I can do it without you, once she's a teenager. Strike that, I think I need your guidance from here on in.*

Ten minutes later, the two kayaks came level in the centre of the bay, bobbing gently about twenty meters apart, now just over a kilometer out from where they'd entered the water, on the beach, opposite the Applecross Inn

'Dad,' Toby called over, 'we've seen loads of fish swimming below us. I'm going in to catch one.'

'With what?' Sean replied, smiling broadly.

Toby shrugged and laughed. It seemed he hadn't thought that far ahead.

Sean felt a fierce stab of pride at the sight of his son. While he looked like a younger version of Sean, a shock of unruly blonde hair topped a strong, well-defined face, with cheekbones any model would be envious of. He had his mother's prominent Roman nose, which even at twelve years of age dominated his face, and her eyes, marine-green with flecks of hazel sprinkled throughout.

Sean called over to his wife, Linz, sitting in the kayak cockpit behind Toby.

'Enjoy that, my love?'

'Toby did most of the work, to be honest, hun.'

She gave Sean the same smile she'd given him the first time they'd met. It had melted him then, and did so, now. He wondered why it took days like this for him to remember how much he truly loved her.

Linz had the same elfin-shaped face that Alice had inherited from her, with almond-shaped, green eyes and a prominent nose. Sean had, on their first proper date, likened her to a Saluki, the ancient hunting hounds of Middle-Eastern kings. The compliment, as he'd intended it to be, hadn't really worked, despite he thought the dogs beautiful and hadn't understood what he'd said wrong. Linz had explained it to him so that he did. They'd still had a second date.

Today, her mane of long, blonde hair was tied up in a ponytail, using a powder-blue scarf that set off a tan that had deepened, it seemed, even since that morning. She seemed to be glowing, as salt-crystals from the sea spray, dried on her skin, caught the sunlight bouncing off the waves, making it look as if she had been sprinkled in gold glitter. She was beautiful, in every sense of the word, a gentle spirit who sparkled for all the world to see. Loved by all for those traits and attributes Sean wished he had been blessed with in such abundance. That she was better for him than he was for her was a given. She made him feel safe and loved in a world he had never felt part of. A love, at times, he'd taken for granted.

'Dad!'

Toby's cry snapped Sean's mind back to the present. The boy had a look of fear on his face he could not, at first, understand.

'What's wrong, son?'

Toby pointed dead ahead of the kayaks. Sean immediately saw what had frightened him. About two hundred meters out, cutting into the bay from the open ocean and heading directly towards them, were two massive dorsal fins.

'Sharks! They're just basking sharks.'

'Are you sure, Dad? They're not great whites?'

'I'm sure, son. Relax! You've clearly watched Jaws.'

Toby smiled, not taking his eyes off the oncoming fins.

'Are they going to eat us, Daddy?' Alice asked, looking back at Sean without any sign of fear.

'No, Princess, they don't eat people. Just plankton and fish-eggs and krill. I think we're going to be fine.'

Alice screwed up her face and tilted her head in quizzical fashion.

'What's a krill?'

'It's a sort of tiny prawn.' Sean tried to turn his daughter's attention back to the sharks as another question formed on her lips. This line of questioning could go on indefinitely once it started. 'We need to be quite quiet, Princess, or we'll scare them off.'

'Okay, Daddy,' Alice whispered, and looked back towards the sharks.

The sharks were moving through the water on a course that would take them between the kayaks. As they got closer, Linz called across at Sean.

'I knew they came here to feed, but I never thought we'd ever be lucky enough to see them.'

'They must have come to wish you happy birthday, Alice,' called Toby, his initial fear replaced with a sense of wonder at nature's drama being played out in front of him.

Sean reached out and stroked Alice's hair.

'They did. I booked them especially for you, Princess.'

'Daddy! You really are a big silly.'

Alice rolled her eyes, amazed at the stupidity of her father. Linz and Toby laughed at her exasperated expression.

'See what I have to put up with?' Sean cried, in mock indignation, then laughed with the rest of his family.

The sharks reached and passed between the kayaks. The white gape of their open mouths and gill slits on either side of their bodies were clear to see, as well as their oddly small and beady, black eyes. The largest of the fish came so close to Sean and Alice they could have reached out and touched it, sliding past them with silent grace, its body mottled and dappled like the sun dried lichens growing on the boulders on the shore. The other shark was shorter, but still longer than either of the kayaks. It passed Linz and Toby almost as closely.

They watched them feed for the next hour, following them in the kayaks, remaining at a sensible distance so as not to spook the gentle giants, although the sharks seemed ambivalent to their presence. It was an hour of shared joy and wonder; a family memory indelibly etched into their hearts and souls.

A couple of hours later, Alice's birthday party was in full swing on the beach opposite the Applecross Inn. Music blared from speakers set at each corner of an open-sided marquee, set up in the private beer garden overlooking the bay. The Spice Girls massive hit, *Wannabee*, had just been put on for the third time, at the insistence of Alice. It was her favourite song in the whole wide world, so she'd informed Sean.

A few of the household staff had come up from the family home, in Edinburgh, to help run the birthday party. Sean had booked all twelve of the Inn's rooms to house them, along with a few close family friends and their children, Linz's parents, Ian and Dorothy, and Sean's mother, Nana Anna, as she was affectionately called by Alice and Toby.

'Right, we've got lobsters, prawns, crab-claws, salmon-steaks, burgers, sausages, potato wedges and chips,' announced Sean, 'please tell me everyone's hungry?'

The cheer that followed told him they all were.

'Any chicken nuggets, Dad?' Toby asked, heading the line at the outside grill Sean and Linz's father were cooking on.

Sean did a double take at the sight of his son. His hair had been slicked back close to his head and it looked as if he was wearing black eye-liner. Combined with a black t-shirt with the name, "Slayer", written on it, and a pair of skinny-fit, black jeans and black training shoes, it gave him a slightly gothic look. Sean opened his mouth to pass a comment, but Linz, standing behind Toby, gave him a look he knew only too well. He and Linz had already had *that* conversation. It would not be a good move to require her to remind him of it. Besides, what the hell did he know about teenage fashion.

'Sorry son, will a cheeseburger do?'

Seemingly appeased, Toby grabbed a burger and headed back down to the beach.

'Well handled,' whispered Linz, piling her own plate obscenely high with grilled prawns then smothering them in tomato sauce. Sean shook his head in dismay.

'Really? Prawns and Ketchup! What a philistine.'

'It's how I like them, hun.'

She gave him a cheeky smile then followed Toby down to the beach.

She was bare-footed and wearing a flouncy, pale blue, summer dress that strained to contain her breasts and showed of her long, toned legs. Her hair was loose and tumbled over her shoulders and down her back in an avalanche of frizzy gold. Sean found himself staring at her as if seeing her again for the very first time.

'Crises averted,' said Ian, looking at his daughter and grandson with obvious pride. 'Of course, she's still too damned good for you.'

He punched Sean playfully on the arm. It was a contact that meant more to Sean than Ian could ever understand.

'I know that, Ian. Trust me, I really do.'

Ian had told Sean the very same thing at their first meeting; a black-tie, reunion dinner at Ian's former school, George Watsons Academy. Sean had got so drunk that he'd thrown-up on his future father-in-law's shoes. It had taken years for that particular *faux-pas* to be forgiven, if not forgotten. Fifteen years on, the reminders were now less frequent and spoken more in jest, reflecting the friendship he and Sean had created between them, forged by their common love of golf and sailing, as well as the three shining jewels in their lives.

'You're a good father,' said Ian, keeping his gaze rigidly fixed on the beach, as if embarrassed to speak so openly. 'I know how much you love them.'

'Thanks, Ian. I do.'

'I know things have been a bit strained between you and Linz, recently, what with the expansion plans for the business and all, but it's the same in every marriage. There are good times as well as bad. But you'll always find your way back to each other, no matter how far apart you drift.'

Linz had obviously spoken to her father about the rough patch they were going through. Instead of being angry, Sean found he was relieved. He knew it had taken a lot for Ian to say what he'd said. For a fleeting moment, he wanted to hug him, but it wasn't either of their ways, and a father's hugs were not something Sean had ever known. A call from up by the Inn took their attention and the moment passed.

Waving at them from the front door of the Inn were Nana Anna and Ian's wife, Dorothy, beckoning one of them, or perhaps both, to come and help with something.

'I best go see what they want,' said Ian, resignedly, 'before they descend on us both.'

He took off his striped chef's apron and handed Sean his serving tongs. Sean stepped aside to allow him out of the serving area, offering a word of advice.

'Don't show any fear, and don't, whatever you do, say it's not your fault, whatever the problem is.'

They both laughed. The line might have been one smothered in dust, but it was *their* dust.

'I'm going out now, Sean. I may be some time.'

Ian smiled, creasing his weather-browned face, and ran a hand through his still-thick head of silver-grey hair, then like an old-time movie-star going out into some desperate last stand, headed up towards the Inn. Sean felt his heart swell. He loved his father-in-law more than he'd ever loved any other man. He was the only father figure he had ever really known. The only man he wished he could be more like. He wished he could tell him that.

The rest of the afternoon passed in blissful sunshine, music and laughter, with everyone, including some of the local children and parents, joining in the festivities. Sean had hired six ponies from a local trekking centre, and rides along the sandy bay were in much demand. At five o'clock, everyone gathered around one of the wooden tables and Alice's special birthday cake was presented. It took two waiters to carry it out, balanced carefully on a large platter. It was a vision in indulgence; a tall, chocolate cake layered with whipped cream, fresh strawberries and strawberry jam, smothered in chocolate sauce that ran down its sides, forming glossy puddles around its base. Seven white candles on the top of the cake, already lit, awaited Alice's attention.

'It's a spoon cake,' cried Alice, unable to hide her excitement. 'Did you make it, Mummy?'

Linz took Alice's face in her hands and gave her a kiss on the forehead.

'Of course, sweetie, it's what you wanted, isn't it?'

'Apart from my new mobile phone, it's the bestest birthday present I could have wished for.'

'A new mobile phone!' Linz's voice did little to hide her surprise. 'My goodness, aren't you a lucky girl.'

She shot a glance at Sean who shrugged and looked back at her as with an expression that said, *I've no idea what she's talking about.* Standing behind Linz, Nana Anna raised a curled pinkie and smiled.

'Right around her little finger.'

'Shut up, old woman, or there's no cake for you,' said Sean, jokingly, knowing full well his mother was right. There was nothing he could deny his daughter. It would, he suspected, ever be so.

'One, two, three . . .blow.'

Alice blew out the candles and Applecross Bay came alive with voices belting out *Happy Birthday to You.*

'Everyone grab a spoon and tuck in,' called Linz.

The resulting melee of jousting spoons, appreciative groans and raucous laughter, at the chaos of eating the cake right off the platter, was one of the party highlights.

The sound of a powerful engine and the crunch of tyres on the gravel road above them took Sean's attention. The car pulled to a stop and was immediately surrounded by locals, who had never seen an Aston Martin Vantage in real life. The luxury sports car was painted glossy maroon and was a study in sleek. Similar, thought Sean, to the man driving it.

Alice rushed towards the car as the driver's door opened and the six-foot frame of Hublot Broussard, QuantumCloud's Operations Director, stepped out. He smiled at her, displaying a set of ivory-white teeth so perfect that only an American dentist could have created them. He wore a fitted, white-silk shirt, open at the neck, which emphasised the athletic build of his daily-honed body, and his shaven head shone ebony black in the sunshine.

'Uncle Hub!'

'Birthday girl!'

Hublot swept Alice up in his arms. She wrapped her arms around his neck and kissed him on the cheek.

'What are you doing here, Uncle Hub?'

'I heard it was your birthday, sweetie, so I came to bring you this.'

Hublot pulled a small but beautifully wrapped present from his trouser pocket. Alice looked back at Sean.

'Please may I open it now, Daddy? I know we've not done the birthday presents yet. But just this one. Please?'

'Go ahead, Princess.'

Sean mouthed a thanks to Hublot and watched his daughter rip the yellow wrapping-paper to pieces.

'Oh, Uncle Hub, I love it. It's exactly what I wanted?'

Alice wrapped her arms, even more tightly, around his neck, hugging him as hard as she could.

'It's a pleasure, sweetie,' said Hublot, touched by the joy in Alice's face. He lifted her into the air above his head and laughed with her. 'I love that you love it.'

He lowered her to the ground and she ran to Sean, holding the present up for him to inspect.

'Look Daddy. It's a case for my new iPhone. Isn't it beautiful?'

'It is, Princess,' replied Sean, realising he had been played.'

The case was a white and green, tropical, palm-print design with the letters "AJ" monogrammed onto it in a bold, black font. It was designed by a company synonymous with the singer, Victoria Beckham, Alice's ultimate style icon.

'It's even got my name on it, Daddy. AJ, for Alice Jameson.'

'It's really lovely, Princess. Why don't you go and show mummy what Uncle Hub gave you. Be sure to tell her it was his idea. She'll be so pleased with him.'

'You are very smart, Uncle Hub,' said Alice, innocently, then ran off to show her mother the special present.

Sean looked at Hublot with much the same look at Linz had given him earlier. Hublot, sensing something was not quite right, defended himself.

'She told me you were getting her an iPhone, man. Said she'd need a cover for it. Told me all about that crazy girl band she loves. Did I screw up?'

Sean laughed and shook his head.

'Not at all, Hub,' said Sean, watching Linz's reaction as Alice bounced up and down in front of her, showing off her present. 'She's just way too smart for us both.' There was, he knew, no way they could refuse her the precious iPhone now. As if to confirm his thoughts, Linz looked across at him and shrugged her shoulders and mouthed the word, *okay*. 'I think we're probably looking at QuantumCloud's future boss.'

'Could do worse, man. She's clearly able to manipulate us all with not much effort. Any idea who she takes that from?'

'I'd say me, but I think it's her mother.'

'I meant you,' said Hublot, 'but I guess you're right.'

'Anyway, what are you doing here?' Sean asked, accepting the bear hug as Hublot encircled him with his massive arms.

'It's good to see you too, bro,' Hublot replied, in a baritone voice that sounded as if he smoked far too many cigars for his own good, when in fact he was a health freak and had never smoked in his life.

'You know what I mean.'

Hublot became serious for a moment.

'Look, I'm sorry to intrude, but you said if I was able to get away then to come on up. So I did. To be honest, there's a situation with the production line in Beijing we need to discuss. So it seemed there were two good reasons for us to make the journey.'

'Us?'

'Hello, Sean.'

Sean turned and stared into the eyes of QuantumCloud's senior lawyer, Judith Sutherland. His reaction at seeing her and the look that passed between them went unnoticed by Hublot.

'Jude, glad you could make it,' said Sean, regaining his composure, 'I've not seen you since Rome. Come say hello to Linz and the kids. Well, say hello to everyone, why don't you?'

He hugged her and kissed her on both cheeks, trying to act as naturally as possible, then took her arm and led her down, along with Hublot, towards the marquee.

'Hub! Judith! Linz exclaimed, on seeing them. 'I'm so glad you could make it.'

'Linz, you look beautiful,' said Judith, hugging her, 'very hippy-chic in that sexy, little beach-dress.'

'Whereas you're still more Armani,' replied Linz, admiring Judith's figure-hugging, cream, silk dress and matching ankle-boots. 'You can take the girl out of Edinburgh, but you can't take Edinburgh out of the girl.' She turned to Hub. 'Thanks for buying Alice the iPhone case. I don't think we can hold off that bit of tech from her any longer.'

'I guess not, girl,' said Hublot, kissing Linz on both cheeks before sweeping her off her feet in a hug that had her beating him off, laughing and gasping for breath.

'Well, you've made her happy, so, as her mother, thank you. I know who else will be happy to see you. Brandy's with the kids, on the beach. She told me you couldn't make it.'

Hub looked down the beach, hoping to see his wife and kids. He spotted them playing frisbee. They clearly hadn't seen him arrive.

'It's not that I didn't want to be here, Linz. She was furious when I told her I was going to miss it. They all were. But it was Sean or me who had to stay behind and hold the fort. The merger, you know?'

Linz held her hands up in front of her and shook her head.

'Don't mention it, Hub, I'm sick of hearing about it. I've barely seen Sean in months. In fact, I think you've both spent more time with him than me.'

She looked at Judith, who nodded in agreement.

'Brandy said the same thing,' said Hub, 'we've all not been home enough. But it's almost done. Anyway, as it turned out, we both ended up here anyway. Maybe she'll talk to me again.'

'You'll be their hero, Hub, no doubt,' said Linz, 'now go and find them and start groveling.'

She hugged him again and let him head off, then turned back to Judith.

'Right, girlfriend, tell me all about Rome. Was it all work and no play, or did my workaholic husband give you some time off for yourself?'

'Yes,' said Judith, hesitantly, 'we . . . I had a little time to look around.'

Linz steered her towards the bar, not noticing her awkwardness.

'So, did you meet a rich count? Or a handsome Italian Prince?'

Judith looked across the marquee to where Sean was standing chatting to Hublot.

'Not really, Linz. I'm not on the market, right now.'

Linz raised an eyebrow.

'Not on the market? Judith! Have you met someone? Or are you ill? Rome! Sunshine! Chianti! Swarthy Latin men! And you're too busy for *that*.'

Judith gave a thin laugh.

'No. It's nothing like that. As Hublot said, we're all too busy with the merger.'

'No shop today, girlfriend,' said Linz, looking across at Sean and blowing him a kiss. Sean raised a hand to catch it and blew one back. 'Let's grab some Champagne and have a good old catch up.'

She led Judith towards the bar, leaving Sean watching after them, intently.

'Sorry Sean,' said Hublot, mistaking the look on Sean's face for one of irritation at his turning up with a problem, 'but I thought you'd want to deal with this yourself.'

'For God's sake, Hub, could you not just have sorted it out yourself? I'm on fucking holiday.'

'That's your call to make,' said Hub, trying not to sound irritated, 'I'm just the messenger.'

'I know, Hub. I know. Sorry. But I'm just back from a week in Rome.'

Hublot put his an around Sean's shoulders.

'Look, let me set up a video call with Kim Jang-Yun, for tomorrow morning, and see if we can work something out from here. If not, I'll head back to Edinburgh and take the first flight out.'

Sean seemed pacified.

'Okay, that sounds like a workable option. But, right now, it's presents time for Alice, and that waits for no man.'

'Agreed,' said Hub, 'and if it's cool with you, I've got a second surprise for her I just know she's going to love.'

'What?' Sean asked, seeing the twinkle in Hublot's eyes.

'I've got three brand new iPhones in the trunk, sorry, in the boot of the car, for some new starts, back at the office. Why don't you and Linz give her one, now, then she can put her new phone cover on it. She'll love you forever and a day.'

'Let me check with Linz, Hub. Somehow it seems to be all my fault we have to give her a phone at all. I'm not entirely sure why?'

Hublot shrugged his shoulders and laughed.

'You're a guy. It's always our fault. At least that's what Brandy always tells me. Check away, I'll go get one, just in case.'

Hublot strode off to his car, while Sean made his way to the marquee bar to speak with Linz, who was chatting and laughing with her parents and Judith.

Sean gave Hublot a thumbs up and Linz flashed him a smile as he rejoined them, phone in hand, helping himself to an ice-cold, alcohol-free beer which he drained in one long draught. He passed the phone to Linz and went off to find his wife and children on the beach.

'I hear you've giving in on the phone.'

Ian looked at Sean and smiled at his daughter. Linz had obviously enjoyed relaying the events surrounding it to her father.

'Seems best for everyone, Ian. But, in my defence, I was coerced and manipulated by intellects far superior to mine.'

Ian raised his glass.

'Women! The smarter sex at every age.'

'We'll drink to that,' said Judith and Linz, clinking their champagne flutes together.

By the time Alice had unwrapped her mountain of presents she was almost apoplectic. She'd been spoiled by Ian and Dorothy, who had bought her a new snowboard and bindings, and collected over two hundred pounds in cash from the birthday cards she'd been given. Nana Anna had given her a drone, which she could use to film herself snowboarding with, in Norway, later that year. Toby was currently flying it out over the bay, looking for the basking sharks.

'This one's from me and mum, Princess,' said Sean, holding hands with Linz.

He handed Alice a small box, wrapped in the same canary-yellow paper that Hublot had wrapped her iPhone case.

'It's something you've wanted for ages,' Linz added, excited to see her daughter's response.

The squeals of delight that filled the air, once the present had been unwrapped, reflected the joy it had given. Alice hugged both her parents, an arm around each of their necks, planting kiss after kiss on their cheeks.

Ceremony over, the music restarted. Hublot took Linz by the hand and dragged her into the centre of the marquee, where they led the dancing, bopping along to *Love me Do*. Sean watched the throng of happy revellers under the fading light of the day, the dance floor lit up by banks of coloured lights blinking and flashing in time with the music. He danced with Alice, feeling at peace with the world, waving to Toby, who had finally plucked up the courage to dance with one of the local girls.

'Princess, have you had a good birthday?'

'It's been fabutastical, Daddy,' said Alice; using the best word she could think of to describe her feelings about the day. 'The bestest birthday of all my birthdays ever.'

'The bestest of all of them all! That good?'

'Yes,' said Alice, looking deadly serious. 'I got my iPhone, so now we can talk anytime you want. Except when I'm at school, of course.'

'Of course,' Sean agreed, equally as seriously as his daughter.

'I've got one more present for you, Princess.'

'Have you?'

Alice's face lit up.

'It's a special one. Just from me to you. Do you want it now?'

'Of course I do, Daddy, you big silly.'

'So! I'm still a big silly, am I?'

'You are Daddy. A big silly.'

Alice laughed at the rebuke. The same rebuke she gave Sean time and again. Their own personal joke that never waned and never would.

Sean set her down and went to fetch a small package that had been hidden away behind the bar. He returned and led her to a quiet table at the edge of the marquee, handed it to her and watched her unwrap it.

'Oh, Daddy,' he's so beautiful,' said Alice, clutching the pale-pink, teddy bear to her chest.

'I know you have lots of them at home, Princess, but this one came all the way from Rome. From a special shop that sells special bears.'

'I love him, Daddy, I really do.' Alice kissed the bear on its rounded snout. 'He's so smiley and soft and pink.'

'What are you going to call him?'

Alice looked pensive for a moment, then smiled as the name came to her.

'Pookie! I'm going to call him, Pookie.'

The dancing continued for another hour or so before Linz made signs to Sean that they should be heading back to their hotel, on Skye. Alice and Toby were both tired from a long day that had been filled with excitement.

'I'll get them ready to go and say a few goodbyes,' said Linz, 'then we can head back to the hotel and get them straight into bed. I'll be back to have the last dance with you in about twenty minutes, if you still have the energy, that is?'

'Absolutely, my love. Shinedown, I take it? *Follow You Down?*

'Our favourite song, hun, what else?'

Sean leaned in and kissed her on the lips. Linz returned the kiss and he pulled her to him. They held onto one other, conscious of their bodies melding together in the way that familiar lovers sometimes forget they once did. Their eyes met and they connected, the distance that had developed between them over the past year receding.

'I've missed you, my love.'

'Me too, hun,' whispered Linz, 'now let me go.' She planted a farewell kiss on his lips and wriggled free of his embrace. 'I'll get the kids ready. Make sure you save me that dance.'

Sean let her go, reluctant to break the emotionally charged moment. He'd missed the feeling of togetherness and the warmth of her love for him. He wasn't good on his own, feeling lost and abandoned without the all-encapsulating love of her. He was only too aware that when she wasn't with him he began to fall apart.

A thick coil of guilt unwrapped itself in his stomach and bit into his gut. He thought of his time in Rome, with Judith, little more than a month ago, and was filled with regret. Linz had to know about it. He needed to tell her, despite the pain she would have to endure would be overwhelming. But he no longer wanted to be the man he had been shaped into.

He and Linz had to talk. Really talk. But that had always been his problem. Talking meant opening himself up to things he'd kept hidden away, buried in a place inside himself. It was all he had ever known. He had been brought up in an environment that was anything but loving, hiding everything, feeling nothing, lying to stay safe. It was how he had learned to survive. But no more, Sean told himself. No more hiding and no more lies. No more running away from his emotions. He couldn't risk losing Linz. He knew he could not live without her. Nor would he want to. He resolved to fix things between them.

And with himself. To do that, he had to go back to Harley Street. He had to finish what he'd started with Jenny Pearce!

Feeling better than he'd done in a long time, he headed up to the Inn and went into the upstairs bathroom, locking the door behind him. From his jean's pocket he took a small, paper wrap, opened it, and stared at the sparkling white crystals, shining like promises, promising nothing. A moment or so later, he headed outside, bumping into Judith at the front door. She was standing by herself, watching the party, still in full swing in the garden below.

'A sunny day and a starry night,' she whispered, huskily.

Sean knew she referring to an afternoon they had spent, together, on the terracotta porch of Sloppy Sam's bar, in the market square of the Piazza Campo De Fiori. A busker with a slightly out-of-tune guitar had played the song, *Vincent*, repeatedly, until Sean had offered him a handful of euros that would keep the young man in cigarettes and wine for at least a week, to move on.

'It's been great, Jude,' said Sean, not wanting to acknowledge the reference.

'Linz seems happy.'

'She is, I think.'

'Of course she's happy, Sean. Why wouldn't she be? It's her daughter's birthday and she's on holiday in one of the most beautiful places in the world. And she has you!'

She took hold of Sean's hand, looking around to make sure no-one was watching them. They stood in silence, for a moment, before he broke the contact.

'It's over, Jude.'

'I know that, Sean. I just wish it wasn't.'

Sean looked down at the dancefloor, wondering where Linz was. He wanted to dance with her. He didn't know what Judith wanted to hear. It wasn't what he said next.

'It never really started.'

'It did for me.'

'You know what I mean, Jude. It could never have gone anywhere. I have the children. And Linz. I love her. I really do. We were a . . .'

'Don't say it, Sean.' Judith cut in. She stared down at the cold, stone road, wishing it were a river of quicksand she could step into and disappear. 'Please don't say it was a mistake. I can't think of us like that.'

'There is no us, Jude. There never was. There was only Rome.'

They stood in silence for a moment before Judith was composed enough to speak.

'One last dance, Sean? One final goodbye, if goodbye this is?'

Her voice was small and sad. Sean found difficult to hear. It was his fault they were in this position. He had hurt her, irrespective if he had meant to or not. Why keep hurting her? At the very moment he was going to refuse, as if the Universe had heard her and sympathised, the opening bars of the Elton John song, *Everybody Falls in Love Sometimes*, filled the air.

'Why not, Jude? Why not?'

He took her hand and led her down to the marquee dancefloor.

Standing behind the partially closed front door of the Inn, Linz watched them walk away. She'd heard little of the conversation, but had seen Judith take Sean's hand in hers. The touch had been more than just friends holding hands. It did not take words to explain what she already knew. The scream inside her was silent, but the world around her trembled.

7

The notorious "Road of the Cows", in Scots Gaelic, the *Bealach na Bà*, is a winding, single-track road built in the year 1822. Engineered in the same way as the great mountain passes of the Swiss Alps, with hairpin bends and viscously steep gradients that seem almost impossible to take on, it boasts the steepest ascent of any road climb in the whole of Scotland. In winter, it is impassable, while for the rest of the year motorists are urged to proceed with extreme caution.

The black Range Rover eased up and into the first of a hundred sharp bends on the mountain pass between the villages of Applecross and Torridon. This was the shallow side of the mountain and the easier to navigate. On the steeper side, the narrow, tarmac road dropped sharply down into the darkness of the glen, over two-thousand feet below.

'Not so fast, Sean,' snapped Linz, turning to check Toby and Alice had their seat belts fastened. Alice was playing with her new phone, holding it to her ear and then to Pookie's, allowing him to take part in the conversation. 'Who are you talking to, my angel?'

'Well,' said Alice, thoughtfully, 'I thought I'd introduce Pookie to Mr Benjamin, Jim-Jam and Spangle. They're all excited to meet him.'

She was talking about some of the other bears in her collection, at home. Toby sniggered.

'They're not real, you know, Ally-Bally.'

'Then how are they talking to Pookie, smarty pants?'

'They're not.'

Alice shook her head at him and held Pookie out towards him.

'Perhaps you should tell Pookie that.'

Toby leaned across and whispered in the teddy bear's ear.

'They're not really talking to you, Pookie.'

'So why are you talking to Pookie, if he's not real, *Tob*ias?'

'Don't call me that,' snapped Toby. Seeing the look his mother was giving him, he acquiesced. 'Alright, if it means that much to you, *Ally Bally*, Pookie *is* real. And the bears at home ***can*** hear him.'

'Thank you, Toby.'

Alice held out Pookie's paw for Toby to shake.

'I'm Sorry, Pookie,' said Toby, taking the outstretched paw.

Peace returned, Linz sat back in her seat, smiling at the sound of her children chatting behind her. Sean reached out to take her hand. She held it, for a moment, then let it go.

'Anything wrong, my love?' Sean asked.

'No. Not really.'

Sean knew better. *Not really,* combined with the tone, was a dead giveaway.

He glanced out of his window at the spectacular view unfolding across Wester Ross. The shadowy outlines of the islands of Skye, Rhum and Raasay were clearly visible. The sun was sinking below the horizon, casting rays of orange fire across the ocean, an indigo sky, following it, descending with the swiftness of a theatre curtain at the end of a dramatic performance.

'Look, guys.'

Sean brought the car to a stop at the top of the mountain pass, allowing them to enjoy the incredible view and the end of what had been an unforgettable day. Darkness shrouded the peninsula. The moon was half-full and low in the sky, though it cast enough light for the shadows of the surrounding mountains to reach out across the *Bealach na Bà* like slumbering giants.

Sean started the descent, heading down towards the pinpricks of orange coming from the village of Torridon. The road became a line of dull silver as it snaked down the mountainside, but the powerful headlights of the Range Rover allowed him to descend quickly.

'It's not a race, Sean.'

The irritation in Linz's voice was clear.

'It's fine, Linz, relax. It's a bendy road but we'll . . .'

'And you've been drinking.'

Sean tutted, drawing a frown from her. She was clearly angry at something. He wished he could figure it out. Only half an hour ago they'd been pressed against each other and making the first real connection they'd made in a long time.

'Hardly at all, my love. No more than four or five ciders throughout the entire day.'

'Anything else?'

'No!'

Sean knew exactly what she'd meant, but he'd poured the cocaine into the sink in the Applecross Inn bathroom without touching it, deciding that, if he really wanted to change, he had to start right there and then.

'Look, Daddy, I'm recording,' said Alice, leaning forward and holding her new phone up in the space between Sean and Linz, videoing the view from the car as it descended.

'So you are, Princess. But it's a bit dark to see much?'

'But it's the *Fairy Road*, Daddy, and fairies glow in the dark, don't they?'

Sean smiled at the innocence of his daughter. She still believed in fairies, Santa Claus, and that her bears were real. It was an innocence, he knew, that would soon be lost.

'They do indeed, Princess.'

He smiled across at Linz, hoping for some glimmer of connection. He got what he wanted, just not the way he had expected.

'Judith looked good, today, didn't she?'

Linz's voice was much less warm than it had been in Applecross.

'I suppose she did,' replied Sean, aware the disconnect between them had returned. Worried at exactly why.

'Perhaps a little overdressed for a beach party, but still beautiful. Don't you think she looked especially beautiful?'

'Look, Mummy,' said Alice, 'Pookie's recording all by himself?'

Alice was holding her phone between Pookie's paws, still leaning forward to video any fairies that might appear.

'Sit back, sweetie,' said Linz.

'Sit down, Alice,' Toby added, irritated at his sister.

Alice sat back, clearly unamused at being asked to do so. Linz turned her attention back to Sean.

'Well, didn't she?'

'Didn't she what?'

Sean knew full well what she meant. But he had the first inklings that something was wrong.

'Didn't she look especially beautiful?'

'I suppose she did, Linz. She's a beautiful woman. You've said it yourself often enough yourself.'

Linz was staring at him. Sean felt her studying his face. She kept picking at the thread.

'Or course, women always look their best when they're in love, don't you find?'

The question was loaded. Sean did his best to avoid a direct answer. He was wondering what had happened to cause Linz to pick this line of questioning. A horrible thought came into his head. *Had Judith told her about Rome?*

'I've never really thought about it, to be honest.'

'Do you find her attractive?'

Sean's senses told him that this was a conversation that could only end badly. He didn't want to have it, but he knew it was one he couldn't avoid.

'What are you asking, Linz? She's my employee, that's all. We work together.'

'Like you worked together in Rome?'

'Yes, in Rome, in Berlin . . . in Paris. She's my lawyer.'

From over his shoulder, Alice spoke to him, giving him some respite.

'Daddy. Pookie wants to get a better view.'

She climbed forward, leaning over the central console between the front seats and pushing the phone past Sean and Linz, towards the windscreen.

'Mum,' said Toby, 'Alice has taken off her seatbelt.'

Linz turned to guide her daughter back into her seat.

'Sit back, Alice, right this minute and put your seatbelt back on.'

'Mummy!' Alice cried, excitedly. 'I think I see a fairy.'

'Alice! Do as your mother tells you!'

Sean's voice was louder than he'd meant it to be, scaring her. She dropped

Pookie into the footwell behind Linz's seat.

'Pookie!'

Sean reached down for the bear, his right arm angled back behind Linz's seat, scrabbling about for it.

'It's okay, sweetie, I'll get him for you.'

'Leave it, Sean,' cried Linz, 'Watch the road.'

She grabbed his hand and pulled it away, the fraught conversation between them making her more forceful than she'd meant. She undid her own seatbelt and reached around to find Pookie.

'For God's sake, Linz, calm down!'

Linz sat back around in her seat, the bear in her right hand. She dusted it down and then turned around to hand it to Alice.

'Here he is, sweetie.'

Alice leaned forward to take Pookie, but was distracted by something ahead of her.

'Look, Daddy, it's a fairy!'

Sean was blinded by a flash of bright white light. Alice had taken a photo on her mobile phone and the camera-flash had gone off. He stamped on the brakes, an automatic reaction. Linz screamed as the car began to skid.

'Sean!'

'It's okay! I've got . . .'

The sudden impact of the car against the safety-barrier threw Sean against the steering wheel. His airbag exploded into his face, driving the breath from his lungs. Linz, her seatbelt not refastened, was thrown against the windscreen with such force that her head cracked the reinforced glass. Alice flew forward, between the seats, directly into her mother's body as it bounced back. Linz slammed against her daughter, the impact knocking her back into the rear seats. Toby screamed in terror. It was the last sound Sean would ever hear from his son.

The rear end of the Range Rover swung round, taking it broadside into the low, corrugated-iron barrier at the edge of the road. It crashed against it, an explosion of metal on metal, like the strike of a blacksmiths hammer on an iron anvil, then tipped onto its offside wheels and dropped into the darkness below.

For what seemed like an eternity, the car bounced down the rock-strewn slope. Like a dark, metal pinball it ricocheted off massive boulders that had lain quiet since the last ice-age, but now, like monstrous, grey teeth, snapped and bit at it as it came careering onto them. The roof buckled inwards, crushing Toby's skull like an eggshell and killing him instantly. The windscreen shattered, the glass torn away like kitchen cling-film, disappearing into the darkness like an enraged Valkyrie. As it somersaulted, Linz was plucked through the open windscreen like a rag doll, her body slamming against one of the boulders with a sickening thud, shattering her spine. Mercifully, she was already unconscious from the impact of her head against the windscreen, so made no sound and knew no pain as she died.

Less than thirty seconds after it had rolled over the safety barrier, the Range Rover came to a shuddering stop against a boulder the size of a two-story building. It was upright, nose down, the front wheels folded underneath the front-end, making it look like a milk cow rising to stand. Every panel was torn and buckled and every window smashed. A violent hiss of steam escaped from under the buckled bonnet, like a dying breath, then there was silence, save for the metallic pinking and ticking of the broken vehicle in its final moments of life.

Sean had been knocked semi-conscious, but his disorientation was only momentary. As he came too, he could smell the acrid stench of spilled diesel from the ruptured engine, then the sweet, coppery taint of fresh blood. It was a smell he knew well from his days in the Army. He raised his hand to his head and felt the wet smear of his ripped scalp, then winced. Disorientated, it had taken a few moments for his brain to register pain, but now he realised where he was and what had happened.

'Linz!'

He wondered why she was no longer in the seat beside him. He undid his seatbelt and turned around to see if the children were all right. A needle of white-hot fire drove into his shoulder, but it was nothing compared to the pain the sight that greeted him caused.

'No!'

He looked away, knowing instantly, from Toby's sightless gaze, that his son was dead. The depth of his loss was visceral and immediate. Alice lay unconscious beside her brother, her face, cherub-like under the cold, blue glow of a moon that lit the scene like a painting by Caravaggio. Sean touched his fingers to her neck. Her breathing was shallow but her pulse seemed strong. She was alive!

'Thank God.'

Spurred on by the realisation that he had to act quickly, Sean pulled on the door handle. Miraculously, it swung open. He stepped down onto the dry, bare earth and picked his way around the back of the car. Save for his shoulder and the cut to his head, he was relatively unscathed. Looking up the steep, boulder-strewn path the car had taken down the mountainside, he had no idea how. Something caught his eye. Lying motionless, a few hundred feet above him, lay Linz, her blonde hair and pale blue, summer dress bleached silver by the moonlight.

'Linz!'

Sean's scream echoed around him. He scrambled up the slope and dropped to his knees beside her.

Linz was on her back, as if laid out by some divine angel, ensuring her dignity as she passed from one world to the next. Her face was unblemished and there were no other obvious signs of injury. It was as if she was in a deep and peaceful sleep. Sean took her wrist, testing for a pulse he already knew he would not find. He lifted her body to him and her arms fell back like broken butterfly wings. He cupped her head in his right hand, supporting her so that he could look at her face, and felt the wet hole in her skull.

'Linz! My love!'

He willed her to come back to him, whispering to her how much he loved her, the ache of the loss of her already unbearable. But then his military training took over. Or perhaps it was simply the protective instincts of a father who knew his child needed him.

'Alice!'

Although he grieved for the loss of his wife and son, Sean fought back the feelings of despair that circled him like ravens around a stillborn lamb carcass. He lay Linz's body on the ground and raced back down the slope, slipping and sliding on shoes designed for the beach, not for mountains, his right arm to his chest as best he could, protecting his damaged shoulder, although the burn of the injury was anesthetised by the adrenaline coursing through this body. Reaching the Range Rover, he practically tore the back door from its hinges and reached for his daughter.

Alice was still unconscious, though, as Sean lifted her clear, she opened her eyes and gave a small but pitiful moan.

'Daddy.'

Her voice was small and faint, but it offered Sean a glimmer of hope. She was conscious and able to speak.

'I'm here, Princess, I'm here.'

He carried her a few paces then knelt to examine her, cradling her in his arms. Alice coughed and a faint line of blackened blood stained her lips.

'It tastes funny, Daddy.'

'I know, Princess,' whispered Sean, 'but it's going to be fine.' He fumbled in his trouser pocket for his phone. It lit up as he looked down at it. 'Damn it!' There was no signal. 'Dear God, please help me.'

Alice tried to lift her head and look around her.

'Where's Mummy?'

'Don't move, Princess. Mummy's with Toby. She's looking after him.'

Sean choked back the tears as his words drove, like iron nails, into his heart.

'Is Toby hurt, Daddy?'

'He hurt his head, Princess. But he's going to be all right. The ambulance is on its way.'

'I'm sore, Daddy, in my heart.' Sean gently touched his daughter's chest with his fingers. Alice screamed. 'Don't, Daddy. Please don't.'

She was still holding onto her precious new teddy bear, and pulled it up over her heart, holding it to her as if it might protect her. She coughed again and a thick spit of black escaped her lips, running down her chin and onto her hands, staining its fur with her blood.

Alice looked down at it.

'Look, Daddy, Pookie's hurt.'

'Don't worry, Princess, we'll fix him. I promise.'

Alice smiled and looked up into Sean's eyes.

'He's not real, Daddy, you big silly.'

The agony of watching his daughter in pain was almost too much for Sean to bear. He was totally helpless. It was a feeling he had never known before. While he was still trying to think of what he could do, Alice gave a moan and Sean felt the life go out of her. As her arms fell back, her fingers lost their life and she dropped Pookie at his feet.

'I know, Princess. I know he's not real,' whispered Sean, holding his face against hers. He could still feel the warmth of her skin and the tease of life below it. 'But then I'm just a great big silly.' He began to rock backwards and forwards, unable to let go of her. A wave of heartbreak and sorrow rose up inside him, a grief that threatened to break him apart. 'Don't leave me, Princess. Please, don't leave me.' He looked up into the silent sky, seeking the only thing he knew could save her, and cried out. 'Bring her back to me, damn you! Bring her back!'

Still holding Alice to him, Sean screamed to the heavens until something inside him stretched past breaking-point and tore free. He felt it the moment it happened. He could not name it, not in words, but something had broken that could never be fixed. He lowered her to the ground then walked away, disappearing into a mist that had risen like a silent, white shroud. Come to hide the dead.

8

Visible from space, Scotland's *An Gleann Mor*, the Great Glen, is a massive valley formed by eroding glaciers during the last European ice-age. Like a savage sword strike cutting a deep wound across the land, the glen runs from the bustling east coast city of Inverness, following a geological fault-line that bisects the mountainous Highlands, down to Fort William, at the head of Loch Linnhe, on Scotland's stunningly beautiful west coast.

A series of rivers and lakes run continuously through the glen, the largest and most famous of which is Loch Ness, home of the fabled monster, *Nessie*. The ancient divide, now a long-distance travelling route for cyclists, kayakers and walkers, passes a great mountain left standing after the ravages of the retracting glacial ice. At over four-and-a-half thousand feet, Ben Nevis is another Scottish monster, although one much easier to find.

Sean glanced up at the sombre mountain as he drove through Glen Nevis, passing the Ben Nevis Visitor Centre, two miles beyond the town of Fort William. He'd taken the afternoon ferry from Skye to the fishing village of Mallaig, on the mainland, then driven the famous Road to the Isles, passing the islands of Eigg and Rhum before stopping for a coffee in the tiny hamlet of Glenfinnan, landing place of Bonnie Prince Charlie at the start of his doomed Jacobite Uprising.

On impulse, he pulled his silver, Mercedes G-Wagon into the *Braveheart* car park, close to the visitor centre, so called, as the movie, a fictional homage to the thirteenth-century Scottish warrior, William Wallace, had been shot largely in Glen Nevis. Out of the car, he made his way up the narrow path towards the Achintree Inn, starting point for the classic hike up Ben Nevis using a pathway called the Pony Track.

Bulbous anvils of cumulus clouds gathered around the mountain's deceptively flat summit like harbingers of doom. Sean felt a chill run through him as he looked up at it. The translation from its Gaelic name, *Beinn Nibheis*, had two meanings, "the mountain with its head in the clouds", and, "malicious mountain". Today, both seemed fitting.

It still had the same effect on Sean it had always had. Ever since he had first trodden its slopes as a teenager growing up in Fort William. "The Ben", as it was commonly referred to by those who lived in the area, climbed from the shores of Loch Linnhe to tower above the town dominated by its shadow. It was where his life had forever changed; where he and Linz had met. He thought back to the day. The memory dragged others to follow. He tried to push them back without success.

They had both been part of an Edinburgh University Climbing Club outing. Young climbers and adventurers eager to take on the challenge of the Nevis Range, travelling on a bus from Edinburgh to the hostel at Fort William, unaware of each other's existence, Sean with his friends, Linz with her then boyfriend, Miles. Split into two groups, they trained on the Ledge Route and Castle Ridge, two of the easier Ben Nevis ridges, although, on a wintery day in Scotland, taking on vertical ascents of over four hundred meters in conditions that saw the temperature drop to minus fifteen degrees, the climbs had been challenging to say the least.

Sean met Linz on the fourth day of climbing, when she'd been added to his team due to a minor injury to one of the other climbers. She had been appointed lead climber, to his annoyance, although the damage had been more to his pride than anything else. That first meeting had been a prickly encounter, but he'd fallen in love with her at first sight.

'I loved you, too, Sean, right from the start.'

Sean turned towards the sound of the voice. Linz was standing on the pathway leading up towards the Achintree Inn. She was wearing her pale blue, summer dress, the same one she'd worn to Alice's birthday party. A golden glow surrounded her, giving her a wraithlike quality.

'Linz!' Her name ached in his heart like new death. He took a faltering step towards her, but she shook her head and pointed up at the mountain. He followed her gaze up to the cloud-smothered, north face and understood what she was telling him. She was remembering the day they met.

'I remember, my love.'

He took another step, but the light around her shifted. The shadows closed in and she began to fade. Her voice carried to him on the breeze sweeping down from the mountain.

'Come home, Sean. Come back to us.'

'Linz! Don't go.'

But she had already gone.

Sad beyond description, Sean tried to force back the feelings of hopelessness and loss. He was totally alone, his life pointless and empty. But Linz had told him to go home. To come back to them. His family were waiting for him. So that was where he would go.

Instead of continuing on up to the Inn, to the comfort of a warm fire and a pint of ale, he headed back down to the car park, stopping only to take a final look back at the mountain, where a smoldering roll of dark cloud descended like a pack of hunting wolves. As he reached the G-Wagon, he turned again, looking back along the shadowy pathway where Linz had been standing. There was no sign of her, only the orange light from the flames of a log fire flickering behind the windows of the Achintree Inn, some half mile away, glowing in the night like the eyes of the oncoming wolves.

9

Merrick sat at the end of a leafy street in an out-of-the-way part of Edinburgh, the kind of street you wouldn't normally drive into unless you already knew it was there. The house was a stone's throw from the Firth of Forth, and the sprawling, two-acre garden backed onto a sandy pathway that meandered along the beachfront, leading to the sleepy harbour village of Cramond, which boasted its own tidal island and had once been inhabited by the Romans.

Sean pulled the G-Wagon into the driveway, stopping to enter the security code on the keypad level with the window. Thankfully, the code had not been changed since he'd last been there the previous June; the day of the remembrance service for Linz and his children, at Cramond Kirk, the local Catholic Church. The high, iron gates swung open and he drove up the tree-lined, granite-chip driveway. Halfway up, he turned away from the hedge surrounding the property and the headlights picked out the white-painted house.

Built over three stories, Merrick was, in the main, designed in the *Art Deco* style of architecture, with a pastiche of other styles, somewhat contradictory but united by a desire to be modern. It had been designed and constructed by a rich industrialist shortly after the first World War, named for his only son who had tragically died in that same bloody conflict. Quite coincidentally, Merrick had also been Sean's nickname while serving with the British Army.

He and Linz had fallen in love with the house when it came onto the market, ten years before, despite its neglected exterior, dilapidated interior and that it was home to a veritable menagerie of rooks and pigeons. They had purchased it without a second thought, along with the winged guests they would eventually have to evict.

It had been Linz, though, who had spent almost every waking hour for nearly two years, dragging the house back to its former glory. With Sean's time increasingly taken up by QuantumCloud's rapid growth, he had let her run free to do whatever she wanted to. The unpaying, winged guests had had their chance, it was her turn to build her nest. It was a marvellous restoration, everyone agreed, when they'd finally been able to throw their first housewarming party. Linz had created a modern but sympathetic exterior, with a much increased in size and modern interior. It was their dream home and the symbol of their journey together. The perfect place in which to raise a family.

Now, the house lay in darkness, or so it first appeared, the latticed windows reflecting the dazzling white lights of the G-Wagon back at him so that he failed to see that the windows on the lower west-wing were lit with a soft, amber glow.

'What the hell?' Sean muttered, finally noticing the light coming from the kitchen.

On the day of the funeral service for his family, Sean had given explicit instructions that Merrick should be vacated. The household staff had been dismissed, with one year's salary and excellent references, but told that they were required to leave that same day. Merrick had been locked and bolted, the security systems monitored twenty-four hours a day by a local security firm run by Sean's closest friend, Miles Gaylord Ronaldson, who also arranged the monthly house-cleaning and watering of the plants.

Abandoning the G-Wagon at the parking area on the west side of the house, Sean made his way around to the front, failing to tread noiselessly on the granite stone chips beneath his feet. Merrick lit up as the motion activated security lights encircling the house switched on, and the Douglas firs, lining the driveway and spread throughout the gardens became a backdrop of shadowy guardians.

As he passed, he peered in through the kitchen windows, but apart from the glow from the six copper, pendant-lights hanging over a kitchen-island that could accommodate a dozen people sitting around it at one time, the room was empty. Although a bottle of red wine and single wine glass had been placed on the island's dark wood top, alongside a silver platter, partially covered with a white napkin.

'Bloody odd,' said Sean, wondering what sort of burglar had broken into his home.

At the front door, he lifted the carbon cover of the security sensor pad and pressed his thumb to the dark glass screen. It scanned his fingerprint and the door unlocked with an almost undetectable click. The handle turned, silently, and he entered the spacious hallway, lit just enough from low-power nightlights set into the white-tiled floor to see there was no obvious sign of intrusion.

From where he stood, Sean could see down the hallway and through to the orangery, which was filled with imported fruitwood furniture and housed a veritable jungle of sprawling plants and leafy palms in massive terracotta pots. The plants stood still and silent, as if they'd been caught out, sneaking around the glassy room. The large kitchen-dining-room, which also opened into the orangery, lay to Sean's left, with the livingroom, library and Sean's personal study housed in the east wing of the house. A white marble staircase climbed to the first-floor landing, turning back on itself at a half-landing to form a mezzanine floor, continuing up to two higher floors, each with its own landing looking down over the entrance hallway.

Sean peered up at the domed glass cupola set into the ceiling at the top of the house. It had been designed to flood the entrance and landings with natural light. Despite his initial reservations, it had been an inspired addition, by Linz. Tonight, only dark storm clouds were visible through the glass. The landings were as gloomy as a morgue. He shivered at a memory of Toby and Alice waving to him from the balcony outside their bedrooms on the first floor, arms and legs stuck through the iron balustrades, happy smiles on their innocent young faces. The suddenness and clarity of it threatened to overwhelm him. He felt his breathing falter and his vision begin to blur.

After that morning's counselling session, Emily had told him that this type of potentially debilitating attack could happen at any time, brought on by emotional stress. It was a normal reaction to the trauma-based therapy he had undergone, as well as a side-effect of his PTSD. The coping techniques he had been taught would be useful when the attacks came. He also had to ensure he took his medication; the medication he'd tossed out of the G-Wagon window on a remote stretch of road between Fort William and Perth, after seeing Linz on Ben Nevis. The Sertraline tablets messed with his body and mind. He'd been prescribed them when he'd first gone to Dunvegan. They'd stopped him seeing Linz when he'd taken them.

He closed his eyes and focused on his breathing, visualising the clock face and the steady sweep of the seconds hand, trying to push down the memory that sought to take control over him. Steadied, he moved towards the kitchen door, sitting ajar, and entered the warmly-lit room, looking around to satisfy himself he was alone. He inspected the bottle of wine under the circle of glowing pendant lights above the island.

'Chateau Musar. A damned fine choice.' The Lebanese wine was one of his favourites. 'Curiouser and curiouser, cried . . .'

He cut the sentence short. It was a quote from the Lewis Carroll book, *Alice in Wonderland*, one he'd often read to the Alice and Toby. Another memory he had no wish to keep.

He turned his attention to the silver platter, lifting the white linen napkin to discover a folded note written on a laid, white paper, unmistakably taken from the desk of his private study. The thought that someone had been in his sanctuary, or in the house at all, other than to clean it, infuriated him. This was the last place he'd been with his family. He had made it clear he wanted absolutely nothing disturbed. Angry, but wondering who had left it, he opened the note and read the handwritten message.

Hi Major,
You're probably wondering who the hell's been here and how they know your partial to Chateau Musar? Well, it's just me! Seeing as I have the code for the door, I thought I'd make sure you didn't come home to a freezing cold house. So, I put the heating on. Blame Judith, she told you might be heading home today. If so, and you're reading this, enjoy. If not, I'll eat the lot myself, tomorrow, and drink your precious wine for my trouble. I'm at the end of the line anytime you need me. Day or night!
See you soon,
Miles

Sean was relieved it had been Miles who had been in the house. They'd been best friends since Edinburgh University, joining the army on graduation and travelling the world together, sharing adventures and more than a few life-and-death moments. They each had a love for the mountains, motorbikes, sailing and whisky, although not all at the same time. He dropped the note back on the island top, feeling guilty for not having spoken to him since the funeral service. But he'd talked to no-one close to him since that miserably wet June morning. After saying goodbye to Linz and the kids, it had been easier for him to be alone, emotionally isolated and removed from all he previously knew.

From being disinterested in eating, the lobster and prawns, washed down with the Chateaux Musar, was devoured with a relish Sean had forgotten existed. He hadn't eaten at all that day, surviving the two hundred mile journey home to Edinburgh on service station coffee and Marlboro cigarettes.

From the kitchen radio, perched on an Ercol sideboard loitering against one of the kitchen walls, tuned as always to Classic FM, flowed the gentle strains of Vaughan Williams' *London Symphony*. The atmospheric music conjured up dramatic images of foggy Victorian streets and the muted honk of foghorns sounding along the River Thames. Despite himself, Sean began to relax. The kitchen was, at that moment in time, a safe place for him to be in the house. To stray beyond it, to venture into the other rooms, was to enter a place of insecurity. But something was telling him he had to. It was, after all, the reason he was there. He had not intended to return to the house, but Linz had told him to come home. She would be here, waiting for him. Somewhere. He climbed off the stool and went to find her.

The living room was a graveyard of ghosts. Sean could see them beyond the doorway. Some were tall and crooked, others crouched and hunched, lurking in the corners and hovering randomly throughout the room, daring him to enter. A hesitant step took him into the semi-darkness. He touched the digital control panel on the wall and the room flooded with light. The ghosts changed form, turning back into chairs, couches and lamps, all of them covered in white cotton dust-sheets. He dimmed the recessed ceiling lights to a low glow and switched on the table-lamps, which were diffused to a soft, ambient glow by the dustsheet shrouds.

To Sean, the room was as familiar as it was foreign. He tried to avoid looking at the large, monochrome prints of himself, Linz and the children, hung on the white walls. Echoes of a past that had faded to whispers. But the echoes would not be ignored. They were everywhere. Calling to him. Forcing him to look. Framed family photographs littered the shelves and side tables around the room. A brass otter Linz had found in a little antique shop on the holy island of Lindisfarne stood on its hind legs, staring at him with an inquisitive look on its face. He couldn't meet its gaze and looked away.

Other bits and pieces from all the days of their lives called to him, each one a sweet memory and bitter regret. Wherever he looked, there was no escaping that the house that had once been their sanctuary was now a tomb.

'Help me,' Sean pleaded, but the God he had always been told would watch over him remained silent.

He reached for an almost full bottle of Caol Isla whisky, sitting on one of the side-tables, knowing that the only spirit that would help him lay in the smoky, Islay malt.

10

The ultra-cool Tigerlily cocktail bar, "Tigers", to its regulars, sits close to Charlotte Square, in the west-end of Edinburgh's upmarket George Street, a wide Victorian thoroughfare filled with designer shops and chic restaurants. The spacious street runs parallel to the world-famous Princes Street, ending at the St Andrews Square, in the east end, under the ever watchful gaze of Edinburgh Castle.

Judith took her tortoiseshell compact from her handbag and checked her hair, lipstick and makeup, despite having already done the important pre-going-out inspection in her car, now safely parked in the central parking spaces that ran the full length of George Street. She glanced back at the sleek BMW coupe and, for the second time, pressed the lock button on the key fob. The orange sidelights winked at her as if to say, *yup, still good*.

The black-suited greeter standing on the pavement outside the bar nodded and smiled as Judith passed him. She returned the greeting and climbed the half dozen steps up to the glass doors leading into the brightly lit front bar. Inside, the bar was colourful and chic, with purple fabric seats, neon lighting and decorative mirrors. She turned right and made her way through the hallway connecting to the much larger main bar at the back of the building.

'Judith, over here.'

Emily was tucked away into one of the semi-circular booths near the back of the bar. She wore the same leather jacket and jeans she'd worn earlier, despite having been back hours before Judith, who'd changed into a navy, Armani trouser-suit, albeit with the same Suzi-Folk boots with the studded heels.

'Hi Ems.'

Emily stood and embraced her, then retook her seat in the centre of the booth. Judith slid in beside her.

One of the cocktail barmen made his way over to take their order. He was in his mid-twenties, tall, with long, dark hair, and both of his arms were covered in tattoos. He carried the same confident, "how you doing", expression that most young men seemed to be able to master almost instantly they'd lost their virginity.

'Hi girls,' he flashed a perfect smile that Mum and Dad had probably paid for. 'I'm Jake. I'll be taking care of you tonight.' He locked his eyes onto Emily like a fighter-pilot fixing the cross-hairs of a gun sight on a potential target. 'What would you like . . . to drink?'

'Well hello there yourself, Jake.' Emily opened her eyes a little wider and tilted her chin down, staring directly up at him. She ran the tip of her tongue over her top lip, wetting it with a thin smear of saliva so that it glistened like a shiny lure. 'What would you *like* to give me?'

Judith watched Jake wilt under Emily's sexually charged riposte, her entire persona shifting from that of a fresh-faced young woman into a bold, sexual predator. It was, she had to admit, wonderfully done.

'I can . . . maybe the . . . espresso martini, or perhaps, white wine? Miss? Madam?'

Jake didn't so much trip over his reply as stumble and fall. Judith looked away, hiding her smile. She had no wish to embarrass the young man any further.

'I'll have the espresso martini, please,' said Emily, switching to her best *butter-wouldn't-melt* look. 'And thanks for being so utterly lovely, Jake. I really *do* appreciate a good service.'

Judith faked a cough to cover her amusement. Jake returned the smile, unsure how best to reply but declining to meet Emily's eyes.

'And you, Miss?' Jake looked at Judith, sheepishly. 'The same?'

It was clear he was desperate to escape.

'Go on,' said Judith, 'why not? It's been a long day. I can get that car service, Scoot, to come and drive me home if we decide to stay out.'

'Thank you, ladies, I'll have your drinks sent right over.'

Jake turned and shot off without a backwards glance. Judith looked at Emily, accusingly.

'What?'

She shrugged her shoulders, but the cheeky smile on her face was a clear admission of guilt.

'That, Miss McGregor, was like watching a cat toy with a mouse.'

'Well, he's good looking, Judith, but he knows it. I've probably done him and a host of future female customers a favour. Anyway, he's about twelve, for goodness sake. I'm all for cougars being cougars, but I've never wanted to be one myself.'

'Cougars! Like Jann Livingston? The vacuous narcissist with the pumped-up tits and lips? I think that's pretty much word-for-word how you described her.'

'*Jay-Lie*!' Emily's *butter-wouldn't-melt* expression turned sour. 'Yes, exactly like her.'

'Claws out then, Ems?'

'It's an accurate description I think you'll find,' replied Emily, her cheeks flushing slightly. 'Christ, she's almost sixty, with a filler-filled face and a neck like a turkey stretching for a bun.'

'A turkey!'

Judith snorted at the bizarre but vivid description. But Emily wasn't finished.

'You've seen her here, Judith, strutting around in her way-too-tight, way-too-short, *almost* dresses, false tits sticking out in front of her like way-too-firmly-set jellies. And don't get me started on those saggy flaps of loose white flesh hanging down under her arms. They might once have been muscles, but now they look more like flappy chicken-wattles.'

Judith laughed at the description.

'So, not still bitter about her stealing Marcus from you?'

'They're welcome to each other,' said Emily, laughing herself, despite that, at the time, she'd thought she'd never laugh again. 'Anyway, Marcus was well into his forties. Way too old for me. I don't know what I was thinking. Now that I've met Connor, I'm completely ambivalent about Jay-Lie's existence.'

'Connor! The new man?'

'Indeed,' said Emily. 'He's bright, smart and as sexy as hell, as well as being a better and much *bigger* man than Marcus ever was.'

She giggled and a flush of blood coloured her cheeks.

'Rich?' Judith asked, ignoring the overt sexual reference but smiling at it all the same.

'He is, not that I give a stuff. I'm not a gold-digger, Judith, unlike Jay-Lie. She'd smother her own mother for an inheritance. In fact, there's a rumour she did.'

'Miaow,' said Judith, then turned her attention to a waitress approaching their table, carrying a tray of drinks.

'Two large espresso martinis, ladies, plus a glass of Prosecco on the house. Jake's compliments. I've no idea what you did to deserve that. Normally, knowing Jake, he'd bring them over himself. I guess, this time, he bit off more than he could chew. Enjoy, you've probably earned them.'

The waitress smiled a knowing smile and walked back to the bar. Emily looked at Judith with a semi-smug grin on her face.

'You see?'

'You were right,' said Judith, acknowledging that what Emily had said about saving some other poor unsuspecting girls from Jake's advances was probably on the money. They clinked glasses. 'So, when do I get to meet this new man of yours?'

'He'll be here in half an hour.'

'Tonight?'

'Yes,' said Emily, 'why?'

'If I'd known, I'd have dressed to impress.'

'Impress! Judith, look at you! You're like a Harvey Nick's mannequin in that suit. Anyway, he'd better only have eyes for me or it'll be more than young Jake who gets the Emily McGregor takedown.'

'Poor Jake,' Judith said, glancing towards the bar. 'He's barely looked in our direction since. And he sent the waitress over because you scared him so much.'

'He'll get over it,' said Emily, 'besides, he was too much like a certain Sean Jameson for my liking. Arrogant and annoying, but still damned likeable.'

'I know what you mean, Ems. I know exactly what you mean.'

The mood shifted at the mention of Sean, inducing a moment of silence that stemmed the conversation, Judith wondering how best to couch the questions she had for Emily, she, in turn, considering what answers she could give if asked.

Judith broke the silence.

'How did it go today?'

'Good, bad and everything in between, said Emily, but before we do this, you need to understand something.'

'Go ahead.'

'While I can't tell you anything, specifically, about Sean's treatment, I can talk about his PTSD in general terms. You already know about that. He's discussed it with you in front of me. I can help you understand where he's been, where he is right now, and what he's likely to experience in the coming weeks. But you can't push me for more than I'm willing or able to give. Agreed?

'Agreed,' said Judith. 'You talk, I'll listen.'

She gave Emily a *thank you* smile.

'A first for a lawyer.'

They laughed and the awkward mood lifted.

'This morning's session was rough, I take it?' Judith asked. Breaking the rules Emily had laid down almost immediately.

Emily shook her head disapprovingly.

'Judith! I thought you were going to just listen?'

Judith ran a pinched finger and thumb across her lips. Emily, appeased, began to talk.

'Well, you actually helped me kick things off with your nineteen-seventies television-series references. Sean and I ended up having a fine old chat about *Donald Duck* and *Taz*, as well as the *Incredible Hulk*. It led to a breakthrough, of sorts, for Sean. For the first time, in all our sessions, he was able to open up and talk about last year's crash.

'That's good, isn't it?' Judith asked, feeling relieved.

She'd expected Emily to tell her something terrible had happened.

'It is,' agreed Emily, 'but only if he continues with a program of therapy. And therein lies the problem. Sean regards all therapy as pointless. He has, right from the start. In his eyes, there's nothing to fix. Or nothing that *can* be fixed'

'What do you mean, Ems, *can* be fixed?'

'Deep down, Judith, he's aware there are other issues from his past to deal with to have any real chance to properly heal, but he simply doesn't want to face them. Even though he opened up to me, today, he was still only dealing with one layer of trauma. Albeit the most recent.

'What are you talking about, Ems? What other layers?'

Emily questioned if she should continue. She'd already given out more than she'd intended.

'Look, Judith, the information I'm about to give you, I only found out recently. By pure chance. I gained access to medical records from a highly respected psychiatrist, based in London. Harley Street, no less. Records that contained details about Sean's past treatment for PTSD.'

'Sean was already being treated?'

Emily could tell Judith hadn't known. She was relieved. Part of her had wondered if she *had* known, but hadn't told her, when she'd initially approached her to take Sean as a client.

'I only found out because the account hadn't been fully settled. I'm guessing it was around the time, last year, when he disappeared.'

Judith knew exactly when Emily was referring to. After attending the funeral service for Linz and the children, Sean had cut off all communication and gone abroad. It had been months before they'd found him. And only after a private investigator hired by QuantumCloud had tracked him down to a suite at the five-star Agavi Hotel, in the beautiful town of Positano, one of the jewels on Italy's incredible Amalfi coast.

'I remember, Ems. Just before his trial. Not a great time.'

'Anyway, a few weeks ago, an administrator from the psychiatrist's office in Harley Street contacted QuantumCloud, seeking payment. Someone there thought it was something to do with me and passed it on. I called Harley Street and found out the truth of the matter. They were good enough to send me Sean's treatment notes, him being legally in my care. I've since spoken to his psychiatrist there, a doctor named Jenny Pearce. What I learned from her was crucial to know for Sean's treatment.'

'What did she tell you?' Emily paused, reticent, it seemed, to divulge more. 'Ems, you can't not tell me now.'

'Okay, Judith, but don't say I didn't warn you.'

'Just tell me.'

Emily struggled with breaking her Hippocratic Oath, but Judith wasn't only his lawyer, she was his friend. And what Sean needed right now was someone who cared about him to be there for him. Judith was as close to family as he had. She decided to put her patient first.

'Sean has deep-rooted issues that stem from trauma suffered in his past. Psychological scars on top of psychological scars. What happened to him, last year, created a new scar, but it also opened up all the old ones. Layers of hidden emotional trauma coming to the surface.'

Judith looked shocked, but her lawyer's mind started processing the information, looking for answers.

'Is it from something that happened to him when he was in the Army? That would make sense, wouldn't it? I've heard about servicemen coming back from warzones suffering from PTSD.'

'It's not only warzones that create post-traumatic-stress, Judith. It can happen to anyone, anywhere, given the right circumstances. The point is, no matter what caused it, and don't ask, because I really can't tell you, Sean had begun to deal with his mental health long before I came on the scene, by seeing Dr Pearce. From what she told me, it was Linz who convinced him to see her in the first place, Linz who made the appointments and Linz who accompanied him to them. Sean had begun the healing process by facing things from a past he had tried to forget, which was a major breakthrough. As brutal as it must have been for him, he faced them for the love of Linz. Unfortunately, he discontinued treatment after only a handful of sessions.'

'Why, Ems? What happened?'

'There were certain moments from his past Sean found impossible to handle. Memories so traumatic, which he'd buried so deeply, that when Dr Pearce started to bring them to the surface, he ran. Despite he'd made some early progress, it was all reversed when he did. In fact, by seeing beginning to open up his past then leaving once he had, he ended up in a worse place than when he'd started. His past traumas came back to haunt him, but he had no-one to help him deal with the fallout. To make things worse, he felt he had quit on Linz. The shame of letting down the person he loved more than anyone else in his world caused the cracks in their marriage to appear.'

'And that,' said Judith, 'is when he had his relationship with me. I was just a sticking plaster over one of those cracks. I've been such a fool.'

Emily, seeing the look of despair on Judith's face, reached over and took hold of her hands.

'Don't be too hard on yourself. Sean's an extremely good-looking man. He's confident, as well as rich and powerful, funny and intelligent, but he can be very manipulative. You would have found it almost impossible to resist his advances once he'd decided he wanted you.'

Judith stared down at the table.

'I couldn't. I tried and failed.'

'I'm not saying he felt nothing for you, Judith, but a man like Sean finds it hard to be without love. Or without sex. Given he equates one with the other. When Sean feels loved, he feels secure and safe. But when he feels *unloved,* he becomes frightened and insecure. His natural instinct is to try to feel safe again. He blocks his feelings of fear and insecurity using alcohol, drugs or women, whichever crutch comes along first. Anything to escape the reality he feels he's in at the time. His perception isn't real, but it's real enough to him, brought on by his PTSD. It's a vicious circle of self-destruction. It's not his fault, it's simply how he's been programmed.'

'I get it, Ems, and I feel so bad, for Sean. I'd no idea what he'd been through. I knew he'd served in the Middle East, but he never talks about it. I guess it was bad. But I still betrayed my friend, Linz. It doesn't make it easier to like myself knowing all this.'

'Don't beat yourself up over it, Judith, we all screw up.'

Judith nodded her thanks and took a deep breath. She wanted to know more about what had happened to Sean.

'So, these past layers of trauma are his main problem?'

'They're part of the problem,' said Emily. The point is, if he doesn't deal with the trauma from his past, he can never properly deal with his current trauma.'

'Jesus, Ems. You make it sound so bleak.

'It was. For Sean, it really was.'

They each sat back and reached for their drinks, taking some time to collect their respective thoughts. Judith decided to push Emily for some answers. Sean needed help. She had to find a way to get it for him.

'So what now? We can't force him to come back to you for more treatment. Not unless you have him committed.' Judith covered her mouth with her hand. 'Dear God, did I even suggest that?'

'Relax, Judith, that won't be happening, not unless he puts himself or anyone else in danger. He's not suicidal, at least he's given me no indication he is. Although it's hard to spot someone who is, even for those of us who are trained. Two-thirds of people who attempt to kill themselves don't leave a note.'

The talk of suicide worried Judith. She thought about Sean and felt uneasy. He hadn't called her after that morning's frosty meeting between them. They'd done that dance before. She knew the steps. He always called!

'Where is he now, Ems, do you know? I'm worried about him. I've got a bad feeling in my gut.'

'He said he was going home.'

Judith couldn't hide her surprise.

'Home! To Merrick?'

'I assume that's what he meant.'

'But he told me he'd never go back there. He said it was a coffin he was not going to climb into.'

Emily shrugged.

'Well, our session this morning was a breakthrough. It was brutal and deeply traumatic, for Sean, but I think it helped ground him. He knows he has to face the reality of his past life if he's going to live again. Perhaps he intended to do that by finally going back to the family home.'

'And you think that's a good thing,' said Judith, sounding skeptical.

'He can't keep living in hotels and floating around the world indefinitely, Judith. That's not going to help him in the long run. Going home is the first step to coming back from his self-imposed exile. His returning to the house doesn't concern me. What does is that we're only weeks away from the first anniversary of the accident. A time when he's more likely to experience an effect psychologists called the *anniversary reaction*.'

'What's that? Judith asked, 'some sort of psychological reaction to the day in the year something awful happened to them?'

'Almost,' replied Emily, 'but not exactly. You see, our unconscious minds have a way of encoding the time of a trauma, date-stamping it in our psyche, if you will, but not quite in the way in which we might expect. Essentially, the anniversary reaction is an individual's response to unresolved grief resulting from a significant loss or devastating life trauma, As the anniversary of the event approaches, the victims of a specific trauma, or from trauma from abuse over many years, experience days or even weeks of anxiety, depression and fear. It's not literally a red-ringed date in the calendar, more the period approaching the date of the trauma itself.'

'And Sean's trauma anniversary is close at hand,' said Judith, 'next month, in fact.'

'Yes.' Emily confirmed.

She sat back and took a sip from her glass of now slightly less than chilled Prosecco.

Judith began to fully realise the importance of what she'd just been told. She looked down into her glass, remembering Alice's birthday and the party at Applecross Beach. The last time she'd seen Linz and the children alive. The day Sean had seen them die. The memory brought her close to tears.

'Oh, Ems, what a mess.'

'Try not to get upset, Judith, Sean's going to be okay. He just needs a bit more time.'

Emily gave her hand another sympathetic squeeze, seeing for the first time how much Judith truly cared about Sean.

'I just had no idea how much he'd been suffering.'

'Who ever does?' Emily replied. 'Mental illness is one of those subjects no one wants to talk about. It frightens people. If we have a cold then we openly share it with all and sundry. When I had that bad flu that was going around, last Christmas, you pitched up at my door with a box of chocolates. And we hadn't even known each other that long.'

'I remember.'

Judith smiled at the memory of Emily, puffy-eyed and with a blocked-up nose, wrapped up in a duvet, on her couch, in her stylish Stockbridge apartment, the previous Boxing Day morning.

'I had people calling me, offering more chicken soup and emotional support than I could handle. And that's my point, Judith. It's socially acceptable to admit virtually any physical ailment and have no stigma attached to you, but tell someone you've got a mental illness and see what happens!'

'I'm ashamed to say it, Ems, but you're right.'

'I wish I wasn't. I've never understood why, when someone finally plucks up the courage to admit to a mental-health problem, they can't expect unconditional love and support. Instead, we're more worried that we'll be judged for being close to that person. Even people with HIV and Aids get more sympathy. How many benefit gigs have we seen, not to mention celebrities wearing pink ribbons, to highlight that? Where are the celebrities wearing mental illness ribbons?'

Judith pondered the question.

'Is there one? A mental illness ribbon?'

'See what I mean!'

'Sorry, Ems. I take it there is?'

Emily took hold of the silver and lime-green pendant, hanging on a chain around her neck, lifting it up in front of her chin to let Judith see.

'I'm wearing one right now.'

Judith stared at the pendant, clearly surprised.

'Your little green fish! I've seen you touch it the same way Sean touches his crucifix.'

Emily giggled.

'A fish? Is that what you thought it was? Well, I suppose it looks like one, with the head on the loop and its tail hanging down from the chain. But look closer, it's the same style as all the awareness loops.'

Judith reached over and took the pendant between her fingers.

'I see that, now, Ems. I never thought it meant anything other than being something special and personal to you.'

Emily's voice took on a melancholy tone.

'It *is* special and personal to me, Judith. It has two meanings, you see. It's the awareness sign for depression and childhood mental health, which I've dedicated my life to helping sufferers of, but it's also used to highlight awareness of lymphoma.'

'Oh, Ems. I'm so sorry.'

Judith was aware that Emily's father, himself an eminent psychiatrist, had died five years previously, after being diagnosed with the stage four blood cancer. She was clearly thinking about him now.

'You weren't to know, Judith, but it highlights my point. There's a judgement attached to mental illness which is anything but the response you need when you are trying to deal with or recover from it. As a result, sufferers hide their illness from their friends and family, covering up their silent shame. People all over Facebook comment on and share posts about mental illness. Most of them simply click on a button to show how caring they are and move on, feeling good about themselves but never actually doing anything to help. To be fair, most people don't really know what symptoms to look out for, let alone try to see them and help.'

Judith looked down at her hands, knowing she was one of those same Facebook button-pushers. Thinking about Sean, and what he was going through, she resolved to not be, in the future.

'So, how will I know if Sean's experiencing any of these symptoms,' said Judith, 'I need to know what to look out for.

Emily nodded.

''Well there's a whole host of behaviour patterns that can come to the fore if he is.'

'Such as?'

'Nightmares, hallucinations, social phobia and difficulty in feeling or expressing emotions are the most obvious. He may avoid wanting to be around the people he loves or cares for, even pushing them away. Then there's self-harm and even suicidal thoughts. The list is a long one, Judith, and nothing on it is anything you'd wish on anyone.

'Even Jay-Lie,' said Judith, smiling thinly.

Emily understood the joke was a standard defence mechanism in times of emotional overload. They'd covered a lot of highly charged topics in the past half hour.

'Even her.'

Judith put a hand to her mouth

'Oh, Ems, that was an awful thing for me to say.'

'No, it was totally normal. It's a coping mechanism we use to convince ourselves that everything is okay. Forget it.'

Judith switched her thoughts back to Sean.

'Sean told me Linz has been speaking to him again over the past few weeks. And you know he really believes he saw her standing beside him on the beach, in Gullane, last year, when he had the episode that eventually brought us to you.'

Emily didn't look shocked.

'Yes, but he was under an enormous amount of stress back then. I'd say it was to be expected, given the circumstances. It was the day after his trial for manslaughter. Can you even imagine how much guilt he felt at being charged for killing those he would gladly have given his life for? His seeing Linz doesn't overly concern me.'

Judith, though surprised, accepted what Emily had said.

'Okay, I just thought I'd mention it. I'm a lawyer, not a psychiatrist. To me it seemed damned concerning.'

'I get it, Judith, but it's really not that unusual to talk to those we've lost. Besides, Sean's covered so much ground, since then, with his treatment, even if he did fight me every step of the way. But it's exactly the kind of symptom we need to watch out for as the anniversary window opens. Did he say he'd actually *seen* her recently?'

Judith shook her head.

'No. Just that he'd been talking to her.'

'That's good,' said Emily, trying to reassure her. 'I still talk to my Dad. He's always there, in my head and my heart. We'll just have to keep an eye on Sean.'

'And that's it, Ems? There's nothing more we can do other than try to keep an eye on a man who wants nothing more to do with me, you, or anyone else, come to that?'

'Sorry, Judith, but I'm afraid so. Unless Sean wants to address his trauma, or puts himself or someone else at risk, there's little we can do.'

Judith shook her head, exasperated with the situation.

'Well, I'm calling Miles.'

'Miles?'

'Sean's best friend,' explained Judith. 'A lovely guy, if a bit mad. But if anyone can get through to him, he can. They've known each other since University. They were in the Army together. Sean neither knows nor trusts another soul on earth quite as much as him.'

'Well, you can try,' said Emily. 'Sean's fighting a battle on two fronts, with different layers of PTSD, one on top of the other, carrying so much damage he won't share and that won't just go away. Talking to anyone would help, but he has to want to help himself. My main concern is that he'll return to using the crutches he's always used to cope when the pressure builds to a point he can't control. It's a classic symptom in cases of children that have been badly abused.

'Abused? As a child?'

Emily covered her mouth with her hand.'

'Shit!

Judith's tears came suddenly and unexpectedly. She used one of the napkins left by the waitress, when she'd brought the drinks, to wipe them away, along with a smear of mascara.

'I'm so sorry, Judith. Are you okay?'

'I'm just stunned,' said Judith, trying to compose herself. Child abuse? Against Sean! It's just such a shock to hear that. You can sometimes see the baggage people carry, but you never get to see inside the bags.'

'Beautifully put,' said Emily, 'and you're right. But I'm sorry if I upset you. It was a stupid mistake for me to make.'

Judith shook her head.

'No, Ems, I'm glad you told me, albeit inadvertently. But now you've got to tell me the rest. I need to know.'

Emily realised she'd opened a conversation she probably had to finish.

'Okay. If you really want to hear about it, I will. There's already an online record of his father's trial, so I'm not telling you anything you can't find out for yourself.'

'Was it bad?' Judith asked. 'His abuse?'

Emily lifted her glass of Prosecco and took a sip, steeling herself, then reached into her bag and took out the twisted, wire coat-hanger. She set it on the table and related the story behind it. By the time she returned it to her bag, Judith was crying so much that Jake had come over to ask if everything was okay?

'It's fine, Jake,' said Emily, 'she's just had some bad news. Give us a minute then bring us each another round. And thanks for caring enough to ask.'

She gave him a warm smile. Jake nodded and smiled back. They both understood it was an apology.

'My God,' said Judith, her sobs subsiding. 'That was harrowing just to hear. I can't believe what Sean had to go through. He was only a child. I can't bear to think of how much he must have suffered.'

'And keeps suffering,' replied Emily, 'that's the real issue. The mind and body interact on every level, so the ripple effect of early childhood trauma leaves a legacy that goes beyond just psychological effects. The biology of the brain and immune functions of children who have been abused are compromised. When trauma and stress happen early in life, the effects are more profound and longer lasting.'

'I can hardly bring myself to think about it. What sort of sick bastard could do what Sean's father did to him?'

It was the first time Emily had ever heard Judith swear.

'It may not be natural to those of us lucky enough to have been raised in an environment of stability and love, Judith, but the environment for many children, sadly, is utterly toxic, and child abuse all too common. Abused children grow into broken adults, lost and alone, unable to understand why what happened to them happened at all. Living in shame and confusion with no one to help them find the way to cope. It's why I do what I do.'

'I know, Ems, and I admire what you do, really. More now than ever. It's something most of us don't think about. Most of us have never experienced anything like that. The thought of a child being hurt, any child, it makes me so bloody angry.'

Judith had no children of her own, although she had two beautiful nieces whom she loved dearly. The thought of anyone hurting those little angels enraged her. She dug the nails of her left hand into her palm so hard that she broke the skin. She used the napkin she'd used to wipe away her tears, moments before, to dab away the blood.

It was what Emily said next, however, that cut the deepest.

'When a child is abused, the child is damaged and is forever changed. The broken child stays inside the adult, and the adult carries the burden and pays the price.'

Outside, a violent burst of thunder split the night, loud enough to be heard over the background music playing in the bar. Judith shivered. It was as if something evil had been listening. Something that was angry at them for their compassion and morality. Aspects of the human condition it cared nothing for. Like those who abuse children.

11

The master bedroom was at the top of the house. The ceiling, formed almost entirely of glass, provided an unrestricted view into the heavens above. Tonight's vista was of storm-black rainclouds, lit in silhouette by a shrouded half-moon, and the sky wept as if it was in a state of mourning. The sound of heavy raindrops falling onto the angled windows above him wakened Sean. It was as if a thousand ghoulish fingers were tapping on the glass, demanding he give his demons entry. For a moment, he remained lost in a dream that had no form or sense or substance, though a faint memory of it lingered tantalisingly out of reach.

He closed his eyes and sleep came for him once more, sneaking up on him when he was certain it would elude him for the rest of the night. But his slumber was restless and fitful, his mind without control of when he might return to the place of dreams. A flash of lightening was followed by crack of thunder, so loud, that it was as if God himself had spoken. The relentless pounding of the storm brought him up to the point of rapid-eye-movement, the point where the delicate line between fantasy and reality becomes blurred.

Like one of Scrooge's ghosts, the dream that came for him carried Sean to somewhere he had no desire to be. He fought against it, tossing and turning on the bed, but still he could not waken. Panic clawed at him like a ghastly succubus, intent on stealing his soul, but still it took him. Bearing him down to another place and time. And the dream came alive.

The room Sean was in was cramped and smelt of untreated wood and old dust. The bare walls and the upside-down steps above his head were vague outlines in the darkness, but a thin lifeline to reality remained at the bottom of the cupboard door. The light in the hallway was still switched on. The darkness he feared had not come. Perhaps, this time, it wouldn't.

From beyond the hallway he heard the dull thud of a fist striking human flesh, and his mother's cries cut him to the core. His father was screaming at her; vile, drunken words filled with malice and rage and hate. Without warning, the door to the livingroom was flung open, banging loudly against the hallway wall. For a moment, Sean was afraid it was his turn. He prayed his father would not come for him and felt the burning shame of wishing his mother to take the beating, instead. But the bruises covering his body, from the beating he'd taken earlier that evening, were still too fresh and painful.

'Leave him alone, you bastard,' Sean heard his mother's cry.

He knew she'd pay for that and his shame deepened. The livingroom door slammed shut and his father's voice receded, still enraged and irrational, made brave by the copious injections of whisky tainting his blood.

Suddenly, Sean realised he could no longer see the cupboard walls or the upside-down steps. The thin line of light at the bottom of the door had been extinguished and the cupboard below the stairs plunged into total darkness. His father had turned off the hallway light! The walls began to recede, turning the small space into the place where all that was malevolent and evil existed; the fork-tailed demons and the dark angels he had been told about. Now, the door into hell would open, guiding them towards him. They would drag him down into a place from which there would be no escape. Where he would burn in the flames of the damned for all eternity.

Sean screamed, desperate to escape the horrors his grandmother had told him of with religious relish. He belonged there because he was a sinner. Because he was bad. Because *he* had killed Jesus. He remembered her words and wept, wondering if, this time, they would come for him.

'Mummy! Let me out. Mummy!'

Sean screamed, knowing the screams, no matter how desperate they became, would go unanswered. He screamed again and then wet himself. The acrid smell spread around him and the shame of it raised tears that no-one would come to wipe away.

In desperation, he scrambled onto his knees, bumping his head on the edge of one of the upside-down steps, and prayed. He didn't want to burn in Hell. He didn't want to be tortured by the demons and the dark angels who were coming for him. He wanted to be with his other grandmother, the one who had been kind and loving. Who tried to protect him when she'd been alive. Everything her own daughter could or would not do. He prayed to God to let him die. To be taken to a place where there would be no more pain or darkness. A place of light, where he would no longer be beaten or screamed at. He begged God to answer him. And He would, wouldn't He? Because God loved him.

Didn't He?

But God had not listened. God had not answered. God had not come.

In that moment, Sean realised he was alone. Somehow, even at five years of age, he knew he would always be. He heard a noise in front of him and screamed again. The demons and dark angels had come. They were sniggering in the darkness. Laughing at his worthless prayers. His prayers turned to screams. And the screams became hysterical.

But, just as he thought he was to be taken, another voice had answered. From somewhere far away, but also very close. A kind and gentle voice. It called him by his name, telling him it would protect him from the demons and the dark angels. From the darkness. From all the bad things that frightened him. Sean followed, as the faraway voice guided him to the empty place, a place, it told him, he could go to whenever he needed. A place where no-one would ever hurt him again. A place of peace and light and silence, where he would always be . . .*Closed! Hidden! Safe!*

12

A shallow sun bathed the headstones in dappled light, filtering through the chestnut trees that ringed the ancient, stone walls separating Cramond Kirk from the main road and impressive houses that bordered it on each side. Behind the church, beyond the graveyard, the golf course was empty, laid white with an early frost that had kept the early morning golfers waiting in the clubhouse, sipping hot coffee and eating bacon rolls, desperate for the sun to burn away the icy glaze and let them play.

As he passed the whale's jawbones arched over the church entrance, a testament to the fishing heritage of the area, Miles glanced out of his car window into the front grounds, where cherry trees stood like penitent mourners either side of the gravel pathway leading up to the double front doors. The trees were alive with colour, new buds bursting on every branch and twig like nature's fireworks. A low, stone wall complemented the surge of life erupting from the grassy verge between it and the main road footpath, regiments of daffodils, crocus and snowdrops standing like bright-painted, toy soldiers, guarding the solemn building behind them.

The irony of such vivid life protecting the dead was not lost on Miles. He could scarce believe it had been a year since he'd stood there, saying goodbye to a woman he'd loved, and to her children, whom he'd loved in equal measure. That he was still unmarried, despite relationships that could have made it past the finish line, was due in part to that unrequited love. *First love, deepest cut.* He pictured Linz, standing between Alice and Toby, waving to him as he drove by. He glanced back in his rear-view mirror but only the flowers watched him go.

'I'll try to look after him, Linz. I promise you.'

He gunned the car, leaving the memory behind him.

A few minutes later, he turned into Cramond Brig Lane, slowing as he drove along the leafy avenue, before pulling into the entrance of Merrick. He stopped at the gates and punched in the security code, then drove up to the house. There were no obvious signs of life, but Sean's G-Wagon was in the side parking area. Miles pulled alongside it, climbed out, and walked across the front driveway, glancing in through the kitchen window but seeing no one. He pressed the doorbell and heard the familiar sound of bells ringing in the hallway. It made him smile, though replayed a precious moment he and Linz had shared.

The sound of the five bells from the Basilica di San Marco, in St Mark's Square, the heart of Venice, had been a personal gift to Sean when she'd redesigned Merrick. Miles recalled her explaining the story behind them when he'd asked why she'd gone to the trouble of having them professionally recorded, in Venice, then set as the welcome to greet visitors to her home.

'They're just bells, Linz. Beautiful, I grant you, but nothing special.'

'*Che bella giornata*,' whispered Linz, with a faraway look in her eyes. 'A beautiful day.'

'Explain,' said Miles, sensing a story behind the words.

'From ancient time, Miles, there have always been five bells at St Marks. Each bell has a special name. The *Marangona*, the largest, at whose sound practitioners of the various crafts began and stopped work, is followed by the peals of the *Trottiera*, so called because, on hearing it, the patricians had to hurry to the Ducal Palace, urging their horses into a trot to get there on time. The third bell is the *Nona*, and rings out at midday, and then my personal favourite, the *Mezza Terza*, which announces important Senate meetings. The final bell and smallest of them all is the *Renghiera*, known as the Evil Deed, which announced an execution.'

'Cool,' said Miles, enjoying the history behind the bells, 'but I still don't get it. Why them?'

Linz touched the gold necklace that lay around her neck, stroking the blood-warm metal as if it were a living thing. Its flattened links were so perfectly formed that it looked like an unbroken strand of rolled gold.

'Sean bought this for me,' she whispered, 'in Venice, on our honeymoon, from a little jewellery shop on the banks of the Canale Grande. We first heard the bells rung that day. Some local procession or maybe just for the thousands of visiting tourists. It's not important. Sean adored the sound of them. We both did. Just being there, together, it was special.'

Miles could see what Linz was describing had been a private and very personal experience for her and Sean. He felt happy for them as well as just a little envious.

'It sounds wonderful.'

'It was, Miles, in so many ways. It's the reason I went to the trouble of recording the bells. Sean gave me the gift of gold, that day, with this necklace. In return, I gave him the bells of St Marks, the memory of that day we shared. A beautiful day, Miles. Or as they say in Venice, *che bella giornata*.'

The sound of the fifth bell, the *Renghiera*, from behind the door, dragged Miles back into the present. He was shaken by the memory and took a breath to steady himself.

'I miss you, Linz. I hope you are with your God.'

He struck his knuckles against the door, having no wish to hear the bells ring again. He could not begin to imagine Sean's pain if the sound of them could open the unhealed wound in his own heart. Again, there was no answer. He peered in through the square, glass panel cut into the door. The hallway was empty, but having seen the empty wine bottle, scrunched-up napkin and empty plate, through the kitchen window, knew Sean was at home. Or at least had been, unless he'd reinstated his daily run along Cramond beach.

Exasperated, he hammered on the door with a force that shook it on its hinges. After waiting two or three minutes, he let himself in. He turned into the living room and crossed to the doorway leading into the library and Sean's personal study, which overlooked the back gardens through a wide expanse of windows behind an oversized glass-topped desk.

The study was a veritable man-cave, with a pair of brown, leather couches and matching club chairs, the shine on the seats and armrests worn away so that the leather was faded and cracked. The white-painted walls were covered in an array of prints, paintings and mounted movie-posters. Sean had clearly been there, for the dust-sheets that had covered the furniture lay in the corner like a crumpled party dress after a good night out.

'Miles!' The voice behind him startled him. Miles didn't turn, as most people would have done. Sean would have loved it if he'd appeared to have given him a fright. 'You're getting careless, old man.'

'I knew you were there from the moment your big clumsy foot creaked the loose floorboard in the livingroom,' said Miles, keeping his voice calm and showing he hadn't been caught unawares, 'I was simply waiting for you to come and see who'd broken into your house.'

'Sure, you were,' said Sean, beaming.

Miles turned and smiled at Sean, then stepped forward to hug him. Sean returned the hug and they clapped each other on the back.

'It's damn good to see you, Major.'

'You too, Miles. I've missed your big ugly face.'

'Miles, is it, now? How terribly formal.'

Sean had always called Miles by his middle name, *Gaylord*. He was the only person alive allowed to use that moniker.

'Well it's been almost a year. Anyway, how are you? Fit and well, I hope? I thought you might have gone soft without me here to keep you on your toes. By the looks of it, you're spending too much time behind a desk.'

'You're looking a bit fuller yourself, Major. When are you due?' Miles immediately realised what he'd said. 'Oh Christ, Sean. I'm so sorry. I'm a bloody idiot.'

'Relax, Miles, you don't have to tip-toe around me. I've had enough of that bullshit. Come on through to the kitchen. I'm hungover as hell and starving. There's eggs and bacon in the fridge. I'm guessing you put them there. You cook and I'll go shower. Deal?'

'Deal.'

'Oh, and Miles, try not to burn anything.'

'One time, Major. I set fire to the mess tent, one time, and you still won't let it go!'

They grinned at each other like schoolboys.

Miles felt a sense of relief. He hadn't been sure how Sean would be. This was as good as he could have hoped.

'Never will, Gaylord, never will,' replied Sean, giving him a broad smile that put him more at ease.

They ate breakfast with relish, chatting between mouthfuls of hot tea, crispy bacon and fried eggs on toast. The conversation was light, with Miles bringing Sean up to speed on everything he'd been doing, recently, from expanding his security company to complaining about the local Edinburgh rugby team. They talked about everything and anything. Anything but the one thing they were both thinking about. Linz and the kids. *That conversation will come*, thought Miles. *When he's ready.*

'What have you been up to, Major? I called, loads of times. I just kept getting your mailbox message. Until that stopped working.'

'I know, Miles. I'm sorry. I just needed some space.'

'I get it, but you're back now, so, you know, anytime you need me. Or you just want to grab a beer and sit in silence.'

'I know that, Gaylord. Thanks.'

'You'll be going back to work soon, I guess?'

'Soon,' said Sean, making a mental note to check that Judith had sold his shares in QuantumCloud. 'I'll probably have to bugger off abroad, possibly even next week, to bring myself up to speed on the merger. Don't be surprised if you don't see me for a while. I'm back, but not for good. You know me.'

Miles nodded.

'One step at a time and one foot in front of the other.'

'Exactly!'

'Are you glad to be home?'

Sean pondered the question for a moment.

'I had to come back. I wasn't going to, but Linz told me I had to. She's here, you know. The kids, too, I think.'

'Of course, they are,' said Miles, nodding in agreement. 'They always will be.'

'I saw her, Miles, yesterday. On Nevis.'

'You were on the Ben?'

Miles looked surprised.

'Above the Braveheart car park, near the Achintree Inn.'

'Where you and Linz first met! Where *we* first met, come to that.'

Miles pictured the day they'd all spent there. It was a good but poignant memory.

'She was there, looking as beautiful as ever.'

'I saw her myself, this morning,' replied Miles, misunderstanding Sean's meaning.

'You saw her!' Sean replied, doing the same. 'Where?'

'At Cramond Kirk. Under the whalebones. I pictured her and . . .'

'Cramond Kirk!' Sean said, not allowing Miles to finish what he was saying. 'I've not been there since . . .'

He buried his head in his hands at the memory.

'The funeral service was rough, Sean. It must have . . .'

Miles stopped talking, unable to properly convey what he was trying to describe. The thought of the heart-breaking day was clearly too much for Sean to bear. *Yet*, thought Miles, *he must face it*. 'Let's go there. You can visit Linz and the kids.'

Sean's face blanched.

'Now? Do you think she'll still be there?'

'Or course she will,' said Miles. 'I've been there to see her myself, many times.'

'How many times?'

Miles was taken aback by the odd question.

'Just a few. To talk to her and the kids. Take flowers. That sort of thing. You know?'

'She never mentioned it.'

Again, the answer confused Miles. He placed a reassuring hand on Sean's shoulder. Sean flinched at the contact, which was not the Sean Miles knew. This was a man who had guided a team of soldiers though enemy lines in the dead of night, not a man who was jumpy or didn't face things head on. He put the odd behaviour down to the strain Sean was obviously under. It was bound to make him a little off kilter.

'I'll drive us there, Major. Don't think about it. Just grab your jacket and let's go.'

Sean hesitated for a moment, unsure what to do. Linz had told him to come home. But she still hadn't come to see him.

'Okay, Miles. Perhaps you're right. Maybe she'd like to meet me there.

Miles parked his jeep just past the entrance to the church entrance and switched off the engine. He and Sean hadn't spoken in the few minutes it had taken to drive there. Sean looked like a man being taken to a place of execution. His face was pale and coated with a light sheen of sweat.

'Let's go, Major,' said Miles, brightly, trying his best to lift Sean's sombre mood. He undid his seatbelt to get out of the car, but Sean placed a hand on his arm.

'Linz and I need to be together, Miles. Just the two of us. She's my wife, after all.'

Miles nodded and patted Sean on the arm.

'Of course, Major. I completely understand. I'll wait for you here. When you're done, maybe we can go for a beer.' He looked up at the sky. 'It's not a bad looking day. We could take the boat out for few hours and sail down the Firth of Forth to North Berwick harbour?'

Sean looked at him as if he was talking Swahili.

"I don't have time to go bloody sailing, Miles! I'm going to talk to my wife. There's a lot we need to discuss.'

'Easy, Major. I know this must be hard for you, but . . .'

'Hard for me? What the fuck do you know about it?' Sean's voice turned cold and hard. 'You spent years being in love with Linz. But she didn't love you, Miles. She loved me.'

Miles could see the anger flushing Sean's face, although he couldn't understand why. He tried to remain calm, despite his anger at what Sean was accusing him of.

'I did love her, Sean, of course I did. But she was my friend, that's all. You know that. Just as *you're* my friend. Linz would want me to be here for you.'

'She doesn't want you, Miles. And I don't need your fucking sympathy. I've done fine by myself, this past year, without you or anybody else to help me. Now, I just need to see my wife. *My wife*, Miles. Not yours!'

Sean got out of the car and slammed the door closed, then stormed off towards the church entrance. Miles called to him through the open passenger window.

'Major! 'What the hell's wrong? Why are you saying these things? Look, I'll wait for you here. Just take as long as you need.'

'Go home, Miles, Sean shouted back, without turning around, 'We don't need you any longer.'

Miles was beyond confused. Part of him wanted to get out and go after

Sean. Another part told him it was a bad idea.

'What the hell's wrong with you. Why are you so angry?'

Sean turned and looked at Miles. It was a look Miles had seen before, in the warzones they'd both encountered, only not directed at him. A look that confused him, for the anger being projected at him was palpable.

'She's not yours, Miles. Linz chose me. Live with it.'

'Sean! What the hell are you talking about?'

'You always wanted her back, Miles, didn't you? You couldn't stay away from her. Always hanging around the house, trying to weasel your way back into her heart. And now you're meeting her behind my back. Trying to take her away from me. Just fuck off, Miles. Fuck off and leave us alone!'

Miles confusion turned to anger. He was furious at what Sean was accusing him of. But he wasn't going to just sit there and take it.

Well if that's how you feel, your wish is my command.'

He gunned the car and drove away, not bothering to look back.

Sean watched Miles go, angry that he had been betrayed by his friend. His chest began to tighten and his vision started to fade. He visualised the clockface and tried to calm himself. He didn't want to lose time. Not here. A voice behind him brought him back.

'Sean.'

He turned to see Linz standing on the footpath in front of the entrance to the church grounds. She smiled at him then walked under the arched whalebones and up the granite-chip pathway, beneath the fawning branches of the cherry trees.

13

Father James Mackenzie, "Mac", to his closest friends, knelt in silence, his head bowed before the outstretched arms of an intricately carved figure of Jesus Christ on the Cross, which dominated the altar wall of Cramond Brig Catholic Church, or "Cramond Kirk", as it was known locally. He knelt, not in adoration or supplication, but because he was trying to erase a red wine stain from the carpet. A spill he'd made when he'd performed a private communion for one of his more important parishioners the previous evening.

Brigadier-General John Murray was a friend of the Archbishop of Glasgow and had always been a generous contributor to the Cramond Kirk coffers in times of need. So, when the Archbishop had called to request Mac open the church doors, despite it being eight o'clock on a chilly Monday night, to provide a private communion for the Brigadier-General and some of his fellow officers due to fly out from the nearby army base the following day, there was no question of the favour not being granted. So, the private communion had gone ahead, and, in due course, Mac had spilt the sacramental wine, his shakier by the day right hand the culprit, the church carpet the victim.

What the Archbishop didn't know was that Mac had served with the then Captain John Murray, some thirty years before, during the Falklands War between Argentina and the United Kingdom, when they'd both been a good deal younger and greener. That same young Captain had saved Mac's life when he'd been wounded on the final push into Port Stanley, the capital of those cold South Atlantic islands.

Mac's right hand still hurt when the weather was cold, but the chest wound he had suffered no longer bothered him. He had been lucky to live.

So many others had not. The near-death experience had been the catalyst for him to devote his life to God, and the reason he'd given up a promising army medical career. So, there'd been no question that he would have refused the Archbishop's request.

'Just didn't want to get you in the shite, Mac,' John had told him later, over a whisky, in Mac's private room at the back of the kirk. 'You know what a pompous old goat he can be. Even God's soldiers have a chain of command.'

At least the carpet is red, mused Mac, although the stain was still visible, despite his efforts to eradicate it.

Resigning himself to defeat, he sat up on his knees and ran a hand through a shock of silver hair that still grew too quickly and made him look a bit like the now deceased actor, Alan Rickman. From the corner of his eye, he noticed someone pass by the window of the side door, where the north transept led out into the Gospel side of the church grounds. Whom it had been, he could not say, for sure, but there had been a certain familiarity to the profile he'd briefly caught.

Sean passed the side door of the church, his feet crunching on the gravel pathway, scanning ahead of him but seeing no sign of Linz.

'Linz!' He called, frantically. 'Where are you?'

'Sean.'

He heard her call, but could not see her.

Ahead of him, a wall, about five feet high, ran from the taller wall of the adjacent house, across the back of the graveyard, joining the main church building. The stone used to build it and its haphazard looking construction suggested it was very old, though it had outlasted the inhabitants buried deep in the ground in front of it. Linz's voice seemed to have come from somewhere close to it.

In the left-hand corner of the graveyard, beyond the gravestones but behind the wall, stood an apple tree. It was in full bloom and heavy with white blossoms. Below its hanging branches, looking directly at him, was Linz, her head and shoulders visible. The sunlight filtering through the spaces in the blossoms dappled her hair in patches of gold. She was as beautiful as Sean remembered ever seeing her.

'I'm coming, my love.'

He stepped off the gravel pathway and onto the grass, passing age-stained gravestones that had shifted, over time, leaving a few of them leaning at random angles. Some had faces so weather-beaten that the original names of the those they stood to commemorate had all but disappeared. Sean rounded one and read the wind-aged words carved into its face, *Custodi in Memoria*, which translated as, if his high school Latin was still to be trusted, Kept in Memory.

Passed it, he looked towards the apple tree, but Linz was no longer standing there. His heart raced and he quickened his pace, rounding the last gravestone and reaching the wall.

A black painted, iron gate topped with *Fleur de Lis* points stood at its centre, it was slightly taller than the wall and surrounded by a stone archway. Beyond it, lay a small courtyard paved with flagstones that looked as old as the ancient church. A narrow flowerbed ran along the back wall, and the same daffodils, crocuses, and snowdrops planted at the front of the church provided a welcome burst of colour. Four iron benches, set in front of the flowers, painted in the same black paint as the *Fleur de Lis* gate, sat empty.

Sean pushed the gate, which swung open, silently, on well-oiled hinges, and passed under the archway into the courtyard. He turned towards the apple tree and walked to the point, beneath it, where Linz had been standing.

'Linz, my love. Where are you?'

His voice faltered, the pain of the loss of her threatening to crush him. He reached out and touched the apple tree, seeking some sort of physical connection. A sudden gust of wind rustled the branches and blossoms fell like flakes of snow, covering his head and shoulders. A strong feeling of premonition swept over him, as if this was a vision of a future he was yet to live.

'Linz, don't leave me, my love.'

'Sean.' Lost in the aching realisation that he was alone, he didn't hear his name being spoken. But the voice came again. 'Sean.'

This time he heard it.

'Linz?'

'You've found our remembrance garden,' said Father Mackenzie.

Startled, Sean turned and looked towards the gate. Finally realising it wasn't Linz he was hearing.

'Mac.'

'Hello, Sean. It's good to see you again. How have you been?

Sean, Mac noticed, was looking around him, as if confused.

'I was just . . . Linz.'

'Shall we take a seat, Sean? I've been kneeling for hours and my knees aren't what they once were.' Mac opened the gate and crossed to the iron bench closest to the apple tree end of the courtyard. He took a seat and looked up at the apple blossoms, then, so as not to show any favouritisim, turned and smiled at the flowers behind him. 'Spring is definitely here, don't you think?'

'Yes,' said Sean, hesitantly, 'I suppose so.'

Mac had baptized Alice and Toby at Crammond Kirk. He'd given Sean and Linz communion, taken their confessions, and been a sounding board for Sean after the death of his father, absorbing the outpouring of anger he had demonstrated for a man he had been made to despise. He and Mac were also former soldiers, which forged bonds like no other.

'Come and sit down, Sean. Let's catch up.'

'But, I'm supposed to . . .'

Sean seemed troubled. Mac guessed why.

It had been a year since they'd last seen each other at the service to commemorate the lives of his wife and children. It was clearly, for Sean, a traumatic return. He kept his voice calm and quiet.

'I love this time of year, when the flowers burst out of the ground like nature's choir, singing away to us that a new season is here and that new beginnings are possible.'

Sean seemed not to have heard him, or, if he had, was too wrapped up in other thoughts. It didn't matter, only that they talked.

'She was here, Mac. Linz was here. Only a moment ago. Didn't you see her?'

Mac nodded.

'I see her all the time, Sean. And there's a bit of her that will always be here. That's good to know, isn't it? Come and sit down. Let's talk for a while.'

'Sure, Mac, why not?'

Sean took a seat beside him, sitting with his hands crossed on his knees, his eyes still fixed on the space below the apple tree. Mac placed his large, weather-beaten hands on top of Sean's, attempting to offer what comfort he could. Sometimes even a human touch was enough.

'She was here,' whispered Sean.

He looked at Mac like a small child seeking reassurance.

Mac nodded, wondering how to best give him that. He had learned early on in his calling that, sometimes, it wasn't what was said that mattered, but simply the act of speaking.

'I really must have the gardeners set some planters out here,' he said, matter-of-factly, 'I think some lavender would be perfect. The bees would love that. We can't live without the bees, can we, Sean? You've got lavender plants up at Merrick, haven't you? Perhaps I could take some cuttings from them to use here. I think Linz would like that. What do you think?'

'Of course,' stammered Sean, 'take as much as you need. Linz *would* love that. She loved her garden.'

He pictured her in the back garden of Merrick, where she'd loved to potter, happiest when creating and nurturing life and colour. She'd always dressed in the same gardening outfit, rain or shine; an old pair of patched-up blue jeans, a grey, Wrangler t-shirt, that had once been his, and scruffy, white baseball boots laced up with lime-green coloured laces.

'Yes, she loved her gardening,' said Mac. 'We had many conversations about what the best manure was for roses. She always swore pig manure was better than horse manure. I never tried her theory out. Still, she told me she was right, and we both know how pointless it was to argue with her once she had her mind made up on something. Isn't that right, Sean?'

Sean seemed to come back from wherever his mind had been. His face changed and he seemed much brighter. It was a subtle change, but one Mac noticed.

'That's why I'm here, Mac. She wanted me to be here, today. She was right there, standing by the apple tree.'

His voice was tight and fraught. He seemed to be almost manic.

'It's all right, Sean. I believe you.'

He was clearly having visions of Linz, thought Mac, which was not unusual. Many of his parishioners had lost spouses yet insisted they had seen them as if they were still alive. Bereavement hallucinations were well-documented and common around the world.

'She led me here.'

Mac nodded.

'Of course she led you here, Sean. And why would she not? She *is* here, as are Alice and Toby.' He stood and took Sean by the hand, leading him the few steps back towards the apple tree. 'Look! Don't you see? Linz brought you here today to visit them.'

Sean looked down at a bronze plaque fixed to the stone wall with four round-headed brass screws. Etched into it were the words:

In loving memory of Lindsay Jameson, Alice Scott Jameson and Tobias Ian Jameson. A daughter, wife and mother. A grandson and son. A daughter and granddaughter. A family together. Always.

'Who? Who did this?' Sean whispered.

'Ian,' said Mac, 'her father.'

'And . . . their ashes?'

'Ian has them. He took them for you, after . . .'

Sean dropped his head in silent shame.

'After I left. After I abandoned them.'

Mac could hear the torture Sean was directing at himself, but couldn't find the words to make it any better for him.

'He waited for months until he did, Sean. He wanted you to be the one to collect them. In the end, he was pushed into taking them by the crematorium.'

Sean knelt and reached out to touch the plaque. The metal was warm, as if some trace of his family's lives remained, trapped in the copper that would carry their names through eternity. He ran his fingers, in turn, over each of the names, seeking a connection with them.

'Linz, my love. Toby, my young Caesar. Alice, my Princess.'

He spoke their names and felt closer to them than he had at any time over the past year. The memory of their faces, the sound of their laughter and their beautiful smiles came back to him. Memories he had banished to the empty place, unable to face them. He pushed them down, still unable to bear them.

'Talk to them, Sean,' said Mac. They're listening.'

Sean bowed his head.

'Forgive me.'

He whispered their names, again, as if chanting a mantra designed to break the spell of death and return them to him. As he spoke, some small part of the pain and suffering of the past year poured out of him, like sand through an hourglass. His shoulders shook as he wept.

Behind him, Mac felt tears pricking the corners of his eyes. If he had not, before, known the sound of true loss, he knew it now. He reached up and held the wooden crucifix he wore around his neck and said a silent prayer. *Dear Lord, help me heal this lost sheep.* He placed a hand on Sean's shoulder, knowing there was nothing he could say to ease his suffering.

Gradually, Sean stopped shaking and became quiet. His fingers still touching the names on the copper plaque.

'I miss them, Mac, so damned much. As I never knew I could. I never knew pain like this existed. I can't bear it.'

'I know, Sean. But you will. You will bear it as others before you have done. You may feel lost, my son, but you are not alone.'

'Then why do I feel so alone, Mac? Day and night. It never ends. I never realised how much I needed them. I always thought it was the other way around.'

'What I am saying, Sean, is that we all feel alone, at times. Especially going through the darker periods in our lives. But someone is always watching over us.'

'God! Is that who you mean?'

Sean spat the words as if purging a bitter taste from his mouth.

'Yes, Sean. He is always with us.'

'Really, Mac? Always with us?'

Sean stood and faced Mac, his face dark with anger.

'He is, Sean. Even if you struggle to believe that.'

'Then where was he the night they died, Mac? Where was he the night Linz was dragged from a falling car and her body broken on the rocks? Where was he when Toby's neck was snapped by a crushed car roof? Where was your precious God when I held my baby girl in my arms and watched her die? If He's always with us, why did he stand by and watch my family die? Because if that's the God you're talking about he's a cruel, heartless God. Not one I want in my life. I'd rather cast him out, as he cast out his own fallen angel.'

'Don't say that, Sean. You're angry, I understand that. But don't blame

Him for what happened.'

'Why the fuck not, Mac? If He's so all-seeing and all-powerful then why didn't He save them? You're the priest, the one with all the fucking answers. Why shouldn't I blame Him?'

'Sean, I can't even begin to try and . . .'

Mac stopped talking. Sean was reeling on his feet. As quickly as his it seemed to have come over him, his rage had evaporated. He fell forward into Mac's open arms.

'I'm so lost, Mac. Lost and alone in a world of darkness and pain. Help me. For the love of God. Help me!'

Mac put his arms around Sean, holding him upright as he collapsed, mentally and physically.

'I'm here, Sean. I've got you. You've found your way home to your family and to God's house. And with His help you will find your way out of the darkness. I swear that to you, Sean. He will not abandon you. And I will not abandon you. I will share your burden and your pain until we find the light. You are not alone, Sean. You are not alone.'

They stood together for some time, beside the bowing apple tree and the silent choir of flowers, Mac holding Sean, feeling his body shake and listening to him weep, like father and a prodigal son.

14

Sean sunk back in the leather armchair in front of the fireplace in Mac's private sanctuary at the top end of the church. The room had originally been part of the sacristy, but at some time in the past had been converted into a quiet place for the priest to relax in before or after church business. They'd entered directly from the Remembrance Garden courtyard, through a side door that Mac had opened with a large bunch of keys looped onto a ring strapped to his waist, hidden beneath the folds of his cassock.

Mac tossed some fresh logs on the burning coals. They snapped and crackled as the flames licked up around them like fiery tongues. He thought to offer Sean a dram, but decided against it, having detected the sour taint of whatever alcohol Sean had obviously imbibed, the previous night, still on his breath. Instead, he rang through to the church kitchens and asked Sister Abagail to bring them a fresh pot of tea and some digestive biscuits. Tea, not whisky, would help best. It always did in such emotional situations.

While Sean ate the biscuits with more relish than even *he* had thought he would, Mac talked about how things had transpired from the last time he'd been in the church, almost a year ago, at the funeral service for Linz, Alice and Toby.

'A week or so after your trial for manslaughter, Sean, something I felt was entirely wrong of the police to bring to court at all, Ian and Dorothy came to see me. They were concerned about you. We could all see how devastated you were and how much the trial had cost you.'

Sean took a deep breath, remembering the shame of the trial he'd been forced to go through.

'They blamed me for the death of their only child and their grandchildren. I could see the accusation in their eyes in the courtroom. They believed it was my fault.'

Mac sat forward in his chair and shook his head.

'No, Sean, that's not true. What you saw was grief and confusion. They were in pain, as you were. As you still are. But they know it was an accident. They don't blame you.'

Sean looked down at his feet, unable or unwilling to take in what Mac was saying. He was subdued and his voice was quiet and shaky.

'The last time I saw them was at the trial. They were witnesses for the prosecution. I've not seen or spoken to them since.'

'I understand, Sean, yet Ian referred to you as *his son*, when he and Dorothy came here, hoping to find out if I knew where you were. They'd gone to your home, only to find Merrick locked and deserted. They'd visited your office, in town, and spoke to some of your colleagues, who knew no more about where you were than they did. They called you and left countless messages, all of which went unanswered. They knew you were in pain. They wanted to help you carry it.'

'I couldn't face them, Mac. Them or anyone else. It was my pain to deal with. My shame to carry. It belonged to me. All of it. Not to anyone else.'

'That's possibly one of the saddest things I've ever heard, Sean. But you're so wrong.'

'Am I, Mac? Am I really?' Sean stared into the flames of the fire, his mind a turmoil of emotions. 'I killed them. I deserve to be in pain for doing that.'

Mac sighed and tried to explain.

'When we share our pain, Sean, that's what makes being human so special. That's when we are at our very best. Supporting each other. Nobody need ever suffer alone. Love is the answer to all our problems and the balm to ease our wounds. Jesus Christ taught us that lesson.'

Sean looked over at Mac, his turn to shake his head.

'That's not my experience, so I guess you don't really understand.'

'Explain it to me then.'

'I've been conditioned all my life, Mac, not to look to anyone else for anything. Even as a child I knew it was the only way to protect myself, hiding my feelings and fear, rather than sharing them. How can you share your pain when there was never anyone to share it with? How can you learn to love anyone when you had no love given to you? I can't just suddenly change how I am or how I feel. It's how I've been made. I don't know *how* to change.'

'I know of your past, Sean. What your father did to you was ungodly.'

'Ungodly! Well that's one way of putting it. I lived with daily violence, constant fear, debilitating loneliness and having to deal with my own shit.'

Sean stared back into the fire, lost in memories that were clearly still torturing him. His speech, Mac noticed, seemed to be slowing. His voice sounded odd and was barely audible.

'Are you all right, Sean?'

'You never shared your problems, Mac. Not ever. There was no point. No-one cared. No-one . . . No one . . . No . . . '

Sean's body seemed to freeze, a look of sadness, or fear, etched into his face. At first, Mac thought he was processing what they'd been talking about. A great deal of emotional baggage had been opened which was being slowly sifted through. But as the minutes passed, it seemed something more. His conscious mind appeared to have completely shut down, as if he had retreated to a place where nothing could touch him. His pupils were massively dilated, the cornflower blue irises turned almost black, his focus far beyond the flames of the fire into which he was staring and his breathing was practically non-existent.

Mac had seen catatonic states before, in soldiers returned home from war, scarred on the inside by the trauma they had witnessed. But this was something else entirely. He remembered his medical training, trawling up information he had long thought forgotten. The dilation of Sean's eyes, *mydriasis,* was a psychological response to fear or surprise, but the fact that he appeared not to be breathing went against that diagnosis. If some dire thought *had* brought back a memory so strong that it had paralyzed him with fear, his heart rate would be racing. He would be breathing heavily and sweating, perhaps even trembling.

Concerned, Mac leant across and placed a hand on Sean's knee.

'Sean, can you hear me?'

Sean recoiled from the touch. His eyes flared wide, the black irises making him look possessed. He slammed a hand down on the back of Mac's hand and screamed at him.

'Don't touch me. Don't you ever fucking touch me again.'

He leapt to his feet and stood over Mac, his face filled flushed and filled with rage.

For a moment, Mac was certain Sean was going to strike him, so he remained still, fearing any sudden movement might bring him onto him like a lion to a lamb. Instead, he spoke, calmly and softly, his voice flat and monotone.

'Sean, it's me. Mac. I'm sorry, I didn't mean to scare you. No one is going to hurt you. You're safe.'

Sean reached down and grabbed hold of Mac's right hand, the grip so powerful Mac could already feel his hand going numb, but as he continued speaking to him, Sean began to release the hold, his eyes turning back from black to blue. In that moment, Mac thought of the book, *Jekyll and Hyde*, knowing he had seen the twin faces of love and hate in the face of one man.

A moment later, Sean dropped his hands, staring at them as if they belonged to someone else. As he held them out in front of him, they began to tremble and his breathing became short and sharp. His confusion was evident. It appeared he was on the verge of some kind of breakdown.

Mac stood and moved, slowly, towards him, reaching out and placing the palms of his hands either side of Sean's arms, attempting to comfort and reassure him. Sean looked at him through frightened blue eyes. Mac smiled at him as if the past few moments had never taken place. Sean was obviously not aware they had.

'Mac! What happened?'

'Nothing, Sean. Nothing at all. You seemed to be in a daydream. Just for a moment.'

It was important, Mac knew, to make light of what had happened, rather than cause Sean any further confusion by telling him what he'd done. His first instinct had been to end the conversation and get away. He hadn't seen violence in a long time, and what had just happened frightened him, but Sean was in pain that went far beyond the loss of his wife and children. Pain, Mac feared, for all his words of comfort, his love, and even with the help of God, he could not fix. But he had asked God to allow him to share Sean's burden. *Had not his prayer been answered?* God had returned the lamb to the shepherd. He would not turn it away. He ushered Sean back into his armchair and sat down opposite him.

A knock on the door startled them both. Sister Abagail opened the door and popped her head in.

'More tea, Father?'

Her voice was sharp and high-pitched, matching the long, thin face on which sat a classic aquiline nose. She peered at Sean through round, wire-rimmed glasses, which enlarged her eyes, making them appear owl-like. Sean smiled up at her, but the firm set of her lips and the accusatory stare did not flicker in response.

'No, thank you, Sister,' said Mac, 'we've still got a few cups in the pot.'

'Very good, Father.'

'Sister Abagail, can I leave it to you to see I'm not disturbed for the next hour?'

'Of course, Father. I'll make sure of it.'

She gave Mac an adoring smile and, with a glare at Sean which left him in no doubt that should he do anything to upset Father Mackenzie it would be her that he would answer to, closed the door.

Mac smiled at Sean and shrugged.

'She's quite protective of me. Sees my comfort and safety as her own personal charge from God.'

Sean returned Mac's smile with one of his own. A smile Mac was glad to see.

'You don't say! I've had warmer looks from people who really dislike me.'

'She's young and shy, but a sweet girl.'

'I don't doubt it, Mac, but I've clearly been warned.'

'I wouldn't cross her, Sean, to be fair.'

'Trust me, I won't. She looked at me like a sparrow-hawk eyeing up a nice fat pigeon.'

They both laughed at the image. Not that it was overly amusing, but because the tension between them demanded it.

Mac took the crocheted tea cozy off the still warm pot and poured them each out another cup. They sat in silence for the next few minutes, sipping their tea, letting the fire warm them and enjoying the peace of the small but homely room. The walls, lined in polished oak, glowed from the flames in the fireplace and the smell from the pine logs was spicy and comforting.

'I couldn't face them, Mac,' said Sean, suddenly, 'them or anyone else. It was my pain to deal with. My shame to carry. It belonged to me. All of it. Not to anyone else.'

'I'm sorry, Sean, what?'

Mac had no idea what Sean was eluding to.

'Ian and Dorothy. We were just talking about them. You told me they came to see you, looking for me. For God's sake, Mac, it was literally just before Sister Abagail knocked on the door to ask if we wanted more tea.'

'Ian and Dorothy! Of course.'

Mac suddenly realised what was happening. Sean had gone back to the conversation they'd had over half an hour before. Prior to having his black-out, for want of a better description.

'Are you okay, Mac?'

'Sorry, Sean. I'm obviously having another one of my grey moments.'

Sean gave him a warm smile.

'Nonsense! We all forget things from time to time. We put them in boxes in our heads and sometimes forget they're there.'

'I suppose we do.'

'Christ! I sound like the bloody lesbian.'

'Like who?' Mac asked, frowning at the reference.

'Emily MacGregor, my psychiatrist. I've obviously been brainwashed by her.'

'It put a smile on your face, Sean, no matter what you meant by it.'

'The nun and the lesbian. Both made me smile inside two minutes.'

'Sean!'

'Sorry,' said Sean, not at all sounding contrite, 'it just struck me as amusing.'

Sean, Mac felt, seemed more like himself than he'd been all morning. Perhaps he should just put what had happened down to him having had to face the full reality of his loss in the Remembrance Garden. Given they'd made some progress, he thought he might push things along a little.

'Tell me, when did you last make a confession?'

Sean gave a low whistle.

'It's been a long time. But why should I bother? It's not as if there's anyone there to hear it.'

'I know you're angry, Sean, with yourself, the world, and even with God. Perhaps you have every right to be. But, maybe as a starting point to getting back to something approaching normal, to continue the healing process, you could begin there?'

'I didn't come back to heal, Mac. I came because Linz told me to. She told me to come back to Edinburgh. She guided me, here, to the church, and led me to the plaque below the apple tree. How else would I have known to go to that exact spot. You told me yourself that you've seen her.'

'I meant in my mind's eye, Sean. I'm sure you *think* you've seen her, and that's perfectly normal. It's called a bereavement vision. But it's not real. It's only your mind trying to comfort you.'

'I saw her,' said Sean, angrily, 'with my own eyes.'

'You wanted to see Linz,' said Mac, 'so you did. Your brain, in a turmoil of emotions, filled in the gaps. But she's dead, Sean, as are Alice and Toby. I know it's painful to accept, but they've passed on to a much better place. Try to take some comfort in that. They can't come back to you, no matter how hard that is to hear.'

Sean went quiet for a moment. Mac was afraid he would retreat back inside himself. Thankfully, it seemed he had simply been reflecting on what he'd said.

'I can't live without them, Mac. Linz understands that. We've talked about. She wants me to join them. It's why she brought me here. She wanted to show me where they were. Where I need to be, too. She wanted me to understand that. And I *want* to join them.'

Mac was aghast at the dreadful implications of what Sean was saying. He was talking, it seemed, about taking his own life; something that went against everything he believed in, not just as a priest, but as a human being.

'That's not why she came to you, Sean, in whatever form she did; ghost, spirit, whatever you want to call it. But the Linz I knew would never ask you to kill yourself to be with her. She loved you. The children loved you. They would want you to live your life, carrying them with you in your heart until it is the right time to join them, in Heaven. You *will* see them again, you must believe that. But your life, here, isn't over.'

Sean leaned forward in his chair, staring into Mac's eyes with a look of almost religious fervor.

'My life *is* over. I need to be with them. You understand that, don't you, Mac?'

Mac took a deep breath, knowing exactly what he had to say to bring Sean to his senses, although he did not relish it.

'So where are they Sean? Where *are* Linz and Toby and Alice?'

Sean looked at him, blankly, struggling to form an answer.

'I…I don't…'

'I'll tell you where, Sean. They're in Heaven, with God, and Heaven is not open to suicides. You'll throw your life away for nothing, if that's what you intend to do. You will never see them again. Never!'

Sean looked like a deer caught in a hunting spotlight. He stared, accusingly, at the large crucifix hanging above the fireplace. He had known that suicide was a mortal sin, of course, but had not thought beyond what he planned to do.

'Damn you, Mac, that's not fair. How can you tell me I can't join them? You say love is the answer, well joining Linz and the kids is surely the greatest act of love possible. How can I be punished for that? It's my life, dammit!'

Mac shook his head and pressed his hands together, as if preparing a prayer to invoke God's help.

'No, Sean, it's not. Our lives belong to God, not to us.' He sought an analogy with which to demonstrate his explanation. 'We are as ships, every one of us, sailing the waters in which He chooses to set us. Through calm and steady seas or raging storms we navigate our ship as best we can, but we are only the captains of those ships, not the owners. Suicide is a mortal sin. A sin against God. The owner of those ships in which he sets us.'

'And you believe that, Mac? Really believe it?'

'It is what the Catholic Church believes, Sean. It's God's law, not mine.'

'Horseshit!' Sean's voice was once again on the edge of rage. 'God no more created that particular law than you did. 'Your church sets rules which you use to keep us all in check. Changing them to suit you on a whim and a bloody prayer.'

'That's not true.'

Mac winced at Sean's colorful language but let it pass. He was becoming more concerned for his mental state. His behaviour was erratic, his emotions swinging wildly from one state to another. What he had said about seeing Linz, about being asked, by her, to join her in death, was beyond normal grief. It was the sign of a mind no longer in full control.

'I'm ready for confession now,' said Sean, taking Mac completely off guard.

'Confession?'

'Confession,' repeated Sean. 'I think you're right. I need to unload the burden I'm carrying. Will you hear it?'

Mac felt a palpable sense of relief wash over him.

'Of course, Sean. I think it will help you. We can go straight to the confessional box. The church should be empty.'

'Yes, Father.'

Sean sounded apprehensive. Something Mac thought was normal for him to feel. But he was clearly taking a step forward, and forward steps were the hardest ones to take when someone was feeling lost.

'Don't be afraid, my son.'

'I'm not afraid,' said Sean, following Mac out through the door that led into the main church building.

Sean sat quietly in the confessional box. It had been a long time since he'd been there, but it was familiar and almost comforting. The same green velvet curtain that had always been there, cutting him off from the world outside, and the smell of old wood and incense adding to the experience. Mac sat in the adjoining booth, separated from Sean by a thin, oak panel with a latticed, reed grill set at face height, allowing them see the vague shape of each other. Less than twelve inches from one another but worlds apart.

'Are you ready, my son?

'I am, Father.'

'May the Lord be in your heart.'

Sean began to speak, although his words were not what Mac had been expecting to hear.

'I did not say I was going to kill myself, Father, only that Linz wants me to join her.'

'That is true, my son, but it seemed that was in your heart. However, we have spoken on the subject and agree it cannot happen. To take one's life is a sin against God and cannot be forgiven.'

'No, Father, we did not agree. I *am* going to end my life. I must be with my family. God cannot stop me. If he wishes to save me, he can try.'

From feeling he had mades some forward progress, Mac felt himself taking a step back.

'You must not speak like this. Not here.'

'Why not, Father? Is my confession not safe with you? Will you not hear it?

'Of course I will, but . . .'

'Then let us speak plainly and truthfully, *Father*.'

Mac heard the emphasis Sean had put on the word, Father, and the underlying anger in it. He had a sense of dark premonition for what was coming.

'I'm listening, my son. Say what is in your heart.'

Sean took a breath, composing his thoughts.

'Let's not forget, Father, that your idea of suicide being a mortal sin came from ancient Rome. Wasn't it Saint Augustine himself who decided on inventing that specific decree. After the rape of Lucretia?'

'Rome's most famous rape! Yes, to a point, you're correct. Although I'm surprised that you know your theological history so well.'

Mac was confused as to where Sean was going, but had no choice but to listen.

'I was raised,' Sean continued, 'if you can call it that, in a strict Catholic family, by a father who saw it necessary to ensure I understood the pain of his religion. It was irrelevant how the lesson was drummed into me, only that it was. Let's just say he was zealous. He, too, believed my life belonged to him. That I was his property, to do with what he wanted. It seemed your God agreed.'

'Your father was misguided, my son. He will be judged in Heaven for his sins.'

'Misguided! Judged in Heaven! You're so bloody typical of the Church, Father dear. You refuse to condemn those blackest sheep that remain inside the fold, but God forbid anyone who attacks them from the outside. Your lot close ranks quicker than politicians fearing an election loss. My father was a fucking psychopath. He deserves no place in Heaven. Yet you tell me he's there That he's been forgiven. How in the name of all that's fucking holy does that work?'

'Sean, please,' said Mac, forgetting he was taking the sacrament and using his Christian name, 'I know you're angry, but enough. Your language!'

Mac heard Sean take a few deep breaths, fighting to control his rage.

'I'm sorry, Father. You're right, I am angry. I think I have good reason. But let's stay on point, shall we?'

'I'm listening, my son. I'm here for as long as you wish to talk.'

Sean's voice returned to a quieter level as he continued to make his point.

'When Lucretia took her own life, unable to bear the pain of her violation, Augustine's response was to develop the notion that, by committing suicide, she had committed an even greater sin. A sin against God himself. But before he decreed suicide was a sin, most Romans considered it a respectable way to exit this mortal coil. Hundreds of Christians, too, were hailed as martyrs for deaths that we would label, today, as suicides; walking into the lion's den and certain death to show the strength of their beliefs. I know how that feels, believe me. I did it every day for seventeen bloody years, except the lion always chose to toy with me rather than finish me off. God was no great help to me then either. He never listened when *I* called.'

'He *was* there, Sean. He is always there.

Sean laughed, but there was no humour in it.

Whatever, perhaps he was just busy when I called. Who cares. But here's the real kicker, Father, the real cherry on top of the fucking religious cake we're fed. Jesus Christ, himself, knew he was going to die, yet freely offered up his life. So, to all intents and purposes, the Son of God committed suicide.'

'That's not true,' cried Mac, stunned at the vehemence in Sean's voice, as well as the attempt to justify his own death. 'Jesus cannot be accused of that. It's a different case entirely.'

'How bloody convenient, Father. Then again, the church always tends to do what's convenient for it rather than what is right.'

'Sean, please, listen to me. I want to explain something . . .'

Mac's attempted to intervene but Sean cut him short.

'The point I'm making, Mac, is that your rulebook is a bloody joke; black on the outside and blacker on the inside. Answer me this. Why, before Augustine's decree, did martyrs and suicides get to go to heaven? And why am I to be refused that same gift, when a man of flesh and blood changed the rules, hundreds of years after the death of Jesus, just because he was pissed off?

'Sean . . .'

'No, Mac, it's my turn to talk, so bloody well listen.'

Mac fell silent, knowing he had no choice but to hear Sean out.

Love is the answer? Really, Mac? Then why is my love not worthy enough? Why should I be denied a place in Heaven? Jesus Christ committed fucking suicide, so why is he not burning in hell?'

Mac was disturbed and confused by the change in Sean. He had seemed to be calming before he took confession, but now it was as if the darker side of him had reemerged. He tried to reach him to bring him back.

'Sean! You must stop! Please. This is blasphemy and highly offensive.'

Sean ripped back the curtain of the confessional box, so roughly, that it tore free from the rail holding it, leaving it hanging limply from the remaining few hooks. He was halfway down the aisle and heading towards the front doors of the church before Mac had extricated himself.

'Sean,' cried Mac, rushing after him.

Sean stopped halfway down the aisle and turned to face him.

'Offensive! You feel offended? Just how in hell do you think I'm feeling?'

'Please, Sean, come back and talk.'

Mac took the few steps down from the alter onto the main nave, but Sean's eyes were filled with such malevolence that it stopped him in his tracks. He looked almost possessed.

'Fuck you, Mac! Fuck you and fuck your Church! And fuck your precious God while you're about it. He's never been there for me, not in all the times I begged Him to come. He took my family and left me here to laugh at. He destroyed my fucking life. And I'm supposed to just smile and accept that? You have the gall to tell me that our lives are His to destroy as he sees fit? Because of his bloody rules? Rules that make no sense. Rules made by petty, controlling men? My father hated his family, Mac. He tortured and persecuted us for years. But, according to you, he gets to go to Heaven. I loved my family more than my own life, but I don't get to be with them because of a technicality. Your religion is fucked up, Mac. So you can keep it. I want none of it.'

Sean reached up and tore the crucifix from his neck, cutting a bloody line into his flesh. He threw it to the floor and stared down at it as if it were something evil. The silver shone bright against the blood-red carpet, like the bloodied, silver spearhead penetrating the flesh of Jesus Christ on Calvary Hill. Mac stared down at it as if realising another lamb was in danger of being slaughtered.

'Sean, please. I'm begging you. Don't leave.'

But Sean was beyond bringing back.

'Jesus wept! Isn't that the saying, Mac? Well, with a father like his, who as good as nailed him to the fucking cross, no bloody wonder!'

Still Mac tried to get through to him.

'God is here for you, Sean. He *will* help you, if you allow Him.'

'Keep your fucking God, Mac. I no longer have need of him.'

'You don't mean that, Sean. You don't know what you're saying.'

I know exactly what I'm saying and who I'm saying it to,' cried Sean, trust me in that.' He looked over Mac's head to the carved statue of Jesus Christ on the Cross, directing his words like the spear that had pierced his side on the day of his crucifixion 'I renounce you, God. Do you hear me? I renounce you.'

He turned and strode down the nave, into the domed narthex.

'Come back, Sean!' Mac called after him, now on his knees in the church aisle, much as he had been when Sean had passed him earlier that morning. Only this time, he *was* praying.

Sean, not looking back, called to him.

'I'm done talking, Mac. To you and your false God.'

He drove his palms into the double front doors, slamming them open against the granite columns on either side of the narthex walls with a force that rattled them on their hinges.

Out in the light, Sean continued down the steps and along the cherry-tree pathway, past a group of shocked, elderly parishioners carrying flowers to lay at the graves of loved ones. Such was his anger he did not register them. His gaze was past them, over the gravestones, towards the white-blossomed, apple tree in the corner of the graveyard.

'Where are you, my love? What do want me to do now?'

But there was no sign of Linz.

He was alone and lost, in every sense of the word. He'd lost his faith, his God, and for the second time, it felt, his wife and children. Nothing could bring them back to him, nor could he be sure to join them if he tried. He walked under the whalebone arch, out onto the street, not knowing or caring where he was going.

15

The taxi-cab ride into Edinburgh city centre was a trip down memory lane, or would have been if Sean had cared to look. The cabbie tried to make small talk, but after a few attempts, which Sean ignored, decided that this was one of those fares that didn't need his views on Edinburgh Council's hatred of all things car and took the fastest route into town. It was a rugby weekend. There were plenty of fares to be had.

The traffic was backed up all the way down Howe Street, the cobbled road that led from the city centre down to Stockbridge, so Sean decided to get out and walk the last half mile.

The old village of Stockbridge, now part of Edinburgh city, was as familiar to Sean as old shoes, although he noticed a few new designer shops and bars had been opened since last he'd been there. He passed the Scran and Scallie Restaurant, where he and Linz had always gone for lunch on the first Sunday of each month to eat what they considered to be the best steak and ale pie in the world. The memory left a bitter taste in his mouth.

As he reached the top of Howe Street and turned right into George Street, he heard the boom of the "one o'clock gun", fired each day from Edinburgh Castle. It was a draw for tourists, but today sent a shell into his shattered heart. The sound dragged his gaze up and over Princes Street Gardens to where the castle stood, some four hundred feet above the city, at the top of a mile-long, sloping crag of volcanic rock.

From its raised portcullis gates, a cobbled road sloped down to the majestic Holyrood Palace, at the bottom of the Royal Mile, from where the ancient kings and queens of Scotland had headed up to the castle on the day they were to be crowned. Narrow streets called, "closes", ran off it on both sides, like veins branching out from the arteries of a beating heart.

Sean remembered taking Alice and Toby out among the maze of the Old Town on one of their much loved, "Daddy Days", when once a month he would take them out in Edinburgh to visit a museum or art gallery, or to explore the city's rich history on foot. It didn't matter where they went or what they did, only that they spent the day together. He had no such memories of his own father to look back on, so had been determined Toby and Alice would never have those empty spaces in their lives. Now they would never remember those days. He could. He wished he couldn't.

Staring up at the castle, trapped in the memory, the image of their last Daddy Day there reappeared like Banquo's ghost to Macbeth; a haunting memory adding to a day that had reached new depths in his already overwhelming sense of loss and shame. He dragged his gaze away and turned along George Street, heading towards Tigerlily cocktail bar.

The bar was busy for just past lunchtime on a Tuesday afternoon. Sean remembered the taxi-driver mentioning it being a rugby international weekend. There were people sporting red and white scarves, clearly Welsh rugby fans here to make a week of it, chattering like frenetic magpies.

He passed the smoking room and headed to the rear of the bar, partially screened off by racks of bottles and glasses stacked in the square serving area. It was a quiet spot from which to sit and survey the comings and goings. Not that he had any intention of surveying anything. He was still reeling from that morning's turbulence. Especially his conversations with Mac. His comment about Heaven not being open to suicides had bothered him. Angry and frustrated, he climbed onto a high bar-stool, A barman with muscular arms covered in tattoos approached him.

'What can I get you, sir?'

'A pint of lager,' said Sean, gruffly. 'Make it Innes and Gunn. And a double Coal Isla. The twenty-year old. No ice. No umbrellas. No straws. And definitely no fucking sparklers. Got it?'

'Of course, sir. Right away.'

The barman gave Sean a well-practiced smile and walked back along the serving area, thinking, *there's always got to be a smart-arse.*

'Student?' Sean asked, as he returned with the drinks.

The bartender set a small ceramic jug of water beside the straight glass with the double shot of whisky in it. Sean smiled, wryly. *At the least he's trained.* Only a philistine took anything other than a drop of water in a fine malt whisky, and this particular Islay malt was a drink that should not be adulterated.

'Final year,' said the bartender, smiling confidently.

Sean found himself despising the boy's eagerness. Life was still a game to him. Everything ahead of him. A future filled with endless possibilities. Unlike Sean, who had only the past to look back at. A past he had no care to see.

'What's your name?'

'Jake.'

'Well, Jake,' said Sean, reaching into the pocket of his black leather box-jacket and pulling out his wallet. 'Here's a card for my tab.'

He removed an American Express Centurion credit card and handed it across the bar.

'Thank you, sir. I'll give you a receipt for it right away.'

Jake stared at the black and gold card. *Holy shit, you have to have deep pockets to have a card like this*! He filed it in a book filled with plastic credit card sized sleeves and handed Sean a paper ticket with a number printed on it.

Sean put it into his jacket pocket without bothering to look at it.

'Can you do me a favour, Jake?'

'Of course, sir. If I can.'

Sean slid a crisp fifty-pound note across the bar, which Jake, after glancing surreptitiously around him to ensure no one was looking, deftly pocketed.

'When either of these glasses are empty, refill them. Don't ask. Don't think. Just do it. Understand?'

Jake smiled and nodded.

'Absolutely, sir. I'll make sure the other bartenders know I'm looking after your needs personally.'

'There's another fifty if you do your job properly. And I'm not in the mood to chat, understand?' Jake nodded. 'And, Jake, call me Sean. I sound like my bloody father when you call me *sir*. And that's the last person I want to be reminded of today. Okay?'

'Okay . . . *Sean*.'

Jake walked away, leaving Sean in peace. It didn't take a genius to see that this was a guy with issues, and who was clearly going to get blind drunk. But with fifty pounds in his pocket and another fifty to come, what did he care?

16

Miles sat in his office and brooded. His secretary, Annie, had seen him come in about an hour before, clearly in a dark mood, given the scowl on his face and the fact that he strode through the office like a pissed-off sergeant-major, ignoring his staff who were sitting behind the computer screens monitoring the client security systems.

'No calls and no visitors, Annie.'

It was a command, not a question.

'Okay, Miles.'

She knew better than to disturb him. On the rare occasion when he was in a mood, it was best for everyone to just keep their heads down and let him be. He normally snapped out of it quickly.

Sitting at his desk, Miles thumbed through a glossy brochure about the upcoming Ryder Cup, the bi-annual golf tournament between Europe and the United States. It was to be played, that coming September, at *Le Golf National* golf course, just outside Paris. He read the same paragraph three times, unable to focus, such was his anger at the way Sean had spoken to him outside Cramond Kirk. Especially accusing him of trying to win Linz back when she'd been alive. He found himself questioning how he really felt about her. Sean was right, in one way, but wrong in the most important way of all.

Miles had loved Linz from the first time he'd met her, falling in love with her, quickly, and out of love, slowly, once it was clear how she felt about Sean. But he'd also fallen in love with Sean. Sure, they'd had their ups and downs, even coming to blows, at one point, but, afterwards, over a pint in the pub, they had laughed at how stupid they'd been. Dare anyone try to hurt Sean,

Miles would have taken them apart. They were brothers, perhaps not by blood, but by choice, which was often a damned sight stronger than familial bonds.

Yes, Miles admitted to himself, he had loved Linz, but it had been a platonic love. What Sean had hinted at was beyond the pale, no matter how upset he might be or how hard things were for him.

'I'm done with him this time,' he said, aloud. A voice in his head asked how many times he'd said that over the past twenty years. On his desk, his cellphone lit up. He'd set it to silent, but it vibrated and buzzed around on his desk like a wingless hornet desperate to get airborne. 'Bugger off, whoever you are!'

Ignoring him, the phone did another flightless circle on the polished glass. He glanced down at the face that had appeared on the screen and picked it up.

The voice that spoke to him was annoyingly cheerful.

'Hello, Miles. It's Judith.'

'Yes, I know. What do you want?'

'Delightful,' replied Judith, 'well I guess there's no need to ask how you are on this bright and beautiful spring day.'

'Sorry, Judith, don't mind me. I'm like a bear who's had his porridge nicked. And not by some gorgeous, forest-dwelling blonde, but by a big, dumb, pain-in-the-ass, other bear.'

'Sean Jameson, by any chance, the other grizzly?'

'Precisely!'

Miles almost laughed, then remembered he was still angry with Sean.

'He has that effect on a great many people,' said Judith, to be fair. It's a kind of special gift. A bit like being a reverse superhero.'

'Like a super-dickhead, more like.'

'Interesting. I can see where you're coming from, Miles. But I really don't think Marvel will buy into that particular franchise.'

Miles laughed. Judith was helping him climb out of his mood. He softened his tone and entered the conversation.

'I suppose you're right. And it *is* a beautiful, bright, if still utterly baltic spring day. So, to what do I owe the pleasure of your call and the sound of your sexy voice? I did what you asked and opened the house up for the git formerly known as Sean Jameson. I even spent a bloody fortune on the bottle of wine you suggested he'd love. I hope it's poisoned him.'

'From Valvona and Croalla, on Elm Row?' Judith asked, laughing at the poisoning remark.

Sean had obviously done something to piss Miles off. She'd no doubt find out what it was in due course.

'The very same,' Miles confirmed. 'It's a great deli, by the way, but bloody pricey. I had some of their gorgonzola and one of the salmon quiche tarts. They really were amazing. You get what you pay for, I suppose.'

'Worth every penny, Miles. I'm sure Sean appreciated it, no matter what you two have fallen out about. And, yes, I am calling about him. Have you seen him?'

'I picked him up from Merrick, this morning, and left him at Cramond Kirk. He told me to bugger off. Kept telling me Linz was waiting for him, as well as saying a few other things I won't go into right now.'

'Did he say he'd seen her, Miles. Like, actually seen her?'

The concern in Judith's voice was evident.

'What is it, Judith?' Miles asked, suddenly feeling an ominous chill. Judith was silent for a few seconds. He could hear her breathing and thinking down the other end of the phone. 'Judith. I can tell something's wrong. Is it Sean?'

'It is, Miles. I need to talk to you about him. He's really not in a good place, and I don't just mean because of losing Linz and the kids. He's got other problems. Problems that go back to his childhood. I thought you might already know about them. You two have been friends a long time.'

'We have,' said Miles, wondering what Judith was referring to, 'he's like a brother to me.' He swallowed hard to keep his voice from faltering. 'Where are you?'

'Just outside the QuantumCloud offices in St Andrew's Square. We could meet in the Antiquary bar if you can come into town. It'll make it easier for you to park from where you're coming from. Assuming you're at your office?'

'I am,' confirmed Miles.

'Good. I'll walk down from St Andrew's Square, which is chock-a-block. There's Welsh rugby fans everywhere, wandering around wearing massive red hats and carrying giant, plastic leeks.'

Miles could hear the sound of singing close to where Judith was obviously standing. He could picture the mayhem of the city centre.

'I'm on my way. I'll be fifteen minutes.'

'Thanks, Miles, that's enough time for me to get there. I'm so worried about him. I'm not trying to scare you, but I'm afraid he might do something stupid.'

'And now *I'm* as worried.

'Try not to be,' said Judith, 'I'll see you soon.'

Miles ended the call, grabbed his combat jacket, and rushed out of his office, past the startled Annie. His mood, she could tell, had lifted, but by the look on his face there was something else causing him concern.

'Tell anyone who wants me I've emigrated.'

'Yes Miles. Don't forget your keys.'

Miles returned her smile as he turned back into his office.

'What would I do without you, Annie.'

'You'd be lost, Miles.'

'I think, Annie, I surely would. You should demand a generous pay rise.'

'I did,' said Annie. 'Last month. You told me to take one.'

'And did you?'

'Yes.'

'Was it fair?'

'Very fair,' said Annie, smiling sweetly, 'if a little generous. But I believe you told me I was worth every penny when you signed it off last month.'

'I believe you.'

Miles wondered how she'd slipped the approval letter under his nose without him even seeing it. Then again, he'd probably not paid attention. It didn't matter, he trusted her implicitly. She'd been with him since the days when his head office had been a single porta-cabin with no toilet facilities on the industrial edge of Edinburgh. Whatever he'd signed off on she'd damned well earned. He made a mental note to check just how much he was paying her, to make sure she'd given herself a large enough increase. She was, he knew, too damned loyal.

Now, he needed to be as loyal.

He thought of Sean, ashamed he'd dismissed their friendship so quickly. *Friendship! Easy when it's easy. Real when it's hard.* He left the office knowing that, if anything happened to him he would never forgive himself.

After parking his jeep in St Vincent Street, an upmarket street in Edinburgh's New Town, Miles took less than ten minutes to reach the Antiquary

Bar, one of the most well-known basement bars on St Stephens Street. He took the half dozen steps down to the wooden doors, pushed them open, and stepped into the warmth of familiarity. He smiled at the blonde-haired woman standing behind the wooden bar counter. They'd known each other for years and dated once, finding out they were better as friends than lovers.

'Hello Avril, long time no see.'

Avril gave him a smile reserved for a chosen few.

'Hello, stranger. Brought your chariot to take me away from all this?'

'Damn, I forgot it, again. But next time I'm down. Promise.'

'I'm counting on it.' Avril gave him a look that said, *I really mean it.* 'Now, what will it be? Oh, and if you're looking for Judith, she's just gone through to the lounge bar. I've just poured her a white wine. Be a love and take it through. Do you want your usual, or is it too early?'

'Driving,' said Miles, holding up his car keys and jangling them in the air, 'so just a sparkling water.'

Judith was tucked away in the corner of the bar, close to the fireplace, beneath the windows, from where you could see up to the pavement outside and watch the shoes of the people passing by, wondering who they were and where they were going

'Miles! I'm so glad to see you.'

'Good to see you too, Judith, it's been ages. You look fantastic, as usual. Miles hugged her then sat down beside her on one of the short bar-stools. 'Now, tell me what's up with our friend?'

He smiled at her, trying to be reassuring.

He wasn't smiling for long.

Judith relayed what Emily had told her. The parts about Sean's childhood abuse enraged Miles, but what scared him most was the part about the anniversary reaction, and that Sean could become suicidal. He couldn't believe it, of course, not Sean Jameson, the decorated soldier and tough-as-nails businessman he knew. But then he'd not known about the abuse or the psychiatrist on Harley Street.

'After we spoke on the phone,' said Judith, 'I spoke to Father Mackenzie. Sean's priest, out at Cramond Kirk.'

'I know who he is and where it is, Judith.'

Judith shook her head at her *faux-pas*. She'd stood beside Miles at the funeral service for Linz and the children the previous year.

'Sorry Miles. Of course you do.'

'I wish I didn't.'

They were both silent for a moment, lost in the memory of a day they would rather forget.

'Well,' continued Judith, 'as you know, Sean was there this morning, and for some time, apparently. From what little Father Mackenzie would tell me, it was one hell of an emotional morning. He hadn't known about the remembrance plaque, or that some of Linz and the childrens ashes had been spread there. Finding out, in Father Mackenzie's own words, had a marked effect on Sean.

'What the hell does, *marked effect*, even mean, Judith?'

Judith shrugged her shoulders.

'All he would tell me was that Sean was highly emotional and not in full control of his own mind. Which is really not what I wanted to hear, given what Emily told me about people with his kind of mental illness.'

'What else?' Miles asked.

'He wouldn't tell me anything more. I'm not sure if he'd even say any more to Emily, to help us, if we were thinking of having Sean committed.'

'Committed? Christ on a broomstick, Judith. That's going a bit far.'

'Miles!'

Judith blessed herself, making the sign of the cross on her chest with her thumb and forefinger.

'Sorry. I forgot you were one of the God squad.'

Judith shook her head in despair.

'And that's just *so* much better. Honestly, Miles.'

Miles looked suitably chaste.

'Sorry. I'm a heathen. What can I say?'

Judith nodded in agreement and carried on.

'Anyway, it's a moot point. Emily wouldn't sign off on anything close to that. At least not without some evidence to back it up. She thinks Sean is making progress. Perhaps she's right, perhaps he is. But, listening to what Father Mackenzie said about Sean not being in control of himself, there was something in his tone, Miles. I can't put my finger on it, but something feels decidedly off. I'm worried Sean might do something to harm himself.'

Miles suddenly wished he'd ordered a stiffer drink.

'What do you think, Judith? Should I go out to Merrick, just in case he *does* do something stupid. Much as I struggle to believe he would. But the thought of it scares the living shit out of me.'

He looked at her, hoping she had the answer.

As it happened, she did.

'Normally, I'd say yes,' replied Judith, ignoring the profanity, 'but let's leave it until tomorrow. Sean needs someone to be there for him. I agree with that. As does Father Mackenzie. Which is why he's going to organise taking care of him, tonight. We can both go round in the morning and take over.'

Miles nodded, looking relived.

'And then I won't let him out of my bloody sight, Judith. And that's a bloody promise.'

17

It was over three hours from ordering his first drink before Sean even looked up, other than to nod his head at Jake, who had replaced his drink every time one of the glasses was empty. The bar had filled in trickles and drabs, and was now filled with office staff from George Street and the hundreds of small businesses that infested the network of cobbled streets and lanes around the city centre, escaping their daytime haunts to find fresh spirits in the bars and restaurants. Thankfully, the row of barstools at the back of the bar had remained empty. That would change when it became crazy busy, later that night. Sean planned to be long gone by then. He had no desire to be among happy, smiling people.

A husky, female voice broke his private contemplation.

'Hello, handsome.'

Sean hadn't seen the woman next to him sit down. She had long, dark brown hair and was in her mid-forties, but trying to look south of that number. Her lips were unnaturally plump, making it look as if she'd had an allergic reaction to something she'd eaten. It seemed to be the trend these days, Sean mused, for women of a certain age to try to turn back the clock when faced with competition from twenty-somethings who could party all night long and still look fresh-faced the next day, but the toll of the ageing bell was measured in lines, blemishes and sagging flesh, and the concept of *less is more* was lost on these nip-and-tuck time-travellers. It had certainly been on this one.

'Natural ageing. You should give it a try.'

'Pardon me?'

The woman had either not heard or understood his acerbic remark.

'Nothing,' said Sean, taking a deep breath, more to hold back a sarcastic reply about her hearing, 'but, trust me, I'm not company you want.'

'Why not, babe? Having a bad day?'

Sean fought the urge to tell her to piss off, his ability to feign any kind of interest at an all-time low. He retained just enough civility to reply.

'More a bad year.'

'And me! So we've already got something in common. I'm Jann, by the way. Jann Livingston.'

Sean took her outstretched hand, more out of politeness than interest.

Her nails were long and polished but the gold Hermes watch on her wrist looked real. She wore a cream leather jacket over a fitted, white blouse, unbuttoned to show of an plastic cleavage, and a short, black skirt that rode high on her thighs as she repositioned herself to face him. Her legs were long and shapely and her black shoes high and strappy. The sagging wrinkles on her neck, however, could not be hidden.

'Sean Jameson. I'd like to say I'm pleased to meet you.'

'Thank you, Sean. You, too,' replied Jann, missing the sarcasm completely.

She was stunning, or once had been, thought Sean, but too much foundation showed she was attempting to mask the truth of her age. She was easily way past fifty. He decided he'd buy her one drink, chat to her for as long as it took for him to finish his, then make his excuses and leave. He didn't want company. He certainly didn't want a middle-aged woman looking for a casual pick-up, which all the signals she was giving off pointed to.

'So, Sean Jameson, what do you do?'

Jann smiled and looked at him with half closed eyes. She probably thought it made her look seductive. It didn't.

'I'm an ex,' said Sean, smiling at his own joke.

'An ex?'

Jann was clearly confused by his answer.

'Yes! An ex-husband, ex-father, ex-businessman. An ex-everything, actually.'

'That bad?' cooed Jann, sounding as insincere as it was possible to be.

Sean was already regretting speaking to her. He tried to let her know that.

'And the rest. Which is why I wanted to be left alone.'

Jann pouted her bottom lip like a four year old, making herself look ridiculous in the process.

'That's not very friendly, *Sean*. I thought you looked lonely. I only came over to see if you wanted someone to make you feel better.'

'You think a lot, don't you?'

Jann smiled, unaware it was not a compliment.

'I try to.'

Sean decided against buying her the drink. He called Jake over and retrieved his credit card, slipping him the additional fifty-pound note he'd promised. Jann's eyes lit up at the sight of the card. She put her hand on his arm. Her touch was more offensive to him than he could have ever imagined.

'A Centurion Amex! Are you a millionaire?'

Sean ignored her question.

'Look, Jann, I need to go. I'm drunk and I want to get drunker. But I want to do it alone. Besides, the bar's getting too crowded for my liking.'

He climbed off his chair pulled on his jacket.

'Oh shit! You're right about that.'

Jann was staring across the bar at something that had clearly flustered her.

'What is it?' Sean asked, checking he had everything before leaving.

'It's a someone. Someone I really don't want to meet.'

'Why not?'

'Let's just say I took something that belonged to her and she didn't like it. As it turns out, neither did I. But that's hardly likely to matter to her if she sees me.'

Sean looked across the bar and saw a face he recognised heading towards him. Their eyes met and Dr Emily MacGregor waved. She headed through the main bar, towards him. The smile on her face was warm and genuine, though it disappeared when she saw who was with him.

'Sean,' said Emily, putting the smile back on, 'I didn't expect to find you here. How are you?'

She gave him a hug and a kiss on the cheek, rather than the handshake he'd been expecting.

'Hello, Professor. I'm good. Well, maybe just okay. But that's good enough.'

'You look good,' said Emily. 'I'm pleased to see you're out and about.' She leaned in closer to him and whispered, 'you can call me Emily, now that we're out of office, so to speak.'

'You look good, too, *Emily*,' said Sean, doing just that! 'Nice biker jacket. I think I've seen it before, somewhere?'

Emily looked down at her jacket, appreciatively.

'Guilty as charged. You know what it's like when you find something too expensive to buy but treat yourself anyway. It's my new favourite thing.'

'Talking of expensive things,' said Sean, 'hows your new office? It's just across the street, right? Up and running yet? Have you started fixing the unfixable among us?'

'Yes, I'm happy to say I have. And it's all thanks to you and QuantumCloud. It's your company, after all. I can help so many more people than I ever thought, and I get to play the big boss.'

Sean gave a wry laugh, partly at the thought of QuantumCloud being *his* company, given he'd cut ties with it, partly at Emily's naivety.

'That, Emily, is sadly overrated. Trust me. Enjoy it while you can. But I'm really glad it's working out for you.'

Emily, to her surprise, found Sean's behaviour towards her, charming. *I can see why Judith fell for him.*

Sean saw her glance past him, at Jann.

'Emily, this is . . .'

'Oh, I know very well who and *what* that is, Sean. We've got one thing in common, haven't we, Jann?'

Jann looked at Emily as if she'd smelt something distasteful.

'Not anymore. I grew bored with your cast off.'

Emily looked back at her with the same look on her face.

'Really? You do surprise me, given the jacket you're wearing. Gucci, if I'm not mistaken?'

'It is,' said Jann, haughtily, glancing down at the sleeves of her leather jacket and holding her arms up to show it off.

'Pre-owned?' Jann's mouth opened and closed like a goldfish as she sought a clever response to Emily's subtle barb, but she was too slow. Emily struck again. 'Yes, I saw you trying it on just the other day in Love Again. It's such a great shop for last year's fashions, and so much cheaper. I'm glad to see you're able to give it another outing. You're so brave. Nice handbag, too. Michael Kors, if I'm not mistaken? I used to have one, back when it was in fashion.'

'You bitch, McGregor,' said Jann, using the best riposte she could find.

Sean felt as if he was in some sort of staged drama. One in which only the two women in front of him knew their lines.

'Sean,' said Emily, turning her attention back to him, 'you should dump this piece of mutton and run. She's bad news. A narcissist, a liar and a user. In more ways than one.'

'How fucking dare you,' screeched Jann, lunging for her.

'Leave her alone, Jann,' snapped Sean, stepping between them.

He turned to face Emily, his face dark with anger.

'Just who do you think you are? We're not at Dunvegan now. And I'm not your bloody patient. At least, not any longer. You can't just decide to interfere with my life. And don't ever tell me who I should or shouldn't be with. I know you're bloody smart, Emily. Smarter than most of the people in this bar, most likely. But you don't always have to fucking prove it.' He turned to Jann and barked, 'come on, we're leaving.'

'Sean! I'm so sorry. You're absolutely right.'

Emily pleaded with him to stay, but Sean brushed past her, heading out of the bar.

'You lose, again, it seems,' hissed Jann, meeting Emily's hostile gaze. 'I'll be sure to let you know how good he was whenever I'm finished with him. You can have *my* sloppy seconds this time.'

She smiled a triumphant smile and tossed her head, then followed Sean out of the bar.

Emily was beyond annoyed she'd let her personal feelings affect her behaviour. She knew she shouldn't have told Sean what to do. That was the best way to get him to do the opposite.

Behind the bar, having stood witness to the catfight, stood Jake. He had a bemused look on his face. Emily looked at him and, for a moment, he thought she was going to have a go at him. She looked angry enough. Instead, she climbed onto the barstool Sean had vacated and rested her elbows on the bar.

'Pour me a vodka and tonic, please, Jake. Make it a large one.'

Jake nodded and gave her a warm but friendly smile.

'Yes, Miss.'

18

The taxi ride back to Merrick took almost half an hour, the streets of Edinburgh like the arteries of a dying heart, clogged with cars trying to escape the city. In that time, Sean had heard almost all of Jann's life story. There was a continuous thread of self-pity woven into each pathetic tale. Every relationship she'd been in seemed to have had the same rosy beginning, turbulent middle, and bitter end, be it man or woman, as she swung both ways, she seemed proud to tell him. None of the break ups, of course, were ever her fault.

Sean had begun to sober up during the journey, and wondered what on earth he was doing with her. He'd been on the verge of making his escape just before Emily had walked in. Now, here he was, sitting at the island in Merrick's kitchen, drinking whisky he didn't need with a stranger he didn't like.

'Fancy a line?'

Before Sean could think to even respond, Jann produced a small paper wrap from her handbag and racked out two white lines on the island top. She was onto hers like a Dyson on dust. It was clearly not her first time. He took the rolled-up twenty pound note she'd handed him and descended back into a hell he thought had been banished from his life.

Twenty minutes later they were pressed together under the dimmed lights of the livingroom. Jann was naked, save for her high-heels, and pulling frantically at the belt on Sean's jeans. Belt undone, she wrapped a hand around the back of his neck, pulling him to her and kissing him passionately. Her skin was covered in a light sweat, a combination of dancing and the effects of the cocaine in her system. The feel of her hot, glistening body against his skin sent waves of pleasure rippling through Sean.

Breaking free from the kiss, Jann's lips worked their way down his body, tracing her tongue down to his stomach and navel, then lower still, encircling him with her mouth. Sean responded, willingly, the needs of his body taking him over. After a few minutes of pleasuring him, skillfully removing his jeans and boxer shorts without Sean even being aware she had, Jann stood up, pushing her mouth onto his and pressing herself against him. Her arms around him, she pulled him down onto the longer of the two couches, knocking over one of the beehive-style lamps sitting on low tables at either end. Sean and Linz had picked them out together, years before, at a closing down sale in Zuzu, a designer lighting shop in Stockbridge.

'Who's a big boy,' Jann whispered, lasciviously.

She took his manhood in her hand, squeezing his hard, needy flesh, then lay back on the couch and put her hands on his naked buttocks, guiding him into her. Sean groaned, overwhelmed by the strength of his arousal and desperate for the comfort of love.

She moved with him, slowly at first, timing the push of her hips to meet his thrusts, then faster, riding the wave of base, sexual desire they were caught up in, her legs around his back, matching the violence of him as he drove into her, until they climaxed in an explosion that left them panting in the aftermath of their urgent lovemaking.

Except, it hadn't been lovemaking. Nothing close. Not for Sean.

The elation he had felt in the brief encounter evaporated and the emptiness returned. It had been sex without love. The love he needed to feel safe. Simply a physical and mental longing to be close to another person. But it was the wrong person. And it *felt* wrong. He'd known it the moment it ended. He rolled off her, onto the floor, kneeling in front of the couch.

'You need to leave, Jann. I'm sorry. This was a mistake. My mistake, not yours.'

'Leave? Are you crazy?'

She looked at him as if he was.

'I shouldn't have brought you here. Not to my family home. Not to the place my wife and children live.'

'Lived, you mean. You told me they were dead.'

Sean dropped his head into his hands.

'They *are* dead. I killed them. And now I've brought you back here and done this.' He looked around the room as if expecting someone to appear. 'What if Linz saw us?'

'Linz, your dead wife! Are you fucking serious?'

Jann sat up on the couch, shaking her head in disbelief. Sean reached for his boxers and pulled them quickly on.

'You need to not be here, Jann. You need to leave. Now!'

'Don't worry, I'm not staying here. You're fucking mental.'

'I'm sorry. It's just that . . . '

Jann stood up, not caring to hear whatever Sean was going to say, retrieving her clothes from around the room before heading into the kitchen to get her jacket and handbag. Sean could hear her talking to someone on her phone.

'What's the address?' she screeched.

Sean called out the postcode and the house name and heard her repeat them. She finished her call and walked back into the living room, her jacket over one arm and her hair somewhat rearranged.

'Jann, can I just say . . . '

Jann held up a hand, dismissing him before he had time to finish trying to explain.

'Save it! I'm not fucking interested. You used me, you bastard. And now you've had what you wanted you think you can just dump me? Well, let me tell you this, Sean fucking Jameson, big-shot businessman and millionaire. I don't fuck for free.'

Sean looked at her, stunned at the dramatic change in her demeanour. It was as if she was two separate people.

'I'm sorry. I don't know what else to say or do?'

Jann laughed.

'You can fuck your sorry. And as for what you can do? Let me give you a heads up on that. I've left my bank details in the kitchen. I've also taken some rather revealing pictures of myself, showing the marks on my body, as well as the cocaine wrap sitting beside your expensive watch. If I don't see a transfer of a thousand pounds, which is my normal overnight rate, into my account, by midnight, the police will be getting the photos and an account of how you brought me here, drugged me up, and then forced yourself on me. See who gets fucked then.'

Sean was stunned at the threat.

'That's a lie and you know it. You wanted it every bit as much as me.'

Jann gave a haughty snort of derision and sneered at him, reminding Sean of the witch from *Snow White and the Seven Dwarves*. The thought made him more ashamed for what it reminded him of.

Jann wasn't finished with her threat.

'Oh, don't get me wrong, babe, the sex was good, and I like it rough, but what you left behind, in me and on me, is enough to have you arrested and charged with rape. The police, these days, over-react to every claim made by a woman against a man, desperate to show they're cracking down on domestic violence, irrespective of the truth of the matter. Even the lawyers know it. It's a standing fucking joke in the law courts.'

Her words brought Sean's own anger to the surface.

'You were all over me from the moment you saw me sitting at the bar. You sat down beside *me*. There's plenty of witnesses to vouch for that. You came onto me, not the other way around. The police would never believe you.'

'Oh but they would,' snapped Jann, 'they're thick as shit and twice as bent.'

'Rubbish.' Sean snapped back.

Jann laughed at him, scorn twisting her face so that she looked even uglier than she was revealing herself to be.

'You think? Believe me, I'm an incredibly good actress when I need to be. Any male officer won't think twice about your guilt once I'm in front of him and crying like a brownie who's failed her sewing badge. I can play the victim, Sean, and I'm a damned good liar when I want to be.'

'I don't doubt it,' said Sean, wondering how he'd got himself into such a mess.

Seeing her words were having the desired effect, Jann delivered the *coup de grace*.

'They'll have you in a cell within the hour, charged with rape and waiting for the court to open, the next day, to give you your trial date. You might even be refused bail and go straight to prison, for months, before that came round. My brother, Dirk, is an ex-cop. Bent as a boomerang, like most of them, but he still has contacts in that big boys club. I've probably screwed half of them. He'd be desperate to get a slice of whatever I sue you for.'

'But . . .'

Sean stopped without finishing his reply. It would make no difference what he said. Not to someone like her. He'd never met anyone like her. Actually, that wasn't true. The image of his father came to mind. He'd also been a narcissist and sociopath.

Jann, seeing the look on Sean's face and realising she had won, smiled at him like a fox looking at a wounded pheasant in an open field.

'See you around, Sean. I'm glad your wife and kids are dead. Why should your life be so fucking perfect.'

She turned and stormed into the hallway, then let herself out of the house, slamming the front door shut with more force than necessary in a parting fit of rage.

Sean crossed to the livingroom window and watched her walk down the driveway, briefly disappearing behind the trees before reappearing close to the entrance gates. She climbed into a taxi that was already waiting. He waited until the taxi had driven off before making his way into the kitchen.

On the island, beside the open cocaine wrap and his unfinished glass of whisky, scribbled on a paper napkin, were the bank details Jann had told him she'd left.

'How could I have been so stupid? She's a bloody prostitute.'

He slumped down onto one of the kitchen barstools and a wave of despair washed over him, the culmination of a day that had been a freefall of emotional plummets. He glanced up at the kitchen clock, which showed almost seven, then down at the half full bottle of vodka he'd pulled from the bar in his study to give to Jann. It stared back at him as if to say, *want to screw up the rest of your night?*

He dropped his gaze to the island top, lost in his thoughts.

The doorbell rang, bringing him out of a momentary daydream. He glanced back up at the clock, surprised to see it showed eight o'clock. Perhaps he'd misread the time when he'd looked at it a moment ago. He winced at the sound of the bells ringing again, immediately resolving to disconnect them, knowing, even as he thought it, he would never be able to bring himself to do so.

'*Che bella giornata*,' he whispered, 'a beautiful day. Ironic or what?' He drained his whisky glass in single gulp, and winced, his anger growing like the flames in his throat. 'If that's that bitch again!' As he passed the silver-framed mirror in the hallway, he glanced at himself. To say he looked disheveled would have been a compliment. His hair was tousled and his face was gaunt. He had no memory of when he'd last showered. 'I look like shit.' But there was little he could do about it right now. 'Who gives a fuck? It's my life.' The irony wasn't lost on him. 'Oh, I forgot, it's not.'

He reached up to touch his crucifix but found it was gone. *Maybe he'd lost it when he'd been on the couch with Jann?* The bells rang for a second time, this time accompanied by the hammer of a fist striking the door. A horrible thought went through Sean's mind. *Could it be the police? No, she would have needed to give a statement before they had an arrest warrant. It had to be someone else.* Whoever it was could bugger off. He would make that clear.

'Hello,' a male voice came from beyond the door.

'Keep your hair on,' hissed Sean, 'for fuck sake.'

He pressed the exit button on the keypad and the door opened. Standing there was the last person he'd expected to see. And the one person he would never ask to leave.

19

His father-in-law looked older than Sean remembered. His face was tanned from days spent on the golf course, in Auchterarder, thirty miles north of Edinburgh, but the wrinkles had deepened and been added to since he'd last seen him. Golf was Ian's passion, despite he was, at best, a middle to high handicapper. He and Sean had enjoyed many days, together, playing at *Machrihannish,* a classic, Scots links on the southern tip of the breathtaking Mull of Kintyre.

As Sean looked disheveled, so Ian looked immaculate. His silver-grey hair was swept back into place with a liberal coating of Brylcream, making him look debonair and distinguished. In his tweed suit and brown brogues, buffed to a gloss at the toes, he looked more like a well-to-do country farmer than a retired naval officer.

'Hello, Sean.'

'Ian,' Sean mumbled, thrown off guard. 'Sorry, I was in the living room.'

'There's no need for explanations,' said Ian, 'it's me that needs to apologise for pitching up unannounced.'

'Not at all,' said Sean, wanting to reach out and hug him, but too afraid to, 'I'm glad you're here. I was going to call. I spoke about you, just this morning, with Mac.'

'I know. He told me. May I come in? It's chilly out here.'

Sean stood back and beckoned his father-in-law into the house.

'Of course. Sorry.'

'Stop apologising, Sean.'

Ian walked into the hallway, immediately turning left into the kitchen, the normal first port of call for anyone visiting Merrick.

The memory of his daughter hit him harder than he'd expected it to. Lindsay had loved to bake, so there was always a range of cakes, breads and other pastries on offer, drawing visitors like honeybees to a flower-strewn meadow. It was the beating heart of the home. Or had been. Until that heart had been so brutally torn out of it. The smell of the kitchen, tonight, was in marked contrast to those happier days.

'Sorry for the mess,' mumbled Sean.

'Been having a party?'

Ian's tone was more acerbic than he'd intended it to be. But he couldn't check the words. He'd arrived with anger in the pockets of his jacket.

'No, I was just . . .'

Sean failed to find an adequate reply, so he looked away, ashamed that the only man he had ever thought of as a father had cause to be angry with him.

Ian already knew Sean had been drinking. He had assumed, at first, he had been drinking alone, but given there were two glasses on the kitchen island that was obviously not the case. One of the glasses had a lipstick smear on its rim and there were lipstick marks on the butts of some of the stubbed-out cigarettes on a dinner plate that had served as a makeshift ashtray. *Lindsay is barely cold in her grave, yet he has the audacity to have a bloody woman in the house! It would have broken her heart.*

The sight of the kitchen, for Ian, was like the feeling a new amputee had of a lost limb. It felt as if it was still there, when, in reality, it was gone. As Lindsay was gone from him. He felt his heart crumble a little more and dragged in a breath to bring his feelings under control. *She was gone! She didn't care. Not any longer!* He looked at Sean, standing in front of him, his head bowed in shame, and could feel his son-in-law's embarrassment.

Suddenly, he felt ashamed.

Christ, how must it feel for him? He pushed the anger back down into his pockets and reminded himself of Sean's loss. *Who am I to judge him for drinking? Or for taking some solace in the arms of another woman? Look at him!*

Sean was not in the best of places. Mac had warned Ian of that on their call, barely two hours since.

'Sean's back, Ian, but facing the most difficult challenge in his life. I am afraid for him.'

Ian had immediately jumped into his car and headed down to Edinburgh. Sean was still part of *his* family. Lindsay would have never forgiven him if he wasn't there for him when she could not be. And Sean needed him now, that much was clear. He had lost his entire world. He was alone and suffering. *No, he does not deserve my anger.* A horrible thought suddenly presented itself.

Perhaps the woman was still here?

'Are we alone?' Ian asked, trying to keep any hint of accusation of judgement out of his voice.

Sean glanced at the glasses on the island and knew immediately what Ian was thinking. He silently berated himself for having left the place in such a state. Thankfully, he had taken the wrap of cocaine and put it in his pocket before answering the door.

'I had a friend over, earlier, but she had to leave to collect her kids.'

Fuck, thought Sean, *what an idiotic thing to say!* The cocaine and whiskey in his system was messing with his brain. He'd also been thrown off kilter by Ian's sudden visit.

'Excellent,' Ian replied. His voice was calm and reassuring, trying to ease the awkwardness of the situation. 'Look, why don't you turn off the music? It's a bit loud. I'll put the kettle on. I always find a cup of tea normally sorts things out.'

Sean became acutely aware of the music playing in the livingroom. He'd not turned it off after Jann had left.

'The music! Of course. Sorry, Ian, my mind's not quite with it. I went to see Linz, at Cramond Kirk, this morning. It's kind of thrown me.'

'I know. I spoke to Mac. It's how I knew you were hone. Go and turn it off. We'll be able to chat better without that infernal racket going on in the background.'

'Be better if it were Wagner, I suppose?'

Sean smiled at Ian for the first time since he'd arrived.

'Eminently so.'

Ian returned the smile and the kitchen breathed an audible sigh of relief.

Sean went through to the livingroom and turned off the music, taking the opportunity to tidy up. He could hear Ian cleaning away the glasses and bottles in the kitchen and was glad to hear some sounds of normal life in the house. He winced at the damage to the beehive lamp that had fallen from the side table and turned it so that the broken part was to the back of the room, satisfied it would pass muster if Ian came through.

Ian was pouring the tea as Sean went back into the kitchen.

'Mugs okay? I can't be doing with dainty cups and saucers. Dorothy would be appalled, of course.'

'Fine by me. But you're right, Dorothy would *not* approve. I think you'd get one of her looks.'

Ian laughed at the thought. Tea, Dorothy had informed him many times since they'd first met, should always be served in teacups.

They stood at the kitchen island, now cleaned and wiped down, sipping their tea. Sean felt like a naughty schoolboy about to get a telling off. Ian was the only man that had ever made him feel that way. Oddly, he enjoyed it. He wasn't quite sure why, but guessed it was how it was meant to feel between a father and son.

'It's been a while since we've seen you, Sean. We've been worried about you. Where the hell did you go? Why the radio silence?'

'How is Dorothy?'

Sean sidestepped the question, knowing the conversation Ian wanted to have, but the answers to the questions he would ask were ones he knew he couldn't give. At least, not answers that would make any sense. For Ian, problems were to be faced head on, not run away from.

'She's fine. I just thought it might be better if I came alone, this time. I don't want you to take this the wrong way, Sean, but I wasn't sure we'd be welcome.'

Sean was appalled that Ian would think that.

'No! That's not what my disappearance was about. It had nothing to do with you or anyone else. You're welcome here. You always will be. This is as much your home as mine. Never feel you can't come here whenever you want to. All the memories of them are here. Linz and the kids. And they're yours as well as mine. There's nothing else left of them. Nothing.'

A single tear rolled down Sean's cheek. Ian almost reached out to him but felt awkward at the thought. He was a loving man in the ways that really mattered, but not demonstrative with that love in the way that modern fathers were able to be.

'No, Sean, that's not true. It's one of the reasons I came here tonight.'

He picked up the leather travel bag he'd been carrying when he arrived, setting it gently on the island-top, then opened it and removed its contents, one by one, setting them down, gently, in front of Sean.

'My God, Ian. They're stunning.'

In front of Sean sat three blown glass vases. Although they appeared to be perfect orbs, a subtly-designed base kept them stable on the island top. Sean immediately knew what they were and what they contained, but could not bring himself to call them urns. They were too beautiful for such an ugly description.

Each vase had a single colour as its base. The first was flamingo-pink, Alice's favourite colour. A vivid lime-green, the colour of the laces in Linz's gardening baseball-boots, the second. The final vase was turquoise-blue, reminding Sean of the beaches of Positano, the town on Italy's magical Amalfi Coast, where the family had holidayed two summers ago. Toby had wondered why the beach at Gullane, where Sean and he liked to wakeboard, was not the same glistening blue and declared turquoise his favourite colour.

Lines of crystal-white, crimson-red and obsidian-black had been integrated with the base colours, laid in swirls around the vases, bringing movement and depth. *The colours of the circle of life*, though Sean. *The birth into light, the blood of life, and the eventual journey back into darkness.* The colours had not been chosen at random, but by someone who had known those whose ashes now lay inside. Sean was mesmerized by their beauty, feeling like a child looking into a kaleidoscope for the very first time.

'Murano?'

He looked at Ian who confirmed his suspicions.

'Well spotted. Venini and Augusto, no less.'

'They must have cost a fortune.'

Sean's response was more a statement than a question. He knew the glass the vases were formed from was created only on the island of Murano, in Northern Italy, within the borders of the city of Venice, Europe's first glassmaking centre and still considered the home of the finest glass in the world. Under Italian law, Murano glass could only be created by the glass-masters that lived and trained on the tiny island. Venini and Augusto were considered amongst the finest of them all. Their astronomical prices matched their reputation.

'What else would be good enough to carry Linz and the children?'

Ian's voice was hushed as he thought of what they contained.

Sean ran his fingers over each vase, connecting with his family as he'd done by touching the brass plaque in the Remembrance Garden, that morning.

'I'll never be able to thank you for this, Ian. I'll pay you back every penny of what they must have cost you.'

'You own me nothing, Sean.'

'But, I can't let you . . .'

'It wasn't me. I didn't pay for them.'

Sean looked at his father-in-law, confused.

'What?'

Ian reached out to touch the vase containing his daughter's ashes, in the touch, sending a private message to her that he missed her more than he could ever say and loved her beyond life.

'Oh, I authorised them, knowing you would want Linz and the kids cared for properly. I knew you'd want the same beauty and colour they brought to our lives incorporated into the designs. And we both know how much Linz loved Murano glass. She spent enough of your money on it.'

Sean smiled, thinly, at the memory and the images it invoked. Linz's collection was spread throughout the house. The most important pieces kept in her private studio at the top of the house.

'You're right. She was obsessive about it. It used to drive me mad. Her and her bloody collection. What I wouldn't give for one more chance to watch her find a new piece and see the joy it brought her.'

Ian took a moment to gather himself, moved by the pain in Sean's voice..

'Her Murano glass and her garden of flowers. She loved the colours of life. What better way for her to be carried, now, alongside her children, inside the colours *of* her life and theirs. Do you approve of them?'

Sean couldn't find the words. None seemed adequate.

He swallowed down the shame that washed over him. For the second time that day he found himself beholding to someone for taking care of things that had been *his* responsibility. To Ian, for the words scribed into the copper plaque at Cramond Kirk, and now to someone else for the beautiful vases that carried the remains of his family.

He looked across at Ian.

'Who?'

'Hublot, Judith and Miles,' said Ian, 'and the board of directors at QuantumCloud. They wanted to do something to show their respect. They'd all been here at one time or another. At a birthday party or a weekend barbeque. Or one of the famous garden parties that Linz loved to host and invariably it rained at. They loved them, too, Sean. Everyone did.'

'And I took them from you,' said Sean, hanging his head in shame.

'No. It wasn't your fault.'

Sean looked up at Ian.

'But, at the trial. You and Dorothy. We didn't even speak.'

'We were witnesses for the prosecution, Sean, but not by choice. The police harassed us from the beginning. They kept saying you had practically murdered Lindsay and the kids. That the story you'd concocted about the flash of light from Alice trying to take a picture of a fairy on her phone was a desperate explanation for a crash you were responsible for. They said that you were probably drunk, which was why you lost control of the car.'

'But it was the truth, Ian, the light *did* distract me. I swear it. And I wasn't drunk. I'd never risk the kids or Linz by doing that.'

'I believe you, Sean, but the police aren't always interested in the truth. Only about finding someone to blame. What happened was an accident. A terrible accident. But an accident none the less.'

'So . . . can you ever forgive me?'

Ian saw the pain in Sean's eyes. It was a pain he had not seen before, but one he knew well. He had been branded by that same iron. They had both of them lost a child. In Sean's case, two. But Ian still had his wife, Dorothy, to share the pain with when it became too heavy a burden to carry alone. Sean had no-one to turn to when the nights were at their longest.

'There's nothing to forgive, Sean. Nothing.'

'I'm sorry, Ian. I'm so damned sorry.'

'Forgive yourself, Sean, or it will destroy you.'

Sean dropped to his knees and wept. Ian's resolve broke and he allowed his own tears to come.

He wept for the memory of his daughter; a daughter he would never again hold. He would never call her, *Princess*, and see her smile at him the way she did when he called her by that childhood name. A name shared on countless dog-walks in the rugged Perthshire hills and woodlands, where Linz had grown up. A name that had passed, from her, to her daughter, Alice. He wept for his lost grandchildren, for the birthday cards he would never write and the Christmas presents he would never watch them open.

After a few moments, Ian wiped the tears away on the sleeve of his jacket and placed his hand on Sean's head, the touch an act of kindness and forgiveness. A forgiveness Sean could not allow himself. Sean reached up, his head still bowed, and touched Ian's hand. A loving touch he had never shared with his own father. One he had so desperately wanted to feel all of his life. His body shook, still gripped in the pain of the loss of his family.

'I miss them, Ian. I miss them so much. I don't know what to do without them.'

'Cry, son. Just cry. I miss them too.'

20

Sean walked Ian to his car, parked in the gravel parking area to the side of the house, beside his own G-Wagon. Above their heads, a frigid, night sky spread out across the heavens, filled with starlight that no longer existed. It had always thrilled Sean to know that the light he could see coming from the closest star to earth, *Proxima Centauri*, had actually shone over four years before, travelling a distance of forty-trillion kilometers to be seen in the present. He thought of Linz, Alice and Toby, wondering if they were somewhere out there, shining a light towards him that he might someday see.

Ian looked up at the night sky and gave a shiver.

'It's a beautiful night, isn't it?'

'It is,' replied Sean, 'but bloody cold.'

'Are you sure you'll be fine on your own? I can stay if you want?'

'I'm okay, Ian, really. I'm going to shower and hit the sack. I'm exhausted.'

'Well, if you're sure?'

Despite having offered to stay, Ian was keen to get home to Dorothy. She was still having a hard time coping with the loss of her daughter and grandchildren.

Sean shook his head and clapped him on the back.

'Just get going. The roads will be icy, once you're out of Edinburgh, and getting worse. So, go, but go easy. Thank goodness you have your Disco.'

Ian grinned as he ran a hand over the car's high bonnet.

'Still the best birthday present ever.'

Sean and Linz had taken great joy in presenting the Land Rover Discovery to him as a seventieth birthday present, three years before. It had been brand new, then, and still looked pristine. Ian was fastidious about keeping it *just so*. He climbed in and started the engine, setting the heaters to maximum and rolling down the window to continue talking.

'Thanks for bringing them home,' said Sean, referring to the ashes in the Murano vases. 'For coming at all. For everything, in fact. I'll never forget what you've done for me.'

There was a melancholy to his voice Ian found saddened him to his core. He tried to reassure him.

'You speak as if I'm leaving for good, my boy, but I'm not going anywhere. If you need me, just call, okay? Besides, I'll see you next weekend. Dorothy too. We need to come and visit Lindsay and the kids, now they're home where they belong, with you. And you're home, too, Sean. I hope you know that?'

'I do, Ian. And it's thanks to Linz. She's here, you know. I saw her at Cramond Kirk, this morning. Mac tells me she's not real, but I know she is.'

'Or course she is. She's watching over you.'

Ian was certain that Sean was, as Father Mackenzie had first thought, referring to her in spirit.

'She told me to come back to Merrick. That's why I'm here. She pointed the way home to me when I saw her on Ben Nevis.'

'And she was right, Sean, wasn't she? Much better for you to be here than wandering around the world like a homeless nomad.'

Sean was relieved that Ian believed him. He'd never had a father to talk to. To ask questions of that only a father could answer. He had longed for that, over the years, eventually locking the sadness and regret away inside himself. Ian, he felt, was giving him that, now.

'What should I do when she talks to me?'

'Listen to her, Sean. I'm sure whatever she's telling you is to comfort and guide you.'

'Do you think so? Do you really think so?'

'I do, Sean, of course. Linz always wanted you to be happy. She still wants that. Do as she tells you for once in your life. As all we husbands should do. Wives always know better.'

He gave Sean a wide smile and laughed at his own words of advice.

'Thanks, Ian, I knew you'd understand.'

Sean reached in through the window to shake Ian's hand. He gave a sigh of relief. He wasn't going mad.

Ian took Sean's hand in both of his, trying to give him the comfort he so clearly needed. The touch, and the look of understanding that passed between them, was the deepest moment they had ever shared. Ian made to say something, but held it back. Sean saw it and knew, without being told, that Ian loved him. He tried to say something that would tell his father in law what he meant to him, but his voice betrayed him.

Ian nodded, as if understanding, and let go of Sean's hand.

'I'll see you next week, son.'

He made the telephone sign with his thumb and pinkie then revved the car and waved farewell.

Sean could not trust his voice to respond. It was the first time Ian had called him, "son"

He watched the Discovery as it headed across the driveway then down towards the already open gates, the bright rear lights shining back at him like the twinkling stars above.

21

The cocaine granules in the open paper packet glistened like icy, morning snow-crust under a winter sun. Sean had taken it from his pocket the moment Ian had left, his parting words about Linz sending him reeling. Ian had believed him when he'd told him he'd seen her. He'd told him to listen to her and do whatever she asked. Linz was here to guide him to where he was supposed to be. Sean had known that, all along, but now he'd received Ian's blessing he was sure of it.

But Mac's words kept haunting him.

Heaven does not accept suicides!

The three Murano vases were sat in front of him on the livingroom table. He'd carried them through, carefully and lovingly. He stared at them with a mixture of emotions; joy that Linz and the kids were with him, unbearable sadness that they were reduced from living flesh to lifeless ash.

'You should be here. If anyone should be dead, it should be me.'

The loss of them raked at his soul and the unbearable pain returned to torment him, bringing more tears.

He was surprised he was crying, again. He never cried. Not since he'd promised himself he would never cry again. And that had been a long time ago. But he couldn't seem to help it. It felt as though some part of him was trying to break free. He wondered what it was and what would happen if and when it did. It was the same feeling that had taken hold of him on Gullane Beach, when he'd had his episode. He took a deep breath, and then another, slowing his breathing and visualising the clock face. Watching the seconds hand count down. He couldn't allow himself to break. He needed to be here when Linz came back. As he knew she would. As Ian had told him.

Sean looked back at the cocaine wrap, knowing, even as he reached for it, even as he told himself he wasn't going to take it, that he would. It had been his crutch so many times before. He looked again at the vases and the pain of his loss reached for him, clawing at his soul. He needed a crutch to make the pain go away. He took one line and then another, until the shiny buzz from the dopamine the cocaine flooded into his blood supply took his fear away.

He drank, straight from the bottle of Coal Isla, not for the enjoyment of the fine, malt whisky, but because he wanted the numbness he knew it would eventually bring. The first gulp burned like an inhalation of flames. The second was easier. By the fifth, the bottle was almost empty. He pushed through until there were only dregs, fighting his body as it tried to purge the whisky from his gut. Comfortably numb, he lay back on the couch, slipping into blissful unconsciousness.

The dream started in black and white; blurred images in his mind. But colours came and the focus sharpened. The marmalade jar was high-up on the shelf in the kitchen cupboard. Twelve year old Sean stood on his tiptoes and got his fingertips to the edge of the lid, trying to tilt the jar towards him so that it would unbalance and roll forward into his hands.

'You stupid little bastard.'

The unexpected sound of his father's voice scared Sean. The jar teetered and rolled towards him, as he had intended it to do, but, instead of catching it, it fell past him, landing with an explosion of shattered glass and sticky, orange marmalade on the ceramic kitchen tiles. He spun round, his heart pounding, It was a little after four o'clock and he'd only just gotten home from school. His father should still have been at work. But he wasn't! And the look on his face told him he was in one of his moods. The moods that changed him from being a violent bully into something much worse.

The first punch took Sean on the left side of the face, sending him sideways into the kitchen wall and dropping him to his knees. He saw stars and felt dizzy, so could not defend himself against the kick that followed. His father still had his heavy work-boots on, a crime for which Sean and his siblings would pay a heavy price if they had committed such a breach of the house rules.

The kick broke a rib on his right side. It was not the first time, so Sean knew immediately it was gone. It felt as if a thin, filleting knife had been driven into his lung, needle-sharp and piercing. He tried to breathe, but it was as if his chest was wrapped in tape, which, ironically, was the treatment he would get later, at the hospital, when he was seen for yet another one of his *falls*. The second kick was into his stomach. Sean rolled into it, wrapping his arms around his father's right leg, stopping him from being able to kick him again. They were too hard to take. Sean knew from experience how to stop them, despite knowing what would follow would be almost as bad.

Stood behind his father, he saw his mother, white-faced and as still as a ghost. Equally as ineffectual. She would watch him take the beating and say nothing, taking a beating herself if she tried to intervene.

Unable to kick him properly, his father punched down at him, but the blows were weak. As any street fighter knew, it was a poor position from which to cause real damage. Instead, he reached down and grabbed Sean by the hair, viciously yanking him up onto his feet.

'Who the fuck said you could help yourself to food?' his father screamed at him, his face flushed with unnatural rage, spraying droplets of spittle into Sean's face.

'No one,' said Sean, meekly, glancing across at his mother. He'd been hungry when he'd returned home from school, as most twelve-year-old boys were. She had told him to go and make himself a sandwich. 'I was just hungry.'

The reply was met by an open-handed slap across the left side of his face. It burst like an exploding firework behind his eyes. He raised his hand to protect himself but his father hit him again, a backhander, splitting his top lip. Sean could taste the coppery blood in his mouth. It was a taste he knew well.

He began to cry. It made his father smile.

'Cry, you little bastard. Cry. I'll teach you some fucking respect.'

He hit Sean again, but this time the blow woke something up. Something that had lain dormant in Sean for years, waiting for the day when it would come back to help him. It whispered to him, now, from somewhere far away.

'Tell him to go fuck himself.'

'Go fuck yourself,' Sean heard himself say. As surprised as his father to hear the words.

Visibly shocked, his father glared down at him.

'What did you say to me, you little bastard?'

He punched Sean in the face; a brutal strike, opening a deep cut above his right eye.

'Tell him he's a bully who can only beat women and children,' the voice inside Sean whispered.

Again, Sean spoke the words, but it was as if someone else was controlling him.

Enraged, his father drove his fist into Sean's face, a harder punch than he normally delivered. It hit like a sledgehammer and something in Sean's left eye burst. The pain was like a shard of glass entering his eyeball. He screamed in agony and would have dropped to the floor if his father had not held him against the wall, by the throat, choking him. It was one of his favourite moves. He liked to see his victim, wife or child, squirming for life in his hands. Sean supposed it made him feel all powerful. Like the God he claimed to love.

'Look at you,' hissed his father, through gritted teeth, 'crying like a little girl. Not so fucking tough now.'

But whatever had come to life inside Sean took away the pain. He wasn't in the kitchen any longer. He wasn't being hurt and feeling scared. He was somewhere else. Somewhere empty. Somewhere far away.

'Your safe now,' the faraway voice whispered, all sticky sweet and marmalade soft.

It made Sean feel safe, watching, from inside, the boy on the outside. He stopped crying and looked into his father's face, staring at him through swollen eyes filled with blood. They would be black by the following morning. He would have to endure another day of being taunted, at school, by the other bullies.

'Tell him,' said the faraway voice, 'that you know he likes to see children crying, but that one day he'll be the one in tears.'

Sean repeated what he'd been told to say, the words strained, his father's hand still tight around his throat, but clear enough to hear. His father froze, free hand raised to deliver another blow. Something had shifted, they both knew it, though neither of them understood it. He let Sean go and backed away, a confused look on his face. It was the first time Sean realised his father was a coward.

Sean slid down the wall, holding his broken face. His father pointed to the smashed jar and the marmalade covered floor.

'Clean that fucking mess up and then go to your fucking room. Don't come down until tomorrow morning. You won't be eating.'

He glared at Sean then stormed out of the kitchen, dragging Sean's mother behind him. It was another of his subtle tortures, not allowing her to comfort Sean or his siblings after a beating.

Sean woke from the marmalade dream, fighting for breath, the choking in his dream turned real. He tried to get up off the couch, but couldn't move. His mind knew what he wanted to do, but his body wouldn't respond. He could hear the ghosts in the room talking to each other in the shadows. The lights had been switched off. He didn't remember doing that. He would never purposefully be in the dark.

Suddenly, the livingroom door swung open and the ghosts went quiet, as if they too could see the figure stood in the doorway, backlit by the light from the hallway. It seemed Sean's dream had manifested into something physical. The figure entered the room and walked towards him.

Sean stared up into the face of a demon. A face that was twisted and rancid and evil. As if a sculptor had fashioned it from wet clay then fired it with so much heat the clay had cracked and split, forming something grotesque. Seething red eyes bored into his, eyes brimming with malice, and the demon spoke to him, its voice filled with contempt.

'You killed them.'

Sean tried to break free of its wasted gaze, desperately looking around the room for someone to help him. But there was no one. There never had been. He begged, wanting it to go away, his voice turning to a pleading whimper.

'Leave me alone. Don't hurt me. Please. Don't hurt me.'

The demon began to laugh. It leaned over Sean, its eyes boring into his soul.

'Cry, you little bastard. Cry!'

Sean tried to scream, but no sound came. He recognised the face of the demon as his years-dead father. Consumed by fear, he plummeted into an ocean of darkness and began to drown.

He woke and tried to draw breath, but the fear that had gripped him in the waking dream tightened around his chest, suffocating him like the bandages wrapped around his broken ribs so many years before, making his heart race as his body begged for air. He looked across to the open livingroom door, half expecting to see his father standing there. Instead, he heard a woman's voice.

'It's okay, Sean. Just breathe.'

'Linz.'

'Sssshhh! You're safe, hun.' Her voice was gentle, like the swooshing sound of slow-breaking waves on a pebble beach. 'I won't let him hurt you anymore.'

And time began to slow.

Finally, Sean drew a breath. Dragging the air into his aching lungs like a free-diver returned to the surface from the depths of the ocean. He sat up, trembling from the culminated effects of the physical and mental pressures inflicted on his body over the course of the past few days. He stumbling into the kitchen and vomited into the empty sink, retching until his stomach was purged. He reached for an empty glass and filled it with water, draining it and refilling it, drinking the second glass almost as quickly.

The dreams had left him badly shaken, the waking nightmare, the worst. He had not experienced anything like that since his University days. He slumped against the sink, exhausted. Despite that he feared sleep, it was one o'clock in the morning and his body was giving him no choice. He made his way up the stairs, into his bedroom, and climbed onto the bed, having neither the desire or strength to undress or to slide under the duvet. He was asleep before he could wonder if sleep would come.

At exactly three o'clock in the morning, the time when the veil between life and death is at its thinnest, leaving spirits free to travel between the two worlds, Sean sat bolt upright. He looked around him, spooked by what he thought he'd heard.

'Who's there?' There was no sound, save for the creaking and cracking all houses make at night in response to changes in temperature. 'More bloody dreams.' He swung his legs round and sat on the edge of the bed. 'Christ, I feel like shit.'

He stood up and went out onto the landing, peering down past the mezzanine into the empty entrance hallway below. It was a still, cloudless night and the light of a the moon flooded in through the cupula above his head, casting an eerie, blue glow over the staircase, lighting it enough to allow him to descend without turning on the lights.

From the fridge in the kitchen, Sean grabbed a small bottle of Pellegrino and drained it. He took a second bottle, intending to take it up to his bedroom, and walked back into the hallway, crossing to the foot of the stairs. Before he could take the first step, a noise grabbed his attention and he looked up. It had sounded like a voice. He peered into the semi-gloom and something caught his eye. He froze, unsure of what he was seeing.

Jesus Christ!

Two dark shadows sat crouched below the banister rail on the first-floor landing, outside the entrance to the children's bedrooms, peering down at him through the iron spindles. Sean wasn't afraid, only confused. For the briefest of moments he imagined it was Toby and Alice. The shadows were in the same spot they used to sit when he came home from work, each night, when he wasn't away on business. He called up to them, but the shadows remained.

'I'm fucking losing it,' he said to himself. But he was certain he could still hear voices whispering up above him. 'Answer me,' he demanded, speaking to them the way any parent would do when their child had been called but failed to answer, somewhere between mild annoyance and growing concern. 'Right, I'm coming up.'

He took the steps two at a time, hearing the sound of light footsteps and children laughing above him. He turned onto the first-floor landing and flicked the light switch, flooding the landings and stairwells with light. His eyes took a second to adjust. He looked at the point where the shadows had been and saw two large teddy bears, *Pooh* and *Paddington*, two of Alice's bears, sitting against the spindle rails. Their legs had been pushed through the gaps in the rails and their furry bodies angled in such a way as to allow them to look down into the hallway.

What the hell? Who did this?' Sean knew he hadn't. *Had he? Had Ian?* He suddenly remembered the lost hour on the kitchen clock. *Is this what it's like to go mad?*

He walked along the hallway, past the silent bears, and turned right onto another narrow landing which separated each of the children's bedrooms. The doors faced each other and both were partially ajar. He knew they'd been closed when he'd arrived at the house the day before. He'd come up and stood in front of them for an hour, unable to bring himself to enter. He pushed open Alice's door and took a faltering first step.

Three walls were painted candy pink, a colour Alice had insisted on choosing herself. A mural of the *Snow White's* seven dwarves took up the whole of the fourth wall. Sean had painted it, himself, in the last month of

Linz's pregnancy, his childhood pastime a skill he still retained, much to Linz's surprise. Alice had loved it, insisting, once she'd seen the film, that Sean add in *Snow White's* evil stepmother, as well as the talking mirror. Now, the haunting gaze of the witch fell upon him, as if to say, *come in, take a bite.* Ignoring her, he took a second step and fully entered the room.

The sight that greeted him was like a physical blow. One that was much harder than any his father had ever delivered. Alice was everywhere. Her wellingtons, red, with white butterflies, that would never splash in puddles again stood in one corner. Teddy-bears were everywhere, piled on the bed, sitting on the floor, and propped up on the little pink stools she'd used when having a teddy-bear's tea-party. All the bears were there, except Pooh and Paddington, still sitting outside, and Pookie, whom Sean had left in the back seat of his car. He'd meant to bring him up but had forgotten he'd brought him back from Dunvegan Castle.

'Alice.' Sean whispered her name. 'Are you there, Princess?'

He knelt down and looked under her bed, but save for her roller skates there was no-one there.

He stood and walked across to her wardrobe, pulling both doors open. A row of clothes hung on wooden hangers, like small ghosts waiting for permission to come out and play. They would never be worn again. The clothes reached for him as he leant forward, gathering them to him in an agonizing embrace. They still carried a faint trace of her essence, preserved in time like a butterfly trapped in amber. But the smell would fade. As would his memory of her. He knew it and could not stand the thought. Sad beyond words, he turned and left, quietly closing the door behind him. The finality of it destroying him just a little more.

Toby's room was the same experience of love and loss. His wakeboard lay against one wall, framed by posters of Emilia Clarke and Maisie Williams, characters from the worldwide television series, *Game of Thrones*. Sean had no idea what characters they played or what the series was about, other than it was something to do with dragons. What he *had* known was that his son had liked both girls. They were *hot*, Toby had informed him. His son had been on the verge of manhood, but would now never become a man. He would never know the heady excitement of having a first kiss, or the incredible yet terrifying experience of first love. Nor would he ever know how it felt to properly fall in love. Or the joy of having children of his own.

Closing Toby's door behind him, Sean went out into the hallway and stood on the landing beside Paddington and Pooh. He turned and looked back at the bedroom doors, knowing he would never open them again. As he climbed the stairs, heading back up to his bedroom, he heard Linz above him.

'Are you ready? Have you seen enough?'

She was looking down at him from the landing outside his bedroom door.

'Linz, my love, I knew you'd be here.'

Sean realised she and the children must have put the bears on the landing. He had heard their voices. He understood now. It was a message to him. They *were* here!

Linz turned and walked into their bedroom, giving him a backwards glance as she disappeared from view. Sean bounded up the stairs behind her. He burst into his bedroom and scanned the room, but Linz was nowhere to be seen. He rushed into the en-suite. Again, the room was empty. Frantic, he made his way back through the bedroom and slid open one of the glass doors to the outside balcony, stepping out into the near darkness. The night was ice-cold and his breath ballooned in front of him. He looked along the length of the balcony but saw no one.

'Hun.'

Sean turned to see Linz, in the bedroom, standing at the end of their bed. She smiled at him then walked through the short, windowless passageway leading from the bedroom into her adjoining private study. Sean rushed inside, following her into a spacious room that looked out over the same balcony he had just been standing on. The glass ceiling in the main bedroom extended over the study, so combined with the same sliding glass doors the room was bathed in light and alive with shadows.

'Linz.' He couldn't see her. 'Dammit, Linz, stop playing with me. Where are you?'

He stared, accusingly, at the Victorian wooden desk set in the centre of the room, as if expecting to see her sitting behind it in the equally antiquated swivel-chair. The chair and the table looked back at him, unable or unwilling to answer.

Sean felt his anger building. Anger at Linz for not being there. At the children for playing tricks on him with Pooh and Paddington. Anger at his father-in-law for having brought their carbon ghosts and causing this to happen. Anger at Mac for threatening him with eternal damnation, and at the prostitute, Jann Livingston, for the way she'd treated him. Mostly, he was angry at himself for having come back to Merrick in the first place.

'Talk to me, Linz! Answer me, damn you!' But Linz was gone. Everyone was gone. 'Why have you all abandoned me?' screamed Sean. 'What did I do? What did I do? What did I do?'

He slammed his fists down onto the desk, knocking a framed picture of himself and the children onto the floor and smashing the glass in the frame. The sound was like a boxing ring bell. The strains and stresses of the past few days became too much to hold in. And like Vesuvius, Sean erupted.

In a boiling rage he swept his arms across the desk, spilling everything on it to the floor. A Tiffany lamp in the form of a pirouetting ballerina, with an exquisite glass shade, shattered as it hit the hardwood floor. A silver ink well and a sheaf of antique pens that Linz had used for handwritten messages were swept aside, the ink bottle spraying its contents onto the *chaise-longue* set behind it. Linz had purchased it from a flea market while accompanying Sean on a visit to QuantumCloud's Paris office, falling in love with the piece on first sight, despite it had been old and tatty. It had been shipped over and recovered in a delicate shade of powder-blue that had brought it back to life. Under the moonlight, the ink seemed like a spray of fresh blood upon the fine, linen fabric.

Like David Banner transforming into *the Hulk*, Sean's mind ceased to see reason, frustration and anger driving him to destroy everything before him. Everything Linz had loved. He put his fingers under the edge of the antique desk and flipped it. It overturned with a crash, landing upside down, leaning at an awkward angle against the *chaise-longue*. He followed the mortally wounded desk across the room, the swivel chair in his hands, swinging it into the underside of the desk and snapping one of the chair legs clean off.

Still out of control, he rushed to the back of the study and vented his fury on the white-painted shelves, where Linz kept her book collection and her favourite Murano glass pieces. He tore the books from the shelves, littering the floor with them, then turned his attention to the Murano glass.

The first piece that bore his anger was an exquisite, yellow glass bowl that Linz had purchased on her first visit to Venice, with her father, as a young woman. It sailed across the room, smashing against the balcony doors and exploding into glass splinters that showered the floor. The bowl was followed by a smiling clown figure that Sean had given her on their fifth wedding anniversary. He wiped the sad smile from its face. Piece by piece the collection was destroyed, until everything was gone and his rage had been vented.

Sean fell to his knees, panting, the red mist draining out of him like pus from an infected wound. In the quiet that followed, he knelt in silence, staring blankly at what he'd done. Then came the overwhelming sense of loss. Some of the most beautiful moments of Linz's life had been eradicated. Now, those precious moments lay on the floor in a rainbow of glass fragments that would never be seen for what they once had been. All the special moments of her life, gone, like tears in the rain.

'Damn you! Damn you to hell,' cried Sean, though who he was damning he wasn't entirely sure. He struck his fists against the floorboards, screaming his frustration, each strike booming through the upper part of the house and out into the silent night. 'Take me! Take me, now, damn you,' he cried, as if invoking something primeval to awaken. Something his ancestors had known about and spoke of, sitting around the clan fires in prehistoric times, fearing the darkness beyond. But Sean knew no such fear. He knew only pain. Pain he could no longer live with. He had to end it. His voice dropped to a whisper, but was no less intense. 'I call on you, Death, to come for me.' 'Take my life. I do not want it anymore.'

Somewhere out over the ocean he saw the flare of two distant lights, as if Death had been awakened to his existence and heard his offer. The lights grew brighter, momentarily, then disappeared.

Spent, Sean's gaze dropped to the desk, collapsed against the *chaise-longue*. It had been badly damaged, its limbs and body broken, but the damage had revealed a drawer built into its underside, a drawer no-one would have ever found unless they had known it was there. The Victorians, he knew, had a penchant for such hidden compartments in their furniture. He had not known it was there, but he'd never used Linz's desk. He wondered if *she* had.

He crawled towards it. There was something protruding from the broken drawer. A book of some sort, it seemed, with a dark brown cover that struck him as being old. He reached for it and pulled at it, trying to wrest it through the gap in the splintered drawer, but the desk held it tight, still trying to protect the secrets it had been entrusted with. Changing tactics, he took hold of the drawer itself, bracing his feet against the desk and pulling with both hands. With a crack like snapping bone, it tore free, and the book fell to the floor.

Sean picked it up, wondering who it belonged to and how it had come to be there. It was a soft-bound, leather journal, about the size of a modern magazine but as old-fashioned looking as the desk. He read the name written in gilt letters on its front, surprised when he discovered whom it belonged to, then opened it and began to read.

He read for hours. Until the first colours of dawn peeked over the horizon, checking that night had gone. He read on as the sun rose out of the ocean, turning its surface to gold. When he finally finished reading, he knew Linz had not abandoned him. She had not abandoned him at all. She had shown him the way!

22

Sean got off the bed and stretched. His body was stiff and sore. It felt early, but his watch told him it was eleven o'clock in the morning. He'd finally gone back to bed, just after dawn, and slept the sleep of the dead. It had been the best four hours he'd slept in weeks, but he was still feeling dusty, inside and out. The past few days had been like riding an emotional roller coaster. It was time to get off!

The massive en-suite bathroom Linz had created had a traditional wooden sauna, tiled steam room, double Jacuzzi, and a large shower-enclosure. Sean tossed the underwear, socks and t-shirt he'd slept in into a wicker basket then pressed the digital on button on the shower control console. He stepped into the steam and a virtual waterfall drenched him from head to toe. The water was preset to a temperature, so hot, that Linz had always refused to come into the shower with him unless he turned it down to something a normal human being could stand. He smiled at the memory and began to feel refreshed.

As he washed, he began to sing the Shinedown song that had always meant so much to them both.

'The first step is the one you believe in, the second one might be profound. I'll follow you down, through the eye of the storm, but don't worry I'll keep you warm.'

It held more meaning to him, this morning, after what he'd discovered in Linz's journal. The first step, he now realised, had been in coming back to Merrick. He hadn't wanted to, but she had guided him here to find it. The second step *would* be profound.

Out of the shower and wrapped in a white towel, he went into his dressing room and opened one of the drawers, selecting a pair of dark blue running shorts, black tee-shirt and a pair of white socks. After lacing up his running shoes, he headed downstairs, glancing at Pooh and Paddington as he passed the first floor landing. He smiled at the bears but they pretended they hadn't seen him. He opened the front door just as Miles was about to knock, hand raised, bunched into a fist.

'Steady on, Gaylord,' said Sean, cheerfully.

He stepped forward and threw his arms around Miles, pulling him into a familiar bearhug greeting.

'Major.' Miles was unable to keep the surprise out of his voice. 'We were just about to . . .'

'Jude!' Sean stepped past Miles to hug her and kiss her on both cheeks. 'You look fantastic.'

'Sean, you're home.'

Judith looked every bit as perplexed as Miles Sean looked her up and down. She was in a pale-lemon trouser-suit worn over a white, silk blouse, with a pair of matching high-heeled shoes that must have made walking on the gravel surrounding the house more than difficult.

'Armani today, Jude, or some other designer I've never heard of? Sexy as hell, girl.' He shrugged, 'Sorry, that probably sounded a bit sexist, but we're still allowed to pay a woman a compliment, aren't we, Miles?'

'Of course we are, Major.'

Miles was confused as to exactly who had answered the door. It certainly wasn't the same Sean Jameson he'd left at the church gates the day before.

'Come on in, both of you.' Sean stepped back and waved them in. 'I was just off for a quick run then was going to have a full chicken coop's worth of scrambled eggs. Except that I don't have any eggs to scramble.' He beamed a smile that drew Miles and Judith into the house. They followed him into the kitchen. 'I've got coffee, as long as you like it black, but little else. Look, why don't I go for my run and pick up some breakfast provisions on the way back. We can have brunch, together, if you fancy?'

Miles and Judith stood, open-mouthed, struggling to form an adequate reply. They'd both been sombre on the way over, expecting to see a different Sean than the one who was practically bouncing around like an out of control *Tigger*. The kitchen was clean and didn't smell of cigarettes or alcohol, which

Miles would have happily staked his house on it being. Judith had been worried about seeing him. How they'd left things at Dunvegan Castle had been horrible, but it was as if he had wiped the memory from his thoughts. She'd also expected to find him falling apart, especially after talking to Emily and Father Mackenzie, but she wasn't going to complain that she'd been wrong.

'Sure, that would be great, Sean.' She reached out to take his hand. 'Are you good? Seriously?'

'I'm better than that, Jude. Coming back here was the right move. You were right. And as someone recently told me, I need to listen to the women in my life a bit more closely.'

'Well it's about bloody time you realised that, Major.'

Miles was overjoyed that Sean seemed to have let go of what had happened at the church the previous morning and was in such bright spirits. He wouldn't mention the altercation. It would be a conversation for another time, if ever. Sean had been under immense stress. He had his best friend back. That was all that mattered.

Sean jogged around the side of the house, through the back garden, and opened the gate onto the narrow pathway that ran between Edinburgh and Cramond Village. He crossed the path and went straight onto the beach, heading down to the waterline. The tide was out and the sand solid underfoot. The sun was low in the sky but the air still chilly.

The beach was empty of people, but the seabirds took off as he neared them, squawking at him, angrily, annoyed they had to leave their feeding ground. He set off at a brisk pace in the direction of Edinburgh, the stiffness in his legs trying to slow him down. Ignoring the acid tears of his muscles, he pushed on, settling into a pace he knew he could keep up for at least ten miles. He had washed off the dust on the outside, now the dust on the inside began to blow away.

A mile ahead of him lay Granton seafront, lined with old, brick-built, two-story cottages and modern flats. Beyond them was the village of Newhaven, busy with tourists and day visitors flowing down to the harbour front. He passed by Loch Fyne seafood restaurant, remembering the last time he'd been there, with Linz, just over a year ago, before they'd set off on their family holiday to Skye. He stopped, watching other couples sitting there, smiling and holding hands. Being in love. He was melancholy, but, after the previous night and the finding of the journal, not as sad.

The run back was as invigorating, but harder and further than Sean remembered it being. His chest began to burn and he struggled to keep his pace, eventually slowing to a jog and then a brisk walk as the cost of the last year, to his body, became clear. The ten miles he thought he could run became half that. He wasn't fit. Not by a long way. The thought annoyed him, especially as he would have need of that fitness in the days to come. But then he remembered what he'd read in Linz's journal and realised it wasn't important. He jogged back to the house at a slower pace, stopping at Cramond Village store to pick up the breakfast provisions he'd promised Miles and Judith he would get.

'Well that was fantastic,' said Sean, draining his second cup of coffee and wiping his plate clean with a piece of sourdough toast that had so much butter on it Judith winced.

'You're a cardiac surgeon's worst nightmare,' she joked.

Sean gave a gusty groan of pleasure as he swallowed the last morsel of the best breakfast he'd had in ages.

'But it's so bloody tasty, Jude. Well done, Miles. I didn't know you could cook so well.'

'Enjoy it, Major, it's your last full cooked. You were exhausted, after that run, so porridge and fresh fruit are the order of the day, from now on. You're going to be joining me at the gym, every morning, too.'

'Every morning?'

Sean looking horrified.

'You can have Sundays off.'

'Too kind, Gaylord.'

They laughed like teenagers looking at their first porn magazine.

Judith studied Sean, wondering if the turnaround in him was for real, or even a good sign. Emily had told her he could seem happy one minute then plunge to the depths of despair the next. He was, it seemed, much more than just okay. And that was what bothered her. While she wanted to know how his father-in-law's visit had been, despite it appeared to have had a positive effect, she was unsure how to broach the subject. Sean pre-empted her before she had to.

'Ian came to see me last night. He brought me the vases.'

'Vases?'

'The Murano vases.'

Judith understood immediately. She made a mental note to ensure she never referred to them as, *urns,* at any time in the future. Vases was actually a much nicer term for them.

'Yes, we saw them on the table in the livingroom. They're beautiful. We've seen them before, of course, when Ian came to collect them from the office.'

'They're so personal, Jude. The colours. I'm guessing that was your doing?

'And Miles,' said Jude. 'He reminded me of your family trip to Italy and Toby's love of the colour of the sea at the beach in Positano.'

Sean looked at Miles and nodded his thanks.

'I can't ever thank you enough. Both of you.'

'It was nothing,' mumbled Miles, embarrassed at Sean's praise.

'No, Miles, it was a great deal more than nothing. I abandoned them. The three people I loved most in the world. I can't begin to think how much they would be ashamed of me for that.'

Miles shook his head.

'They would never be ashamed of you, Major. They loved you.'

'Anyway, it wasn't just us,' added Judith, realising for the first time that Sean was carrying such guilt. 'Hublot and the entire board were involved. Hub took time out to come with me to Venice to organise them being made. He used some of his personal business contacts to ensure we got to speak to Venini and Augusto at all.'

Sean knew how much time that must have taken out of Hublot's hectic schedule with the merger in full swing.

'I'll call him and thank him.'

'He'd really appreciate that, Sean. We just wanted to do something nice for them, as well as for you. Everyone understood how you felt and why you left.'

'She's right, Major. I don't know that I would have handled it any better.'

'Nonetheless,' said Sean, 'I was deeply moved. I've treated you both so badly, recently, and said some things that were out of order. I'm sorry for that. Truly. Can you forgive me?

'Nothing to forgive, Major. Absolutely nothing.'

'Same here,' said Judith. 'What are friends for if not to abuse when you're feeling down.'

She gave Sean a bright smile.

'I did love you, Jude. As much as I could have done. I'm sorry I said I didn't.'

Judith climbed off her stool and came around the island to hug him.

'Thank you for that, Sean. I know you did. In your own way.'

'Let him go, for feck sake,' said Miles, 'the man's turning blue.'

They all laughed and the somberness of the moment disappeared.

'And another thing, Jude,' said Sean, 'would you try to stop the sale of my shares. Although I'm probably too late. I'm an idiot for wanting to hurt the company.'

'I didn't sell them,' said Judith, hoping it wasn't going to send him into a rage. 'I wanted to give you time to cool off and reconsider. I'm sorry I disobeyed your instruction.'

Sean sighed in relief.

'Honestly, Jude, I'm glad you did. I don't want that on my conscience. Hublot is the right man for the job, I always knew he would be. He'll lead the company forward.'

'Aren't you going to go back when you're ready?' Miles asked.

'Of course. That's what I meant,' said Sean, 'but not anytime in the near future. I've lots to sort out.'

'Such as?'

'Just that I'm going to take time to think about my future, Jude. About where I want to go and what I really want to do. I read something, the other day, that made me think about that. I'm going to take the advice of the person who wrote it.'

'Who was?' Judith asked.

Sean knew she was diving for pearls. He wanted to give nothing away about what his actual plans were.

'I can't remember. I think it was an article in one of the magazines in Emily's treatment room. It was about finding yourself, through travel, after a period in your life that's been rough.'

'Sounds like good advice,' said Judith, pacified, for the moment, it seemed.

'Good idea,' said Miles, enthusiastically, 'what about some sailing? We always talked about doing the Mediterranean. What an adventure that would be.'

'It's certainly something to consider, Gaylord. An adventure is exactly what I think I need. But, right now, I'm going to stick the dishes in the dishwasher, if I can figure out how to start it, then I'm off to Cramond Kirk. I need to speak to Mac.'

'That's great, Major. And while I'm the last person to give you any advice on religion, I think it's a good thing. We'll head off and let you get on with it.'

At the front door, Judith stood with Sean while Miles walked around the side of the house to get his jeep.

'I'm glad you're okay, Sean. You are okay, aren't you?'

'I'm fine, Jude, stop worrying. Say hello to Hublot for me. Tell him I'm sorry and I'll come see him soon.'

Judith looked up into Sean's face, seeking any signs she might have missed. He seemed fine, but a little bit too fine.

'He understood why you wanted to dump the shares. He's not angry, but he'll be relieved to know you changed your mind. Now, if you need me, call me. Promise?'

Sean smiled down at her, knowing she was looking for him to give himself away.

'I promise.'

'I'm so proud of you, Sean. For the way you're handling things. Linz would be proud of you too.'

'She is, Jude. She is.'

Judith wrapped her arms around his neck and hugged him

'Of course she is. I know you saw her at Dunvegan, but have you seen her since?'

The tone in Judith's voice set Sean on the defensive. She'd been asking him leading questions for the past half hour.'

'Only in my dreams.'

'That's good, Sean, really good.'

She hugged him again and then let him go, as Miles brought his jeep around to the front door.

'Goodbye, Jude,' said Sean, waving her goodbye, 'take care of you.'

He turned and walked back into the house, giving her no chance to answer him. Inside, he looked up to the first floor landing. Standing between Pooh and Paddington, looking down at him, was Linz.

'Hi, hun,' she called down to him.

'How did I do, my love?'

Linz smiled and nodded her approval.

23

There were three men in Sister Abagail's life; God, Jesus and Father McKenzie. She loved them all. Not equally, of course, that would be impossible, but almost as much. She'd been an orphan since she could remember, so there were no images of the faces of her parents for her to recall, but she had a family that had given her the love and joy that made up for a mother and a father who could not. She knocked on the door of Father Mackenzie's private rooms at the back of Cramond Kirk. He was her number three, behind God and Jesus Christ, of course.

'Come in.'

Mac's voice was sharp.

'Father Mackenzie, I'm so sorry to disturb you, but . . .'

'What is it, Sister?' He was annoyed she'd knocked. He'd explicitly told her he wanted no intrusions. 'I'm writing my homily.'

'I know that, Father, and I deliberated on interrupting you, but . . . '

'It's fine,' said Mac, softened his voice. 'What's wrong?'

'The man who was here the other morning, the one who was shouting at you and damaged the front doors when he stormed out. He's in the Remembrance Garden. He asked me to . . .'

'Sean! He's here?'

Mac scrambled to his feet and brushed past Sister Abagail, who went from being afraid of his reaction to feeling pleased that she'd done the right thing.

'He's in the Remembrance Garden, Father,' she repeated, 'not in the church.'

'Why didn't you say so?' Mac smiled at her as he turned back into his room. 'Now, go back to your duties and we'll chat later.

'Of course, Father.'

'I'm glad you told me, Sister. He is in a difficult place, deserved of our care and forgiveness.'

'I thought about it, Father,' said Sister Abagail, bowing her head, penitently, 'and almost didn't. But I am an instrument of God. If He has guided this troubled soul to His house then who am I to question His judgement?'

She turned and walked off, leaving Mac thinking he had been blessed when this beautiful soul had been sent into his keeping. He crossed himself then opened the side door and stepped down into the flagstone courtyard, wondering just what version of Sean he was about to meet.

It was past one in the afternoon, but the sun still hadn't warmed April's icy breath. Sean was by the apple tree, looking down at the copper memory fixed to the wall. He was dressed in a black fleece and had a dark, woolen scarf wrapped around his neck to keep off the chill. A pair of camouflage army-trousers and tan Timberland boots completed the ensemble, making him look like an outdoor adventurer. But he was clean-shaven and looked a damned sight better than he'd looked the other morning.

'Mac,' said Sean, turning to face him. 'Thanks for coming out to see me. I thought you might not, the way your warrior nun looked at me when she found me.'

'I told you, Sean, I'm her mission.' He gave Sean a warm smile. 'You should have come into the church. But I guess you'd rather be here with Linz and the kids. Do you want to come in now? I've got a fire going.'

'No thanks, Mac, I'd rather stay here if you don't mind. I won't keep you long.'

'I've nothing better to do, Sean, take as much time as you want.'

Mac took a seat on the same iron bench they'd sat on the morning before. Sean sat down beside him.

'Just don't preach to me, Mac. Okay? I only want you to listen to what I'm going to say then tell me the truth about something.'

'Whatever you want,' said Mac. I'm just glad you want to talk. And that you're here.'

'I'm here to say goodbye.'

'Sean! We talked about this. About taking your own life.'

Sean shook his head.

'I'm not going to kill myself.'

Mac pressed his hands together in a silent thanks to his maker and gave a sigh of relief.

'Thank God! I've been worried sick about what you said about joining Linz and the children.'

'You don't understand. I said I wasn't going to kill myself and I meant it, but I'm still going to be with them.'

Mac's look of relief changed to immediate concern.

'What do you mean? I'm not following you.'

'I saw Linz, again, last night,' said Sean, drawing a look of surprise from Mac. 'She showed me something I needed to see. I knew she was here to guide me. And she has.'

'Guide you, Sean? In what way?'

Sean recounted what had happened the previous night, starting at the point where he'd dreamt about his father, Linz appearing to him, and the destructive rage that had come over him in her study.

'She guided me there, Mac, knowing I'd vent my anger when she disappeared. I found something as a result of that anger. Something she wanted me to find.'

What?,' Mac asked, drawn into the story despite being concerned that Sean's bereavement visions were becoming more sinister than they should be.

'This!'

Sean reached inside his fleece and pulled out the leather journal. He handed it to Mac.

'Lindsay Melville,' said Mac, reading aloud the name on the cover. 'Is this her diary?'

'Sort of,' said Sean, 'maybe more of a record of those days that were important to her. The places she'd been and the places she still wanted to visit. She seemed to have started it when she first left home to come up to university. She talks about meeting Miles, her classmates, her love of

Edinburgh and of joining the University Climbing Club. She mentions me, and how we met. I knew she'd fallen for me, but says she knew she was going to marry me from the moment she'd first spoken to me.'

'She got her man, didn't she?'

'She did, Mac. Perhaps the wrong one.'

'No Sean, never think that. Linz loved you. You were always meant to be together. Linz knew that long before you did.'

She fought to keep us alive, Mac, even when I buggered off to the army for eight years. I owe her for that, or I'd have missed out on her. On finding real love. The only shot I was ever going to get at it. I never really understood it until she was gone.'

'Sean you will find . . .'

Sean's face darkened.

'Don't tell me I'll find someone else I won't. She was the love my life. I don't want to find anyone else. I want her!'

'I understand, Sean. I'm sorry.'

Mac resigned to keeping his platitudes to himself. They'd gotten him nowhere, the day before, so why would that have changed? Sean was calmer, but his skin was paper thin and a brooding anger was crawling beneath its surface. He let him continue. It was clear he needed to talk.

'She was so happy when we were married. When we went to Venice on honeymoon. When we found Merrick. But the kids were the greatest joy of all. I knew that, of course, but reading how she felt about them in her own words was deeply moving. I almost felt as if I was intruding, but Linz wanted me to see these things. She wanted me to find the journal, to finally understand what she wants from me.'

Mac felt the same sense of foreboding he had felt when Sean had told him Linz had wanted him to join her in death. But he needed to let Sean finish before he could try to intervene.

'Go on.'

'Sure, there were things about me that annoyed her. The past year or so we hadn't been as tight, not like we once were. But they were getting better. She was so damned proud of me when I chose to face the demons that had haunted me from my childhood. Getting psychiatric treatment in

London. She was there for me, supporting me, every step of the way. But I gave up on the treatment, Mac. I thought I didn't really need it. But the memories I'd buried deep down in myself, so far down I thought they were gone, were still there, destroying me from the inside out. I was keeping them there, thinking I could control them. Not realising that they were controlling me.'

'And how does all this make you feel now?'

'I feel ashamed, Mac. Ashamed for giving up on the treatment. At not fighting tooth and nail to become the man she always wanted me to be. The man she knew I could be if only I would just allow myself. I let her down. I let them all down. And then I killed them. But I won't fail her again. Not now she's shown me what to do. In there!'

'And that is?' Mac asked, tentatively. 'And what's it got to do with her journal of journeys?'

'Journal of journeys! Sean exclaimed. 'I like that. I like that a lot. It's closer to the mark than you probably meant it to be. Here, let me show you.'

Sean took the journal and opened it, flicking through the pages until he found what he was looking for then handing it back. Mac hesitated to look down at what was written in the pages.

'Are you're sure you want me to read this? It's filled with Lindsay's personal thoughts and emotions.'

'There's nothing much on those two pages,' said Sean, 'just about our holiday together in France. We were on the Mont Blanc Circuit, one of the greatest treks in Europe. It encircles Mont Blanc, the highest mountain in Europe, passing through Italy, Switzerland and France. One hundred and seventy kilometers of ascents and descents that are as beautiful as they are breathtaking, with hilltop towns and villages dotted all along the way.'

'It sounds amazing, Sean. You both loved your adventures, back then, didn't you?'

'We did,' said Sean, seeing the memory, 'we just stopped having them after we got married. We forgot all about them. At least, I did. Linz wrote them down to ensure she didn't. But she's shown me the way forward now.'

'I'm not following you,' said Mac, glancing down at the journal.

'Look at the list on the right-hand page.'

Mac looked at the page Sean wanted him to read. There was a list, written in Lindsay's handwriting.

Climb Ben Nevis North Face (the Observatory Ridge)
Trek to Mount Everest Base Camp (as high as we can get)
Summit Mont Blanc (dance in the snow)
Walk the Camino De Santiago (get seriously spiritual)
Climb K2 (don't get caught in an avalanche)
Ride motorbikes across the Himalayas (from Pakistan to China)

'That's the list of adventures you and Lindsay wanted to do?'

'It is,' said Sean. 'Our unfinished adventures. We made the list on that holiday to Mont Blanc. I remember it like it was yesterday. It was early summer, so we decided to go do something wild. We just packed our gear and headed to France. We had so few responsibilities back then.'

'Didn't we all.'

'We sat in our tent, one night, during a storm, near the Grand Col Ferret, the highest point on the trek, close to the border between Switzerland and Italy, eating cold sausages, fresh tomatoes and crumbly, goats cheese. I think we had a baguette and a couple of French beers. We were listening to the storm and talking about all the adventures we were going to have together. This is the list we came up with. Linz must have written them into her journal when we got back to Scotland. They were important to her. To us both. That's why she showed them to me last night.'

Mac's eyebrows furrowed.

'I still don't understand, Sean. Ae you saying you're going to do them now? For Linz? Because, if you are, I think it's a great idea.'

He was relieved that Sean had found a purpose. It was exactly the kind of journey that could help him heal.

'It all makes sense, Mac, don't you see? Linz pointing to the mountain, when I saw her on Ben Nevis, then telling me to go home. She *wanted* me to come back to Merrick to find her journal.'

'Perhaps you're right. Who can say.'

Mac, despite his answer, was still unclear about what Sean was trying to tell him, but had wanted to show support. Sean, however, was not.

'Of course I'm right. Why else would she have done all this? She led me here, Mac, to find you! Heaven doesn't accept suicides, isn't that what you told me? You made me realise that killing myself wasn't the way to be with her. She brought us together to let you tell me that.'

'I must admit, Sean, it's been playing on my mind since you told me.'

Mac was relieved on one hand, but Sean, he noticed, seemed not to be really listening.

'Linz wanted me to go back to Ben Nevis, once I'd found her journal and spoken with you. She planned it all. When I saw her, there, I thought she was pointing to the part of the mountain where we'd first met. Showing me our past. But she wasn't. She was pointing somewhere else. She was showing me our future.'

'Where was she pointing, Sean? And what future are you talking about? I really don't understand.'

'She was pointing towards the north-east face, Mac. The first adventure on the list in her journal. The adventure we were supposed to do together but never got to start. But we can do it now.'

'So, are you saying you're going to carry her ashes with you, Sean? Is that what you mean? You and her doing these unfinished adventures together?'

Sean shook his head.

'You still don't get it. Mac.'

'What, Sean? What don't I get?'

'Linz wants me to join her and the kids.'

'But, I thought you said you weren't going to kill yourself.'

'I'm not going to kill myself, Mac. Someone else will.'

If he had been confused, before, Mac was even more so. Sean was making no sense.

'Who would do that, Sean?

'Death,' said Sean, his face deadly serious. 'I asked Death to come for me, last night, in Linz's study. I offered myself to her. I think she heard me.'

Mac was stunned. Rather than changing his mind, Sean had clearly lost a little more of it.

'Sean, you can't think like that. Death can't hear you, or be commanded.'

'Perhaps not commanded,' agreed Sean, 'but maybe she can be helped along.'

'Sean, you're not making any sense. Come inside and . . .'

Sean shook his head.

'No! I'll never go into a church again, Mac. I came her for one reason, to ask you a question. One you promised to answer truthfully.'

'I did, Sean. And I will, if I can.'

'Then answer me this. If I die doing something dangerous. If I fall from a mountain face or get caught in an avalanche, or I'm mortally injured or die of hypothermia. Will I go to heaven?

'Sean, you're still telling me you're going to kill yourself. Only by another means.'

'No, Mac, I'm not. And that's the point. I'm *not* going to kill myself. I'm going to put myself in the hands of Fate and let her decide. The north-east face of Ben Nevis has some of the most difficult and dangerous climbs in the world. Linz knows that. She knows I probably won't make it. She understood that was how I could be sure to come to her. It's why she led me to you and the journal. Its why she pointed to the Observatory Ridge on Ben Nevis.'

'I see.'

Mac sat, quietly, contemplating the enormity of what he'd heard. Although he could not agree with what Sean intended to do, it was still, perhaps, a step forward from him admitting he was going to commit suicide. Despite he had renounced God, perhaps God had not abandoned him. Perhaps the challenge he was about to embark on *was* part of God's plan.

'So? Answer me, Mac.'

Mac knew he had to answer truthfully.

'If you die in an accident, Sean, even if you have put yourself in the way of harm, as long as you do not purposefully attempt to die, and as long as you fight to live, you will be judged in Heaven. If you die in that manner you *will* join your family.'

Sean looked relived. He stood and readied to leave.

'Thanks Mac, that's all I needed to know.'

'Sean, please. Let me give you communion. If you are going to do this I won't try to stop you, but take God with you on your journey.'

'He's not *my* God, Mac. Not anymore. I need to be with Linz. And she needs me. He separated us. I will not speak with Him again. I've asked the Universe to decide what happens.'

'God *is* the Universe, Sean. I hope you discover that out there.'

'I doubt it, but thanks.'

Mac resigned himself to accepting that Sean was going to do what he had threatened. There was little he could do to stop him. Rather than trying, he thought to give him the only protection he had to offer. He reached inside his cassock and removed something from the pocket of his shirt.

'Before you go, wont you take this back?'

In the palm of Mac's hand lay Sean's silver crucifix.

'Linz gave this to you. Despite how you feel about God, I think she would want you to have it.'

Sean looked over at Linz, standing below the apple tree. She smiled at him and nodded. He took the crucifix and put it into his pocket, then offered a hand, which Mac took, clasping it in both of his and saying a silent prayer to God to keep him safe.

'Thanks for all you've done for us over the years, Mac. You've been a positive in our lives. Linz wants you to know that too.'

He turned away and walked to the *Fleur de Lis* gate, opened it, and walked out among the gravestones. The sun cast an ethereal, white glow around him, as if he had already turned from flesh to spirit. Mac watched him until he was out of sight then stood and walked towards the side door into the church. He had a homily to finish. He knew it would take longer to write than he had originally thought it would.

24

Sean started out from Edinburgh mid-afternoon, shortly after talking to Mac at Cramond Kirk and getting his permission to die, so to speak. Not that he felt he needed permission, he had already renounced God, but getting that clarification had been necessary to move ahead with Linz's plan. After packing his climbing gear, he placed the Murano vases back on the kitchen island along with a letter addressed to Miles, telling him he was climbing in Glencoe, and a further letter to Mac, asking, in the event of his death, to spread his ashes beneath the apple tree in the Remembrance Garden at Crammond Kirk.

After taking the A9 motorway north towards Stirling, he headed west on a beautiful section of winding road that passed the village of Balquidder, where Rob Roy McGregor had been laid to rest in the year 1734, at the little kirk, looking across Loch Voil. The highlander had spent his final days among the hills and forests he loved, overlooked by the dramatic mountain terrain of the Braes of Balquidder. Linz and the kids had joined Sean on a mountain bike ride among those same low mountains when they'd holidayed in the nearby village of Strathyre, a few years back, biking, kayaking and climbing. He shook the memory away and tried not to give in to his returning despair.

Onward, he drove, climbing higher with each mile, the land around him changing from rolling hills to lowland mountains. Most of the higher peaks were still smothered in snow, their sides winter white, as if the mountain had been dusted by a giant icing-sugar shaker. He passed through the village of Callander, its main road lined with tourist shops and restaurants, where more such memories reached for him.

Twenty miles on, he entered the village of Crianlarich, a few miles north of the head of Loch Lomond, stopping at the Artisan Café, inside the old Strathfillan Church, to purchase a cappuccino and a bread roll filled with cheese and tangy, lime pickle. He sat outside, at one of the wooden tables, admiring the views.

The land around him was filled with stunning mountain peaks. Sean and Linz had climbed there, many times, over the years. Their last trip together had seen them take on *the Cobbler*, a dramatic mountain with two summit peaks that looked like the Devil's horns. The kids had been here many times, too. Sean gazed down the glen and remembered one such time.

'Is this village famous for making bread, Dad?'

'I don't think so, Toby. Why?'

'Because the sign over there that says we're in Breadalbane. I thought it might be because they were famous for making bread.'

Sean smothered a smile. Linz was watching, clearly about to enjoy the coming explanation.

'It makes sense, I suppose, son. But it means something different in Scots Gaelic. Can you see the yellow writing below the word, Breadalbane?'

Toby looked up at the sign. Printed below the name of the town was another which said, *Braghad Albainn.*

'Sure, Dad, but what does it mean? I know its Gaelic, but I can't read it. We don't get taught that in school.'

'More's the pity,' said Sean. 'Well, the ancient language was the language of *Alba*, as our country was known by the Romans. It means high ground of Scotland. Look around and you can see why.'

'Lots of mountains,' said Toby.

'Exactly,' said Sean, and ruffled his son's hair.

Linz smiled at them, moved by the simple but loving interaction between her husband and her son.

The image lingered for a moment then the ghosts disappeared, leaving an empty feeling it the pit of Sean's stomach. He tossed more than half of the bread roll into a waste-bin and headed back to the car park, needed to escape the torment.

The memories of his family and moments they'd shared were becoming more frequent and harder to block with every mile he drove towards Ben Nevis.

He wondered why, then understood. It was because they were with him. He'd taken some of their ashes from the vases before leaving Merrick, despite he found it traumatic, pouring a little of the ash from each vase onto a flattened piece of paper, creased along its length, then transferring the mix into a round, silver hipflask with the image of a stag on its front, in bronze, a gift from the children which he'd never used. It was a sad irony that it now held them. The hipflask lay inside the pocket of his climbing jacket, next to his heart.

A few miles past Crianlarich, the tiny village of Tyndrum came into view, Sean drove through it, passing the Green Welly Stop, one of the most well-known rest areas on the west coast of Scotland. Normally, he would have stopped, but it would only bring memories he did not want.

Just outside the village, the road split, heading to two of the most iconic areas in the highlands of Scotland. The left fork headed west towards the coastal town of Oban, at the mouth of Loch Linnhe, from where ferries sailed to the islands of Mull, Jura, and Islay. The right fork led north, higher into the mountains, the road cutting through Glencoe, a barren area steeped in the darkest Scottish clan history, before descending to the ancient town of Fort William.

Sean passed through Glencoe as dusk fell. The shadows of a coven of mountains known as the Three Sisters loomed over him as he reached the highest point on the glen, their gaze following him as the road dropped down on the other side. Not long after, he entered Fort William. It was like stepping back in time. He passed the hospital, a place he knew well, ignoring the mental image of his mother standing there, stone-faced and silent. *Same as you ever were*, he thought, and pressed on, feeling guilty for blaming her. She had done her best. It was not her fault his father had been a monster she could not fight.

Through the town, he turned east, heading down through Glen Nevis on the same road he had driven only four days ago after leaving Dunvegan Castle, when he'd been heading nowhere. It seemed so long ago and so much had happened since. Now, at least, he knew where he was headed.

Halfway along the glen he turned into the Braveheart car park. The orange lights of the Achintree Inn were visible through the trees. It was dusk, but still light enough to pick his way up the stony path. Ten minutes later, he pushed open the Inn door and stepped into the open reception area, dropping his leather overnight bag at his feet. A red-haired girl, standing behind the bar and pulling a pint, called over to him.

'Be over in a second.'

'No worries.' Sean called back.

The Inn was warmed by a log-fire set in an old, stone fireplace which looked as if it might have even been around in Bonnie Prince Charlie's days. In front of it were rustic looking couches and club seats that didn't match but looked comfortable. Hung on the bare stone walls were loops of old climbing rope, rusted-iron crampons, pitons, and old climbing boots, telling you exactly where you were; in the heart of Scotland's climbing country.

'Mr Jameson?'

The girl came towards him with a smile as warm as the log fire. Sean returned the smile as best he could.

'How did you know?'

'Well, it's quiet tonight,' she replied, 'but it's early in the week. We get busier at the weekends. So, there was only you to come. You booked earlier, didn't you?'

'I did,' said Sean, pulling out his wallet to offer his credit card.'

'I'm Sandra, by the way. I'm here all night. If you need anything, let me know.'

'Call me Sean.'

Sandra stepped behind a small reception area and looked down at a book lying open on the desk.

'Are you on holiday, Sean?'

'Sort of. I'm climbing tomorrow.'

Sandra studied Sean as she filled in some details in her check-in book. He was well-spoken and polite, but either shy, pissed-off, or just not a great talker. *Men, it's like drawing conversation from a parrot with learning difficulties.* She loved her job, and one of the things she most loved was chatting to the people that frequented the Inn. They were mostly climbers, like her, and she loved the camaraderie and banter. Most were only too happy to chat, especially before a climb. This one, though, was icy-cold. Although she knew some climbers got so focused they zoned out into their own worlds.

'On the Ben?'

'Yes. I'll be up and away before breakfast.'

'We do breakfast, early, for the climbers,' said Sandra, 'from six. If you plan to leave before that, I can get the chef to make you something up to take with you or to have in front of the fire before you go. Of course, the fire won't be lit, not that early, unless you want to light it when you get up?'

'Pretty relaxed, here, aren't you?'

Sandra shrugged.

'We're not some fancy hotel in Edinburgh, Sean, we're in the highlands of Scotland. Surely you know about our legendary hospitality and trusting nature? It's just a fire.'

'Thanks, Sandra, I'll have breakfast, here, if you leave it out. Can I pay now? That way I can beat the rush in the morning?'

'Funny,' said Sandra, laughing politely and taking Sean's credit card. 'Just staying with us the one night?'

'Yes.'

'What route are you thinking tomorrow? The Pony Track?'

'I'm thinking more the Tower Ridge,' replied Sean, 'all the way up.'

Sandra looked surprised.

'Won't you need two nights?' Most people that take on the Tower start out early and come back late, ready for a hearty supper, a wee dram to celebrate, and a well-earned night's sleep.'

Sean shook his head.

'I'll be fine with one night, thanks. I won't be coming back.'

Figuring he didn't want to talk anymore, Sandra handed him an old-fashioned mortice key hung on a silver carabiner.

'I'm sorry to hear that, Sean. Well, good luck tomorrow. You're in room three, along the hallway and up the stairs. Come down when you're ready and have a bite to eat.'

'I'm not really that . . .' Sean made to refuse but changed his mind. Even a condemned man had the right to a last supper. 'I'll be down in ten minutes. Would you choose something for me? I'm not a fussy eater and I've got pointy teeth, so meat's fine. In fact, it's preferable.'

'Sure thing, iceman.'

She gave Sean a parting smile and headed to the kitchen, leaving him pondering what she'd meant.

25

Sean left the Achintree Inn a little before six in the morning, after a broken, dream-filled sleep. Sandra had been good to her word and left a large bowl of porridge next to the microwave. He'd eaten it mechanically, rather than with any real enjoyment. She'd also set out a selection of fruit, energy bars and filled rolls for him to help himself to. He stuffed some of them into his rucksack and, while driving to the car park on the other side of Fort William, where he would begin his climb, ate a couple of bananas, loading up on slow release carbs he knew he would be glad of later.

A little after six-thirty, he began the ascent up via the *Allt a Mhuilinn*, a winding trail following a stream, or "burn", as the Scots called it, flowing down from the top of Ben Nevis. It was cold, so he zipped his fleece up to his neck, pulled his felt beanie down over his ears, and started to walk. It was still dark, the light of the coming morning a thin hope on the horizon, so he used the head-torch on his climbing helmet to help light the path. There was no need to force his pace, so he stopped for a break, about five-hundred feet up, taking a seat on a wooden bench by the side of the path.

As he gazed over the surrounding mountains and glens, the glow of dawn lit up Loch Linnhe and Loch Eil, turning them from expanses of indigo ink to mirrors of molten silver. The view was stunning, but didn't fill Sean's being with the wonderment such views normally did. Since the accident, the ability to engage with the world around him was gone. Something inside him was dead, and even the beauty of nature's palette could not bring it back to life.

He thought about what he was there to achieve and was at peace with the thought. The past year had been beyond his worst imaginings of Hell.

He could not face another trapped in that sadness. Death *was* his peace. He stood and walked on, trying not to think of all he'd lost.

The sun began its slow climb into the heavens, making it possible for Sean to switch off his head-torch. A glassy rim of thin ice lined the edges of the burn like salt on a margarita glass, and the pathway beneath his feet crunched with every step. The world was turning colder and whiter the higher he climbed.

At seven hundred feet a wooden signpost reading, *North Face and CIC Hut,* came into view, rising on the pathway like an icy, skeletal reaper. Sean passed it and stopped at a picnic table that afforded another magnificent view towards the islands of Rhum and Eigg. He'd sailed there, once, with his father-in-law; a memorable five-day jaunt.

At fifteen hundred feet, a mist dropped down to cloak the mountain in a translucent shroud, although visibility was still good enough to see the pathway. The cold was biting and the wind had picked up, lowering the temperature further. Sean pulled on a pair of fleece-lined mitts to warm his hands and walked on.

An hour later, now above the tree-line, he scanned ahead, looking for the hydro-dam he knew sat at the head of the "corrie", a steep-sided hollow at the head of the glen. He had to turn right there to head towards the Nevis ridges. He didn't want to pass it in the mist. Forty minutes later, two thousand feet up, the dam came into view.

As suddenly as it had arrived, the mist lifted and the land opened out in front of him, transforming into a wide vista of gleaming snowfields, sharp-pointed pinnacles and a jaw-dropping series of buttresses and gullies. The five great ridges of Ben Nevis came into view, rising out of the glen like giant Celtic warriors. The panorama was even more stunning than Sean remembered, but any joy he might have felt was dampened by the reason he was there.

He crossed a bridge over the burn, heading towards the famous CIC Hut, a private shelter for mountaineers and the only alpine-style hut of its kind in Scotland. It had saved the lives of many stranded climbers, over the years. It stood at the foot of the Tower Ridge, standing high and foreboding, starkly silhouetted against the sky. It was where he and Linz had first met.

'Linz, my love. Would that you were here with me.'

As if the Universe had heard his prayer, nature presented him with a gift that only those who venture into these remote places can ever hope to be given. A herd of wild deer appeared, to his right, cresting a rise then stopping to survey their domain. The lead stag, a canny fourteen-pointer with antlers measuring almost six feet across, sniffed the air and coughed a warning to his herd, a mix of hinds and fawns.

Sean stood deadly still, appreciating it was the last time he would see such a magnificent sight. A minute passed, and another, but the herd remained motionless. Finally, assured there was no danger, the stag coughed an all clear and they moved on, trotting across the open glen, back to higher ground. He watched them until they had disappeared from view then walked on towards the base of the ridge he had come to climb.

The Observatory Ridge, regarded as one of the most technically challenging climbs in the world, was a climb that killed, and climbers who attempted it had to have the stamina and skill required to conquer it. Doing it alone, in semi-winter conditions, was the most dangerous and demanding time of all. Sean was an experienced climber, but he was forty-five years of age, and his last serious climb had been years ago. He was also out of condition, if his run along Cramond beach had been anything to go by. It was madness to think he could climb it and survive. He reminded himself he was looking at it through the eyes of a mountaineer, seeking a safe and successful ascent, which was the last thing he was aiming for.

From his rucksack, he unpacked his climbing harness and stepped into the leg openings, pulling it up to his crotch so that the loops fitted snuggly around his upper thighs. He clipped the belt part of it around his waist and hung his safety gear from the metal carabiners already fastened to either side. He looked like a gunfighter, only, instead of six-guns on each hip, wore bunches of slings and pegs on one side and his axes on the other. He looked up at the ridge then wished he hadn't. The almost sheer face of ice and ragged black rock stared down at him, as if asking him what the hell he thought he was doing.

The scale of the challenge was daunting. Sean doubted he'd get even halfway up before something drastic happened. His worst fear was of having the accident he wished for, but not dying. He could fall and be severely injured, left as a vegetable in a human wheelbarrow, in a grubby and sterile hospital ward, his life in the hands of machines, breathing for him and feeding him.

Dying was acceptable, living like that was impossible to contemplate. If Hell existed, for Sean, that was surely it.

'Ready or not, here I come.'

The words made him think of Toby and Alice, hiding on the landing outside their bedrooms, waiting for him to come home. He wondered if they were waiting for him to come to them now. The thought steadied him. He took a deep breath and prepared to climb.

The ridge started at a point just under three thousand feet up the north-east face of Ben Nevis, taking a direct line up to the summit plateau, fifteen hundred feet above, where the crumbling remains of an old, scientific observatory still stand. Sean planned on making nine pitches, climbing in defined stages until he reached the summit. Not that he considered he would get there.

Normally, he would need multiple safety anchors set in place in case he fell. If that happened, his rope and harness would save him. He decided he would only set safety anchors where to not do so would be considered reckless to the point of suicidal. Apart from that, he would free climb the mountain, at least until he fell. He reached out and touched the rock, sending a benediction to the mountain. And to Death.

'I will climb you, mountain, to the best of my ability. I will not purposefully give up my life. But when you take me, Death, take me swiftly.'

The first pitch was relatively straightforward, the rock a mix of gabbro and basalt. He recalled his first climbing instructor explaining the particularities of both on their first serious climb together.

'If you don't know the difference yet, Sean, you soon will. Gabbro is like climbing a cheese grater. It's skin-shreddingly tough and can draw blood from your fingertips almost instantly. Basalt, on the other hand, is treacherously slippery, particularly when wet, and while it won't cut you, it will still kill you.'

Sean climbed slowly at first, ensuring three points of contact on the mountain at all times before contemplating his next move, placing his hands and feet on the ledges and holds to test they were solid before moving on. Within twenty minutes, he was over one hundred feet up, almost at the top of the first pitch. Reaching it, he took a break, resting on a narrow ledge, leaning back against the mountain with his legs dangling over the void. His breathing was steady but he was already sweating from the exertion. He unzipped his climbing jacket and took a few gulps of water from his water bottle.

Looking down at the rocky scree at the ridge base, Sean was amazed how effortless climbing it had been, but it was set at an easy angle and filled with good hand and footholds. It had needed little real climbing ability. He turned his gaze to Tower Ridge, on his left, standing tall and bleak, devoid of any signs of life, and pictured himself, Linz and Miles on it, as once they'd been, shouting encouragement to each other as they practiced on its lower reaches. He nodded to the ghosts then zipped up his jacket and stood up, gazing skyward at the second pitch.

The north-face of the mountain had remained in shade since the previous day, so the rock was damp and slippery. There was little *névé* on the lower pitches, the rock-hard ice that forms when snow melts and refreezes, into which ice-screws could be placed. Wave-crests of thin ice cascaded over the rocks around him. The slightest tap would see them collapse. Even the turf that was visible, in patches, between the rocks, was only partially frozen, and although the handholds and footholds were plentiful, climbing the initial part of the pitch would be difficult.

Halfway up the pitch, two hundred feet up the ridge, came a point where the route was open to variation, with the choice of using an *arête*, an almost vertical edge of flat rock jutting out from the ridge, which would require solid climbing technique and strength, or climbing a slab of black basalt that looked like a flat tombstone set into the mountain. The *arête* seemed the easier of the routes. Initially, Sean decided it would be the safest route to take. But then remembered why he was there.

'Temptress,' he called up at the mountain, 'lifting your skirts for me.'

His cry echoed off the walls of the other ridges, so that it seemed he was being watched by an audience of taunting demons.

Choosing the basalt slab, he crabbed along a narrow seam to get to it, leaning into the rock face, which lay close to vertical. At his back, lay open space to the rocks below, but he refused to place any safety gear. The slab was fifty feet high and half as wide, as if a knife stroke from the gods had sheared it away from the mountain. There were few handholds, but a vertical crack provided the perfect route up to another smallish ledge and the end of the second pitch.

Sean pushed his left hand into the seam and made a fist. With his hand wedged into the gap, ignoring the burn of the rock against the skin, he leaned back and looked up, studying the route, assessing the hand and foot placements possible. There were few. He would have to use sheer strength to climb it. He began to climb, bunching a fist in the seam then using his feet to push himself up, reaching up with his free hand and bunching *it* higher up in the seam, repeating the move until he reached the top of the slab and climbed onto the ledge. The skin on both hands was red and scraped. Oddly, the pain served to make him feel alive. He had not felt that way for a long time.

Sitting with his legs hanging over the top of the slab, rubbing his hands to stimulate the blood-flow, Sean looked out to the Western Isles. He could make out the Isle of Skye, in the far distance, its mountains rising into the clouds like horny ridges on the head of a mythical sea dragon. He ate a banana, relishing the sugar surge. He was thirsty, and normally would have rationed his water more carefully, but knew he would probably not need it much longer. Ironically, he was feeling strong and beginning to enjoy the climb. The old skills were still there. Not as sharp, perhaps, but he felt a certain satisfaction at having made it, so far, without incident.

'Pride comes before a fall,' he said to himself, knowing Fate would have whispered that should she have heard him.

The third pitch was short and uncomplicated, apart from a *gendarme*, a mass of rock protruding from the ridge face, forcing Sean up and around it before reaching a platform that jutted out over the climb-line. The platform was several paces wide and deep, the perfect place for a proper break. He took off his climbing pack and stretched his arms and legs, walking around in tight circles to alleviate the lactic acid building up in them. A look at his watch showed he was already two hours into the ascent. *Hardly the fastest climb.* But then speed was of no importance.

The sun had finally risen high enough to shine onto the face of the ridges, lighting them up like vertical blades of bright steel. He looked beyond them, out over the Western Isles and across the sea to the point where it became mist white and confused itself with the sky. The best days of his life had been spent out there, with his family. He realised he was procrastinating, due, largely, to the fact that the next pitch was the one that would probably end his life. It was one thing to reconcile yourself to dying, quite another, the closer you came to it happening. He hoped he would be brave enough to face it. The thought made him wonder if Linz was watching. It gave him the courage to move on.

Refocused, Sean shrugged on his climbing pack, tightening his safety harness to the max, though only out of good climbing practice. Despite the severity of the pitch, he was still going to free-climb. It wasn't breaking the promise he'd made, to Mac, to fight for his life. Others had free climbed it and succeeded, risking all for the thrill of the climb. Why not he?

As he was assessing the first move, a high-pitched scream echoed down the ridge face. Silhouetted against the sky was a giant bird of prey. At first, Sean thought it might be a buzzard, but it was far too big, and the wide wings were squared off at the wingtips. It could only be a golden eagle. This part of Scotland was the domain of the great birds.

'Is that you?'

The eagle banked towards him, then, catching a thermal, it turned, away from the ridge, circling directly over the climb-line Sean was set to take. It shrieked, again, as if calling to him. Urging him on. Sean called back to it, knowing in his heart it was Linz.

'I hear you, my love. I'm coming.'

The pitch was easier to begin with than he had anticipated, but the ridge-face soon became vertical. It took monumental skill and effort for Sean to cling to the rock. At one point, he was forced to climb out into the void, gravity trying to pluck him from the mountain. A couple of times the ridge narrowed to the width of a person, with sheer gullies on either side, where the feeling of exposure was almost overwhelming. He climbed on, passing option after option to place safety gear, continuing to pit his skill and life against the mountain.

About halfway up, he reached a ledge no wider than his boots, but was wide enough to allow him to take a break. The ridge face had narrowed to the point that there was no alternative escape route. It was climb up, here, or climb down. Sean had no intention of doing the latter. He studied it for a full five minutes, regaining his strength. There was a seam in the rock that would allow him to place a "cam", a spring-loaded, safety device he could jam into it, which would open, further, if he fell. Instinct told him to use it.

Above him, the eagle continued to circle, its shadow visible against the cloud-filled sky. He called up to it once more.

'Are you waiting for me, my love?'

But the eagle remained a silent watcher.

Lifting his left foot up onto a thin edge of rock, Sean pressed down with the toe of his boot, testing its integrity. The foothold was firm. It would give him the leverage he needed to propel himself up. He picked out the handhold he was aiming for. It was higher than he would have liked it to be and dusted in frozen snow, but appeared wide enough and deep enough to allow the move he had in mind. He would spring up, hooking the fingers of his right hand over it, simultaneously lifting his right foot onto a horizontal smear of protruding rock just below his current eye-line.

Sean played the move out in his mind one final time, took a deep breath, then pushed down, hard, with his left leg, propelling his body up in an explosion of movement, at the same time, punching his right arm up above his head, so that he looked like *Superman* flying up the face of the mountain. The fingers of his right hand curled as he reached for the hold, hooking over it, as he'd planned. He felt the ice on the handhold crumble as he touched it, breaking away like sugar frosting on the edge of a cake. The last thing he heard, as he dropped into the void, was the haunting scream of the eagle.

CLAUDIA

26

Plymouth Light stands at the head of Gurnet Point, at the entrance to Plymouth Bay, close to the quaint little town of Duxbury, in Massachusetts County. Built in the year 1768, a wooden structure, as all early lighthouses were, it remains one of the very oldest of its kind. The two-storey house beside it, which had served as home to the lighthouse keepers and their families, over the years, originally had a lantern hung at either gable end, making it America's first twin-light lighthouse.

The sun passed its zenith as Claudia Montgomery meandered the last few hundred yards up to the old lighthouse tower. She had expected it to have changed since she'd last been here, but it hadn't. It was exactly as she'd left it; tall and silent, gazing out to sea. The beam from its light had been extinguished years before, but it had guided her to it, today, lighting up a hundred stored memories as she approached.

An offshore breeze welcomed her as she crested the rise on the landward facing side of the tower, just above the sandy car park. She tightened the knot on the white, silk scarf holding her long blonde hair in place and zipped up her navy-blue, sailing jacket to keep off the early-April chill. After a cold, grey start, the sun was doing its best to warm the day. The storm clouds that had gathered like crowds at a car crash had all but dispersed and the sky was an ocean of blue above the blue of the ocean.

As she walked the last few paces up to the tower, Claudia traced her fingers over the fence points, a ritual that took her back to childhood walks she'd taken there. The knee-high, picket fence leading up to the tower was broken in places, the white paint flaked and crackled under the ravages of a thousand summer suns and winter days. She reached the lighthouse, stopped, and closed her eyes, listening to the screams of the herring gulls floating overhead. She'd always loved the sound of them. As had Paul, though, if he still did, she could not honestly say.

You should be here!

She wished they hadn't argued. The memory of the fight drew tears to the corners of her eyes, but she refused to let them fall. It was ironic, she realised, that she'd felt the urge to come back to the old lighthouse. Today of all days. She didn't really know why she had. Or maybe she did, but didn't want to admit it to herself. It was alone. So was she. Perhaps that was the reason it had called out to her soul that morning.

She'd driven down from her home, in Lexington, an upmarket suburb, north of Boston, travelling south on the Pilgrims Highway, passing through the seaside town of Duxbury and out along the narrow isthmus towards the lighthouse.

Claudia had been born in Duxbury and had lived there for the first seventeen years of her life. A not too exciting, not too boring, normal childhood. She'd gone to school during the week and worked weekends in the local art gallery before going up to study Contemporary Art at Boston University. Her parents had lived in the town all their lives, until her mother had died from cancer, six years ago. Her father had moved out west, shortly after, and was now remarried. Her sister, Margot, still lived in the family home with her husband and their five children. All girls. All still under the age of fifteen.

Lexington, where Claudia and her husband, Paul, now lived, was a beautiful old town filled with colonial houses that rubbed shoulders with newer but just as exclusive and pretty, modern houses. It had the dubious honour of being where the first shot of the American Revolution had been fired. The gravestones in the old cemeteries still bore the names of some of the original colonial families. They'd been overjoyed when they'd found their house in Robinson Hill, a six-bedroom house set in ten acres of gardens filled with flowering shrubs and surrounded by cypress and pine trees. A new start for them, Paul had assured her, five years before, and the perfect place to raise their family.

But the new start had changed little for them, other than that Paul was now away for most of the week, and, lately, most weekends. Even when he was home they seemed to spend little time together, and their time together spent arguing. The family had not come and, at forty-two years of age, Claudia felt that ship was fast sailing. They had both been tested and the results had been normal, whatever that meant? There was, according to the doctors at the fertility clinic they had chosen to help them conceive, no reason why she had not fallen pregnant.

Six rounds of in-vitro fertilisation treatment in the past three years had been difficult for them both to endure. The cost had not been in dollars, but in emotions, the rainbow of hope that rose, each time they tried, fading like a mirage on the barren sands of failure. The most recent treatment had been four months ago. They were both still suffering the after effects of *that*. It's what had caused the fight. It didn't matter, Claudia had tried to tell herself.

Only that it *did* matter. It mattered a lot.

Claudia sensed Paul no longer had the desire to be a father. Either that, or he had simply given up on the idea that it was ever going to be possible. He was, instead, more focused on his new career. Already an internationally published author, a west-coast based television studio had approached him with the idea of taking his series of books about a history teacher and his dog, who, between them, solved any number of unsolvable, historically-based mysteries, to the screen. Paul had jumped at the chance.

Lately, he'd been spending a lot of time in Los Angeles, working on the scripts for the upcoming series. It was a fantastic opportunity, apparently. But an opportunity for what? Claudia had asked. They already had enough money for their needs. What use was money when they spent less and less time together? They were supposed to be concentrating on having a family. The question had turned into an argument and Paul had stormed out of the house. That had been four days ago. She hadn't seen him since. He was at the house of some famous producer on Ocean Drive, at least, that's what his last text had told her. He'd said he loved her and was sorry about the fight. He was sick of fighting and assumed she was too. They needed to sit down and talk about their future. He hadn't mentioned their sixteenth wedding anniversary. Which was today.

Standing by the old tower, Claudia reminded herself that this was where their story had started. Their first date, twenty years before. A walk along the beach and a picnic of crude cheese sandwiches and refined champagne.

Like the light from the lighthouse, their love had once burned bright, but that light had dimmed to the point it was almost extinguished. The truth was, they had begun to live separate lives, Paul absorbed in his new-found success, she, locked away in her studio at the bottom of their garden, where, at times, even when he came home, she chose to sleep.

Her home studio was a single storey of glass and steel. Mainly glass. A modern, open white-space that flooded with light each morning. It looked out over Robinson Hill, which, although only a thousand feet in height, provided a sanctuary of walkways and trails, though, increasingly more importantly, solitude. Claudia found she was spending more time there, instead of painting and sculpting, having lost her passion for the one thing that always made her feel alive. The trees and the birds and the meandering river had become her confidants. She was sure the birds and trees were growing tired of her constant complaining. The river, like Paul, seldom spoke.

Their journey from a one-bedroom apartment in Boston to sprawling house in Lexington had been made with Paul by her side. But that journey seemed to be coming to an end. She knew if they wanted to save their marriage they would have to fight for it. But the distance between had stretched to breaking point.

Perhaps today was the breaking point?

She stopped and leaned against the lighthouse tower, looking up at the round glass dome at its top, visible through the underside of the latticed, iron gantry surrounding it. The old lady stood still and silent, staring out to sea, as if seeking sight of some passing sailing ship to call out to. Needing a purpose to still exist.

'I don't have a purpose, either,' whispered Claudia.

She ran a hand over the white-painted, wooden boards, connecting with it. But the tower didn't answer. Stoic in its loneliness. Maintaining its dignity.

Beyond the lighthouse, the headland curved away to Claudia's left, forming a natural sandy bay. A scrubby, winding pathway, above the beach, led down through the dunes to a high outcrop of rock she knew was called the "Point", due to the fact it resembled the bow of sailing ship jutting out into the sea. She followed the pathway down towards it.

The lightkeeper's house, a hundred yards down the pathway, below the lighthouse tower, had been abandoned. At least, it looked that way, to Claudia, as she passed it. The building seemed solid enough, if unloved, its paintwork, like the fence posts around the tower, was cracked and peeling, needful of attention. The glass in the windows was intact, but the eyes of the old house were caked in a layer of dried salt. They seemed to blink, the rolling ocean waves, beyond it, reflecting in the hazy glass. Claudia moved past it, feeling its gaze upon her back, pleading, perhaps, to be loved again.

Someone was standing at the base of the Point, now, only a few hundred metres ahead of her. Close enough for Claudia to see it was a woman. She was wearing some bright yellow windcheater and three-quarter-length white trousers. What was most noticeable about her, though, was her mane of long red hair, streaming out behind her in the breeze. She reminded Claudia of the actress, Maureen O'Hara, in the John Wayne movie, *The Quiet Man*, one of her favourite movies. *It's like an old-fashioned movie scene*, she thought, *the beautiful woman waiting for her lover to return from far-off lands.*

'You're such an old romantic,' she said, to herself, and the sadness that she'd partly shaken off returned.

Claudia realised it was spending her anniversary alone that was making her so melancholy. Instead of walking on up to the Point, as she'd intended to do, she left the path and headed across the dunes, down towards the beach, taking care not to stand on the clumps of willowy daisies that rocked back and forth among the sea grass, just above the sand line. She would not tread on a flower or a bug. It was something Paul had always teased her about.

But life was life.

As she neared the water's edge, Claudia stopped and removed her deck shoes and white, ankle socks, stuffing the socks into the shoes and tying the laces together to allow her to sling them round her neck. She rolled her white linen trousers up to just below her knees and walked towards the water. The sand was warm. She relished the feel of it, underfoot.

'One of life's little gifts,' she whispered, the sun and the sand warming her heart as well as her body.

Claudia wandered back in the direction of the lighthouse, letting the waves wash over her feet. The shallow bursts of rolling foam sent chills of satisfaction through her, awakening her to the beauty of a place that had once meant so much to her.

Her father and mother had brought her and her sister here so many times, over the years. Family walks with Sparky and Brooke, their long-since departed golden Labradors, and Seabiscuit, a white highland-terrier who had been the most annoying but fun dog. She and Paul didn't have a dog. Paul always resisted her attempts when she raised the subject. Perhaps he'd thought she wanted it as a substitute for a child. *Perhaps he was right.*

The childhood memories made her feel bad for not having stopped to see her sister when she'd passed through Duxbury. But she couldn't take seeing the disappointment on Margot's face when she learned she was spending her anniversary alone. Margot's life was a constant whirlwind of cooking and cleaning. But her family was her life. She always had a glow of contentment when she talked about her children. Claudia had seen it, and, at times, resented her for it, much to her shame.

Why her sister had been blessed with five beautiful children and she not been able to produce even one, Claudia could not understand. But the pain it caused her, on those days she thought about it, was almost unbearable. She had not cared to remind herself of that failing today. It was enough she was feeling the loss of her husband and her marriage without feeling the loss of a child she had never had.

In the distance, out to sea, two sailboats cut through the waves like giant swans skimming along the surface.

'Swans mate for life,' she said aloud, and her sadness deepened.

Too many thoughts were running through her head for her to deal with. She found herself evaluating her entire life. The sum she arrived at amassed to little that gave her any solace. She'd never felt so alone.

'Hello.'

Surprised, Claudia spun round, almost losing her balance.

'Oh . . . it's you.'

The woman smiled and the crow-lines at the edges of her eyes crinkled like concertina bellows. She was in her mid-to-late sixties, her skin tanned from days spent walking on the beach. Her eyes were bright aquamarine, like the shallowest part of the ocean on a sky blue, summer's day. Claudia had never seen such piercing eyes. Above all, they were kind eyes.

'It is me, you're right.' The woman laughed. It put Claudia immediately at ease. 'Do you know me? I must confess I'm at an age where anyone could be familiar.'

'Yes,' said Claudia, 'I mean . . . No, I don't know you.'

She thought she must sound like a complete idiot. She'd been lost in her thoughts and the woman had taken her by surprise.

'Well, do you, or don't you? I'm confused, myself.'

'I saw you earlier, is what I mean,' replied Claudia. 'You were at the Point. I was heading up there, but you looked deep in thought, so, I didn't. I wanted to give you time.'

'Give me time? I like that expression. Did you just make it up?'

'Yes,' said Claudia.

'You should be a writer.'

'My husband is.'

Claudia felt a tear threaten but held it back.

'Is he famous?'

'Sort of. I'm Claudia Montgomery, my husband is . . .'

'*Claudia!* Your name is Claudia?

The look on the woman's face was one of pleasant surprise. As if the name meant something to her.

'Yes.' Claudia replied. 'Why?'

'It was my husband's favourite name.'

'Oh! I see.'

Claudia smiled, not quite sure how to respond. The woman smiled back, but the look on her face made Claudia feel sad. She wasn't sure why.

'So, your husband is Paul Montgomery.'

Claudia hoped she wasn't a fan. She couldn't take having to talk about him. Not today.

'That's right.'

'I know his books. The ones about the history teacher and his dog. They solve unsolvable crimes from the past.'

'Professor Joey Amato and Moldova the beagle,' said Claudia, 'a bit of a madcap premise, but his fans love them.'

'I haven't read any of them, but I know who he is. Quite the celebrity around Boston.'

'I suppose,' Claudia replied, shrugging her shoulders.

The woman looked behind her, as if expecting to see someone else, wandering around.

'He's not here with you?'

'No! He wasn't able to . . .' Claudia was about to lie when the tears came. 'It's our anniversary,' she blurted out, 'and . . . and I don't even have a bloody hanky.'

The woman reached out and took Claudia's hands in hers, holding them pressed together and kissing her fingertips as if it were the most natural thing in the world to do. Like a mother might comfort a child. Oddly, to Claudia, it felt that way.

'Well, in that case, Claudia Montgomery, I guess the only thing to do is to have a cup of tea and find you one.'

Claudia dabbed her tears away on the sleeve of her jacket.

'I'm so sorry. I feel so stupid.'

The woman laughed.

'That's okay, my dear. I feel stupid at least once a day. Now, let's go and have that cup of tea. Do you see the cottage set back from the beach?'

She pointed up the beach, towards a small, wooden building at the foot of the sand dunes, almost directly below the wooden lighthouse tower. Claudia followed her gaze and nodded.

'Yes. I grew up in Duxbury. I've been walking past it all my life.'

'Excellent, well that's where I live. I've not spoken to anyone for weeks, and may be going a touch stir crazy, so even if *you* don't want to chat, I do. Would that be fine with you?'

'I'd love to,' said Claudia, with only a slight wobble in her voice. 'Thank you so much . . .'

'Hannah, my dear. My name is Hannah Thomas. I'm the lighthouse keeper. Or the keeper of the lighthouse, to be more accurate. And this little feral, at your feet, is Sylkie. I found her wandering along the beach, not more than a year ago. Or perhaps she found me? Who knows? Sometime those we need come into our lives at exactly the right time. I know Sylkie did.'

Claudia looked down at the scruffy but utterly adorable looking brown terrier at Hannah's feet and smiled for the first time that day.

27

The porch steps walked right down onto the sand from a covered hardwood porch, where two Adirondack chairs, a low, wooden table set between them, faced out across the beach to the bay beyond. Claudia settled into the one with a blue-checked blanket spread over its back. For colder days, she guessed, but not today. Nestled down among the dunes, the cottage was sheltered from the breeze, and the sun had turned the air warm enough to allow her to remove her jacket and sit comfortably in her faded, denim shirt.

'I'm a real morning person,' said Hannah, 'up with Sylkie at early o'clock, shine or rain. I like to beachcomb, she likes to dig for crabs. I find lots of flotsam, she's yet to find a crab. Then again, perhaps she's not really looking for crabs at all.'

'Perhaps not,' said Claudia, relishing the simple life Hannah seemed to have living right on the beach. 'Perhaps she just likes digging holes.'

Hannah chuckled and reached down to tickle Sylkie's head. Sylkie snuffled her fingers, hoping there was a morsel on offer. Disappointed to find there was not, she dropped her head down onto her paws, looking up at Claudia with pleading, brown eyes, as if to say, *she doesn't feed me, you know!*

The planked walls of the cottage were painted a pale, duck-egg blue, hung with pieces of fishing net, lobster-creel floats, and adorned with seashells. The paint was faded, but only served to make it more quaint and homely. Wooden window-shutters, painted a slightly darker blue, were held in place against the outside wall with bits of orange cord, and a stack of old crab-pots were piled up, on the sand, against the right-side gable end. Strings of seashell windchimes hung, overhead, along the porch front, playing nature's own music as they brushed gently against each other.

Claudia gazed over the sand to the shimmering ocean and thought it was possibly one of the most beautiful places she'd ever been. *Six bedrooms in Lexington and I'd swap them all to live here.* Hannah seemed to sense her thoughts.

'It's a great place to live, my dear, but it gets wild. Especially during storm season. Sometimes, I just sit here, listening to the thunder and watching the lightening flash across the sky. You can feel the pounding boom of the surf run though you when the waves smash against the shore. But the Beach Shack always keeps me safe and sound.'

'The *Beach Shack!*' Claudia exclaimed, loving the name.

'She is what she is,' said Hannah, reaching up and patting the porch-rail beside her seat.

'Do you live here by yourself?' Claudia asked, sipping her Earl Grey tea and wondering why she didn't drink it more often.

'My husband, Jonathon, passed away two years ago. So now it's just me and Sylkie.'

'I'm sorry, Hannah, I shouldn't have pried.'

Hannah, if she was upset by the question, didn't show it. Instead, she took the question as an invitation to chat.

'I remember hating this place when we first came. I was a city girl, you see, from San Antonio, home of the Alamo. We arrived here the same day the Apollo rocket fired into the sky, heading for the moon, sixteenth July sixty-nine.' She looked out at the beach as if the memory of the day was being played out in front of her. 'It was John F Kennedy who started that race. There's a museum dedicated to him, on Cape Cod, about thirty miles across the bay as the crow flies. Or should that be as the seagull flies?'

'Seagull seems more appropriate,' said Claudia, returning Hannah's smile.

'Jonathon and I used to sit here and watch the sky, wondering if we'd see the spaceship coming home.' Hannah seemed to realise that she was doing all the talking. "Sorry, my dear, I'm wittering on and not letting you get a word in edgeways.'

Claudia settled back into her chair.

'Don't stop. Witter away.'

Hannah was exactly the company she craved at that moment in time. She was pleased when Hannah took up the offer.

'We met in San Antonio, after Jonathon was posted there with the United States Air Force. I was eighteen, fresh faced and innocent. He was twenty-one, handsome and dashing in his uniform. I refused to go out with him, three times, before I finally went to the drive-in with him to see *The Sound of Music.*

'I love that old movie,' said Claudia, picturing the actress, Julie Andrews, surrounded by snowy mountains and singing her heart out.

'I wasn't bad looking, myself, back then.'

'You're still beautiful,' said Claudia, and meant it. 'Your eyes! And your hair is amazing. You remind me of . . .'

'Maureen O'Hara,' said Hannah, pre-empting her.

Claudia smiled, surprised.

'How did you know?'

'Jonathon always said the same thing. But the hair is silver-grey under this dye. He always loved my hair. Said it was the first thing he noticed about me. We started walking out together after the movie night. My parents fell in love with him. I did too. He was kind, attentive and considerate, with the kind of manners that would considered old-fashioned, nowadays.'

'Old-fashioned, maybe,' said Claudia, 'but who doesn't love a man with good manners. There's nothing sexist about having a door held open for you and being treated like a lady. Carry on, please. I'm really enjoying this.'

Hannah didn't need to be asked twice.

'We were due to get married in the summer, but Vietnam happened, so we decided to marry before he left. We had one night together and then he was gone. He promised he'd come back to me, but made me swear that, if something happened to him, I'd live the rest of my life the way I was supposed to. He said I was to marry someone else and have the family he knew I'd always wanted to have. He told me to love my life and to live the hell out of it.'

'But he came back, didn't he?'

'Four years later,' said Hannah, a memory smile on her lips, 'almost to the day.'

'Four years apart! That must have been awful for you.'

'It was. But he kept his promise and came home to me. Only, he wasn't the same man. He'd been captured, you see. Shot down on a bombing raid over Hanoi. He got burned down one side of his face. I didn't care. He was still the man I'd fallen in love with. The only man I've ever loved. The man I still love.'

'Oh Hannah. I'm so sorry, said Claudia, feeling her eyes filling with tears as the memory caught in Hannah's voice.

Hannah took a moment before speaking again.

'He was due to work in my father's law firm, but he just couldn't be around people anymore. So, we found this place, bought it, and moved out here, all in the space of a four weeks. It's where we've been ever since.'

I can't say I blame you.' Claudia looked around her. 'I love your Beach Shack. It's like living in paradise. Imagine being able to own buy your own little slice of it.'

Hannah gazed over the beach to the bay beyond and nodded in agreement.

'You're right, it is marvellous. It's been the best place to live. It belonged to someone my father had worked for. That's why we came to see it in the first place. Although we didn't expect to end up with an old lighthouse tower and the lightkeeper's house, to boot.'

Claudia couldn't hide her surprise.

'You own the lighthouse *and* the house, as well as this?'

'And all the land around it,' added Hannah. 'Mind, it was cheap when we got it. The lighthouse wasn't used any longer and the "big house" was broken down, filled with sand and ghosts. There was a lot of work needed to make them both habitable. But Jonathon loved the solitude of the dunes, the one road in and out, and the sound of the waves at night. It put him at peace. We mended the tower, and the big house, then turned this place, which was no more than a broken-down fishing shack, into this little oasis of calm among the dunes.'

'But what did you do to survive, financially, I mean?' Claudia asked, then immediately covered her mouth with her hand. 'I'm so sorry, Hannah, that was rude of me.'

'It's just being naturally inquisitive, my dear,' said Hannah, laughing at Claudia's embarrassment. 'Anyway, I like talking to you. I've not talked about this before. Don't ask me why, but, today, you're just what I needed.'

'Me too, Hannah. You're just what *I* needed.'

'Well, to answer your rude but perfectly acceptable question, we had Jonathon's air force pension and three years of back pay from his time in Vietnam, to start with. Daddy passed away, back in the early eighties, and

Momma, a year later, so I inherited their house and the law firm. There was an offer on the table from a competitor, in San Antonio, that was too high to refuse, so, I sold it. We had more than enough money to live on, here, for the rest of our lives. Jonathon had always loved carpentry, so he began making furniture in his workshop up in the lighthouse. We sold what he made, but, to be honest, it was more about his love of making it than making money.

'I'd love to see some of his work.'

'You're sitting in one of his chairs, my dear.'

Claudia ran her palms along the arms of the chair and felt closer to a man she'd never met, but was getting to know through Hannah's story. It was an odd but warm feeling to know he had put his love into something that, in a small way, connected them now.

'They sold well, too,' Hannah continued, 'in stores from Cape Cod and all the way up to Gloucester. As for me, I continued painting, something I'd taken up when Jonathon had been in Vietnam. I sold them in the art galleries in the same towns as he sold his furniture. Mostly, I took care of my man. And although it might not be okay to say so, in this crazy world we live in, I was happy doing that. He loved me and needed me. I loved him and needed him right back.'

Claudia was silent for a moment, reflecting on the tale she'd been blessed to hear. She was envious of the love Hannah and Jonathon had so obviously had for one other, and the simple life they seemed to have lived, together, by the ocean.

'So, you're an artist?'

'Was,' said Hannah. 'I don't paint as much as I used to. Not since Jonathon died. And the arthritis makes it harder to hold the brushes, these days. But I still love it. It grounds me and makes me soar, if that makes sense.

'I'm an artist, too,' said Claudia, 'so it makes perfect sense.'

'What a coincidence. *Another* thing that connects us.'

Claudia wasn't sure what Hannah meant. It didn't matter. She felt an even stronger connection with her, a woman she'd met only a few hours before but felt she'd known all her life.

'I have a gallery, in Lexington, called ***Sans Cera***. Paintings, mainly, and some large-scale sculptures. I did a lot of corporate commissions in the past, and earned good money, but over the past five years I've been pleasing myself about what work I take on. The paintings have gotten bigger and the sculptures grown smaller.'

'Where do you work?' Hannah asked.

'I have a studio, at my home, on the outskirts of Lexington. It's at the back of my garden, overlooking a mountain, well, a hill, really. There's lots of light and white space, and nobody bothers me, which is just what I need when I'm creating.'

'It sounds perfect,' said Hannah. 'Mine's perhaps not as spacious as yours, but it's got the best views in the world. And the light surrounds me. Would you like to see it?'

'Yes please,' said Claudia, 'is it here?'

'It's behind us, actually,' replied Hannah, 'up in the tower.'

'In the lighthouse? Hannah, I'd love to see it.'

They made their way through the dunes at the back of the Beach Shack, taking a set of steep steps cut into the hill that lead directly to the lighthouse tower. Claudia told Hannah about Paul, her failure to get pregnant, and the argument that had ultimately brought her to the lighthouse in the first place.

'I'm so sorry to hear that, my dear.'

'There's such a distance opened up between us, Hannah. I'm not sure we're going to be able to close it.'

'Do you still love him?' Hannah asked, taking Claudia's arm as they climbed the steps.

'I do, but it's getting harder to love in one direction. I don't think he's interested in me any longer. It's our anniversary, and we've not even spoken. Perhaps if we'd had the family we always wanted it might have helped us now.'

'Perhaps,' said Hannah, 'but I loved Jonathon and he loved me, despite we didn't raise any kids. When you love someone unconditionally, you mend the gaps before they become chasms that can't be bridged. Perhaps you both just need to work a little harder and talk a lot more. Having a family is one part of loving someone across the years, but it's not the be all and end all. At least that's what we found. I wanted a child to raise. I still think about how that would have been. That unconditional love.'

'I know you're right,' said Claudia, 'but I so desperately want to know that kind of love.'

They reached the top of the steps and stood in the shadow of the lighthouse. Hannah turned and looked north, over the isthmus, towards Duxbury, some three or four miles away.

'You said you have five nieces living in town?'

'Yes.'

'Then you should be taking joy in their lives, my dear. Seeing them when you can and loving *them* unconditionally. They're part of your family. All children are precious. They all need love. Just like flowers need the rain. It doesn't matter which way the wind blows the rain in, as long as it falls on them.'

Hannah's words resonated with Claudia, making her feel ashamed. She knew hadn't seen her nieces as much as she should have.

'Your right, Hannah, I do need to try harder. As should Paul. And you're right about my beautiful nieces. I've gotten so hung-up on having my own child I've neglected seeing them. That's going to change from her on in. Now, enough of the drama and melancholy. Show me your studio.'

28

Claudia stood on the metal gantry surrounding the top of the lighthouse, imagining sailing ships of old finding their way home by the light from the old wooden tower. The metalwork was solid, but the latticed, iron railings were beginning to rust and the black paint that remained clung on in flaky patches. The circle of glass that made up the lamp-room was streaked with rain from a hundred storms, and clumps of green sprouted from the red, tin roof where sea-grass seeds had taken root, but the view was magnificent!

She looked west, across Plymouth Bay, and could see the old fishing town only a few miles away. She turned her gaze past the yachts lying at anchor, to Duxbury, on the adjoining bay, where memories of balmy, summer nights and stolen, teenage kisses made her smile, then walked around the gantry until she was looking east, over Cape Cod Bay, to Provincetown, a grey smear in the far-off distance, robbed of definition but still visible.

'It's beautiful up here, Hannah.'

Hannah stood beside her, looking out at the same blue-green vista. The wind had freshened. It tossed her auburn-red hair so that it streamed behind her like the hair of the women who used to wing-walk on the upper foils of biplanes back in the days of black and white television. There was something almost angelic about her, thought Claudia, as if she wore her soul around her rather than carrying it on the inside.

Claudia had covered her own head, with her scarf, to stop it blowing around her face. She removed it and let her hair fly free. It rippled around her like the mane of a galloping, Palomino mare. The feel of the cool wind and the fresh iodine tang of the sea engaged her senses and she felt alive and vital.

Something shifted and changed, inside her, and the mist that had shrouded her heart, all morning, had disappeared.

Although she had no religion to speak of, Claudia had a firm belief in the power of the Universe. That was good enough and god enough for her. The Universe had guided her to the lighthouse, and to Hannah, and it was speaking to her now.

'I'm listening,' she said, and closed her eyes.

She thought she heard a voice call to her from somewhere far out in the ocean, as if the wind had carried a message of time to come, of journeys to make and adventures to be had. She smiled and wondered why she was being so silly, caring little that she was. Her sprits had lifted, reason enough for such fanciful thoughts.

'Come inside,' called Hannah, over the breeze. 'Let me show you where I work.'

The studio was hexagonal and formed from glass, giving it a magnificent three hundred and sixty degree view out over the ocean and the surrounding land. Claudia hadn't stopped to appreciate it properly when they'd climbed the spiral, cast-iron staircase that wrapped around the inside of the tower like an inside-out helter-skelter, Hannah having taken her straight out of the glass door at the top of the stairs and onto the metal gantry.

'Wow!'

It was all she could think to say, although it was as good a description as could have been made.

'Welcome,' said Hannah, 'to my world of blue and white. Occasionally grey, but never dull.'

'Now I see why you said it was surrounded by light,' said Claudia, 'it's utterly amazing.'

The afternoon light flooded the room, refracting through and then bouncing off the inside of the circle of glass windowpanes. The dispersed rays lit up miniscule dust particles floating in the air, making them seem like microscopic flakes of floating gold, giving the room an almost ethereal luminescence.

'I told you about the light,' said Hannah, unable to hide her pride.

'And it's much more spacious than I thought it would be.'

'Two reasons for that,' replied Hannah, casually flicking though a stack of canvases lying against one of the windowpanes. 'The space in the bottom floor of the tower is pretty decent, and the walls of the tower are actually quite steep, so the size of my Glass Menagerie doesn't change as much as you think it might when you stand at the bottom and look up. It's still only half the size of the ground floor, but there's plenty of room, don't you think?'

Claudia agreed entirely. She'd already fallen in love with the place. And the name Hannah had given it, the *Glass Menagerie*, was perfect.

'You said there were two reasons why it seems larger than I'd expected it to be.

'Look around, my dear, what's missing?'

Claudia searched the room but couldn't figure it out. She looked down at the wooden floor and noticed a circular patch, not quite the same shade of the floorboards in the rest of the room. They seemed newer, or had been covered by something, in the past.

'Of course! The lamp!'

'Well done,' said Hannah. 'Jonathon dismantled the old lantern to give me extra room to work. He worked downstairs. I worked up here. We got our own space and the quiet we craved, but got to meet for lunch, up here, every day.'

The studio smelt of oil paint and thinners, a smell Claudia knew well. An array of brushes exploded out of the tops of glass jam-jars and tin pots sitting on part of the wooden seat surrounding the inside of the room, and half-squeezed tubes of oil paint lay like sleeping toy soldiers waiting to be called into battle. A large artist's palette, covered in crusted blobs of oil paint, lay on a three-legged, wooden stool, beside an easel holding a large canvas, placed so that Hannah could look out over the ocean as she worked. The canvas was covered with an off-white muslin sheet, so Claudia couldn't see what the subject of the painting was. She was intrigued to find out.

Laid against each of the windows were stacks of finished canvasses, all of them were seascapes, at least the ones Claudia could see at the front of each stack were. They showed storm ravaged skies, sailing ships and rolling, white breakers on angry seas. In the middle of the room, inside the circle of patchwork floor where the old lamp had once been, was an antiquated, two-seater couch. The round armrests were stained with fingerprint smudges of different coloured paint. Claudia flopped down into it. It was super comfy.

'Do you like my couch of many colours?'

Claudia rubbed at the paint stains and inspected her fingers, but the smudges were long since dry.

'It's absolutely perfect, Hannah. I could sleep here.'

'You should have seen Jonathon and Daddy trying to get it up here. They cussed me all the way up. Well, Daddy did, anyways.'

She smiled at the memory, picturing the two men who had filled the significant moments in her life, one, as she grew up, the other, as she grew old, sweating and panting for breath after manhandling the heavy couch up the helter-skelter stairs.

'I'll bet,' said Claudia, imagining how difficult it must have been. 'But definitely worth it.'

'God, Claudia, but Jonathon loved me. I miss him terribly.'

Claudia found herself envying the woman she'd just met. She couldn't imagine Paul ever doing something like that for her. Maybe once, but not anymore.

'Can I see the painting?'

Hannah followed Claudia's gaze towards the covered canvas on the easel. She didn't answer and seemed somewhat reluctant.

'It's not finished.'

'What is it? Another seascape?'

'Not this time. Something completely different. Inspired by a recent adventure. I started it a few months ago. The painting, that is, not the adventure.'

'Give me a clue,' said Claudia, wondering at Hannah's melancholy tone and faraway look.

Hannah thought about it for a few seconds before answering.

'Let's just say it's a question of perspective at the end of a journey. You'd really have to be there to fully understand it.'

'That's not really helped me much,' said Claudia, now more intrigued than ever.

'I've struggled to complete it, to be honest,' said Hannah, not being drawn into explaining more. 'I've had to spend quite a lot of time dealing with my...'

Hannah's discomfort was obvious. Claudia didn't push her to finish what she'd been going to say. Instead, she moved the conversation.

'I know how you feel. I've got an exhibition to get ready for at the end of May, at my gallery. My business manager is going nuts at me to finish the new work for it, but I've been so wrapped up in my own problems that I've just given up on everything. That is, until today. I think you've inspired me to stop wallowing.'

'Then I'm glad you came, my dear. I've never shown anyone else my studio. Only Jonathon and Daddy. Now you.'

Claudia was shocked. It was such a personal thing for Hannah to have done. Especially for a total stranger.

'I don't know what to say, Hannah. I'm so grateful. I feel ashamed, after being so pathetic on the beach, having a poor me day. You've been through so much more in your life than I've ever had to deal with.'

Hannah shook her head.

'I was having one of my own, my dear. Meeting you snapped me out of it.'

Claudia hauled herself out of the couch of many colours and began flicking through the stacks of paintings, noting that, although the subject matter was similar, seascapes or views of the lighthouse, there were a great many of the Point, as well as views of the lighthouse tower and the ocean which had clearly been painted from there. She looked out to where she'd first seen Hannah standing, at its base, where, now, the waves were rolling in and breaking upon the dark wedge of rock.

'I saw you looking out to sea. You seemed far away.'

Hannah moved over to stand beside Claudia, who was looking at another canvas, a painting of the lightkeeper's house, and the sandy pathway out through the dunes, heading down to the Point. The high viewpoint showed it had been painted from the Glass Menagerie.

'I was at the end of the earth, my dear. Quite literally.'

'And where exactly is that?' Claudia asked.

Hannah turned her gaze towards the Point.

'Finisterre.'

Claudia lifted an eyebrow.

'Finis-where?'

'Finisterre,' Hannah repeated, 'is in northern Spain. Like us, here, it overlooks the Atlantic Ocean, only from the other side. It was once thought to be the most westerly point on earth, back when the Romans ruled the known world. It's from the Latin, *finis terrae,* meaning the end of the earth.'

'Sounds a touch ominous,' said Claudia.

'Well it is on a coastline called the Costa del Morte, which is Spanish for Coast of the Dead. From the Point, about three thousand miles away. That's where I was looking out to when you saw me.'

'Any specific reason why?'

'I was thinking of Jonathon. Part of him is there.'

Claudia looked at her, confused.

'Part of Jonathon is at Finisterre? I don't understand. I thought you said his ashes were scattered up at the Point.'

'They are, my dear, at least, half of them are. But the other half lie in Spain, at Finisterre. I put them there myself, last year, when I walked the Camino de Santiago. Have you heard of it?'

'Can't say I have. What is it?'

'That would take a day of tea and cakes to explain,' said Hannah, 'but, in short, it's a medieval pilgrimage that begins in a picturesque little town called Saint Jean Pied de Port, in the southwest corner of France. It climbs up and over the Pyrenees, into Spain, then crosses the whole of the country to the Cathedral of Santiago de Compostela in the city of Santiago. It's an epic journey of almost eight hundred kilometres.'

'You walked eight hundred kilometres?'

Claudia was more than impressed.

'Last year,' replied Hannah, looking proud of herself. 'It took me forty days. I took Jonathon with me, in my backpack. It was a dream of his to do it, after we watched the Martin Sheen movie, *The Way*, which is also what the Camino is sometimes called. We planned to do it together, one day, but then he got sick and one day never came. Until last summer. I decided it was now or never.'

'It sounds amazing, Hannah. But eight-hundred kilometres. I could never do that.'

'Of course, you could. I did. And you've got over twenty years on me.'

Claudia wondered if she could make it. She loved trekking, but that far was a daunting thought.

'It does sound like quite an adventure.'

'It truly was,' said Hannah, 'in so many ways I can't even begin to explain. It was the journey of my life. My biggest adventure.' She looked at Claudia. 'When was your last adventure?'

'Not sure I've ever had one.' Claudia laughed, but inside she knew it was true. 'When's your next?'

'Sadly, the Camino was my last.'

Hannah's voice quieted and she seemed a little upset.

'Your last.' Claudia asked, sensing her sadness. 'Why your last?'

Hannah answered. Her words spoken softly. As gentle as spring rain but as brutal as rape.

'I have cancer. Stage four. I've only got a few months left.'

A wave of grief hit Claudia harder than she could have imaged it doing only a few hours before. Hannah had been sad and lonely when she'd first seen her. Thinking about Jonathon. His ashes lying on a coastline far across the ocean. Yet she'd interrupted her own grief to care for a total stranger, expecting and asking nothing in return.

'Hannah, I'm so sorry.'

Claudia stood and hugged Hannah to her. She did not try to stem the falling tears.

'It's okay, my dear,' whispered Hannah, stroking Claudia's hair and holding her as she wept, 'there's no need to cry. I'm just moving on, that's all.'

'But I've just found you, Hannah. I'm sad that we have so little time left to share. Can I come and see you again?'

'Of course. I'd like that very much. As often as you want. I can tell you all about the Camino, if you want. I might even show you that infernal thing.'

Hannah tilted her head towards the covered canvas on the easel. Claudia laughed and took her head off Hannah's shoulder, delving into her pocket and wiping her eyes with the hanky Hannah had given her earlier.

'I'll hold you to that.'

'You can, my dear, and that's a promise.'

Claudia took Hannah's hands in hers and gave them a squeeze of affection.

'I'm so glad we met today, Hannah. I really am.'

Hannah smiled and nodded.

'You know, my dear, people sometimes meet each other in the strangest of circumstances, But it's always for a reason. Most times, that reason is never revealed, and the Universe moves on, wondering, what if? Perhaps it brought us together, today, for such a reason. We just need to figure out what it is.'

'We will,' said Claudia. 'Somehow, I know we will.'

29

It was past four in the afternoon by the time Claudia climbed into her car and headed back to Lexington. Hannah had become tired and needed to take her medication. Claudia had insisted on walking her back to the Beach Shack, ignoring her protests that she was fine. They'd hugged goodbye, Claudia promising to visit again the following week.

She felt strangely drawn to the older woman who had suddenly stepped into her life. She imagined that it might have had something to do with the loss of her own mother. A mother she had loved, dearly, but had struggled to connect with. The feelings continued as she headed up the Pilgrims Highway, towards Boston.

Just as she turned onto interstate ninety-three, Claudia's phone rang. She clicked the hands-free button on the steering wheel and smiled as she heard the voice of her best friend and her art gallery manager, Isabella Stamford.

'Hey there, honey, how's your day been?'

'Hi, Isabella, still hard at work?'

'I've got a tough boss, honey. I can't just slope off for a glass of vino whenever I feel like it. Always better to drink *at* work.'

Claudia laughed and felt her mood shift.

'I'd quit if I were you.'

'I just might,' said Isabella. But, seriously, where are you? I thought you might have come into the gallery this afternoon, then I remembered it's your wedding anniversary. Has Paul been lavishing you with sparkly gifts and multiple orgasms?'

'Chance would be a fine thing,' said Claudia, 'but a little difficult to have either when he's not even on the east coast.'

'He's not here?'

Isabella sounded shocked and slightly angry.

'No, he's in Los Angeles. We had another fight.'

'His fault, honey, I'm sure. Honestly, he can be such a dick.'

Claudia stifled a laugh.

'Come on, Isabella, give him a break. He's working. This television deal's important to him. It's his dream to see his books come alive on the screen. Anyway, the fight was as much my fault as his.'

'That's all well and good, honey, but it's your bloody anniversary. He could take at least one day off to be with you. But, I'll leave it alone. So, what are you up to then? Anything exciting or bad?'

'I've been down at Plymouth, visiting an old friend.'

'An old flame! What's his name?'

'No-one you know. And *he,* is a *she*. I'll tell you about her when I see you.'

'Where are you now?'

Claudia glanced up to take a bearing.

'About fifteen miles south of Lexington. Want me to stop in at the gallery?'

'Well, it's been pretty busy here, but it's gone dead,' said Isabella. 'Why don't you come into town and park up near Harry's Bar? I'll close up and head over to join you. We can have a drink to celebrate your anniversary. That is, if you don't mind celebrating with me instead of your erstwhile husband.'

Claudia considered for a moment. She didn't really want to rush back to an empty house.

'Okay, sounds good. I'll see you in half an hour.'

'And don't be too downhearted, honey. I'm sure Paul will probably turn up with some roses and a beautiful bottle of white wine. He might be a man, but he's not stupid enough to expect his wife to dress up as a cheerleader if he doesn't.'

'And just how do you know about his cheerleader fetish, Isabella Stamford?'

'I think you've mentioned that more than a few times in passing, honey.'

'I guess I have,' said Claudia, laughing again and thanking her lucky stars for having such a wonderfully irrepressible best friend as Isabella, 'but the cheerleader outfit has more chance of being ravished by moths than by Paul. Anyway, I'm not sure I could squeeze into it any longer. I've put on a few pounds, recently, comfort eating and sitting on my fat ass after the last bout of IVF. I've always been a size ten, but now I'm a size ten and a bit.'

'No action in the bedroom then?'

Claudia tried to remember the last time she and Paul had made love, but couldn't remember. She couldn't hide the sadness in her voice as she answered Isabella's question.

'Not for months. Paul's tried to come onto me a few times, but I keep finding an excuse not to let it go anywhere. I think he's given up bothering. I'm beginning to think he's having an affair. He's been guarding his phone, lately, as if it contains the launch codes for a nuclear missile.'

'Don't jump to conclusions, honey. Maybe you're right. Maybe he is tired, what with all the travelling he's been doing, back and forth to the City of Angels. Still, he needs to get . . .'

'Hello! Isabella, are you still there?'

For a moment, Claudia thought they'd been cut off, but then heard a man's voice in the background. Isabella was speaking to him. She came back on the line.

'Honey, I've got to run. We've got a customer here who needs me. A handsome one. Excuse me while I go and flirt outrageously with him and try to sell him something expensive.'

'Okay, have fun.'

'I'll see you at Harry's Bar, unless he wants me to go home with him. He's not wearing a wedding ring, not that I'm fussy about that any longer.'

The call disconnected and Claudia laughed to herself, imagining Isabella fawning over some poor client who would have no idea he was dealing with a recent divorcee with a newfound freedom and a tendency towards nymphomania.

They'd met at a University fraternity party, in Boston, almost twenty years ago, and stayed in touch. Claudia had poached her from an exclusive gallery in Boston, two years ago, and their friendship had been rekindled, becoming closer than ever before. Isabella knew everyone in the art game; not just in Boston, but across America and internationally. The prices Claudia was getting for her work had increased significantly under her shrewd stewardship.

Yet, despite the success Isabella had brought her, Paul still had a problem with her. Claudia could not understand why. Recently, the friction between them seemed to have intensified. Perhaps Isabella was too strong for him, too gregarious and outgoing, as well as being highly intelligent. Paul liked his women to be less outspoken and forthright. She wondered what that said about her.

With only a few miles to go before she hit the outskirts of Lexington, Claudia thought about heading home to change before meeting Isabella. In between making her decision, the phone rang again.

'Have you scared him off already?'

'Pardon?'

Claudia put her hand over her mouth to stifle a laugh.

'I'm so sorry. I thought you were someone else. I was just on the phone to my friend.'

'No problem, mam. I've made the same mistake myself.'

'Okay, so now that I've embarrassed myself completely, who are you and what can I do for you?'

She thought it might be one of her corporate clients, although she didn't recognise the voice.'

'My name is Robert Smith, from AT&T, your phone company. I'm in your apartment, in Boston, if you're Mrs Claudia Montgomery, that is?'

'I am indeed, Mr Smith. So, you're in the apartment?'

'Yes, Mrs Montgomery. One of the security guys let me in, on your husband's instructions. Your husband ordered a new leased line. I'm connecting it to your phone system in the apartment.'

Claudia finally understood the call.

'Yes, he mentioned there was something was being done, but I've really no idea about it. He's the one you should be talking to. I don't use the apartment. It's more his downtown office and overnight flop when he has an early flight out.'

'That's fine, Mrs Montgomery, there's nothing I need from you. I'm only calling because I can't get hold of your husband. He put your number down as a secondary contact on the account.'

'He never said. How can I help?'

'I just wanted to let you know the new line is connected to the iPBX. I've had to reboot the system so it's wiped the pre-set options. I'm not allowed to reset them, that's something your husband has to do for himself.'

'I won't pretend to understand a word you've just said,' Claudia replied, 'can you say it again in English?'

'I'm sorry, Mrs Montgomery, what I mean is, I had to switch the telephone system off. It's back on again, now, but if you could tell your husband he needs to set up the add-on services he wants, like call-waiting, hiding the telephone number when he's making calls, call recording, and so on, that would be great. I'll leave a note along with the paperwork, but I just wanted to give you the heads up its been done.'

'That's kind of you, Mr Smith. I'll certainly pass it on to my husband.'

'Have a nice day, mam.'

'You too.'

Claudia disconnected the call and took the turnoff for Lexington.

The parking around Lexington town common, more often referred to as Battle Green, was busy. After circling a couple of times, Claudia found an empty space and parked up. It took her ten minutes to walk to Harry's Bar, which was a few blocks from her gallery on Massachusetts Avenue. She looked in through the wide glass frontage and saw it was quiet. It was Wednesday afternoon. The college students didn't normally fill the bars to bursting until Thursday night, when their weekends really got started.

The bar was cool and bright, with lots of exposed brickwork covered in bar paraphernalia and neon signs. There were high tables and chairs set throughout, as well as lower-seated booths. Claudia chose a booth near the front and slid along the red leather, bench seat. A fresh-faced waitress with her hair in bunches, dressed in a white t-shirt with a Harry's Bar logo and wearing a short, denim skirt and cowboy boots that emphasised her *Daisy Duke* legs took Claudia's order of a glass of Shiraz. The girl's perfectly-rounded bottom strained against the skirt as she walked back to the bar.

Claudia remembered a time when she could carry off such an outfit. *Yeah, right, about a hundred years ago.* Perhaps she was being too hard on herself? She wasn't a twenty-something, anymore, she was a forty-something, albeit an *early* forty-something, which was almost like being a thirty-something, wasn't it? She smiled at the thought and reminded herself that she did an hour of yoga every morning and walked up Robinson Hill most days. She was a size ten, almost, with breasts that needed no support and smooth skin that benefited from a healthy diet. Still, she envied the girl's most-likely effortlessly toned body and unmade-up, unblemished face. At that age, you didn't have to work so hard to look good.

Two oversized TV screens, wall-mounted at either end of the bar, were streaming music videos, playing the song, *Written in the Stars*, by the singer, Jack Savoretti, about two lovers torn apart by circumstances the song didn't make clear. Claudia had forgotten to be sad. The song lyrics and haunting voice reminded her.

'Thanks Jack,' she whispered, hoping he wasn't going to do an encore.

As the song ended, the bar door swung open and Isabella Stamford walked in.

'Honey!'

Isabella strutted towards Claudia, her black, high-heeled shoes clicking sharply on the wooden floor. Her long, auburn hair, was, today, piled up on her head. It made her neck look long and elegant. Her skin was pale but glowing. She removed her horn-rimmed sunglasses and her blue eyes sparkled as she met Claudia's gaze. Her voluptuous lips, painted in her trademark bright red lipstick, formed a smile that was wide and genuine. Claudia smiled back, forgetting Jack and his sad song.

As usual, Isabella looked immaculate. She was a fan of the fashion of the nineteen-fifties, her style icon being the Italian superstar from that period, Sophia Loren. Today's clothing ensemble was comprised of a tight, cream pencil-skirt and matching fitted jacket worn over a black, silk blouse, unbuttoned enough to expose a red bra that fought to contain her full breasts. A wide, patent-leather, black belt, nipped around her waist, and a white silk scarf, spotted with black polka dots, tied over her head and knotted under her chin, completed the outfit. She exuded style, grace and movie-star sex-appeal. Every man in the bar, as well as most of the women, noticed her entrance.

'You look fabulous,' said Claudia.

Isabella leaned down to give her a hug and a peck on the cheek that missed her by at least six inches, but the intent was there.

'I represent you, the gallery, and your incredible work,' said Isabella, sliding into the seat opposite Claudia. 'I have to reflect the style, flair and overall *joie de vivre* you get when you purchase an original Claudia Montgomery artwork.

You sell for a lot of money, honey. I need to reaffirm that price in everything to do with the gallery, including myself. I've gotten you many a commission and sale looking like this. Don't knock it.

'I wasn't,' said Claudia, laughing at her friend's outrageous candour. 'The business is growing, month on month, so, wear what you want to wear if it keeps the profits up.'

'Besides,' said Isabella, 'I dress for me. You know I love that whole fifties thing. It's so powerful and feminine. I like to dress up for work, not slouch around the gallery looking like some lefty lesbian wrapped in a shapeless smock and open-toed sandals. We sell aspiration, honey, not asparagus.'

'Bizarre comparison,' said Claudia, laughing at the description, 'but you're absolutely right. Anyway, how was the hunk you left me for when you hung up? He obviously didn't whisk you away.'

'Sadly, no, but I flirted with him outrageously, so who knows? He's from Boston. Some computer company owner looking for a new piece of artwork for his reception area. Half our age, but damned cute. I've booked him an appointment to meet with you in a few weeks from now, prior to the exhibition. Oh, and the date's set for that. Second weekend in May. How does that work, for you?'

'Your call, Isabella. You bring in the clients and you run the show. I'll be sexy, artsy and flamboyant, if I still can.'

'You know you can, honey, but just so long as you're there. The buyers like to meet the artist when they spend their hard-earned cash. On that subject, will the new paintings be ready anytime soon? You promised me four. So far, you've only delivered one.'

'I know,' said Claudia, shaking her head. 'I hope so.'

'You hope so?' Isabella looked concerned. 'I need you to be a bit more positive than that, honey. Seriously. I've got people coming from all over the county, as well as international gallery owners who are looking to expand their portfolios.'

'I'll get right back on it, Isabella. I promise.'

Isabella looked dubious, but knew there was little point in pushing.

'Okay. I'll leave with it you.'

'Thanks.'

Claudia sipped her drink and wondered how Isabella would react when she told her that, at best, she would have only two of the pieces she had promised ready in time.

'While we're at it,' added Isabella, not noticing the doubt on Claudia's face, 'for the love of all that's holy, come into *Sans Cera* and meet my new assistant. She's quite the catch for us. Young, smart and sexy. If I was ever going to experiment with the other side, she could probably turn me.'

Claudia shook her head and laughed.'

'Pervert.'

Isabella nodded.

'Guilty as charged.'

They chatted for a while, discussing the exhibition and the guest list, before Claudia's mind slipped away to Hannah and the things they'd talked about that afternoon.

'I need an adventure.'

'Me too, honey. I'd like mine about six feet tall, as rich as Bill Gates, and look like Bradley Cooper.'

'Isabella, honestly, what are you like? No, I mean a real adventure, to clear my head of everything that's floating around in it. Mainly Paul and me growing apart. Not having had the family we wanted. All the stuff that's making me feel so bloody low.'

Isabella reached across the table and patted Claudia's hands.

'I know you want children, honey. It's been hard on both of you. But maybe it's just not meant to be.'

Claudia tutted.

'You sound like Paul.'

She stared down into her drink. No matter what anyone said, her biological clock was still ticking.

'What sort of adventure are you thinking about?' Isabella asked, trying take Claudia's mind elsewhere.

'I don't know,' said Claudia, 'I've not really thought about it yet.' On impulse, she said, 'maybe the Camino de Santiago.'

She began to tell Isabella about meeting Hannah at the lighthouse.

'I want a Jonathon,' said Isabella, once Claudia had finished telling her

Hannah's story. 'It's so romantic and beautiful, but also sad. To think she's dying, all alone, in that little shack by the sea.'

'It's a beautiful place, Isabella, really, it is. More importantly, its where Hannah wants to be. She's got no self-pity, either. That's one of the things I admired most about her. She still loves her life, despite the cancer. She embraces it, bad and good. I need to do that more. I might not be able to do the Camino, but what say you and I go up to the White Mountains next weekend. Let's go hiking.'

Isabella patted Claudia's hands, condescendingly, and flicking her gaze away from the table towards another part of the bar.

'Count me in, honey. But enough about you and hiking. Look at those cute guys at the bar. They've been eyeing us up for the past twenty minutes. What say we go over and let them chat us up. I'll be all coy and virginal. You try not to depress them. What do you say?'

Claudia did a surreptitious glance behind her and winced as she made eye contact with one of them. She looked away, embarrassed she'd been caught.

'Christ! They're about twelve years old, Isabella. And as for you being coy and virginal, that ship sailed a long time ago.'

Isabella feigned a look of outrage.

'Don't be so ageist. The taller one's at least twenty-two. And how dare you. I can still do coy.'

'No way,' said Claudia, grabbing her keys and purse from the table. 'I'm going home for a bath and good night's sleep. I need to be up early or there'll no new paintings for the exhibition.'

She slid her bottom along the leather bench seat and stood up, ensuring she didn't look behind her. She could feel the eyes on her. Isabella gave her a wink and looked over at the guys. She licked her lips, making Claudia laugh.

'Agreed. You go on home, honey. I'll stay and see who talks to me first.'

Claudia left her perfecting her coy and virginal look, wondering which of the eager looking young men she would be going home with that night. Knowing Isabella, it might just be both.

30

Claudia drove the few short miles from the centre of town up to her house in Robinson Hill. She'd been feeling down when she'd first arrived at the bar, but Isabella's infectious and irreverent character had cheered her up considerably. She'd come out of her divorce much stronger than Claudia felt she herself would have done, starting a new life in Lexington, as much to work with Claudia as to escape her ex-husband, Gerrard, who was still a partner in the same prestigious Boston art gallery where Isabella had worked.

The divorce had come as a shock to Claudia, who'd always thought her friend's marriage solid. Although she hadn't known Gerrard all that well, he'd seemed a decent and kind man, clearly devoted to Isabella. Perhaps they'd simply spent too much time together, living and working with each other twenty-four hours a day. Something she and Paul didn't have to worry about. These days, they were like proverbial ships in the night.

The security lights lit up and the garage door automatically opened as she pulled into the driveway. She parked her Porsche Boxster in the garage, letting herself into the house through the door connecting into the kitchen. She could hear music playing. It was coming from the conservatory, at the back of the house, overlooking Robinson Hill. She'd taken breakfast there before making the snap decision to drive down to Plymouth Light.

'Dammit. I left the radio on.'

She walked into the dining room and stopped, confused at what she saw.

The room was encircled in already-lit, tall, white candles, giving it a warm glow. The Bert Bacharach song, *This Guy's in Love with You*, oozed out of the speakers mounted in each corner of the room, and in the oversized fireplace, a stack of burning, pine logs gave the room a spicy, sensuous smell. The dining table was laid with a white-linen tablecloth, at its centre, a crystal vase filled with long-stemmed red roses. Beside the roses was an uncorked bottle of white wine, jammed into an ice bucket overflowing with cubes of glistening ice.

The glow from the candles, reflected in the full height windows, bobbed like paper lanterns floating on a dark lake, surrounding Claudia's own ghostly reflection. She stared at the spectre of herself then gave a frightened gasp as another moved up behind her. She turned, looking up into the face of her husband.

'Hello, sweetheart.'

'Paul! You gave me a fright. I thought you were in Los Angeles.'

Paul smiled down at her, enjoying her surprise.

'Turns out I didn't want to be there. Not without you. Especially not tonight.'

Claudia was happy to see him, but hid it. She tilted her head to one side, coyly.

'What's so special about tonight?'

'Sweetheart, did you really think I'd forget our anniversary?'

Despite being adamant she was not going to get emotional, Claudia's voice trembled.

'Well you didn't call me, Paul, or even send a text. Not all day. What was I supposed to think?'

Paul kissed her full on the mouth, lingering just long enough to deliver the message of intent, his body pressed against hers. Claudia felt her heart beat a fraction faster as he looked into her eyes. He was a good-looking man, and while his coal-black hair was the envy of many men his age, his eyes had always been his best feature, dark grey with flecks of cobalt blue that sparkled when he was angry or aroused. She broke free of the embrace, knowing how he wanted things to progress.

Sensing her reticence Paul let go of her, busying himself by pouring them each a glass of wine. He handed her a glass and they clinked them together.

'Happy anniversary, sweetheart.'

'Happy anniversary, Paul.'

Despite he had called her *sweetheart*, Claudia had not yet melted enough to allow herself to respond as she normally would. The ice in the wine bucket might be melting, but the ice in her heart was still to be thawed.

Paul continued trying.

'Sixteen years. Who'd have thought it?'

'I know,' replied Claudia, still a little surprised at Paul's appearance, 'I'm glad you came home to celebrate it. I thought perhaps you wouldn't? Not after our fight. I thought I was going to spend it alone. It hurt, being by myself, today. We've never not been together on our anniversary.'

'I'm sorry, sweetheart. I didn't *want* us to be apart. I guess neither of us did. We both know why it happened. It's this damned treadmill we've both been trapped on, trying to get pregnant. But we've never missed celebrating our anniversary. So, I caught the early afternoon flight out of Burbank.'

He stroked her cheek and kissed her on the forehead. Claudia responded by raising a hand to cover his. Allowing the ice to melt.

'I'm glad you did, my darling, really I am.'

She smiled up at him, her eyes softening. Paul took her hand and kissed the back of it, then led her over to the table.

'Well then sit down and let me feed you. I stopped in Boston to pick up your favourite food from your favourite store. You can tell me all about your day by the sea. I assume that's where you were?'

'You know me too well,' said Claudia, looking down at the feast Paul had laid out, 'there's nothing like being by the ocean, when you're down, to lift you right back up.'

Rather than eating at the table, they sat by the fire, enjoying the two lobsters and dozen prawns that Paul had stopped to buy from Red's Fish Market and savouring the delicious dry white wine he'd brought back from Los Angeles. Claudia told him about Hannah and her day at Plymouth Light. Paul, in turn, told her of the progress of the television series.

'They begin shooting the pilot, the day after tomorrow.'

'Paul, that's wonderful. You must be over the moon? It's what you always dreamed of.'

'Who knew it would be Professor Joey Amato and Moldova the Beagle who would give me that prize. I still can't believe it.'

Paul opened a second bottle of wine and, as they drank it, Claudia began to feel herself truly relax with him for the first time in months. She was open with him about struggling to deal with not having had the child they wanted, and her irrational anger at him getting on with his life, embracing his passion while she had lost hers. Painting seemed unimportant when what she wanted, more than anything else, was a child of her own.

'I wanted a family, too, sweetheart, you know that.'

Claudia ignored he had said *wanted*, assuming it had been a slip of the tongue.

'I know that, my darling, but you seem to handle the failure of not having one much better than me.'

'We don't have to give up.'

Claudia leaned into him, closing her eyes and enjoying the feel of him against her. She'd missed him so much and was glad he'd said what he'd said about keeping trying.

'I'm so glad you feel that way.'

'I do, sweetheart. I always have. And you're right, I've gotten caught up in my work, recently, but it's an incredible opportunity to bring my books to a wider audience. But it's only the start. Once the series becomes as successful as the producers tell me it's going to be, so many more doors are going to open. I'm not writing about Joey Amato and Moldova the bloody beagle for the rest of my life, but, right now, they're getting me where I want to be. We'll never need to worry about money again.'

'How much money do we need, Paul?'

'Enough that I can spoil you. Like this.'

He stood and walked across the room, retrieving something from his brown leather shoulder-bag, laid on one of the conservatory sofas. He sat down beside her, holding a flat box covered in black velvet.

'Paul?'

'Happy anniversary, sweetheart.'

Claudia took the box and stared at it. She suddenly felt ashamed she hadn't bothered to stop and get him a card. She hadn't really expected to see him.

'Oh, my darling. I didn't get you anything.'

'I've got my new Ferrari, sweetheart, Hollywood fawning all over me, and you! What more could I possible want?'

Claudia couldn't help but notice that his car and Hollywood were above her in his list of what was important. She decided she was being ungrateful. He'd at least thought about her and got her a present.

'I still feel bad.'

Paul shook his head.

'Don't! Now, go on. Open it.'

Claudia opened the box, tentatively, as if afraid something was going to pop out at her, but the surprise was a good one. Lying on a purple felt baize was a rope of twisted silver flecked with delicate strands of gold. It was as thick as the tip of her pinkie. She took the necklace from the box and held it, draped over her open palms like a strand of warm liquorice. Hanging at its centre was an emerald the size of a small bird's egg, encrusted around its edge with diamonds, held in place by a dragon's claw fashioned from bright silver.

'Paul. It's absolutely stunning.'

She held the necklace up to look at it more closely. It was light and delicate, despite the thickness of the chain, and the emerald glowed as the flames from the fire danced inside it like iridescent fireflies in a frantic courtship dance. Paul knew, from her face, he'd chosen wisely.

'It's supposed to be Peridite,' he said, 'for a sixteenth wedding anniversary, which is a semi-precious stone known as the evening emerald. But I thought a real emerald would be a far better choice.'

'Since when did you know so much about semi-precious stones,' said Claudia, laughing at him.

Paul shrugged his shoulders and laughed with her.

'Okay, you got me. But I'm only repeating what the girl in Quadrum told me.'

'Quadrum!' Claudia's mouth dropped open. 'Up on Chestnut Hill?'

She gave the necklace a more studied appraisal.

'Boston's finest jewellers,' said Paul, 'or so I'm reliably informed by someone in the know.'

Claudia was more than impressed. She hoped she'd get the chance to thank whoever his friend had been. It was a truly special gift.

'I know they are, my darling. I've often passed it and stopped to look at some of the amazing creations in their window. I've never dared go in, though, it's so damned expensive. Paul, really, you shouldn't have.'

'Well, now you own one of them. And it's a one of a kind, my darling, just like you. Here, let me help you put it on.'

Paul climbed to his feet and held out a hand.

Claudia allowed him to pull her up. She handed him the necklace, turning her back to him and unbuttoning her shirt so that it fell open to her navel. Paul fastened the chain around her neck then followed her to the mirror hung on the wall opposite the fireplace. Claudia studied her reflection, loving the glimmer and sparkle of the silver and stone creation around her neck.

'It's absolutely stunning. I love it, Paul, I really do. But you shouldn't have spoiled me like this. I don't feel I deserve it.'

Paul, standing behind her, slipped his hand inside her open shirt and lightly dragged his fingernails across her stomach and kissed her on the back of the neck, sending a shiver of anticipation through her.

'You always wanted an emerald, Claudia. I promised I'd give you one, when we were both poor students.'

'We might have been poor, Paul, but we were in love. It didn't matter to me if you brought me diamonds and pearls or tea and biscuits, as long as we were together. I've missed that togetherness.'

She turned and kissed him on the mouth, running her fingers through his hair, then led him back to the fireplace and guided him down onto the soft woollen rug.

'You don't have to do this, sweetheart.'

He seemed reticent, which surprised Claudia, but it had been some time since they'd been together as man and wife. She put her fingers to his lips to stop him saying anything more.

'I know, my darling. But I want to.'

She kissed him again, this time more passionately, sliding her tongue into his mouth and feeling a warm tingle run down to between her thighs. Although she felt nervous, she wanted to give herself to him. She knew he needed it. Perhaps, she thought, so did she.

31

Paul was in the shower, singing a song Claudia had never heard him sing before. He sounded happy. She was too. They'd had sex, twice, the previous night, but had not made love. The joining of hearts and souls, as well as of bodies, had simply not been there. *Probably more my fault than his.* She made a note to talk to her doctor about her libido. It was practically non-existent. Loss of sexual appetite was a side-effect of the fertility treatment process, but it had been months since the last failed attempt.

Naked, but for a towel wrapped around his waist, Paul came out of the bathroom and walked over to the window, pausing to look out over Robinson Hill. Claudia noticed some scratches on his back that had cut his skin and looked raw and fresh.

'Looks like I've marked you, my darling.'

Paul tried to look over his shoulder. Unable to properly see, he went back into the bathroom to use the bathroom mirror.

'You have indeed, you little wildcat.'

'I didn't notice myself doing that,' Claudia called through to him. 'I think that's a first, for me.'

'Neither did I,' replied Paul, re-emerging from the bathroom. 'But I'm sure it's not the first time.'

He tugged away his towel, using it to dry his hair.

Claudia couldn't help but notice the bobbing erection. He was always horny in the morning, despite that she, invariably, was not. This morning, she decided he could have his wicked way with her.

'Coming back to bed?'

She patted the space beside her and let the duvet fall away, revealing her breasts and tossing her hair in a coquettish manner that she felt said, *come and get me big boy*.

'Actually, sweetheart, I thought I'd do us some breakfast. I don't know about you, but I'm absolutely starving. I used up a lot of energy last night.'

Claudia was relieved, if a little surprised. *At least I offered.*

'Sounds good, my darling.'

'Scrambled eggs with buttered toast, crispy bacon, fresh orange juice and hot coffee,' said Paul, hopping on one foot as he pulled on a sock. 'What do you think?'

'Perfect!' Claudia got out of bed as Paul continued to dress. 'I'll grab a shower, if you're happy to do the cooking and serving?'

'Of course. See you at the dining table.'

Paul pulled on a pair of grey jogging pants and a black t-shirt and headed out of the bedroom

Claudia crossed the floor and looked out of the window. The sun was shining and the sky was blue and cloudless. It was a beautiful day and her mood, from yesterday, was in a much different place. She wanted to keep it there.

'Paul,' she called after him, 'why don't we eat in my studio instead? It's a beautiful morning. The views from it, over Robinson Hill, will be lovely.'

'Okay, sweetheart,' Paul, already halfway down the stairs, called back, 'make it half an hour and I'll bring it out to you.'

By the time Claudia had showered and dressed, then made her way out of the house and down the garden path, Paul had laid out breakfast on the white, formica table on the ground floor of her studio. It was an oversized piece of modern furniture that she used for laying out canvasses and project plans. They parked themselves at one end, sitting diagonally across from each other at one corner. Claudia slid open the floor to ceiling sliding glass doors and they ate to the sound of the river and the birds. Today, she mused, they would not have to listen to her complain.

'This is delicious, Paul. Again, I don't know what I've done to deserve such special treatment. And your cooking is much improved.'

'I just wanted to say sorry for storming off on you after our fight. I really am, sweetheart. As for my cooking, I got lucky. Don't get used to it.'

Claudia laughed and leaned over to kiss him, but Paul's attention had switched to his phone, lying by his plate. It had just buzzed with an incoming message. He picked it up, opened the message, and frowned, then set the phone back on the table, face down.

'Problem?' Claudia asked, wiping up the last of her eggs with her remaining corner of toast.

'Not really. It's just Sam.'

'One of your producers?'

'Yup! She's always on my case about something. With the pilot due to shoot, tomorrow, she's even more up-tight than normal.'

'She? I thought Sam was a man.'

Claudia wasn't sure why she was so surprised, or concerned. Paul seemed non-plussed.

'Nope! Sam is Sammy. Most definitely a girl.'

'Is she pretty?'

Claudia wondered what had made her ask.

Paul gave her a quizzical look.

'No more than any of the other girls out there. sweetheart. Every second one of them seems to be an aspiring actress. You know how it is.'

'No, I don't, actually.'

Claudia's voice had a bit more edge to it than she'd meant it to have. Paul laughed and shook his head at her.

'Claudia Montgomery! You're not jealous are you?'

'No! Not really.' Claudia heard the huff in her own voice and realised she was. 'I'm sorry, Paul. You work with women. Of course, you do. Just as I work almost exclusively with men. At least, it seems that way when it comes to my corporate commissions. Ignore me, it was a stupid thing to say.'

Paul reached over and squeezed her hand.

'Look, we've both had it rough, recently, sweetheart. In fact, the past few years haven't been easy on either of us. Like you said, we've allowed ourselves to drift away from each other. What say we make some changes and to try to drift back?'

Claudia attempted a smile and nodded. Paul was right. And wasn't that just what Hannah had told her? *The harder you both worked at being married the easier being in love and staying in love got.* She was being stupid and knew it. She leaned over and gave Paul a peck on the cheek.

'Well, now I've got you all to myself, what shall we do today? What about a trip down to the lighthouse? I so want you to meet Hannah. You'd love her, Paul, really.'

Paul winced and shook his head.

'I'd love to, sweetheart, but I'm on the six o'clock out of Logan Airport, tonight, back to Los Angeles.'

Claudia was unable to hide her disappointment.

'Tonight? Paul! So soon?'

'It's the pilot shoot, tomorrow, Claudia. I told you that. I want to be there for it. I need to be. It's a truly special moment for me. I thought you understood that.'

His phone buzzed again. He read the message and typed out a reply. Claudia stood up and began to clear away the breakfast things.

'More hassle from *Sammy*?'

She tried to hide the sarcasm in her tone, but failed. Paul, if he'd noticed, didn't show it.

'It's constant, sweetheart, believe me. Look, I need to get the script. It's in my folder out in the car.'

Claudia didn't want this to be the prelude to yet another fight. It had the potential to be. She needed to be supportive. The pilot *was* a big deal to Paul. Of course, he had to be there for it. It would be like her having an exhibition of her artwork at *Sans Cera* and not bothering to turn up. She needed to stop being stupid.

'I know it's a big deal for you, my darling, and you deserve it to be a success. I'm just sad you're leaving again so soon. But I do appreciate you came three-thousand miles for me, yesterday.'

Paul kissed her on the forehead.

'Thanks, sweetheart. It was worth it, wasn't it?'

Claudia watched him walk across the garden towards the house. His phone buzzed again. He'd left it on the table. Normally, he wouldn't let it out of his sight. She told herself she wasn't going to look at it, even as she reached for it. There was a message on the screen from someone with the initial "S", which Claudia guessed was shorthand for Sammy. It didn't mean he was having an affair with her, but the extravagant necklace he'd given her and the cooking of breakfast, not to mention the refusal of morning sex all added up to something. *Or am I being paranoid?* He'd told her Sam was a girl. He hadn't needed to admit that.

'Listen to yourself, Claudia. Admit to what?'

She still opened and read the message. *Looking forward to seeing you later. Big day tomorrow. Kisses!*

The wave of anger that washed over her was as sudden as it was profound.

On impulse, she clicked back to view all of Paul's messages. There were none, yet hadn't she just seen him texting Sammy? He'd obviously deleted his entire message log. She clicked through to his phone calls. There was only one, a call he'd taken the day before, mid-afternoon. Claudia's anger turned to confusion as she realised whom the number belonged to. Her business manager and best friend, Isabella Stanton!

Why the hell is her number there? They don't even like each other that much.

Claudia looked up and saw Paul coming back across the path. She replaced his phone, face down on the table, as he'd left it, then stepped away.

'Well here's the pilot script,' said Paul, retaking his seat. 'I know what Sam wants me to look over. I'll flick through it and then we can decide what we're going to do with our day. I thought we could take a hike up Robinson Hill then maybe grab some lunch in Boston, down by the wharf.'

'Sure. Sounds great.'

Claudia only just managed to get the words out. Her mind was in turmoil. Not only at the lovey-dovey message Paul had gotten from Sam, but at the discovery of his call from Isabella.

'You okay?' Paul asked, reaching out and taking her hand. 'Look, I'm sorry I need to go back tonight, sweetheart.'

Claudia tried not to flinch at his touch.

'I'm fine, Paul, really.'

She knew her voice was tight and probably sounded odd. She couldn't help it. She was angry and had so many questions she wanted to ask. But she needed to formulate them first. Paul knew she was far from fine. He assumed she was upset about him having to leave so soon after getting home, but there was nothing he could do about that. He read the script as Claudia took the breakfast things into the house. By the time she returned, he'd composed and sent his response to Sammy and was ready to go.

They walked down the pathway that continued from their garden onto the north side of Robinson Hill. An army of rhododendron bushes clustered around them as they entered the park, gigantic, green blobs adorned with bursts of orange and pink and white. After crossing the iron bridge over the silent river, they took the steeper of the two pathways heading up towards the summit. Paul reached for Claudia's hand. She took it, tentatively, and they walked up the dirt pathway admiring the colours of the new season.

'Slow down, Paul,' said Claudia, pulling him back, 'you're striding ahead like you're on some sort of mission.'

'I'm just walking at my normal pace, sweetheart. I've taken to having an early morning run along Manhattan Beach. I guess I never have anyone else with me to slow me down so I go at my own pace.'

Claudia nudged him with her shoulder.

'That came out well.'

Paul realised how it must have sounded and immediately sought to limit the damage.

'Sorry. I didn't mean you were too slow or unfit.' The look on Claudia's face made him realise he was still digging. 'What say I just stop talking.'

Claudia shook her head, laughing at his discomfort.

'Good idea. But I need to be honest with myself, Paul. I've put on a few pounds.' Paul said nothing. Claudia knew he was being polite. She was more than aware she was out of condition. But she needed to talk. *They* needed to talk. 'I've lost my desire. For everything, it feels.'

Paul stopped walking and turned to face her.

'I know that, sweetheart, but I don't care if you're a few pounds heavier or not, you're still an incredibly beautiful woman.'

Claudia mock punched him on the arm.

'I really think you need to work on your chat-up lines, my darling. You've just agreed with me that I'm getting fat, then told me that I'm *still* beautiful. Can I just tell you, you write way better than you speak.'

Paul shook his head at this own stupidity.

'It's not what I meant, sweetheart. I just mean that, for all you've gone through, putting on a few pounds isn't that much of a big deal.' Seeing the look on incredulity on Claudia face, he put his head in his hands. 'Shit, I'm really putting my foot in it this morning.'

'I'm only teasing you, my darling.'

Paul blew a sigh of relief.

'Well I guess I deserved it. Now, at the risk of being sexist, let me help you the rest of the way up.'

Claudia took the crook of his arm in hers and they walked on up the hill. She began to relax, enjoying the beauty of the forest and the cool, clean air.

'Anyway,' she said, a determined steel in her voice, 'I'm going to do something about the things I've lost about myself.'

'Like what?' Paul asked.

'I'm thinking of going up to the cabin and doing some hiking. You're away for a month, after today, so I may as well use the time to get myself back on track.'

'Great idea, sweetheart, but won't you be a bit isolated up there? The cabin's pretty much out on its own.'

'I thought I'd ask Isabella to come and join me. Maybe just a couple of days during the week. Her new assistant can take over at the gallery when she's up there with me.

Claudia watched Paul's response out of the corner of her eye, waiting to see if he gave anything away, but there was nothing in his face that told her anything. However, he hadn't said he'd met Charity. The question of *why not,* bothered her. *Was it because he hadn't wanted to admit he'd gone to Sans Cera to meet Isabella?*

'At least she'll keep the bears away with that perfume of hers.'

'Paul! Honestly!'

Claudia acted shocked, although she was relieved to hear his disparaging remarks about Isabella. *They couldn't be having an affair. It made no sense. There must be a logical explanation for her calling him!*

'Sorry, sweetheart, that was a cheap shot. I know she's your best friend.'

'I couldn't run the gallery without her, Paul. She's the one driving it forward. I've let her completely take charge over the past months, to be honest.'

'I'm sure she's loving the autonomy.'

Claudia decided to bait the hook.

'Have you seen her recently?'

Paul shook his head.

'Isabella? No! We don't really see eye to eye. You know that. Why?'

'No reason. I just wondered if you had. She's looking really good.'

'Divorce obviously agrees with her.'

'It does seem to,' said Claudia, and took the hook out of the water.

Nothing in Paul's voice seemed to suggest that he was feeling uncomfortable. She decided to leave it, for the moment. They had precious little enough time left together, the last thing she wanted was another argument.

They walked on for a few minutes, hand in hand, stopping from time to time to admire the new life bursting on every branch and bush and the sounds of the birds and insects helping nature in its endeavours.

'Have you ever thought about opening another gallery?' Paul asked, breaking the easy silence.

'God no! One's enough. Besides, I'd need another Isabella. I can provide the artwork, but I need someone to manage the business side of things. That's become crystal clear since she came to *Sans Cera*. What prompted *that* question?'

Paul stopped walking and turned, again, to face her.

'I'm going to be spending more and more time out in Los Angeles. I like the team I'm working with and Sam's already lined me up with an idea for a script she wants me to develop after the television series is done. But there's so many more opportunities out there, Claudia. It's why I want to move there, permanently. I want *us* to move there. The fresh start we talked about this morning.'

Claudia couldn't hide her surprise.

'Like Lexington was meant to be five years ago.'

'We were different people back then, Claudia.'

'Yes, Paul, I suppose we were.'

She let the statement hang in the air between them. Paul pushed it aside.

'So, what do you think?'

The idea had come so far out of left field Claudia didn't really know how to answer.

'I can't leave my gallery. Besides, our lives are here, Paul. My sister and my nieces.'

Paul shook his head. Claudia's answer was clearly not the one he'd wanted to hear.

'Sweetheart, you just said that Isabella practically runs the gallery. Besides, you can open a new gallery out there and keep the one here. She'd love the opportunity to expand and manage business on both sides of the country. All you would need to do is paint and sculpt, the things you most love to do. As for your sister and your nieces, be honest, you rarely see them.'

'I plan to change that,' replied Claudia, equally as annoyed, 'besides, that's not the point.'

'Then what is?'

Claudia didn't have an answer to hand.

'How long has this been in your mind, Paul?'

'A while now, I suppose. I've looked at some properties on Santa Monica beach. A few I think you'd really like.'

Claudia was shocked at the revelation. She couldn't understand why he'd gone behind her back on something that would fundamentally affect both their lives.

'You've already *found* somewhere to live!'

'I've looked online, Claudia, no more. And it's for both of us, not just me. We need to put the past behind us and move on. We wanted to start a family, but it doesn't look like it's going to happen. We both know that, however hard it might be to finally admit it.'

'But, last night, Paul, you said you wanted a child. You said we didn't have to give up trying.'

'I said I wanted a child, Claudia. We *both* wanted one. And we've tried, God knows we've tried. We've paid that damned clinic a fortune and spent years going through fertility treatments that have been worthless and made us both feel like crap.'

Claudia scowled, her disappointment evident.

'I should have known it would be about the money.'

Paul's face darkened at her accusation.

'That's not fair, Claudia, and you bloody know it. It's not about the money, it's about you and me. I'm sick of the feelings of loss we *both* go through every time another treatment fails. It leaves you depressed for months on end and me feeling like a failure. Like I've somehow let you down. It's pushed us further and further apart and all but ruined our sex life.'

'So, you're not getting enough sex, is that it?'

'Dammit, Claudia,' snapped Paul, his voice raised in anger, 'stop putting words in my mouth. That's not what I'm saying, but you've barely let me near you in the past six months.

The fight went out of Claudia. She knew what he was saying was true.

'It's not my fault, Paul. I don't mean to push you away, I just . . .'

She began to cry. Paul put his arm around her shoulders and hugged her.

'I know that, sweetheart. But surely you can see it's time to get off this merry-go-round and get onto a new ride. A different ride, perhaps, but one where we're no longer going around in circles, hanging on for grim death. I'm throwing myself into my new career, one I've dreamed of having since I was a kid, but I can't keep flying back and forth across America to live it. And I can't keep on coming home to this. It's destroying us both.'

Claudia shrugged away his embrace and walked ahead of him before turning to look back.

'Then perhaps you should just go, Paul. Go and find a house for you and your slut to live in.'

The words were out before she could check them.

'What do you mean, *my slut*?'

Paul's face was pale with shock, or anger, Claudia wasn't sure which.

'Sammy! Your sexy little girlfriend out in Los Angeles. She sent you another message when you were getting your script from the car. It's obvious something's going on between you. She sent *kisses* and says she can't wait to see you tonight. You didn't want to come back to bed with me this morning. Perhaps you're saving yourself for her?'

Paul looked at his phone and read the message from Sam. He looked back at Claudia as if wondering who she was.

'You read my messages?'

Claudia had expected an explosion of anger, but his voice, as he spoke, was quiet, as if he couldn't fathom the betrayal of trust. She hated herself for what she was saying, but she couldn't seem to stop herself

'All one of them. The rest were conveniently deleted.'

'I delete my calls and messages every day, Claudia, that's why. Apart from the ones I need to action or keep. Otherwise I end up with hundreds of them clogging up my inbox. Did you think about looking in my saved folders, you'd have found everything there if you had, all carefully filed for you to investigate?'

Claudia's anger disappeared like floodwater over a waterfall. She felt they had reached the lowest ever point of their relationship. It made her beyond sad.

'No,' she replied, sheepishly.

'Well you should have. Not that I've anything to hide. But that's beside the point. What the hell where you doing looking at my messages anyway? If you wanted to check up on me, all you had to do was ask. I'd have given you the damned phone and helped you do it.'

Claudia, although feeling awful, was unable to let it go. Despite she had opened the box, he had to shut it.

'Answer the question, Paul.'

'What bloody question?'

'Are you screwing Sammy? Just tell me. I need to know the truth.'

Paul took her by the shoulders, forcing her to look at him.

'Don't be so bloody stupid, Claudia. She's twenty-six and engaged to a great guy who's a damned sight younger and more handsome than me. Christ, they're getting married, next month, after she finishes work on the pilot. As for her signing off with some kisses, it's Los Angeles, *everyone* sends hugs and kisses to each other, even the damned men. It's less than meaningless.'

Relief washed over Claudia. She fell against him, sobbing into the folds of his jacket.

'Oh, Paul, I'm so sorry. I've never looked at your phone before today. I've felt so down, recently. I was frightened I was losing you. I keep thinking stupid thoughts and I acted on one of them. Can you ever forgive me?'

Paul pulled her to him, stroking her hair as she wept against him.

'You *never* have to ask for my forgiveness, sweetheart. I know it's because of the strain you've been under. And much of it is my fault. I've left you alone here for too long, not really considering how you've been feeling after yet another damned fertility treatment went wrong. I'm the one who should be asking for forgiveness, not you.'

Claudia let her tears fall freely, the stress and strain of the past months finally releasing.

'Oh, Paul. I don't know what's happening to me. To us. I'm so frightened we've lost ourselves and won't find our way back to one another.'

'I know, sweetheart, I know. I feel the same way. That's why I want you to come out to Los Angeles with me to find somewhere to live. To try to start again.'

'*Can* we start again, Paul?'

'Of course, we can, sweetheart.'

'And . . . what about having a baby?'

Claudia looked up at him, willing the answer she so desperately needed.

'If it happens, Claudia, then it happens, but as it should, naturally, through making love. Then we'll know it was *really* meant to be. I can live without a child, but I don't want to live without you. I just can't keep on going like this.

Claudia held onto him as if letting go, now, would somehow seal their fate. A fate she already sensed was somehow inevitable.

'Me neither.'

'Well this is where we are headed, sweetheart, if something doesn't change. We don't have to give up, but we do have to give in. Especially when it comes to the fertility treatments.'

'I know that, my darling. I know.'

'So, will you come with me, out west, to our brave new world?'

Claudia was silent for a moment. What he was asking was for her to change her entire world. She felt she shouldn't have had to hesitate and wondered what that might mean.

'I can't answer that, Paul. At least, not yet. I don't know *what* I want, to be honest, but I'm losing myself and I'm losing you. We both know that's true.'

Paul tilted her face up to his and kissed her gently on the lips.

'I don't want to lose you, Claudia, but I want my Hollywood dream. The wish I made, years ago, is finally coming true, and I can't put the genie back in the bottle.'

The birds and insects around them seemed to have fallen silent, as if shocked at the interruption to their day, and a shadow drifted across the hill as a bank of cloud obscured the sun. Claudia felt a chill and buried her face into Paul's jacket, clinging to him as if afraid there was some darker meaning to it. Perhaps a message from the Universe she did not wish to hear.

32

After parking close to Lexington Battle Green, Claudia walked down past the Minuteman Memorial, a life-sized, bronze statue of a colonial farmer holding his musket, facing the route of the British advance on the day of the Battle of Lexington, during the American War of Independence. The farmer was Captain John Parker, the Lexington militia leader in the year 1775. Turning onto Bedford Street, she paused to admire the Buckman Tavern, where the militia had gathered, awaiting the oncoming British Redcoat troops. The old tavern had seen many such dramas played out over the centuries. The irony was not lost on her, given she had her own personal drama to be played out when she reached her gallery.

She and Paul had finished their walk lost in their thoughts, the realisation they had come to some sort of impasse, clear. They'd driven down to Boston in their own respective cars to lunch at the Atlantic Fish Company, one of their old haunts from their time living there as students.

Lunch had been like meeting each other again, recounting the stories lovers tell one another to add a deeper layer to the initial physical connection. Stories told and retold, over time; shaped and polished until they resembled something approaching the truth. Memories brought back to life and viewed though rose glass. Claudia had wondered why they had been like that. They had kissed goodbye, she, telling him to love every moment of the filming of the pilot television show, he, urging her to rediscover her passion for painting. Paul had then headed out to Logan International Airport, Claudia back to Lexington to speak to her best friend.

Ahead of her, Massachusetts Avenue opened out on both sides. Claudia turned left along it, passing busy boutiques, shops and cafes. Downtown Lexington was blessed with wide streets and walkways, a popular place of relaxation and interest for visitors who came up from Boston at the weekends. It was a family town, with lots of open green spaces and well preserved streets and places of interest, filled with down-to-earth people. Why on earth would she want to trade it for the madness of Los Angeles? Finding no answer, she walked on, pushing the question to the back of her mind.

Sans Cera gallery stood at the east end of Massachusetts Avenue, a red-brick building with a wide *façade* and tall, arched windows on all three floors. Built in the late nineteen-hundreds, and close to Boston Harbour, it had originally been a tea warehouse. Claudia felt a sense of pride when she looked at the gallery name on the windows. It meant a sculpture carved without blemish, with no cracks or chips hidden by sand and glue, the way the ancient artists had covered up such mistakes. Perfection, in other words, which is what she always strived for in her own artistic creations.

She pushed through the double, glass doors and stepped into a world of white; white walls, white furniture, white reception desk and white card and print racks. In fact, anything that was not Claudia's artwork, was white, even the large, neon letters spelling out *Sans Cera* on the wall behind the spacious reception area. The redesign had been Isabella's idea, the first major change she'd effected after taking over the running of the gallery. Overhead, twin rows of aluminium spotlights were spaced out along thin, wire tracks, perched like white chickadees watching the world below them.

The gallery was bright, airy and *very white*, thought Claudia, seeing it for the first time in almost two months, but it oozed serenity and calm, complementing the large bronze, iron and stone sculptures wandering the floor like lost chess pieces, and was the perfect backdrop for the colourful paintings adorning the walls.

When it came to her painting style, Claudia was more Picasso than Pissarro. Post, rather than *pre*-impressionist. She had fallen in love with Picasso's tour de force painting, *Guernica*, at first sight, after seeing it at Boston's Institute of Contemporary Art. She also admired the work of Gustav Klimt. His painting, *Woman in Gold*, was, she considered, a study in genius, and its journey from Vienna to New York's Neue Gallery, after being stolen by the Nazis, during

World War Two, was fascinating. They were two incredible paintings and histories linked by Fascism and the atrocities of war.

'Mrs Montgomery. How lovely to finally meet you.'

The young woman approaching Claudia was seriously attractive and had legs that any catwalk model would have envied. She was taller than Claudia by a good five inches, although her high heels made the difference more noticeable. She was wearing the same sort of fifties-style, pencil skirt that Isabella favoured and her breasts strained against a black, silk shirt, raising little creases of fabric around the buttons. The clothes were chic and expensive. A long mane of auburn hair bounced almost as much as her breasts, and she walked with the slow, languid grace of a giraffe. Her smile was full and expensive, but there was intelligence and strength behind her clear, blue eyes. She wore little make-up, not that she needed to, given her twenty-something year-old skin was as flawless as fine English porcelain.

'Hello,' replied Claudia, unable to help but return the girl's infectious smile.

She remembered Isabella's joke about her new assistant being the woman who could finally *turn* her, and understood why she'd said it. She was movie-star stunning.

'I'm Charity Appleton, Isabella's new assistant,' the girl announced, in a voice that was cultivated, polished and refined. 'I've been here for a few weeks, but we simply keep missing each other. I'm a big fan of your work, Mrs Montgomery, and of the gallery. You've created something quite aesthetically and culturally beautiful here.'

Clever, clever girl, thought Claudia, liking her immediately.

Charity had been at the gallery for almost a month, yet she'd implied they must have just *missed* each other. She'd also praised Claudia for the design of the gallery when she must have known it was Isabella's doing. It was subtle and smart. Claudia took the outstretched hand. Charity's touch was cool and firm, without the slightest trace of uncertainty.

'It's lovely to meet you, Charity. Sorry it's taken so long to come and introduce myself. I can only blame my new works in progress for the upcoming exhibition.'

'Of course, Mrs Montgomery. I understand completely. Can I just say how privileged I am to be given the chance to work here. I graduated, last year, from Boston University, with a first in Art History. I've been holding out for the right position since then.'

'A first,' said Claudia, 'very impressive.'

'I have no idea how I managed to scrape that result,' said Charity, somehow looking as if she had really meant it.

And self-effacing too!

'I'm sure you worked hard for it, Charity. Never ever apologise for your achievements.'

'I won't in future.'

Charity gave Claudia a smile that would render anyone, male or female, immediately smitten.

Claudia was impressed by Isabella's choice of assistant. Quite apart from her fashion model looks, she was clearly a formidable young woman, and obviously of breeding, given her name, if nothing else. It was so colonially derived it would be hard to find another to match it. She had a heady combination of intelligence, beauty and poise, as well as clearly being from old money.

'Have you settled in, Charity? Oh, and please call me Claudia. Mrs Montgomery is so formal. It also makes me feel ancient.'

'I have, *Claudia*,' replied Charity. 'I'm working with some of your existing clients, pulling in pieces for the upcoming exhibition. It's a baptism of fire, but I like the heat turned up.'

I'll bet you do, Miss Appleton, thought Claudia, already pitying any potential client that might come into the cross hairs of Charity's sights. She'd make the gallery a fortune if she was as good a saleswoman as she looked and sounded.

'Do you live locally, Charity?'

'I have an apartment on Newbury Street, on Back Bay.'

'How lovely.' Properties in the exclusive Boston seafront area, Claudia knew, started at a fortune and worked their way up to "don't even ask". *Mummy and daddy's money for sure.* 'I was there this afternoon, having lunch with my husband.'

'Mr Montgomery. Such a lovely man. He made me feel so welcome.'

Claudia couldn't hide her surprise.

'You've already met him?'

'Yes,' said Charity, 'a few weeks ago. He didn't stay long. We had coffee while he waited for Isabella. I'm a big fan of his books. He was telling me about the new television series. You must be very proud.'

'I am, absolutely.' Claudia wondered why Paul hadn't mentioned meeting her. More importantly, why had he come to see Isabella. She decided to find out. 'Is Isabella in?'

'She's in the storage rooms with John and Caleb,', replied Charity. They're unboxing some of the on-loan paintings and sculptures that came in this morning.'

'I see,' said Claudia, trying to compose herself. 'Well, it's been lovely to meet you, Charity. We must have lunch. Allow me to really welcome you on board. Soon, I promise. Now, I'll go find Isabella and let you get on.'

'Of course, Claudia. I look forward to our lunch.'

Charity turned and walked back to her desk at the reception area. Claudia turned to head to storeroom at the back of the gallery. She stopped, on impulse, changing her mind, and turned back to followed Charity towards the reception area.

'On second thoughts, it sounds like Isabella's really busy. I won't disturb her. I'll call her later tonight. It wasn't that important anyway. I just popped in to say hello.'

'Of course. Shall I tell her you called?'

'Do that, Charity, thanks.'

Claudia left *Sans Cera* and headed along Massachusetts Avenue, wondering just how long it would be before Isabella called her.

33

The massive canvas set against the wall of glass in Claudia's studio had a blank look on its face, but little paint. The image in her head remained unformed. The more she tried to force it out the less clear it became. The one thing that had never been a problem for her had been the ability to create something from nothing. Normally, when she painted, she stopped being a physical, sentient being, her hand guided by some instinctual force. But not today.

Dammit! What the hell is wrong with me?

Her phone, on the studio table, buzzed. She cursed it but was glad of its interruption. The paint-laden palette knife was growing heavy in her hand. More metaphorically than physically.

'Claudia Montgomery, ex-artist.' She barked her name like a dog annoyed by a stranger approaching its gate, then softened her tone before the caller replied. 'How can I help?'

'Hi, honey. Creative juices not flowing?'

'Isabella!' Claudia's tone tilted back. 'Sorry, I'm in the studio trying to find my muse. She's seems to have abandoned me.'

'Your muse is a woman?'

'I've never really thought about it, to be honest. I guess yours would be a man if you were at all creative.'

'Ouch!' Isabella picked up the first signs that something was bothering Claudia. 'You were at the gallery this afternoon. Why didn't you come say hello?'

Claudia wasn't ready to explain. The thoughts in her head, bubbling under the surface, were not good ones.

'I met Charity.'

'So! What do you think?'

'She's everything you told me was and more. Beautiful and all business. You've hired a younger version of yourself, it appears, only she's that bit brighter. Got a first from Boston, I believe.'

'Again, ouch!'

Isabella could hear the edge in Claudia's tone and wondered what was wrong. Perhaps it was that she'd interrupted her while she was trying to paint. Claudia realised she was being bitchy, but a flush of anger had washed through her as soon as she'd heard Isabella's voice. She reminded herself that her thoughts were only suspicions at present.

'Only joking. Sorry, Isabella, I'm not in the best of moods.'

'That's okay, honey. Want me to come over? Charity is more than capable of managing the place. She's already got John and Caleb eating out of her hand. She's currently having them move one of the loan paintings that just came in. *Vertigo*. You know the one.'

Claudia visualised the massive painting in her head, a study on perspective in a hundred hues of purple. It had sold to one of the big Boston law firms for over a hundred thousand dollars.

'I remember the piece. It took me months to create, once I'd started.'

'I guess that's the key, honey, starting.'

'Point taken,' said Claudia, holding back the response she wanted to make.

'Anyway, I can come over, if you want?'

'She met Paul,' replied Claudia, ignoring Isabella's offer. 'At the gallery. I didn't know.'

'She did,' confirmed Isabella. 'Only briefly.'

'Why didn't you mention it?'

'I guess I didn't really think it was all that important. Are you sure you're fine, honey? You sound funny.'

'I don't feel very funny, Isabella. Why was he at the gallery? He doesn't normally come to see me, even when I am there. Not that I've been there for a while.'

'Try a month,' said Isabella, then immediately took it back. 'Not that I'm complaining.'

Claudia did.

'That's my point. I'm normally here at my studio. Paul knows that.'

'I suppose he popped in on the off-chance you were there. Maybe he was passing and just wanted a look in. He's not disinterested in your work, honey.'

'Didn't you see him?'

Isabella began to sense there was something bothering Claudia that included her.

'He was gone by the time I got back.'

'So, you've not spoken to him, recently?'

Isabella hesitated long enough for Claudia to know that she had. Her heart sank at the thought that some betrayal had taken place between her husband and her best friend.

'You know we don't really get on that well.'

Isabella was avoiding giving a straight answer. Her veiled denial made it even more obvious something had.

'That's not what I asked.'

Claudia's voice was steely cold.

'Well,' said Isabella, hesitantly, 'I guess, since you're asking, you know I have.'

Claudia felt an overwhelming desire to attack the blank canvas with the palette knife. Her knuckles were white with the force of her grip on it. She had suspected Paul was having an affair. She'd said as much to Isabella, on the phone, driving back up from Plymouth Light the day before. Thinking about it, now, Isabella had defended him. She cast a line out, hoping she would offer herself up to be caught.

'You're right, Isabella. I *do* know!'

'It's not what you're obviously thinking, honey. I swear on my life. I'd never do anything to hurt you like that.'

'Really? Then why didn't you tell me you'd spoken to him? He was talking to you while I was crying on the beach, where he should have been. What the hell's going on, Isabella?'

'Honey, why don't I come over and we can clear this up? You're not thinking straight. I know you're upset, but . . .'

'Upset!' Claudia hurled the palette knife across the room. The umber oil paint smeared across the canvas like the blood from an open wound and the knife fell to the floor. 'I'm more than bloody upset. My husband comes home late on our anniversary and tells me he wants to live three thousand miles away, and that I need to come with him if our marriage is to survive. He no longer wants to try for a baby, something he knows means more to me than almost anything else. He meets your stunning new receptionist but forgets to tell me they had coffee together. And now, my best friend, who apparently doesn't even like him that much, tells me they've been chatting on the phone behind my back. Upset, Isabella! You think?'

Claudia only just resisted the urge to hurl her phone after the palette knife. She was breathing heavily and her heart was racing. Isabella, shocked by her outburst, tried to explain.

'Claudia, please, listen to me for a moment. Let me explain.'

'Go ahead, Isabella, explain! But it better be bloody good, because I'm on the verge of coming down there and . . . well, I don't know what I'm on the verge of doing, but it won't be good.'

Okay, honey. Yes, I did call him, but only to remind him it was his wedding anniversary. I told him to get himself home, preferably with something ridiculously expensive, and to pay you some attention. You've been so down, over the past few months, and how many times have you cried on my shoulder about how things have become between you two? I didn't want to have to pick you up again, today, if he forgot.'

Claudia felt the anger flushing through her dilute at what Isabella had said. She softened her voice.

'Then why didn't you just *say* something to me, in Harry's Bar? You're my best friend in the world. Why didn't you just tell me the truth about speaking to him.

Isabella gave a derisive laugh.

'Really? Tell you I'd called your husband to remind him to buy you flowers on your anniversary? To turn up, even? Like that would have made you feel *so* special. What would you have done if the situation had been reversed?'

Claudia felt the weight of the past twenty-four hours fall from her shoulders. She hadn't wanted to believe Isabella would betray her in the worst way possible. The relief that she hadn't was overwhelming. Her voice, as she answered, was tired and small.

'You're right. I would have done the same for you.'

'I know that, honey, which is why I did it for you.'

Claudia felt ashamed at having treated her friend without even meeting her and talking it over, face to face. She'd acted badly and immediately regretted it.

'I'm sorry I shouted at you, Isabella, and for practically accusing you of having an affair with Paul. It sounds so stupid, now we've spoken. Can you forgive me? I'm so messed up, right now. It's as if the ground beneath my feet is turning to quicksand and I can't find a solid path out of it.'

'Honey, there's nothing to forgive. I'm sorry if I overstepped. But you know I would never betray you like that.'

'I do know that, Isabella. Really, I do. Look, I can't say I'm happy you felt you had to cajole him into remembering our anniversary, but I get why you did. Although Paul should have known that for himself.'

'He should, but he's a man,' said Isabella, laughing.

Claudia laughed with her. Just a little laugh. But a laugh.

'You're right. What can we expect? They're bloody useless, most of the time. I don't know why we bother with them at all.'

'Because they occasionally rise to the occasion,' replied Isabella, lasciviously.'

Claudia laughed a little more.

'You never stop, do you?'

'Never. Anyway, tell me, did you like your present?'

'I loved it,' said Claudia. It's an emerald and diamond necklace.'

'Expensive, I hope?'

'It's from Quadrum.'

'Wow,' exclaimed Isabella, 'I know the store. One of the girls who works there is a friend of mine. We share the same taste in fifties clothing and men.'

'Isabella, honestly.'

Claudia began to relax a little more. The dark cloud of betrayal had lifted from over her head.

'So, you got your jewellery *and* a decent white wine?'

'And more besides,' said Claudia, suggestively. 'Candy the cheerleader didn't come out to play, but her older and more sensible sister did. Paul and I had sex, twice, no matter if it wasn't the mind-blowing, over-the-moon, in love sex we used to have. And he turned me down, this morning, when I offered myself to him, which wasn't like him.'

Isabella went quiet for a moment. Claudia wondered if she'd shocked her with her admission. But this was Isabella, and that, she knew, was almost impossible to do.

'Okay, honey, I've got the picture, let's just leave it there. At least you got some. Look, do you want me to come over for a while? We could share a bottle of white wine.'

Claudia wandered over to the now not so blank canvas, forming a picture in her head from the image created by the stain on it from the hurled palette knife. An image of a holy man dressed in a silk robe and wearing a bejewelled, golden crown, kneeling at the foot of a bloodstained, wooden cross, offering a Roman soldier a coin to finish off the victim nailed to it. The name of the painting she had yet to create came to her immediately. *Betrayal.* She smiled at the irony.

'No, I'm fine, Isabella. I'm glad you called and allowed me to vent my anger at someone. I'm just sorry it was you. All the numbers in my head were adding up to the wrong answer. I'm fine, here, by myself. Let me try to paint.'

'Fair enough, honey. I've got a lot on at the gallery anyway. There's more pieces arriving every day, from existing clients, for next month's exhibition.'

'I'm glad you're down there taking care of things, Isabella. I think, without you, the way I'm feeling, right now, I'd close the gallery down if you weren't.'

'I love it, honey. It's great to be able to run things the way I know they should be. I was never able to have that autonomy at my last gallery.'

'You can do what you want at *Sans Cera*, Isabella, you know that, don't you?'

'Thanks for the vote of confidence. It means so much to me. I love *Sans Cera* as if it were my own.'

'We'll, on that note,' said Claudia, 'I promised you a twenty-five percent share in the business when you came on board. You've far exceeded the uplift in turnover we set as the target for that to happen. So, I'm going to give you it now.'

'Honey, you don't need to do that.'

Isabella was taken aback, but Claudia had made her mind up.

'No, you've earned it. I'll get the paperwork sorted out and sent over for you to sign. Anyway, it's as much in my own interests as yours. I want the gallery to thrive and I can't do it without you. If I *do* decide to head out west, with Paul, I need to leave it in capable hands. And your hands are more than capable.'

'So I've been told.'

'Tart.'

'Guilty as charged, honey.'

Claudia's mood had brightened. She decided she did want to see her friend, face to face, to apologise properly.

'Look, what about coming over and having a glass of wine with me, tonight? We could watch an old black and white movie and stuff our faces with popcorn.'

'Actually, I can't, honey.' Remember the taller of the two young guys from Harry's Bar? Well, it turns out he's twenty-seven, so he's close enough to my age to not count as baby snatching. We're having dinner, later, in Boston, near the wharf. Want to double-date?'

Claudia laughed.

'No thanks. But you go enjoy your man-child.'

'Okay, but seriously, if you need me, call me. I'll drop whatever I'm holding and head over.'

Claudia snorted at the suggestive reply.

'Enjoy your night. I'll come down to *Sans Cera* tomorrow. You can tell me the sordid details then.'

'If you're sure.'

'I am. Now go. Work hard then play harder. And Isabella...'

'What?'

'Thanks for being a such a good friend.'

'Always, honey.'

After a supper of salad and the remains of the lobster from the previous evening, Claudia decided on an early night. The entire day had been stressful from start to finish. Her conversation with Paul, on Robinson Hill, had left her feeling vulnerable and confused. He no longer saw a child as the most important thing for them. She could not feel that way. She didn't blame him. She knew how hard the fertility treatments had been for her, but had not really considered that he was hurt, too, every time they'd tried and failed.

She put down the book she'd been trying to read. It was just gone seven but she felt she could sleep forever. As she reached across to switch out her bedside lamp, her phone rang. She answered it without reading the name of the caller.

'Claudia Montgomery.'

'Sweetheart.'

'Paul? Oh, I'm so glad to hear from you.'

She pushed herself up against the headboard, pulling the pillows from Paul's side of the bed in behind her and plumping them up behind her back.

'It's just a quick call,' said Paul, 'to thank you for a wonderful anniversary. I'm glad we talked. It was overdue.'

Claudia felt bad for thinking he had been having an affair with Isabella. It sounded so stupid now.

'I know, my darling, I feel the same. We both needed to get a few things off our chest. I've been so wrapped up in my own thoughts, for so long, I didn't really think about how *you* felt about everything. I'm sorry for that.'

'No need to apologise, sweetheart. But we need to keep talking, albeit by phone, over the next month, while I'm stuck out here.'

'Absolutely,' agreed Claudia, 'we will. Anyway, where are you? Are you calling from the plane?'

'No, I'm still at the damned airport. The flight was cancelled due to some technical issue. The airline's sending another aircraft up from somewhere down south. We take off at midnight, apparently.'

'Paul, that's awful. Could you not come home and catch an early flight in the morning?'

'And miss my big day? No way. I'll get into L.A. by two in the morning, western time. Sam and her fiancé are going to pick me up from the airport and let me stay at their apartment for a few hours. I'll get some sleep on the plane and in their spare room before we head out to the set.'

'At least she's looking after you.'

Claudia tried not to sound churlish at hearing Sammy's name.

'What are you up to sweetheart?'

'I'm in bed,' replied Claudia. 'I was about to switch the light out when you called. I tried to paint, this afternoon, but it was pretty much a total loss.'

'I'm sorry about that, sweetheart. Perhaps it will start to flow tomorrow.'

'That's why I'm in bed. Isabella's not going to be happy if I don't deliver something new for the exhibition. I had an idea for a new painting, so at least I've got something to work on.'

'Good. Well, I'll let you sleep then. I'll call you from movieland after the shoot.

'Okay, my darling, speak to you then. I love you.'

'Me, too,' said Paul, a little too perfunctory, thought Claudia, as he disconnected.

She was glad he'd called her. He didn't normally. She'd thought about mentioning Isabella having spoken to him, about their anniversary, but what was there to gain? Only another argument. So what if he'd been reminded to buy her an anniversary present? How many men forgot stuff like that? He'd come home long before Isabella had called him and he *hadn't* forgotten their anniversary, that was what was important. But something was still eating at her. She just couldn't put her finger on it.

For no reason, she clicked through her call log and realised that Paul hadn't called from his mobile phone. The call had been made from a landline number. Claudia knew she recognised it. Then it hit her. It was the number from their apartment in downtown Boston. The engineer who'd called her on her way home from the lighthouse had said the services on the telephone system needed to be reset. She was sure one of those services was hiding the phone number of the apartment when an outgoing call was made. She'd forgotten to mention it to Paul. She hit redial on her phone and the call connected, taking her straight thought to Paul's answering service at the apartment.

She tried again, without success.

Confused and feeling sick to her stomach, Claudia climbed out of bed and pulled on a pair of Timberland boots, jeans and a sweatshirt, then went downstairs, heading through the kitchen and out into the garage. *Paul was at the apartment! Why hadn't he said so*? There was no choice. She had to find out the truth of the matter, even if that meant going there to confront him and whoever he was with.

Claudia drove her Porsche through downtown Lexington, heading north-west on Massachusetts Avenue towards Depot Square, passing *Sans Cera*. The gallery lights were out, save for the glare of the spotlights in the front window, illuminating a large-scale painting she'd named, *Seven Shadows*, an artistic meander into the world of Dante's seven levels of hell, which reminded her of the painting that had formed in her head earlier that day, *Betrayal!*

Although she tried to stop it, her mind created pictures of Paul with another woman, in bed, in their apartment. She imagined how she would catch them together and what she would say when she did. The images only served to fuel her anger.

She slipped right, driving a little too quickly, onto interstate ninety-five, lost in the gut-churning feeling that comes with a serving of deceit. On impulse, she scrolled though the illuminated display of names in her list of contacts until she landed on Isabella's. She hit the call button and waited.

'Hello, Isabella Stamford. Sorry you can't reach me. Leave a message and I'll get . . .'

Claudia ended the call without waiting to listen for the beep.

Isabella had said she was going on a date, into Boston, somewhere on the wharf, with the young guy she'd met in Harry's Bar. Paul, instead of being at the airport, was at their apartment, close to the waterfront. *Coincidence?* She didn't want to think she had been lied to, by them both, but everything seemed to be adding up to confirm her worst fears. She hated how she was feeling. She'd never been the jealous type. Now, it smothered her.

'What the hell am I doing? This isn't who I am.'

Claudia started to doubt herself. There was a perfectly good reason for Paul being at the apartment. It was close to Logan Airport and he'd had an eight-hour delay. It made sense to go there. He could work on his script rather than spend hours at a busy airport. She almost took the next exit, intending to go home, but something stopped her. *If there was nothing to hide, why hadn't he told her where he was?* It was the third thing he'd hidden from her in the past twenty-four hours; coffee with Charity, secret telephone calls from Isabella, and now this!

Five miles out of Boston, Claudia took the exit towards the Government Centre then turned onto John F Fitzgerald. The traffic was light but the streets were busy with students, tourists and locals heading down to the bright lights of the wharf. She turned right into State Street then down Congress. Their apartment was on Pearl Street, close to the Boston Tea Party Museum, less than five minutes away.

Pulling up to the gate of the building's underground parking, Claudia pressed the fob on the keyring. The gate opened and she drove down to the first basement level, parking close to the lift. There was no sign of Paul's car, but there was another level below this one. If he'd come here, earlier, he might have had to use it. The thought that he'd left her only a mile or so away, after their lunch together, to meet someone, here, sent her anger skyrocketing.

The lift descended and the doors swished open. Claudia pressed the button for apartment seventeen. The landing lights came on the moment the lift doors opened on their apartment floor. She looked across at herself in the hallway mirror and wondered who the woman staring back at her was. She almost didn't get out, loathe to find out if her instincts were right. Equally as afraid not to.

The apartment door was locked, as Claudia had expected. She pressed the fob to the entry pad and it unlocked with a quiet click. She entered and walked through the livingroom, out into the hallway connecting to the bedrooms. There was enough light coming in through the windows to allow her to not switch on the main lights. The master bedroom door was ajar, only slightly, but enough for her to see the bedside lamps were lit. She pushed the door open and stepped into the room. The sight that greeted her confirmed her worst suspicions.

34

The wooden lighthouse tower stood stark against a frigid sky layered with early-morning cloud that had yet to decide to stay or go. Below it, on the Beach Shack porch, Hannah looked out across the bay, wondering if she should close the shutters and prepare for one of those springtime storms that rolled in from the Atlantic Ocean and raged across the entire eastern seaboard. The wind had freshened even in the hour she'd been on the beach with Sylkie, who was looking up at her as if to say, *it's coming*.

Back inside, shutters closed, she was busy making breakfast when Sylkie began barking. Hannah looked towards the door, wondering if someone had knocked. She hadn't anything. Then again, the aria, *Un Bel di Vedremo*, from Puccini's great opera, *Madame Butterfly*, was blasting out of the radio on the kitchen worktop. She took the frying pan off the stove and turned the radio down a touch before opening the door.

'Claudia! How lovely to see you.'

'It is? I wasn't sure,' said Claudia, suddenly feeling a bit abashed. 'Hello Sylkie.'

She bent down and ruffled Sylkie's ears, sending the little terrier into a frenzy, licking at her hands and wagging her tail as if greeting an old and much-loved friend.

'Of course, it is, my dear,' said Hannah, taking Claudia's hands in hers. She could see she was upset. 'I was just fixing breakfast. Have you eaten? I'm guessing not. It's only eight-thirty. You must have left Lexington when it was still dark to get down here so early.'

'You're sure it's not an inconvenience?'

'Not at all. Now, come in out of that wind, it's getting blowier by the minute.'

Hannah ushered Claudia inside, taking her windcheater and hanging it on one of the cast-iron coat hooks fixed to the back of the door.

The kitchen was bright and airy and smelt of fresh-baked bread and coffee. The walls were bare wood planking, the colour of sand, although the back wall was made up of built-in shelves, partially screened off with vibrant orange, batik sheets, rather than doors. A square table and four matching chairs, formed from bleached driftwood, dominated the centre of the room. The Beach Shack was as laid back as Claudia had expected it to be. More importantly, it was warm, welcoming and homely.

'What brings you here again so soon?' Hannah asked. 'Not that I'm not happy to see you, but I'm guessing something's upset you rather than it being just a social visit.'

'That obvious?'

'Just a bit.'

'Honestly, Hannah, I'm not even sure how I got here. I just got in the car because I needed to get out of the house. Somehow it drove me down here.'

Hannah gave Claudia a smile that wasn't fully returned. Her sadness was like a shawl that needed to be taken off and hung, with her windcheater, on the back of the kitchen door.

'What a clever car. Well, now that you *are* here, what say I make us both some breakfast and we can have a chat.'

'I'm not really hungry,' replied Claudia.

Her answer was largely ignored by Hannah, who proceeded to cheerfully inform her of what was on the menu.

'I've got a fresh-baked loaf in the oven and a pot of coffee on the stove. I'm doing crispy bacon and over-easy eggs. You can eat, or not, but I'll be mortally offended if you don't.'

Claudia tried for a smile. Hannah could tell it was forced. She carried on trying to cheer her up, undaunted.

'Thanks, Hannah. I think you're just what I needed.'

'Good. And after breakfast we can go for a walk up to the Point. You can tell me everything. What do you say?'

A real smile crept onto Claudia's face and she felt the sadness start to lift.

'How can I refuse such a great offer?'

'You can't,' said Hannah, ushering her towards the kitchen table, 'now, sit down, relax, and enjoy the music. Chat to me or not, it's up to you. Milk in your coffee? Or do you prefer cream?'

'Cream, please,' replied Claudia, taking a seat. 'I think I'd rather talk *after* breakfast, if that's okay? I've had so much running around in my head for the past twenty-four hours I'm not sure I know where to start.'

'Suits me,' replied Hannah, edging the volume button on the radio up a smidge, 'I'm enjoying the music anyway. Puccini is such a wonderful storyteller. Always sad, but in a good way.'

'Can't say I know him, to be honest,' replied Claudia. 'I've never really been a fan. Actually, that's not true. I've just never had the chance to *become* a fan.'

'Listen and learn then, my dear. This is one of his best. *Madame Butterfly*, no less.'

Hannah made breakfast, slicing the bread, straight from the oven, into unladylike slices, lathering them with butter and piling them high with fried eggs and smoky-bacon. Claudia found herself salivating at the glorious smell. It turned out she was hungry after all. They ate in quiet contemplation, listening to the music.

'That was wonderful,' said Claudia, polishing off the last mouthful then draining her glass of freshly squeezed orange juice. 'I think I'll need to walk a bit further than the Point to work that off. Thank you, Hannah. So much.'

'My pleasure. I have no fear of calories or cholesterol, for obvious reasons.'

'Hannah! Don't say that.'

'Why not? It's true. I'm not going to lie to myself about how much time I've got left. And I'm going to enjoy everything, no matter how bad it is for me, right up to the end. You, on the other hand, will definitely need to work it off.'

Claudia scowled in mock indignation and ran a hand over her stomach.

'Agreed.'

Hannah stood and began to clear away the breakfast things.

'Right, let's get the washing-up done and then we'll walk. Wash or dry?'

'I'll dry,' said Claudia, helping her, your skin's already old and wrinkly.'

'*Touché*,' replied Hannah, and laughed, helping Claudia's mood climb fully out of the dark place it had been trapped in since the previous evening.

Twenty minutes later, they were walking along the beach, arms linked, jackets zipped, wearing woolly hat's that Hannah had ferreted out of a blanket box set beside the kitchen door. The bay had turned seaweed-green and the sky darkened to a hue of smelted iron, as if some impending war between them was brewing, the rising waves rolling onto the beach like refugees trying to escape the coming battle. Claudia shivered. More of apprehension than of cold.

'Can you feel it?' Hannah asked.

'I've got goose-bumps,' replied Claudia, 'and the hairs on the back of my neck are standing up.'

Hannah wiggled her fingers and rubbed her hands together.

'My hands are getting stiff and achy and my body's all tingly. It always happens when there's a storm coming in.'

'It's that sixth sense we have,' said Claudia. 'That feeling you get deep down inside you. It chills you but thrills you at the same time.'

'That's because we're all connected to the earth, my dear. It's how our ancestors were. Although they were so much more attuned to their environment than we are now. It's the voice of the Universe. We can still hear it, even if it's a distant echo of times long gone. But it still guides us, I believe that for sure.'

Claudia nodded.

'You're right. And I think I need to listen to it more.'

Hannah decided it was the perfect point to continue the conversation they started at the beginning of their walk.

'So, you went to the apartment and found it empty. Surely that was a relief?'

Claudia took a deep breath, preparing herself, mentally, to recount what had happened the previous evening, when she'd reached the apartment.

'It was. I guess, but the bed was unmade and the lights were left on. It had definitely been slept in.'

'By one or two people.'

Claudia shrugged

'Who knows? I'd gotten myself so worked up I didn't really notice. I just turned and left. I forgot to check the sheets and the pillows. All the evidence a detective would look for at a crime scene.'

'But *was* it a crime scene?'

'I'm not sure, Hannah. I'm really not. The point is, Paul had been there, and he'd hidden that fact from me. Why would he do that? The only reason that makes any sense is because he had a woman with him.

'It doesn't mean he did.'

Claudia fell silent, so Hannah left it.

They meandered along the sand, moving up to the path leading through the dunes to avoid the waves that were breaking further and further up the beach. Claudia recounted what had transpired between her and Paul over the past few days; his conversation with Isabella, his desire to move to Los Angeles, and that his main focus in life was no longer on having a child.

'Maybe I should just forget about having a baby.'

Claudia's voice was filled with a sadness Hannah couldn't miss.

'What is the voice of the Universe telling you to do, my dear? The one you say you need to listen to more closely.'

Claudia thought on it for a moment before answering.

'I think it's telling me to figure out what the hell I want from the rest of my life. To go and find it instead of moping around. I've never felt so adrift and alone, Hannah, not ever.' She took hold of Hannah's hand and stopped to face her. 'Apart from having you, that is. I know we hardly know each other, but, no matter how weird it sounds, I feel connected to you in a way I've never felt before.'

Hannah smiled and gave Claudia a hug that left her feeling teary.

'We are connected, my dear. Much more than you know. We can both thank the Universe for that.'

'I do,' said Claudia, wondering, not only at Hannah's words, but the strange tone of her voice.

Hannah tucked the crook of her arm into Claudia's and they walked on.

'I know how you feel, though,' said Hannah, 'about being adrift. I was there, myself, not so long ago. Just after Jonathon died. And once before that. A time when I felt more alone in the world than I'd ever been. When everyone, including God, it seemed, had abandoned me.'

Claudia looked at her, tilting her head, asking without asking, but Hannah didn't explain further.

They had almost reached the Point, where the pathway re-joined the beach and the high cliff, on their right-hand side, ran down across the sand to meet the ocean. Hannah led them towards the cliff, following a narrow, shingle track that ended abruptly at a rounded rise of black granite. She clambered up and over the boulder, sliding down the other side of it so that only her head was visible, then took a step to her right, disappearing.

'Hannah, where did you . . .'

Hannah stepped back out from behind a vertical shear of rock that stood slightly proud of the cliff face; a hidden cleft in the cliff face parallel to but hidden from the shingle path they'd just walked along.

'Still here, my dear. Now, climb over and follow me. I want to show you something.'

Claudia clamoured over the bulge of granite and followed Hannah into the narrow passageway. It was as if one part of the entire cliff had sheared away, forming an open seam that ran deep inside. She looked above her and realised the cliff face angled out over them, hiding the passage from anyone looking down on it from the clifftop above.

'Wow, this is cool, Hannah. You'd never guess it was here.'

'Jonathon found it, years ago, quite by accident. It's the only way up to the clifftop. We never allowed anyone to come here before. It's a very private and personal place. But there's something you need to see.'

At the end of the passageway they climbed a set of naturally formed steps which opened out onto a flat, grassy bluff, overlooking the beach, almost a hundred feet below. It resembled the pointed hull of a ship, sailing out into the open ocean ahead of it. Claudia followed Hannah onto the grass.

'This is amazing. What a cool place to come and hang out. You've even got a bench to sit and look out from. That must have been difficult to get up here.'

'Jonathon brought the materials up and built it himself.'

Claudia noticed Hannah had a faraway look on her face. A mix of sad and happy.

'Hannah, I'm so sorry. I'm acting like a kid in a sweet shop, not thinking about what this place means to you.'

Hannah shook her head and gave Claudia a thin smile.

'It's fine. You're acting like I did the first time Jonathon brought me up here. I'm glad I can finally share it with someone else. Someone who'll understand this place for what it is. It's one of the most special places to me in the whole world.'

'It's a wonderful thing to have . . .'

Claudia started to speak, but Hannah shook her head, silencing her.

'You said, earlier, my dear, that you felt alone and adrift. I told you I knew the feeling well. That I'd felt the same way, twice in my life.'

'When Jonathon died,' whispered Claudia, sensing she was about to find out something deeply personal.

'Yes. When Jonathon died. That was the second time. But there was a time before that. Many years before. The worst time of my life, in fact. A time when I felt like a boat adrift in a stormy sea, being rocked so violently that at any moment I might be swamped and the boat would sink. The waves were so high I couldn't see any sight of land, or find a light to guide me to safety. I could see only darkness. Hear nothing but the ceaseless rage of the wind. I called for someone to help me, but I was alone in an ocean of despair. Forever would be, or so I thought.'

'What changed?' Claudia asked, captivated by Hannah's story, hearing the pain still carried in her voice.

Hannah, after a few moments, continued.

'The boat wasn't swamped. And I didn't drown. In time, the wind stopped screaming and waves began to settle, rising lower, each day, until the ocean around me was calm and flat. And then I discovered something wonderful.'

Claudia was no longer aware of anything but the sound of Hannah's voice, as if her story had calmed the growing storm and only *they* existed in the whole of the world.

'Tell me, Hannah.'

'I discovered I wasn't alone. All around me, as far as I could see, were hundreds of other little boats, all with someone sitting in them. People just like me, looking at the boats that had become visible to them, all of them realising they had never been alone, only that the waves had been too high to allow them to see each another, and the wind too loud to hear their cries for help. They were never alone and adrift at all. Someone was always with them. They just had to wait for the storm to be over and the waves to fall to find that out. I came out of the storm to find Jonathon waiting for me. As he had been all along.'

Claudia's eyes filled with tears.

'That's so beautiful, Hannah. It makes me sad for you but lifts my heart at the same time.'

'Come. There's something you need to see.'

Hannah took hold of Claudia's hand and led her across the grass to the bench sitting at the point of the clifftop. There was a flat stone set into the ground in front of it with some words carved into it. Claudia looked down and read them.

"Betsy Claudia Thomas. Born 27th March 1974. Passed into the arms of Jesus the same day."

'We buried her here,' said Hannah, quietly, kneeling beside the stone, 'so she would always be close to us.'

'Your daughter?' Claudia whispered, knowing instinctively it was.

Hannah nodded and ran her fingertips across the name carved into the stone memory.

'Our little angel. Hello, Betsy, momma's here again. I've brought a friend to meet you.'

Claudia fell silent, overcome with emotion at hearing the love Hannah so obviously still felt for her daughter. She laid a hand on her shoulder, offering some comfort.

'Oh, Hannah, I'm so very sorry.'

Hannah was silent for a few moments. Claudia did not interrupt the silence. She almost felt as if she should walk away, giving her the privacy she felt the moment deserved. But something made her stay. Finally, Hannah spoke.

'It's funny, you know. No matter it's over forty years ago, I still miss her. I think about her every day. I got to hold her for a while before she passed. She was so perfect. Ten little fingers and ten tiny toes. A button nose and tiny pink lips that looked like the most delicate rose petals you've ever seen. I've always remembered her face.'

'That's why you acted so surprised when I told you my name,' said Claudia, fighting back her tears, 'when we met on the beach. I share hers.'

Hannah, still kneeling, lifted a hand to her shoulder, touching Claudia's fingers.

'Yes, my dear, you do. It was as if the Universe had sent you to me. I'd come to see Betsy, to tell her I'd soon be with her, when I saw you on the beach. I was drawn to you, despite I didn't know why. You listened to the Universe, too, that morning. It drew you to the lighthouse for no reason you could understand. We were both of us guided to each other, neither of us knowing why.'

No matter how it sounded, Claudia knew it was true.

'Do you think we ever will?'

'Perhaps one day, my dear. But it's out of our control. We may dance, knowing the steps to take, but it's always the Universe that calls the tune.'

They were both silent for a few moments, Hannah kneeling beside her daughter's grave, Claudia looking out over the ocean in silent contemplation.

'What happened, Hannah? Can you talk about it?'

Hannah stood and turned to look back at the lightkeeper's house. The old building was still and sombre, as if ashamed of its part in the coming story.

'She was born over there. In the big house.'

Claudia finally understood why the house was empty and neglected.

'That's why you don't live there! Why you and Jonathon moved down to the Beach Shack.'

Hannah looked away from the house, as if the seeing of it reminded her of the ghosts that still haunted it.

'I couldn't be there. Not afterwards. I haven't been inside since. I never will. It was a lovely home, for a while, but it's not a home any longer. Perhaps it will be, again, one day, for another family.'

'I understand, Hannah. I really do. And I'm so glad you've shared this with me. It's such a deeply personal thing.'

Hannah turned to face Claudia, taking hold of her hands, her expression deadly serious.

'There's a reason I did, my dear, and you need to listen and understand it, even if you don't at first believe it. You were ***always*** meant to be right here. It was already written in the stars. I think one of the reasons the Universe brought us together was for you to know about Betsy. Bringing you here, in a sense, answers the question you've been asking yourself.'

Claudia looked at Hannah, blankly, not picking up on her meaning.

'What question?'

'You asked me if it was worth it, having a child?'

Claudia remembered. She'd asked it, not half an hour ago, while they'd been walking along the beach.

'Well, was it, Hannah? Was it really worth it? For the pain you've suffered in losing her.'

Hannah stared into Claudia's eyes, a fierceness blazing in her own.

'I had my child, Claudia. I held her in my arms and talked to her for an hour before she left me. It was the most important hour of my life. Betsy saw me and I saw her. We were together, mother and daughter. I would give *anything* for one more minute with her. Just one! Long enough to tell her that she has always been loved. That she is with me, in my heart and soul, every moment of every day. That she will remain there for the rest of my life, until I hold her in my arms once more.'

'Oh, Hannah.'

Claudia could feel the depth of Hannah's loss. It was palpable, visceral and raw. But she was smiling, as if, even in the pain of the memory, there was some greater comfort.

'You ask if it's worth it, Claudia. Having a child? It is!'

35

By the time they'd passed the lighthouse and walked down the steps to the Beach Shack, the wind was whipping the sand across the beach so hard it stung the exposed skin on their hands and faces. Arm in arm, shielding their eyes from the grainy storm, they stumbled the last few paces towards sanctuary. Behind them, the pounding waves, crashing onto the beach, seemed like the incessant roar of some demented sea monster. They tumbled through the front door and Hannah leant against it to force it shut. Suddenly, a massive burst of thunder that seemed to come from directly above them, exploded, making them both jump.

'Jesus Christ,' cried Claudia.

'I didn't know you were religious, my dear.'

'I'm not. But I'm willing to rethink.'

They stared at each other, wide-eyed at the suddenness and severity of the thunderclap, then burst out laughing, a laugh that left them both gasping for air, tears streaming down their cheeks. Sylkie's tail was going ten to the dozen, confused at their strange behaviour but happy to see them returned.

'That was as loud a thunder burst as I've ever heard,' said Hannah, divesting herself of her hat, scarf and gloves, as did Claudia, putting them back in the wooden box by the kitchen door.

Outside, the sound of the storm was louder than ever.

'I'm glad we headed back when we did,' said Claudia, 'it's gotten mad out there, all of a sudden.'

'It's how it happens, here,' said Hannah. 'I did warn you.'

'You did, I remember.'

'Well you're going nowhere, my dear, even if you had planned on getting back to Lexington.'

'I'll have to leave at some point,' said Claudia, not really caring to think about it.

'You don't. Not really. There's a spare bedroom. You're more than welcome to stay. Now, more importantly, let's get the kettle on.'

Claudia wanted to stay more than anything. The thought of driving back to a large, empty house was less than appealing.

'I wouldn't want to impose,' she said, hoping she wasn't being convincing.'

'Claudia! Don't be silly! I'd appreciate the company. Look, it's almost one o'clock. Let's check the forecast and see what it's saying. But I think tea and scones are required, first, if you fancy.'

Claudia thought it over for a split second then nodded her approval.

'I really shouldn't. But why not?'

'Okay, you make the tea. The kettle's on the stove. Teapot and cups on the shelves at the back. There's half a dozen fresh scones in the bread-bin. Just pop them in the oven to heat them up a bit. There's butter, jam and cream in the fridge. I'll switch on the radio and we'll see what's what.'

'It might be on the weather channel.'

'It probably is, my dear, and if I had a television set that would be a good idea.'

'You have no television?'

Claudia looked like a teenager who'd had their phone taken away from them. Hannah looked back at her like a parent who couldn't see the problem.

'It broke, last year. Or the year before. I can't honestly remember. I didn't replace it, or even miss it. Besides, I have my faithful old transistor radio to listen to my classical music, and a shortwave radio-set to call the coastguard, when I need to.'

'What more could you need, I guess,' said Claudia, still struggling to believe Hannah lived without a television.

Hannah switched on the kitchen radio and the sound of a piano filled the room, making it a much cosier than an interfering television set would have, Claudia conceded. Hannah conducted the music with her fingers, waving them in the air at the invisible orchestra she pictured.

'Mozart's piano concerto number two, if I'm not mistaken.'

Claudia smiled and shrugged her shoulders, pleased to see her happy after the sombre mood they had both been in on the way back from the Point.

'I wouldn't know. I like classical music, but I rarely know who wrote it or what it's called.'

Hannah looked over to the imaginary violin section, waving her fingers at them to slow them down a touch.

'Jonathon and I loved our classical music. It stirs the blood and feeds the soul. Now, talking about feeding, get the scones into the oven. You'll find plates and cutlery easily enough. Just act like it's your own place. We'll eat through in the snug, in front of the fire. I'll get a few logs on and we'll be like proverbial bugs in no time.'

'The *snug,*' said Claudia, looking through the open doorway leading from the kitchen into a small but cosy looking living room, 'it so suits its name.'

A pair of matching two-seater couches, separated by a low, wooden table, waited for them in front of a large, stone-built fireplace. The fire seemed dead, but a glow of orange showed it was still breathing. Hannah wandered through and added some logs from a stack piled against the wall. The window shutters were closed, but, after switching on a couple of lamps, the glow from the rekindled fire and the lamplight gave the room a soft, amber glow, making them feel even more sheltered from the storm.

'Tell me about the Camino,' said Claudia, licking her fingers, before tucking into her second jam and cream smothered piece of scone. 'These are delicious,' she tried to say, spluttering as a crumb went down the wrong way.

'I can see that,' said Hannah, 'but I thought you were just having one.'

'I didn't want to be rude. Besides, there were two on each plate.'

Hannah laughed at her.

'May I remind you it was you that put them there.'

'Oh, of course,' replied Claudia, 'I forgot.'

Hannah gave her a look that said, *really?* She was, though, pleased to see her looking happier than she'd been when she'd first arrived.

'Eat away, my dear. I enjoyed breakfast, but my appetite comes and goes. I still love to bake, so it's nice to see someone enjoying the fruits of my labour.'

'I'll do my best,' said Claudia, preparing the remaining half of her scone. Probably be better if it was fruit.'

'Do you want to hear about the Camino De Santiago?' Hannah asked.

Claudia looked up from her plate, an excited gleam in her eyes.

'Absolutely! I've been thinking about it ever since you spoke of it. I even looked it up on the internet. It's got quite the history.'

'Well,' said Hannah, setting her teacup down on the table and settling back into her couch, 'the Camino, which means *path*, in Spanish, dates back to the eighth century, when the remains of St James the Apostle were discovered in northern Spain.'

'St James. Wasn't he beheaded by King Herod?'

'Apparently,' said Hannah, 'and his remains found their way back to the province of Galicia, where he preached the gospel after the death of Christ.'

'You know your Camino, Hannah.'

'Well, when you walk almost eight hundred kilometres, passing through the whole of northern Spain, you learn a bit about it.'

Claudia pictured flower-strewn fields and gently-rising mountains beneath a warm summer sun.

'It sounds wonderful. And terribly romantic.'

'Yes, it does, but, believe me, it's bloody hard going. Your feet pay the price, especially in the beginning. Twenty kilometres, or more, every day, for over a month, is hard work.

'Wow, that's pretty hard going for anyone,' said Claudia. Seeing Hannah frown, she apologised. 'Sorry, I'm interrupting again.'

Hannah's frown turned upside down and she carried on with her story.

'During the Middle Ages, the Camino was responsible for the largest movement of people in Europe. Rich and poor making their way to the cathedral of Santiago de Compostela, where the pilgrim mass and the certificate of pilgrimage would ensure less time spent in purgatory.

'The scary Catholic Church,' said Claudia, 'always wanting a price to be paid. I'd rather follow the stars.'

Hannah gave her a knowing smile.

'Interestingly enough, it does. It's thought the ancient route followed the Milky Way.'

'That's cool, Hannah. Religion *and* the Universe. I think I like it more, now. I'm not a believer in God, as you can probably already tell.'

Hannah shrugged.

'You don't have to be, for good things to happen, my dear. Anyway, it fell out of fashion towards the end of the Middle Ages. The first person to do it in modern times was Father Elias Valina, the priest of a Galician village called Cebreiro, who marked out the ancient route with the symbol of a yellow scallop shell on a blue background, thus allowing modern day pilgrims to find their way.'

'So, you started in St Jean Pied de Port? In France?'

'I did,' said Hannah, proudly, 'then climbed over the Pyrenees and down into Spain.'

Claudia refilled her cup and ate the remaining bits of scone lying on her plate, then sank back into her couch. She was loving spending the day with Hannah and hearing about the Camino. She wanted to hear more.

'Where was the most beautiful place you visited?

Hannah looked skyward, pulling in pictures.

'Oh my, what a question. Well, I loved St Jean, where the Camino begins, it's such a pretty town and everyone is a pilgrim, so it seems. It's got such an air of excitement about it, everyone waiting to begin their trek. I loved Puenta de Orbigo, for its amazing Roman bridge and the story of the knight who lived there and fought three hundred jousts in the name of the woman he loved. Then again, the architecture of Leon was incredible, especially the stained glass in its cathedral. Santiago, itself, was amazing. Arriving there was highly emotional, for everyone, after making the journey of their lives. Of course, placing some of Jonathon's ashes at Finisterre was one of those special moments. I finally let him go, there, by the sea. But I promised I'd come back, one day, to join him.'

'It sounds wonderful, Hannah. I'd really love to do it myself.'

Claudia stared into the fire, imagining what such a journey might be like.

'Perhaps, my dear, you will.'

'Maybe,' said, Claudia, ruefully. 'If someday ever comes.'

The clock on the wall struck four, almost at the same time as another boom of thunder shook the house. Claudia stood and walked to the window, peeking out through a gap in the shutters to see how bad the storm.

'I take it it's still as bad?' Hannah asked, as Claudia gave a shiver.

'Worse, if anything, but it still might pass.'

Hannah looked doubtful.

'I'll go check with the coastguard again. See what they say.'

'Okay,' said Claudia, I'll stick a few more logs on the fire while you do.'

Hannah went through to her bedroom. Claudia could hear her speaking to someone on the short-wave radio set, although she couldn't make out what they were saying to each other.

'It looks like you *have* to stay now,' said Hannah, coming back into the snug. 'The coastguard says it's on for the duration. He advised against travelling anywhere up the coastline. There's trees down and traffic accidents all over the place. So, that's that! The spare room's already made up. You can keep me company.'

'Are you sure, Hannah? I feel I've kind of pushed myself upon you today, uninvited.'

'Claudia! Seriously! You can come here anytime you want to. Anyway, listen to it. Do you really think I'm going to let you go out there in that? No, it's settled, you're staying with me.'

'Fine with me,' said Claudia, tossing another log on the fire. 'I'd be at home by myself anyway. No one's expecting me. Oh, God, that sounded pathetic.'

She laughed at herself.

'Just a bit,' replied Hannah, laughing with her.

Suddenly, Hannah fell forward, leaning against the back of the couch with one hand, the other shooting to the centre of her chest. It looked as if she was having a heart attack. Claudia rushed to her aid, placing a steadying arm around her shoulders. Hannah was moaning with each laboured draw of breath.

'Hannah, what is it?'

'It . . . it's fine. Give me a moment.'

Her words were forced. She was clearly in severe pain. Claudia rubbed her back, trying to help, not knowing how to.

'What can I do?'

Hannah looked towards the kitchen doorway.

'My pills. They're in my bag. Two bottles. One from each.'

Claudia rushed through and grabbed the handbag. She found the pill bottles and took a pill from each, poured a glass of water, then headed back through to the snug.

'Here.'

Hannah swallow her pills. Slowly, her breathing returned to normal and her moans became quieter. Claudia helped her back onto her couch, unsure if she needed to call a doctor. Hannah looked up, giving her a reassuring smile that only half worked.

'Don't look so worried. I'm okay.'

Claudia, sitting on the edge of the table between the couches, took hold of Hannah's hands.

'You weren't a moment ago.'

'Well, I am now, so there's no need to fuss. Sit down, you're making *me* feel nervous.'

Claudia sat down on her couch, finding she was a bit shaky. The incident had scared her.

'How often does that happen?'

'Sometimes*.'

Hannah's reply was elusive, but Claudia was determined to get to the bottom of what had just happened.

'Every day?'

'Perhaps. Yes, it does seem to be getting that way.'

'You should be in hospital.'

'No!' Hannah said, firmly.

'But you're sick. It's obvious.'

'I'm not sick, Claudia. I'm dying. There's a bloody big difference.'

'But . . . surely they can make you more comfortable?'

Hannah was adamant in her reply.

'Where's more comfortable than my own home. And I'd not be able to visit Betsy.'

'But surely . . .'

Hannah sat forward, despite it was an effort, and stared straight at Claudia.

'I am not going into a hospital, Claudia. Not while I can still look after myself. Don't let's talk about it anymore. Or you can leave if you can't do that.'

Claudia was shocked at the tone of Hannah's voice.

'Do you want me to go?'

Hannah's voice softened as she replied.

'No, my dear, I don't, but I'm not going to hospital. I'm not leaving here. You just have to accept that.'

Claudia realised she was fighting a losing battle. Hannah was clearly fixed on the subject.

'Okay, Hannah, it's your call. I need to respect that, even if I don't agree with it.'

'Good. Now, pour me a whisky.'

Claudia was shocked at the request.

'But . . . you've just had your tablets.'

'And I'm fine, Claudia, really, but if I have to give up my afternoon whisky then I may as *well* be dead. It's in one of the shelves in the kitchen cupboard. A bottle of Glenmorangie. You'll find glasses in . . .'

'In the back cupboard,' said Claudia, 'behind the crazy lady's hippie, batik curtains'

'Yes,' said Hannah. She looked up at Claudia and gave her a thin but welcome smile. 'And the crazy lady would like a three-finger slug with a few drops of water. Have one yourself. You still look like you've seen a ghost.'

'You scared me half to death.'

'One of these days I'll scare myself fully to death,' said Hannah, 'until then, I shall live how I like, and like how I live.'

Back on their respective couches, they sat quietly, listening to the strains of Elgar coming from the kitchen radio, enjoying the warmth of the fire and the taste of the whisky. Hannah hadn't spoken more about what had happened. Claudia decided it would serve no purpose to try to get her to talk about it further. Instead, she asked about the whisky that, despite thinking she wouldn't like, she was loving.

'This is Scottish whisky, right?'

Hannah held her glass up to the fireplace, enjoying the golden dance of the flames behind the whisky.

'It is. All the way from the east coast of the Scottish Highlands.'

'So, why the love of this whisky, Glenmorangie?'

Claudia pronounced it, *glen-more-**a**ngie*, making Hannah wince.

'To begin with, my dear, as any Scotsman would be at pains to point out, it's pronounced *glen-morrange-ee*, so if you ever meet one, remember that, it might well save your life. They take their whiskies very seriously, so I'm told. Just remember there's a *glen* at the beginning with an *orange* in the middle and a *gee*, like in gee-whizz, at the end. Just run the three syllables into one another and you have it.'

'I'll try to remember that,' said Claudia, 'not that I expect to be meeting one any time soon.'

Hannah raised her glass above her head and looked up.

'Don't let the Universe hear you say that.'

'Plot away, Universe.' Claudia raised her own glass in salute, before taking another sip. The whisky warmed her as she swallowed, leaving the subtle taste of lemon-zest and vanilla-cream, combined with delicate hints of ginger and nutmeg, on her tongue. 'This is bloody good, though. Who knew?'

They sat quietly for a few minutes, savouring the whisky, listening to the rain hammering on the roof of the cottage and the relentless howl of the wind.

'Anyway,' said Hannah, 'to answer your question about why *this* whisky, Jonathon introduced me to it after he'd come back from Vietnam. He had a friend who went by the not very subtle moniker of *Scotty* who introduced Jonathon to it and he developed a taste for it. He passed his love for it onto me when he returned. So, I sit and sip this, every evening, remembering the nights we supped it together.'

'What a lovely memory.'

'It is indeed. I do miss those nights.'

Despite knowing it was pointless trying to get Hannah to speak about her cancer and how she had decided to deal with it, Claudia couldn't help feeling concerned about her. She decided she was going to help in any way she could.

'Can I talk to you, Hannah? Seriously?'

'Only as long as it's not about me being ill. I want to be happy for as long as I can.'

'It's more practical than anything else.'

'Fire away then.'

'Don't you have any other family around, anywhere? I'm worried about you being here on your own. I understand you want to be here and not in some sterile hospital. If the situation was reversed, I'd probably feel the same.'

Hannah shook her head.

'There's just me. I was an only child, you see. As were both my mother and father.'

'So, you really are alone?'

'I've got Sylkie.'

Hannah reached across and patted the little dog's head. She'd jumped up onto the couch after her episode, as if knowing her mistress was in pain and wanted to be near her.

'And you have me,' Claudia added.

'Thank you, my dear, but I don't want to be a burden on anyone. Especially not you.'

'Too late for that, you already are. And you're not getting rid of me, so don't bother trying.'

Hannah held her hands up in submission.

'I'm not going to.'

'Good! Because I'm going to help you any way I can. By being here as much as you want. Don't fight me on this, Hannah. Okay?'

Hannah could see the determined look in Claudia's eyes.

'Okay.'

'Now, I've been thinking about how best to help, while we've been sitting here.'

Hannah gave a pretend shiver.

'Sounds ominous.'

Claudia ignored the jest and carried on.

'Paul's away for the next month. It's not like I *have* to work. I want to help out. So, if there's anything I can do, anything at all, just ask. I mean it. Anything.'

'Well . . .'

Hannah hesitated. There was clearly something on her mind.

'What is it, Hannah? Tell me. I said anything and I meant it.'

'Well, I've been putting off thinking about what needs to be done before I leave. And stop looking so sad when I say that, Claudia. I need to be practical. If you really *do* want to help me, you need to pull yourself together and accept what's happening to me.'

Claudia knew she'd just been told off. She took a deep breath.

'You're right. I'm not going to be any use to you if I can't even talk about it. Consider me firmly pulled together.'

'Excellent!' Hannah sat forward on the couch. Claudia could see the familiar sparkle had returned to her eyes. 'Now, amongst other things, I need to sell the property.'

'The whole thing?'

'Yes. I've no idea if I should sell it in one lot or split it up. But I absolutely will *not* sell the land at the Point. I want my ashes there, well, at least half of them, to be with Betsy.'

'I'm sure that can be arranged by your estate agent. It's your land, Hannah. How much do you think it's all worth?'

Hannah shook her head.

'I've no idea. We paid twenty-five thousand dollars for it, but that was in the sixties. We've worked on all three properties since then.'

Claudia was surprised at how little it had originally cost, but it had been almost fifty years ago, long before property prices had gone insane. She threw a figure out, based on nothing concrete, but one that she felt Hannah could realistically achieve.

'It's got to be worth a million, at the very least. Perhaps more. You need to get a valuation done and to speak to a real estate agent on the best way to sell it.'

'I know. I just haven't felt like bothering, having no one to pass it on to. But I don't want the government to take it, so selling really seems the only way to stop that. I thought I'd use the money to provide a home for Sylkie for the rest of her natural life. Perhaps pay someone to keep the land around the Point safe and maintained.'

'Good idea,' said Claudia, 'we can surely find someone to do that easily enough. A local, maybe, from Duxbury. Right, what's next on the list.'

'Well,' said Hannah, warming to the task, 'there's a lot of Jonathon's furniture stored up in the lighthouse. A ton more up in the big house. It all needs to find a home.'

'But to where?' Claudia asked. 'That's the problem.'

Hannah looked at her as if she should have given her the answer, not asked another question.

'No idea, my dear. Have you any bright ideas?'

Claudia began brainstorming. She could only find one that made any sense.

'What about selling it? Jonathon must have had a list of shops that he sold to?'

'I suppose so,' said Hannah, 'but it's been a few years since he sold anything. After he got sick, it just wasn't something he could have done, even if he'd wanted to. But you're right, I guess they might. If we can find his old records. They'll most likely be somewhere in his workshop, up in the lighthouse.'

'Okay, that's the second thing taken care of.'

'I love your enthusiasm, my dear.'

'Anything else?' Claudia asked, hoping there wasn't.

Hannah looked at her, sheepishly, almost as if she was afraid to tell her there was.

'Well, as well as his furniture in the lighthouse ground floor, there's his workbenches, tools, motorbike, two cars and a heap of other stuff he collected over the years. It's lying around, everywhere, including the lighthouse basement.'

'There's a basement in the lighthouse?'

'Under the ground floor of the tower. Jonathon used to take goods in lieu of payment when he first started selling his furniture. There's all sorts of collectables hidden down there. It's the same size as the ground floor.'

'Wow.'

Claudia baulked at the thought there was more than twice what she had originally thought they would have to get rid of.

'And, of course,' Hannah added, 'last, but not least, I've got over a hundred paintings up in the Glass Menagerie. And some larger pieces stored up in the big house.'

'Anything else, Hannah? Can there be?'

'Just one more thing.'

'What's that?'

Claudia dreaded the reply, realising the job she had offered to undertake was growing legs. Hannah smiled a wry smile.

'Only my funeral.'

'Oh!'

Claudia felt herself welling up and tried to hold back the tears. Hannah could see she was upset.

'Don't cry, Claudia. You promised. You're no bloody use to me as a weeping mess.'

'I'm not going to cry, Hannah. I won't cry again. At least, not until after you leave. Is that okay?'

'Deal.'

'So,' said Claudia, trying to lighten her own mood, 'will you be having a Viking funeral.'

Hannah laughed.

'I was thinking more a sky burial. I've always wanted to go to the Himalayas to see Mount Everest. I love the thought of the vultures feeding on me then pooping me out over the mountains.'

'I'm not sure we can do that,' said Claudia, shuddering at the prospect, 'but all else is possible. How long have we got?'

'Eight weeks. Maybe ten.'

Despite her promise, a single tear ran down Claudia's cheek. She stood and moved around the table, taking a seat beside Hannah.

'It's just not bloody fair.'

'No, my dear, it's not.'

Hannah smiled but her eyes, too, were teary.

'But,' said Claudia, hating that she was perhaps making Hannah upset, knowing she had to be strong for them both, 'we're not going to sit here blubbing. We need to get started on that huge to-do list.'

Hannah nodded and wiped the tears that had sprung her by surprise away on a hanky she pulled from the sleeve of her cardigan.

'Honestly, I don't know where to even begin. I'm not sure I'm up to it either, physically or mentally.'

'That's why you're going to let me do it,' said Claudia, making the decision without even asking Hannah's opinion. 'I can stay with my sister, in Duxbury, and come here every day to help.'

'No! I don't want you to do that.'

Claudia couldn't hide the disappointment that Hannah was refusing her help.

'But, why not? I thought you said you wanted me to help.'

'I did, my dear, and I do. But I have one condition.'

'What?'

'Come and stay with me, here, at the Beach Shack. You can keep an eye on me as well as help me get everything done. Maybe just a few days a week, if you didn't want to be here all the time. Just think about it.'

'I have,' said Claudia, eagerly, 'and I'd love to. I'll go home in the morning and pack a few things to bring down, if that's okay?'

'Bring all you want,' said Hannah, clearly excited about the prospect. 'It'll be great to have company. But I don't want to impose on you. Don't feel you *have* to do this.'

'I'm not being kind, Hannah. I'm being selfish. I already love it here. It'll be more like a holiday.'

Hannah leaned forwards and picked up her glass of Glenmorangie, raising it to Claudia.

'Well, on that note, I formally welcome you to my humble home.'

Claudia reached for her own glass and clinked it against Hannah's.

As they'd been talking, the fire had died down and darkness had settled around the Beach Shack. The storm had eased, but still blew hard, and heavy rain continued to fall. Claudia threw a few more logs on the fire and the creeping shadows slunk back into the corners.

They talked until late, stopping only for Hannah to make a supper of cheese and tomato on home-made, sourdough toast, spread liberally with English mustard and washed down with cups of milky tea.

'Okay, I'm exhausted,' said Hannah, once she'd finished eating, 'let me show you to your bedroom.'

'I can see it from here,' said Claudia, looking at the side-by-side doors at the back of the snug.

'It's bigger than it looks. It's got an en-suite bathroom with an old cast iron bath-tub. It looks a bit old fashioned, but works fine.'

'I'll be more than okay, Hannah. Don't worry. I'm going to stay up, for a while, if that's okay.'

'It's more than okay, my dear.'

Hannah went through to the kitchen to let Sylkie out. Sylkie ventured out, slowly, looking back at Hannah as if to say, *don't forget about me,* and was back scratching at the door in minutes. She scampered back into the safety and warmth of the kitchen as soon as Hannah opened the door.

'Not liking the storm, Sylkie?'

Hannah peered out into the darkness. The clouds were doing their best to hide the glow from the moon, but it was bright enough to see the sea, black as oil, silver crests of surf exploding against the slate-grey sand. Sylkie, as if to agree, scampered through to the snug and jumped up onto the couch, straight into Claudia's lap.

'I think I've made a friend, Hannah.'

'I think she's welcoming you here.'

'Well,' said Claudia, tickling Sylkie's head, 'if truth be told, I'm glad I'm going to be staying'

'As long as you're . . .'

'Don't even say it, Hannah. It's a done deal.'

'Okay, my dear. I'll be happy to have you here. I'll head off to bed. I've had far too much excitement for one day.'

Hannah stood and headed towards her bedroom door, waving away Claudia's attempt to help her.

'Sleep well, Hannah.'

'You too.'

Later, Claudia fell asleep to the sound of the storm still raging outside her window, wondering why the Universe had placed her there, knowing that, irrespective of why, she would go with it. It felt right. Besides, there was simply no way she was going to abandon Hannah. She felt connected to her in a way she didn't really understand. *I hope I sleep.* It was her last thought before closing her eyes and floating away.

36

Claudia began rising earlier than she'd done in years. She and Hannah settled into a routine that started with a dawn walk along the beach, followed by breakfast, weather permitting, on the Beach Shack veranda. She lived in jeans, t-shirt and sneakers. Hannah continued to have her *episodes*, but they were infrequent. With her medication, which Claudia ensured she took as directed, she seemed able to deal with them. They grew closer, each day, their bond becoming more like mother and daughter than friends. Hannah gave her free reign to do as she thought best. Claudia threw herself into the tasks with a fervour she thought long-since lost.

They began their list of tasks by cataloguing Jonathon's furniture, Claudia using her iPad to create a spreadsheet of the inventory. Her first decision was to move the furniture stored in the lighthouse up to the lightkeeper's house; the "big house", as Hannah preferred to call it. She borrowed John and Caleb from the *Sans Cera* gallery to help move the heavier pieces. Hannah showed her a track that led from the car park, just below the lighthouse, up to the rear of the big house, which was why Claudia had decided to make it the store for everything. When the time came for Jonathon's furniture to be taken to the shops, it could be loaded directly into the van she would use to transport it.

Hannah was assigned to cataloguing her paintings, as well as Jonathon's smaller collectables stored in the ground floor and basement rooms of the lighthouse. She also started to spend more time in her studio, which Claudia encouraged her to do.

'You're working on *that* painting, aren't you?' Claudia asked, one evening, as they sipped a whisky in front of the fire.

'I am, if you must know. But don't you dare sneak a peek at it. Not until it's finished. Promise me.'

'I promise,' said Claudia, crossing her heart.

'I want it to be a surprise. It's a special painting, to me. I hope, one day, it will be as special to you.'

Claudia could see the mischievous look on Hannah's face as she said it.

'What do you mean?'

'Mañana.'

Hannah was giving nothing away. Claudia accepted she would just have to wait.

Two weeks later, sitting back into the couch of many colours, beside Hannah, in the middle of her almost empty studio, Claudia announced they had reached an important waypoint.

'Well, it's taken a lot of work, but that's the tower almost cleared. Do you want to hear the grand total of what you've got?'

Hannah gave a shiver of nervous anticipation.

'Having seen it all being moved, I feel like Jonathon and I were hoarders.'

'There's certainly more than I'd been expecting,' replied Claudia, taking a bite from one of the tuna mayonnaise sandwiches Hannah had prepared for lunch, 'but it's all beautiful stuff. I wish we didn't have to sell it.'

'I want you to take whatever you want, my dear. I've seen the way you look at the driftwood table and dining chairs. The one with the cast iron legs. They're yours, and I won't take no for an answer, so don't bother saying it.'

'I do covet those particular pieces,' said Claudia, pleased to be offered them. 'I'd like them for my own studio, to be honest. They'll fit in there perfectly, and they'll always remind me of my time at the lighthouse.'

'Good. It's nice to know a little bit of Jonathon and I will be with you every day. Now, tell me. What's the count?'

Claudia pulled up the spreadsheet on her iPad.

'There are forty-eight chairs and six dining tables, although one set is now mine, twelve bar-stools, eight lamp tables, four Adirondack seats, six coffee tables and two sideboards.'

'That's a lot of furniture,' said Hannah, 'I hope we can sell it.'

'Let me worry about that,' Claudia replied, with more confidence than she felt. 'Have you put together the list of shops Jonathon supplied?'

Hannah brandished a sheet of paper with the names and addresses of all the buyers Jonathon had worked with over the past thirty years.

'I've got it here.'

'Pencil and paper. Hannah, how terribly quaint.'

Hannah shrugged her shoulders and stuck her tongue out at Claudia before replying.

'Still works without a battery.'

'You're right,' Claudia conceded. 'Now, apart from the paintings and the furniture, there are six of Jonathon's wood-working machines. I called a friend of mine, from Lexington, Barry Gibson, who's coming to see them tomorrow. He has a construction business and a team of guys who build furniture and take on woodworking projects. I'm hoping he'll help us identify what the machines are, what they're worth, and where we night be able to sell them. Oh, and the real-estate guy you arranged to come will be here the day after tomorrow. We'll finally get some idea of what the place is worth.'

Hannah nodded, but looked neither happy or sad.

'I hate to think of it being carved up. But I guess it's how it has to be.'

Claudia shook her head in disagreement.

'Hannah, if you don't want to sell it then don't. It's entirely down to you. This is your home. You done *have* to do anything with it you don't want to.'

'No. It's fine, my dear, really. I'm just being sentimental. I won't be here for much longer, so there's no point me being stupid about it.'

Claudia stood and took hold of Hannah's hands.

'You're *not* being stupid. Don't even think that. This place has been your sanctuary for a very long time. It wouldn't be normal if you didn't feel like this.'

Hannah gazed out towards the Point, a melancholy look on her face. Claudia knew exactly what she was thinking.

'I guess so. But I'm keeping the part I want to keep. The only part that really matters to me. I hope you'll come visit me, there, from time to time?'

'You know I will,' whispered Claudia, 'you *and* Betsy. Now, before I get emotional, let me finish the list.'

'Right, what else is there?'

Claudia inspected her iPad and continued.

'There's twenty-two metal and ceramic signs, a host of other collectables, a motor bike, and Jonathon's old Volkswagen convertible, which I've managed to not look at yet, although only because you asked me not to. I don't know why you're being so secretive about it. Oh, and the Ford pick-up.'

Hannah blew a noiseless whistle.

'It sounds like an awful lot. What the heck will we do with it all?'

Claudia shrugged.

You're right, it is a lot, but I've called a company that specialises in collectables, Rare and Vintage, based in Boston, and they're coming to look at it all on Monday morning. I photographed everything and sent the pictures to them by email. Their owner offered to buy the entire stock there and then. I promised no-one else would see them before he did, so he was happy to wait. Phil Bannister, his name is. He's bringing a truck with him, so I'm fairly sure he wants to make a deal.'

'God, Claudia, I don't know what I'd have done without you.'

'I've had fun doing it, to be honest, Hannah. As well as just being here. It's really helped me start finding myself again. Finding my happy.'

'And what about Paul? Is he still part of your happy?'

Claudia looked slightly forlorn at the mention of her husband

'We've barely spoken, despite he'd said we'd talk more often after our anniversary weekend. He'll be back for the exhibition opening in a few weeks. We'll talk then. For now, we're both taking time out from each other. Perhaps it's for the best.'

It was Hannah's turn to take Claudia's hands. She pushed them together and kissed the top of her fingertips, as if a mother making a promise to her child.

'It'll work itself out, my dear, it always does. Perhaps this time apart *will* help you both.'

'I miss him, Hannah. That's a good sign, isn't it?'

Claudia looked as if she didn't know if it was or not.

'Of course,' replied Hannah, wondering if indeed it was.

'Okay, onto the last item,' said Claudia, busying herself to avoid thinking about Paul and her marriage.

'Which is?' Hannah asked, knowing not to pursue the conversation further.

'Your paintings. You have over one hundred canvasses. All finished works, all of them stunning.'

'You're flattering me, my dear.'

'Not at all. You're an amazing artist.'

'So many,' said Hannah. 'What am I going to do with them?'

Claudia smiled at her, impishly. Hannah could see the look on her face and wondered why.

'I've got a plan.'

'You do?'

'Yes.' Claudia replied, clearly itching to share it.

'Claudia! Tell me.'

'They're all going to one gallery.'

Claudia looked like the cat that got the cream, seeing the surprise on Hannah's face.

'One gallery? How? Where? What's it called?'

'It's in Lexington,' said Claudia. 'It's my gallery, *Sans Cera*.'

'Your gallery?'

Hannah looked upset. For a moment, Claudia thought she was angry with her.

'Just hear me out, Hannah. I know you probably think I'm doing this out of pity, but I'm not.'

'Are you sure, Claudia, I don't want . . .'

'No, Hannah, don't even think that. I've already sent some of the images of your paintings to Isabella. She's agrees they are exceptional. We've got a third floor that is currently empty. We'd already discussed introducing some new work alongside mine. It might take time to sell them all, but we have great footfall from all the visitors to the town, and your work is vastly different from mine, so there's no artistic conflict. So, if you agree, that's where they're going. What do you think?'

'I think you are an angel,' said Hannah, throwing her arms around Claudia and hugging her, her initial concerns swept away, 'a guardian angel.'

'So, you're happy for me to do this?'

'Of course, I am, my dear. It's perfect. But your gallery has a reputation to think about. Are you certain they're good enough?'

'Hannah, really! I'm doing it because I love your work. Anyway, I'm going to charge you a huge commission on each sale. At least twenty dollars.'

'Steep, but I accept,' said Hannah, laughing gaily. 'But, seriously, I'll agree only if you take whatever percentage from them you need to cover your costs. As well as your normal profit.'

'We'll do it at the standard rates of any other gallery, if that makes you happy?'

'It does. So, I'll agree.'

Claudia clapped her hands together, pleased her idea had been so well received.

'Perfect. I'll get one of our vans down next week. We can take them all up in one go. You'll need to come and see them when they're hung.'

The look on Hannah's face was almost childlike, filling Claudia with as much joy.

'How exciting. I just wish Jonathon could have be there to see them with me. He always said I should have my own showing. I never thought I would.'

'I'm excited for you, Hannah. I really am!'

The next week was busier than they could have imagined. Hannah's paintings were sent up to *Sans Cera*. The feedback from Isabella and Charity had been better than Claudia could have hoped for.

'The woman is gifted,' said Isabella, when Claudia had called. 'I think, if you'll agree, we'll show them as a second exhibition, the week after yours.'

Claudia agreed wholeheartedly.

Phil Bannister, the owner of Rare and Vintage Collectables, almost passed out when he'd gone through the shop signage and other bits and pieces Jonathon had amassed over the years. He agreed a sum of thirty-thousand dollars for everything, loading and transporting the lot to their new home, in Boston, that same day.

'I thought it was all just junk,' said Hannah, when Claudia handed her the cheque. 'Jonathon would have said, *I told you so*, if he could have been here to see this.'

'He *is* here, Hannah. I'm sure of it.'

'And laughing at me, no doubt.'

The following day, Barry Gibson arrived to review the workbenches and machinery. Everything was in excellent order, he told Claudia, old but sought-after pieces of branded equipment from a time when America had made its own tools. He offered a price Claudia thought high, but was happy to take. He also purchased the old motorbike and Ford pick-up, loading both onto a trailer attached to his own pick-up truck, while his workmen loaded the equipment into their van. Hannah took a walk up to the Point, unable to watch another part of Jonathon being taken away from her.

'It's like watching a life you created, over decades, being dismantled in just a few hours,' she explained to Claudia, later that evening.

Claudia understood perfectly but could offer no comfort, other than to be there to talk to, if needed.

The realtor from Chamberlain and Belloite, one of Boston's premier real estate companies, came by, two days later. The young man who represented them introduced himself as Kenneth Chamberlain, a partner in the firm. Both Hannah and Claudia wondered how someone still in his twenties had risen to such a position, but when he revealed that his great-grandfather had started the firm, almost a hundred years before, they'd understood. He wandered around the properties, taking measurements with a digital measuring device and photographing everything. When pressed for a valuation, he assured them they would have one by the following day. The issue of keeping the Point was not an obstacle.

The following afternoon, Claudia and Hannah climbed to the top of the lighthouse and stood, facing each other, in the Glass Menagerie. Claudia opened the email, on her iPad, and read the preliminary report, which, Kenneth Chamberlain explained, was representative of what the property was worth, sold as one lot, excluding the Point. Hannah was as anxious as a child on Christmas Eve.

'Don't keep me waiting. What's it worth?'

'Guess.' Claudia teased.

'A million dollars.'

'I think you'd best sit down, Hannah.'

'Not as much? I thought not,' said Hannah, glumly. 'I really should have looked after the place better.'

'Hannah, sit down, for goodness sake.'

Hannah took a seat on the couch of many colours. Claudia sat on the arm of the couch, beside her.

'Okay, tell me the worst.'

'Well,' Claudia continued, 'the view of the young . . .'

'And attractive,' added Hannah.

'Yes, I suppose he was attractive. I didn't notice.'

'Really?'

Claudia ignored the sarcastic tone and Hannah's raised eyebrow.

'The view of the young *and* attractive, Mr Chamberlain, is that selling the entire property in one land parcel will fetch a price somewhere in the region of . . .'

'Claudia! Spit it out.'

'Four million dollars!' Claudia leapt off the couch, her excitement too much to contain. Hannah flopped back on it. For a moment, it looked as if she was having another of her episodes. 'Hannah, are you all right?'

'Give me a moment, my dear. I'm in shock. Can you repeat that figure for me? For a moment, I thought you said four million dollars.'

Claudia held the iPad out for Hannah to see.

'I did. Here, look for yourself.'

'I haven't got my glasses,' said Hannah, still shaking. 'It's fine, I believe you.'

'Four million dollars,' repeated Claudia, and gave a whistle. 'Technically that makes you a multi-millionaire, *mam*.'

She curtsied to Hannah in mock deference.

'Stop it,' said Hannah, laughing, as the reality sunk in. 'But I suppose you really *should* call me Lady Hannah from now on, don't you?'

'Absolutely, your ladyship.' Claudia looked at the email again, reading it in more detail. 'It says if you sell the property off in separate parcels you might get another million.'

Hannah shook her head.

'It's not what Jonathon would have wanted. Nor me.'

'I get it,' said Claudia, 'it's just an option.'

'An option we won't be taking.'

'Agreed.'

'So, finally, everything's gone from the lighthouse that needed to go,' said Hannah, 'apart from one last thing.'

She held out a hand, beckoning Claudia to help her stand up. Claudia reached for it, knowing exactly what she was talking about.

'Then what say we go downstairs, Lady Hannah, and you can finally let me look at this old Volkswagen of yours? I've no idea why you've kept it such a secret from me.'

'Okay,' said Hannah, laughing at Claudia's address. 'I'm excited for you to see it. And talking about secrets, you've not sneaked a peek at the painting?'

Claudia looked over at the canvas, still covered by the muslin cloth. Hannah had been working on it, religiously, over the past few weeks.

'Not once. Despite I've been tempted.'

'Good! It's nearly finished. You'll see it soon enough.'

'It's so wonderful that you're painting again, Hannah. I've abandoned my own. I'm supposed to give three new paintings to Isabella, for the exhibition. I don't know how I'm going to break it to her that I've not even done one.'

'Don't fret, my dear. I'm sure she'll understand. Your muse will come back to you when it's the right time. I didn't paint for almost two years, myself. I just lost the desire to.'

'That's where I am,' Claudia replied, ruefully, 'but I'm not going to let it bring me down. I've loved being here, helping you, instead. We've done so much in such a short space of time.'

Hannah shook her head in disagreement.

'*You* have, you mean. I've just watched. I owe you a great deal, Claudia. Thankfully, I know exactly how to repay you.'

Claudia stopped and turned to face her. Her turn to disagree.

'No, Hannah, you own me nothing. I was so down when we met. Getting to know you and to fall in love with this wonderful place has been a joy for me. It feels like home, now, the home I always wanted to have. One that fills my heart and soul with joy. It's brought my happy back, and that's a priceless gift.'

Hannah hugged her and kissed her on the cheek. It took all of Claudia's resolve not to cry.

'Right,' said Hannah, 'let's finally look at this old wreck you've been so eager to see.'

'Lead the way, your ladyship.'

Down on the ground floor, Claudia undid the knots on the ropes holding the dusty tarpaulin over the car. She slid if off and heaped it into the corner of the now almost empty room.

'Well,' said Hannah, running her hand over the bonnet, 'here she is.'

She couldn't help but smile at the look of surprise on Claudia's face.

'Hannah, you literally just called her a wreck.'

'Did I?' Hannah grinned at Claudia. 'She was when she first came here, but I think I also said it was an unfinished project. Granted, I didn't say what needed to be done to finish it. What do you think?'

'She's beautiful,' said Claudia, almost reverently. 'Mind if I take a closer look?'

'Be my guest.'

Claudia walked around the car, tracing her fingers over its feminine curves. It appeared to have just rolled off the production line. Its panels were perfect and the doors opened and closed with a satisfyingly solid clunk. The paintwork was a flat sky-blue, with cream leather seats that matched the new canvas hood. The carpets were a deeper shade of the same cream, and, like the chrome bumpers, hubcaps, door-handles and trim, in showroom condition.

'It's a nineteen sixty-five convertible,' said Hannah, admiring the car alongside Claudia. 'A classic Beetle. Jonathon finished it just before he got sick.'

'He obviously put a lot of time into it.'

'He did,' said Hannah, sounding a little sad, 'but it was a labour of love. His family owned a garage, you see. He worked there from he was knee-high to a cricket. Knew all there was to know about cars and fixing them up. The new paintwork, the hood, and the new interior, were all done by a company that specialised in that sort of thing. Jonathon did everything else. Even putting in the new engine. Fitted right here.'

'It doesn't *look* like an unfinished project,' said Claudia. 'What more is there to do?'

Hannah nodded her head towards the rear of the Volkswagen.

'Fix on the number plates and we're legal. They're in the trunk.'

Claudia opened the trunk lid, looked inside, and then laughed. Hannah watched her, a knowing smile on her lips.

'Hannah! You tricked me. I forgot the engine's in the trunk.'

Sorry, my dear, couldn't resist it. I made the same mistake the first time Jonathon brought her here.'

Claudia went around to the front of the car and popped the bonnet. The white plates were painted with dark blue letters and numbers, below which the word, "California", had been painted in a flowing, red script.

'Well? Do you like her?' Hannah asked.

'I love, absolutely *love* her', said Claudia, admiring the beautiful little car in front of her. It oozed style and old-school cool.

'Finish her, then. For Jonathon.'

Claudia hesitated, feeling emotional at stealing a moment she felt belonged to someone else.

'You're sure you want me to do this?'

Hannah nodded.

'You've earned the right. Jonathon would agree with me. There's a screwdriver in the trunk.'

'Okay, I will.'

Claudia found the screwdriver and began to fit the plates. Hannah took a soft dust-cloth over the paintwork, removing what little dust there was. Plates fitted, Claudia opened the double lighthouse doors and the light flooded in. They both stepped back and admired the car. The white number plates really had finished it off.

'She looks even better in the natural light,' said Hannah, finally seeing the Volkswagen as it had been meant to look and feeling emotional herself. 'Beyond pretty.'

'Shame we can't drive her.'

'Says who?'

Hannah's had an impish grin on her face. Claudia was confused as to why.

'The battery will be dead as a dodo.'

'It would be, my dear, if one of the mechanics from the garage in town hadn't fitted a new one when you were visiting your sister and nieces last Sunday.'

Claudia looked no less confused.

'Well, that's one thing, but we'd still need to be sure that the wheels turn. The brakes have probably seized, and we'd have to check the fluids levels, too, just to be on the safe side.'

'Yup! All taken care of.'

The look on Hannah's face had changed to one of joy. She laughed and clapped her hands together, finally able to reveal the secret she'd been keeping for the past week. Claudia finally realised she'd been well and truly set-up.

'Last Sunday, I assume?'

Hannah's smile answered her question. She reached into the front pocket of her faded-blue dungarees and fished out a black leather key fob with the shiny "VW" logo letters at its centre, a jangle of shiny keys hanging off it like Christmas baubles. She tossed it to Claudia.

'Jonathon said all I had to do was fit the plates and turn the key. Although, he knew I never would. I can't drive, you see. Go on, Claudia, get in and give her a try. I know you're dying to.'

'You planned this all along, Hannah, didn't you?'

Hannah gave Claudia a look of complete innocence.

'*Moi*? Now, quit stalling, pardon the pun, and jump in.'

Claudia popped the clips on the windscreen and folded the hood back behind the rear seats, then eased herself into the newly sprung and recovered leather driver's seat. She took a hold of the polished-wood steering wheel and looked out through the windscreen.

'Feel good?' Hannah called to her, waiting for her outside the tower doors.

'Amazing,' whispered Claudia, stroking the polished wooden wheel.

The key slid into the ignition barrel like a knife into butter. Claudia turned it forward and the instrument panel lit up. She turned it further and the engine coughed like an old man coming awake after a long sleep, then burst into life, plumes of white smoke billowing out of its chromed exhaust. She slid the car into gear and drove out into the late-afternoon sunshine.

'She's alive,' cried Claudia, pulling up beside Hannah.

'Of course, she is,' said Hannah, proudly, 'Jonathon built her.'

'Hop in then, Miss Daisy.'

'Now?'

Hannah looked dubious.

'She's road legal,' said Claudia. 'Besides, we'll not go far. Just up to the Pilgrims Highway.'

'I've not got my handbag.'

'Get in and stop fussing, old woman, or I'm heading off by myself.'

'Honestly, you young folk,' said Hannah, opening the passenger door, 'just wild with abandon.' She climbed in beside Claudia and put on her seatbelt. 'Okay, let's go.'

They drove down from the lighthouse to the car park, bumping over the uneven ground and laughing like children on a fairground ride, then headed along the beach road, towards Duxbury. Hannah switched on the radio, which crackled to life, and the song, *Good Vibrations,* began to play. They passed through Duxbury, singing at the top of their voices, reaching the Pilgrims Highway about ten minutes later.

'Well?' Claudia asked, looking over at Hannah.

'Well what?'

'I know you don't have a television, but have ever seen *Thelma and Louise*? The movie with Susan Sarandon and Geena Davis.'

'The ultimate girlie road movie? I may be old, Claudia, but I'm not completely out of touch.'

'What I mean is,' said Claudia, 'I'm not suggesting we go as far as Mexico, but we could take a trip down the seaboard. Just as far as Sandwich. We can have a walk around the old harbour. Sylkie's in the Beach Shack and she'll be fine. I've got my credit card, so, if you're lucky, I'll even buy you a milkshake.'

Hannah took a millisecond to decide and answer.

'Okay, *Thelma*, hit the gas. I need another adventure.'

'You're on, *Louise*.'

Claudia turned left and headed down the empty highway, accelerating the car to fifty miles an hour.

'Not too fast,' cried Hannah, her flaming red hair billowing out behind her.

Claudia laughed at her.

'No need to worry, a car like this isn't built for speed, it's built for cool. And she oozes that, don't you, Sky?'

'*Sky!* Is that what you're going to call her?'

'Just for today. She's your car, Hannah. You need to give her a name All cars have names. It's lucky.'

Hannah looked over at Claudia and put a hand on her arm.

'No, my dear, she's yours to name, and Sky fits her perfectly. I can't drive her, remember? And I'm not selling her to someone I don't know. Besides, I want to think about you driving her when I'm gone, hood down and the wind in your hair. And don't bother saying no, you're taking her. Anyway, I already registered her in your name, so it's too late to refuse.'

Claudia didn't speak. Not immediately. Only because she couldn't. But the tears rolling down her checks told Hannah how she was feeling.

'You made me cry, again,' said Claudia, accepting a tissue Hannah pulled from the chest pocket of her denim dungarees.

Hannah patted her knee in a reassuring and motherly way

'I'm sorry, my dear. I didn't mean to. Now, wipe your eyes and get me to where we're going. I fancy that milkshake.'

'Hannah, are you sure about . . .'

'Claudia, I swear to God, if you ask me one more time am I sure about anything, I'm going to report you to . . . well, to whoever deals with scurrilous suggestions about one losing one's faculties. You're keeping Sky, it's not up for discussion. Anyway, I can afford it. I'm worth millions, don't you know. Although, I still have a price for her.'

'Which is?'

'The price is that you visit me, once a month, down at the Point, after I leave. And bring me fresh roses, you know how much I love them. Come down and say hello to me, Betsy and Jonathon. At least, that way, we'll have someone to remember us.'

'I would have anyway.'

Claudia's voice was choked with emotion and fresh tears slipped down her cheeks.

'I know, my dear. Now, no more tears or I'm driving us home. Trust me, you and poor Sky don't want that.'

Claudia laughed and her tears stopped falling.

'I promise, Hannah. And thank you for Sky. She's the best present I've ever been given. I accept.'

Hannah, giving Claudia a derisive snort.

'Like you had a choice. Now, drive on, Thelma. Let's see if we can't find ourselves a Brad Pitt to sit in the back.'

37

Over the last week in April and though the first week in May, Claudia delivered furniture to galleries and gift shops, from Duxbury, all the way down to Cape Cod. The list of stores that had stocked Jonathon's furniture had proved priceless. All of them remembered him with fondness. Many had wondered why he'd stopped contacting them. Once Claudia had explained the situation, they were more than happy to take his furniture back into stock. It had, they'd all advised her, always sold well.

Hannah had taken over dealing with the estate agent, Mr Abercrombie, aided by her long-term lawyer, Abernethy MacLelland, from the law firm she and Jonathon had always used. He was also a trusted friend. Abernethy, under Hannah's instruction, was arranging the specific details regarding the sale of the lighthouse and other properties, including the separation of the land around the Point. He was also taking care of her will.

Although she seemed to have been energised with the clearing out of the lighthouse tower and the big house, Hannah was still becoming weaker each day. Her episodes were becoming more frequent, the pain she was suffering, at times, leaving her unable to move. Kevin Chancery, head of the Oncology Department at the Massachusetts General Hospital, in Boston, had spoken to Claudia, informing her that aside from Hannah taking the medication he'd prescribed, there was little else that could be done. All Claudia could do was to be there for her and ensure she continued her medication.

Hannah decided she would use the money from the sale of the properties to fund some charity work. She was also still considering turning the lightkeeper's house into a home for dogs, to ensure Sylkie always had a home she loved and would be properly looked after. Claudia had offered a different solution.

'I love her,' she said, one evening, sitting by the fire, sipping room-warmed Glenmorangie, with Sylkie lying contently across her knees. 'I can't see her going anywhere she won't be treated right.'

'Spoiled rotten, you mean,' said Hannah, 'as little Sylkie always is.' She smiled as Sylkie lifted her head and looked at her across the coffee-table. 'Are you sure? It's a big commitment?'

'More than sure,' said Claudia, 'if you're happy for me to have her. I promise she'll be well taken care of. We have a huge garden she'll love playing in, and Robinson Hill is a great place to go walking. It'll get me off my fat ass, too. Even if we move out west, I'll make sure we have a garden for her to run around in. Although, now that I've lived by the beach, I think I might have to insist Paul finds us a property next to the ocean.

'I agree,' said Hannah, 'but not that you've got a fat ass. You've lost weight, that's easy to see. Not surprising, given the number of times you've climbing the lighthouse stairs. Not to mention the amount of furniture you moved.'

Claudia looked down at herself and thought she was leaner around her hips and thighs. Her stomach, too, was flatter than it had been in some time.

'I must admit, I'm feeling fitter and healthier than I've done in years, despite your scones and cakes.

'Paul will notice, I'm sure. He's back, soon, isn't he?'

'He's back for the exhibition opening, a week past this Saturday,' replied Claudia. 'I'm looking forward to it. I'll bring him down to see you, unless you've changed your mind and want to come up to it.'

'No thanks, my dear. It's time you need to spend with your clients, schmoozing and being the centre of attention. Anyway, you'll be going back home with Paul, afterwards, or out for a fancy dinner in Lexington. I won't be the gooseberry to you two lovebirds.'

'Let's hope we *are* lovebirds.'

'You will be. Wait till he sees your new look, all lithe and tanned with your sun-bleached, blonde hair. He'll be all over you.'

'Now *I'm* blushing.'

'Claudia Montgomery, whatever is going on in that mind of yours?'

'Nothing I care to share. I might shock you.'

Hannah eyes glinted mischievously as she replied.

'I could tell you a few things about Jonathon and I that would curl your toes. If the beach and the Beach Shack could talk, what scandalous tales they'd tell.'

Claudia looked over at her and laughed.

'Hannah Thomas! Now who's blushing!'

They sat and talked for hours in front of the fire, as they had done each night since Claudia had arrived. She most loved hearing Hannah's tales of the Camino de Santiago. They painted pictures in her head she wanted to bring to life. They talked about everything and anything, watching the shadows rise and fall as the flames died in the hearth, like the memories they spoke of.

38

Sylkie scampered after the stick, leaving a line of paw-marks in the wet sand, waiting until a slow-breaking wave had receded before collecting it and ambling back to Claudia, wagging her tail as if to say, *okay, I brought it back again, now stop throwing it away.*

'Good girl, Sylkie.'

Claudia looked up and saw Hannah, sitting on the Beach Shack veranda, watching them, and waved to her. She waved back and Claudia breathed a sigh of relief. She hadn't seemed herself, that morning. It was the first time she'd not managed their regular walk along the beach. Sylkie, tired of chasing stick, decided to go and dig up a crab. Within moments, her furry bottom was sticking up out of the sand, tail wagging furiously, as she excavated a hole big enough to hide half her body in.

Claudia walked up towards the Beach Shack, stopping at the bottom of the steps to give a whistle, which Sylkie ignored. She climbed the steps, dropped into the seat opposite Hannah, and looked out across the bay. The sea was like a pool of molten silver, stretching into the far distance, and the sun burned white in a cloudless sky, making it difficult to distinguish where one element stopped and the other started.

'How was the walk?'

'It was lovely,' said Claudia. 'It's beautiful out there, today. Just look at the view. The sky and the sea seem to be merging into one. It's as if you can see forever.'

'They call it the *skiether*,' said Hannah, 'in some parts of the highlands of Scotland, so Jonathon once told me. The place at the limit of our vision where you can't really tell what's what and where's where. The place between heaven and earth. It's where our souls go, first, after we die, to get ready for a new journey, still close to home but one step closer to God.'

'What a lovely thought,' said Claudia. 'I love the name for it, the *skiether*. I might not be religious, but I'll remember that.'

Hannah made to stand.

'Let me get you some breakfast, my dear, that was a long walk you took.'

Claudia stood up, wagging a scolding finger at her.

'You'll do nothing of the sort, crazy lady. You're not well. I'll do it myself.'

Hannah settled back in her chair, the tartan chair-rug draped over her knees, despite that the air was warm. Claudia noticed but said nothing.

'Well, if you're sure? I *am* still a bit tired. There's a fresh loaf in the oven. It should be ready by now. Honey and butter already out on the table for you. I've not got an appetite, this morning, for some reason, so none for me. I must have picked up a bug.'

She smiled at Claudia, who smiled back, although could not hide the worry.

'Give me five minutes. I'll bring some out for you. Even if you're not *that* hungry, you still need to try to eat something.'

She got up and gave Hannah a hug, then headed into the Beach Shack to prepare breakfast.

'I'll do my best,' said Hannah, and closed her eyes to take a five-minute nap.

Claudia looked down at her, lying wrapped in her blanket, and wondered if she should be as worried as she felt. She went inside to make breakfast, unable to stop.

'Mmmm. So good.'

Claudia closed her eyes as she chewed a piece of Hannah's home-made wheaten loaf, liberally smeared in butter and running with golden honey.

'Always tastes better after a walk along the beach,' said Hannah. 'The sea air sharpens the appetite and you really feel you've earned it.'

'Absolutely. I could stay here forever and eat the same thing every day and not complain.'

Claudia licked the creases at the corners of her mouth, snaring the last sticky crumbs and drips of honey. Hannah smiled over at her, thinking about how on earth she would ever have coped without her, as well as how much she loved her.

'Sorry I wasn't up to the walk this morning. My get up and go had got up and gone.'

'How are you feeling now?'

Claudia looked over at Hannah, glad to see she wasn't quite as peely-wally as she'd looked earlier.

'I'm fine, my dear, really. I'm going to go up to the studio, later, to work on the painting.'

'The unfinished masterpiece! When will I get to see it?'

'Monday morning, after your weekend back home.'

Claudia was surprised and excited.

'Really?'

'Yes! I've been working on it every day, pretty much, while you've been out selling Jonathon's furniture. Oh, and on the subject, there's a hundred dollars in the envelope on the kitchen table. It's for the boys from your gallery, just to thank them for their help.'

'You didn't have to do that, Hannah.'

'I know. I wanted to.'

'That's kind of you. I'm sure they'll be moved by the gesture.'

'You'll be off soon, my dear, heading home for your big weekend.'

'I thought I'd head out soon. I want to stop and say hello to my sister and nieces, first. They're off school, today, and I promised I would visit.'

'That's wonderful. I'm so glad you're seeing them more.'

'Me too, Hannah. And it's thanks to you.'

'Nonsense! Anyway, are you looking forward to your exhibition, tomorrow? And seeing Paul?'

'Both,' said Claudia, with a look of trepidation on her face. 'I'm not sure which one makes me more nervous. Tomorrow's only for business clients, the ones spend the big bucks. The exhibition's in Isabella's hands, but she's done so many of these sorts of events before, so I know it'll be perfectly organised. She's forgiven me for not delivering on the new paintings, but we've had so many pieces in from existing clients, as well as raiding my stock of older, finished projects, in the gallery basement. Charity's been working on the merchandise, creating prints, t-shirts and mugs for the public to buy when it opens to everyone on Sunday.'

'It will be a roaring success,' said Hannah, 'I know it. I'll come up and see it next week.'

'I so want you to see your own work on the new floor,' said Claudia, excitedly. 'All of your paintings are already hung. I can't wait to see them myself. The New Artists Gallery at *Sans Cera* will be open to everyone, next weekend, with you there to cut the red ribbon.'

'I'll be so proud, my dear. And so very grateful to you.'

'You deserve it, Hannah. Now, are you sure you're going to be fine here by yourself. I don't like that you missed your walk, this morning, and you've eaten practically nothing of your breakfast. I know you're still in pain after last night's episode. Don't pretend you're not.'

Hannah shook her head at Claudia's worried look.

I'm fine, Claudia, please don't fuss. Besides, I've got Sylkie to keep me company. I'll miss having your around, of course, but I'm going to spend the weekend up in Glass Menagerie, painting. I'll take a walk out to the Point, at some stage, to say hello to Betsy and Jonathon.'

'Be careful climbing up, I don't want you to . . .' Claudia stopped talking, seeing the exasperated look on Hannah's face. 'Okay, I get the message. I'm shutting up.'

'Good! Now, get yourself ready and get going. I'll see you on Monday morning. If you're sure you want to come back, given I've worked you so hard over the past month?'

'Of course, I do,' Claudia replied, 'I've enjoyed it no end. Oh, and don't forget, Abernethy MacLelland is coming here, tomorrow morning, for you to sign the paperwork selling the properties and splitting off the land around the Point.

'I won't,' said Hannah. 'Everything is organised. Now, if you'll make me one last cup of tea before you go, I'll love you forever.'

'It's on its way. Your ladyship. And you'd better.'

Hannah watched Claudia as she stood and walked across the Beach Shack veranda. She whispered to her, too quietly for Claudia to hear, but her hearing what she had said was not important. It was how it made Hannah feel in the saying of it.

'Always.'

39

Standing outside the entrance of *Sans Cera* gallery was a large, bronze figure of a seated woman. Her hands lay on her lap, one on top of the other, fingers pointing down forming a "V" shape that covered her pubic area. Her breasts, however, were exposed for all the world to see, and although her head was tilted onto her right shoulder, as if she was sleeping, her eyes were open. A flow of wavy hair tumbled down her back, curled around her front, over her thighs, spilling out over her crotch. The look on her face was one of serenity, as if uncaring that she was displaying her nakedness and sensuality, the left side of her face, formed in the shape of a penis, accentuating that.

The sculpture was Claudia's homage to Pablo Picasso's masterpiece, *Le Reve*, which was every bit as sexually charged as the great master had intended the painting to be, showing the fifty-year-old Picasso's mistress, twenty-two-year-old, Marie-Therese Walter, in exotic reverie. It was a libidinous portrait of sexual desire and expression, and while not worth the one hundred and fifty-five million dollars recently paid for Picasso's painting, had still sold to a firm of private bankers for an impressive two hundred thousand.

'Hello!'

Claudia had been so focused on the sculpture she'd not seen Charity come out to greet her. She was dressed casually, in a white t-shirt and close-fitting jeans that showed of her long legs and hourglass figure.

'Hi, Charity. I didn't see your there.'

Charity gave Claudia a hug and kissed her on both cheeks.

'I love this piece. It's based on *Le Reve*, isn't it?'

'It is. My interpretation of Marie-Therese, not Picasso's.'

'You make her a more liberated woman than the painting does. More sexually confident, rather than how he intended her to look. And naming her, *La Eve*, I love that.'

'I did get a few complaints from the local God squad, to be honest,' said Claudia, 'when she first went on show. Thankfully, she sold inside the first few days and was moved to Boston.'

'I suppose she is ever so slightly irreverent,' said Charity, 'if you think of her in biblical terms; Eve, the temptress, portrayed though time as the woman who caused the downfall of man. Your sculpture reinforces that portrayal.'

Claudia nodded, impressed by Charity's intuitiveness and interpretation. She wondered if Isabella had been coaching her.

'Exactly as I intended it to. She's powerful and sexually confident, as Eve would have been, if a woman had written the Bible.' They studied the sculpture for a moment. 'Is she safe out here?'

Charity ran her hand over Eve's head, then gave her a solid push.

'I wouldn't worry about it. It took a forklift to unload her from the truck. Besides, there's manned security cameras monitoring her twenty-four hours a day, and an overnight guard for good measure.'

'Good. I wouldn't want her stolen from Eden for a second time.'

A voice behind her made Claudia turn.

'Hello stranger, you look fantastic! Give me a hug and let me see you properly.' Isabella grabbed a hand and twirled Claudia around. 'You've lost weight, and I love the beach blonde hair. Have you been to some health club I don't know about?'

'Long walks on the beach, healthy eating, not much alcohol, and lots of hard physical labour,' said Claudia, returning Isabella's hug. She found she was pleased to see her friend. 'Hows the exhibition looking?'

'It's looking great. Charity and I were just going over the final details for tomorrow. Come and look.'

'No thanks. I just stopped to say a quick hello, on my way back up from Duxbury, in my new car.'

Claudia turned and looked at Sky, sitting in one of *Sans Cera's* private parking bays. The late afternoon sunshine made her chrome and paintwork sparkle and shine.

'Wow! I always wanted a convertible Beetle,' said Isabella, ambling over to take a closer look. 'She's so cool. And she looks brand new. Wherever did you find her?'

Claudia followed her over and ran a hand over Sky's bonnet.

'She was a gift, from Hannah.'

'That's one hell of a gift, honey, but I know you'll have deserved it. I hope she's well?'

'She's doing fine. Just taking one day at a time. She's really looking forward to next weekend, seeing her paintings in the gallery.'

'They're already hung. Up on the new floor. Charity did most of the hard work. Wait till you see what she's created, it's amazing.'

'It was so good of you both to allow me to take on the project,' said Charity, coming over to join them by Sky.

Claudia shook her head.

'I'm sure you've don't a great job, Charity. I look forward to seeing it in the morning. But, right now, I'm heading home to check the house is still standing and to wait for my erstwhile husband to show up.'

'Paul's back, tonight?' Honey, that's great news.'

Isabella looked surprised. Claudia wasn't sure why she would be.

'He is, but not till late.

'How lovely for you to have him here for your exhibition,' said Charity.

Yes,' said Claudia. 'it *will* be nice to have him here with me, tomorrow. I've not seen him in a month.'

'Don't let him keep you up all night, if you get my drift,' said Isabella. 'I need you here, bushy-tailed and bright-eyed, in the morning.'

'Isabella! Not in front of young Charity!'

'Absolutely,' said Charity, putting a hand over her heart, 'I'm still as pure as driven snow.'

All three of them laughed at her mock look of indignation.

'Don't worry,' said Claudia, 'I won't be late.'

She gave them both a hug then climbed into Sky and drove off, heading home for the first time in over a month.

After a hot bath, where she shaved her legs and, on impulse, her mind on the night ahead, everywhere else Paul might enjoy shaven, Claudia made a supper of tuna-mayonnaise and salad. It was a simple meal, light enough to stop her being too full for whatever Paul might want to do to her, enough to give her the energy she might need to do it. She felt horny, which surprised her. Perhaps it had been looking at the sculpture of Eve that had started her mind down the road to temptation and the needs of the flesh.

Whatever it was, it led Claudia to her dressing room and into the bottom drawer of her dresser, where she fished out Paul's favourite outfit for her to wear during sex; a tight-fitting *New England Patriots* football shirt that came down to the top of her thighs, almost, and a pair of white socks, pulled up to just below her knees. A pair of white Converse sneakers completed the ensemble. She tried the outfit on and was pleasantly surprised to find it fitted perfectly. The month at the beach had definitely paid off.

She stood in front of her full-length bedroom mirror and smiled at "Candy", the sexy, high-school cheerleader, who gave her a knowing wink. Tonight, Claudia decided, Paul could play with Candy's pom-poms for as long as he wanted. Happy with the outfit, she lay down on the bed. It was seven-thirty and getting dark outside. Paul's plane would land in half an hour. By nine o'clock, he'd be in the house, and five minutes later, if she had anything to do with it, he'd be in her.

After scrolling through her iPod for a few minutes, Claudia selected a Dean Martin playlist and lay back, listening to the ultimate Italian crooner. She'd relax for a while then surprise Paul at the top of the stairs and let him chase her.

She wouldn't run too fast.

The sound of her phone ringing on the bedside table woke Claudia. She sat up, disorientated, wondering why she was dressed as a cheerleader, and smiled as she remembered. She grabbed the phone and answered it.

'Paul. Have you landed?'

'Claudia! I've called you twice in the past hour and left you two messages. Where have you been?'

Claudia checked her phone. There were two missed calls showing.

'I'm sorry, darling, it was on silent. I must have dozed off. Where are you?'

'I'm still in Los Angeles.'

Claudia noticed the time on her phone. It was after ten. She'd been asleep for hours.

'But, you're meant to be here!'

'I missed my flight. We over-ran at a meeting with the execs from MGM. They've come in with an offer to take over the series and to turn it into a movie. It's Metro Goldwin Mayer, Claudia. Everything I've ever dreamed off. Aren't you pleased for me?'

'I'm lying in our bed, dressed as a cheerleader, Paul. Waiting for you. So, no, I'm not pleased. I'm bloody furious.'

'Sweetheart, be reasonable. I can get an early flight out, tomorrow morning and be there early afternoon. We can have tomorrow night and all of Sunday together.'

'Don't bother, Paul. I may not be here. Candy *definitely* won't.'

'And what's that supposed to mean, Claudia? You won't be at our home?'

'*Our* home! Seriously, Paul, since when has it been *our* home? You live in Los Angeles, now, as far as I can tell.'

Claudia's anger was beginning to simmer. Paul ignored the warning signs and tried to defend himself.

'It's where my work is, Claudia.'

'You're a writer, Paul. You can work from anywhere.'

'I know I'm a bloody writer, but I don't just want to write novels, any longer. I want to be involved in screenwriting. I always have. You know that.'

Paul was becoming angry. It was evident in the tone and volume of his reply. Claudia was silent for a moment. He was right, of course, and if MGM had come into the mix, she knew he couldn't just walk away. But it didn't help dilute her own anger.

'That doesn't change the fact that you should be here. It's the opening day of my new exhibition, tomorrow. That's important to *me*, even if it's not to you.'

'As this is to me, Claudia. I'm actually *working,* out here. Can you say the same bloody thing?'

'And what the hell's that meant to mean?'

Paul hesitated for a moment, then said what was on his mind.

'Only that Isabella's set up your exhibition almost single-handedly, at the same time as running your gallery. For Christ's sake, Claudia, you didn't even deliver the new paintings you were meant to have been working on. Instead, you've been off wandering around old lighthouses and playing nursemaid to your new friend.'

Claudia's hands began to tremble.

'Playing nursemaid! How bloody dare you! Hannah has stage four cancer, not the bloody flu. And I've worked damned hard to help her get ready to die. And so what if I am taking care of my friend? It's a damned sight more important than painting a few new pictures. I've got time, she hasn't.'

'Taking care of your *friend!* You hardly bloody know her, Claudia. What is it, three or four weeks since you met?'

His words took Claudia's anger from simmering to boiling point.

'How long do you have to know someone to care about them, Paul? Answer me that, damn you. You and Sammy seem to have gotten pretty close, pretty damned quickly. Or is that different?'

'For Christ's sake, Claudia, I've already told you there's nothing going on with her.'

'I know that. It's not what I meant. What I mean is, how much time needs to pass before you're allowed to care about someone in the world according to Paul bloody Montgomery?'

'That's not what I meant, either,' Paul shouted back.

The argument was fast becoming overheated, but Claudia was finding it hard to pull back from it.

'And as for my gallery and how I see fit to run it, that's my business. Did I moan and complain to you all the times in the past you couldn't write, because it just wasn't flowing?' Did I?'

'No, you didn't,' said Paul, backing off a step.

'That's right, Paul, I didn't. I went out to work while you stayed at home waiting for your bloody muse to return.'

Realising what he'd said about Hannah, and how it must have sounded, Paul tried to step back. His voice softened.

'Sweetheart, all I meant was . . .'

Claudia was beyond listening. Paul had told her to follow her heart. To do what she needed to get her confidence back. And she'd done that. What was worse, though, and what was fizzing through her head, was that he'd obviously been speaking to Isabella. How else would he know the new artwork had not been delivered? Isabella being left to run ***Sans Cera*** by herself was something they'd also clearly discussed. Perhaps even that night at the apartment, in

Boston, when Paul's flight had been delayed. If it even had been? Whatever the facts were, it was clear they had continued to talk to each other behind Claudia's back. Once more, the pieces of the jigsaw were falling into place, and the picture they were forming was becoming clearer and darker.

'Look, Paul, it's obvious we need more time apart for you to begin to value me as much as your bloody television series, or whatever else is keeping you there. I'm your wife. You should be here for me.'

'Just like I asked you to be here with me, Claudia. I practically begged you to come out to Los Angles and at least see the place. Did you come when I asked?'

He was right. Claudia knew it.

'No, Paul,' she whispered, 'I suppose I didn't.'

They were both silent, realising, perhaps, they were heading for dangerous ground. Ground that could at any moment give way under their feet, dragging them down into an abyss from which they might not climb out. At least, not together.

Paul broke the silence.

'I wanted to come, Claudia, if only to show support for you. But it's your gig, and this is mine. It's not like you'd want to come to the studio and spend time mooching around the set while I'm working, would you?'

Claudia was suddenly too tired, emotionally and physically, to keep fighting.

'You're right, Paul, I probably wouldn't.'

'I love your work, sweetheart, but it's not as if you'd have time for me. I've been at these events of Isabella's, she practically has you on her arm all day. Which is as it's meant to be.'

'I know that, Paul. I know you're right. I just wanted you here with me. I wanted us to be together.'

'I want to see you too, sweetheart. Look, why don't you fly out here for a few days next week? You've done all you needed to do to help Hannah. I'm proud of you for that. I didn't say it, but I am. I'll take some time off and we can enjoy the madness of the City of Angels together. I can still come home, tomorrow, if you want me to?'

Claudia took hold of the olive branch.

'I'll think about it. Coming out to you, that is. Don't come back tomorrow. There's little point when you'd have to fly back twenty-four hours later. I'll be at the exhibition all weekend. And you're right, Isabella *is* demanding, isn't she?'

The olive branch had been sharpened and turned into a spear. Paul, despite being poked with it, didn't flinch.

They made small talk for the next few minutes, but the conversation was awkward and stilted. What had promised to be an evening of reconnection had been reduced to distant words on a lifeless line. In the end, Claudia told Paul she was tired and had to sleep. He hadn't fought to keep the conversation alive. He hung up without saying that he loved her. Candy, like Claudia, didn't really care.

40

Claudia arrived at *Sans Cera* earlier than she'd planned. After a fitful night's sleep, she'd woken as dawn broke and spent the first hour in her studio in a strenuous yoga session. The sun had risen over Robinson Hill, streaming in through the windows and lifting her mood. Combined with the endorphins pumping around her bloodstream, it had left her feeling energised and filled with anticipation for the day ahead.

'Where's Isabella?' Claudia asked, climbing the second set of stairs, just ahead of Charity.

'She's up there already,' said Charity, 'we both got in early to make sure everything was ready for you to see. She's super excited for you to give the new gallery your seal of approval. Me too.'

'Don't be nervous, Charity, I'm sure you've done a great job.'

'I know it means a lot to you. Your friend, Hannah, is a gifted artist. I think it benefits *Sans Cera* to have a space for other artists.'

'My thoughts exactly,' said Claudia, warming to Charity even more. 'Now let's see this creation of yours. Lead the way.'

Charity passed her and climbed the final few steps, turning, at the top, to wave Claudia into the new space.

'Welcome, Mrs Montgomery, to the New Artists Gallery at *Sans Cera*.'

Claudia took a few paces into the room and looked around. Where once had been old wooden boards, was a white, tiled floor, which reflected the light from the angled, glass skylights, flooding the entire room with natural light. The brick walls had been plastered and painted white. Stud partition walls had been added, coming off the walls, creating mini-galleries for visitors to progress through, turning what had been a large rectangular room into an architecturally and aesthetically more interesting space. The studs were only just above head height, keeping the whole floor open and airy.

Hannah's paintings had been arranged by the date of their creation, painted below her signature on the lower right-hand corner of every canvas. Set against the pristine white walls, they looked stunning, the vibrant colours in her palette both startling and soothing to the eye.

Claudia turned and hugged Charity, catching her off guard.

'You've done an amazing job. I'm seriously impressed.'

Charity was clearly relieved.

'I'm so glad you like it. I wanted to create something beautiful for you and Hannah. As well as for the gallery.'

'You've succeeded in all three, Charity. I love the new skylight glass. Translucent white, rather than clear.'

'Isabella's idea, to be honest, but I agree, it really diffuses the natural light so much more. Much better to view the paintings.'

Isabella emerged from one of the mini-galleries close to the centre of the room, her high heels clicking on the tiles. She hugged Claudia and kissed her on both cheeks. Claudia hugged her back, if a little stiffly.

'What do you think, honey?'

'An amazing transformation,' said Claudia. 'So much better than I thought it could ever be. And Hannah's paintings look amazing. I've only ever seen them stacked up in her lighthouse.'

'She'll love it, too, don't you think?'

'I just said that to Charity.'

'There's one or two things still to do,' said Charity, 'but it's as good as finished.'

Isabella gave her a knowing look.

'I told you not to worry, didn't I?'

'You did.'

'Now,' said Isabella, 'enough praising ourselves. Time to get ready for the main event. Let's get down to the ground floor and make sure everything is as it should be. It's exhibition time, girls.'

They walked down the stairs together, Isabella giving them their allotted tasks as they walked.

'Charity, you check on the bar, it's still being set up. Make sure the bartenders know they don't serve drinks from the bar, only via the waiters and waitresses. Claudia and I will check on them to make sure they know their responsibilities.' She looked at Claudia. 'We drafted in some of the local students to serve food and drinks.'

'Good,' said Claudia. 'It all seems well organised. I'm looking forward to it. I thought I wouldn't be.'

Isabella hugged her. A hug, Claudia couldn't bring herself to return with as much warmth.

'Of course you should be. It's your day, honey.'

Charity went off to finalise the bar while Isabella introduced Claudia to the students, who gave them precise instructions on what was expected of them.

'Perfection,' said Claudia, 'your end-of-day bonus depends on it.'

'What time's Paul getting here?' Isabella asked, as she and Claudia took a last-minute stroll through the ground floor, inspecting the artworks.

'He's not coming.' Claudia replied, unable to keep the coldness out of her tone. 'Didn't you know?'

'What?' Isabella looked genuinely shocked. 'Why the hell not? And how the hell would I have known?'

'Sorry. I just thought you might have called him to ensure he didn't let me down again.'

Claudia immediately chastised herself. It was the wrong time and place to start down that line of discussion. She went on to recount most of the conversation she'd had with Paul, the previous night, omitting the part that included Isabella.

Isabella, though, seemed to take his side.

'Well, I can understand him to a degree, honey. I guess you don't turn down a meeting with MGM. But he should still be here.'

'So, you didn't call him, this time?'

Isabella looked shocked at the suggestion.

'I'm not making that mistake again. Once bitten and all that.'

Claudia was more sad than angry, knowing her closest friend was lying to her. The question of *why*, remained unanswered. She took a deep breath and pushed the thought away. It was her exhibition. The way she was feeling, it might well be her last.

'Okay, let's get this show on the road. I'm still going to enjoy today.'

'That's the spirit, honey.'

Charity came in through the front doors.

'All good?' Isabella asked.

'All good. I was just picking up some information cards from the printers. I noticed a couple of typos on the ones we got yesterday. I'll go sort them out and then get changed out of my jeans and t-shirt.'

'We need to get into our party frocks, too,' said Isabella, turning to Claudia. 'You got your little black number and heels?'

'As instructed. Hanging in my office.'

'Right girls,' said Isabella, 'back here in fifteen minutes, looking like the three witches from Macbeth. The sexy versions, that is. Ready to cast a spell over whoever comes before us.'

'Hubble bubble,' said Claudia, following Isabella through to the backroom offices to change.

The clients began to arrive and were greeted, in turn, by the three witches, given their name badges and exhibition catalogue, then led into the ground floor gallery to mingle and chat. The waiting staff served an unending supply of bucks-fizz and soft drinks, alongside sushi and vegetarian entrees.

'Senator Goulding,' said Isabella, recognising Boston's newly elected republican senate member, David Goulding, coming through the front doors. 'How lovely to see you. I'm so glad you decided to accept our invitation.'

The senator was in his late forties. His shoulder-length, dark hair was immaculately cut and flecked with silver. He was tall and tanned, and someone who obviously looked after himself. His white linen suit and pale yellow shirt, combined with Ralph Lauren, tan leather loafers, made him look more like a well-heeled tourist. Isabella knew she hadn't sent him an invitation, so was confused as to how he was there, though happy to see him all the same. His attendance would look great in the gossip columns of the Boston magazines and newspapers covering the exhibition.

The mystery was solved a moment later.

'Uncle David,' cried Charity, coming back into the reception area, having deposited another important guest into the gallery. She threw her arms around the senator and kissed him on both cheeks.

The senator hugged her back, lifting her off her feet.

'How are you, little girl? Are your folks here, yet? I've not seen them since last Thanksgiving.'

'They're arriving soon, Uncle David. I'll let them know you're here when they do. In the meantime, I'd like to introduce you to the artist, Claudia Montgomery. She's my boss, so be especially nice to her. And remember to buy something expensive.'

Charity took the senator by the crook of the arm, guiding him past an open-mouthed Isabella, towards Claudia.

'Mrs Montgomery.'

The Senator's voice was deep, musical and refined. He had clearly cultivated his diction in the best schools and Ivy League universities.

'Call me Claudia, please, Senator. I'm meant to be a hip and cool artist, if that's at all possible. Mrs Montgomery sounds as if she bakes cakes.'

The senator gave Claudia a warm smile and shook her hand. His grip was firm and cool.

'You carry off both with aplomb, Claudia. Hip and cool, that is. I've no idea about your cakes, but I'd be more than happy to find out. Call me David.'

Claudia returned his smile.

'Thank you so much for coming to my exhibition.'

'Not at all. I'm pleased to meet the woman who's given my niece her dream job. If I can ever be of service, please, don't hesitate.' He reached inside the pocket of his jacket and extracted a crisp, white business-card that had his name embossed on the front and contact details on the reverse. He handed it to Claudia. 'It's my personal number. Call me, anytime.'

'That's most kind of you, *David*.'

Claudia felt herself blush and wondered what the hell was wrong with her. Candy, it seemed, was still lingering in her psyche.

'And now,' said the senator, turning to Charity, 'take me inside, little girl. Show me some of these pieces you've been telling me would look great on my office walls.'

Charity led the senator off, chattering like a magpie that had found a silver ring.

'Call me *David*. It's my personal number.'

Isabella whispered in Claudia's ear, mimicking the Senators slow drawl. Claudia gave a lascivious laugh and held the senator's card up in front her.

'Behave, or I won't give you his card.'

'Charity's uncle,' said Isabella, taking the card out of Claudia's hand, 'the senator. Who knew?'

Claudia shook her head and laughed as Isabella popped the card, under her dress, into her bra.

'That girl, Isabella, is worth twice whatever you hired her for.'

'She's certainly a smart girl, our Charity,' replied Isabella, looking over at Charity and her uncle, who were standing in front of a large painting entitled, *Expression*; a monochrome study of the face of Mary Magdalene looking up at Jesus Christ on the cross, a sly, almost knowing, smile upon her face. 'I'll need to watch her.'

'Worried she'll take something that doesn't belong to her?'

Claudia's voice was laced with sarcasm.

'Should I be, honey?'

Isabella, if she'd picked up on something from Claudia's acerbic remark, didn't show it.

Claudia wondered if, perhaps, she was wrong in what she was thinking. *Could Isabella and Paul really be having an affair?* She might just have called him to apologise for reminding him about the anniversary, and mentioned, in passing, the new paintings not being done, as well as having now practically running the gallery by herself. *She had a point.* Claudia knew she had shirked her own responsibilities in that regard. In fact, remembering the walk she and Paul had taken on Robinson Hill, on their anniversary weekend, hadn't she, herself, told him she hadn't been to the gallery in months?

'Only joking,' said Claudia, softening her tone. 'Just don't bring your toy-boys anywhere near her. Then again, she's still just a child.'

Isabella laughed and the awkward moment evaporated.

'She might be young, honey, but he's turning into a big girl. We'll *both* have to keep an eye on her. I think that whatever Charity sets her sights on, Charity gets.'

Claudia looked back over at Charity, who clearly had her uncle eating out of her hand.

'You may be right.'

Isabella turned to welcome another guest who had travelled all the way from San Francisco.

'Brett, how lovely to see you. How was the flight? Please, let me introduce you to the star of the show, the artist and owner of *Sans Cera*, Claudia Montgomery. She turned to Claudia and primed her. 'Brett purchased one of your paintings. last year, *Firewall*, I think it was.'

'Sure was,' said Brett. 'Everyone in the office loves it.'

Claudia gave him an iceberg-melting smile and took his outstretched hand.

'Brett. How lovely to finally meet you in person. Isabella tells me you have one of the most discerning eyes she's ever seen. Please, let me show you my new work, personally.'

She hooked arms with an obviously pleased Brett and led him into the main gallery floor. If she had anything to do with it, *his* firewall would be breached and another expensive painting heading back to the East Coast with him that very night.

Half an hour later, Isabella concluded her opening speech and called upon the senator to declare the exhibition open. Charity told him he *had* to do it. In the end, Isabella practically had to drag him off the stage, albeit to a thunderous round of applause from all watching. He had, however, made the first purchase of the day, Charity proudly putting the first green dot of her career on the painting of Mary Magdalene.

'It'll look marvellous on my office wall, Claudia,' said the senator. 'I hope you'll personally deliver it and help me hang it?'

Claudia assured him she would be honoured to.

'Maybe you'll get to see his majority,' Isabella whispered in her ear, 'I hear it's quite large.'

Claudia almost sprayed the Senator with a mouthful of champagne at the comment.

Charity's parents, Faith and Teddy, arrived and were introduced to Isabella and Claudia. They were delightful people and doting parents. Teddy purchased a sculpture entitled, *Deliverance*, a seven-foot tall, bronze stick-man holding a balloon, in the shape of an apple, while he gazed up into the sky. It was a play on technology having replaced God. Claudia knew Charity loved it and was certain she'd coerced her father into buying it for her. At a shade over sixty-five thousand dollars, it was an expensive present to give his daughter. However, Charity's family were obviously wealthy. The present was simply daddy taking care of his little princess.

A little after four, Charity locked the front doors. Claudia and Isabella paid all the staff, including a generous one-hundred-dollar bonus for each of them.

'What's the verdict?' Claudia asked, as the three of them plonked themselves down into one of the white leather sofas in the main reception area.

'Well,' said Isabella, totting up the figures, 'in terms of green dots and including commissions on which we've already had down-payments, as well as prints sales and other merchandise from the shop, we've sold over three-hundred thousand dollars of paintings and sculptures. The revenue from the new commissions, once completed, will bring today's tally to a little over half a million.

'Wow!' Claudia exclaimed.

'All in all, honey, a much more successful day than I could ever have hoped for. I think we've firmly established *Sans Cera* as one of the most successful galleries on the east coast of America, and Claudia Montgomery as one of the finest artists.'

'I'm so happy for you, Claudia,' said Charity. 'I knew I'd chosen the right gallery to work for.' She immediately looked at both Claudia and Isabella, her face aghast. 'Oh, I'm so sorry, that sounded awfully arrogant.'

'Don't be,' said Claudia, 'not at all. You knew what you wanted and you went and got it. Don't ever stop doing that. Besides, we're glad you chose us. You had other offers. We're both aware of that, aren't we, Isabella.'

'We are. And I agree with Claudia. If you want something, grab it with both hands.'

'Thanks,' said Charity, blushing. 'It means so much to me to hear you say that.'

'Well,' added Isabella, 'I hope what I'm about to tell you makes you even happier. The sale of *Deliverance* and *Expression,* to your uncle and your father, gives you a personal commission of twelve thousand dollars. Your other sales take that figure up to over twenty thousand. I'm so pleased for you. It's just reward for all your efforts. I couldn't have done without you these past few weeks.'

'I'm happy about the commission,' said Charity, looking as if it meant nothing to her, 'but I'm more pleased at how the day went. It was my first exhibition, ever. It was such fun. I wasn't sure Uncle David would make it, which is why I didn't say anything. If I had, and he hadn't come, I'd have felt I'd let you both down.'

Claudia put an arm around Charity's shoulders and gave her a supportive hug. 'I knew it was something like that. But you shouldn't have worried. Nothing's ever guaranteed when you hold events like these.'

'Next time don't keep it to yourself,' said Isabella. 'I would have gotten way more coverage from more exclusive magazines if I'd been able to leak he might have been here. Still, the photographer we hired sent the images of your uncle and his purchase to the news desks in Boston and New York, we'll get great publicity from them. Again, well done, you've become a much-valued part of the *Sans Cera* team.'

'Absolutely!' Claudia raised her glass of champagne. 'To Charity, for raising our game.'

'To Claudia,' said Isabella, raising hers, 'for being so incredibly talented.'

'To Isabella,' said Charity, following suit, 'for giving me the chance to be here in the first place. And to *Sans Cera* for being the best gallery in all Massachusetts.'

They clinked their glasses together.

'*Sans Cera.*'

41

The Pilgrims Highway runs south, from Boston, down to the town of Plymouth, the landing site of the first voyage of the ship, the *Mayflower*, which carried the first settlers, or "pilgrims", to America, in the year 1620. The pilgrims, religious outcasts, in the main, were said to have first set foot on American soil at a place called Plymouth Rock, on December the twenty-first, at the end of their monumental Atlantic crossing. Claudia wondered what it must have been like, landing in, quite literally, a new world. Were they happy or sad? Did they miss their old lives back in England and Scotland? The thought of home, and where that home, for her, now lay, swirled around in her head as she turned off the highway and headed east towards Duxbury.

The smell of the sea grew stronger and the sound of screaming gulls filled the air, loud, even above the steady throb and chug of the Volkswagen's engine. Despite it had no way near the power or panache of her own Porsche, she had already fallen in love with the little car. It brought her a joy of driving she had never felt. Sky had character and style. She also fitted Claudia's own new world, here, down by the sea.

Through Duxbury, she crossed Powder Point Bridge and headed out along the isthmus towards Plymouth Light. She waved to Alec and Roddy, two fishermen she'd met, a few weeks before, when she'd purchased the most beautiful fresh fish from them. They waved back and Claudia felt a warm sense of familiarity and belonging. It lifted her soul in a way Lexington did not.

While pleased at the success of the exhibition's first weekend, she still felt flat, especially after spending Saturday and Sunday night alone. She and Paul had spoken on the Saturday night, once she had dragged herself from

Harry's Bar, leaving Isabella, Charity, and the waiters and waitresses they'd worked with that day, partying harder than she could ever remember doing. The conversation had, though, been easier than the previous night. She'd agreed to fly out and see him after visiting Hannah.

The lighthouse rose ahead of her, stark against a cloudless sky. Bypassing the car park, she took the sandy track from it up to the wooden tower. The doors were closed, although, looking in through the windows, she could see the lights were switched on, a sure sign Hannah was up in the Glass Menagerie. Inside, it was eerily quiet, save for the creaking of timbers as the early afternoon sun warmed the tower. Claudia climbed the helter-skelter stairs to the first-floor landing and called up into space above.

'Hannah' No answer came. 'Hannah, are you up there? I'm home.'

Hannah clearly wasn't there. Likely she would be down in the Beach Shack, preparing lunch. It was after one-thirty, after all. Besides, Sylkie would have barked if she'd been up in the studio. The little dog followed her mistress everywhere.

Claudia stepped back out into the sunshine and looked towards the Point, squinting her eyes against light. It was too far and too bright to see anyone standing there. Had it really been only a month since she'd first seen Hannah, standing there? It felt as if she'd been here all her life.

Suddenly, as if a mist had lifted and allowed her to see things clearly, she realised that what she'd called up to Hannah, about being home, was true. She'd driven down, that morning, feeling excited about arriving. The house in Lexington no longer made her feel that. Perhaps it had, six years ago, when the thought of a family to fill it had made it seem that way. But it no longer did. Not in the reassuring way that coming home should feel. Claudia felt it, here, at the lighthouse. *I am home*, she thought. She wondered what she was going to do about that.

As she reached the top of the steps leading down to the Beach House, she heard Sylkie barking and smiled. She'd missed the scruffy little feral. The wind was light, though it still disguised from where and from how far away the bark had come. She hurried down the last of the steps and looked up and down the beach. There was no-one to be seen. The Beach Shack, too, was empty, but Hannah had left a note saying she was heading out to the Point. She would then head back to the lighthouse to resume work on her painting. The note had the time scribbled on it. *Twelve thirty. An hour ago*, thought Claudia, *she must still be out at the Point.*

The tide was in and the water lapped almost over her feet, as Claudia took the hidden passageway, at the base of the cliff, then clambered up the rock steps up to the grassy bluff. She broke out into the sunshine and looked across to the wooden bench, expecting to see Hannah. She wasn't there, but a bunch of fresh, white roses lay on top of Betsy's stone.

'Dammit. I should have gone back to the lighthouse and walked down by the big house. We've passed each other.' Claudia looked back towards the lighthouse and spied Hannah standing on the iron gantry at the top of the tower. 'Hannah, I'm here!'

Claudia called and waved, knowing it was unlikely Hannah would see or hear her from so far off. She was, though, looking down towards the Point, no doubt having seen Sky, parked, and knew Claudia was back.

As if to confirm her thoughts, Hannah turned and went back into her studio. Claudia headed across the grassy triangle and back down the cliff steps, looking forward to telling her what she's just discovered. No matter how crazy it sounded, she knew, without any doubt, she wanted to be here for the rest of her life.

Heading up the pathway through the dunes, she stopped at the big house, looking at it more closely than she had done before. It was beautiful, even if the paint was flaked and patchy and the garden wild and overgrown. It would be an amazing property to bring back to life. She began to daydream about how she would put her own mark on it, designing the garden in her head, planting rose bushes around a white picket fence. *Am I being crazy? 'No, I'm not? The Universe is telling me I'm supposed to be here.'*

Sylkie, barking at her from the base of the lighthouse, brought her back to the present and the house in her head faded. She headed on up towards the lighthouse, eager to speak to Hannah and find a way to make it work.

'Hello, Sylkie. Have you missed me?' Clearly Sylkie had, for she was jumping up against Claudia's legs and wagging her tail excitedly. 'Calm down, girl. I'm home. Let's go upstairs and break the news to mummy that I'm staying.'

She climbed the stairs, pausing to look down at the now fully empty ground floor. It seemed massive, now that Jonathon's life had been taken from it.

'Hannah!' Claudia called, as she climbed the last few steps up to the studio. 'I'm here. I saw you from the Point. You obviously couldn't see or hear me. I'm a bit later than I meant to be. Sorry, but I've got something I need to tell you about. I've decided that ... Hannah!

Claudia's anguished cry echoed around the tower at the sight that greeted her. Hannah was lying in the middle of the floor, between her easel and the couch, face down and motionless. Claudia froze, her mind trying to process what her eyes were seeing, then rushed across the floor, dropping to her knees beside Hannah and gently turning her over. Sylkie stopped barking and stood, quietly, as if knowing something was very wrong.

After checking she was breathing, Claudia tried to remember what she was supposed to do in this situation. She thought to lift Hannah onto the couch, but decided against it. Instead, she grabbed one of the cushions and placed it under her head. Hannah was barely breathing, and her skin was as cold as ice, but she was still alive.

'Oh, Hannah, I'm so sorry I wasn't here for you. Please don't go. Not yet.'

As she said it, Claudia felt her heart breaking.

Regaining her composure, she pulled out her phone and dialled the number Hannah's doctor had given her for the Boston ambulance service. A voice answered after only two rings.

'Emergency services. How can I help you?'

The operator was cool and calm. She asked if Hannah was conscious? If she was breathing? Was her airway clear? Who and where the patient was? After Claudia had explained that Hannah was suffering stage-four cancer and was under the care of Doctor Kelvin Chancery, the operator advised that an ambulance was on the way, and that she should try to keep Hannah as comfortable as possible until it arrived.

Claudia sat on her knees, supporting Hannah's head in her lap, stroking her hair and talking to her, unsure if she could hear her or not. Suddenly, Hannah opened her eyes.

'Thank God,' said Claudia, 'Hannah, can you hear me?'

Hannah smiled and spoke, but her voice was small, as if the life force she had always had in abundance was fading.

'Claudia, my dear. I'm so glad you're here. I was waiting for you. I think I must have fallen. Can you help me up?'

'Don't try to move, Hannah. The paramedics are on their way to check you out. But you're going to be fine. Just be still, for now, and let me hold you.'

Hannah reached up to touch Claudia's face.

'You're so good to me, my dear. You know I love you, don't you?'

Her hand dropped back to her side, the effort, too much.

'I do, Hannah, I do. And I love you. You've been like a mother to me. Oh, Hannah, there's so much I want to tell you.'

'I know, my dear. But there are things I need to say to you, first. Hold my hands, will you.'

Claudia's took Hannah's hands in hers.

'Just hold on, Hannah. Try not to talk. You can tell me later.'

'I don't think there's going to be a later, my dear. And there are things I need to say to you, now, so let me.'

'Okay, Hannah. Okay.'

Claudia nodded, struggling to speak, the reality of what Hannah had just said was almost too much to bear.

Hannah spoke to her, gently, but determinedly.,

'I never had the chance to watch my own child grow. I never heard her first words or put a plaster on a cut knee and kissed it better. I never got to take her to her first day at school, or watch her go to her prom in a dress Jonathon would have complained about. I never walked along the beach with her and collected seashells, or went paddling in the ocean on a hot, summer day. I never had the chance to watch the lines of her life unfold alongside the creases of mine. To know her as a daughter. As a woman. As a friend.'

A wave of pain ran through her. She gasped and her body stiffened.

'Sssshhh. Don't speak anymore,' whispered Claudia, 'you'll be walking down to the Beach Shack to have a Glenmorangie with me in front of the fire in no time.'

Even as she said it, Claudia had the image of a solitary glass and the silence of a room that had lost its soul and heart. Hannah's breathing eased and she spoke again.

'But I had that chance with you, my dear. I had the journey I missed, with

Betsy, with you, however short, as my daughter. It is a gift I can never repay you for. That priceless time. And your love. If I have been as a mother to you, it is only because you have allowed me to love you like one. I'm going to miss that. So very much.'

Claudia tried not to cry, but Hannah's words had been too much for her to hear and not be moved by. She spoke back to her, through her tears.

'The ambulance is coming. Try to hold on.'

Hannah smiled up at her.

'I don't think it's going to be fast enough, my dear. But I'm where I'm meant to be. And I'm happy. You need to let me go. But I want you to be happy, not sad.'

Hannah's breathing had become almost non-existent. Claudia could feel her slipping away. She prayed for the ambulance to hurry.

'Don't leave me, Hannah.'

Claudia's tears fell onto Hannah's face.

'I can't see you, my dear. Are you crying?'

'No, not crying.'

Claudia wiped her face with the sleeve of her jacket.

'Remember. We agreed. No tears.'

'No tears,' whispered Claudia, 'I remember.'

Hannah gave a shiver. Claudia held her closer, trying to warm her. Her body felt small and fragile. She looked past Claudia, her eyes focused on the blue painted ceiling of the Glass Menagerie.

'It's cold. Are we outside?'

'Yes,' whispered Claudia, 'we're at the Point. Where you love to be.'

'Describe it to me, my dear, will you?'

'The sun's shining on the sea,' said Claudia, struggling to keep her voice from breaking, 'and the sea is so wide and blue that you can see almost all the way to Finisterre.'

'Finisterre.' Hannah whispered. 'I was there, you know? With my Jonathon.'

She smiled and her eyes misted, as if seeing herself, there, in another time.

'That's right,' said Claudia, gently.

She was still holding Hannah's hands in hers. They were colder than before, her breathing desperately shallow. In the distance, she could hear approaching sirens.

'What else can you see, my dear? Tell me.'

Claudia struggled to speak, but knew she had to fight the sadness threatening to overwhelm her. She understood this might be the last time they spoke, and wanted to paint a picture Hannah could see, in her mind, as she passed on to wherever she was going to.

'The tide's going out and the gulls are landing, looking for whats been left. They look funny, hopping across the sand, chasing the crabs. There's a flock of pelicans skimming the waves out towards Cape Cod, probably heading out to the sandbanks to feed.'

'I see them,' said Hannah, 'I see them. It's so beautiful up here, isn't it?'

Claudia heard the ambulance tyres skid to a stop on the sand. It must have driven right up the tower.

'It *is* beautiful, Hannah. So very beautiful.'

'We always loved this place, didn't we?'

Hannah's voice was as slight as a whisper of breeze.

'I do love this place, Hannah. I really do. I just figured out how much, out there, at the Point, looking back at you standing on the balcony. You saw me, didn't you? I know you waited for me to come home before you left. Well, I *am* home. That's what I was going to tell you. You brought me here. And now I never want to leave. Not ever.'

Claudia wasn't sure if Hannah could still hear her, or knew what she was saying, but knew it was important to speak to her.

'Jonathon!' Hannah turned her gaze towards the stairwell. 'What are you doing here? I thought you were working up at the lighthouse. Look, Betsy, your father's here.'

'I see him, Momma,' whispered Claudia, 'I see him.'

'Say hello to your father, my dear.'

'Hello, Daddy.'

Claudia stumbled over the words, her heart already broken.

'Always take care of each other, you two,' said Hannah, 'it's the most important thing in the world, loving your family. Even if you get angry with each other from time to time. You only get one family. So be good to each other. Always. Promise me that now, Betsy.'

Claudia gently squeezed Hannah's hand.

'Yes, Momma. I promise.'

'You're such a good girl. I love you so much.'

Hannah's hands went limp and her eyes closed.

Claudia felt her go. She looked down at Hannah's face and thought she had never looked quite so beautiful. Her skin was glowing, the sunlight dust gathering around her like miniature specs of gold.

Still kneeling, she looked out towards the Point, and then beyond it, to where the ocean and the sky met in a blur of blue and grey, so that she couldn't tell where one stopped and the other started. She remembered Hannah had told her it was called the skiether. The place where the souls of the newly passed go before leaving on the next part of their journey. She wondered if Hannah was looking back at her from it.

'Anyway,' said Claudia, stroking Hannah's hair, 'as I was saying, I've decided I'm going to stay here, with you. No, there's no point arguing, I'm not leaving you. I'm just not. I love you, you see. Do you hear me? I love you.'

She held Hannah to her, rocking her back and forth, telling her how much she loved her and thanking her for the time they had spent together. She held her as the medics rushed up the helter-skelter stairs and into the Glass Menagerie and tried to bring her back. And when the medics told her they were sorry, she held her still. She held her for a long time, afterwards, unable to let her go.

42

The old church on the hill overlooking Plymouth Bay had seen many funerals over the course of its existence. It had been built by the first pilgrims who had landed there. Above its doorway, carved into a thick piece of oak, were the words, *"Whomever you are and wherever you might be on life's journey you are welcome here."* They were apt, thought Claudia, looking up at them, for Hannah. Her life hadn't ended. She had simply made one part of her journey. Today was just another staging point.

The service was a quiet affair, attended by Claudia, Paul and few of the local townspeople. Abernethy MacLelland, Hannah's lawyer, sat at the back of the church, weeping into a hanky and blowing his nose at regular intervals. Hannah, Claudia knew, if she was looking down, would be laughing. She was glad Paul was with her. He'd flown in immediately she'd called him, shortly after the medics had taken Hannah's body from the lighthouse. He had been supportive and kind, which had surprised her, initially, but then their problems were not that they did not care for one another.

The minister spoke of Hannah and Jonathon's love for each other. Although they had kept largely to themselves, they had been regular churchgoers with a strong sense of faith. Hannah would be welcomed into the Kingdom of Heaven, to be with him, he had assured the congregation. Claudia had not shared Hannah's religious views, but hoped that, if there was a God, he was part Scottish, and would make sure she had a plentiful supply of Glenmorangie.

After the service had ended, the minister approached Claudia and Paul, who were standing in the church gardens looking down over the isthmus to the ocean beyond.

'Mrs Montgomery?'

'Father? Minister?' Claudia stumbled over her words. 'I'm sorry, I don't really know how I'm supposed to address you. I'm not religious.'

'James is fine. I'm not Catholic, so *Father* isn't right. Minister would do, but plain old James is better. And we are all of us religious in one way or another, Mrs Montgomery. Sometimes we just don't know it.'

He held out his hand. Claudia took it. His grip was gentle, as were his light grey eyes. She immediately liked him.

'Then you must call me Claudia.'

'Thank you, Claudia.'

James turned to Paul and offered his hand.

'Mr Montgomery.'

'Paul, please. Glad to meet you, James, albeit under these sad circumstances.

James nodded.

'Indeed. Did you know Hannah well?'

'I'm sorry to say I never had the chance to meet her.'

'Then you missed meeting a remarkable woman. She was someone quite special.'

'My wife tells me so.'

Paul took hold of Claudia's hand and gave it a gentle squeeze. James looked back to Claudia.

'You spent quite a bit of time with Hannah over the past month or so. She told me all about you.'

'She did?'

It was a shock for Claudia to hear Hannah had spent *any* time at church. She had never mentioned it. But then Sunday was the day Claudia visited her sister and nieces.

'Well,' James continued, 'I just thought you might like to know that she considered finding you one of the most wonderful things the Universe ever sent her.'

'Oh, I never thought . . .'

Claudia stopped talking, not quite sure what she was trying to say. James, seeing the look on her face, offered explanation.

'Don't look so shocked. Believing in the Universe and believing in God are not mutually exclusive. The Universe is God, and God is the Universe. And God, above all else, is love. Hannah believed that to be the one great truth. She loved you. You clearly felt the same way about her. That's all that really matters in the end.'

'Thank you,' said Claudia, 'that's very kind of you. Your words have helped me so much more than you know. I've been so down since . . .'

Seeing she was on the verge of tear, James took one of Claudia's hands in his.

'I'm glad if I have helped. It's my job. And while you may not believe in God, Claudia, He believes in you. I'll say a prayer to help guide you to where you need to be. But, now, I'll bid you good afternoon. Hannah's coffin is due to be taken to the crematorium. All the arrangements have been long since made. She was nothing if not efficient, as well as being very specific about how things were to be done.'

Claudia smiled, but felt the tears prick at the corners of her eyes at the mention of Hannah's coffin. It made it all seem so much more real, as well as final.

'She was, wasn't she?'

'Speaking of what Hannah wanted,' added James, 'I believe her lawyer, Mr MacLelland, wants a brief word. I'll send him over, if I may.'

Claudia nodded and gave him a smile of thanks.

'Of course. And thank you, James.'

'Good day, Claudia. I'll see you here again, I'm sure. I'm here to talk to you anytime you need me.'

He nodded to Paul then headed back towards the front of the church.

Claudia suddenly felt very fragile. Paul put his arm around her shoulders and kissed her on the cheek.

'I'm going to miss her so much.'

'I know you are, sweetheart. She had become a big part of your life. I see that now. I'm sorry I missed meeting her. If I'd only come back for your exhibition, I might have had the chance.'

Claudia shook her head and gave a sad sigh.

'My exhibition! It seems so irrelevant, now. Hannah's own exhibition was supposed to open, today. She was so excited to see it. Now she never will.'

'Not to mean to be insensitive, but what will you do with her paintings? Continue to show them?'

'Of course,' said Claudia, 'I want them to be her legacy. I'm going to keep most of them in the gallery as a permanent collection of her work.'

'Perhaps that's what her lawyer wants to see you for. There's quite a lot of money's worth. It'll go to her family, I guess.'

'She had no family, Paul, not as far as I know.'

'Money has a way of tempting the insects out of the woodpile, Claudia.'

He saw the look of disapproval on her face and immediately regretted saying it.

'Honestly, Paul, since when have you become so unkind? The more time you spend in Los Angeles, the less tolerant and cynical you seem to become.'

Before Paul could answer, a tall man in a long, grey overcoat and dark charcoal hat approached them. He was in his late sixties, possibly older, with a gaunt face that matched the coat.

'Mrs Montgomery. I'm Abernethy MacLelland. We spoke, briefly, a few weeks ago.'

'I remember, Mr MacLelland. It's nice to finally meet you in person.'

Claudia offered her hand and introduced Paul.

'Delighted to finally meet you, Mrs Montgomery. Firstly, I want to express my condolences. Hannah Thomas was a long-term friend and client. Friend first, client second. I was also a friend of her husband. It is a very sad day.'

'Thank you. Mr MacLelland,' said Claudia, 'she spoke very highly of you.'

'Indeed,' he replied, then turned to address Paul. 'I wonder, Mr Montgomery, if I might have a few moments alone with your wife. Some private matters. I hope you understand?'

'Certainly,' said Paul. 'I'll take a walk around the church grounds.' He kissed Claudia on the cheek. 'Take your time, sweetheart. Good afternoon, Mr MacLelland.'

Abernethy raised his hat.

'Good afternoon, Mr Montgomery.'

Paul walked off in the direction of the church gates. Abernethy waited until he was certain he would not be overheard before turning his attention back to Claudia.

'Mrs Montgomery, may I begin?'

'Claudia, please. And, please do.'

Abernethy smiled a lawyer's smile.

'Would you mind awfully if I kept it to *Mrs Montgomery?* I'm a bit old-school, I suppose, but I am, after all, acting under the instructions of my client. It took me twenty years before I finally called Hannah by her first name.'

'I think I like old-school,' said Claudia. 'Call me what makes you feel best.'

Abernethy looked relieved.

'Thank you, Mrs Montgomery. Now, I have a letter to deliver to you, from Hannah. It was entrusted to me, last weekend, with the instruction to put it into your hand when this time came. We both know it was always a matter of *when*, and not *if*, this was going to happen, due to Hannah's illness, which I know you were fully aware of.'

Claudia nodded, smiling to herself. Hannah had always been one step ahead of everyone when it came to managing her life, and, as it was turning out, her death.

'What does it say?'

Abernethy looked as if Claudia had asked him to remove his clothing.

'It is an extremely private and personal matter, Mrs Montgomery. I have no *idea* what the letter contains. I was instructed to pass it to you. I am keeping my promise to do so. The only thing I would add, no matter how strange it may seem, is that Hannah asked me to tell you to open it when you were alone. I suppose she understood why. You probably will, too, once you read it.' Her reached into his coat pocket and took out a white envelope, handing it to Claudia. 'Now, I will bid you good day. Again, I am sorry for your loss. It is quite clear that Hannah was an excellent judge of character. I hope to see you again, sooner than later.'

'You too, Mr Abernethy. One thing more, if I may?

'Yes?'

'I need to know what I'm supposed to do with Hannah's paintings. I don't know if you are aware, but . . .'

'I am indeed, Mrs Montgomery, fully aware. I'll be in contact regarding Hannah's will reading, next week. I believe you have a small bequeathment.

It would be a pleasure to be able to hand it over to you in person.'

'Hand it over? So it really *is* a small bequeathment?'

Claudia smiled, trying to lighten the moment for them both.

'I can say no more, Mrs Montgomery. But I believe it will fit in your handbag. And now that I have broken my vow of client privacy, I shall retire and think on my failing.'

For a moment, given the look of concern on his face, Claudia was worried she had pushed for too much information.

'I'm so terribly sorry,' began Claudia, 'I only meant . . .'

Abernethy's face creased into as wide a grin as it could stand.

'I'm only joking, Mrs Montgomery.'

He reset his face and raised his hat, then turned and walked off, leaving Claudia laughing for the first time since Hannah had died. It had been wonderfully delivered and just what she needed. She wondered if Hannah had put him up to it.

'I'll bet you did, you crazy lady.'

Claudia stared at her name, written on the front of the letter in dark blue ink and in beautiful flowing script. The kind of writing taught to a different generation. Another of humanity's growing losses. She longed to read the message it contained, but assumed it would leave her feeling emotional. Today had been emotional enough. Instead, she went in search of Paul. She wanted to go home.

It was dusk by the time they got back to Lexington. Paul dropped Claudia off at the house and immediately headed down to his club for a workout, after which, he had business calls to make, which he would do from there. Although he had been at home for five days, he'd said little about his television series. Claudia, to be honest, was glad. She found it hard to care.

After pouring herself a glass of wine, she went up to her bedroom and lay on the bed, cocooning herself in a nest of pillows. The letter was whispering to her, as it had been since she'd been given it. Whatever Hannah wanted to say to her could not wait. She slipped her thumbnail under the open fold at the top right corner of the letter and ran it along the stuck-down flap. It opened easily. She removed the letter, unfolded it, and began to read.

My dearest Claudia,

If you are reading this, I am already gone. I am with Jonathon and Betsy, but I'm also still with you. I always will be. I won't tell you how much I love you, I think you know that already. You've been like a daughter to me. I wish I'd told you that sooner. Sometimes, my dear, you need to be far away from the things you think you most cherish to realise how much you love them and need them. Or to realise that you do love them, but don't necessarily need them. I hope that makes sense.

After Jonathon died, I hated living by the lighthouse. I almost sold up and left. Thankfully, I realised, in time, it was my home, as well as Jonathon and Betsy's resting place. I needed to be where they were to be truly happy. On the Camino, I carried a little part of Jonathon with me, to leave at Finisterre. It was my last adventure. Now, my dear, you need an adventure. And I need be with him.

So, I have left the lighthouse, and all else, to you. My parting gift. I know you will love it, as I have. To think of you there, painting in the Glass Menagerie and sitting in my couch of many colours, brings me joy. Abernethy MacLelland has everything in place. He will hand you the deeds, in due course. They'll fit into your handbag. I hope he shared that with you! It made me laugh to see his face when I asked him to use those exact words. You may sell the lighthouse or live there, whatever you wish. But I would love to think you will take over looking after it. All I ask is, if you do sell it, retain the Point and visit, once in a while, to say hello. Take care of little Sylkie. Love her as she loves you.

If you do decide to take me on one final adventure, and do one of your own, then walk the Camino de Santiago. It will change your life. Trust me in that. Place some of my ashes at the Point, but take some of me to Jonathon, at Finisterre. He is waiting there for me. Go and have your own adventure, Claudia. Find out what you 'need' in your life, along the way.

I told you, once, that people meet each other for a reason. Most times that reason is never revealed and the Universe moves on. We both wondered why it brought us together. I think we found out. Don't you?

You have my love. Always.

Hannah.

HANNAH

43

A shriek from high above his head brought Sean back to reality. The image of himself lying dead on the rocks below was still clear in his mind's eye, Death hanging over him, whispering her greeting. He pressed himself against the face of the mountain and visualised, instead, the train station clock, counting down the seconds. His breathing slowed and the adrenaline stopped washing through his bloodstream. He took a breath and went over what had happened.

The move had been risky, but not impossible. He could not have been blamed if he had fallen. Looking up at the eagle, just before he'd made it, had caused him to lose time at a moment when losing time meant almost certainly losing his life. He'd tried for the handhold, above his right shoulder, but the ice had crumbled. He'd fallen, just managing to grab hold of the ledge he'd been standing upon as he dropped past it. Hanging there, he'd thought about letting go, but that would have been suicide. Against God's rules.

He looked up and saw the eagle, still circling, looking down at him like death's harbinger. It was Linz. It had to be.

'I'm sorry.' His voice bounced back off the adjacent ridges, multiplying into an eerie chorus. 'I didn't have a choice.'

He clicked the carabiner on his safety harness into the metal piton already driven into a narrow fissure in the rock face. He hadn't noticed it before. *Or had he?* If he fell, again, this time the rope would hold him in place. He realised he'd been given the chance to die, but not taken it. Some part of him, perhaps his body's instinct for survival, had saved him. He wondered if he could fight that instinct should he fall again. Having no answer, he placed his left foot onto the crease of rock he'd used as the launch point, minutes before, and looked up at the handhold.

An hour later, at the top of the fourth pitch, Sean pulled himself onto another ledge that allowed him to sit and rest. After taking a long draught of water and eating one of the filled rolls he'd carried in his pack, he waited for his body to recharge. He leaned forward, looking down between his knees at the climb line he'd taken, wondering how the hell he was still alive, then gazed over to Tower Ridge, and to Carn Dearg, further off, as the sun cleared the top of the mountain. On any other day, the sight would have been a joy to behold, but today was not another day, and he was far from joyful.

Across on Tower Ridge, two climbers appeared. Dots of movement, more than anything else. They'd been hidden from him by one of the massive buttresses. They were slightly below his altitude, near the Douglas Boulder, a semi-cone of rock separated from the main ridge by gullies on both sides. He watched them for a few minutes before they were, once more, hidden from view, before moving on.

During the next couple of pitches, the climbing became easier but the protection sparser. Sean climbed on without safety placements, unless some part of the pitch demanded them, hour after hour, adopting the same routine; assess, climb, rest and repeat. He stopped thinking, climbing mechanically, spurred on by instinct. Ironically, that which he had wondered how to control should he fall again.

Towards the end of the seventh pitch, his attention was taken by the sound of an approaching helicopter, the *thump-thump-thump* of its heavy blades chopping into the air, unmistakeable. He looked round and saw it, a mile out, hanging in the sky like a fat, yellow honeybee seeking a patch of flowers. It was a coastguard helicopter, most likely from the base at Torlundy. For a moment, he wondered if Mac had opened the letter he'd left for him. *Would he have contacted the police?* Suicide, after all, was still a crime.

The helicopter came closer and closer to the point where Sean was resting, standing on a thin ledge, halfway up the fifth pitch, his body pressed against the ridge face. He could feel the wind from the rotors and the noise became almost deafening, but then it banked sharply right, heading over towards Tower Ridge. It stopped, hovering directly across from him, and a crew member was lowered down alongside a wire rescue-basket. They were clearly taking up an injured climber. Perhaps one of the two he'd seen earlier. He hoped the climber was alive. If the mountain wanted a death, he was only too willing to give it one.

After watching the helicopter crew bring the climber on board, Sean climbed on, listening to the sound of it as it flew off, until, once more, save for the breeze, there was only the sound of silence.

A couple of pitches from the top, he felt his blood sugar drop to a dangerous level. He recognised the coppery tang in his mouth and his body felt sluggish. After a short rest, where he drank his remaining water, despite having no food to replenish his body, he felt rested enough to go on.

The final pitch was from another ledge, the only protection being a sling wrapped round a point of rock that would probably be unlikely to hold him in a fall. Still, he was doing what Mac had told him was required of him, by not taking risks he knew would most likely kill him. He climbed on and reached a stark slab of rock, pointing to the heavens like a monolith to success, but which afforded no protection whatsoever. It was, he felt, the last chance for Death to claim him. Death, however, seemed to have no intention of doing so.

After seven hours of solo climbing, Sean entered the final boulder field, just below the summit, to amazing sunset views across the highlands from the highest point in Scotland. He walked up to the old ruins and looked back at the edge of the Observatory Ridge, unsure of how to feel about having completed the climb. Feeling nothing, he turned and walked away, taking the Pony Track, down towards Glen Nevis.

It was dark and the path was steep, with only the light from a half-moon showing him the way. Sean was exhausted and struggling to go on. He hadn't drunk or eaten in hours, and his body was weak to the point of collapse. Halfway down the mountain, he stumbled and fell, landing heavily. Stretched out on the freezing stone, he wondered if he could go on. The temperature had dropped below zero and the cold was a constant ache. He would die of exposure if he just stayed where he was. It would be relatively painless. More importantly, it wouldn't be his fault. This was his way out. He closed his eyes and gave in.

The sound of footsteps surprised Sean. He turned his head and looked back up the pathway at an approaching figure, a woman, surrounded by glowing light. She stopped by his side and looked down into his face.

'Hello, Sean.'

'Linz! You're here.'

'I always was, hun. I was waiting for you.'

'I didn't see you, my love.'

'Yes, you did. I'm everywhere. A bird or a stag, or a mountain butterfly. You just need to watch for me.'

'I knew it was you. The eagle?'

'The eagle,' said Linz.

She stood tall and stretched out her massive wings. She tossed her head and her golden hair became a wide rack of pointed antlers. She looked so beautiful. Sean was happy she'd come to collect him.

'I can join you now, my love.'

Linz shook her head and her antlers sprayed golden glitter all around her, making her look like a Christmas card angel.

'Give up, you mean? Is that who you really are, Sean?

Linz's voice was stern and sharp. Sean knew she was angry at him for what he'd said.

'I just want to be with you, my love.'

'You can, hun. Just not yet. Not like this. You need to get up.'

She looked at her wings then folded them back behind her. Sean dropped his forehead onto the back of his hands. He didn't want to move. He didn't want to go on. He wanted to be with Linz.

'Come for me now,' he whispered.

He wondered if Death was close by and could hear him. But he only heard Linz's voice.

'Didn't you listen to Mac?'

'Take me with you, Linz. Please!'

'Get up, Sean. Fight! Or lose me!'

'Linz!'

He looked up, but Linz was already gone. The glitter that had fallen from her antlers was still there, a trail of it leading back up towards the summit.

She had been there!

Two hours later, Sean stumbled into the *Allt a Mhuilinn* car park, where his day had begun almost twelve hours before. He climbed into the jeep, at the point of hypothermia, his hands so cold he was barely able to turn the ignition key. The car heated up and his body warmed. He ate a filled roll and drank a two-litre bottle of water, feeding like a ravenous animal afraid its kill would be stolen.

Warmed but exhausted, he stared at himself in the car mirror, barely recognising the haggard face looking back. His skin was desiccated from the relentless gusts of icy air he'd endured as he'd descended. He hadn't covered his face, as he knew he should have. He'd not cared enough about himself to do that.

'I look like Death.'

He knew, as he said it, this was not how Death looked. Death had peeked at him, on the mountain, when he'd almost fallen into her arms. He'd seen her and knew what form she took. He knew she was aware of his existence. She had heard his call to her and wanted to collect what had been offered.

He closed his eyes and lay back in the car seat.

'Close, hun, so close,' Linz whispered, from the seat next to him.

Her wings and antlers had gone, but she was still surrounded by golden light. She still looked beautiful.

As Sean's eyes closed and sleep took him, another voice came from the seat directly behind him. A voice he would not have recognised, but would have known.

'Next time.'

44

Sean slowed the car to a standstill and stared across the garden at Merrick. The house brooded below a sky that looked like an upside-down Arctic landscape. The windows that had blinked him farewell, only a few days ago, stared straight ahead, pretending they could not see him, then glanced down at him as if to say, *I thought you weren't coming back*?

'Me neither,' said Sean.

Paddington and Pooh hadn't moved from the balcony. They stared at him with glassy eyes, saying nothing, but Sean could feel their judgement. He walked into the kitchen. There was no smell of fresh baked bread. The handwritten note addressed to Miles and the letter to Father Mackenzie were still propped against the vase containing his Linz's ashes.

'Hi guys. I'm sorry. I tried.'

He ran his hand over each of the vases them and felt them with him. It was as if they had collectively spoken to him, forgiving him for not being with them. A wave of relief washed over him and, with it, tiredness, falling on him like a heavy, steel net, so that his legs almost buckled. The force of will that had carried him up and down Ben Nevis, then back to Merrick, had finally burned out. He made his way up the stairs to his bedroom and collapsed onto the bed.

At first, there was only grey. Then then the colours came. Slowly. Washed out. As if too much water had been added to an artist's paint-blocks, flooding them into a rainbow puddle. But the colours grew stronger and became more defined, until the dream in his mind began to play out and make sense.

Sean saw his fourteen-year-old self, rushing home from the old pier building in Fort William. He'd been fishing, but had forgotten to keep an eye on the time. He was late. And he was afraid. Despite having caught a dozen mackerel, and knowing his mother would be glad of them, he had broken the rules. His father, if he was home, would be angry. Not out of concern for his son's welfare, only that Sean had broken the golden rule. The rule of absolute obedience.

He knew he might take a beating. He'd had them before. A weekly occurrence from as far back as he could remember. He could take it. But he did not want his mother or his brother or sister dragged into it, having to pay the price for his sin. It was how his father operated, corrupting and leveraging love.

Sean ran as fast as he could up Belford Road, passing Saint Mary's Catholic Church. He wondered if his father was still there? He usually was, on a Saturday afternoon, lying to his God. He turned into Alma Road and saw the house. He scanned the street, looking for his father's car, but couldn't see it. The driveway was empty. His father was still at church.

'Thank you, God.'

For once, it seemed, He had answered.

Sean opened the front door to the house, not knowing what would be behind it. After storing his fishing rod in the cupboard under the stairs, he made his way into the living room, his fishing bag still slung over his shoulder. He planned to clean the fish and put them in the freezer. Halfway across the room, he stopped dead.

'Mum. I thought you were out?'

He smiled at his mother. She didn't smile back. The look on her face enough to tell Sean why. His heart sank and his stomach lurched. He knew what was coming. Or thought he did.

Today would be different.

'Sean. You're late'

The fear in her eyes was like the amber warning lights on the safety-crossing outside his school gates. Sean held up his fishing bag in explanation.

'Only by half an hour. I caught a dozen mackerel.'

He sensed movement behind him and turned, too late to defend himself from a punch that caught him on the right side of his face. He dropped to his knees as the pain burst in his head, blinding him with white light. He didn't have to be able to see to know it had been his father who had struck him. The hatred in the voice did that.

'Where the fuck have you been?'

Sean tried to stand, but another punch, driven into his stomach, doubled him over. He dropped back to his knees, gasping for breath, and the fishing bag fell from his shoulder, spilling the wet fish over the carpet.

'I was just fishing.'

He heard the pleading tone in his voice and hated himself for the weakness. It was pointless. He should have known better. His father would only enjoy hearing it.

'Now look what you've done, you little bastard.'

'I wish I to fuck was.'

It was a wish Sean had often made, but never said. Until today. He didn't know why he'd said it.

The words sent his father into an instant fury. He bunched his fist and hooked Sean on the left side of his face, knocking him sideways onto the floor. The smell and the taste of the oily fish he'd fallen onto made him gag. As he lay, helpless, his father kicked him in the face, breaking Sean's nose, so that a gush of hot blood mingled with the cold fish slime. He felt something else break, in his neck, and lost all feeling in his body and the ability to move.

'I told you to be back here at five o'clock,' his father screamed, spittle dabs flying, his face distorted with righteous rage. 'What gives you the right to disobey me? Did Jesus Christ disobey his father when he was ordered to be nailed to the cross?'

Sean knew this argument well. It always appeared to make sense to his father. It was also the prelude to more suffering. He tried to crawl away, but his body still didn't seem to be responding properly to what he wanted it to do. He knew he had to answer, no matter the pain. Silence would only anger his father further.

'No.'

'So why the fuck did you disobey me?'

There was no answer he could give, Sean knew, that would make any difference. His father was already past the point of no return and in the mood to hurt someone. Someone weaker than him. The reason why was irrelevant.

'Gordon!'

Sean's mother screamed at her husband, but took a backhanded punch to the face for daring to intervene. She fell back, her lip split and bleeding.

Sean looked up at her and managed to shake his head. Her trying to help him would only make things worse. He also could not stand by and watch her beaten, again, the shame of watching it and not being able to help her was worse than any pain his father might inflict upon him.

'Leave it, mum.'

Behind her, he saw his younger brother and sister. They'd come into the room at the sound of their father's screams, frightened of what might happen to them but not wanting to abandon their brother. They both started to cry. Sean glanced over to them and tried to smile. He hated seeing the fear in their eyes. He was their big brother. He was supposed to keep them safe.

'*Leave it, mum,*' his father said, in a whining voice, mocking Sean. 'You and your precious fucking mother. Both of you, fucking liars!'

He grabbed Sean by the hair and dragged him up onto his feet, then out into the hallway. Sean, his senses returned, lashed out at his father, but not yet physically developed enough for it to count, the punch was ineffectual. But the very action of his son fighting back lit the fuse to his father's anger, and the hatred that lived inside him exploded. He punched Sean in the face, half-closing both his eyes as the flesh puffed up around them.

Sean felt himself being dragged upstairs. To save his hair being ripped out of his scalp, he stumbled up the steps, behind his father, and then across the landing into his own bedroom. A brutal punch to the face knocked him to the floor. As he stood, another equally savage blow sent him sprawling backwards onto his bed, unconscious.

Sean woke, naked, apart from his underpants, face-down on the bed. His hands were bound to the wooden headboard with two of his own church-day neck-ties, and one of his father's hands was around the back of his neck, pushing his face down into a pillow. The taste of copper in his mouth from a split lip made him gag. He struggled to breathe and passed out again, coming too, moments later, still bound.

Panicking and disorientated, Sean pulled against the binds on his wrists, but the knots had been tied cruelly tight. His hands were beginning to tingle from restricted circulation. He lay still, wondering if his ordeal was over, but the hope died as he turned his head and looked up at his father, standing over him, staring down at him with a face Sean did not recognise as being even human. His father's eyes glowed red with hatred and his smile had become a demonic sneer. He held a wire coat-hanger in one hand, crushed and twisted to form a single, thicker strand, the hook part crudely wrapped around it, protruding slightly. The sight of it confused Sean, initially.

'I'll teach you to obey me, you little bastard.'

His father's voice was filled with hideous intent. Moreso than Sean had ever known it before. But it was nothing to the sound that came next.

The hiss of the coat hanger wire cutting through the air would live with Sean for the rest of his life, the blur of the silvery whip the opening act to a beating that would redefine pain. The first strike took him across the small of his back, the wrapped strands cutting into his flesh and leaving an angry purple welt. He screamed, high and shrill, the cries growing louder and more desperate with each subsequent strike.

'Cry you little bastard. Cry,' his father screamed at him with each lash of the wire, his voice growing louder and more hateful as he warmed to his task.

Sean tried desperately to escape, but with his hands tightly bound, could only swing his legs and the lower part of his body off the bed, so that he was kneeling, as if saying his goodnight prayers. He looked round and the whip took him across the face, sending a white-hot burn across his left eye and partially blinding him. His father moved towards him and punched him on the back of his head, then dragged him back up onto the bed.

'Move again and I'll go downstairs and kill your precious, fucking mother. I'll do it, this time. I swear to God.'

Sean went silent and stopped fighting, afraid that this time his father might carry out his oft repeated threat.

And the torment proper began.

His father lashed him, again and again, crisscrossing the strikes so that Sean's back soon resembled a painting by Jackson Pollock, only these were brushstrokes of blood, not paint. Despite the pain, Sean didn't cry, keeping the promise he had made to himself, two years before, on the day of the marmalade jar and the faraway voice. He screamed, with each strike, and when the pain became almost too much to bear, he begged for mercy, sending a silent prayer to God to help him.

But God did not answer!

Sean understood, in that moment, that God *wanted* him to suffer. As His own son, Jesus Christ, has suffered, nailed to his wooden cross, betrayed by a father he'd loved.

But then came the voice.

'I'm here, Sean. I won't let him hurt you anymore. You're safe.'

He turned his head and looked up. Linz was standing behind his father. She was surrounded by light. She looked like an angel.

'Linz! Help me!'

'Shut up, you little bastard,' his father cried, lashing down at him, lost in his madness.

Linz stepped past him, spreading her wings and holding out a hand to Sean. Her antlers were a glittering crown of gold upon her head, like the crown of thorns Jesus had worn. Sean reached out and took her hand, the ties that bound him falling away. As he walked with her, past his father, Sean turned and looked back at the boy on the bed. Despite he had lost consciousness and his cries had stopped, his father kept beating him, the hissing wire slapping against bloodied flesh.

'Come with me, hun,' said Linz. Don't look at it anymore.'

'But, what about . . .'

Linz smiled and touched Sean's face. Her fingers were soft and warm. She shook her head, showering him in golden glitter, then spoke to him, her voice blocking out his father's screams and the hiss of the coat hanger whip.

'He's going to be okay. He's going to find me. Don't you understand this yet?'

'I'm not sure, Linz. I don't understand.'

'You will, hun. In time.'

There was no more pain. There was no more fear. He felt loved. He felt safe.

45

Sean rolled out of his bed, onto his knees, leaning against the bedframe as if preparing to say his goodnight prayers. He was out of the dream but still trembling from the ordeal of it. The beating he had received that day had been the worst of his life. The memory of it had remained locked away in the empty place, until now, like the other memories that had been coming to him, recently, in his dreams. He had thought himself protected from them and knew, with the reawakening of them, something profound was happening to him. The empty place wasn't protecting him any longer. He needed something to lash out at and chose the God who had always failed him.

'Why are you torturing me? Is it because I renounced you? Are you that fucking petty that you bring these memories to me, now, when I sleep? When I can't defend myself. Why have your forsaken me? Christ, but Jesus must have fucking hated you.'

He pressed his face into his pillow and wept. As he should have wept twenty-five years earlier. When he'd been betrayed and abused by his own father.

The whisky seared Sean's throat but helped to calm him. He settled back into the livingroom couch and shook himself free of the remnants of the dream. He would not go back upstairs to the bedroom, fearful of what might come for him if he fell asleep again. He had never been plagued by such visceral visions and wondered why they were coming now. They always seemed to happen, here, at Merrick, the home he had shared with Linz. She was the only person who knew what had happened to him. The only one who knew about the empty place and the bad things he kept hidden there. The thought brought with it a startling realisation. Finally, as she had told him he would, he understood what was happening.

Linz's love for him had helped him keep the door to the empty place closed, safe from the awful memories he'd buried there when he'd followed the faraway voice to it in the past. The things the faraway voice had hidden from him to keep him safe. Without her, he could no longer keep the bad things away. Linz had come to protect him in the dream, just now, taking him away from the pain. She *still* wanted to protect him! She still loved him and wanted to make sure the bad things would not hurt him. And they would, without her here to stop them. Linz wanted him to come to her not just to *be* with her, but to keep him safe!

He knew what he had to do to help her.

Sitting at the desk in his study, Sean woke his iMac and went online, searching for flights from Edinburgh to Delhi. He found one departing Edinburgh at two-thirty that afternoon, with a connecting flight from London Gatwick later that evening.

'Four hours from now,' he said to himself. 'Can I make it?'

He looked over his desk, at Linz, sitting in one of the club chairs.'

'You can, hun.'

'Are you coming with me?'

'I'm always with you, hun. I told you that before, remember? Butterflies and birdsong. I'll be waiting.'

'On Everest, my love? We always wanted to go there, didn't we?'

Linz smiled then stood and walked over to a picture of herself and Sean standing on the summit of Schiehallion, one of the Munro's they'd climbed together, years before the children had been born. Sean remembered the day well. They had been so in love. They'd found a bush filled with little blue butterflies that had taken off when Linz had brushed past it. They'd flown all around her, as if they knew she was a special soul and not to be afraid of.

'And now we will, hun.'

'Number two in your journal, my love. I'm so glad you showed it to me. I'd forgotten about our list.'

'I hadn't, hun. I'll see you there.'

Linz spread her butterfly wings. They shimmered, gold and blue, under the bright sunlight coming in through the study windows. She was beautiful. Sean couldn't remember seeing her look *so* beautiful. Except, perhaps, the sunny day in Applecross Bay, sitting in the kayak, when the sun had shone on her hair and lit the salt on her skin to gold. Their last day together! He looked at his computer screen, and when he looked back, she was gone. *Probably gone up the children's rooms to say goodbye.* Feeling safe and loved, he booked the flight to Delhi, adding an onward connection to Kathmandu and booking a room at the Radisson Blu hotel, close to the city centre.

The next two hours were spent packing, Sean stuffing enough gear for a minor expedition across the Himalayas into his yellow, hundred-litre duffle-bag. The old North Face bag had accompanied him around the world on many climbs. It felt good to be dusting it down once more. He was excited, he realised, to be leaving for somewhere he and Linz had always longed to visit. He retrieved his passport from the safe in the wall, making sure he had his international driving licence and inoculations booklet. He'd travelled extensively, over the past few years, so knew he was covered for pretty much anything. He also had international travel insurance, not that he would need it, but the authorities, where he was going, could be sticklers for paperwork.

His mind turned back to the nightmare he'd just had. Perhaps it had been in his head from the day Emily showed him the coat hanger, during their last counselling session. On a whim, he decided to call her. She would be pleased to learn he'd faced it. He found her number in his phone and made the call.

'Emily MacGregor.'

Her voice was bright and cheerful.

'Hi, Emily,' said Sean, his voice a reflection of hers.

'Hello. Who's speaking?'

'Really! After all our time together. I'm hurt.'

Emily recognised his voice.

'Sean! Are you all right? Has something happened?'

Emily's concern showed in her voice.

Sean sought to ease it.

'I'm fine. Actually, I'm better than fine.'

Although surprised, Emily was relieved to hear from him.

'It's good to hear from you, Sean. I've been worried about you. I wanted to call you after what happened at Tigerlily, with Jann Livingston, but I wasn't sure you'd talk to me.'

'Forget it, I should have listened to you about that psycho. It should be me apologising, not you.'

Emily breathed and audible sigh of relief.

'Good! Then we'll leave her as a horrible memory.'

'Best place for her.'

So, tell me Sean, how are you coping, now you're back at home? I'm here for you, you know, anytime it gets tough.'

'I do. And I really appreciate that you are. I'm doing fine. Just back from a climb. I was up at Ben Nevis.'

'You're climbing again! Sean, that's wonderful.'

'It's done me good. It was so beautiful up there. I see things a lot more clearly now. I'm going back into the mountains, today, as it happens. But I'm calling to tell you something else.

'What's that?' Emily asked, pleased to hear him sounding so upbeat.

'The coat hanger you showed me. Remember?'

Emily immediately understood what Sean was referring to. She was surprised he was bringing it up. It was something she'd still hoped to talk to him about, but he really needed the help of a professional to deal with *that* psychological minefield. But any step forward was a step in the right direction. But she wasn't going to rain on his parade.

'You're certainly talking like I've never heard you do before, Sean. Why is that, do you think?'

Sean paused, thinking about his response.

'You were right all along. I had to face the memory of my father and what he did to me. It was the only way to begin to deal with it and hope to finally let it go. I can never be where I'm meant to be with him still lurking inside of me.'

Emily, if surprised, still took it as a positive step. Although she was still a little concerned he'd taken it alone.

'Sean, that's truly wonderful to hear. It does seem that you're making progress. You always deflected the questions about your father when I asked before. What's changed, do you think, to allow you to face it now?'

Sean didn't so much answer as follow the thought unravelling in his head.

'He was damaged, you see. He couldn't love anyone, not even himself. I don't know why. He blamed his children for taking his wife away from him, thinking, if she loved us, she couldn't possibly love him. He was so needy and narcissistic, just like Jann Livingston. I guess that's why she was sent to meet me. I needed to see another face of evil to help me see the true face of my father. I hate to say it, but I'm like him in some ways, I think.'

Emily, while reticent to get into any deeper discussion about Sean's father, still felt the need to try to help him now.

'No, Sean, you're not. You only feel like that because you survived the accident. It's called survivor guilt and it's perfectly normal. Trust me, you're nothing like him, and you *don't* deserve to suffer. Accidents happen. It's a part of life. What's important for you to think about is that you loved Linz and she loved you. You loved your children and they adored you. You were part of a happy, loving family. You didn't let *anyone* down, like your father did you and your family.'

'Perhaps,' said Sean, but I still feel guilty for leaving them. But I won't for much longer.'

Sean's answer worried Emily. The tone of his voice was odd. She knew she needed to speak to him, face to face, and soon.

'Look, Sean, no matter how much you're improving, you still need some help dealing with these memories. They're clearly reawakening in your psyche. That's not easy to deal with. Especially not alone.'

'But that's just it, Emily, I'm not alone.'

'That's good. Who's with you? Is Judith there? Or your friend, Miles?'

'No, it's Linz! She's taking care of me. She always has. I understand that now.'

Emily felt a chill on the back of her neck.

'Linz! Your wife, Linz?'

Sean laughed.

'Don't sound so surprised. Yes, my wife, *that* Linz. She's here, now. Do you want to talk to her?

Emily hesitated, half afraid for what it might mean to agree. She decided to push Sean a little further to see how far gone he was.

'Sure, that would be great.'

She heard him call out, the phone clearly held away from his face.

'Linz! Come and speak to Emily.' A few moments passed. 'Sorry, Emily, she was here a minute ago. We're heading off soon. She's probably getting a few things together, now we're finally getting to do the adventures we planned.'

Emily had no idea what he was referring to, but his behaviour was sending warning bells ringing.

'That's great news, Sean. It must be nice to see her again. I know you missed her when we chatted about her at Dunvegan Castle.

'She was at Dunvegan,' said Sean, 'I'm surprised you didn't see her. She was with me on Ben Nevis, too. She wouldn't let me give up and die. She made me come back to Merrick to face my father, to make me understand why I didn't have to be afraid of him anymore. She's looking after me. She always has been. I just didn't understand it properly.'

The warning bells in Emily's head became deafening.

'She wouldn't let you die! Did you *want* to die, Sean?'

Sean didn't hesitate in his reply, making what he said all the more frightening.

'I have to.'

He said it way too calmly for Emily's liking. Her blood ran ice cold. He was sicker than she'd realised. She kept her voice calm, not wanting to alert him to her growing concerns.

'Sean, who told you that?'

'Linz explained it to me. Mac wouldn't listen. He said I had to stick to God's rules. But how could *he* understand?'

'Mac?'

'Father Mackenzie. We were in the garden at . . . Cramond Kirk. 'We were . . . standing by . . .'

Emily noticed his speech begin to slow.

'Sean! Are you okay?' There was no answer. 'Sean, talk to me!'

She could hear him breathing, but there was clearly something happening to him, physically as well as mentally. His voice sounded odd and he seemed distant. Finally, he spoke.

'By . . . the apple tree. Linz was . . .'

He stopped speaking, his breathing fading away to nothing. Emily knew what was happening to him and tried to fight the panic rising her herself. She needed to get to him. Fast! She kept her voice as steady and calm as she could.

'Sean, are you going to be at home all day? I thought I might come over and see you.' There was no answer. Emily feared he'd gone. A minute passed and she began to fear he'd ended the call, but then she heard him breath. 'Sean. Talk to me. Please. Are you okay?'

'Hello, Professor, is that you?'

Sean answered as if he'd just picked up the phone. He sounded different, his voice was harder, more like the voice Emily had become used to. He'd called her *Professor*, when only moments ago he'd been calling her by her name.

'Yes, Sean, it's me, Emily. I thought I'd maybe come over to see you and Linz, today, if it's convenient?'

'Linz?'

'Yes,' replied Emily. 'I've not met her yet, despite all the times we've talked about her. It would be good to talk to both of you together.'

'Is this some kind of strange therapy, Professor?

Sean was angry and it showed in his voice.

Emily was disturbed by the dramatic change in his behaviour. She was annoyed at herself. She should have recognised his symptoms. He was clearly in a state of psychosis. His PTSD was affecting him badly. She'd really thought he'd been making progress. She'd been wrong. Very wrong. She thought about how to handle the situation.

'I'm sorry, Sean. I didn't mean to upset you. Look, if it's not convenient, then perhaps some other time when you . . .'

Sean cut her off.

'Look, it was nice of you to call, but I'm totally fine. And after what happened at Tigerlily, frankly, I'm surprised to hear from you at all. Why don't you just leave me alone to get on with things.'

'Sean, perhaps if we could . . .'

Sean hung up, wondering why she'd bothered calling him. She was making no sense. He stood up, deciding to shower and then head straight to the airport. He'd spend an hour relaxing in the British Airways Lounge before his flight to London.

Emily tried to call Sean back, but there was no answer. Instead, she called Judith, but the call went straight to voicemail. Deciding she had to do something, she made her way out through her office, ignoring the frantic waves from her receptionist.

Out on a busy George Street, she turned right, heading towards St Andrews Square and the QuantumCorp office. Judith might be in a meeting. The only thing she could do was to get there and find her. Failing that, she'd head out to Sean's house, by herself. Just as she crossed Frederick Street, her phone rang.

'Hi Ems, sorry I missed your call.'

'Judith, thank God.'

Judith could hear the fear in Emily's voice.

'What's wrong?'

'It's Sean, Judith. And it's bad. Where are you?'

'I'm in the Dome Bar, with Miles. What's wrong with Sean? You sound scared.'

'Leave, Judith. Leave right now. Get up and get out onto the street. I'm on George Street. Stay on the castle side and walk towards my office, we'll find each other.'

'We're on our way, Ems. But you're really scaring me.'

Miles and Judith met Emily outside the Assembly Rooms, where some of the best comedy shows in the Edinburgh Festival took place every year. The worry on their faces was in stark contrast to the usual happy smiles of the festival goers. Judith quickly introduced Miles to Emily.

'What's happened?'

'Sean called me,' said Emily, her voice tight with worry, 'not long ago. He's having a psychotic episode. I need to have him sectioned right away. He told me he was with Linz. Actually *with* her. Apparently, she's been telling him she wants him to die. Part of Sean thinks it's real. It's as if his personality has almost split in two.'

'Jesus Christ,' said Miles, 'I knew he was acting odd when we saw him.'

He avoided Judith's accusing glance.

'He's more ill than I thought,' said Emily. 'It's my fault. I should have realised it sooner.'

Miles pointed to a black, Mitsubishi Jeep sat in one of the central parking bays

'My car's right there. Let's go.'

The three of them rushed across the road and piled into the jeep, causing a look of concern from more than one or two other drivers and pedestrians as the wheels spun on the tarmac and headed off along George Street.

Sean pulled out of Merrick's driveway for the second time in as many days. He looked back at the house where he had spent so many happy times with Linz and the children. There was nothing left of those times, and nothing there for him to care about. He said a silent goodbye, knowing, this time, he would never return.

Twenty minutes later, Miles reached Merrick, having driven as fast as the traffic would allow. He pressed the code into the front door keypad, letting the three of them into the hallway. The house was still and silent. Judith and Emily went into the kitchen. Miles headed into the lounge, hoping to find Sean in his study, although he already knew he was probably out as his G-Wagon hadn't been in the driveway.

'Miles!' Judith's voice echoed through from the kitchen. Miles rushed through to find her holding up an envelope. 'It's addressed to you.'

He took the note and tore it open.

'Sean said he was going back to the mountains,' said Emily, as Miles read it. 'He said he'd been on Ben Nevis, a few days ago, and almost died. I think he's heading back there.'

Miles handed Emily the note.

'According to this, he's heading to Glencoe. He'll be on the road to Stirling, by now, but I can catch him. He won't be chasing as hard as I will. I'll have to leave right now.' He looked at Emily and Judith. 'You'll both have to get a cab back into the city.'

'Forget it,' said Judith, 'there's no way I'm not going to be there for him if he needs me.'

'I'm coming too,' added Emily, 'this is my responsibility. He's still my patient. You might need me to help calm him down, as well as to speak to the police if we need to stop him from harming himself.'

They looked at each other, understanding and fearing the possibility that Sean might, unless they reached him.

'Fine,' said Miles, 'let's go.'

Less than an hour later, as Miles' jeep sped past the Green Welly Stop, where the road to the islands divided, heading north, Sean was five thousand feet above them, climbing fast, heading south.

46

At a height of just under ten thousand feet, Lukla's Tenzing-Hilary Airport was one of the highest in the world, and one of the most dangerous to fly into. As well as being short, and perched perilously on the edge of a two-thousand-foot drop, it had no air traffic control, so landings were left to the skill and experience of the local pilots, who landed by eye. Sean caught a glimpse of the airstrip as the plane banked right, beginning its final approach.

'Two minutes to landing.'

The pilot in the open cockpit, less than two feet in front of Sean's seat, struggled to be heard over the roar of the engines.

After only a slightly bumpy landing, Sean stepped onto the tarmac and took a breath of icy air, filling his lungs and snapping his senses alert. Although the sky was blue and cloudless, and the sun shining brightly, it was not much above freezing. He was glad of his gloves, fleece, and Merino wool hat. He looked around him, taking in the first sights and sounds of the Himalayas.

The landing strip was busy with climbers and Sherpas, filled with an array of rucksacks, duffle-bags and a host of other climbing gear. Most of the serious climbers attached to teams planning to summit Everest, as well as those heading only as far as Base Camp, began their journey at Lukla. Oxygen levels were fifty percent less than at sea level, so the twenty-four-mile trek to the base of Everest helped with the acclimatisation process everyone had to go through.

'Mr Sean!'

A Sherpa guide, wearing an orange puffer-jacket and sporting a similar black beanie to Sean's, approached him, hand outstretched and a warm smile upon his round, weather-beaten face. Sean couldn't place his age, but guessed he was in his late thirties. His eyes were as brown as old tobacco and the lines on his weather-beaten face had been earned over many climbs.

'Kamal?'

Hello, Mr Sean, I am most pleased to be meeting you on such a glorious day as today surely is.'

'How did you know it was me.'

'The hotel, Mr Sean, were very kind to send me a copy of your passport.'

Although he'd planned to climb alone, on arrival at his hotel in Kathmandu, Sean had been informed it was impossible without a licenced guide. Reluctantly, he had accepted the constraint, allowing the hotel travel desk to organise a local Sherpa. Despite having been forced into hiring him, Sean was pleased to see him. He took Kamal's hand, wincing at the strength of the grip.

'Good to meet you, Kamal.'

Kamal looked over at the plane Sean had just got off, where a swarm of Sherpas were hovering around the growing pile of luggage and equipment, ferrying it off like worker ants raiding a rival colony's nest.

'Mr Sean. You must wait here, please. I will collect your pack. Do not wander off unless you wish us lost to each other before our journey has begun.'

Kamal smiled, again, revealing a set of perfect white teeth and making Sean smile back. He oozed happiness and contentment with his life, be it what it was, in a way that westerners seldom did.

'I won't move, Kamal. It's a yellow Mont Blanc. My name's printed on it in black letters.'

Sean watched Kamal retrieved his duffle-bag from the plane, hoisting it onto his back as if it were filled with balloons, instead of the thirty-five kilos it weighed. Sherpas were unnaturally strong and exceedingly fit, their physiology different from virtually any other race on earth, allowing them to operate with ease at heights where normal men would falter. Sean had fully intended to carry his own pack, but said nothing as Kamal re-joined him, picking up his own only slightly smaller pack and strapping it onto his chest. This was, after all, his livelihood.

There were lines of tea rooms and shops bordering Lukla's cobbled main street, filled with chattering trekkers, climbers and local people. The general sense of excitement was palpable.

'Do you wish to stop for tea before we head out of the village, Mr Sean?'

'No thanks, Kamal. I had breakfast in Kathmandu. I'd rather we got ahead of the crowd.'

'Onwards, then, to our Earth Mother, *Chomolungma*.'

Sean didn't recognise the name.

'*Chomolungma*? I thought the Nepali name for Mount Everest was *Sagarmatha*?'

Kamal, just ahead of him, stopped and turned.

'It is, Mr Sean, and you are most wise to know this. But in the tongue of the Sherpa and the Drokpa Tibetans, who are born in her shadow and live under her divine protection, she is known as *Chomolungma*, Goddess of the Wind.'

Sean looked around him as they made their way through and out of Lukla. The town was small and the buildings low and ancient looking. It felt was as though he had stepped back in time. There were intricately-carved, prayer wheels everywhere. Passing a set, he reached out a hand and spun one, wondering which particular god he'd invoked. Strands of coloured flags were strung across the streets, tied to buildings, and fluttering from every bridge and high monument. There were five colours, some printed with images and texts he could not decipher.

'What do the flags mean, Kamal?'

'They are prayer flags, Mr Sean, and so very important for us all. They are arranged, always, in the same order, from left to right.

Sean looked up at a string of flags, crossing the street from one building to another.

'So they are. I hadn't noticed until you said.'

Kamal's smile made it seem he had been blessed for revealing, to Sean, some great, cosmic secret. He enlightened him further by explaining what the colours meant.

'Blue represents the sky above us. White for the air that surrounds us. Red is for the fire that warms us, and green the water that gives us life.'

'And yellow,' said Sean, interrupting, 'represents the sun?'

The expression on Kamal's face was one of unbridled joy. As if Sean had miraculously become spiritually enlightened.

'Ever it is so, Mr Sean. May it shine on all living things.'

'Do they carry your prayers to your gods, Kamal?'

'That is what many people think, Mr Sean, but it is not so. The prayer flags are but to promote peace, compassion, strength and wisdom. Our prayers and mantras are carried by the wind, spreading good and compassion into all of the world around us.'

Sean looked back at the string of flags, seeing them, now, for much more than he had first thought.

'It makes a damned sight more sense than our western gods, when you put it like that.'

'Mr Sean?'

'Never mind. I just liked what you said.'

Kamal pressed his hands together, as if about to pray, and bowed his head.

'Namaste!'

Sean had found a certain peace in Kamal's words. He began the trek, feeling his sprits lifting as they walked.

Trains of lumbering yaks passed them, returning from the villages, high above, as well as from Everest itself. They were smaller than the domestic cows back home in Scotland, Sean noted, but burly and well-muscled with a spread of horns that threatened to sweep him from the narrow pathway.

'Keep the beasts to the valley side when they pass, Mr Sean,' called Kamal, 'and yourself to the mountain.'

Sean made a mental note to remember the advice.

The yak trains, apart from the Sherpas, were the only way to transport supplies and equipment. There were no roads, only ancient tracks and paths cutting through the valleys, leading into the mountains. Helicopters flew back and forward from Everest to Lukla, throughout the day, but at a cost of four thousand dollars per one-way trip, were mostly reserved for the professional climbers and medical emergencies.

Kamal and Sean followed the Dudh Kosi river, crossing swaying suspension bridges and climbing switch-backed paths dotted with pink rhododendrons, stopping for lunch at one of the many teahouses that lined the route, in a village called Padking. The food was delicious, Sean had to admit, as he tucked into a spicy, goat curry, scooping the food up with buttery, fried flatbreads.

After lunch, he sat outside the tearoom, on a wall, overlooking the tree-lined river. A small butterfly flew towards him, landing on a bush growing beside him. It sat, opening and closing its powder-blue wings, warming them in the sun. He held out his fingers towards it.

'Is it you, my love?'

The butterfly took to the air, fluttering past Sean's face so closely that he felt its wings brush his cheek. It rose up, behind him, like a piece of coloured paper attached to an invisible thread, flying over the orange tiles of the tearoom roof and out of sight. But it had kissed him. He knew it was Linz.

A little after two o'clock, they resumed the trek, reaching the village of Monjo just as the sun began to fall away, and checked into the Yeti Mountain Home, a circle of wooden buildings with prayer flags strung over the doorways and between the buildings. It had a common bar and a garden for its guests to relax in. The bedrooms were wood-lined with comfy beds, private bathrooms and plenty of electric points. All in all, it was more than Sean had been expecting.

Sitting on his bed, relieved to be out of his climbing boots, he stared out of the open window, listening to the sound of trekkers chatting in the garden and the cowbells of passing yak-trains. He was tired but content with his first day. He'd seen Linz, which had lifted his spirits more than anything else. She was here. As she'd promised she would be.

'Butterflies and birdsong. Isn't that what you told me, my love?'

Supper was goat stew and dumplings, followed by rice pudding and jam, which, despite being delicious, Sean struggled to get down.

'Not hungry, Mr Sean?'

'It tastes great, Kamal. I just don't feel as hungry as I should.'

'It is because we are so high, Mr Sean. But you will be need to be eating ten thousand calories a day if you are to survive the climb up to Chomolungma.'

Sean winced. He'd been at altitude before, and knew he had to fuel his body, but what Kamal was suggesting bordered on ridiculous.

'Ten thousand! That's four times what I normally eat.'

'Your body will be working harder than normal, Mr Sean. It must be fed. The altitude will take away your appetite, but you must eat, no matter you do not wish to.'

Sean forced down another spoonful of rice pudding, which clearly pleased Kamal, who advised they would continue their trek just after sunrise the following morning and that Sean should get as much sleep as possible. He would waken him in good time for breakfast. Already not relishing the thought of eating again, Sean went up to his bedroom and was asleep in minutes.

The next day began under another blue and cloudless sky, bitterly cold and with a bracing breeze, heading up towards the first great marker on the route, the twin suspension bridges just below the entrance to Sagarmatha National Park. They marked the official entrance to the Everest region and were the last in the series of such crossings before reaching Namche Bazaar, their stop for the night. They would cross the higher of them, the Hilary Bridge, four hundred feet above the river. Reaching them, Sean stared up, remembering when he had last seen them, at the cinema, with Linz and the kids, watching the movie, *Everest*. They had all wondered what it would be like to make that crossing, swaying in the wind and looking down into the open void. His heart ached for the chance to watch another movie with them.

Kamal led them across a long section of mixed, rocky terrain that followed the line of the river, then up a steep climb through the surrounding forest. They reached the Hilary Bridge and Sean followed him out onto it. Ahead of them, halfway over, another set of trekkers were crossing with less calm and confidence. With every step they took, the bridge bounced and the groans from those who were finding the ordeal terrifying filled the air. Sean let them move on before reaching the centre himself. He stopped and looked down the valley.

'I hope you all can see this,' he whispered, but the ghosts of his family remained silent.'

Sad that he was alone, he walked on across the bridge.

The joy and relief in the faces of the group that had just crossed made Sean angry. He strode passed them, not stopping, ignoring the smiles and greetings being sent his way. Watching him, Kamal was troubled. They had barely spoken since breakfast and Sean remained withdrawn and uncommunicative. His aura was an angry crimson streaked with pale, sickly blue, showing he walked with the bad spirits. Whatever the reason for him being there, he seemed to take no joy in his surroundings, or in the trek, itself.

The terrain beyond the bridges grew much steeper. Kamal set an easy pace, but it was a long, hard climb into Namche Bazaar. By the time they arrived,

Sean's legs felt like lead and his head was pounding.

'We will spend two nights here, Mr Sean,' said Kamal, as they collected their room keys.

'I really wanted to head on, tomorrow, Kamal. I'm a bit tired, but that was a hard day's climbing. I'm sure I'll be fine after a good night's sleep.'

'You are tired, Mr Sean. You must acclimatise as everyone who reaches Namche does. It is not an option. It is most required.'

'Must we? I'm keen to finally see Mount Everest.'

Kamal gave Sean his usual happy smile.

'You can see *Chomolungma* from here, Mr Sean, at the Norgay Tensing Memorial. It is no more than ten minute's up and out of the town. But we cannot go any higher without resting properly. I'm sorry. But you will enjoy a day, here, in Namche.'

Sean tried to hide his annoyance. There was nothing he could do. Kamal was adamant. He could stop him from carrying on if he felt he was not physically capable.

'You're right, Kamal, I probably *do* need a break. I'll take a rest and have a shower. I'll see you later, at dinner.'

'Most excellent, Mr Sean.'

Kamal was glad Sean had not pushed further to resume the climb. He could see he was struggling, but that was normal for almost everyone who came to the Himalayas and climbed so high. It was the climbers who were reckless he was more concerned about. Sean, despite the burden he so obviously carried, did not seem to be one of those.

After a better than expected night's sleep, there was little for Sean to do except explore the Sherpa capital. Although he was feeling ill and his mood was already dark, he walked down into the town to explore.

Namche Bazaar was built on the slope of an arch-shaped mountain. The houses climbed the hillside like the semi-circular seats of a Roman amphitheatre, their multi-coloured, tin roofs spread like scatter-cushions. In its past, it had been a historic trading hub, famous for yaks' milk cheese and butter. Sherpas from neighbouring villages and traders from Tibet would gather to barter goods. It was famed for its ancient culture, traditions and heart-warming hospitality. Now, it was more known as the staging point for expeditions to Everest and the other great Himalayan peaks surrounding it, although the hospitality of the Sherpa people was no less diminished. They were, Sean discovered, the happiest and friendliest people he had ever met. Irrespective of his headache and his demons, he could not help but fall in love with their smiling faces and joyful disposition. Linz, he knew, would have loved them every bit as much.

Sean meandered around the town centre, stopping to browse the craft shops selling Tibetan artefacts, trekking clothing and mountaineering equipment. The narrow streets were busy with locals going about their business, as well as trekkers and mountaineers readying themselves for the next part of the climb. He took a late lunch in the open town square, drinking condensed milk sweetened tea, encircled by dark-forested mountains that rose and fell like the crenelated spine of a snow dragon. It was mid-afternoon before he climbed the hundreds of stone block steps back up to the tea room, where Kamal was sitting on the front porch, chatting to some of the other Sherpas.

'Mr Sean! Have you been enjoying our beautiful town?'

'It's an incredible place, Kamal, but I'm more looking forwards to getting on up to Base Camp.'

'Of course,' said Kamal, wondering why Sean was so fixated on getting there. 'How are you feeling? No symptoms of altitude sickness?'

'None,' said Sean, lying.

His headache was perpetual, despite the paracetamol he was taking with alarming frequency.

'Then we will head on tomorrow, Mr Sean. But we must first do an acclimatisation climb, this afternoon, up to twelve thousand feet. We may do it now, if you wish? As soon as I finish my tea.'

Sean had not desire to do any acclimatisation climb.

'Actually, I met some other trekkers who are doing the same. They asked me to join them, visiting the Tensing Norgay monument, to get our first sight of Mount Everest. After that, they're heading up to the Hillary Memorial. That should be high enough. Yes?'

'It would be just so, Mr Sean.'

'Then just relax, Kamal. Enjoy your tea and chat to your friends. I'll catch up with you later.'

'Are you sure, Mr Sean? It is so important to make these types of climb, however short they may seem. They will help you be ready to go higher. Climb high and sleep low, it is the only sure way to manage the mountain sickness.'

'I know that, Kamal,' said Sean, curtly, 'but, as I said, I'm going to go up with the friends I made down in the town.'

'If you are certain, Mr Sean, then very well. But please let me know you have returned.'

'Okay. I'll see you later.'

The monument was ten minutes above Namche, the first place where trekkers coming from Lukla could see Mount Everest. Sean stood below the statue of Sherpa Tensing Norgay, the "Tiger of the Mountains", who had accompanied Edmund Hilary on its first successful ascent in 1953, gazing at the mountain of mountains. A horizontal wisp of white blew off its summit, thirteen kilometres away. He felt suddenly overwhelmed. It was an emotional moment, seeing one of the world's greatest natural wonders.

'Linz, my love, it was a dream of ours to stand here. I'm glad we finally got to live it.'

Reaching into the inside pocket of his jacket, Sean removed the hipflask containing hers and the children's ashes. He unscrewed the top and poured a little of them into the air, watching as the dust was carried off on the breeze like the fine-blown spindrift on the top of Mount Everest. He turned and walked away, heading back down to Namche, the sense of loss too much to bear. He wanted to sleep and to never wake.

Ignoring his initial reservations, given how pale Sean still looked the next morning, Kamal commenced the climb, leading him past the Tensing monument he'd stood at the previous afternoon. The first few hours were relatively easy, traversing the left-hand side of the valley high above the river. At one point, the trail descended sharply downhill towards the water, where they had a lunch stop at another small teahouse.

Despite having lied to Kamal about the acclimatisation hike, Sean felt no worse for not having done so. In truth, he felt his strength returning. So much so that he strode out ahead of Kamal, that afternoon, covering the remaining few miles up to Tengboche monastery in under two hours.

'You are clearly feeling fine, Mr Sean,' said Kamal, as they approached the monastery, shortly after dropping their bags off at the teahouse they were staying in that evening. 'The rest at Namche has been most excellent for you. As I told you it would be.'

'You were right, Kamal. I feel much stronger for the rest. Let's press on, hard, tomorrow.'

'We shall, Mr Sean, have no fear. We will reach the great temple of Tengboche, by nightfall, tomorrow. It is a most holy place. I am glad you will be seeing it.'

'Just as long as you don't expect me to pray,' said Sean, under his breath.

Tengboche monastery lay in the heart Khumba valley, almost thirteen thousand feet up. Regarded as one of the most beautiful in the entire world, the main temple building sat upon a knoll at the foremost point of a long spur of rock, overlooking the Imja river. Gathered around it were quaintly constructed houses, antiquated in appearance. Ancient Tibetan scriptures referred to the valley as a sacred and deeply spiritual place. That sense came over Sean as he gazed out over the rooftops to mountains that seemed, despite their great height, to have crept up around him. Tensing Norgay had lived in the village and seen these same great peaks, every day. *Little wonder,* Sean mused, *he had thought to conquer them.*

'You wish to visit the monastery, Mr Sean?'

'I have no god to pray to, Kamal.'

'Then do not pray, but light a candle for those you no longer have in your life. The monks will say a blessing for your safety.'

'Perhaps later,' said Sean, with little conviction.

He had no need for any such blessing. He could see Kamal looking at him as if he knew exactly what thoughts were in his head.

Ignoring his initial reservations, Sean decided to visit the monastery, lighting three candles before taking the time to explore the rooms inside the ornate building. Beyond a set of arched, red-lacquered doors, he noticed half a dozen monks clothed in yellow-ochre robes, seated on a raised dais, waiting for the line of visitors to enter before making their blessings. On impulse, he joined the line, removing his boots and sitting cross-legged on the floor once he'd entered the prayer room.

The room was filled the sweet tang of incense, a heady smell designed to soothe the senses. The monks began to chant, a slow, rhythmic sound, deep and guttural, using their unusual nose and throat singing style. Sean had meditated before, with Linz, and always found it relaxing. He closed eyes, his mind taken over by the combination of the sounds and smells, and felt her presence with him, giving him a rare moment of inner peace.

The next morning, Kamal started them out early, leaving the tearoom as the sun swept into the sky, lighting the mountains in a burn of vibrant gold.

'The terrain's a bit up and down today,' said Sean. His mood was brighter after another dreamless sleep and the sense that Linz had been with him in the monastery.

'We call it Nepalese flat,' said Kamal. 'It can feel like you are making no headway at all, but we are getting higher, Mr Sean. We will be at sixteen thousand feet by the end of today.'

'How much further until a stop?'

'We will be reaching the village of Pangboche in less than one hour, Mr Sean. It is a short walk from there to the settlement of Shomare, where we will have the most excellent lunch. My sister has a tearoom there and will make us the most excellent goat stew.'

'More goat stew! Most excellent, Kamal.'

'I am glad you are liking it, Mr Sean,' said Kamal, missing the sarcastic inflection in Sean's voice.

They trekked on through vast swathes of open, boulder-strewn land, the mountains around them, white giants with dark frowns, looking down on them as if wondering what insects had come among them. Inside the hour, they reached Pangboche. Kamal was glad to see Sean was in high spirits. They had chatted more than on any other day. It was a good sign, he thought, although his aura was still tinged with by the dark spirit he carried.

Pangboche was one of the villages on the trail that had suffered most from the earthquake that struck Nepal two years before. The resulting avalanche at Everest Base Camp had killed over twenty people, Sherpas and climbers alike. The devastation across the region, however, had been biblical, with nine thousand dead and countless more injured. Kathmandu had been laid almost entirely to rubble and the country shattered.

The devastation was still evident as they entered the village.

Kamal stopped to light incense outside the remains of some houses that had been demolished. He chanted a prayer and took time to speak to some of the village people. Everyone seemed to know him. Sean walked ahead. While he felt for the village, he had not known the people who died. He had his own souls to mourn.

After lunch, at Shomare, where Sean had conceded that Kamal's sister *did* made the best goat stew he had ever tasted, much to her delight, it was a gradual up-hill trek towards the Imja Valley, passing the great mountain, Imja Tse, better known as, *Island Peak*, the name given to it by the British Everest Expedition that had included Edmund Hilary and Sherpa Tensing. An hour later, they arrived in the village of Dingboche, sixteen thousand feet above sea level.

'Our lodge is at the top of the town, Mr Sean,' Kamal announced, cheerfully. 'We spend all of tomorrow here. Our very last night of acclimatisation.'

Sean, feeling the effects of the long hike, as well as the increasing lack of oxygen, didn't have the strength to complain.

The next day, Sean explored the land around the town, enjoying amazing views of Ama Dablam, Imja Tse, Lhotse, and the other surrounding mountains, each name famous amongst climbers the world over. The weather was unusually calm, with cloudless, blue skies and warm sunshine throughout the day. His senses seemed heightened by the incredible beauty on show. He wondered why that should be the case, and then it dawned on him.

'There is no breath quite as sweet as the last breath,' he whispered to the mountains.

By the following morning, the weather had changed for the worse. The sky was heavy with pregnant clouds that promised snow, the wind gusting hard and the overall going ice cold. Each step was a step hard won. Within the first hour, Sean was exhausted. He'd eaten almost no breakfast, though had made a show of twice going back to refill his porridge bowl, returning to his room to pour it down the toilet.

Onward, they climbed, passing the tiny settlement of Lobuche, heading up towards the Khumbu ice flow, the world's highest glacier, on a slow trek across a long, elevated route, rock-strewn and treacherous to walk on. A few hours later, they stopped at Dukla, no more than a single, stone teahouse set back from the pathway, serving soup, sandwiches, and offering a place to rest before taking on the challenge of the Dukla Pass. Sean forced himself to eat, not wanting Kamal to know that the effects of altitude sickness were really taking hold.

As they entered the Dukla pass, after lunch, Sean began to falter, despite they were climbing more slowly than they had done over the past week. His legs and arms felt oddly heavy and his breathing was becoming laboured.

'Are you fine, Mr Sean,' called Kamal, walking slightly behind him, allowing Sean to set the pace.

'I'm fine, Kamal,' replied Sean, feeling anything but.

It took another hour for them to reach the top of the pass and enter an area known as Chukla Lare, where cairns, prayer flags and memorial monuments honoured the climbers and Sherpas who had died trying to conquer Everest. The place had a sombre feel to it, as if the dead it sought to recognise were watching those still living pass, bound for the same fate that had befallen them.

Sean wondered at the risks those dead climbers had taken to reach their personal goals. Giving their lives to climb a mountain for the love of something others could not understand. Their bravery was honoured, their names carved into the stone monuments. Would his death be any less honourable? Was his love for his family any less than theirs had been for the mountain?'

'How are you, Mr Sean,' Kamal asked, as Sean flopped down on a boulder and dropped his head onto his hands.

'I'm okay, Kamal. Just a bit tired.'

But his skull felt as if it was being compressed by a giant vice and his heart was racing.

'I will take your oxygen level, Mr Sean, if I may?'

Kamal took a portable pulse-oximeter from a pocket in his jacket. Sean was about to argue, but knew it was pointless. Kamal would likely not carry on if he refused. He allowed him to put the monitor clasp onto his middle finger and hoped it would not cause a problem.

'Well?' Sean asked, expecting the worst.

A normal reading, taken at sea level, would be around ninety-nine percent of the oxygen breathed into a climber's lungs being transferred into the bloodstream. But, here, where the air was so thin, it was harder to maintain that level. If it fell below seventy the patient was already dying.

'Seventy-four,' replied Kamal. 'It is low, but it is not bad. Do you have any other symptoms?'

'No,' said Sean, relieved the reading had been better than he'd expected. 'I'm good to go on.'

'Fine, Mr Sean. We will keep checking.'

'Sure, Kamal. How much further to go?'

'We will be reaching Gorak Shep in only a few hours, Mr Sean. Rest for a while longer.'

Sean felt a wave of relief as Kamal turned away and headed across to talk to a group of Sherpas descending from above. He knew he was feeling the first signs of hypoxia. Worried that the next time Kamal took a reading, he would be feeling even worse, he reached into the pocket of his climbing jacket and pulled out a slim, white plastic wrapper with six tablets in it. He punched two of them through the foil backing and swallowed them down with a gulp of water from his water-bottle. The Diamox tablets would counter the effects of hypoxia.

Many climbers used the drug, but as well as helping prevent the symptoms of hypoxia, it could also mask them, allowing a climber to keep pushing his body until something gave. Treatment, after that point, was crucial to survival. If Diamox had already been taken, it was important for those around the climber to know. Sean had no intention of letting Kamal know he had taken it, or that he had been since leaving Namche Bazaar.

'Just get up to Gorak Shep,' he said to himself. 'One last push.'

They reached the top of the Dukla Pass and crossed into an area of loose boulder fields and glacial moraine. The landscape was unique and beautiful. The Diamox Sean had taken kicked in shortly after leaving the monument valley and he began to feel better. Kamal took another reading and found his blood oxygen level had risen to eighty-two.

'Impressive, Mr Sean. You are getting to be stronger as we are getting higher.'

Sean forced a smile as he replied.

'I think it was just the climb up to the pass that blew me out. It was bloody steep. I think I might have also eaten too much of that porridge for breakfast.'

'It has worked, has it not, Mr Sean. For we are almost there.'

The up-and-down trail into Gorak Shep took three more hours. They finally reached the settlement at the edge of a frozen lake just before darkness descended.

'Seventeen thousand feet,' said Kamal, as he checked them into their rooms for the night and handed Sean his key. 'Base Camp is another six hundred feet up. We shall trek there in the morning. The weather will be better and the views will be most beautiful to behold.'

'Can't wait,' said Sean, almost out on his feet. 'I'm going to get an early night in preparation. I'll come down for supper. But don't wait for me, Kamal.'

'Are you sure you are feeling fine, Mr Sean?'

Kamal noticed he was paler than he'd been earlier.

'All good. Just dog-tired. That was the hardest day yet.'

'The hardest work is done, Mr Sean. Tomorrow will be easier.'

'Excellent. I can't wait to get there. I'll see you in the morning.'

Even after another Diamox tablet, Sean was feeling bad. He took a shower and lay on his bed, hoping to sleep, but sleep would not come. His head was throbbing, his fingers tingling and his breathing was laboured. He rushed to the bathroom to vomit a rush of black water, a sign his blood had been oxidised by the acids in his stomach. He was dying, and realised it. From his bedroom window, he looked out across the frozen lake and felt a longing to walk out onto it, but knew he would be seen. He had to bide his time to do what he had come so far to do. He lay back on the bed, trying to meditate himself into a place of calm.

It was after ten when Sean woke and the room was in semi-darkness. He left the building, slipping out of the main door of the accommodation block, into the night, heading towards the Khumba Glacier, directly across Gorak Shep's dry lakebed then up over the glacial moraine towards Everest Base Camp. A blanket of stars was spread out above his head, the lack of any light pollution giving him a view of the cosmos most people on earth never got to see. He struggled to appreciate it. Each breath was hard won and the pain in his head was growing. He tried to ignore it. It would soon be irrelevant.

The trail reached the top of a ridge, where a sharp spine of rock led towards a *cul-de-sac* at the end of the glacier. Ahead of him, nine thousand feet higher,

Everest rose like a white, shark fin between its lesser brothers, Khumbutse and Lhotse. All three summits were over two miles above the point where Sean was standing. Another world of extreme and deadly altitudes. Despite his pain, he was entranced by the magnificence of his surroundings. If he had to choose a place to draw his final breath, this would always be it.

He trudged on across the moraine, the pain in his head becoming almost totally debilitating. Disorientated and confused, he stumbled and fell. He stood, unsure of where he was and which way he was supposed to be going. A moment later, he fell again, cutting his knees on the sharp rocks, but the pain was nothing compared to the burning in his chest. His lungs begged for air and he was having trouble standing, his legs refusing to do as he asked them. Somehow, he dragged himself up, but tripped almost immediately, dropping to his knees. He looked up into the star-filled sky.

'Linz! Where are you?'

There was no sign of her. He called again, his voice growing weaker.

Fat blobs of snow began to fall. Lightly, at first, dusting Sean's face, freezing on his eyelashes and blurring his vision, but as the snowfall became heavier the land around him began to lose definition, as if a gossamer shroud had been draped over his face. He tried to stand, but his body would not respond. He was numb, mentally and physically, and what thoughts he had were disjointed and confused. He lay, face down, too tired even to remain kneeling. Within minutes, he began to shiver, his body trying desperately to keep itself alive in the sub-zero cold. There was only one thought in his mind, however. He held onto it. *Where are you, Linz!* He lifted his head and looked up, the very action of it, exhausting,

'Linz.'

His voice was less than a whisper.

'Sean.'

He thought he heard her call him, but struggled to see anything through the gossamer veil. He called again, fighting to be heard above the worsening snowstorm.

'Linz.'

'Sean'

This time Sean was certain he had heard her call to him. He called back to her, or imagined he had, and looked up to see a bright light coming towards him across the open ground of the lake bed. As it neared, the light split, becoming three glowing balls of white; silent, glowing buoys, floating across a frozen ocean. The lights reached him. Although his vision had almost gone, he recognised the voices and stretched out a hand towards them.

'My angels.'

The lights hovered over Sean, filling him with a joy he had thought forever lost. He began to cry.

'Don't cry,' said Linz, taking hold of his hand. 'We're going to take care of you now.'

Sean closed his eyes and gave himself up to his family. Billowing white clouds began to fold around him. Wrapping him in a warm embrace. Keeping him safe and making him feel loved.

47

Claudia strolled through the Piazza Delle Erbe, the historic city square in the centre of Verona old town, pausing to browse the market stalls filled with farm grown produce from all over the province. The square was packed with locals and tourists, and alive with the cries of stallholders beckoning all to sample their wares. It was a scene that had been played out, daily, for over a thousand years. She caught the eye of one of the merchants as she passed his stall.

'Bella Signora. Viene, prova le migliori olive di tutta Verona.'

'What's he saying, Maddy?' Claudia asked, returning his smile.

'I think it was, something to do with you trying the best olives in all Verona,' said Maybelline Anderton, 'although I think he means to offer you something quite different.'

She smiled at the beckoning merchant and shook her head, taking Claudia by the arm and leading her on through the maze of colourful market stalls.

'Oh, I see,' said Claudia.

She flushed and turned back to have a second look, but the merchant was already fawning over another woman who was paying him and his olives more attention that she had.

Arm in arm, they reached the other side of the market and turned along the Via della Costa, stopping to look at the statue of Dante Alighieri in the adjoining Piazza dei Signori. Maybelline looked up at the stony face of the great writer, poet and politician.

'He doesn't look happy, does he?'

'Well,' said Claudia, walking around the statue's base, 'you know his story, don't you?'

Maybelline shrugged her shoulders.

'I know he wrote a book called *Inferno* and took a trip through Hell, but that's about it.'

'He did,' replied Claudia, studying the face of Dante. 'But he also wrote a wonderful poem called, *The Divine Comedy*, which was his declaration of love for a woman called Beatrice. She lived in Florence, as did he. The only problem was she was married to someone else. It didn't stop Dante loving her, though. He loved Beatrice all of his life.'

Maybelline rolled her eyes.

'Tell me they got together in the end? I can't take another story of lost love. Not after standing beneath Juliette's balcony, this morning, listening to the ill-fated story of her and Romeo. What is it with the Italians and their desperate tales of forbidden love?'

'Sorry, no can do, Maddy,' said Claudia, laughing at Maybelline's exasperation. 'the story ends in tragedy. Beatrice died young, at just twenty-four. Dante never got over the death of his one true love. His masterpiece was written in her honour, preserving his unrequited love through all of time.'

Maybelline looked up at Dante with a new respect.

'Very sad, but *trés* romantic. I want someone to love me like that.'

'Don't we all,' whispered Claudia.

She thought back to the week before, to the lighthouse, the day Paul had visited it for the first time. The day everything between them had begun to change, although she had not thought it then.

'Well, what do you think?' Claudia asked, as she and Paul stood at the Point, gazing out over the ocean. She'd laid some fresh flowers on Betsy's stone and whispered hello to her and Hannah. Oddly, she did not feel Hannah's presence, despite she had been sure she would.

'It's kind of remote, but beautiful,' replied Paul, turning to look back over the dunes to the lighthouse tower. 'I can see why you love it. The place is incredible, even *if* the lightkeeper's house needs work.'

Claudia gazed across at the big house.

'Mostly just redecoration. Perhaps some remodeling.'

She pictured herself and Hannah walking along the sandy pathway, heading up to the lighthouse, as they had done so many times over the past six weeks. Her eyes moistened, despite having promised herself she would not cry, but this was the first visit she'd made since her death. The memories and feelings were still vivid. Joy for what had been, sadness for what was lost.

'I suppose.'

'We can start a fresh life here, Paul. It would be an amazing place to bring up a child.'

'What about your gallery?'

'It's an hour away. As is the airport.'

'So you still won't consider moving out west?'

'I went, as I promised I would,' said Claudia, 'and last week *was* fun; seeing where you work, meeting Sam and her boyfriend and getting to watch the actors do their thing. But it's just not me. I love it here. I feel free and at peace. It would be a wonderful place to bring up a child. And I do want to keep trying for a family. Don't you?'

'As I said before, sweetheart, if it happens, it's meant to be. More to the point, I don't see why you want to move out of Lexington. To here!'

'I don't love Lexington like I do here. I take it from that you still plan to live in Los Angeles?'

'I have to, you know that,' replied Paul, sounding annoyed that Claudia had even asked. 'I can come back once a month, perhaps more often, but we need to be honest with ourselves. Can we live like that? Can we still have a marriage that works? It feels like we're so far apart from each other, even now, that I'm just not sure we could.'

It seemed they both felt the void opening up between them. As if recognising it, and being afraid, they held each other.

'Tell me it's not the end, Paul.'

'I want to, Claudia. I don't want it to be the end.'

'Then why does it feel like it might be? I'm afraid for us.'

'I'm afraid too.'

Claudia looked up into his eyes. She could see the sadness she felt, reflected in them.

'We need to try to harder. Both of us.'

Paul pulled her closer to him, feeling her heart beating against his chest.

'I want to try, sweetheart.'

'Then we need more time together, my darling. Or we won't make it.'

It was, Claudia felt, a make or break moment in their marriage. She wanted him to commit to trying for a family, whatever that took. Even adoption. She wanted them both to live in the big house, despite he might only be home every second weekend. She would fight for him to ends of the earth, but would he fight for her? Paul, it seemed, had read her mind.

'Look, sweetheart, I know you're going to leave some of Hannah's ashes here, today, and that you want to take some of them to . . .'

'Finisterre.' Claudia reminded him.

'Right.'

Thinking he was angry, Claudia pleaded with him to not fight her on the decision she'd made after reading Hannah's letter, after the funeral the previous week.

'I told her lawyer that I was going to honour her wishes. I have to. I hope you didn't mind.'

'Of course not, sweetheart. I understand completely.'

Claudia hugged him, relieved there was not going to be an argument. She had already made her mind up on flying to Europe, and nothing would change that.

'I'll only be gone a week. I can fly into Madrid and get a connecting flight up to Santiago. From there, it's only a couple of hours to Finisterre, by car. I have to do it. I couldn't live with myself if I didn't take her to be with Jonathon.'

Paul shook his head.

'That's not where I was going. It's the right thing to do. She gave you all this. And it's one hell of a gift. The place is worth millions.'

Claudia frowned, annoyed, again, that everything in Paul's life seemed to be measured in terms of money.

'I don't care about that, Paul. I love this place. Almost as much as Hannah did. She knew I wanted to be here even before I did. I wanted you to love it too, for us both to be here.'

Paul, realising he'd stepped onto shifting sands, tried to make amends. He took hold of Claudia's hands.

'I know that, sweetheart. And perhaps we both can.'

Claudia wondered what he meant.

'Really? Do you mean that?'

'I do. But we need to work us out first. Which is why I was about to suggest something that might help to do that.'

'What? Tell me, Paul. I'll do anything to make us work again.'

Paul looked down at her, a wry smile on his face.

'Well . . . what if we were *both* go to Finisterre?'

Claudia's face lit up. She was surprised but ecstatic at his suggestion.

'Paul! Do you really mean it?'

'I do, sweetheart, but listen to what I'm suggesting and see if it works.'

'I'll be quiet, my darling. I Promise.'

Paul outlined the plan that had just come to him. One, he hoped, that would give Claudia the opportunity to take Hannah's ashes to Finisterre, as well as given them the time together they so obviously needed.

'What I'm suggesting is that, instead of leaving for Europe, next week, you wait a few weeks longer and we go together. We could have that second honeymoon we always talked about. We can finally visit Paris and Rome, even Venice, if you fancy. We could go to one of those operas Hannah introduced you to. We can easily fly into Spain, while we're there, and go to Finisterre.'

Claudia threw her arms around him.

'Are you sure?'

'I need to show you I'm committed to us, Claudia. It's a promise. I won't break it, no matter what.'

Claudia was so happy she felt she might burst.

'You've no idea how much this means to me, my darling. I thought you didn't love me any longer.'

'I do love you, sweetheart. Perhaps I've forgotten to show you that, recently. I promise I won't forget again.'

Claudia planted a kiss on his lips, shocking him by sliding her tongue into his mouth and turning the kiss into something more passionate.

'That's all I need to know,' said Claudia, as Paul broke free from her embrace. 'I'll try not complain so much when you have to go away, and I'll be as slutty in the bedroom as you want me to be when you come home.'

Paul pulled Claudia to him.

'I think I like that. Especially the slutty part.'

They both laughed and kissed again, connecting with each other in a way that they had not done in some time.

'We *can* make it work, Paul, can't we, being here?'

'We can, sweetheart, just as long as you don't expect me to do any of the redesign work. This is your place, now, to do with what you want. I'll be happy to come home and be a part-time lighthouse keeper, if this *is* where you really want to live.'

'Oh, I do, Paul. I really feel this place will be where we raise our children.'

'One step at a time, sweetheart. You need to get pregnant first.'

Claudia looked up at the lighthouse, remembering the day she'd come back to it, only a few short weeks ago. She knew it was going to be her home for the rest of her life. She felt, too, truly loved by Paul. For the first time in a long time, she began to feel at peace.

'Thank you, my darling, for coming here with me today. For choosing me. For choosing us. Let's have a second honeymoon. Maybe I'll get pregnant in Paris or Rome.'

As she said it, Claudia sent a silent prayer to the Universe, asking for that.

'We can try, sweetheart. Now, why don't you do what you came her to do. Hannah's watching you, I'm certain.'

Claudia closed her eyes.

'She is, even if I can't feel her here, yet.'

'I'm sure she is, sweetheart. I'll give you some time alone.'

Paul kissed her on the forehead and headed back across the grass, taking the steps down through the cliff to the beach below.

Once he was gone, Claudia took a small, wooden box from her shoulder bag and carefully opened the lid. There was no wind and the sky was blue and cloudless. One of those "stilly" days, as Hannah called them, when the whole world seemed to pause for breath.

'Farewell, my dearest Hannah, know you are missed and loved. Thank you for everything you've given me, as well as for what it still to come. You've one more adventure to take, crazy lady. We both have. I might not be walking your beloved Camino, but I *am* taking you to Finisterre.'

She took a handful of Hannah's ashes in the palm of her hand and sprinkled them over Betsy's stone. The tears she cried were for the thought she had joined mother and daughter once more.

Claudia had already moved down to the lighthouse and was staying in the Beach Shack, with Sylkie her constant companion. At first, the little dog seemed to miss Hannah, searching for her everywhere, but the searches grew less frequent as each day passed. Claudia loved her and enjoyed her company, especially when the lonely nights came. She'd also started to visit her sister and nieces in Duxbury more often. The girls had loved Sylkie at first sight and spoiled her rotten.

The week before she and Paul were due to fly to Rome, Claudia started organising the refurbishment of the big house, hiring a local company to do all of the work. The project manager, Ben Stillman, was clearly a professional. Everything could be left in his capable hands while she and Paul jaunted around Europe. The house would be finished by the time they returned. Paul, she told herself, would grow to love it as much as she did. She would have a family to share it with. Somehow, she knew it.

Paul, true to his word, surprised her with plane tickets to Rome, departing on the fourteenth of May. They would see all of the sights there were to see, and more. Claudia's anger, when he had, two days before they were due to fly, told her he had to delay their trip, had been profound. She had refused, point blank, telling him that, if he failed to be at the airport, she would be on the plane alone. In the end, he had not come, imagining, Claudia felt, that she was bluffing. She had thought so, too, but had recalled Hannah's words about finding out what she *needed* in her life. It was clear what was most important to Paul. It wasn't, Claudia realised, her.

Rome had been amazing to visit, even alone. She'd almost been able to forget about Paul's betrayal. She thought of it as such. Their last phone call, less than twenty-four hours ago, the day she had travelled up to Verona, had gone very badly, reinforcing that view.

'You said you wanted to fix us, Paul. You suggested this holiday in the first place. This second honeymoon, so called.'

'Honey, I bought the tickets. It was all planned. But this new deal came right out of the blue. Why couldn't you have waited just a few more weeks?'

The insensitivity of his answer infuriated Claudia.

'There will always be another deal and a few more weeks to wait, Paul. I could have spread Hannah's ashes at Finisterre, by now, and been home. It was you who delayed me. You did this to us. Not me.'

'Honey, give me a week, I'll fly out and join you in . . .'

'Don't bother making promises you won't keep. I'm not waiting for you, Paul, not anymore. Do what you want. I'm doing what I *need*. Anyway, I doubt you'd be able to find me.'

'They have airports all over Europe. I'm sure I'll be able to find you, wherever you are.'

'Not where I'm going.' Claudia snapped, her disappointment in her husband at an all-time low.

'And where's that?' Paul replied, a huff in his voice that turned her disappointment to anger.

'I'm going to walk the Camino de Santiago.'

It was a spur of the moment decision, for Claudia and it clearly shocked Paul.

'But, I thought you were just going to *drive* to Finisterre.'

'Things change, Paul. You of all people should know that.'

'Don't be stupid, honey, you can't just up sticks and walk across Spain. You've not trained for it, and I doubt you packed your trekking gear? Christ, you could hardly even get up Robinson Hill, last month.'

Paul laughed, finding what he had said, amusing. It wasn't, to Claudia. Added to what he'd just said, it was the worst thing he could have done. Touchpaper lit, she exploded.

'Fuck you, Paul Montgomery. We'll see who's fit enough. Stay at home and build your new career, it's obviously more important to you than I am. And don't bother coming out. I'll see you when I feel like coming back. And when I do, I want an answer to a very simple question.'

Paul was taken aback at hearing Claudia swear, as well as at the tsunami of anger she was directing at him. An anger he had not known existed within her.

'Which is?' he asked, meekly, no longer seeing any funny side.

'Do you want to remain my husband or not?'

'Honey! Be reasonable.'

'Reasonable!' Claudia screamed. 'You utterly, selfish bastard. I've bent over backwards to be reasonable. But I'm done with that. Decide what you want and tell me when I get home. Until then, don't bother me.'

'Honey! How will I know where you are?'

'I'd send you a bloody postcard, Paul, if I knew where you lived.'

'You know exactly where . . . '

Claudia was past the point of hearing anything more he had to say. And something else was bothering her. Something that took her back to Lexington. To Isabella and *Sans Cera*.

And another thing. I don't get why you've started calling me, *honey*, because in all our years together you never have. Perhaps your mixing me up with someone else.'

'Claudia. It's just an expression. Perhaps I picked it up out here, you know what they're like.'

'No, Paul, I don't. Anyway, I have to go. Someone's waiting for me. See you around, *honey*!'

She hung up and switched of her phone, fighting the urge to toss it under a passing tram.

For the first few days in Rome, Claudia had been absorbed in the Eternal City. She visited the Galleria Borghese, one of the most famous and prestigious museums in the world, marvelling at the collection of fifteenth to eighteenth century paintings and sculptures, especially those by Bernini, Canova, and another of her personal favourite artists, Caravaggio. A day trip to visit the Trevi Fountain and the Spanish Steps, organised by her hotel, though, had been the highlight of the trip.

She'd met Maybelline, "Maddy", as Claudia had decided to call her, in the world-famous Babbington's Tearooms, at the foot of the steps. They'd shared a table and hit it off immediately. She was the same age as Claudia, but a widow, taking a tour of Europe, looking for a new husband, preferably someone from the Italian royalty. She sympathised with Claudia's predicament, but urged her to persevere, if she still loved Paul. When Claudia confirmed she still did, despite being as angry with him as she had ever been, Maybelline had offered to become her chaperone, protecting her from the unwanted advances of the hot-blooded gigolos wandering the streets, day and night, seeking vulnerable women like them. Claudia had only just stifled her laugh at Maddy's description.

One night, though, she'd danced on the rooftop garden of their hotel, looking out over Rome, and been chased by a middle-aged Italian banker who was there for a convention. She'd drunk too much red wine and allowed him to kiss her, but declined his invitation to join him in his private suite. Maddy had scolded her, the following morning, for not introducing him to her.

After a few days of sightseeing, in Rome, she and Maddy had taken the train to Verona, visiting one of the most romantic cities in northern Italy, where they now stood, beneath the statue of Dante. Maddy was visibly melting in the heat, her make-up losing the battle it had been fighting for the past hour. She dabbed her brow with a cooling wipe and decided enough was enough.

'Let's get back to the hotel,' said Maddy, 'I need a glass of chilled white wine and a late lunch. Then we can take a nap before tonight's show.'

'Sounds perfect,' replied Claudia.

She was also feeling the effects of a searing, mid-afternoon sun. They'd been sightseeing since early morning, and hadn't eaten anything since breakfast.

'I can't believe it's your first ever opera,' said Maddy, as they wandered through the maze of narrow streets leading to the luxurious Due Torri Hotel, in the shadow of the church of Saint Anastasia, in Verona's old town, 'you must be tremendously excited?'

'I am, Maddy. I can't actually believe it. If you'd told me three months ago I'd be in Italy, going to the world famous Arena di Verona, to see a live opera, I would have called you crazy.'

'Well you *are* going. And what a first one to see. *Tosca*, by the great master himself. Puccini.'

Claudia pictured a poignant memory and tried to smile, but the smile would not come.

'It means so much that it's that one. Hannah introduced me to opera through *Tosca*. We listened to it sitting by the fire, one night, during a raging storm, sipping Glenmorangie whisky.'

'What a great way to hear your first opera. I'm sure she'll be with you tonight.'

'I'm certain I'll feel her. She'll be in my handbag. Part of her, anyway. I'll bring her wooden box out and set her on my lap.'

Despite herself, she felt a little sad that Hannah would not be with her, enjoying the opera for herself.

'She will,' said Maddy, taking Claudia's hand. 'Now, no more melancholy. Let's go have that glass of wine.'

The opera began on time, at eight o'clock, beneath a soot black sky filled with bright stars, watching the scene below with the same interest as the audience seated in the ancient colosseum. Claudia marvelled at the sheer scale of the set and the glorious opening backdrop. She took a sharp intake of breath as the music began, and wasn't sure she'd breathed again during the entire performance. At just past eleven, at the end of the third and final act, the singers took their final standing ovation to the raucous cheers from an exuberant audience. Claudia came down from the cloud she'd been sitting on since the first aria. *Tosca*, performed live, was as dramatic a love story as she could ever have hoped for, bittersweet and deeply moving. The orchestra and opera singers had been beyond spectacular.

'I'm on my last tissue,' said Maddy, like Claudia, unable to stop the tears from falling.

Claudia dabbed her eyes with the hanky offered to her by an older gentleman who had felt sorry for the weeping woman sat next to him all evening.

'My God, Maddy, that was beautiful, but so sad. The aria in act two almost did for me. I thought my heart was breaking.'

'*Vissi d'arte*,' replied Maddy, blowing her nose loudly. 'One of the most famous arias of all time. *Tosca*, praying to God, asking him why He has abandoned her. It's spellbinding and intense. I was almost apoplectic.'

'I noticed,' said Claudia, 'as did everyone around you.'

Maddy smiled and began to reapply some make up to her tear-stained face. Satisfied she was presentable, she returned the tortoise-shell compact back in her clutch bag.

'The ending, though, was the worst of all. I so wanted Tosca to live. I couldn't believe it when she killed herself.'

'Me neither,' Claudia agreed, 'honestly, it was so sad.'

'Heartbreaking.'

Maddy stood up and straightened her dress, preparing to leave.

Claudia, looked down at the little wooden box containing Hannah's ashes, sitting in her lap, where it had been throughout the entire performance.

'Thank you for that. I hope you enjoyed it too.'

She pictured Hannah's face and, this time, was able to smile back at her.

'Tosca didn't want to live without the man she loved by her side,' said Maddy, checking her seat to make sure she'd not left anything behind. 'When he died, her heart broke, and she died, too, inside.'

'But would you really die for love?' Claudia asked, following Maybelline along the aisle. 'I can't imagine a love so deep that I'd want to kill myself if it were ever lost. Even Dante lived on after the death of Beatrice.'

'I don't know, Claudia. *I've* never felt a love like that. I wish I had. Perhaps it could exist. I think it would be amazing to love someone so much you felt you could never love again. And what point is a life without love? In the end, it's the greatest gift we are given. The ability to love and be loved, completely and unconditionally.'

Claudia looked up into the star-filled.

'Would that I could find that? Maybe the Universe can fix it for me?'

As she said it, the Universe, she felt, from paying her no particular attention, turned its gaze upon her. It made her shiver. She laughed at herself and the night, once more, turned warm.

48

Sean woke to a world of silent white. His body had no weight to it, nor any substance. Not that he could discern. He was of spirit, not of flesh. His senses not quite gone but somehow changed. He tried to speak but no longer had a voice with which to form words. He thought his question and it came back at him from out of the billowing clouds surrounding him.

'Is this heaven?'

He heard another voice. Close by, but somehow also far away. As if the person speaking was at the end of a long tunnel.

'It's not heaven, Sean. Not really.'

'Linz!'

His own voice echoed back at him.

'Yes.'

Her voice was crisp and clear. Closer to him than before.

Sean thought he saw a glow of golden light ahead of him, but it came and went, lasting a moment and all of time. He couldn't quite understand how that was. He knew it meant something.

'Where are you, my love? I can't see you.'

'Don't worry, hun. I'm still here.'

Sean felt Linz beside him. All around him. In him. She was everywhere and nowhere. Everything and nothing. All at once. But he felt safe and loved, knowing she was there with him. Watching over him. As she always had done.

'Where is this, my love?'

'Sssshhh! It doesn't matter. But you can't stay, hun. You have to go back.'

Her voice began to fade. The essence of her began to disappear.

'Linz. Don't leave me. Please.'

'It's okay, hun. Don't be frightened. I'm always with you. Butterflies and birdsong, remember?'

The clouds closed in before Sean could answer, smothering him and taking away what little sense of reality there still was.

And then there was nothing.

49

The view from the sixth floor of the Medicari Private Hospital, on the outskirts of the sprawling city of Kathmandu, was probably one of the best in the world. Sean woke and looked over at the windows, screwing up his eyes against the brightness. He was no longer in the white clouds, but the memory of them, and of Linz, was as clear as the water in the jug by his bed.

I'm alive!

A crushing weight of disappointment pressed down on him like avalanche snow. He stared up at the white-painted ceiling and wondered if he'd been dreaming. He felt numb and empty, and his thoughts were disjointed and unclear, as if he'd been drugged. He was attached to an intravenous drip that fed into his left arm, and a digital monitor which showed his heart rate, blood pressure and oxygen levels. He was in a hospital, that much was obvious.

He struggled to sit up, arranging his pillows against the steel bars of the bedhead as best he could with hands that were heavily bandaged. They looked like two fat blobs of white candy floss. With some difficulty, he propped himself up into a sitting position. The effort of it left him dizzy and breathless. He stared at his bandaged hands and tried to wiggle his fingers. There was no feeling in them. He wondered, for a moment, if he still had them? He'd seen the effects of frostbite before. Climbers he knew had lost fingers and toes to it. The thought scared him. He pulled back the blanket and saw that his feet were similarly bandaged.

He couldn't feel his them either.

Trying to remain calm, when all he really wanted to do was detach himself from the machines and remove the bandages, Sean gazed out of the windows to the Himalayas, some distance away but easily visible. The memory of being there, on Everest, came back to him. He remembered walking out onto the frozen lakebed at Gorak Shep. He remembered the biting cold and the blinding gossamer veil. Above all, he remembered seeing Linz and his children, as angel lights. Beyond that, there was only a vague notion of a dream he couldn't quite form into a lucid image.

'Mr Jameson!' A voice from over by the door startled him. A nurse, dressed in standard whites, smiled at him. 'You're awake. I'll fetch the doctor.'

'Nurse!'

Sean's call halted her departure. She turned back to him..

'My name is Uyen, Mr Jameson. I'm the nurse looking after you. I'm so glad to see you awake and well. I know you will have questions, but the doctor will explain everything, I'll fetch him. Give me a moment, please.'

Nurse Uyen made off down the corridor, returning, a few minutes later, accompanied by a white-coated doctor who had a bald head, round, wire-framed glasses and a face that looked as if it was in a permanently state of happiness. He was Indian, or perhaps Nepalese, Sean couldn't tell which. He looked at Sean and shook his head, tutting like a headmaster admonishing a naughty schoolboy.

'Mr Jameson, awake at last. You gave us some moments of concern.'

The doctor took a look at Sean's chart, hung on the end of the bed, while nurse Uyen checked Sean's his and fussed around him, plumping up his pillows and helping him sit more upright.

'Are you hungry, Mr Jameson,' she asked.

'I don't think so.'

'I'll fetch you something anyway.'

She bowed her head to the doctor then left the room.

'I am Bikash Sharma,' said the doctor, 'one of the consultants here in the Medicari Hospital. If you please, you may call me Bikash, or Doctor Sharma, I will answer to either. As you please. How do you feel? Are you up to chatting?'

Sharma had a remarkably gentle and comforting voice, Sean thought, and wondered if it had been cultivated to be so over many years standing by hospital bedsides.

'Sure. I feel fine, just a bit groggy. But good to chat. Is *doc* okay?' Sharma nodded his head. 'And call me Sean.'

Sharma dragged a chair from over by the window across to Sean's bedside and sat down.

'Do you know where you are?

'In a hospital?' Sean replied, sarcastically. 'I'm guessing, from the sight of the Himalayas, somewhere in Kathmandu.'

Sharma nodded and looked down at the hospital chart.

'Correct on both counts. You were brought here over twenty-four hours ago, suffering from frostbite and severe hypoxia. Your readings are better than they were then. By a long way. You are most fortunate not to be lying in a morgue.'

'Lucky me.'

Sharma looked annoyed at the flippant comment. His face took on an expression of deadly seriousness.

'I don't think you quite understand, Sean. Another few minutes and you'd have been beyond bringing back.'

'*Bringing back*?'

'Yes! This may come as a shock to you, but you died up there.'

'I . . . *died*?'

Sean struggled to take in what Sharma had said.

'For all of two minutes, before you were resuscitated.'

Sean shook his head in disbelief. He began to laugh. Sharma had seen others he had broken the same news to react in odd ways. Laughter was simply the mind's defence mechanism kicking in, releasing a fake happy-hormone to calm and reassure the person. He tried to offer some comfort.

'You're fine, Sean. There's no lasting damage to your heart or brain. But the news must be upsetting.'

'Sorry for laughing, doc, it's just that, well, if you understood, you'd laugh, yourself. Someone's just played a great big joke on me.'

Sharma nodded, misunderstanding Sean's meaning.

'Do you need some time alone? Perhaps you wish to talk to one of our excellent psychoanalysts? We even have a priest, should you wish to speak to a holy man? News such as this can be very debilitating, mentally and spiritually.'

Sean shook his head.

'No! I'm just astounded to hear I actually died. It feels kind of unreal, though. I wasn't aware of it, I don't think.'

'Of course,' said Sharma, 'it's a normal way to feel.'

Sean was stunned by the irony of the situation, but had no need to talk about it with anyone. He was more interested in why his hands and feet were bandaged, or more what lay *beneath* the bandages.

'What about the rest of me?'

'You have responded well to the medication,' said Sharma, 'although the best medication for altitude sickness is always less altitude. As I'm sure you already know. I understand you had been taking Diamox.'

'I had,' said Sean, trying not to look guilty, 'just as a precaution. I guess it didn't work that well for me.'

'Clearly not,' said Sharma.

He wondered why Sharma had mentioned it. Lots of climbers used it when they were at altitude. It was no big deal. But there was something in his voice that told Sean the conversation wasn't over. He tried to deflect any further discussion about it by holding up his bandaged hands.

'So, tell me the worst. Will I ever play the violin again?'

'You are a violinist?'

'Sorry, doc, I was being sarcastic. What I mean is, do I have all my fingers and toes?'

Sharma nodded.

'The bandages are purely precautionary.'

'That's something, anyway.'

Sean was relieved, if nothing else. Dying was okay. Losing bits of himself under the knife was definitely not.

'There is *some* damage we must discuss, however,' said Sharma, 'but first, tell me what you remember. You were found lying in the snow, just below Base Camp. What were you doing out there, at night, and alone?'

Again, the tone of Sharma's question, as well as the question itself, put Sean on the defensive. Was he trying to assess his mental state? Was he suspicious that he had purposely tried to kill himself? Although he was in Nepal, he was in a modern, private hospital, and any accidents that occurred on Everest had to be reported to the Nepalese government officials, along with a medical or coroner's report, and would be investigated. Sharma could, he was certain, keep him here against his will if he considered him a danger to himself.

'I remember going for a moonlit hike, doc. It was just so incredibly beautiful, up there. I wanted to be out in it, under the stars. I'd never seen anything quite like it before. Stupid, I guess, thinking about it now, but I really didn't think there was any immediate danger. I wasn't going that far from the accommodation block, and the weather was good, at least, it was when I started out. Apart from that, I can't really remember anything else, other than it started to snow. I think I must have lost my way as it got heavier.'

Sharma nodded.

'It was incredibly dangerous *and* stupid. You took a risk with your life in one of the most extreme environments in the world, where the weather can change in minutes. You're clearly an educated man, so I can only put it down to the altitude sickness you were already suffering, which makes judgement poor, at best. You most likely wouldn't even have known you were suffering from it.'

'Like I say, doc, I don't really remember anything other than thinking it was an amazing place to be. You're right, it must have been altitude sickness clouding my brain.'

'It happens, Sean. To the best of climbers.'

Sean felt a sense of relief. It seemed Sharma accepted his explanation and would record it as a simple accident due to hypoxia. He quickly steered the conversation on.

'Who found me, doc? Who saved my life? And how the hell did I get down to Kathmandu?'

'You were seen walking out of the camp by your Sherpa guide.'

'Kamal?'

'Yes, Kamal. He went out after you with two other Sherpas. They almost lost you when the snowstorm started. It is a miracle they found you at all.'

Sean gave a sarcastic laugh.

'I don't believe in miracles.'

That's as may be, Sean, but it seems they believe in you. Kamal told me it was divine intervention that saved you. I have no idea what he meant by that. You may ask him that yourself. He's been here since you were brought in, waiting for you to regain consciousness.'

Sean couldn't hide his surprise.

'Why? Surely he has better things to do.'

'For a Sherpa guide to lose a client, Sean, is the worst thing that can happen to them. They are responsible for your life, up there. Kamal did not recognise how sick you already were when he took you up to Gorak Shep. Even though it was he who found and resuscitated you, he blames himself for what happened to you.'

'It wasn't his fault, doc. I hid the fact I was taking Diamox from him. I didn't want him to know I was struggling. It was all my own fault. I can't have him blamed.'

Sharma shrugged.

'That may be so. And you were foolish to do that. But quite apart from the fact he feels responsible, it reflects badly on his ability to do his job. He almost lost you. It may have implications for his ability to gain future clients.'

Sean felt an overwhelming sense of guilt at causing Kamal any distress. He'd been more than a good companion, no matter how it had come about. He'd tried to look after him when he had not cared to look after himself.

'Christ, what a bloody mess. The last person I would want to have caused trouble for is Kamal.'

Sharma, seeing Sean's anguish, patted the edge of the bed and gave him a reassuring smile.

'Don't worry, I will see to it that my report reflects what you have told me. I will ensure it is known Kamal has been absolved of all blame. But you owe him an apology, as well as your thanks for saving your life.'

'When I see him,' said Sean, 'it'll be the first thing I do.'

Seemingly pacified, Sharma moved on

'Now, let us discuss the injuries you have sustained.'

'First, doc, tell me how in the hell I got here, given the last thing I remember is being at eighteen thousand feet, at night, in the middle of a snowstorm. One moment I'm dead, the next, here, alive, in Kathmandu'

Sharma nodded, understanding Sean had questions that he needed answers to. He decided he would provide at least one of them.

'Okay, but I must be brief, I have other patients to care for.

'Fine, doc, just tell me something.'

'From the little I know, after you were taken back to Gorak Shep, by Kamal, your hands and feet were bathed in warm water and a steroid injection administered. You were then put on oxygen until first light. One of the hospital helicopter pilots, a young Canadian, Ryan, I believe his name is, took off in semi-darkness, risking his own life to reach you. You were brought directly here from Base Camp. Kamal never left your side from the moment he found you out on the glacier.'

Sean hung his head in shame.

'I've caused a lot of people a lot of trouble. I put their lives at risk, as well as my own.'

Sharma, seeing Sean was genuinely upset, offered him some solace.

'You *could* look at it that way. But accidents happen when man confronts the beasts of nature. There is no greater beast than *Chomolungma*. You're not the first person this has happened to. You won't be the last.'

Sean sat silently for a moment. He realised that his plan to die on Everest, from the outset, had been flawed. He was supposed to go there to meet Linz, alone. He had not considered anyone else being with him. If he had not had been forced into taking Kamal, he would now be with her.

'I should have been more careful.'

'Perhaps,' said Sharma, again missing Sean's meaning, 'but you survived.' He glanced up at the clock on the wall above Sean's bed. 'Can we get to your injuries? I really must get on.'

'Okay. Tell me the worst.'

'Well, you will not be climbing again any time soon. Two months. More likely three. You have stage one frostbite in your toes, more commonly referred to as . . .'

'Frostnip! I'm a climber, doc. I know the terminology.'

'Good, then you also know to expect pain and discomfort when we take you off the mediation currently being administered into your system. It's why you might feel light-headed and have some moments of confusion.'

'I can live with pain, doc, that's not a problem for me.'

Sharma continued, again not getting Sean's meaning.

'Your fingers were slightly worse off, given you were not wearing gloves.'

Sean was surprised.

'I'm sure I had them on when I left Gorak Shep.'

'Irrespective of that, you have stage two frostbite, which you will know is classed as superficial frostbite, on your fingers and hands, which is why they are bandaged. When Kamal found you, they were turning blue and badly swollen, from the ice crystals forming in your skin.'

Sean shuddered. The thought that he might have woken up without his hands and feet scared him more than anything else. He held his bandaged hands up in front of him, relieved to hear he damage was minimal.

'As long as they're all still there.'

Sharma gave him a reassuring smile.

'They are, do not worry. But there will be blisters. They will need to be drained and the dressings changed each day. Nurse Uyen will take care of that. Again, it will be painful.'

'I get it, doc. It's fine.'

''So,' added Sharma, 'we will continue a course of antibiotics and you will recover fully. You may struggle to use your hands for the next month, perhaps longer. You'll will need to do plenty of physiotherapy to get them working properly again. In short, you need to take it easy. No more mountains.'

Sean nodded, annoyed, but accepting what he was being told.

'Fair enough. But how soon will I be fit to leave. I don't like hospitals.'

'Seven days, Mr Jameson,' said Sharma, standing up and hooking Sean's chart over the end of the bedframe. 'Until then, you must rest. Can you do that?'

'Sure.'

'Good! And now I really must attend to my other patients. I will ask nurse Uyen will come to redress your hands and feet.. She's here to take care of you, Sean, so let her. Your insurance company have already been informed. Kamal provided us with the necessary documents you gave him before your climb. They will cover the costs. Someone from administration will bring the paperwork for you to sign, once you are able to.'

'It's fine, doc, I'm lucky enough to not to . . .'

Sean stopped speaking, mid-sentence, staring over at the windows. Sharma followed his gaze, but could not see what had taken his attention.

'Are you feeling all right, Sean?'

Sean didn't answer. Not right away. When he did, he seemed confused.

'It's . . . nothing.'

Linz was standing by the window, looking out towards the mountains. She turned her head and looked at him. Sean found it hard to meet her gaze.

He was distracted by Sharma, who was looking at him with growing concern on his face.

'Are you sure?'

'Sorry, doc. I was miles away. Just thinking about all that's happened. It's a lot to take in.'

'Of course,' said Sharma, 'but there is nothing to be concerned about. Just rest, we will speak again.'

He bowed his head and left the room.

Linz walked over and sat down in Sharma's seat. Sean was beyond happy to see her. He thought she might have been angry with him. As usual, she knew what he was thinking.

'Linz! I thought you'd abandoned me. I thought . . .'

'Don't upset yourself, hun. I'm not angry with you. And I won't ever abandon you.'

'I came to meet you, my love. Like we planned.'

'I saw you, hun. I was with you, don't you remember.'

Sean nodded. He remembered she was there. He'd seen her light.

'Why didn't you take me with you, Linz? You were supposed to take me with you.'

Sean wished he could reach out and touch her. He felt the sadness that lived inside him threaten to overwhelm him.

'It's okay, hun. You don't have to be sad.'

Linz smiled at him. It pushed the sadness back down inside him. She made him feel the way she'd always made him feel. Safe and loved.

'I'm sorry, my love.'

'For what, hun?'

'For failing you. Again.'

Linz shook her head, spraying gold glitter over her shoulders and down the front of her pale blue, summer dress.

'Perhaps you're not meant to be with me, hun. Not yet.

'Don't say that, Linz. Don't you *want* me to be with you?'

'Of course I do. You know that, hun. Perhaps there's somewhere else we have to go, to be together.'

'Can we be, my love?'

'We will be, hun. In the end. Don't worry.'

She stood and walked over to the windows, then turned back to face him. The sunlight made the glitter on her sparkle. Like the sunlight reflecting off the waves onto her skin had done, at Applecross Bay.

'Promise?'

Linz nodded and spread her wings. She looked like an angel.

'Mr Sean.'

Startled, Sean turned to see someone standing in the doorway.

'Kamal!'

'You were talking to her, again, Mr Sean.'

Sean looked over to the windows, but Linz was gone.

'Talking to her?'

'To your wife, Mr Sean. You went out onto the glacier to be with her, I think.' Kamal came into the room and closed the door behind him. He walked up to the seat Linz had just been sitting in. 'May I sit?'

Sean nodded.

'I wasn't talking to anyone.'

'It's okay, Mr Sean, do not be worried. I will not mention it to anyone. It is not so strange to speak with those we have lost yet still love.'

Sean realised Kamal knew about Linz. Part of him was glad to be able to share her being with him.

'Did . . . did you see her, Kamal?'

'Alas, Mr Sean, she appears only to you. Her spirit and yours are joined. But she was with you on *Chomolungma*. Of that I am certain. She led me to you when you were lost.'

'What do you mean, she led you to me?'

'When the snowstorm started, Mr Sean, I lost sight of you. I searched, with the other Sherpa's, but you could not be found. But then the light of your torch guided me to you. Only I saw it. I cannot explain why that might be so.'

Sean's face blanched.

'I had no torch, Kamal.'

'This I now know, Mr Sean. Yet there was a light that guided us to where you lay. It disappeared as we reached you. You were lying on the ground, already covered in snow. Ten minutes more and we would not have been able to save you. I did not understand it, at the time, but I am now most certainly sure your wife was with you. She was the light I saw.'

Sean looked at Kamal and saw only honesty in his eyes.

'Thank you, Kamal. I'm so very sorry for putting your life and livelihood at risk. It was not my intention. I hope you can forgive me. I will try my best to make amends.'

'Please, Mr Sean, it is a blessing upon me that I was able to save you. I knew that a dark spirit had been following you. I should have spoken to you about it. It is I who have failed you.'

Sean shook his head.

'Don't say that, Kamal. It's not your fault.'

'I prevented you from joining your most wonderful wife, Mr Sean, that is what I am sorry for. But my religion forbids me from allowing harm to come to any living thing. I had no choice but to save you.'

Kamal bowed his head, as if ashamed, making Sean feel even worse than he already did.

'I should thank you, Kamal, for the gift of my life. Despite it's a gift I do not care for. But there is no forgiveness required, from you, my friend.'

They sat in silence for a few moments, each of them reflecting on what had happened.

'Will you tell me of your wife, Mr Sean? Of your family? I should very much like to hear of them, now that I have become part of their story. We are all of us connected, the living and the dead, as one family under the love of Buddha.'

'I owe you that much, Kamal,' said Sean, 'seeing the truth in his words.'

He recounted the details of the accident on the *Bealach na Ba*, a mountain, ten thousand miles away, much smaller than Everest but equally as dramatic. He spoke of the loss of his faith and his anger at an uncaring God. Of how Linz had guided him to her journal, and of the list of adventures she wanted him to undertake. The bridge that would allow them to reach one other.

'I have also suffered such loss,' said Kamal, his almost permanent smile fading for the first time since Sean had met him at Lukla airport. 'My two sisters and mother were lost in the great earthquake. We passed their house, in Pangboche, on our way to Gorak Shep.'

Sean remembered the moment.

'I saw you light incense there, Kamal, and say prayers. I didn't know it was for your family. Forgive me, I was too wrapped up in my own pain to see yours.'

'It is fine, Mr Sean. A personal thing. I did not wish to burden you. I spoke with them. They were concerned for you and told me to watch over you. It is how I knew to remain vigilant the night we reached Gorak Shep. My mother told me it was not your time. You have another journey to make. One that will end with a new beginning. A new life.'

'Your mother was clearly a kind and wise soul, Kamal, but she is wrong about that. There is no new beginning for me. My life is over.'

'Perhaps,' said Kamal, 'sometimes she was. I miss her and my sisters every day, Mr Sean. Their spirits will stay with me until they find new bodies to go to.'

'But you still have your wife and children, Kamal, don't you?'

'Yes, Mr Sean. They were not harmed in the earthquake.'

'How would you feel if you had lost them? Would you not wish to join them?'

Kamal was silent for a moment, considering the question, as well as his reply

'I would, I think, Mr Sean, for it would most terribly break my heart. But I would go on living, for them. I would see them, still, as you see your wife. I am also forbidden to take my own life. It is against my religion.'

'And that is where we differ,' said Sean, resignedly. 'I have no religion. Not anymore. I have only the pain of their loss. A pain I am forced to endure each time I wake, and through each day, until I sleep. They are my first and last thought. I cannot live with that pain, Kamal. I cannot live without them.'

Kamal studied Sean's face, seeing the sadness smothering in his soul. His aura still pale blue and streaked. The bad spirit was still attached to him. It seemed he was determined to join his wife and children in death.

'What will you do now, Mr Sean?'

Sean considered the question for a moment.

'I really have no clue. I suppose I will have to wait until I am recovered enough to face another challenge and offer myself to Death.'

'Why must you wish for this, Mr Sean?' Kamal asked, saddened that the man whose life he had saved wanted to throw that gift away. 'It is the belief of all Buddhists to refrain from such a thing. To do so risks being reborn into a sorrowful realm, because of dark, final thoughts.'

Sean shook his head in disagreement.

'But that's just it, Kamal. If it happens, and Death comes for me, Linz will be with me. My final moments will be with her. They will be moments filled with love.'

'So, you truly welcome Death, Mr Sean?'

'I called for her, Kamal. She heard me. It is for her to decide when she takes me. Perhaps the journeys I have undertaken, so far, are her gift to me, showing me the beauty of the life she will finally take from me. Or perhaps they are part of my path back to Linz. The tests I must face before I am worthy of joining her. I want to be with her. I want to see my children again. So I will go on. I will continue to be tested.'

'I would very much like to have met this wife of yours, Mr Sean. I hope you will find your way back to her.'

'I will, Kamal. I love her beyond my own life.'

'I love you, too, hun,' said Linz, once more standing by the windows. 'And you're right about the journeys. They are a test.'

Kamal saw Sean looking towards the windows and the smile upon his face.

'She is with you now, Mr Sean?'

'Yes.' Sean whispered. 'She is.'

Kamal stood and turned to face the windows. He pressed his hands together and raised his fingertips to his forehead, then bowed to Linz.

'She likes you, Kamal. I can tell.'

'I do like him, hun.'

Kamal walked to the door and opened it. He stopped and turned, bowing to Sean.

'Farewell, Mr Sean. May you be forever blessed. And may the life you need become the life you find. Namaste.'

50

The train rumbled into view as Sean climbed the steps and joined a hundred other backpackers waiting on the platform for its arrival into the pretty French town of Bayonne. Like a herd of nervous wildebeest waiting on the bank of a crocodile infested river, they shuffled towards the edge of the track, eager to claim their space on what was sure to be a crowded train to St Jean Pied De Port. There, they would begin another journey, to the city of Santiago de Compostela, a trek of almost eight hundred kilometers across northern Spain.

After a long flight from Kathmandu to Paris, Sean had taken a connecting Air France flight to the elegant seaside city of Biarritz, acclaimed for its beaches, thalassotherapy centres and gastronomy, as well as being the gateway to the Basque Country. He'd spent the night in a small hotel, more tired than he'd imagined he could be. Doctor Sharma had told him to expect that after the massive amounts of antibiotics he'd required to ensure his frostbite had not become infected.

The train left Bayonne, on time, through a valley of cypress trees, high unkempt hedgerows and open farmlands, climbing slowly but steadily into the hills. Around him, the nervousness in the faces of the other travellers gave way to smiles, introductions and excited conversations. For most, the journey had been planned long in advance, their reasons for being there, varied and personal, although now that they were so close to the start of their adventure they wanted to share their stories, meet new friends, and to know they were not alone on that journey.

Sean avoided any attempt to speak to him, impervious to the general state of excitement around him. Today, of all days, was, for him, one of sadness, not joy.

In truth, he had almost not come at all. There was no danger to it, so it would be pointless. But Linz had told him had to, at the hospital in Kathmandu. So he would walk the Camino for her, his focus on its ending rather than the journey they had dreamed of doing together. He withdrew his mind to the darkness feeding inside him, staring out of the window, seeing nothing of the beauty around him.

A dozen or so carriages down, close to front of the train, Claudia chatted to two Dutch women she'd met on the platform. They had introduced themselves as Babette and Robyn.

'So, Claudia. You are travelling alone?'

Babette offered her a macaroon from a box she'd purchased from a little bakery on the banks of the Adour river. Claudia picked out a green one and bit into it. She screwed up her face at the tart taste before replying.

'Yes. I'd hoped my husband would be with me, but his work commitments kept him home, in Los Angeles.'

'What flavour did you get?' Robyn asked, declining Babette's offer to try one with a wave of her hand.

'Apple. As tart as it is sweet. But delicious.'

'And you've just been to Rome and Verona,' continued Babette, 'how adventurous of you, a beautiful woman travelling around Europe, alone.'

'I was never in any danger,' said Claudia, laughing, 'except, perhaps, from the advances of the Italian men.'

The look on Babette's face showed she clearly agreed.

'They *are* incorrigible, and *so* forward. Not like our Dutch men, who are every bit as handsome, but taller and much cooler. Although we do hope to meet many men of many nationalities on this trip of ours, don't we Robyn?'

'Speak for yourself,' said Robyn, her nose stuck in a book about the history of the Camino. 'I'm here to find inner peace and keep you out of trouble.'

Babette threw her a cheeky grin.

'Good luck with that. Tell me, why are you walking the Camino, Claudia?'

'Tell her to leave you alone if you'd rather.'

Robyn shook her head at Babette, who shrugged her shoulders.

'No, it's fine, Robyn. Really. I'm glad to have company.'

Babette stuck her tongue out at Robyn.

'See!'

Claudia smiled at her and answered the question.

'Well, I had the most amazing time in Italy, and then wondered where to go next. I'd heard about the Camino from a friend who'd walked it last year. So I thought, I'm here, in Europe, why not? There's supposed to be some beautiful cities along the way, not to mention all the little towns and villages I'll pass through.'

Robyn looked up from her book.

'There are, Claudia. I'm most looking forward to visiting Leon. And walking into Santiago, of course. Can you imagine the feeling when we walk into the city on the last day? If we make it, that is. It's a long way.'

'We'll all make it,' said Claudia.

'I'm looking forward to being everywhere and seeing everything,' said Babette, 'just being out there in the countryside and away from reality. I'm not seeking anything other than what the Camino provides.'

'Well that's the most famous saying of all, isn't it?' Robyn saw Claudia's puzzled expression and explained. 'They say that, whoever *they* are, that whatever you need, the Camino provides.'

Claudia remembered what Hannah had said to her, in her letter, about finding what she *needed*?

The train began to slow.

'Oh look, ladies. I think we're here.'

'I'm still a girl, actually,' said Babette, grinning at Claudia.

It was infectious. Claudia couldn't help feeling drawn to her.

'And she's no lady,' added Robyn, making them laugh.

The train pulled to a stop with a metallic grating and series of puffs and wheezes, throwing everyone off balance as they tried to retrieve their rucksacks from the overhead storage spaces, butting each other like sparring mountain goats as they tried to haul them onto their backs. The melee was good natured, though, and eventually everyone was ready to disembark.

Claudia had already sent most of her luggage onto her hotel in Paris. She planned to travel there after completing the Camino, to spend a final few days sightseeing before flying home to Boston. She'd purchased a new rucksack, in Verona, which was small enough for her to trek with and still carry all she would need. It had little in it, at the moment, other than some underwear and socks, a couple of t-shirts, basic toiletries, her sneakers and a pair of jeans. Looking around at all the other trekkers, carrying bulging packs, she felt somewhat intimidated. *What the hell am I doing here*, she thought, as the doors slid open and the crowd spilled out onto the platform.

'Would you like to walk with us?' Robyn asked, helping Claudia down from the train carriage. 'You look a little shell-shocked. Trust me, there's nothing to be afraid of. Babette and I have been here before, so we know how it can make you feel first time round.'

'Yes, we got as far as Pamplona, last time, before we had to go home,' added Babette, 'but enjoyed it so much we knew we had to come back and do it all. Come on, Claudia, say yes. Join us for a day. Or a week. Whatever you feel like. We can keep you company until you find your feet?'

Claudia considered it for all of a second.

'Yes please! I must admit I'm feeling a bit out of my comfort zone. But I don't want to impose on you two.'

Babette took her by the arm.

'You're not. This journey is one best done shared. It's one of the great gifts of the Camino, meeting new people. If you want company, you have it, every step of the way.'

'Enough talking,' said Robyn, 'look behind us. There's ten carriages emptying onto the platform. We need to get ahead of them or the queue at the Pilgrims Office will be hellish. I want to get my Compostela passport and be able to have some dinner. And before midnight, this time, if possible.'

'I remember,' said Babette, 'we had to wait for hours to get it, last time. You know what we're talking about, Claudia?'

'Yes. The pilgrim's passport. The card that we get stamped along the way to prove we've actually walked the Camino.'

'That's it,' said Babette, waving her walking stick ahead of her like a knight's lance. 'Okay, let's go. As you Americans say, fast foot forward.'

'I think,' said Claudia, 'it's first foot forward, but I know what you mean.'

They crossed over the railway line and headed through the outlying streets towards the town centre. Twenty minutes later, they passed under the arch of the original west gate, part of the ancient walls that had once protected the city's inhabitants from attack by Spanish and Moorish raiders.

Inside St Jean's old town, the buildings changed dramatically, the cobbled streets narrowed and the timber framed houses shuffled closer together, shading the line of new pilgrims from the light of the sun. Claudia ran her fingertips along the white plaster walls of one of them. She could almost feel the history of the ancient town in her touch.

After walking along the Rue de France, they turned left up the steep Rue de Citadelle. The street was lined with quaint looking shops. Claudia peered into the latticed windows of one selling trekking gear. The oak lintel above the door was black with age. At its centre was the roughly carved image of a scallop shell. There were also bunches of real scallop shells, hanging on hooks, outside the shop doorway, each with a red cross painted on its front.

Claudia took one of the shells in her hand.

'What's the deal with the seashells?'

'*Madame*. May I be of assistance?'

She started at the voice, not having seen or heard the shopkeeper come up behind her. He was old and slightly bent, with a weathered face, but his chestnut-brown eyes still contained the fire of life and his smile was broad and welcoming, below a prominent, Gallic nose.

'I'm sorry,' Claudia stammered, 'I was just . . .'

'There is no need to apologise, *Madame*. You are checking my wares. It is what they are set out here for, *n'est-ce pas*?'

'*Oui*,' said Claudia.

The shopkeeper smiled at as if she'd just told him he was the most handsome man in the world.

'*Vous parlez francais, joliment, Madame. C'est merveilleux. Puis, je peux vous raconter l'histoire de Saint Jacques et de la coquille?*

'Oh!' I don't really . . . I mean, I can't speak much French. In fact, I don't speak French at all. Other than a few words.'

Claudia put the fingers of her free hand to her lips, clearly flustered. A fact not missed by Babette and Robyn, who were enjoying her discomfort. Babette translated, nodding a greeting to the shopkeeper.

'He said you speak French, beautifully, and asked if you would like to hear the history of the shell.'

'The shopkeeper gave Babette the same warm smile he'd just given Claudia.

'You speak my language well, *Madame*. May I ask where you are from?'

'We are from Amsterdam,' said Babette, nodding towards Robyn.

'And I'm from Lexington, close to Boston,' said Claudia, regaining her composure. 'It's in America.'

'Yes, *Madame*. I am aware Boston is in America.'

The shopkeeper rolled his eyes and tilted his head at Claudia.

'I'm so sorry, *Monsieur*,' said Claudia, feeling she was making a complete fool of herself, 'I didn't mean to . . .'

'Ah, *Madame*! You apologise more than I do to my beautiful wife.'

'I'm so . . .'

Claudia almost apologised, again, but caught the automatic response in time. The shopkeeper gave her an even wider smile.

'I jest with you, *Madame*. Please, forgive me.' He took hold of the shell in Claudia's hand. 'May I?'

'Please do. I keep seeing these shells everywhere. Hanging from everyone's backpacks, on the top of their walking sticks, and in virtually every shop window.'

'Allow me, first, to introduce myself. I am Xabier Aristizabal, from a long line of Basques of noble birth. Alas, no longer a knight, now but a lowly shopkeeper.'

He bowed theatrically and swept a hand low to the ground, in a greeting dating from the Middle Ages. Claudia curtsied, enjoying the play between them.

'And I am Claudia Montgomery, descended from somewhere in Scotland, from ancient warriors, so I believe. Now, but a lowly artist and sculptor.'

'The honour, Claudia, is mine.'

Xavier took Claudia's hand and kissed the back of it, making her blush.

'You are too kind, sweet knight.'

'Honestly, what are you both like,' said Babette, laughing with Robyn at Claudia and Xavier. She blushed, herself, when Xavier took her hand and did the same.

'So, Claudia,' said Xavier, after kissing Robyn's hand to ensure she didn't feel left out, 'you are a *peregrino*? A pilgrim? You walk the Way of St James, to Santiago?'

'I suppose I am,' Claudia replied. 'And, yes, I *am* going to walk to Santiago.'

For the first time, she said it with confidence. She *was* going to walk it. She found she was relishing the journey ahead.

'And this is your first time in Saint Jean?'

'Yes. I've never even been to Europe before.'

Xavier looked shocked at such a scurrilous admission.

'Then, Claudia Montgomery, you are doubly fortunate. For as well as being in my beautiful town, you get to walk the Camino de Santiago. It is an ancient pilgrimage, as you no doubt already know.'

'I don't really know *that* much about it, Xabier, but I'm excited about doing it. You can feel a real sense of anticipation in the air. Everyone is so happy. I've never felt anything quite like it.'

'Then I am happy for you, Claudia, for it is a life changing journey you will undertake. Allow me to tell you of the prophet and the shell. I will not take long. My wife, Marie-Claire, will already be watching me from inside the shop, wondering why I am talking to three such beautiful women.'

'I don't see her,' said Claudia, 'and I'm sure she will be used to you talking to many such beautiful women.'

'Perhaps you are right,' said Xabier, giving Claudia a mischievous wink. He held up the shell between them. 'Now, let me recount to you the history of the *Coquille de St Jacques*.'

Babette interrupted him before he could begin proper.

'Xabier, we know the story, if you will excuse us, Robyn and I will head up to the Pilgrims Office. Claudia, come and join us when you're ready. It's just up there. Look, you can see the queue.'

'Okay,' said Claudia, 'I'll see you soon.'

Xavier bowed to Babette and Robyn.

'It has been a pleasure meeting you both. *Buen Camino*.'

'You too, Xabier,' said Robyn and Babette together, then headed up the street to join the growing line of pilgrims.

Claudia turned back to Xabier.

'You're sure you have enough time, Xabier? Your shop looks busy.'

'I have my beautiful wife, Marie-Claire, to serve them. Besides, I love to talk. I am lifted by your joy in being here. The Camino and the pilgrims are our lives, Claudia. We like to share in all their journeys.'

'Have you walked it yourself.'

'Fifteen times,' said Xabier, in reply to Claudia's question. 'I shall walk it again before I go to the land of eternal wine, women and song.'

Claudia smiled at one of the women inside the shop, behind the counter, watching the exchange. She was in her late sixties and had a kind face. She rolled her eyes and shook her head at Claudia, a gesture unseen by Xabier who had his back to her.

'Fifteen!' Claudia replied, stifling a laugh.

Xabier turned and looked into the shop.

'*Mon Dieu!* I knew I could feel Marie-Claire's eyes on us.'

His wife blew him a kiss then turned away to speak to a customer. Xabier turned back to Claudia, shaking his head.

'That woman! *Que dois-je-faire?* What am I to do?'

Despite the theatrical protests, he could not hide his smile.

Claudia could see they were still very much in love. She felt a flutter of sadness at the thought of her own marriage. She remembered a saying she'd heard, recently, which seemed to fit the moment, and spoke it, without meaning to.

'A smile is a thought that comes from the heart.'

'Un sourire est une pensée qui vient du cœur,' said Xabier, translating it into his native French.'

'I think I like it better the way you say it,' said Claudia, and her melancholy lifted.

'It is beautiful in any language, Claudia. Now, where were we?

'You were telling me the history of the scallop shell.'

Xabier looked back to the scallop shell and went back to his story.

'The apostle, James, four hundred years after the death of Christ, went to the north-westernmost part of Spain to convert people to Christianity. After returning to Palestine, years later, he was taken prisoner by Herodes Agrippa and tortured to death. His disciples stole the body and brought it, aboard a small boat, back to Spain. Alas, the sea drove the boat onto the Spanish coast. The Apostle was then buried at a secret place in a close-by wood.'

Claudia was enthralled.

'I had no idea the story was so dramatic.'

'Indeed, Claudia, and more so. Centuries later, a hermit heard music coming from the same wood, and saw a bright light shining among trees. In Latin, that light is known as *Campus Stellae*, meaning, the Field of the Star, which, over time, became the word, *Compostela*.'

'I did wonder at the meaning,' said Claudia, enjoying the history of the journey she would make.

'And so,' Xabier added, 'the tomb was discovered. In time, the Spanish King, Alphonse, declared James the patron of his empire and built a chapel at the site of the wood. From that time on, pilgrims have followed the *Holy Way of Santiago* to the original chapel, which became the cathedral of the new settlement. The city of Santiago de Compostela.'

'And the shell, Xabier, why did it become his symbol?

'The legend, Claudia, recounts that Saint James' body was washed ashore surrounded by scallop shells, Hence, it became his symbol. You will see them painted on walls and streets all the way from St Jean to Santiago.'

Claudia took Xabier's hands in hers.

'Thank you so much for taking the time to tell me all this, Xabier. It really has brought the Camino to life for me so much more.'

Xabier placed the scallop shell into Claudia's hand.

'Then, you must take this.'

'Xabier, I couldn't. Please, let me pay you for it. You've given me so much already, in your story.'

'*Mais non!* I will not hear of it. It is a gift. A good luck charm for you to carry on this wonderful journey. Your smile is payment enough. I have enjoyed your company, Claudia Montgomery. If there is anything you need, before you depart, you may visit my shop.'

Claudia, turned sideways to show Xabier her rucksack.

'You must have noticed my almost empty pack. I do need a few things.'

'Marie Claire and I will be waiting to serve you. Until then, *buen camino*.'

He bowed and went back into his shop, leaving Claudia to head up the hill to join Babette and Robyn, feeling even more excited about her impending journey.

Some twenty minutes later, Sean passed by Xabier's shop. He noticed the scallop shell carved into the wooden lintel above the doorway. It was simpler in design than many he'd seen walking up from the station, and clearly hundreds of years old. For a moment, he thought about going inside, but decided, instead, to find the albergue he had booked for the night. He walked on, up the busy street, passing the Pilgrims Office, where Claudia and her new friends were standing in the queue, chatting happily, oblivious to all around them.

The Gite de la Porte albergue was easy to recognise from the daub plastered frontage and latticed windows, as well as the exposed stonework around the heavy oak door. It had looked the same on the website Sean had used to find an place to stay for the evening. After checking in, he left his pack in his room and headed back down the hill, joining the queue for the Pilgrims Office, ensuring no-one would talk to him by putting his headphones in his ears. After a shorter wait that he'd thought it would be, he entered the building and stood in the first of four lines of people waiting their turn. Before long, he found himself at the front of his and took a seat at the desk. The young woman seated opposite gave him a warm smile he did not feel inclined to return.

'*Bonjour!* Hello! My name is Francine.'

'Hello,' said Sean, gruffly.

Francine pressed on, her jovial outlook unchanged. There were many people that passed through the office. Most were of a happy disposition. Some were not. This one was clearly of the latter group.

'May I have your name? To register you as a pilgrim.'

'Sean Jameson.'

'And you are walking the Camino, Sean?'

'That's why I'm sitting here, *Francine*.'

'Of course. Why else?'

Francine smiled, again, hoping her joke would be acknowledged. It was a hope in vain.

'Sorry,' said Sean, seeing the exasperated look on her face. 'I'm not really in the mood for conversation.'

'I understand. How far do you intend to go, on the Camino?'

'Santiago.'

'Excellent, it is a wonderful journey to undertake. Life changing, I think you will discover.'

'I doubt it.' Sean muttered, under his breath.

'Are you walking or cycling?'

'Walking.'

'Alone? Or do you have some . . .'

'Alone.'

Why am I not surprised, thought Francine. *Merde! He is a miserable one.*

'Of course, Sean. That is wonderful. Many people seek the solitude and time for inner reflection that the Camino offers. And may I help you with any accommodation?'

Sean tutted, becoming exasperated with Francine's pointless questions.

'Look, Francine, I'm sure you're a lovely girl, but I don't want any help with anything. I'm perfectly capable of looking after myself. Can you just give me what I need and deal with the people behind me?'

Francine bit her tongue. She was done trying to be nice to this sullen, albeit handsome man. She filled in the forms she needed and took a copy of Sean's passport, then handed Sean a folded card, a little smaller than a paperback book, with the picture of a scallop shell printed on its front.

'This is your Compostela passport,' said Francine, the warmth she had greeted him with, gone, 'you need to have this stamped along the way. All of the albergues, as well as most of the bars in the villages and towns, can do that. One per day. Two, from Sarria to Santiago.'

She put the card into a clear, zip-lock bag, along with his other documentation; the maps and accommodation guides for the villages in the regions he would cross, then handed it across the table.

As Sean reached for it, Francine noticed his hands. They'd been hidden in his lap, behind the desk. Three fingers on his left hand were individually bandaged. He also had a bandage wrapped around his right hand, from the first joint of his fingers up to and under the cuff of his fleece jacket. The exposed skin on both hands was red and inflamed. Whatever accident had befallen him, she realised, he must still be in some pain. She was immediately angry at herself. *You do not know why people come here, Francine. Some carry burdens we cannot see. Forgive me, Father, for being ungodly to this poor soul.* She reached up and touched the small crucifix hung around her neck.

'Thanks,' said Sean, noticing. 'I have one, too.'

He reached into his right pocket and, with only a little difficulty, pulled out his own silver crucifix. He'd carried it with him since leaving Edinburgh, not yet able to bring himself to wear it around his neck. Linz had given it to him. It remained a memory of theirs he wanted to keep. But it meant no more to him than that.

'It is very beautiful, *Monsieur*.'

'My wife gave it to me. On a happier day.'

The sadness on Sean's face was obvious. Francine felt tears spring to the corners of her eyes. She offered a silent prayer. *Watch over him on his journey, Father.*

Sean put the crucifix back into his pocket and stood up. He could see the pity on her face. It repelled him. He wanted no sympathy. Francine saw the shift his eyes and knew he had pulled away from her. But she had connected with him, if for only the briefest of moments. *The Camino provides.* She hoped it would provide for him.

'Go with God,' she said, as Sean turned away.

He turned back to face her, anger now the dominant expression.

'God is the last person I wish to travel with!'

He turned and walked out of the office, leaving an impression on Francine she would never forget.

Out in the warm, early evening sunlight, Sean began to panic. The girl's kindness had caught him unawares. He had allowed himself to open up to her by showing her his crucifix, and with that connection felt something other than the detachment and isolation he wore as armour. Kamal had almost died by being close to him. He could not risk allowing anyone else to become involved with him in any way. His chest tightened and his breathing became difficult. His vision began to blur.

No! Not here! Not now!

Sean walked across the cobbles and leant against a high wall, behind which he could hear the sound of children playing. The sound of them only added to his distress. Images began to appear in his mind. Images he had not care to see.

'Not today! Please! I don't want to remember.'

He pressed his head against his forearms and tried to force the memories away.

'Breathe, Sean. Breathe.'

He heard Linz's voice and looked up the hill. She was standing no more than twenty yards away.

'Linz.'

His voice was barely audible. He closed his eyes, sucking in deep draughts of air.

'Are you alright?'

Sean felt a hand on his upper arm and heard a woman's voice beside him.

He answered without looking at her.

'I'm . . . fine.'

'Well you don't look fine.'

'I am. Just give me a minute.'

The woman wouldn't take no for an answer.

'Look, why don't you come and sit down? You're welcome to join us for a cup of tea. That might help.'

Sean shrugged off her hand and turned to look at the woman who had come to his aid. She was a good five inches shorter than him, with shoulder length blonde hair, tanned skin and green eyes.

'Tea? Really? Look, lady, why don't you go back to your happy gathering and leave me the hell alone.'

Claudia was shocked at the vehemence in Sean's voice and the look of anger on his face.

'I was only trying to . . .'

Sean was having none of it. The anger on his face stayed put.

'You damned yanks! Always sticking your bloody oar in where it's not wanted.'

He pushed himself off the wall and made his way up the hill towards where Linz had been standing. She was no longer there. Claudia sat back down at her table and watched him go, visibly shocked.

'What a horrible man,' said Babette, scowling at Sean's back.

'A real *Klootzak*,' said Robyn, 'an asshole, I think you Americans say.'

'He seems troubled,' said Claudia. 'Did you see the bandages on his hands?'

'Maybe he got in a fight,' said Babette. 'With an attitude like his, I wouldn't be surprised. Forget him.'

'Babette's right, Claudia, forget him,' said Robyn. 'Come on, we're on the Camino. Nothing can be allowed to dampen our spirits.'

'You *will* still walk with us in the morning, Claudia?'

'Of course, Babette. We're all in the same room tonight and on the same road in the morning.'

'Up and over the Pyrenees, then down into Spain,' Babette replied. 'Lord help us. That climb out of here. It's bloody exhausting.'

'The hardest day of all,' agreed Robyn, 'but we'll make it.' She lifted her teacup. 'Here's to the Camino. May it bring us whatever we seek.'

'Cheers,' said Babette, raising hers.

'Slanje,' said Claudia, then turned her gaze, up the cobbled street, to the man she had tried to help.

He was standing between a gap in the buildings, looking out over the meadows and mountains. It reminded her of seeing Hannah standing at the Point, looking towards Finisterre and longing for Jonathon. This man had the same sad countenance about him. She hoped, if he had suffered some loss, he would find what he was looking for. She turned to chat to Babette and Robyn. When she looked again, he was gone.

51

Early morning birdsong greeted Sean as he stepped off the cobbled street and crossed the tarmac road, passing the signpost telling him he was leaving St Jean Pied de Port and had seven hundred and ninety kilometres to go until he would reach Santiago de Compostela. Reaching behind him, he touched the spot in his rucksack where the box containing the ashes of his family lay.

'We're on our way,' he whispered.

He closed his eyes and pictured them, then took the first of the million steps he would take to get there and began to climb.

A few hundred feet up, Sean stopped and looked back over the high walls of St Jean's ancient citadel. As if called by some unseen pied piper, from every doorway, it seemed, a trickle of people began to emerge into the streets. The trickle grew into an ever-widening stream, becoming a flood of humanity headed across the river and up the Rue de Citadelle. But the eight kilometres climb up to Orison, the only rest stop on the day's climb, was steep. The bunched army would disperse into a broken line, age and will sorting the wheat from the chaff.

He turned back and looked up to where he was headed. The sky was a rolling bank of cloud stretching across the mountains separating France from Spain. Charlemagne and Napoleon had once marched their armies up and over those same mountains, and now their ghosts challenged him to follow them and do the same. Three hours, at the most, according to his map, then he'd be able to rest and have some food. He'd skipped the communal breakfast at the albergue, not wanting to be dragged into the inane chat that would undoubtedly be served. He folded his map, replacing it in the side pocket of his rucksack, and climbed on.

'What a gorgeous view,' said Claudia, looking over the valley they'd climbed out of that morning, two thousand feet below. The early cloud has gone and the patchwork of green fields and yellow meadows stretched into the distance, still and silent beneath the blue, until the land met the sky at the point where they both lost their colour. 'I can see the skiether, Hannah,'

They'd started early, taking breakfast on the hoof to avoid the crowds Babette and Robyn assured her would follow, climbing slowly, taking plenty of stops to enjoy the view as well as to rest. Their bodies were not as conditioned as they would become by the time they reached the end of the journey.

The Camino, Xabier had told Claudia, the previous evening, when she'd gone back to his shop to buy the last few things she needed for her journey, was done in three parts. The first third of the journey was physical, although the pain she would suffer would soon go. The second part was more mental, where she and her fellow pilgrims would really begin to enjoy and appreciate the beauty of the journey. The final third would be deeply spiritual, when the questions she had come to have answered would be revealed.

'It is beautiful, isn't it,' agreed Robyn, shrugging off her rucksack, dropping it next to a table on the paved verandah belonging to the Orrison Refuge café.

'I'll be able to appreciate it in a minute or two,' Babette added, 'once I get my breath back. That was harder than I remember.'

Robyn laughed at her and helped her with her pack.

'Agreed, my friend. But it's not over yet.'

'How much further?' Claudia asked, turning back from the railing and taking a seat. 'We must be halfway up by now, surely?'

Robyn checked her ever present guide book.

'Another fifteen kilometers and two thousand feet to climb. But it's not nearly as steep as this morning. It's just after midday, so we'll have quick lunch here then head over the mountains into Spain. We'll hit Roncesvalles by five o'clock and get a bed in one of the monastery dorms.'

'Excellent,' said Claudia, 'now, let's order some food, I'm ravenous.'

They devoured the pilgrim's meal of beef stew flavored with roasted tomatoes and red peppers. For dessert, they had *arroz con leche,* a creamy, rice pudding dusted with cinnamon, a favourite, in Spain, so the waitress that served them had said. Babette introduced Claudia to *cervesa con limon*, a lemon-infused beer that was cold and tangy and slaked the thirst she'd built up climbing up to Orisson.

'What's so important about Roncesvalles?' Claudia asked, as they digested their lunch and enjoyed the sun on their faces, looking out over the valley.

Babette nodded towards Robyn.

'Ask her, she's the cultured one. Always making me visit museums and art galleries when I'm perfectly happy with a nice wine bar.'

'Philistine,' hissed Robyn.

She began to tell Claudia some of the history of the religious settlement.

'Well, the most compelling legend tied to Roncesvalles is that of the great French army of Charlemagne. About thirteen centuries ago, after lifting the siege in the town of Zaragoza, his army set out to regress through the same passage they'd entered Spain, over the mountains we're crossing today, but they were attacked by the surrounding Spanish tribes. It was a bloody encounter. Thousands of French and Spanish soldiers died up there.'

'Cool,' said Claudia. 'It kind of makes you see this place a bit differently than just a religious trek.'

'The mountains are meant to be filled with their ghosts,' said Babette, 'so we better not disturb them.'

She laughed as Robyn threw her a pretend punch on the arm.

A steady stream of walkers flowed in and out of Orrison. The mood, despite everyone finding the initial going tough, was of excitement and anticipation for what lay ahead. They got talking to a couple of people who joined them at their table. Mark, a Texan, freshly retired from his job as an engineer, lived in Boulder, Colorado. He normally hiked on his doorstep, in the Rocky Mountains, but had always dreamt of trekking the Camino. His walking companion, whom he'd met only that morning, Wendy, was in her early twenties and from Amsterdam. She was tall, blonde and willowy, with a beautiful smile. She was due to meet her boyfriend, in Santiago, at the end of her trek. Babette and Robyn chatted with her in *hundred-mile-an-hour* Dutch

'Nice guy,' said Claudia, waving goodbye to Mark and Wendy. I love his Texan drawl. But too gung-ho for me. He almost got up before he sat down.'

Babette, scraping the last of her rice pudding from her bowl, nodded, watching Mark heading off at a pace she knew she could never match. Wendy, taller than him by at least four inches, kept pace easily.

Robyn began re-lacing her hiking boots, which she'd taken off to let her feet breathe.

'Ten minutes ladies, then we'll need to move. I think we can . . .'

Babette interrupted her.

'Don't make it obvious, but look, Claudia, there's that guy that was rude to you in St Jean.'

All three of them looked across the verandah to see Sean heading up towards the café. He was wearing a black t-shirt, olive-green army-trousers, tan-coloured hiking-boots, and sporting a pair of teardrop, aviator sunglasses. His pack, Claudia noticed, was even smaller than hers. She wondered if he was only doing a section of the Camino rather than the entire trek. Sean saw them and glanced over. Instead of turning her face from him, as Robyn and Babette instinctively did, Claudia smiled and waved. Sean met her gaze, but looked away without acknowledging it.

'Claudia! Did you just wave at him?'

'I was being polite, Robyn. He saw us staring at him. He must have felt embarrassed.'

'Did he wave back?'

'No, I think he was a bit shocked.'

'Perhaps he's just rude.'

'Rude or not,' said Babette, looking at Sean, now past them and heading towards the *café*, 'he's a handsome man. And *that*, ladies, is a lovely bottom.'

They all stared, then started giggling like schoolgirls.

'Yes, he does looks fit,' said Robyn, 'more like a soldier than a pilgrim.'

She was right, Claudia had to agree. But it was more than just his look that set him aside from the other travellers. She couldn't say exactly what it was. There was just something about him.

Sean stopped at the serving hatch at the front of the *café* and ordered a filled baguette and a large bottle of water. When the waitress returned, he put the food and water into his pack and headed out of Orrison.

'He's walking on,' said Babette, 'not even stopping to sit and chat, like everyone else. No surprise there.'

'Perhaps he has his reasons,' said Claudia. 'I have the feeling he's got some problems he's dealing with. Maybe he's here to work them out. Who knows? He might even be carrying someone's ashes. Just as I am.'

'You're carrying someone's ashes?' Robyn and Babette replied, looking shocked and bemused.

Claudia nodded, surprised by their surprise.

'My friend, Hannah. She died about a month ago. I'm taking her to Finisterre to be with her husband. She carried his ashes there a year ago after *he* passed.'

'How romantic,' said Babette, 'tell us everything.'

Robyn gave Babette a withering look for her insensitivity.

'Only if that's okay with you, Claudia? If it's not too hard to talk about. Isn't that right, Babette?'

Babette looked suitably chastised.

'Sorry, Claudia. I didn't mean to pry.'

'It's fine, Babette. I *want* to talk about her. If I do, it makes it seem she's here with me. Does that make sense.'

'Perfect sense,' said Robyn.

Babette nodded in agreement.

'She left me a lighthouse in her will.'

'A lighthouse.' Babette's face lit up. 'Now, I'm really intrigued. This Hannah of yours sounds like a remarkably interesting lady.'

'She was.'

'Right,' said Robyn, 'let's move. Claudia, start at the beginning and miss out nothing, it'll take our minds off the climb.'

'Let's not catch the *Klootzak* up.'

Claudia scowled, annoyed at Babette's comment.

'Don't call him that. This is a supposed to be a journey of love, after all.'

'Sorry, Claudia, you're right. Okay, I promise not to call him any more horrible names. Instead, we'll call him . . . Major Tom.'

'Major Tom?'

Claudia failed to see the connection.

Babette sang a line from the song, *Space Oddity*.

'Ground control to Major Tom. David Bowie, you know? Out in space, floating in a tin can. Lost and alone.'

Claudia, laughed, the penny dropping.

'Okay, I get it. That's a better name, if still somewhat sad. Although we'll probably never see him again.'

'Probably not,' said Robyn, 'now, come on, you two. Move!'

She started on ahead of Babette and Claudia, but they quickly fell into place alongside her.

'Right,' said Claudia, 'let me tell you about my friend Hannah. I met her on a beach, near an old lighthouse, on the day of my sixteenth wedding anniversary. She had wild, red hair and looked like a white witch.'

Babette and Robyn listened, enthralled, as they headed up towards the summit, high above them.

Sean looked back and saw Claudia and her friends following him They were, though, already some way behind him. He'd seen them staring at him as he'd walked into Orrison, and noticed her wave. He'd almost gone over to apologise for the previous day, but he was done with people trying to help him when he hadn't asked for it. He'd rather they all just left him alone. He pressed on, pushing hard to reach the top of the mountain, ensuring they wouldn't catch him.

The gradient steepened and he stopped to rest. He was breathing hard and could feel his heartbeat in his temples. He was tired, a combination of jet-lag and the antibiotics he was still on. But his hands were healing well. He wouldn't have to be on them much longer.

'Come on, Sean. Not far now.' He looked up and saw Linz standing at the top of the pass. 'I'm coming, my love.'

Fifteen minutes later, he stood on the summit. Despite the afternoon sun, the wind-chill raised goosebumps on his naked arms, so he dropped his pack to allow him to shrug on his fleece. He looked around and realised he was alone, but knew Linz was watching him from somewhere. The mountain was quiet, but alive with invisible history. Behind him, lay France, ahead and below him, the Spanish border, guarded by a solitary vulture circling overhead. It screamed and banked down towards him, turning away at the last moment, A mock dive, perhaps, to scare him away from a nest that might be close by.

As it rolled, the vulture screamed again, reminding Sean of the golden eagle he'd seen on Ben Nevis.

'Butterflies and birdsong,' Sean called out to it in reply. 'I know it's you, my love.'

The cloud of sadness and anguish he'd felt, today, a day he hated more than any other day, momentarily lifted. He looked around him and saw the ghosts of a thousand, long-dead soldiers lining the mountaintop, their faces turned towards him.

'Allez vous! Seguir! Spain awaits you,' they called to him.

Urging him on.

He nodded to them and took the first step down to Roncesvalles, four thousand feet below, where the bells of the mission began to ring out, calling its pilgrims home.

52

Sean watched the swallows twist and roll under a mauve-pink sky as he made his way into Pamplona, three days after leaving Saint Jean. He'd spent a night each in Roncesvalles and Zubiri, paying more for private accommodation rather than sharing a dormitory at the public albergue, where up to a hundred people slept in shared dorms, in long lines of cast-iron bunk beds.

Entering from the north of the city, he passed the bull ring and headed on through the busy narrow streets, following the metal scallop shells set into the paving stones and the yellow arrows painted on the walls of the buildings until he reached the Plaza de Castilla, the great square in the heart of the city. It was already past eight o'clock and the lights of the bars around the square twinkled with promises, the loud chitter-chatter of the Spanish patrons like a menagerie of manic parrots.

One bar, in particular, caught Sean's eye. One he had heard of and wanted to experience for himself. The Café Iruna. It was the favourite bar of one of his few heroes; Ernest Hemingway. Pamplona had great significance for the renowned American writer. His novel, *The Sun Also Rises*, was set there, and Ernest had loved the place, even if it had not, while he was alive, returned that love. Now, it happily embraced him for the money his fame brought the city in his death. Sean's hotel was a stone's throw from the square. He decided to check in before heading back.

Showered and changed into fresh clothes, Sean pushed through the revolving door and entered the Iruna Café. The main bar was larger than he'd thought it would be, but it still managed to retain the cosy mood of a bygone age. It was an Art Deco world of low-lights, chequerboard floor-tiles, leather seats and ornate mirrors. Amber-coloured, glass lamps hung from a high ceiling, casting an ethereal, orange glow throughout. It was every bit as stylish as he had hoped it would be. It was easy to imagine Hemingway, there, during the roaring twenties, drinking and laughing, being the great boor he was reputed to have been.

Being a Wednesday night, it was quiet. Most of the visitors seemed not to be Spanish, but the bar was a famous stop on the Pamplona tourist trail, so he was not surprised. A middle-aged waitress with crimson-red lipstick and jet-black hair, swept back into a pony tail, approached him. The badge on her white shirt told him her name was Rafaella. Her face was severe, with sharp-painted eyebrows and high cheekbones. *All angles*, thought Sean, *like a Picasso painting*, but her voice was gentle and her smile inviting.

'Welcome *signor*. You have come to eat?'

'*Si*,' said Sean, 'but I'd also like to see Hemingway's bar. Would that be possible?'

'In the corner, on the right.' Raphaella pointed to the back of the room, at a door that connected to a smaller bar, where, Sean knew, Hemmingway had liked to ensconce himself when he was here. 'Would you like to eat there?'

'That would be even better, Rafaella. You sure?'

'We are not busy, tonight, *signor*. It is fine. Will I bring you a menu or will you trust me to choose for you?'

'Go ahead. I'm more interested in seeing through there.'

Sean nodded towards the door to the side bar.

'Of course. You Americans love your great writer. However, I prefer our own literary genius, Miguel de Cervantes.'

'Who wrote *Don Quixote*,' said Sean, drawing a look of admiration from Raphaella. 'A wonderful book, I grant you, but you can't compare the two writers. I agree with you when you say he was a genius. You're clearly too intelligent to be waiting tables.'

Raphaella smiled a wry smile.

'I thank you for the compliment, *signor*. This is my father's café. I help him out from time to time. I am a teacher, for my sins, at the Universidad de Navarra. A Professor of Literature.'

Sean nodded and smiled at her. Feeling a little foolish.

'Which is why your English is so good. Apologies for my stupidity in suggesting that waiting tables is not a worthwhile profession.'

Raphaella bowed her head and looked up at Sean with hooded eyes that sparkled with interest. Her smile was warm and forgiving.

'When you go through, ask Jorge, behind the bar, for a *Hemingway Daiquiri*. It was one of your hero's favourite drinks. Tell him Rafaella is taking care of you, personally. I will bring you some of our finest *pintxos* to sample.'

'*Pintxos*?'

Sean tilted his head. Raphaella gave him an answer she'd clearly given many times before.

'*Si*, though you may know them as *tapas*.'

'Ah, of course. Thank you, Rafaella. By the way, my name is Sean. And for the record, I'm Scottish, not American.'

'Sean, then,' said Raphaella, huskily. 'I apologise for not having the ear to tell where you are from. I love your country very much. I studied in St Andrews, for one year. You have many wonderful castles. As do we Spanish.'

'I agree,' said Sean, enjoying the interplay between them, 'although your country is equally as beautiful, from what little of it I've seen, so far.'

Rafaella moved closer to him. Only a fraction, but enough to create an intimacy between them. She gazed up at him, her irises flaring, hazel brown with flashes of gold, and placed a hand on his bare arm, tracing her fingernails along his skin. Her touch as gentle as that of a slow-moving tarantula spider, but, to Sean, it was as if he had been touched by fire. He recoiled from it, pulling his arm away and stepping out of the space they shared. He saw confusion in Rafaella's eyes. Then anger in her face.

The shift in her brought Sean's mood crashing down around him.

The closeness of her had brought back the image of the prostitute, Jann Livingston, and his shameful betrayal of Linz. Suddenly, Sean did not want to be there. The room closed in around him and he felt his chest tighten. His heart was beating wildly and his vision blurring. He had to escape! He turned and stumbled back towards the main door of the bar, bumping into a few tables and spilling the drinks at one of them. As he reached the door, it opened, and in walked Linz. Behind her, were other people he did not recognise.

'Linz.' He reached out to her. 'I'm sorry. I wasn't . . .'

Linz reached for him, but, in that moment, her face changed.

It wasn't her!

Sean's panic heightened as she spoke to him.

'What's wrong?'

Claudia put her hands on either side of Sean arms, thinking he was going to stumble. He was ashen-faced and seemed to be struggling to breathe. Her first thought was that he was seriously ill.

'Don't touch me!'

The venom in Sean's voice scared her. He pushed past her, bumping her with his shoulder and knocking her back against the doorframe.

'Hey, watch what the hell you're doing, man,' said one of the men coming in behind her, an American with a bald head and a silver goatee beard.

He grabbed Sean by the lapels of his jacket.

Instinctively, Sean took hold of Mark's wrist and rolled it anti-clockwise, making him cry out in pain and let go of the jacket, which stopped Sean from completing the move and breaking his wrist. He had been a professional soldier, trained in close combat. Mark was in his sixties, five inches shorter and physically smaller. It would not have been a fair fight, if a fight had been what Sean had intended. But he only wanted to escape the panic gripping him.

It was that panic that had dictated his next action.

As Mark's grip fell away, Sean drove his shoulder into the centre of his chest, sending him sprawling backwards through the doorway and out into the square. He landed heavily on the paved front of Iruna Café. Passers-by stopped, shocked by the commotion.

'Mark,' cried Babette. She followed Sean out through the front door and pushed him in the back. 'Leave him alone, you bloody bully.'

Claudia, recovered from the shock of Sean's push, came out of the bar like a tiger chasing an antelope. She stopped in front of him and stared up into his face, her gaze afire with anger. Not so much at what he'd done to her, but what he'd done to her friend.

'What the hell's wrong with you?'

'I'm . . . I'm sorry.'

Sean was looking all around him, his eyes filled with fear and confusion. The look on his face calmed Claudia. *He's terrified.* Her anger melted like fresh snow kissed by sunlight.

'I'm calling the police,' shouted Rafaella, who had followed the fracas out into the street.

Claudia turned to her as she began to punch in a number on her phone.

'No. Please don't. I'll pay for any damage. We're all okay, aren't we?'

Everyone looked at her as if she'd taken leave of her senses.

Babette, seeing the look on Claudia's face, backed her up.

'Sure, why not?' We're all good.'

'Mark nodded, but looked at Sean as if he wanted to kill him. Raphael, seeing the looks on the faces turned towards her, capitulated.

'If you insist, *senora*. But he,' she said, her voice bristling with anger, 'must leave. Now! My father may have already called the *Guardia*.'

Claudia turned back to Sean.

'Go! Before you get yourself into real trouble.'

'I'm sorry,' Sean repeated.

He could see the shadows all around him, watching from beyond the orange streetlamps set round the square. Waiting for him to leave the light and come to them. Claudia could see the fear in his face. It confused her. She wondered why he was so afraid.

'It's all right,' she said, gently, 'don't upset yourself any more. We're all in one piece. At least it gives us something exciting to talk about over dinner.'

Sean stared into her eyes. They were filled with concern for him. For some reason, he wasn't angry seeing it.

'Tell them I'm . . .'

Claudia's voice softened further.

'Don't worry about it. I don't think you really meant it, did you?' Sean shook his head. Claudia smiled up at him. 'I'll forgive you for bumping me *and* for snapping at me, yesterday, in Saint Jean. Although, I'm not sure my friends would be as generous. But it's better to be kind, isn't it?'

'I don't deserve kindness.'

Sean's words, and the way in which he'd said them, touched Claudia's heart so deeply that she almost reached out to him. In that moment, she felt they had connected in the way that, sometimes, when two people meet, something bigger than them is shared. She wanted to help him. She didn't know why it was important to her. It just was.

'You should go,' she repeated, her voice catching as she spoke. She didn't want him to leave.

Sean's suddenly felt calm and safe. Unsure why that might be.

'I'm going. I *am* sorry.'

Almost reluctantly, as if he had felt the same connection, he turned and walked away.

Claudia lost sight of him as he merged with other people she didn't know, before walking back towards her friends. She looked back into the square, seeking sight of him, but he was gone. She felt a sense of loss, which confused her. She hadn't asked his name and wished she had. She turned to see Robyn staring at her, a perplexed look upon her face.

'Claudia?'

Claudia shook her head as she passed her, heading back into the Iruna Café, where the oft-troubled Ernest Hemingway had once stood, attempting to drink away the demons that tortured him.

53

Claudia, Babette and Robyn looked out over a sea of yellow and green, listening to the *whoosh-whoosh-whoosh* of the blades from the line of giant wind-turbines stretching around the mountainside and relishing the baguettes filled with ham, cheese and tomato they'd picked up from La Posada de Ardogi, the little bar in the village of Zariquiegui, halfway up the mountain. They'd just made the ascent to the top of Alto de Perdón, along an uneven, boulder-strewn track, climbing to an altitude of almost two thousand feet. The mountain was one of the most famous on the Camino de Santiago and provided an amazing view over Pamplona and the Pyrenees.

'It's hard to believe we crossed them,' said Claudia, surveying the ragged line of mountains stretching across the horizon.

'I know what you mean,' replied Robyn, 'but that's what the entire journey's going to be like. You look at the distance you need to travel each day, wondering, will I make it? But you always do.'

Claudia stepped back to better see the line of sculptures lining the flat summit of the mountain. The silhouettes were cut from sheet steel only a few millimetres thick, but were strong and rigid, able to stand against the winds that blew constantly through the valley and over the mountaintop.

'And just look at the reward.'

Robyn followed her gaze.

'Cool or what?'

Claudia opened her arms, embracing the view, as if trying to gather it.

'As a sculptor, this was one of the things I really wanted to see. Do you know much about them?'

Robyn flicked through her Camino guide.

'There's not much here other than a picture telling me they're here. Don't you?'

Claudia walked back over to the iron statues and ran her hand over the nose of one of the steel donkeys. The surface was completely rusted. It felt like running her hand over rough sandpaper.

'I know they were created by an artist called Vincent Galbete, who wanted to immortalize the pilgrims, so he created this line of travellers and their donkeys crossing the mountain on their way to Santiago. Simple in design, beautiful in that simplicity. There's supposed to be . . .' She walked along the row of figures and stopped. 'Yes, here it is. Look.'

Babette and Robyn followed her over to a solitary, life-sized figure of a man, a stick over his shoulder and his body stooped as if he were trudging, heavily burdened, both physically and spiritually. Babette read the words carved into the steel in her best Spanish accent.

'*Donde se cruza el Camino del viento con el de las estrellas.* You speak a little Spanish, Robyn. What does it mean?'

'Where the path of the wind crosses with the stars, if I'm translating it right.'

'What an apt name,' said Claudia, 'I'd love to see it at night. It must be beautiful.'

'And cold,' said Babette. 'Come on, we've rested long enough. That wind's chilly, even if it is sunny. Let's get moving. The climb down from here will be as hard as it was coming up. My feet are *still* aching.'

'Blisters?' Claudia asked. 'I've got two myself. Only small ones, but I'm keeping an eye on them.'

'I've no blisters, said Babette, at least, not yet. I'm just not used to walking so far for days on end. I can't wait to get to our stop and soak them. Where are we headed again?'

'It's a decent sized town called Puenta La Reina,' said Robyn, studying her guidebook, 'another fifteen kilometres. But we can stop before then for a glass of lemon beer, at a village called Uterga.'

She saw the look of relief on Babette's face and laughed.

They hoisted their backpacks onto their shoulders and walked past a tall, wooden signpost covered in direction arrows, the names of various world cities painted on them in bright colours, giving rough directions and distances to them from where they stood.

'New York,' said Claudia, looking up at the sign. 'Three thousand six hundred miles. I'm so far from home, yet I don't feel as lost as I've felt for such a long time.'

'I thought you lived in Boston?' Babette asked.

'I do, but it's not on the signpost. New York's close enough.'

The path down towards Uterga was every bit as steep and rocky as Robyn had suggested it would be. The landscape was open and wild, with random swathes of woodland interspersed with fields of swaying grass and wildflower meadows. They continued down through a steep gorge, careful not to miss their step and fall. Eventually, it opened back out to woodland and the track widened, flattening as it meandered through the trees.

'I really enjoyed Pamplona,' said Robyn, 'it was such a beautiful city.'

Claudia, walking beside her, agreed.

'Mark and Wendy should have taken a day off and stayed, instead of pressing on. The museum was amazing. So was the gallery.'

Babette, ahead of them, turned, her mouth half full of the remaining baguette.

'The only down was Major Tom.'

She choked, then laughed at herself, making herself cough even more.

'That's Karma,' said Claudia, catching up with her and patting her on the back.

Robyn looked at Claudia, raising an eyebrow.

'I noticed you were keen to make sure he didn't get in trouble when the waitress made to call the police. Care to explain why?'

Claudia hesitated for a moment before replying.

'I was just being kind. Besides, you didn't see the look on his face. He seemed afraid of something.'

Babette snorted, clearly not agreeing.

'Afraid! It was us who should have been afraid. Did you see how easily he overpowered Mark? That move, where he twisted his wrist. It was like watching a trained assassin.'

Claudia nodded.

'Like from a James Bond movie.'

'James Bond isn't a bully,' said Babette, 'or a drunk. Major Tom has a problem. I'll be only too glad if we never see him again.'

Claudia felt differently.

'I don't think he's a bully, or was drunk. I saw something else in his eyes when I went out into the square after him.

'What?'

'I'm not sure now, Robyn. But, when he looked at me, he came back from wherever he'd been. We had some sort of strange connection.'

'Perhaps it was love striking you both in the same moment in time,' said Babette. 'You hear about that happening in the oddest of places. Love at first sight.'

It was Robyn's turn to snort.

'More likely just the adrenaline in your system, after all, he'd just knocked you against the door.'

'Yes,' said Claudia, not at all convincingly, 'you're probably right.'

She walked on ahead, not wanting to be drawn further into the discussion.

She had thought about him more than once, since that night. *Sean!* That's what the waitress from the Iruna Café had said his name was. Perhaps the connection she'd felt with him *had* been imagined. She tried to put the memory of him out of her mind.

For the next five days, they crossed ragged, windmill-topped ranges and passed through lush meadows, where the heady smell of golden rapeseed not just filled but overwhelmed their senses. The Basque region of Navarre was a never-ending twist of undulating beauty. Ten days after leaving St Jean, at the end of the first week in June, they entered the city of Burgos, crossing the bridge over the River Arzanlon and passing through the high stone gate into the Plaza Mayor, under the imposing shadow of the Santa Iglesia Cathedral Basilica de Santa Maria de Burgos.

Claudia stared up at the nobbled spires, awestruck.

'Wow! You can understand why people, hundreds of years ago, were so afraid of the church. Imagine coming here from your little village, where nothing was over two stories high, and seeing *that*. It must be two hundred feet tall. We have to visit it.'

'We've got tomorrow set aside as a rest day,' said Robyn, so we can. We're booked into the Abba Burgos Hotel for two nights. It's got a swimming pool, a steam room, a sauna, private showers and fresh clean sheets.'

'I need a bit of luxury,' said Babette. 'You can keep your culture. I'm not walking another step once we check in. I'm going to sit by the pool and drink cocktails.'

Robyn shook her head.

'Philistine.'

Babette stuck out her tongue.

'Guilty as charged.'

'Okay,' said Robyn, looking back at her street map. 'The hotel's just off the square. Let's find it and have all have a quick dip in the pool before dinner, then we'll come down and eat in the square. We can allow ourselves a few glasses of wine without worrying. We can lie in as long as we want in the morning.'

'Then what are we waiting for?' Babette asked, heading off in the wrong direction.

54

Brooding and demanding of attention, the shadow of the Cathedral Basilica de Santa María de Burgos loomed long across the square below it, as it had done since the year 1221. A millisecond in terms of human evolution, but forever in the spiritual timeline of the people of Burgos.

Claudia, dressed in a white linen shirt, matching trousers and a pair of white sneakers, descended the granite steps on its western side and walked out onto the Plaza de Santa María. It was a little after ten o'clock and the square was beginning to waken. The sun, already up for hours, played its light across the cathedral's limestone façade, making it look as if it had been painted in shimmering gold leaf.

She'd slept like a baby in her king-sized bed, on soft cotton sheets, beneath a light duvet, supported by plump pillows. The air conditioning had been an extra luxury after the past few nights in albergues, where air conditioning was an open window. She'd risen, early, and after a refreshing and invigorating swim in the hotel's outdoor pool, taken a light breakfast before heading down into Burgos old town.

Babette and Robyn were still in their rooms, but they'd agreed to go their own way for the rest day. They'd meet for dinner at the same restaurant they'd eaten at last night. The food and company had been fantastic. They'd met up with Wendy and Mark, who introduced them to a lovely French couple, Romano and Helena, both in their mid-twenties, from the French city of Orleans, who were walking the Camino for the first time.

Claudia lowered her gaze to study the pointed arches of the Portal of Saint Mary. She had researched the cathedral's history, over breakfast, and knew the three intricately decorated, hand carved portals had been inspired by the facades of the great cathedrals of Paris and Reims. The central arch, which dated back to the thirteenth century, was known as the Door of Forgiveness. Its iconography, dedicated to the Virgin, was considered the most important sculptural manifestation of Gothic art in the province of Castile. She walked under it, running her hand across one of the carved figurines, then entered the cathedral.

Rather than being quiet and reverent, as she had expected it to be, the cathedral was filled with noisy pilgrims surveying the exhibition of power and wealth. It was as impressive on the inside as it had been looking at it from the square. The sweeping gothic architecture was both awe inspiring and humbling. *Created to be so*, thought Claudia. *There were none so willing to be saved than those in fear for their mortal soul.* She stopped and gazed up at the circular Rose Window, ten thousand pieces of medieval, coloured glass set high above the south transept, depicting the image of a pious Saint. It was, she had to admit, beyond stunning.

'No wonder this place is a World Heritage Site.'

Everywhere she looked were paintings, religious icons and gold or silver treasures. Amassed over centuries. Offerings from those who came to serve their God, or as payment for the saving of a soul, provenance disregarded as long as the assets flowed into the church.

After an hour or so, Claudia had seen enough. She left, declining to pay to view the Gaudi exhibition in a room at the back of the church, close to the main exit. It reinforced her long held views on the church, that any religion that took money from its followers to build its shrines, then charged them to look upon them, was no religion worth her time. *Churches are supposed to be open to all, not only those who can pay to enter.*

Back in the sunlight, she walked across the square, turning left along the Paseo del Espalon, a wide, tree-lined footpath running parallel with the river. Choosing the first little café she came to, she ordered a cold drink from the bar, took a seat at an empty table, outside, and relaxed, soaking up the sunshine and the atmosphere, watching a constant stream of pilgrims and cyclists pass her by.

She pulled out her map of Burgos city centre and opened it.

'You are looking for somewhere special to visit, *Senora*?'

A waiter in a black waistcoat, matching trousers and white shirt, carrying an oval tray that had the word, "Bacardi", written across it, picked his way between the tables, towards her, carrying her mineral water. He was half her age, at least, but gave her the same cheeky grin the Italian waiters in every café in the centre of Rome flashed when they talked to a woman. Age, it seemed, not relevant, only the chase. *Clearly a European thing.* She returned his smile. *When in Rome!*

'I'm looking for the Museum of Evolution.'

'It is close by, *senora*,' said the waiter, and proceeded to give her directions rather than look at the map. 'Along the river then across the next bridge. You cannot miss it. Alas, I cannot accompany you, but should you wish to return, this evening, I can show you some of the best local *tapas* bars. The ones the tourists do not visit. You are a tourist, No?'

He set the water on the table, along with the paper bill.

'I'm walking the Camino, actually,' Claudia replied, 'just having a rest day in your beautiful city.'

'A *peregrino*!' He picked up the bill and theatrically ripped it up. 'Then your drink is a gift from one pilgrim to another. I have also walked the Way of St James. It is an experience you never forget.'

Claudia was surprised at his reaction. A moment ago, he'd been hitting on her. Now, his demeanour had totally changed.

'Are you sure?'

'Of course. It is nothing. This is a deeply spiritual journey you are on, *senora*. I hope you find the peace you are looking for.'

He bowed his head and headed back into the café, leaving Claudia bemused.

'Well,' she said to herself, 'they clearly take their Camino very seriously. Either that or I'm losing my sex appeal.'

She finished her drink and gave the waiter a wave, which he returned, then headed along the river towards the museum.

The Museum of Human Evolution is a modern, rectangular reflection of glass, steel and stone; a large, open and airy space of white *feng-shui* style with a wide, glass roof and floor-to-ceiling windows that flood its spaces with natural light. It sits on the opposite side of the river from the cathedral, the two iconic buildings facing each other down, as if dismissive of the other's claims for the ascent of man.

Sean had been there for an hour. He'd started, as the guide at reception had advised him, at the top of the building, on the third floor, where there had been some amazingly well-created interactive displays on the development of the earth and of man's place upon it. Now he was admiring a display of skulls that showed the physiological progression from the earliest humanoids to more modern Homo sapiens.

He'd decided to spend the day in Burgos, taking a well needed rest. The museum, despite his misgivings about visiting it alone, was beautiful, inside and out. Today, it was almost devoid of people. At least, of living ones. There was an almost religious solemnity about the place, where the bones of a hundred of humankind's oldest skeletons were laid to rest in open glass coffins.

He moved on, stopping to listen to the audio commentary at one of the information stations beyond the display of skulls, fascinated by what was being said. It was a reference to the notion of God and the evolution of humanity.

'Hello. I thought it was you.'

Sean, slightly startled, turned. He'd been so lost in the commentary that he hadn't notice someone standing next to him.

'You!'

'Yes. Me Claudia.' She laughed, putting the fingers of right hand to her lips. It was a natural reaction, childlike, in a way, but one Sean found strangely appealing. 'Sorry, I couldn't resist that, given where we are. You know? Apes and men and all.'

'I get it,' said Sean, returning her smile. 'Me Tarzan.'

He shook Claudia's outstretched hand, glad his bandages were gone and the scars from his blisters all but disappeared. She didn't seem to notice. Or if she had pretended not to. He wondered why he cared. Her hand was soft and warm. He let it go before she did.

'Sorry,' said Claudia, 'I didn't mean to make you jump. I was just wandering around and this was next in my path. It's pretty interesting, isn't it, the whole thing?'

She looked up at him, sending his senses spinning further.

'Yes, I suppose it is.' Sean wondered why she was talking to him. More, why he was talking back? While he was still wondering, he introduced himself. 'I'm Sean, by the way.'

'I think I'd far rather be where I am now, *Sean*, evolutionally speaking, that is. Imagine living in a cave and being constantly worried about being picked off by a sabre-tooth tiger or giant bear.'

'I suppose so.'

Sean was unsure if he should walk away or let her move on. She didn't move, so he spoke, although felt more than a little tongue-tied.

'I'm sorry about what happened in Pamplona. I didn't mean to bump into you.'

Claudia smiled and nodded.

'You said so at the time. Don't you remember?'

Sean nodded. But didn't.

'And your friend. The guy who grabbed me. Is he okay?'

'Mark! Yes, he's fine. He's an American, like me. We're used to people wanting to attack us.'

'Oh, I see,' said Sean, completely missing the joke. 'I was just trying to get him away from me. I never meant to hurt him.'

Claudia could see he was genuinely sorry. She was pleased he felt the need to apologise.

'Seriously, don't worry about it. It was only his pride you dented. Anyway, he's a Texan, so as tough as an old boot.'

'Good.'

'You seemed in a bit of panic. What was wrong?'

'I was just . . .' Sean began to feel uncomfortable. 'Look, it's been nice to meet you, Claudia, but I'd better let you get on.'

Claudia was surprised at his abruptness. She didn't want him to rush off again before getting to know him a little better. Not that she knew why.

'But you've not finished your visit. Please don't leave on my account. Stay and enjoy your day off.'

'Day off?'

'Yes. From walking. You're on the Camino, like the rest of us. Aren't you?'

Sean shrugged his shoulders.

'I suppose so. I'm here, anyway.'

His answer was confusing. Claudia wondered why he'd said it as he had. It intrigued her about him even more. She tried to keep him engaged in conversation.

'Well then you need to enjoy today. It's another long walk, tomorrow., and I don't know about you, but my feet could do with a longer rest. I've got a few blisters just starting to show.'

'You need to know how to tape them up properly. Your feet.'

Sean looked at Claudia as if she should know exactly what he was talking about.

'I guess,' said Claudia, having no clue.

They stood in silence for a few moments before Sean broke it.

'I'll show you, sometime. If you like.'

'That would be handy,' said Claudia, 'or *footy*, more like.'

She smiled and waited for Sean to respond. It seemed the joke had not been that good.

'Of course,' said Sean, flatly.

Trying to engage in conversation with him, Claudia realised, was like catching soap bubbles. She almost walked away, but something made her reach out to him again. There was an air of sad and lonely surrounding him as she'd never felt before. She couldn't turn her back on him. It simply wasn't in her nature.

'Look, I was just about to go to the café, downstairs, to grab a coffee. Would you join me? I'm on my own. It would nice to have some intelligent company.'

She saw him hesitate. *He's going to say no. At least I tried.*

Sean surprised her.

'Okay. But I'm not sure I'll be any good to talk to. I've not really talked to anyone for a while.'

Well that's brutally honest, if a little sad, thought Claudia. *Thank God he's not trying to chat me up. Now why on earth did you think that?*

'I'll risk it,' said Claudia, 'and it's my treat. I'll even stand you to a pastry.'

'Coffee's fine, thanks,' said Sean, and followed her to the lift.

They got their coffees and sat down, choosing a table overlooking the river and Burgos old town. The spires of the cathedral stood high above every other building.

'Have you been to visit it?' Claudia asked, looking towards it. 'I was there this morning. It's a beautiful building.'

'It's not somewhere I want to be.'

She wasn't quite sure how to respond. There was some dark backstory in his words she felt she should keep away from.

'Are you married?' *Christ! I must sound like some sort of desperate woman.* 'I'm sorry, Sean, that was a really personal question. It's kind of automatic, at our age.'

'It's fine, Claudia. Don't worry about it.'

'Well, as you already know,' said Claudia, trying to appear nonplussed, 'I'm American. Where do you hail from?'

'Scotland.'

'Scotland! How wonderful. I was introduced to your whisky, recently, by a friend. She loved a whisky called Glenmorangie.'

Sean looked at Claudia with genuine surprise on his face.

'You said it right. Most people pronounce it wrongly.'

'I was told you just need to remember to say *orange* in the centre and *gee* at the end,' Claudia replied, thankful the conversation was now a bit more normal. 'My friend, Hannah, said I shouldn't get it wrong if ever I met someone from Scotland. Apparently, you take your whisky seriously.'

Sean smiled.

'We do.'

Claudia remembered an evening she'd sat with Hannah, in the Beach Shack, by the fire. The first time she'd tasted Glenmorangie. She'd told her she doubted she'd ever meet someone from Scotland. Hannah had told her not to let the Universe hear that. A chill ran down her spine at the serendipitous memory.

Sean studied Claudia more closely, trying to ensure she wasn't aware he was. She was beautiful, he could not help but notice that. Her blonde hair framed her face, making her look a bit like the actress, Jennifer Aniston. She was more tanned than she'd been when he'd first seen her in St Jean, her white linen shirt making it more pronounced. Her skin, though, was flawless, and she had the most mesmerising green eyes he was trying to avoid looking into. There was, too, a gentleness too her that could not be missed. She was, he felt, a good soul.

'What happened to your fingers,' Claudia asked, noticing Sean's eyes on her and suddenly feeling conscious of how she looked, 'it looks as if you burned them. Tell me to mind my own business if you want.'

'No, it's fine, they're almost better. I got frostbite.'

'Where?'

'Mount Everest,' said Sean, studying his fingers. 'I was there before I came here.'

Claudia was impressed. She'd never met a climber before, let alone one who'd been to Mount Everest.

'Wow! That's cool.'

'More cold than cool, to be honest,' replied Sean, grinning at her and making her heart beat a little faster. 'I got lost on a glacier, pretty high up. And I lost my gloves.'

He held his hands up and wiggled his fingers.

Claudia blew on her steaming coffee then carefully took a sip. Sean's eyes were drawn to her lips. They were a delicate shade of pink, full and moist. He wondered what it would be like to kiss them. Unsure of why he had thought it, he looked away, pushing the weakness back down inside himself.

'Are you a professional climber?'

'No.'

Claudia sensed he didn't want to talk about what had happened in any depth, so moved the topic.

'Are you enjoying Spain? Or are you missing home?'

'I don't have a home. Not any longer.'

Sean left the statement hanging, leaving Claudia wondering, apart from what he'd meant, what else she could say that would lighten things. She'd never met a more difficult person to talk to in all her life. She'd noticed his watch and the way he spoke. He was obviously an educated and successful man, but something of an enigma, annoying but equally as intriguing at the same time. *And so damned handsome.* She felt her cheeks flush and feigned a cough, hoping she hadn't been obvious.

'I live in a lighthouse, by the ocean,' she said, 'trying to cover up the minor embarrassment.

Sean, it appeared, hadn't noticed or didn't care.

'Best place for a lighthouse, I suppose. I lived in a tree, once, for an entire month.'

Claudia laughed, expecting him to explain. He didn't.

'I'd like to hear about that, sometime.' *But then you don't want to tell me about that, do you?*

Sean, confirming her thoughts, moved the conversation elsewhere.

'Your friend. You said her name *was* Hannah?'

He saw the pain flicker across her eyes. He knew the emotion well. He wanted no-one else to feel it. Especially not her. *Why do I care how she feels?*

'Yes. She died. A couple of months ago.'

'I'm so sorry, Claudia.'

'It's fine. She was a beautiful soul, Sean. And so brave. She fought to enjoy her life, right up to the very end.'

'Good for her.'

'Life has to go on, though,' said Claudia, resignedly. Which is kind of why I'm here.

Sean looked away, his gaze set over the river towards the spires of the cathedral.

'Does it?'

'Of course, it does. Hannah taught me that. No matter what, we live on, despite our losses. Only a coward gives in. Life is wonderful and meant to be lived. Like we're both doing, here on the Camino.'

Sean shook his head and his expression changed to one of sadness.

'Sometimes life is not the answer, Claudia. Sometimes it's too hard to keep living when your reason to live is gone.'

Claudia gestured to the exhibits beyond the café.

That's not true, Sean. Look around you. Everyone here fought for the gift of life. Christ, they fought bears with fire-hardened sticks to survive. As a species, we took life by the scruff of the neck and lived it. Where would we be if our ancestors had given up when things got tough?'

'You don't know what you're talking about.' Sean's voice was raised and his face had darkened. 'Sometimes life *isn't* worth fighting for. You're only talking about your own experiences.'

Claudia was confused by the sudden change in his behaviour. Almost as if he was two completely different people. The same way the waitress in Pamplona had described him being to *her*, that night.

'What's wrong with you, Sean? What happened to you to make you feel like that? 'Why are you so down on everyone and everything?'

'Who says I am?'

Sean's mood was fast slipping back to where it had been before Claudia had turned up to bother him.

'I've seen you, Sean, always alone. Never engaging with anyone else. Seeming to be at odds with the world. Don't you *want* to enjoy the experience of the Camino with your fellow travellers? It's one of the main points of doing it, I'd say.'

Sean stood up, pushing his chair back, violently.

'You don't know me, Claudia. Go preach somewhere else. I don't need you to be my friend. I don't need *any* new friends to walk the bloody Camino with.'

Claudia fought to keep hold of her own temper.

'You know, Sean, one of the girls I'm walking with . . .'

'*Girls!* Well that's a bloody stretch.'

Claudia ignored the childish insult.

'She gave you the nickname, Major Tom. Want to know why?'

Sean thought he didn't care, but still asked.

'Why?'

'It's from the David Bowie song.'

'*Space Oddity*. Everyone knows that.'

'Well,' Claudia continued, 'Major Tom is all alone, floating in space, surrounded by nothing and wishing he was with his wife and those he loved. You're surrounded by people and by love, yet all the time you seem to be wishing you were surrounded by nothing.'

Sean looked her in the eyes. His voice dropped to a whisper.

'You couldn't be more wrong if you tried, Claudia.'

He turned and walked away, not looking back.

Claudia watched him go, confused at what he'd said and angry that they'd fought, seemingly over nothing.

'Damn him. I was clearly in a state of confusion in Pamplona, *and* again, today. I want nothing more to do with him. Babette was right. He is a bloody *Klootzak*.'

Outside, Sean wandered across the bridge, heading back along the path towards the historic centre of Burgos. He walked quickly, seething with anger. *Who was she to lecture him? What the hell did she know about anything? She'd lost a friend, big deal. He'd lost his entire reason for living.* He felt the familiar panic begin to come over him. He slowed, breathing hard, his vision blurring.

'Help me,' he whispered.

He felt Linz beside him.

'She annoyed you, didn't she, hun?'

'Yes.'

'Forget her. She doesn't know you.'

Sean looked at her. She was so beautiful. Her hair was gold, lit by the early afternoon sunshine, and her pale blue, summer dress fluttered in the light breeze that blew in across the from the surrounding Spanish hills.

'I miss you, my love.'

'I know. I miss *you*, hun.'

'Do you, Linz? Really?'

'Always.'

Sean knew she was about leave. He didn't want her to go.

'Don't go.'

'I'm never gone, hun. I'm always here when you really need me. You know I am, don't you?'

Sean nodded.

'You always know when I need you, my love. And you always come to me when I really need you. I just miss you.

He started to feel afraid and unloved. His panic threatened to take a firmer grip of him. Linz knew and tried to calm him.

'Breathe, hun, just breathe.'

In his mind, Sean watched the second's hand on the station clock ticking down. His breathing eased and his vision returned to normal. Linz was gone, but it was okay. She loved him and she'd made him feel safe.

Feeling better, he turned and looked back at the Museum of Evolution, wondering if Claudia had followed him out. There was no sign of her. To his right, stood the cathedral, its tall spires rising over the riverside buildings. Its face was in shadow, the sun directly behind it, making it look dark and imposing. It screamed at Sean, referring to the Museum that went against the word of its God.

'You went there! You looked at its lies! Now look at me! Look at the truth!'

Sean scowled at it and called back.

'You don't exist for me anymore! You abandoned me, remember?'

True to form, there was no answer.

55

Sean entered the sleepy little town of Carrion des los Condes, which, according to another traveller he'd passed, who'd insisted in engaging in conversation, had been a town of great importance at the time of the old pilgrimages to Santiago de Compostela. Its medieval origins were obvious in the historic buildings and in the old town, Sean had to agree. After walking through its centre, which was filled with chattering pilgrims, he stopped for lunch and a cold beer at a little bar on the outskirts, near the medieval bridge and the monastery of San Zoilo.

The bar owner was an Irish rugby fan, for reasons Sean didn't understand, given his limited English and Sean's even more limited Spanish. That aside, they'd talked about their respective teams whilst the bar owner's wife looked on, bored, having no doubt heard the conversation a hundred times before. She served Sean a rabbit ragout, which was delicious, and a zesty lemon tart, for desert. He left, promising the owner he would return, some day in the future, to drink with him and talk more about rugby.

It had been five days since he'd departed Burgos, passing though the villages of Fromista and Castrojeriz, each day spent under a clear, blue sky. His strength was returning and he felt physically better than he had in a long time. The daily dose of sunshine and exercise had healed his body, if not his mind. He'd thought, each day, about his run in with Claudia at the Museum of Evolution, replaying their conversation in his head, still angry that she had felt it necessary to bother him with her opinions. But, as he walked, the memory of her became something different. She had been kind to him, for the third time. He wondered why he kept bumping into her. But then they were both walking in the same direction, headed for the same destination.

After following a winding pathway through a steep-sided valley filled with pine trees, alone in the world, or so it felt, Sean heard someone up ahead. As he rounded a bend, sitting on a fallen tree, set back from the path, was a young girl. She had short blonde hair and looked familiar, although he didn't know why. Her pack was against the tree and she had her head in her hands, sobbing. For a millisecond, he thought about walking past her. It was none of his business. But then he thought of Alice, imagining her sitting there, sad and alone. He turned and walked back.

'Hello.'

The girl almost fell off the tree at the sound of Sean's voice.

'Hello,' she replied, in a wobbly voice, looking up at him through frightened, blue eyes.

'Are you okay?'

'Yes.'

The girl stared down at her feet. Sean almost turned and left, but Alice whispered to him not to.

'Really?'

'No, I suppose not,' she said, sounding utterly forlorn.

She started to cry again.

Sean spoke gently, not wanting to frighten her. He'd seen her look around, nervously, when he'd first approached her, perhaps realising she was alone in the middle of a forest with a strange man. Not that Sean thought of he was in any way strange, but he understood.

'Look, why not tell me what's wrong. I'll see if I can help. If not, I'll leave you alone.'

The girl looked up at him, seeking kindness in his eyes. She found it and relaxed.

'Okay.'

'Good,' said Sean. Now, what's your name?'

'Wendy. I'm from Amsterdam, but my name is from England.'

Sean offered a hand.

'Pleased to meet you, Wendy from Amsterdam. I'm Sean, from Scotland, but my name's from Ireland.'

Wendy shook his hand, looking slightly less afraid.

'We met before, in Pamplona. You knocked over my friend, Mark.'

'Oh! That! Sean looked suitably contrite. 'It was a complete accident, Wendy. I didn't mean to.'

Wendy smiled up at him and nodded.

'My friend, Claudia, said that, at the time. She said you weren't well.'

'Did she now?' Sean muttered. 'Claudia! It seems I can't escape her. We met, again, a few days ago, in Burgos.'

'I know. I had dinner with her and her friends. She said you were a . . .'

Sean held up his hands.

'Let's just leave it there, shall we? Although she was probably right, whatever she said.'

Wendy laughed.

'I think she likes you. She kept talking about you.'

Sean laughed with her.

'I doubt it. I've given her no reason to. Look, I'm sorry if I scared you, that night. I'm not a bad person, I was just having a bad night. Will you accept my apology?'

'Of course.'

'Good. Now, tell me what's wrong.'

Wendy looked down at her boots.

'It's my feet. They're so sore. I had some blisters and put some Band-Aid plasters on them, but now they're really hurting.'

'Where's your friend, Mark? He didn't leave you like this, did he?'

Wendy looked affronted that Sean would suggest such a thing.

'Of course not. He would *never* do that. He went ahead of me, this morning. We wanted some alone time. What am I going to do, Sean? I don't think I can go on.'

She seemed about to start crying again.

'It's okay. I won't leave you here. Even if I have to carry you to wherever our next stop is.'

'Sahagun. It's about ten kilometres on.'

'Sahagun, of course. Listen, Wendy, it's all going to be fine. Do you believe me?'

'Yes.' Wendy's voice was weepy, but she gave an apprehensive smile. 'You're kind. Claudia was right.'

'Whatever,' said Sean, not wanting to continue along the Claudia conversation. 'Now, I used to be in the army, so I've got some medical training.' He hoped that would further reassure her. 'The first thing I need to do is to get your boots off, just to see how your feet are looking. Can you let me do that?' Wendy nodded, although Sean could see she was still afraid. 'I'll be very gentle and I'll go slowly. Just shout if you want me to stop. Okay?'

Wendy nodded.

'Okay.'

Sean took of his pack and set it beside hers. He knelt in front of her and lifted her right boot onto his knee. As he undid the laces, he chatted, trying to keep her mind off what he was doing.

'What age are you, Wendy?'

'I'm twenty-three.'

'Really? I thought you were younger.'

Sean looked up and smiled, thinking he'd paid her a compliment. Wendy looked back at him as if him thinking her younger was some sort of ageist slur.

'I'll be twenty-four in August.'

'Really old then,' said Sean, deciding to keep his opinions to himself from now on. He slipped her boot off then started on the other. It came off without any problem. 'That feels better, I'll bet. Having the boot off?'

'So much.'

Wendy was wearing light-blue woollen socks. There were bloodstains showing on each of them, at the toes and under the pads of her feet. He was worried about what he'd find once he took them off. He explained what he had to do next.

'I need to take your socks off, Wendy. I'm going to soak them with some water, before I do. It'll cool your feet as well as help get them off. They might be stuck to your blisters, but it'll really help.'

'Okay. Will it hurt?'

'I'll try not to let it.'

'Twenty-three or not, to Sean, she was just a frightened little girl. He looked up at her face and saw Alice looking back. Without warning, his chest began to constrict and his vision blurred.

Wendy could see something was bothering him.

'Are you okay?'

'I'm fine,' replied Sean, picturing the clockface and counting the seconds, forcing the air into his lungs. 'You just reminded me of someone. My daughter. Alice. She died. Last year.'

The tear came without warning, spilling from the inside corner of his right eye and tracing a wet line down his cheek to the corner of his lips. He licked at it with his tongue and wiped his face with the back of his hand. Wendy, seeing it, looked every bit as upset.

'Oh, I'm so sorry, Sean. I didn't mean to upset you?'

'No, it wasn't your fault. It's just that . . . well, I've not thought about her for a while. I've not allowed myself to.' He saw the sadness on Wendy's face and forced a smile. He didn't want her to be sad. It helped pull him back. 'I'm fine. It just took me by surprise.' He took a deep breath. 'Okay, let's get these socks off.'

The water soothed and cooled Wendy's feet as Sean had promised. Her socks came off without any problem. He spent a few minutes examining each foot before offering his prognosis.

'How are they?' Wendy asked, still sounding afraid.

Sean looked up and gave her his best reassuring smile.

'Well, the good news is that they are not too bad, but the bad news is that they're not too good. You'll need to see a doctor when we get to . . .'

'Sahagun! Why can't you remember it?'

'I'm old,' replied Sean, shrugging his shoulders, 'that's about the size of it. One day you'll know how it feels.'

Wendy laughed at and with him, and the mood around them lightened.

'But, I'm okay, Sean? I can still do the Camino?'

'You should be fine, after some rest and proper treatment.'

Wendy looked more than relieved.

'Thank goodness.'

'What size are your feet?' Sean asked, looking at her boots while cupping the heel of her right foot in his hand.

'I'm a thirty-nine, normally.'

Sean immediately understood the issues the boots had caused her.

'These boots are a thirty-nine? And they look brand new.'

Wendy confirmed his suspicions.

'I got them in Amsterdam, just before I flew out.'

'Okay, so the first problem you have is that they're not broken in. The second, is that they're at least one size too small.'

'But they're my normal size,' Wendy protested.

'Yes, they are, but you don't normally walk twenty or more kilometres a day, do you?'

'No,' said Wendy.

'That's what I'm getting at. When you're hiking, especially such a distance, your feet swell, You need boots that are worn in, as well as at least one size bigger. That's why you're getting blisters. Added to that, you're not taping your feet up before you walk. I'll bet you're not taking proper rest stops either.'

'Oh.'

The sheepish look on Wendy's face confirmed everything Sean had just said.

'Okay, well, from now on, you need to stop and take your boots off every two hours. Sit with your feet above the level of your heart. It makes a massive difference.'

'I will, Sean, I promise. So, what do we do now?'

Seeing the look on her face and hearing the plaintiff tone of her voice, Sean realised she'd given up all decision making to him.

'First, I'm going to clean your feet with antiseptic wipes. I'll put some blister pads on the worst affected areas. Then I'm going to take the insoles out of your boots, to give your feet more room. That should hopefully be enough to get you to Sahagun. I'll carry your pack.'

'But you've got your own pack to carry.'

Sean looked at Wendy as if, now, *she* had committed the ageist slur.

'I may be old enough to be your father, but I'm perfectly capable of carrying both.'

Wendy looked back at him with a mixture of admiration and awe

'I don't know what I would have done if you hadn't come along, Sean. Claudia was right. You are a good person. Wonderful, in fact.'

Sean didn't know how to respond. He felt good. Needed, even, for the first time since the night of the crash. He thought of how he'd failed his own children, then focused on what he needed to do, for Wendy, to keep the thought away.

'Just sit there and let me get you ready. It's going to hurt a little, getting your boots on, but it'll get better once you start walking.'

Sean was halfway through putting on the first blister pad when he heard someone calling Wendy's name. Still kneeling, his back to the pathway, he looked round.

'You!'

'Me Tarzan,' said Sean, smiling up at Claudia.

Claudia smiled back, despite trying not to, then dragged her gaze to Wendy.

'What happened?'

'Hi Claudia. My blisters got worse. I had to stop walking. Sean stopped to help me. He was a medic in the army.'

Claudia looked down at Sean, who carried on tending to Wendy's feet.

'Were you?'

'Not quite. I was *in* the army. I have some medical training. There's a difference.'

'Are you sure you're managing?'

Sean lifted an eyebrow.

'Want to take over?'

Claudia apologised, realising how it must have sounded.

'No, of course not. I'm sorry. You're obviously doing a great job. Thank you for helping her.'

'What do you *think* I'd do, Claudia, leave her out here all alone? I couldn't have her ending up like poor old Major Tom.'

'Touché.' Claudia replied, unable to supress her grin.

Sean turned his focus back to Wendy, not wanting Claudia to see he was also grinning.

'Well, I don't want to be known as Major Tom who also hates children. Do I now?'

Wendy gave Sean a look of indignation

'I'm not a child. I'm a young woman.'

'Sorry, Wendy, that's what I meant.'

Claudia couldn't help but notice that Wendy was staring at Sean as if he had rescued her from being devoured by a dragon. *She's a little bit smitten with him.* She wondered why she felt jealous.

'Where's Mark?'

'He pushed on ahead of me this morning,' said Wendy, dragging her eyes away from Sean. 'Where's Babette and Robyn?'

'Same. I wanted some *me* time. They left just after dawn. I'm surprised you didn't see them.'

Wendy shook her head.

'Right,' said Sean, putting Wendy's socks back onto her feet. 'We're almost done. Let's get your boots back on.'

For a moment, Claudia wished he were holding her naked foot and putting *her* socks back on. Sean caught her gaze and she looked away, hoping he hadn't read her mind.

With the insoles removed and the laces loosened, Wendy slipped her right foot into her boot, pressing it down against Sean's thigh. He constantly reassured her, telling her how brave she was being.

He's so kind and gentle, thought Claudia, seeing a side to Sean she had not expected. As if he was used to dealing with children. *He probably has his own. He's wearing a wedding ring, after all.* She wondered what his wife looked like then shook the thought away.

'That's so much easier now the insoles are out,' said Wendy. 'You're so clever, Sean. I'm glad you found me.'

'I told you, didn't I?' Sean helped her into the left boot and tied them both. 'Now,' he said, holding his hands out to her, 'take my hands and stand up. It might hurt, at first, but the blister pads and the numbing from the antiseptic ointment should help.'

Wendy stood and took Sean's hands. She stepped forwards a pace then fell against him.

'Careful,' said Sean, catching her in his arms.

Claudia felt the green-eyed monster tapping on her shoulder. *She's definitely acting up for him.* She gave Wendy a look that said, *I know exactly what you're doing.*

'Try and stand by yourself, Wendy.'

'I'll try,' said Wendy, meeting Claudia's eyes in a challenge they both understood. She flicked her eyes back to Sean. 'But I'll just hang onto you a little bit longer, Sean, if that's okay? Until I'm sure I can walk properly.'

She threw the challenge back to Claudia with a thinly veiled smile.

Sean, oblivious of the game being played in front of his nose, still holding Wendy's hands, walked her backwards.

'It's fine. Hold onto me as long as you like.'

Wendy followed him, tentatively, staring into his eyes.

'That feels so much better. It's still a bit sore, but I think I can walk. Maybe with just a little more help to begin with.'

Sean looked over at Claudia.

'Can you take over, just until she's steady on her feet? We need to get moving if we're going to get to Sahagun before nightfall. I really want a doctor to look at her.'

'Sure,' said Claudia, hiding her smile as Wendy reluctantly let go of Sean's hands, 'but what about her pack?'

Sean answered her by putting on his own, then wearing Wendy's on his front.

It took four more hours to reach the village of Sahagun, where, after being seen by the local doctor, who spoke excellent English, Wendy was advised to rest up for at two or three days. One of her blisters was slightly infected and she needed to start a course of antibiotics immediately.

'What am I going to do now,' Wendy asked, tearfully?

'There's a good hotel back in Carrion de les Condes,' said the doctor. 'You could rest up there. You can take a taxi back. If you don't, you won't finish the Camino. I'm sorry, but you *must* follow my advice or you will make things worse for yourself.'

'I've just come from there' said Wendy, fighting back tears. 'Besides, my budget doesn't run to taxis and hotels.'

Claudia put her arm around her, giving her a motherly hug.

'Don't cry, sweetie. We'll work something out.'

'Who shall I make out the bill to?'

'I'll take it,' said Sean, following the doctor through to her office. He turned to Claudia. 'Give me a minute.'

Wendy looked after him and tried to stand.

'But . . . Sean!'

'It's fine, Wendy. Just get yourself ready. Okay?'

'Okay,' she replied, clearly a little embarrassed.

'Right,' said Sean, coming back into the treatment room, 'let's go to the bar next door and work out what to do next.' He turned to the doctor. 'Thanks for all your help. We'll make sure she rests up.'

The doctor bowed her head.

'*Buen Camino.* I am sure you will all make it. Just ensure your daughter rests.'

No one corrected her.

At the bar, next door, Sean ordered lemon beers and they took an outside table, enjoying the cool, early evening air. It was almost seven and the sky was surrendering to the coming night, turning a rich peach and casting a soft glow over the white plastered fronts of the houses along the street.

'You paid the doctor,' said Wendy, looking at Sean.

She was sniffling, but no longer crying.

'It's nothing. Don't worry about it.'

'It's not nothing. I won't ever forget what you've done for me, Sean. Not ever. But what am I going to do?'

She looked on the verge of breaking down again.

Sean took hold of her hands, across the table.

'I have a plan. It's the only option you have, frankly. But it will mean you can still do the Camino.'

'Really?'

Wendy looked dubious.

'Yes, really.' Sean gave her a smile that said he was. 'Just hear me out before you say anything. And that means both of you.'

'Okay,' said Wendy and Claudia.

Sean outlined his plan.

'I think this is the best option for us.'

'Go on,' said Claudia, moved by Sean referring to them as, *us!*

'The doctor's right, Wendy, you can't walk for at least a few days. Not if you want to continue on the Camino. Which you do. Right?'

Wendy nodded in agreement.

'Right.'

'Then you *have* to go back to Carrion de les Condes.

'But, I wanted to . . .'

'Wendy, let Sean finish,' said Claudia, gently but firmly.

'Sorry, Sean. Go on.'

'Okay. So, while I was in her office, the doctor called the hotel she told us about. They've got a room booked and ready for you. It's a beautiful old building, close to the centre, a converted monastery overlooking the old town. You've got a suite with a bath, a shower and a view over the gardens. It's even got an outdoor pool. There's a hotel doctor who's going to check your feet each day. I've booked you full board, so you can eat there. You need to stay off your feet as much as you can. Just chill out, relax, and get your feet in better shape.'

'But . . . Sean.'

'Wendy, you promised you'd trust me.'

'Let him finish, Wendy, for goodness sake,' said Claudia.

Wendy gave them both an apologetic smile.

'I'm sorry. I promise to shut up.'

'I've booked you in for five days,' continued Sean, 'just in case you take longer to heal. They have my credit card details. Whatever you need, just order it. There's a sports shop in the town, and the hotel manager is going to organise a selection of new hiking boots to be brought to you to choose from. The ones you have are too small to go on in. Just remember to buy at least one size larger than normal and to tape up your feet at the start of each day. I'll show you how. Oh, and last but not least, when you're ready to go again, the hotel car will bring you back right here. Now, how does all that sound?'

Claudia was open mouthed at everything Sean had arranged in such a short space of time, albeit with the doctor's help. His generosity, too, towards someone he didn't even know, was staggering. She felt ashamed she'd misjudged him.

'Sean, that's amazing. Isn't that great, Wendy?'

Wendy was overcome and started to cry. If Sean had saved her from a dragon, before, now he'd saved her from an army of monsters.

Sean teased her, trying to take away the tears.

'I thought you'd be happy. But, if you want, I can cancel everything and you can just try to . . .'

Wendy smiled and the tears stopped.

'No, it's just that . . . It's too much. I can't let . . .'

Sean held his hands up in front of her.

'Don't even think about saying no, Wendy. Anyway, it's all arranged. The taxi will be here in about ten minutes. Claudia and I will come with you to see you settled in and make sure you have everything you need.'

Sean looked across the table, at Claudia, who nodded in agreement.

'Absolutely.'

Wendy reached over and threw her arms around Sean's neck.

'I didn't think people like you existed. You're like an angel. A guardian angel.'

'Trust me, I'm not,' said Sean, 'but I'm glad to be able to do something good for a change.'

Claudia picked up on his last three words. There was a story in them. She was determined to find out what it was.

A moment later, a white Mercedes with a green light on its roof pulled up in front of the bar. The driver called to them through this open window.

'*Signor*, you have ordered a taxi for Hotel Real Monasterio San Zoilo, in Carrion de Los Condes?'

'Yes,' Sean called back, 'can you help the girls with their luggage. I'll join you in a minute.'

The driver got out and began to load the rucksacks into the boot of his car.

56

Sean and Claudia checked Wendy into her hotel room. It was bright and warm, had a flat-screen television, an old-fashioned desk and looked out over the beautiful hotel gardens. She would be more than comfortable for the few days she was there. Claudia went to the shop, at reception, where she purchased pyjamas, magazines and a couple of books for her to read. She bumped into the French couple, Romano and Helena, whom she'd had dinner with, in Burgos, who were also staying in the hotel. Helena was also having problems with *her* feet, so they'd decided to take a couple of days off. They promised to look in on Wendy and keep her company.

Back in Sahagun, Claudia sat in her room at the private albergue she'd booked into for the night, across the street from the bar they'd left a couple of hours before. Her phone battery had run out. She stared at it, waiting for it to come back to life. It took only a few minutes to light up and start pinging. There were eleven missed calls and as many messages, all from Robyn and Babette. She suddenly realised they would be worried about her. To confirm her thoughts, Robyn's last text message mentioned calling the American consulate, as well as the local police.

Claudia called Robyn, who answered on the second ring.

'Claudia?'

'Hi, Robyn.'

'Thank God.' Robyn sounded more relieved than angry. 'Where the hell have you been? Are you all right?'

Claudia heard Babette in the background.

'Put her on speaker. I want to hear.'

'I'm in Sahagun,' said Claudia, 'in a little albergue. I'm absolutely fine.'

Robyn breathed an audible sigh of relief.

'Thank God! We're ahead of you. In a village called Ranero. Claudia, we called and called when you never turned up. We've been so worried. We called the police, but they said you'd probably got tired and just stopped for the night, somewhere else. Apparently, it happens a lot. Is everything okay?'

There was genuine concern in Robyn's voice.

'Believe it or not,' said Claudia, feeling a little guilty. 'I've been with Sean.'

'Sean!' Robyn's concern turned to confusion. 'Sean who?'

'Major Tom,' called Babette, laughing. 'You're telling me we've been worried about you being abducted, or eaten by a bear, and all the while you've been hanging out with Major Tom?'

'I suppose I am. Sort of. It's a long story.'

Claudia realised how it must have sounded.

'Why am I not surprised?' Robyn snapped. 'Is he there? I want to give him a piece of my thoughts.'

'I think you mean a piece of your *mind*, Robyn.'

'Whatever,' said Robyn, clearly not amused. 'Give him the telephone.'

'I would, if I could, and he could explain things, but I'm not with him now.'

Robyn's tone became accusatory.

'Really! So why couldn't you have called to let us know you were hooking up with him.'

'It's not like that, Robyn, not at all.'

'Well something happened between you two in Pamplona. And in Burgos. Don't deny it. I might not know you that well, Claudia, but I know what I saw and heard in your reaction to him. Both times.'

'Robyn, that's nonsense. Up until this afternoon, I thought he was the most annoying guy I'd ever met.'

'What happened to make you change your mind?'

Babette had clearly moved closer to the phone and had her own set of questions to ask. Claudia could picture the smile on her face.

'Don't think were not both still angry with you for scaring us half to death,' said Robyn, 'but Babette's right, for once. Tell all.'

Claudia recounted how she'd found Sean tending to Wendy, and of the drama that had ensued, as well as the part he'd had played in sorting out everything to allow Wendy to continue the Camino.

Robyn's tone and opinion changed instantly.

'He's been amazingly kind. And so generous.'

'Maybe he's a reclusive billionaire,' said Babette. 'I always liked him.'

Claudia heard Robyn gasp at the other end of the phone.

'Liar! You said you couldn't stand him.'

'He's not what we *all* thought,' said Claudia, refereeing.

'I feel bad for the things I said about him,' Babette added. 'I'll make it up to him the next time I see him.'

'Goud graver,' Claudia heard Robyn say.

'What?

'It means, gold digger,' explained Robyn, over Babette's denials.

Claudia tried to move things back onto a more even keel.

'Anyway. I'm staying here, tonight. I'll walk on tomorrow morning.'

'We'll wait for you.'

'No, Robyn, just head on into Leon. Get us a nice hotel and I'll catch you up later in the afternoon.'

'Are you staying with Major Tom?'

The meaning in Babette's voice was obvious.

'Babette!' said Robyn, sharply, 'that's none of our business.'

'Sorry, Claudia.'

'But, are you?' Robyn asked.

'No, it's not like that,' protested Claudia, feeling that, no matter what she said, Babette had her mind made up on what really had happened.

Babette confirmed her thoughts.

'*Commencing countdown, engines on,*' she sang, twisting the words from the *Space Oddity* song then laughing, lasciviously. 'So, he's not coming to your room to tuck you in?'

'No! I'm really not with him,' said Claudia, forcefully. 'To be honest, I don't know where he is. We got out of the taxi and he walked me to the albergue, just to make sure I could get a room, then said goodnight and walked off. Seriously, after all we'd just gone through. I can't understand him.'

'He's a man,' said Robyn, 'don't try.'

'Sure,' said Claudia, 'but one minute he's chatting away, being the nicest guy you could hope to meet, taking care of Wendy as if she were his own daughter, the next, he clams up again and buggers off like we're nothing to each other.'

'But you *aren't* anything to each other, Claudia.'

Robyn's voice was dripping with sarcasm and innuendo.

'I didn't mean it like that, Robyn.'

'Of course, you didn't'.

'Bugger off, Robyn. Anyway, I'm tired and I need to sleep. I'll enjoy walking on my own again, tomorrow, after today's adventure.'

'No problem,' said Robyn, stopping teasing. 'We'll see you in Leon. I'll text you where we are.'

'See you there.'

'Claudia,' she heard Babette call, 'if anyone knocks on your door in the middle of the night, be sure to let them in.'

'Honestly, Babette, what do you take me for?'

Claudia hung up before she could tell her.

Her phone pinged, almost immediately. She was surprised to see a message from Paul. She opened it and read it to herself.

Hi sweetheart, sorry I've been hard to reach. I've seen a few missed calls from you and tried to call you back. You're probably in some remote area in the mountains. Things are going great here. I'll tell you about it when we chat. Love you.

She checked her phone but there were no missed calls. *And wouldn't he have left her a voice message?* Babette and Robyn had. Maybe there was some issue with the phones. Then again, maybe she was making excuses for him. She sent a message telling him she'd be in Leon the next day then switched out her light and closed her eyes. The last image in her mind was of Sean's face. She lied to herself that it was only a random thought brought on by the day's turn of events.

57

Claudia started walking a little after nine o'clock the next morning, leaving Sahagun and making her way up a steep hill before heading down through a patchwork of rolling fields that could only be described as heavenly. She'd taken breakfast in the little bar across the street, wondering if she might see Sean. She told herself she didn't care if she saw him or not, but was disappointed when he hadn't appeared.

It was a quiet morning on the Camino, most pilgrims already well on their way. A group of cyclists passed her, calling a chorus of, *buen camino*. She called back to them, feeling the joy in a truly special camaraderie she had never before experienced. She looked at her phone, wondering if Paul had texted her back. He hadn't. There was, however, one from Wendy, who said she was relaxing by the pool with Romano and Helen and feeling much better.

Around midday, she stopped at a local farm and bought bread, cheese, and delicious smelling tomatoes, along with a large bottle of home-made lemonade. The farmer's wife was fat and jolly and spoke no English, but hand signals and smiles sufficed to allow the exchange. Claudia packed the food in her rucksack and headed on, the beauty of the surrounding countryside and the sunny weather lifting her soul to new heights. She thought of Hannah, picturing her walking just ahead of her.

'I'm so glad you sent me here. I never knew it was going to be like this. Maybe I was supposed to come here and do this. Maybe this is what I needed.'

'Hello, talking to yourself? Or is there someone I can't see?'

Claudia's heart skipped a beat. She spun around to see Sean sitting a little way back off the pathway, among a copse of trees, at a rustic wooden table and chairs.

'Jesus Christ, Sean! I nearly jumped out of my skin. I thought you'd be miles ahead of me.'

She was suddenly conscious of how she looked, and began fiddling with her hair, then, aware she was doing it, stopped.

Sean tried not to make it obvious he was looking her up and down, admiring her legs and the shape of her body. Her breasts were straining against a short-sleeved, white shirt. The sight made his breath catch. He focused, instead, on her face, which didn't help. There was a flush to her cheeks that made his heart beat a little faster. Her hair, today, was the colour of golden wheat, and her eyes, which he thought her best feature, were even more sparkling green than normal. He tried to sound normal, failing utterly to do so.

'Sorry. Didn't mean to frighten you.'

He looked away, hauling his pack up onto his lap, pretending to look for something, wondering what the hell was happening to him.

'You must have left early,' said Claudia, regaining her composure.

She had no idea what had come over her at the sight of him. She resolved to be polite and to chat, for a few moments, before moving on. There was no harm in that.

'I did,' said Sean, still fiddling with his pack. 'I just stopped to watch the birds.'

'You're a bird watcher?'

Claudia was unable to connect the dots. She thought he looked more like an old-time, safari guide, from right out of one of Wilbur Smith's African adventure novels.

'My wife was. We used to go . . .'

Sean stopped talking and looked away, as if staring at a memory that had appeared without warning.

The words had resonated with him, Claudia could see, but they had also resonated with her. Mostly because of the abject sense of loss he had projected. She knew, instinctively, his wife was dead. Her heart ached for him. She wanted nothing more than to give him a hug. She knew she couldn't leave him.

'Mind if I sit down at your table?'

She shrugged off her pack before he could refuse.

'It's not my table. It was here as I was passing.'

If it had been a joke, Claudia couldn't tell. Sean hadn't smiled. But at least he hadn't said no to her sitting with him.

'Wendy's fine, by the way,' she informed him, 'enjoying being by the pool.'

'That's good.'

'You were incredibly kind to her, Sean. She was scared, no matter if she didn't show it. You took that fear away. I was impressed.'

'I didn't do it to impress you, Claudia. I did it because it was the right thing to do. She's just a kid.'

'Of course. Sorry. I didn't mean anything by it.' *Bloody hell, I'm on eggshells with him every time we speak.* She sat down on the seat beside him. 'Have you had lunch?'

'Not yet.'

Claudia offered him an olive branch, instead of hitting him with a metaphorical one.

'Share mine, if you like.'

'No, but thanks, Claudia. I was just about to head on.'

Claudia reached into her pack and brought out three brown paper bags and the bottle of lemonade. She laid everything out on the table before he had a chance to say no.

'Come on, Sean. You're just being polite. Really, I've got too much for one person. You'd be doing me a favour. I got it from a farm, a few miles back. Cheese, bread and baby tomatoes, all washed down with,' she lifted glass bottle up and inspected it, 'I'd like to say, chilled, but it's verging more towards cool, homemade lemonade. Simple fare, but fresh off the vine, or bushel . . . or goat.'

She gave Sean a smile that made it impossible to refuse and began sawing at the cheese with the oddest piece of cutlery he had ever seen. It had the scooped end of a spoon, the tines of a fork and, along one edge, the serrations of a knife. It took his mind off leaving.

'What the hell is that?'

'It's a spork,' said Claudia, holding it up and looking at it herself. 'I bought it from a lovely man called Xabier, in Saint Jean. It's fantastic, isn't it?'

'If you say so,' said Sean, allowing himself a smile and deciding to stay.

Claudia offered it to him and he used it to cut some slices of cheese and tomatoes for them both. He followed her lead in tearing off a chunk of baguette and making a crude sandwich. He ate it slowly, relishing each bite.

'You were obviously hungry,' said Claudia.

Sean looked back at her and nodded in agreement.

'I think I was. This is delicious. Sometimes, I just forget to eat, to be honest. Until I'm starving.'

'We need all the strength we can get on this crazy trek of ours.'

Claudia watched him eat, glad she'd joined him and that he'd stayed to share her lunch. Sean, watching her, felt strangely at ease.

'Where are your friends? The two girls I keep seeing you with.'

'Babette and Robyn,' Claudia replied, nibbling at her sandwich and fighting the urge to remind him of his sarcastic reply when she'd called them, *girls,* before, in Burgos Museum of Evolution. 'They called me, last night, worried sick. I think they thought I'd been eaten by bears or something. They're up ahead, waiting for me, in Leon. We're all so looking forward to being there. It's meant to be a beautiful city.'

'It is.'

'Have you been there?' Claudia asked.

Sean shook his head.

'No, I just meant, I've heard it is.'

'Well, I sure guess we'll see,' said Claudia, accenting her accent and sounding more like Mark, the Texan.

'You're American, aren't you?' Sean asked, smiling at her self-effacing joke.

'For my sins.'

'First time in Europe?'

'It is,' said Claudia, enthusiastically, 'and I absolutely love it. There's a real sense of history here. It's in the very stones of the buildings. A history we just don't have back home. I've not been to that many places, but I was in Rome. It was amazing. And I visited Venice and Verona.'

'Verona,' said Sean, wistfully. 'One of my favourite places in the world. I've been there, many times.'

'Really? Well, this is probably not up your street, but its where I saw my first opera. My only opera, actually. At the Colosseum de Verona.'

'Which one?' Sean asked. His interest genuine.

'*Tosca*, it's about . . .'

Sean nodded, knowingly.

'Yes, it's a good one to start with. Poor *Tosca*, she never really stood a chance against Baron Scarpia. I prefer *La Boheme*. It's another of Puccini's tragic love stories. Set in Paris. *La Ville Lumière*, or the City of Light, as it's known.'

'*You!* Like opera? Really?' Realising how it must have sounded, Claudia immediately apologised. 'I'm so sorry, that was remarkably rude of me to suggest someone like you wouldn't like opera.'

'Someone like *me*?'

'I only meant that, well, you're just not . . . you don't seem as if . . .'

Claudia stumbled over what she was trying to say. Realising she was still digging the hole she'd gotten herself into, she stopped talking.

'Relax, Claudia. I'm just teasing you.'

Sean laughed at her, making her laugh at herself.

Claudia looked into his eyes and lost herself in him a little more. It felt as if the Universe had reached down and gently nudged them closer together. She could feel a tension building between them, like the feeling in the air before a wild storm. She suddenly felt tongue-tied and flustered.

'Do you still go. Yourself? To see it? Opera, I mean.'

'I used to,' said Sean, huskily. Like Claudia, he was struggling to gain control of his emotions. 'I've not really cared to, for a while.'

'Why not?'

Sean looked away.

'It doesn't matter. Look, I'd better go. Thanks for the food, Claudia. I'm grateful. It was really kind.'

Claudia couldn't hide her disappointment. They had taken a step toward each other, but Sean seemed, now, to have become uncomfortable. As if meeting with her on an emotional level had frightened him. She had no idea why it was important for her not to let him go, but something told her it was.

'Don't just leave like that, Sean. Can't we walk together for a while? It was a nice lunch. It seems a shame to just part now. Anyhow, I need someone to protect me from the bears.'

Sean mulled it over for a moment.

'Well, I don't think there *are* any bears around here, but I'd hate you to have to take the chance and not be there to help. So maybe for a while. I usually like to walk alone. I'm not the best company.'

'You said so, in Burgos, before you left the museum.'

'Sorry, Claudia. I seem to say that to you a lot.'

'It's fine, Sean, I get it. You're complicated. No big deal. We're just two pilgrims having a day on the Camino. Let me get my pack on and we'll go. We don't have to talk. It's a lovely day. We can just enjoy the sunshine and the beauty of Spain.'

'Okay, Jane! Let's go.'

'Right behind you, Tarzan!'

They smiled at one another then looked away, busying themselves with putting on their packs, afraid of meeting the other's gaze. Whatever force was bringing them together, time and again, was connecting them, now, at some level they could not understand or control.

For the next hour, they strolled past endless furrows of ochre-brown fields studded with gnarled and twisted olive trees, bursting from the earth to stand like sun-charred statues reaching into a cornflower blue sky. Sean was quiet and contemplative, although there was a peaceful, easy feeling between them. Claudia walked ahead of him, turning every so often to check he was still there. Each time she turned, their eyes met. She knew, like her, he felt the charge passing between them, and when she had her back to him could feel his eyes on her. It excited her. She hadn't felt that "whooshy" feeling for a long time. Sean, trying to stop himself from watching the undulating roll of Claudia's pert bottom, felt much the same.

'You walk like an assassin,' said Claudia, letting him pass her as she bent down to tie a lace that wasn't loose. She couldn't take him being behind her any longer. 'Your tread is almost silent.'

'Years of night patrols in the Middle East,' said Sean, 'when I was in the army. My best friend, Miles, was way better than me. He always referred to me as Merrick. You know, from the film, *The Elephant Man*?'

'The one with John Hurt. I absolutely loved that movie.'

Claudia took her turn following Sean, not trying at all to stop herself looking at *his* bottom. It looked firm and had a lovely round shape. She wondered what it would be like to hold

'Yes,' said Sean, 'he played the lead character, John Merrick.'

'But what's that got to do with you walking so . . . Ah, I get it,' said Claudia, catching the proverbial penny, 'you were trying to walk quietly because you were out on patrol and didn't want to get caught.'

'Exactly,' replied Sean, looking back and catching the direction of her gaze. He smiled and looked away as Claudia's tan turned a shade redder, 'he always told me I was as noisy as an elephant, hence the nickname. Miles thought it was funny.'

'It is.'

Claudia wondered what Sean would look like in an army uniform. *Pretty damned good*, she imagined.'

'Oddly,' Sean continued, 'I bought a house with the same name.'

Claudia was puzzled.

'Elephant? Bit of an odd name for a house.'

Sean couldn't help but laugh at her mistake.

'Don't be daft. *Merrick!* The house is called Merrick.'

'Ah, now I see. Merrick! It's a lovely name.'

'It was a lovely house.'

They walked on in silence for a few moments. Something had bothered him, thought Claudia. She tried not to let the progress they had made slip away.

'Tell me about Merrick.'

Even though he was ahead of her and Claudia couldn't see his face, it was obvious he was fighting some battle inside himself. He'd opened up to her, over the past few hours, but now it seemed, at the mention of his former home, a home he had clearly loved, that the armour of ice he constantly wore had reformed. She remembered him telling her he no longer *had* a home. There were so many unanswered questions with everything about him. Sean closed the door to any further attempts to find any answers.

'I don't want to talk about it, Claudia. I'm sorry. Look, if you don't mind, I'm going to get a move on. I've been taking it easy, because of you, but I prefer a harder pace. I like to be alone. It's just the way I like to travel. You understand, don't you?'

'Don't let me keep you,' said Claudia, feeling a little hurt at the clumsy way he'd put it.

'Thanks. I enjoyed walking with you. And thanks again for the food.'

He headed off and, within minutes, was hidden from view on a winding pathway bordered by woodland, leaving Claudia wondering what the hell had just happened. He'd acted like an elephant, all right, she thought. One of those big bulls that caused mayhem wherever it roamed. Always alone and always angry, blowing dust out of its nose and scaring all the other elephants away.

'Damn him! Let him go. He's nothing to you,' she said to herself, as she walked.

'Maybe not,' said Hannah, popping into her head, 'but you like him, don't you?'

'No, I don't bloody like him. Anyway, who asked you, old woman?'

Hannah laughed at her.

'Just saying.'

Claudia vented her anger on a hapless stone, sending it rolling down the pathway with a kick. It bounced up into a leafy bush, sending a cloud of white butterflies into the air They flew up and around her as she passed, fluttering haphazardly, like the thoughts in her head. She walked on, determined to enjoy the sunshine and solitude, stopping only to slip on her headphones. She smiled as Bob Marley gave her the best advice she could have received.

'Don't worry, about a thing.'

58

At the end of the nineteenth century, a young architect from Barcelona crossed the Spanish peninsula to build a textile warehouse in León. His name was Antonio Gaudi and the building was *Casa Botines*. What he created would be a unique work that cities from all over the world would dream to emulate, becoming part of an itinerary that any traveller wanted to experience when visiting the great Spanish city.

Claudia made her way up Calle Ancha, entering Leon from the north, and stopped to admire the gothic architecture of the spectacular building. Its red brick façade glowed under the late afternoon sunshine, the angular towers and round end-turrets giving it the appearance of a fairytale castle. She had discovered Gaudi, years before, at school, before deciding that art, rather than architecture, would be her greatest passion. However, he had retained a special place in her heart. There was, she felt, no history of either discipline that ignored Casa Botines originality and contribution to the world of construction. She felt overwhelmed by emotions she had not expected to feel.

'I can't believe I'm actually here. I've seen this building so many times in magazines and books. I've admired it and been inspired by it all my life.'

'It's a beautiful building,' said Brendan, the young Irish guy she'd met just outside of Leon. He was a student, studying something Claudia could not now remember. 'Gaudi's first major work, you said.'

'He was nineteen years old when he designed this, Brendan. Nineteen, can you imagine? A true genius. There's never been an artist who knew how to unite technique and aesthetics like Gaudi.'

In the paved square below Casa Botines was an iron bench with a life-size bronze of the great man sat upon it. Tourists and pilgrims were having their picture taken sitting alongside him. Brendan took out his phone and turned to Claudia.

'Let me take a picture of you with him. He's one of your heroes. You can't come all this way and not preserve the moment.'

Claudia dropped her pack and wandered through a flock of pigeons that were strutting around the square as if they owned it. She took a seat beside Gaudi, slipping an arm around his back. The metal was cooler than she'd expected it to be, given how sunny it was.

'Great to finally meet you,' she whispered, to the old, metal man.

Gaudi stared straight ahead, looking at his first masterpiece, his pose for the camera unaltered.

'Done,' said Brendan, showing Claudia the picture.

'Looks great, you need to send it to me. I'll give you my number before you head off. Right, I think the Plaza de Regla is just up the street, next to the cathedral. According to Robyn's text message, she and Babette are at a café close to it. I can't miss them, apparently.'

'Lead on,' said Brendan, helping her back into her pack.

They walked on up the busy street then out into a massive, paved plaza bordered by shops and cafes on all four sides. The cathedral, at its centre, dominated everything.

'Wow! I thought Burgos Cathedral was impressive, but this is something else,' said Claudia, gazing up at the thirteenth century monument to God.

With a pale grey façade, boasting three richly sculpted doorways and two soaring towers that rose like the fingers of a giant hand, into the heavens, the cathedral exuded an almost luminous quality. The main entrance was lorded over by a scene of the Last Judgement, whilst an extraordinary gallery of *vidrieras* was wrapped around the entire building. The kaleidoscope of stained glass was breathtaking from the outside. Claudia could only imagine what the windows must be like viewed from within.

'It's truly incredible,' said Brendan, equally as impressed. 'I've never seen anything like it.'

Claudia nodded in agreement.

'They call it Spain's gothic masterpiece and Leon's spiritual heart. Now I know why.'

'Claudia!'

She turned to see Robyn, stood at a little café on the west side of the Cathedral, waving to her. She rushed over and gave Claudia a hug that left them both laughing.

'Robyn, it's so good to see you.'

'You too. I know it's only been a day, but I've missed you.'

'Me too,' said Claudia. There was no feeling, she felt, like seeing a friendly face in an unfamiliar place. 'This is Brendan. He's a student, from Ireland. We met a couple of hours ago and kept each other company walking in.'

'Hi Brendan.'

Robyn smiled and gave him a warm hug.

'Have you been drinking?' Claudia asked, noticing Robyn's flushed cheeks and bright demeanour.

'I may have had a few glasses of wine, but we're on a longer rest day than normal. It's allowed. Come on over, we're sitting with some friends you'll recognise.'

Claudia followed Robyn and, as she approached the table, recognised Mark. He stood and hugged her.

'Good to see you, Boston,' he said, in his familiar slow drawl, using the nickname he'd given her some weeks back.

'You too, Mark. Wendy sends her love. She says she'll see you in Santiago.'

'I'm glad you were there to help the little lady.'

'It was mainly Major Tom,' said Claudia, 'he was wonderful to her. But as it turns out, Babette was correct. He is a *Klootzak*.'

'Well that's going to be awkward,' said Robyn, giving Claudia a wry smile and a look she couldn't understand.

'Why?'

Before Robyn could answer, Babette came bursting out the café.

'Claudia, darling. I'm so relieved to see you. Look who we found.'

Following Babette out of the bar, carrying a tray full of drinks, was Sean. Claudia stood, open mouthed, looking at him. Sean, trying not to catch her eye, made his way to the table and served the drinks

'That was a large Jack Daniels with ice, Mark, wasn't it?'

'Sure thing, cowboy,' drawled Mark, smiling up at Sean as if they were old drinking buddies.

'We saw Sean walking in about an hour or so ago,' explained Robyn, to a clearly confused Claudia. 'We couldn't just let him pass without saying thanks for everything he did for Wendy.'

'Nope!' Mark added, his nose turning even redder from the Jack Daniels he'd been drinking for the past few hours. 'He said you were a ways behind him. Couldn't keep up with him. Isn't that right, Sean?'

'Did he, now,' said Claudia. 'Well, I suppose he's right. He *is* hard to keep up with.'

She shot Sean a glance as if to say, *what the hell?*

Babette put her hand on Sean's forearm.

'It's been really lovely to finally meet you.'

A rush of jealousy flowed though Claudia's veins. Her shock at seeing him, combined with her anger at the way he'd left her, earlier that day, guided her actions. She took hold of Brendan's arm and hugged her head against his shoulder.

'Everyone, this is Brendan. He's from Ireland.'

Everyone greeted Brendan and he shook hands with each of them, including Sean.

'Sit down son, and have a drink,' said Mark, rescuing the slightly awkward moment without knowing he had.

After chatting for half an hour, Brendan stood up and announced it was time he was leaving. He was meeting friends at the public albergue, not far from the cathedral. He hoisted on his backpack then turned to head off.

Claudia stood up and stopped him.

'Don't forget to take my number, Brendan.'

'Oh, of course, for the . . .'

'Yes,' said Claudia, ensuring everyone could hear her, 'you can text me later tonight.'

'I will. It was good to meet you, Claudia. I really enjoyed our walk.

Claudia hugged him and planted a kiss on his cheek.

'Me too, Brendan. It was *really* lovely.'

Brendan turned and headed off across the square.

'What a nice boy,' said Robyn, as Claudia retook her seat, giving her a look that said she knew exactly what she was up to.

'He is,' gushed Claudia, 'and so handsome.'

She thought she saw Sean smirk and immediately wanted to throw something at him.

The conversation and wine kept flowing, although Sean, Claudia noticed, drank only mineral water. She began to relax, despite being confused as to why he was sitting with them, given he'd told her he hadn't wanted company. Although not joining in as much as he could have, he was polite, and clearly able to hold his own in all of the conversations being struck up. He didn't talk about himself much, other than to say he owned a telecommunications company he was taking a break from. Everyone, it seemed, had warmed to him.

'So, you're a millionaire businessman,' Babette asked, looking decidedly merry from the amount of wine she'd drunk, 'trying to find yourself?'

'Not so much, Babette. I found myself long ago. I guess I'm trying to get lost again.'

He looked across at Claudia and a moment of understanding passed between them.

'Like on Mount Everest?'

'I suppose so,' said Sean, angling himself more towards her. 'Pretty cool place to do that. Don't you think?'

'More cold than cool, I'd say.'

They laughed, remembering having said the same words to each other in the Museum of Evolution café.

'You got me back,' said Sean, sending an apology in his smile.

Claudia grinned back at him.

'I did. I knew I would.'

'Somehow, Claudia, so did I.'

'So, how are the fingers?'

Sean held out his hands to her.

'You tell me.'

Claudia took them in hers, turning them over and inspecting them. The touch sent little jolts of electricity firing thought her body. She looked up to see him looking directly into her eyes. Her heart was beating wildly and her face suddenly felt unnaturally hot.

'They seem . . . much better.'

'Do you think so?'

Sean's voice had become low and husky.

Claudia struggled to reply.

'Yes. Don't you?'

'I think,' whispered Sean, 'that being here agrees with me.'

His words were nothing close to what he'd meant. They both knew it.

She let go of his hands, missing the touch of him almost immediately. Suddenly aware of the silence that had descended over the table, she turned to see everyone was watching them, with looks of bemusement on their faces.

'Sean climbed Mount Everest,' said Claudia, a little too quickly, trying to cover up the awkwardness she suddenly felt. 'He got frostbite. In his hands. He's a mountaineer.'

'Of sorts,' said Sean, trying to hide his own amusement.

'Mount Everest,' exclaimed Mark, 'that must have been one hell of an adventure.'

He proceeded to question Sean while Claudia tried to regain her composure. She could see Robyn staring at her across the table, the question in her eyes, obvious. She stood, intending to escape to the bathroom for a few minutes. As she stepped away, her phone, sitting on the table, began to buzz. She picked it up, answering it without looking at who the caller was, relieved to escape Robyn's gaze.

'Claudia Montgomery.'

'Claudia. It's me.'

'Paul! I didn't expect to hear from you.' She walked a few paces into the square. 'What time is there?'

'Six in the morning. I'm just getting up.'

'It's seven at night, here. I'm in Leon.'

Claudia glanced over at the table and noticed Sean had stood up and was putting on his pack.

'Goodbye,' Sean said, to Mark. 'I'm glad I was able to apologise for what happened in Pamplona.'

Mark stood and hugged him, looking almost tearful at his impending departure.

'Don't matter none to me, son. Been great to meet you under more cordial circumstances. If you're ever in Boulder,' he drawled, 'you make sure you come visit. My wife, Janell, would just love to meet you. She makes a mean pot-roast.'

'Thanks, Mark, I will.'

Sean shook Mark's outstretched hand then hugged Robyn.

'Maybe we will see you again along the way.'

Sean shook his head.

'Probably not, Robyn I'm going to push on pretty hard, from here on in. But thank you for a lovely afternoon. It's been a while since I had one as good.'

'It was lovely to meet you,' said Babette, looking up at Sean with *Bambi* eyes. Sean gave her a hug that he had to finally break free from.

'Likewise.'

Claudia was talking to Paul, but her head was spinning. Sean turned from table and looked across at her. He mouthed *goodbye*. She sent him a look that said, *don't go*, then tried to reply to something Paul had said. Sean shrugged his shoulders and smiled at her, then turned and walked away, heading out of the square, down towards Casa Botines. She watched him leave, losing him in the maze of people wandering the busy street. A quiet sob caught in her throat as she almost said his name.

'Are you okay?' Paul asked.

Without waiting for her to answer, he continued to tell her about the new deal he'd just signed, and that he'd put a deposit on a house in Los Angeles.

'I'm fine,' said Claudia, 'that sounds wonderful.'

Her voice was quiet and filled with sadness. For more than one reason.

'You'll love it here, Claudia. I do.'

'I'm sure, Paul.'

Her voice had dropped to a whisper. She was choking back emotions she could not understand.

'Right, honey' said Paul, not noticing anything was wrong, 'I've got to go. Got an early meeting.'

Claudia barely noticed what he was saying. He'd called her *honey*, again, but she could not have cared less. Her eyes remained fixed on the street, hoping

Sean would appear. She said goodbye and returned to the table.

'You missed Sean,' said Babette, cheerily, as Claudia retook her seat. 'What a nice guy.'

Claudia smiled, thinly, struggling to reply. She felt empty, inside. As if some part of her being had been cut away.

'I saw him go.'

Babette pressed on about the phone call.

'How's Paul?'

'Happy. He bought a new house.'

'Where?' Babette asked, not seeing how Claudia was feeling.

'Los Angeles.'

'But, I thought you loved your new lighthouse? Isn't that on the other side of America? How's that going to work?

Claudia was on the verge of tears, wishing Babette would give her a moment.

'I didn't ask.'

'Hadn't you discussed it.'

'No.'

She was struggling to think straight. Only just holding back the scream building up inside her. Babette was relentless.

'But, how are you going to . . .'

'Claudia.' Robyn interrupted, coming around the table. 'Can you give me a hand with the drinks?'

'Sure.'

Claudia stood, her mind in a daze of emotions and feelings she could not get hold of. She allowed Robyn to take her by the arm and guide her away from the table.

'Are you all right?

'No, not really,' whispered Claudia, leaning against her for support.

'I knew you weren't. It's Sean, isn't it? What's going on? Has something happened between you two?'

Claudia shook her head.

'No! Nothing's happened. We had lunch together, earlier today, that's all. We walked and talked for a while, afterwards, but then he wanted to be alone, so he left me and walked on. That was the last I saw of him until I walked into

Leon and saw him with you.'

'Then why are you so upset? And what the hell was going on when you took his hands.'

'You noticed?'

Robyn laughed.

'Noticed! Are you serious? The whole damned table noticed. We could all feel it. Even Mark, and he's a man, as well as being half-drunk.'

'There's nothing between us, Robyn. Nothing.'

Even as she said it, Claudia knew it wasn't true.'

'But you like him, don't you? A lot.'

Claudia scarcely trusted her voice to answer.

'But, I'm married, Robyn.'

'Yes, to a guy who just bought a house thousands of miles from where you live without even discussing it with you. A guy who should be here with you on a second honeymoon. If he's got time to go buy himself a house, Claudia, he's got time to come and be with his wife. I'm sorry to be so blunt, but you know I'm right. Anyway, it's clear there's something special happening with you and Sean.'

Claudia looked shocked to hear Robyn had seen it, but knew, deep down, what she was saying was true.

'I don't *know* what's going on, Robyn. There's some sort of connection between us. I can feel it, every time we meet. I know he does too.'

'Connection? You think? Christ, Claudia, if I had half as much of a connection and a quarter of the sexual tension with a man, as you clearly have with Sean, I'd already be pregnant.'

Claudia laughed and wiped away the tears forming at the corner of her eyes. She took a breath and felt the scream that had been building up inside her begin to evaporate.

'It doesn't matter now, though, does it? He's gone. I'll probably never see him again. Perhaps it's just as well.' But the thought of not seeing Sean again immediately made her heart ache. 'Robyn, what the hell's happening to me?'

Seeing Claudia was still upset, Robyn put an arm around her shoulders.

'Lightening, sweetie. Plain old lightening. You never know where it's going to strike, or how hard. Now, there's no point staying upset. Come on, let's go and get Babette away from the bar. We're going for *tapas*, tonight, at an open-air restaurant in the old town. We need to get you checked into the hotel. Once you're showered and changed, you'll feel better.'

'You're right,' said Claudia, pulling herself together, 'there's no sense in being glum. Besides, even if I don't understand what's going on with my heart, I'm here to have fun. I promised Hannah I would. And we *do* need to get *her* moving. Look!'

She pointed over at Babette, dancing with Mark to some Spanish guitar music being played on the *café* speakers.

'We may be too late to save her,' said Robyn, laughing, 'but we can still save Mark.'

Claudia followed Robyn back towards their table, which Mark was encouraging Babette to climb onto. She couldn't help but look to the empty street, beyond, hoping against hope to see Sean's face.

59

The clock at the entrance to the *Barrio Humedo*, the nickname given to the oldest part of Leon, concentrated within the ancient Roman city walls, struck ten as Claudia, Robyn and a now sober Babette headed into the Plaza San Martin. They'd met up with Mark, at the cathedral, a ten-minute walk away, who had a couple of American ladies in tow, travelling the Camino from Leon to Santiago. Bonnie and Clyde, which they assured everyone was their real names, were in their fifties, but acted as if they were teenagers, so were a welcome addition to the group.

'Right, we're looking for the Taberna Oriente Medio, on the Calle de Juan,' said Robyn, 'it's meant to be just off this square.'

Bonnie pointed at a street sign that said, *Calle de Juan*.

'There!'

They were seated at one of the outside tables, eating the most marvellous *tapas* any of them had ever tasted, taking turns to drink red wine from a *porron*, a triangular-shaped, glass bottle with a pointed spout, from which a thin jet of wine spurted out whenever it was tipped up. The trick was to aim the jet of wine into your mouth. The waiter made it look easy. They all took turns with some successes and some drastic failures, Bonnie spilling wine over her white dress and Babette pouring it into her eye, but they didn't let it spoil the fun. Robyn was glad to see that the only tears in Claudia's eyes were tears of laughter.

After dinner, they headed back to the Plaza San Martin, where some sort of event seemed to be taking place. A wooden dancefloor in the centre of the square was busy being prepared for something. After choosing one of the overlooking bars, they ordered drinks and stood with the gathering crowd, mainly tourists and pilgrims, waiting for whatever was going to happen to begin.

A collective murmur went up as four young, female dancers, dressed in full-length, red, flamenco dresses walked out into the centre of the dancefloor, followed by four men dressed all in black, each carrying an acoustic guitar. The crowd hushed as the dancers lined up, readying themselves for the performance.

'I think its flamenco dancing,' said Robyn.

'How wonderful. I wasn't expecting this. Did you know?'

'Not at all. I was just following the advice of the concierge at the hotel. He told me the Barrio was the place to come for food and nightlife. Seems he was right.'

Suddenly, the guitarists began to play; sweeping bursts of staccato that filled the square, creating a fast-paced, pulsing rhythm, accompanied by the rapping of wooden castanets being played by the dancers. A lone male dancer dressed in black waistcoat, red shirt and tight, black trousers emerged from the crowd, strutting into the centre of the dancefloor. He clapped his hands, once, as if to announce his arrival, then began to dance, using intricate toe-and-heel clicking steps, with well-defined and aggressive dance movements.

'He's doing a *Zapateado*,' Robyn announced, excitedly, recognising it. 'It's a typical men's flamenco dance. I've seen it on television.'

'He looks like a sleek, black bull,' said Claudia, swept up in the passion of the moment, 'baiting the women to come to him.'

At the taunts of the male dancer, the female dancers began to dance. They started slowly, with purposeful, well-controlled movements, grabbing the ruffled fronts of their dresses in one hand and pulling them up to show their tanned and shapely legs, stamping the wedged heels of their dance-shoes into the boards, other hand high in the air, accompanying the guitarists with sharp raps of their castanets. They were hypnotic, sexual and sensual. The crowd cheered and clapped, caught up in the heady mood and the smouldering heat of the night.

Claudia was mesmerised by the dancers. One, in particular, grabbed her attention. She was taller than the others and easily the most beautiful. Her skin shone like muted gold under the lights dotted around the square. Her face was almost symmetrical, with sloping, almond shaped eyes and voluptuous lips, painted to match her dress, her hair, black as coal, hanging down to the small of her back, flicked and tossed like the tail of an Andalusian stallion as she danced.

As she watched, Claudia suddenly noticed another face on the opposite side of the square.

'Sean,' she whispered, shocked at the strength of her reaction to the sight of him.

He was watching the dancers, unaware she had seen him.

As if her whisper had been a scream that only he could hear, Sean looked past the dancers and met her eyes. A rush of blood coursed through Claudia's body and her breath caught in her chest. She wanted to go to him but was unsure of how to negotiate the crowd, packed tightly together and pushed up to the edge of the dancefloor. As she tried to figure out what to do, the music stopped and the dancers left the stage, to wild cheers and thunderous applause. Everyone remained where they were, waiting to see what happened next.

Claudia looked back across the square, seeking sight of Sean, but she could no longer see him. As she thought how to push her way through the crowd and try to find him, a lone figure walked out into the centre of the dancefloor. He was tall, slim and bearded, with shoulder length, black hair. Under one arm, he held what looked like a set of Scottish bagpipes. He took a seat on a short stool, set out for him by one of the bar owners, who spoke to him briefly then turned to face the crowd.

'It is Pablo's turn to entertain us,' he called, in heavily-accented English.

The crowd quietened and the square fell silent. There was an expectancy of something amazing about to happen.

Seated, the bagpipes laid across his knees, Pablo closed his eyes and began moving his right elbow up and down, pumping the bag full of air. A monotonous drone filled the square, like the hum of a massive beehive, and a single, haunting note rose up over the hush of the crowd, building in intensity, then falling, only to begin once more. Each time, new notes were added, woven into the emerging melody.

Claudia found she was holding her breath. Every face was turned to Pablo, mesmerised by the voice he brought from the pipes. The music was intoxicating, its essence, the lingering memory of love's lost regret, the phrasing of each refrain somehow more glorious than the last. She scanned the other side of the square, desperate for sight of Sean. Finally, she found him. He was looking right at her. Their eyes locked and she found it hard not to go to him, such was the emotional turmoil building inside her.

Suddenly, the tempo of the song shifted, becoming faster and more dramatic. From the side of the stage the guitarists and dancers walked out, arranging themselves around Pablo. The guitarists began to play a pulsing accompaniment, supporting the cry of the pipes, lifting the pace and the mood of the music. The dancers stamped their feet and clapped their hands, and the beat changed once more. Pablo pushed the melody, changing the rhythm of the tune, taking it into a joyous flamenco. The dancers moved towards the edge of the crowd, choosing people at random and dragging them onto the dancefloor to join them, until everyone, it seemed, had become part of the dance.

'Come on,' cried Babette, grabbing Robyn and Claudia by the hands and pulling them towards the melee taking place.'

'Not me,' called Mark, 'I'll grab a table.'

He laughed at the look on Claudia's face as she allowed herself to be pulled out into the throng.

Reaching the centre of the dancefloor, Claudia immediately let go of Babette's hand, pushing her way towards where she'd last seen Sean. She found him, watching from the edge of the crowd but taking no part, and made her way towards him. Reaching him, she held out a hand.

'Dance with me.'

'Claudia. I'm not . . .'

Sean hesitated, his eyes filled with apprehension. Claudia moved closer to him.

'You said you wanted to get lost, Sean. Get lost with me.'

Claudia's eyes bored into his, pleading with him to take a chance. Sean took hold of her hand, following her out onto the dancefloor.

They danced, tentatively, at first, bodies lightly pressed against each other, then closer, led by a deeper desire Claudia knew they shared. She felt his breath on her bare shoulders and the smell of him when he pulled her to him, his stubble rough against her cheek. They were so close, at times, it seemed they had to kiss. Claudia wanted to, but sensed that, if she made the first move, it would destroy what they were slowly building. She felt at ease in his arms, as if it was the most natural place in the world for her to be. She knew, in that moment, he would be part of the rest of her life. She could not explain why she felt it so strongly, or how it might even happen. But she knew.

An hour later, after dancing themselves to a stop, they were slumped into the seats at a table, with Mark, drinking ice-cold, lemon beer. They were joined by Robyn, who had also had enough.

'That was mad,' she cried, struggling to be heard over the still frenetic music.

'It was bloody exhausting,' said Sean. 'I think climbing mountains is way easier.'

Robyn looked at Claudia, leaning against him. She was glowing, as much from what she was obviously feeling, as well as from dancing.

'You two looked like you were having fun.'

Claudia looked at Sean and the air sparkled around them.

'Sean's going to walk with us, tomorrow.'

Robyn smiled a knowing smile.

'Marvellous,' said Mark, 'but I'll be way ahead of these girls, partner. Feel free to break away from them at any time if it gets too much. One of them never seems to stop talking.'

'Are you *really* going to join us?' Robyn asked, shooting Mark a pretend look of annoyance. 'I thought you preferred walking alone.'

Sean looked at Claudia.

'Blame her. I was forced into agreeing on the promise we could stop dancing. Although, I normally like to leave later in the morning to avoid the crowds.'

'Just get up early for a change, it'll be worth it,' said Claudia, giving him a mock punch on his shoulder, 'we're finally going to reach the Bridge of Lances, so Robyn tells me.'

'Bridge of Lances, what's that?' Sean asked.

'A long Roman bridge over a river,' explained Robyn, 'where a famous Spanish knight fought three hundred jousts over his lost love.'

'I look forward to hearing about it.'

Claudia stared into Sean's eyes, wondering how he had captured her heart. It appeared the feeling was mutual.

'I'll tell you the story when we get there.'

'Deal.'

Sean couldn't remember when he had last spent time enjoying life with other people, then remembered it had been at Alice's birthday party, the previous year. He suddenly pictured Linz. He had promised he would dance with her, that night, but she'd not come back to the dancefloor. If he had known it would have been the last chance they would ever have to do so, he would have found her and danced.

Claudia saw the flash of sadness cross his eyes and wondered what had caused it.

'What's on your mind?'

'Nothing. I've just not danced in a long time.'

'I'm sorry, I didn't mean to pry.'

'No, it's not you. Claudia.'

'Doesn't she ever stop,' said Robyn, pointing at Babette, who had accosted the black-clad, male dancer and was gyrating wildly against him.

'She's too interested in having fun to care,' said Sean. 'And why not? You never know when it might be your last chance to dance.'

The sadness in his voice was obvious. Claudia took hold of his hand and kissed his fingertips. He pulled his hand away and shook his head. He stood, surprising her, and nodded to Mark and Robyn.

'I'll say goodnight. Thanks for letting me to join you.' He looked down at Claudia, who was clearly somewhat taken aback by the sudden change in him. 'I enjoyed our dance. I truly did.'

He turned and walked away, pushing past the crowd of happy dancers at the fringes of the dancefloor, heading out of the other side of the square.

'What the hell just happened,' Robyn asked, seeing how utterly dejected Claudia looked.

Claudia, still watching after Sean, shook her head.

'See what I mean? He's like two different people. All the time. I don't know which one is Sean and which one is Major Tom.'

'Are you okay?'

'I'm fine, Robyn. But I'm going back to the hotel.'

Claudia was too saddened that the night had ended as it had, to stay any longer.

'Want me to walk with you?'

'No, but thanks. I'd rather be by myself for a while. I'll see you and Babette in the morning.'

'Are you sure? If you want to talk?'

'I'm fine, Robyn. Just leave it, please.'

Claudia said her goodnights then headed off in the opposite direction to Sean, wondering what she was going to do about how she was feeling about him. As she passed the cathedral she looked up at its windows. The glorious colour was gone and the stained glass now dark and sombre, reflecting her mood.

60

Claudia sat on the north side of the river, dangling her feet over the edge of the ancient stone wall and looking over the Bridge of Lances towards the medieval town of Hospital de Orbigo. The orange tiles of the roofs were baking hot and heated air rose from every building, making the village shimmer like a desert mirage. The village took its name from the hospital the Knights Templar had founded by the winding River Orbigo, built to assist the medieval pilgrims taking the old Roman road from Leon to Astorga, becoming more famous for the bridge that crossed it, though more the story behind it.

They had walked, that morning, she, Babette and Robyn, from Leon, accompanied by the two Americans, Bonnie and Clyde, Mark having elected to walk on ahead at his usual brisk pace. There had been no sign of Sean at the cathedral. In truth, Claudia hadn't really expected to see him. They'd reached the bridge around two in the afternoon. She was still confused about what had happened the previous evening, but the confusion had slowly turned to anger.

'He needs to explain a few things to me,' she'd told Robyn, who had just tried to convince her not to wait for Sean to come by, 'and he's bloody well going to.'

'Are you sure you want to wait? He might be ahead of us.'

'He likes to walk late in the morning, Claudia snapped, not meaning to, so he can avoid having to speak to anyone. The bloody weirdo.'

'If he's such a weirdo, why do you want to see him again?'

Babette's question drew an exasperated look from Robyn.

'If I knew that, I'd tell you,' said Claudia, shaking her head. 'But we met on the first day, in Saint Jean, and we *keep* meeting. It's like we're *meant* to meet. I know it sounds crazy. You don't have to tell me.'

Babette shrugged her shoulders.

'What the hell do I know? I'm twice divorced and still waiting for the perfect man to walk into my life. For all you know, he's walked into yours. Are you sure you don't want us to wait for you on the other side of the bridge?'

Claudia looked back down the pathway running parallel to the river.

'No, but thanks. He has to pass here at some point. Unless he's going to swim across.'

'He might, if he sees you,' said Babette, laughing at her own joke.

Claudia laughed with her, momentarily lowering her anger levels to just under boiling point.

'Look, I need to have this out with him. You two just head on to our stop for tonight.'

Robyn took Babette by the arm.

'It's only a few kilometres from here. Over the bridge and keep walking. A hostel called the Albergue Verdun. Its right on the Camino trail. It's a good stop for us to then head into Astorga, tomorrow, through some of the most beautiful countryside on the entire Camino.'

'Thanks, Robyn,' said Claudia. 'Now, go on, both of you. I'll see you soon.'

It took another hour for Sean to appear. He was walking alone with his head down, dressed in his olive-green army pants and black t-shirt. He'd acquired a new stick and had a green bandana tied over his head to keep the sun off, his eyes hidden by his aviator Ray-Bans. He reached the bridge and stopped when he saw Claudia.

'Are you waiting for me?'

He removed his sunglasses.

Claudia kept hers on.

'Whatever gave you that idea?'

'Oh! Okay then.'

He replaced his sunglasses and made to walk past her, out onto the bridge. Claudia jumped off the wall, not quite believing he was simply going to leave.

'Are you *seriously* going to leave me sitting here?'

Sean turned back, as if he was behaving perfectly normally.

'I thought you said you weren't waiting for me. I thought, perhaps, you were waiting for your Irish friend. The one you gave your phone number to, in Leon.'

'Brendan?'

'That's him,' said Sean. 'Nice boy.'

Claudia removed her sunglasses and glared at him.

'He's young enough to be my son.'

'I did wonder,' said Sean, 'but I'm not one to judge. You hear about cougars and their taste for younger men.'

His comment drew a look of utter indignation from Claudia.

'Well this is one woman who doesn't share that taste. I only gave my number to him so he could send me a photo he took of me, outside Casa Botines.'

'The Gaudi grain store? Yes, I took a look around it this morning. It's a wonderful piece of architecture. He was young, too, when he designed it. Seems to be a recurring thing with you, liking younger guys.'

Claudia could tell Sean was joking, but refused to acknowledge it. Then he smiled at her and she forgot to be angry.

'Funny guy.'

'Not normally.'

'You don't say, Sean Jameson.'

Sean continued to smile at her. *Damn him, he really annoys me*, she thought, then lost herself in his smile and cornflower blue eyes. She couldn't help but smile back. Sean, seeing the olive branch being waved, decided to reach for it.

'Okay, what say we call a truce, Claudia . . . whatever your name is?'

'What terms?'

'Any you want,' said Sean, enjoying the game.

Claudia considered, for a moment, before offering.

'Okay. My terms are that you keep me company for the next ten kilometres. Maybe I *will* tell you my surname, just in case you ever need to find me in the future.'

'Done!'

Sean offered his hand to seal the deal, which Claudia purposefully ignored. He knew he deserved the snub, but stifled a laugh all the same. She shrugged on her pack and they walked out onto the bridge.

The bridge was a wide pathway of brick-red, paving stones with a line of larger stone strips laid along its centre, worn smooth, in places, by the feet of the innumerable pilgrims who had gone before. A row of antiqued, iron streetlamps stood to attention over the nineteen arches, watching them cross. Much as they had done for hundreds of years.

'It's beautiful, said Claudia, looking along its length.

'Yes,' Sean agreed, looking at her then bac to the bridge. 'Beautiful.'

Claudia wasn't sure if he was referring to it, or to her. She felt flustered, but tried not to show it. They reached the centre and stopped to look down into the slow-flowing water.

'So,' said Claudia, composure regained, 'this is the famous Bridge of Jousts. Do you want me to tell you the story of how it got its name?

'Tell away.'

'Okay, but don't interrupt me or I'll forget everything Robyn told me.'

'I won't.'

'Right, so, hundreds of years ago, a knight called Don Suero, the son of a noble family of Leon and a self-proclaimed prisoner of love, swore to break three hundred lances in a jousting tournament.'

'Why?' Sean asked. He held his hands up as Claudia gave him a scolding look. 'Sorry, go on.'

Claudia shook her head and tutted, theatrically, before carrying on.

'Poor Don Suero fell in love with Lady Leonor, who sadly didn't return his affections. He displayed his heartbreak by donning an iron collar, to show himself as a prisoner of love, but this wasn't enough to get over Leonor's rejection. So, in fourteen hundred and thirty something, I can't remember the exact date, the still love-struck Don Suero announced that he would joust any knight brave enough to fight him on the bridge of Hospital del Órbigo. The one we're standing on. Once he'd had won three hundred jousts, he would remove the collar and be free of his affliction. This became known as the Tournament of the Honourable Passage. Anyone who didn't feel like a joust had to throw a glove on the ground, fording the river instead of taking the bridge.'

'And did he?' Sean asked.

'Did he what?'

'Win three hundred jousts?'

'Sadly, no,' said Claudia, 'the king stopped him after he'd won only two hundred. I think he was getting complaints from people just trying to cross the bridge and not really wanting to fight. Don Suero's collar was removed and he went on a pilgrimage to Santiago instead.'

'And did he win back the lady Elanor's hand?'

'It's Leonor,' said Claudia, 'not Elanor. Haven't you been listening?'

Sean rolled his eyes.

'Well, did he win back *Leonor's* hand?'

'I've absolutely no idea,' said Claudia, laughing at the look on Sean's face, 'but I like to think he did. He went to an awful lot of trouble for her with all those jousts, the iron collar *and* his pilgrimage.'

'He did, but some women are worth that much pain and suffering.'

'Maybe they are.' Claudia understood Sean was talking about something entirely more personal. 'Anyway, that's the story of the bridge.'

Sean looked across the bridge, imagining the jousts that had taken place on the very stones on which he stood. He understood Don Suero's motives and sacrifice. He felt sad, but not overwhelmed, at the link they shared across the bridge of time.

'Nice to know the history, Claudia. I'm really glad you waited to tell me that.'

'I'm glad I waited for you, Sean.'

She gave him a smile they both understood was an offering of forgiveness and walked on, over the bridge, stopping to read some further information about the history of the village at a large information board on the other side of the river.

'Do you fancy a drink?' Sean pointed to a bar just ahead of them, by the end of the bridge. 'I'm parched after all that walking. And it's getting hotter. We could get a cool beer and take a seat by the river. Besides, I owe you for the guided tour.'

'As well as for leaving me like you did last night.'

Claudia looked at him, the hurt in her eyes, real.

'Yes. For that. I'm sorry.'

'And for the time before, in Burgos.'

'Yes,' said Sean, 'and for that.'

'And for . . . Shall I go on?'

Sean hung his head. He looked genuinely remorseful.

'Please don't, Claudia. I get it. I've been a pain.'

'You have, Sean Jameson, but buy me a cold beer and we'll call it quits.' Claudia held out her hand. 'And it's Montgomery. Claudia Montgomery.'

'It's a deal, Claudia Montgomery.'

Sean ordered them both a *cervesa con limon*, which the waiter brought to their table along with some small plates of tapas. Claudia popped a piece of bread with a thick slice of sausage on it into her mouth, eating it with relish.

'I love the free snacks you get at the bars. I don't know what this dark sausage is, but it's delicious. I've been eating it since we left Saint Jean. Every bar and café seems to have it.'

'It's called *morcilla*,' Sean told her, 'but it has a different name where I'm from.'

'*Morcilla*. Sounds quite beautiful. What do they call it in Scotland?'

'It's not quite as romantic. We call it black pudding. Don't you have it in the United States?'

'Not that I've ever seen.' Claudia took another piece from the plate. 'Black pudding. What an odd name for a sausage. It's not black and it's not a pudding. So, what's it made from?'

'I'm not sure I should tell you,' said Sean, trying to hide his amusement.

'Why not?'

'The answer might not be what you're expecting.'

'Come on, Sean, how bad can it be?'

Sean held up his hands, giving in.

'Well . . . it's also known as blood sausage.'

'Blood sausage!' Claudia looked bemused. 'Is that because of the colour?'

'No, it's because of the blood. It's made from pig's blood.'

Claudia stopped chewing and her face paled. For a moment, Sean thought she was going to be ill, but she took a long draft of beer and swallowed the mouthful down.

'Don't tell me anything more about anything I'm eating, Sean. I don't want to know.'

'To be fair, Claudia, you did ask.'

'Yes, but you didn't have to tell me.'

'Noted for the future. Are you sure you're okay?'

'Im good,' said Claudia, giving a shiver, 'but let's not talk about it. Tell me about Scotland. I need to put my mind somewhere else. I've heard of one of your animals, which sounds interesting. I think it's called a haggis.'

Sean couldn't stifle his amusement.

'Why are you laughing?' Claudia asked. 'Did I say it wrong?'

'It's not that,' replied Sean, 'it's just that you told me not to tell you anything more about things that you might eat.'

'You eat haggises?'

'In a way,' said Sean, wondering how best to answer her question. 'But I can't tell you any more than that. Not unless you want to feel ill again.'

I don't! Just tell me about your homeland. Anything to forget about weird food.'

'Okay, I owe you a story, I guess.'

'You do, now talk, tell me about Edinburgh Castle.'

Claudia felt she was really seeing him for the first time since they'd met. He seemed genuinely relaxed and happy. She was still falling for him. She knew she should try not to fall too hard. She wondered how best to do that and came up with nothing that helped.

'Why don't I tell you about Nessie, instead,' said Sean. 'The Loch Ness monster, you know? That's a far better introduction to my country for you, apart from whisky, of course.'

'Okay, but first I need another beer.'

After the waiter had brought them refills, Sean began to tell Claudia about the mystery surrounding the monster.

'It all began hundreds of years ago with a medieval monk. An Irish saint called, St Columba, by the banks of Loch Ness, the longest, deepest loch, which is what we call a lake, in Scotland. Now, poor old Saint Columba saw a monster's head peering at him from out of the water, so naturally he began to . . .'

By the time he had finished telling Claudia his stories of the mythical creatures still found in the mountains and forests of the Scottish Highlands, the sun had sunk fully into the river, turning the surface of the water to gold as it disappeared. They were hours spent in easy conversation and, for once, nothing seemed to get in the way or ruin the moment.

'I suppose I'd better get going,' said Claudia, not wanting to, but noticing three text messages from Robyn.

Sean had booked himself a bed for the night, the bar having an unoccupied private room, overlooking the river, but insisted on walking Claudia to her albergue. He carried her rucksack and they walked in easy companionship, listening to the sounds of the Spanish night.

'So,' Claudia asked, as they reached her albergue, 'are you still going to walk with me tomorrow?'

'Didn't we walk together, today,' replied Sean, taking off her rucksack and handing it to her.

'Across a bridge, Sean, and a fifteen-minute walk in the dark. It's hardly the same.'

'Okay, I suppose you're right. But I'm not the best . . .'

'Yes, I know,' said Claudia, pre-empting him, 'the best company. Let me take the risk of that.'

Sean held up his hands.

'Okay. I give up. I'll meet you, right here, in the morning. At nine, okay?'

Claudia almost leaned in to hug him, but fought the urge.

'Perfect. Thanks for today. It was fun.'

'Goodnight, Claudia Montgomery. I hope someone someday fights three hundred jousts for you.'

Sean turned and headed back towards the town. Claudia watched after him until the darkness swallowed him then called after him, despite she knew he probably wouldn't hear.

'Goodnight, Sean Jameson. I'd let *you* fight for me. But I fear you have other demons to battle.'

She turned away and opened the gate into the albergue, wondering why it was she already missed him.

61

The world was wet and damp as Claudia left the albergue. The Camino was the colour of wet sand and smattered with puddles of ash brown water, where yesterday there had been empty scoops of pale, bone-dry dust. Robyn and Babette had left an hour earlier, when it had still been raining, but now the rain had stopped and an advancing line of white sky battled the grey rainclouds into retreat, allowing the troops behind, in blue and yellow, to advance and claim the day.

Sean was waiting at the gate, where he had promised he would be. Claudia had convinced herself he wouldn't be there, so was surprised though delighted to see him, albeit there was a sullen look upon his face, rather than the smile he'd given her when he'd left the previous evening.

'Good morning,' said Claudia, brightly, 'that was quite the thunderstorm last night. I hope you didn't get caught in it on the way back to the bar.'

'I did, but it's only water. Are you ready to go?'

'All good.' She looked up. The sun was peeking down at them, warming the air. 'It's going to be a nice day, I think.'

'No storms, no rain. No rain, no rainbows.'

Claudia smiled at Sean's reply.

'I've not heard that before, is it yours?'

'Someone else said it to me, a long time ago,' said Sean, not offering further explanation. 'Come on, let's go. We've a long walk to get to Astorga. About twenty-five kilometers. Six hours, if we have a break or three.'

Claudia was unable to hide her surprise.

'You're going to walk all the way with me?'

'Well, I thought about what you said last night, about me up and leaving you twice before. I won't promise much stimulating chat, but I won't leave you, today, even if we argue about something.'

'I'll try not to annoy you.'

'You don't have to dance around me, Claudia. I'm not some sort of ogre.'

'On that note, *Shrek*, let's walk.'

'*Shrek*, the green ogre?'

Claudia smiled and stuck out her tongue.

'If the cap fits.'

'Child,' said Sean, moving ahead of her to hide his smile.

They walked the first hour in relative but easy silence, enjoying the warming sunshine and the clean, fresh air of the new day. Sean even replied to some of the pilgrims cries of '*buen camino*', surprising Claudia further. The countryside around them was pretty, but not the stunning scenery Robyn had promised. After a quick stop at a roadside campervan selling coffee and cakes, run by a lovely Dutch couple who looked like old hippies and insisted on playing guitar and singing them a rendition of the Nancy Sinatra song, *These Boots Are Made For Walking*, they climbed a zigzag pathway up a steep hill, where a new and altogether different vista lay before them.

'What an amazing view,' said Claudia.

'It is beautiful, isn't it,' agreed Sean.

They land below them fell away to a wide valley laid to a vast patchwork of rolling grass fields, corn-yellow meadows and golden sunflower fields, the Camino cutting through it like a slow-winding river of dust.

'I think this is among the most beautiful of all the countryside we've been through,' said Claudia, enjoying the feel of the sun on her face and the heady smell of the countryside, 'although every region has its wonders and its high points. Even the barren, red plains of the Meseta we've just gone through.'

'Hard to say,' said Sean, 'I haven't seen it the way I maybe should have. I should have stopped and looked around more than I've done.'

Claudia nodded in agreement. Thinking about the journey they'd made from Saint Jean and the land they'd covered.

'It's made me realise there's so much more in the world to be seen. So much more to experience than just working to live. I live such a dull and sometimes solitary existence.'

'I doubt your life it dull and solitary, Claudia. I've seen you with your friends. They all love you and love being around you. It's obvious.'

Claudia looked at him and smiled.

'You know, Sean Jameson, you can be so nice when you want to be.'

Sean gave her a pretend scowl.

'Don't tell anyone. It's taken almost four hundred miles and twenty-something days to create moody old Major Tom. I don't want anyone to think differently of me.'

'Your secret's safe,' said Claudia, wishing she could reach out and take his hand, 'but I don't think you want to be alone. Not really.'

'I don't.'

Sean suddenly thought about Linz. He missed her and still wanted to be with her, but he was becoming more confused about things than he'd been before he started the Camino. He pushed the thought away. He wanted a day without the continual torture of dark memories and guilt. Just one day of peace. Claudia seemed to sense him slipping away. She tried to ensure it didn't happen.

'Let's keep moving.'

'Good idea,' said Sean, 'I don't want you seizing up on me.'

Claudia laughed and nudged him, playfully, bumping her shoulder into his arm. It seemed to snap him back to the joy of the day.

The path dipped and meandered as they walked through the valley, surrounded by bushes and hedgerows filled with the chitter-chatter of birds. The colours of the land were a great deal more vibrant after the previous night's rain had washed away the dust from weeks of continuous sunshine. They stopped, again, to gaze over a massive field of sunflowers, stood to attention like yellow-hatted soldiers, their sun-browned faces turned skyward, looking in the direction Sean and Claudia had just come from.

'I've never seen so many sunflowers in one place,' said Claudia, standing a little ahead of Sean, 'there's millions of them, and they all look so happy. Isn't it funny how they all face the sun? All except that one. The one in the middle of that big clump in the centre. The slightly taller ones. Look! Can you see it?'

She pointed out across the field.

Sean followed her gaze and, sure enough, the tallest of the sunflowers seemed to have turned away from the sun, as if it looking for something it had lost or left behind. It wasn't as bright as the others, its petals a paler yellow and its face a lighter brown, as if the rain had failed to wash away its dust. It was bent, as if carrying an invisible weight. He stared at it for a few moments then turned and walked on, heading in the direction the lone sunflower was gazing. He spoke to Claudia as he passed her.

'Not all flowers face the sun, Claudia.'

His voice was devoid of joy, like the wilting yellow petals of the lone sunflower. She knew he was referring to something else. Something deeply personal. The invisible burden he carried with him wherever he went. She felt his sadness and it saddened her.

'Please don't say that, Sean. I don't want to think like that. Not today.'

But he was already some way ahead of her, following the winding pathway, his face, like the sunflower, turned away from the sun.

For the next hour, Claudia gave him space, walking a little way behind him, trying to enjoy the quiet solitude and the early summer countryside. Suddenly, Sean stopped and knelt down on one knee. He turned and looked at her, waiting for her to catch up. She reached him and could see he was staring at something on the pathway just ahead of him.

'What is it?' she asked, not seeing what he was staring at.

'Look. Just ahead of us. Can't you see them?'

Claudia looked down at the dusty path and finally saw them. A few paces ahead of them, an army of green caterpillars was moving, *en masse*, from one side of the pathway to the other. There seemed no obvious reason for them to be doing so. The bushes and trees on both sides looked the same. Claudia laughed and clapped her hands like a child seeing a circus tent being put up, knowing the clowns were coming.

'What are they doing.'

'I've no idea,' said Sean, looking almost as excited at seeing them as Claudia. 'Perhaps all the boy caterpillars live on one side of the path and the girl caterpillars live on the other. Maybe it's time for them to get together and make baby caterpillars?'

'How lovely,' said Claudia. 'A mass love-in.'

'Lucky them.'

'Absolutely.'

There was a slightly awkward silence as they pondered on what the other had meant.

'We'd better get on,' said Sean, clearing his throat and letting the moment drift away.

Claudia watched, bemused, as he picked a careful path through the caterpillars, avoiding treading on any of them. He was, she thought, an utter contradiction. An ex-army mountaineer, tough and strong, obviously able to handle himself, yet, here he was, tip-toeing around a line of tiny caterpillars, being careful not to hurt them.

'You're very considerate to them, Sean. Another of those caring traits you try to hide from everyone?'

'Normally I'd pick them off the path and make sure they were safe, but there's hundreds of them. Far too many to rescue. So, I'll do what I can do to...'

He stopped speaking and knelt down again, scooping something up into his hand.

'Now what?' Claudia asked.

'Look,' Sean whispered.

He turned to face her, opening his hand, palm up, the way you would feed a horse a sugar cube.

Sitting there, staring up at Claudia, was a little frog, its spotted, grass-green back in stark contrast to the off-white underside. Its bright orange eyes bulged in its head, as if it was wondering what sort of strange creature had captured it. And if it was going to be devoured.

'Sean, he's lovely.'

Claudia lowered her voice so as to not frighten the little creature. The frog, though, seemed totally nonplussed.

'Want to kiss him? He might turn into a prince.'

'I wish,' said Claudia, purposefully avoiding looking into Sean's eyes.

After a few moments admiring the little creature, Sean stepped off the path and set the frog down in the long grass. He returned to the path and walked on, still taking care to avoid the caterpillars.

'Why the love of caterpillars?' Claudia asked, following Sean's lead and stepping around and between them.

'Butterflies and birdsong,' said Sean. 'I used to tell my daughter that butterflies were fairies in disguise, and that they could turn themselves into butterflies to allow them to sing with the birds, in the dawn chorus. Birds being afraid of people, even little people, it was the only way the fairies could join them without scaring them away. The frogs, too, were always part of the early morning choir.'

'Oh, Sean, what a delightful story. She must have loved it. What age is she now?'

Sean stopped dead in his tracks. He made to speak, but the words would not come. The pain on his face and grief in his eyes was shocking for Claudia to see. He shook his head and looked away, then walked on ahead of her.

Claudia was confused, for a moment, before realising what had happened. *Oh my God, he's lost his daughter too.* She immediately thought of Hannah, and of Betsy, the daughter she had lost. She had carried the pain of that loss all her life. A pain, she remembered Hannah telling her, that never went away. The same pain was evident in Sean's eyes. *What have I said.* She let him walk ahead of her, giving him, and her, time to recover.

Less than fifteen minutes later, Sean stopped and let her catch up with him at a bubbling water-fountain, close to some ruined buildings.

'Sean, I'm so sorry.'

'It's fine, Claudia. Just leave it. You weren't to know. But I don't want to talk about it.'

They walked on in silence, Claudia feeling awful but having no idea how to reset. They'd gotten closer over the past few hours. She didn't want to lose that. She tried to find a way back.

'So, your country, Scotland, is green and it rains a lot.'

'Almost every day. Except when it snows.'

Sean gave her a smile. Claudia was relieved he'd replied.

'Not like Spain. Here, it rains only on the plain, or so the saying goes.'

'Almost, but not quite,' said Sean, correcting her. 'The rain in Spain falls mainly on the plain is the correct saying. But it actually falls mainly in the mountains.'

'Then why do the Spanish have that saying if it's not true?'

Sean gave a laugh.

'It's not a Spanish saying, actually. It's English.'

'English! Claudia said, surprised. 'Well that makes no sense.'

'It depends in what context you try to understand it, to be fair. The sentence itself, the rain in Spain stays mainly in the plain, was conceived because some people in England were irritated by other people in England speaking with a Cockney accent.'

Claudia screwed up her face and raised an eyebrow.

'What's a Cockney?'

Sean thought about it for a moment before explaining.

'It's a neighbourhood in London where they speak with a particular accent which can be difficult to understand. But, if you say the rain in Spain sentence, repeatedly, every day, your accent will go away, apparently. They tried it on us Scots, too, for hundreds of years, but the English still couldn't understand us. They still can't, on the whole, for that matter.'

'Thanks for that,' said Claudia, 'although I'm not sure I'm any the wiser.'

'So, how come you're on the Camino?' Sean asked, the mood between them discernibly lighter.

'My friend, Hannah, the one I told you about, who died of cancer. I'm carrying her ashes with me.'

'What are the chances,' said Sean, shaking his head.

'What do you mean?'

'Nothing. Only that it's a bit like that movie, *The Way*.'

Claudia's face lit up. It was one of the movies she'd watched after deciding she was actually going to walk the Camino, back in Verona. She'd streamed it on her phone, on the plane, on her way to Spain.

'The one with Martin Sheen, where he carries his . . .'

'Tell me more about this lighthouse of yours,' said Sean, not letting her finish. 'The one your friend, Hannah, left you.'

Claudia told him all about how she'd come to the lighthouse tower, the big house and the Beach Shack, the journey she and Hannah had made, as well as what she had decided to do with the place while she'd been walking the Camino.

'I'm going to turn the tower into an art gallery and cafe, using the ground floor and basement, as well as the first floor, for the artworks. I'll keep the glass room, at the top, for myself. It was Hannah's studio. She called it her

Glass Menagerie. She'd love to know it was still being used. The views over the ocean are breathtaking, and it's so utterly peaceful.'

'It sounds amazing, Claudia. A great place to paint, I'm sure.'

'I've not painted there, yet. But I will. I've gotten my muse back. Especially after the other night in Leon.'

'What happened in Leon?'

Despite knowing Sean knew full well what had happened, Claudia said something else, unsure how to say what she actually wanted to.

'The flamenco dancers. One especially. She was so colourful and alive. I just got the urge to try to capture her movement and vitality on canvas.'

'I'd like to see that, when it's done.'

'You'll have to visit me then, at the lighthouse, won't you?'

Claudia said it before she could stop herself. Sean looked at her, wondering if she'd meant to say what she'd said. She looked a little flustered. He guessed she had.

'What about your husband? Will he live there too?' Aware he'd asked such a personal question, he apologised. 'I'm sorry, that's none of my business.'

Claudia, if she cared, didn't show it.

'Paul. My husband's name is Paul.' It felt odd to her, saying his name, given how she was feeling about Sean. 'He's a writer. Quite successful, as it happens. We've been married for sixteen years.'

'You don't have to tell me anymore, Claudia.'

'I want to, Sean. I need to talk. Do you mind?

'Not if you don't.'

'Fine, then you walk, I'll talk.'

As they walked, Claudia spoke of Paul and of their lives together. How they'd made the journey from poor students in one bedroom to rich strangers in six. She talked about her gallery and Paul's books, her desire for a child and the failed fertility treatments. She told him, too, of the growing distance between them and his desire to move to Los Angeles to become a full-time scriptwriter. Sean understood that desire. It had been the same calling for him to join the army.

'I can't say I blame him for wanting to follow his dream. It's clearly important to him.'

'I *don't* blame him, Sean, but he's going ahead with or without me. He was supposed to be here, with me, but didn't come. He doesn't seem to care about what I want, anymore, only what he wants.'

'And what *do* you want, Claudia? What do you need in your life?'

'What do I *need*?'

Claudia looked at Sean, wondering why he'd said it that way. Sean noticed and wondered what he'd said.

'What?

'Hannah asked me that very same thing, in a letter to me, just after she'd died. It's why I'm here at all. She told me to go and find what I needed most.'

'Which is?'

'More than anything else, I want a child. But Paul doesn't. Not really. He says he does, but I know he's only saying it because he thinks it's what I want to hear. He's not interested in continuing the fertility treatments.'

Hearing the sadness in her voice, Sean put his arms around her and gave her a supportive hug.

'Don't upset yourself. It's going to be okay.'

Claudia became very aware of him. She could smell the warm, musky scent of him and hear his heart beating in his chest. She felt herself melt into him, more than just physically. Sean, too, became aware of the closeness of her. He found he wanted nothing more than to protect her and make her feel safe. Claudia, despite feeling she should pull away from him, pressed herself closer to him and continued talking.

'Hannah told me that having a child was the most amazing gift we could ever be given. She held her baby for an hour before she died. Can you imagine that, Sean? She told me it was the most important hour of her life. I asked her if it had all been worth it; a lifetime of painful memory for a fleeting moment with her daughter. She told me it was. I think it must be the most wonderful feeling in the world to hold your own child and to look into its face. To feel such unconditional love.'

Suddenly, Claudia felt Sean's body convulse against her and heard the agony in his voice as he spoke.

'It is.'

She looked up and felt his tears on her face. Her own melancholy instantly forgotten, she stepped back, free of his embrace, taking his hands in hers. Seeing his pain was unbearable.

'What is it, Sean?'

'I have . . .' He stopped and took a deep breath. 'I *had* a daughter. Her name was Alice. She was seven years old and the most beautiful little girl in the world. And a son. Toby. He was thirteen. They died, last year, with their mother, in a car crash. It was my fault. I'm carrying their ashes with me.'

Claudia was shocked but finally understood something Sean had said earlier.

'So that's what you meant when you said *what were the chances*.'

Sean nodded.

'I couldn't talk about it. I've not really talked to anyone about it. I don't know how to.'

'Do you want to talk about them now, Sean? You've listened to me. Let me be here for you. I won't say anything. I'll just listen.'

Sean was fighting to stay in control. Speaking his children's names threatened to bring on a panic attack. He couldn't let himself fall apart, but part of him needed to say the words he carried like stones in his shoes.

He took a breath and began to talk.

'It was Alice's seventh birthday, last year, on the twenty-seventh of May.'

Claudia realised the significance of the date. It was the same day she had arrived in Saint Jean, about to start the Camino, one year on. The day she had first seen Sean, leaning against the wall.

'Oh, Sean. No wonder you reacted to me the way you did.'

'She loved being seven, Claudia, and feeling all grown up.' Sean allowed a sad smile onto his face at the memory of the day. 'We were on the west coast of Scotland, on holiday, in a tiny village called Applecross. The sea was so blue that morning . . .'

He told Claudia everything. How the accident had happened, his guilt at having survived, his trial for manslaughter, and the resulting treatment he received on the Isle of Skye. He revealed his shame at having had an affair with Judith, of seeing Linz on Ben Nevis, and of how she had led him to her journal. He spoke candidly of his abuse at the hands of his father and losing his faith in God. He spoke, too, of the night he had brought the prostitute, Jann Livingston, to Merrick.

Claudia listened, shocked at times, angry that he'd suffered abuse at the hands of his father, frightened for him when he spoke of his desire to join his family, more so when he'd described his recent climb on Mount Everest.

'You could have died there.'

'I should have.'

Claudia took his hands in hers and looked up at him, desperate to reach him.

'Please don't say that, Sean. I can't bear to hear you say that.'

'I wanted to, Claudia. I really did.'

'Tell me you don't still want that?'

'I . . . I'm not sure anymore. I owe it to them. To Linz.'

Claudia was still trying to deal with what he'd told her about trying to die. That he was still unsure was more than concerning.

'She wouldn't want you to die, Sean. Not if she truly loved you.'

Sean shook his head and looked down, clearly filled with guilt. Claudia's heart ached for him. He was in so much pain. Haunted by a brutal past and carrying the blame for the loss of his family.

'I can't betray her again. I can't do that to her.'

Something became much clearer for Claudia.

'Sean, is that why you pulled away from me when I kissed your fingertips, in Leon? Did you feel you were betraying Linz then? And before, in Pamplona, did something happen there, too?

Sean nodded.

'The waitress, at the bar in the square. She was flirting with me. I couldn't let her. I'd already let Linz down so badly with . . .' The image of Jann Livingston, came into his mind. 'I thought . . .'

'You thought you were being unfaithful to Linz. *That's* why you were looking around you when you were with me in the square. In case Linz had seen you with the waitress.'

'I love her, Claudia. I miss her every moment of every day. I failed her when she needed me most and betrayed her with Judith. I live with the shame of that, every single day. But I can't keep carrying it. I can't keep living with it.'

'I understand, Sean. I get it.'

Sean took a deep breath and seemed to pull himself out of the hole he had allowed himself to fall into. A few minutes later he seemed able to speak again.

'I'm sorry. I don't know why that all just seemed to come out. I shouldn't have burdened you with my problems.'

Claudia shook her head.

'Never apologise for being honest about how you feel, Sean. About telling the truth. It's the most important thing in the world to do. And as for burdening me, you didn't. You shared. There's a difference. Perhaps you just needed a friend to talk to and I happened to be there. Maybe the Universe brought us together to help us both get through the tough times we seem to be facing.'

'I guess so. I'm glad you're here, Claudia. But what about you? Are you okay?'

'Christ, my problems are nothing compared to yours, Merrick. I'm just ever so slightly nuts. You're a complete fruit cake.'

She laughed, lightening the mood for them both.

'Well, I guess we both know each other's problems now,' said Sean, laughing with her, and with the laugh feeling some small part of the weight he had been carrying from Saint Jean begin to lift.

'I think, Sean, we've both made a friend to share those problems with. Now why don't we just walk this damned Camino and see if we both don't get some sort of answers when we finish?'

Sean felt as if something had changed inside him. He felt almost at peace, a feeling he had given up as lost to him.

'Good idea. I don't know what the hell happened to me there, Claudia, but I blame you completely. Now what say we get on to wherever the hell we're meant to be getting on to.'

'I accept full responsibility,' said Claudia. 'I started it, after all, breaking down on you like that. And we're headed to the town of Astorga. It's meant to have an amazing Templar Knights castle.'

'It's *Knights Templar*,' actually, said Sean, correcting her.'

'Whatever. Anyway, it's only a few more hours walking if we don't lollygag.'

Sean looked at her, incredulously.

'Lollygag? What the hell sort of weird word is that?'

'It means to take our time,' Claudia explained, 'lollygagging along.'

'Honestly, you Americans and your crazy treatment of our beautiful English language.'

'It's American English.'

Sean rolled his eyes to the heavens.

'Don't even get me started on that one. Let's just crack on.'

He then had to proceed to explain the saying to a confused Claudia.

From Astorga, for the next five days, they walked together, the routine always the same. Although Sean stayed in a different hotel or private albergue, he would meet Claudia, Babette and Robyn the following morning. The days were long and hot, lived under golden suns and clear blue skies. They ambled through the lush countryside and farmlands of Galicia, traversing the hilly landscapes of the final region of the Camino, the air scented with meadow wildflowers and the heady aroma of wild garlic, growing at the sides of the path, heavy with glossy white pearls.

They reached Sarria on a Sunday evening, to the sound of three sets of church bells enticing the different factions of penitents to prayer. Sean, as tired as any of them, decided to stay in the same hotel. Claudia, despite being ribbed by Robyn and Babette, who were convinced that she and Sean were already lovers, assured them they would not be sharing a room.

'We're just friends. Trust me on that, Robyn,' said Claudia, as they sipped a glass of cold white wine at dinner, that night. 'There can't be anything between us. I'm married. Besides, Sean has his own issues to deal with.'

'What kind of issues?'

'I can't say, Robyn, I simply can't. But they're difficult ones for anyone to deal with. I wish I could help him. He might have joined us, but he still won't let anybody in. Not fully.'

'What the hell happened on the way into Astorga, Claudia? Something did, so don't tell me it didn't. You two made some sort of deeper connection. And if it's not sex, what the hell is it?'

'Don't keep asking,' said Claudia, becoming annoyed at Robyn's questions. 'It's for Sean to tell you, although he won't. All I *will* say is that he's suffered a terrible loss and is still in a great deal of pain. If I were you, I'd not push him on it.'

'Okay, I won't.'

'Good.'

'Just one last thing.'

'Honestly, Robyn, you're infuriating.'

'Tell me you're not in love with him?'

'I'm not in love with him,' replied Claudia, unconvincingly, 'I care for him, that's all.'

Robyn flicked her eyes skyward then looked at Claudia with an incredulous look on her face.

'Well maybe you should tell him how much you are *in care* with him and see what happens. In another five days we'll be in Santiago. You won't have the chance to tell him after that. Not once he's gone.'

Claudia hadn't thought of the day she and Sean might say goodbye to one another. Thinking about it, now, she felt a profound sadness come over her.

'Okay. I hear you. Perhaps I will. Not that there's anything to really tell. Now drop it, he's coming back to the table.'

From Sarria, the final push to Santiago de Compostela began. They spent a night in the medieval town of Portomarin, one of the jewels of the Camino Frances, a picturesque village that overlooked the river Miro from the top of a long, Roman-style staircase. They drank cold lemon beer and ate spicy beef stew laced with tomato and *morcilla*. Claudia decided to forget what Sean had told her about how it was made. It tasted far too delicious.

After a night in Palace do Rei, where they drank wine and ate plates of chargrilled *pulpo*, the delicious octopus dish the region was famed for, they headed west, passing through Casanova and Leboreiro, stopping for lunch in the village of Melide, where they ate an incredible array of *tapas* and struggled to get back to their feet for the afternoon hike to Aruza, their destination for the night. The Camino followed a winding, forested track, marked, every kilometer, with concrete distance markers showing the scallop shell of St James and the distance to Santiago.

Late in the afternoon, Sean and Claudia held back, allowing Babette and Robyn to get ahead of them. They were chatting away about nothing in particular when Claudia stopped walking, her attention taken by one of the markers telling them they were forty-five kilometers from Santiago.

'What is it?' Sean asked.

'Right,' said Claudia, looking around her, 'Robyn told me this was the one we needed to find. Now we just need to find the signpost.'

'What signpost?

Claudia ignored the question and continued searching.

'There! That must be it.'

She pointed to a track leading off the Camino, partially hidden from view by the surrounding long grass, and headed over to inspect it more closely.

'That must be what?' Sean asked, following her.

Set back along the track was an old, wooden signpost with the word, "*Molino*", carved into its single direction arrow. The arrow pointed deeper into the forest.

'It's where an old flour mill used to be, apparently,' explained Claudia. 'There's meant to be some sort of enchanted glade.'

'Enchanted glade? What are you, six?'

Claudia stuck out her tongue and walked off the main pathway and into the trees.

'Come on, Sean, where's your sense of adventure. Let's see if it actually exists. What's the worst that can happen?'

Sean shrugged, knowing the decision had already been made.

The track was narrow and the trees set back from it, initially, but the deeper Sean and Claudia got, the more they huddled together. The forest became gloomy, shaded from the daylight by thick, leafy branches that merged above them into an umbrella of green and reached for them like woodland giants.

'It's getting spooky in here,' said Claudia, glad Sean was behind her, 'but Robyn insists there's a grassy glade filled with snowflowers.'

'What the hell are snowflowers?'

Claudia shrugged her shoulders.

'No clue. Maybe she made it up. But when we find the fairy glade, we'll find the snowflowers.'

'Fairy glade and snowflowers!' Sean said, sounding entirely sceptical. 'Sounds like more like a fairy story.'

'Her words, Sean, not mine. Come on, keep going. It's an adventure.'

They pressed on through a forest, a procession of birds flitting in and out of the foliage around them. Claudia watched, in wonder, a battalion of red squirrels leaping effortlessly through the branches, playing some kind *of catch-me-if-you-can* game. Just as she was about to admit defeat and suggest they turn back, the trees stepped back, revealing what they'd been searching for.

'Look, Sean, it's so beautiful. What a little oasis.'

In front of them was a wide, circular glade carpeted in lush grass and blanketed in delicate white daisies, ringed by a canopy of tall trees and lit by bright sunlight. The branches, overhead, opened to a form a circle of clear blue sky, below which ran a stream with gently sloping sandy banks, the sound of water adding to the magical ambience. The trees were covered in large, white flowers.

'And there's your snowflowers,' said Sean. 'Looks like I owe Robyn an apology.'

'I'm sure she'll let you off.'

As they looked up, a sudden gust rustled the treetops and thousands of flower petals floated down around them, landing on their upturned faces like warm snowflakes and transforming the glade into an enchanted, wintery woodland. It looked, to Claudia, like something out of a Walt Disney movie. She held out her hands to catch the falling petals, as did Sean.

'They're like big dandelion puffs,' said Sean 'You know? When the yellow dandelion flowers turn into puffy white balls. The ones you can pick and blow, sending the fluffy bits off on the breeze.'

'They are,' said Claudia, excitedly. 'I used to love doing that when I was a kid. We called them fairy parachutes, because of the bits that floated off when you blew them. Fairies would hang onto the stalks and float off to wherever they wanted the wind to take them. Fanciful, I guess, but we were just kids.'

'They're actually called *pappi*, 'the dandelion seeds.'

'Hark at you the expert gardener,' said Claudia, and began to pirouette across the grass, arms outstretched, twirling like a ballerina in an on-stage snowstorm. 'No matter what they're called, they bring back special memories.'

She looked happy in those memories, thought Sean, but then some people did have childhoods worth remembering.

From out of nowhere, he pictured himself standing in the Remembrance Garden at Cramond Kirk, the day he'd seen Linz, when the apple blossoms had fallen on him in almost the same way the snowflowers were doing now. Almost as if it had been a premonition of today.

Claudia stopped spinning and looked over at him, his head and shoulders were covered in the white flower petals. He looked like a handsome mountaineer caught in a snowstorm. Something shifted in her and she moved towards him, slowly, not wanting to scare him.

'Look,' she whispered, 'there's one on your nose.'

Without thinking, she reached up and picked off the petal, lifted it to her lips, and blew, sending it floating into the air between them. She saw the same uncertainty she was feeling in his eyes.

'Did you make a wish?' Sean asked.

His voice was husky and he seemed to be breathing slightly heavily.

Claudia struggled to answer him, such was the tension in the air between them. She felt a warm tingle run through her body.

'Yes, Sean. I did.'

She moved closer to him, the small space between them disappearing as their souls reached out to touch.

Sean stood still, lost in the emotional connection between them. He could feel it and knew Claudia did too. Her eyes were doe-like, the pupils dilated so that they were more black than green. He felt her breath, gentle on his face, and her fingertips as she laid them on his arms. Her touch was like hot wax dripped on his skin. Time seemed to slow, and then stop. He heard himself moan, as if something buried deep inside him had come awake.

Claudia lifted her face and parted her lips, running her tongue across them to moisten them. Her eyes narrowed, becoming cat like.

'Sean.'

Her voice was more an emotion than a sound.

Sean touched her, drawing his fingers lightly across her arms, his hands mirroring her touch on him, as if a prelude to a dance. Her skin was soft and warm. Understanding he was giving her permission, Claudia pressed herself against him, sliding her arms around his waist, her desire for him overwhelming. The butterflies in her stomach opened their wings and prepared to take flight.

'Claudia.'

The simple sound of her name on Sean's lips touched her in a way she could not have prepared for. She was lost in him and suddenly afraid of where this would lead her. But it was too late for such concerns.

'Kiss me, Sean.'

She opened her mouth, lips parting more, showing him she wanted him. Their lips touched, the slightest of *almost* touches. And it seemed the stars had aligned.

'I can't do this.'

Without warning, Sean stepped back, breaking free of the embrace. Claudia reached for him, unsure of what was happening. Still needing him.

'Sean?'

'I'm sorry, Claudia. I'm sorry'

He buried his face in his hands then looked back at her, clearly distraught. He had the same frightened look on his face as he'd had when she'd seen him in Pamplona, outside the Iruna bar. Her confusion turned to concern.

'It's okay, Sean. I'm sorry. It's not your fault.' She remembered her conversation with Robyn, only a few days ago, about telling him how she felt about him. She realised she had to do it now. 'Look, I'm not sure if you want to hear this, but . . .'

'Claudia, don't . . .'

'Don't tell me not to, Sean. We've been brought together from the first moment we met. You know that. Time and again we're dragged towards each other. Time and again we get pulled apart. It's like the Universe is playing some sort of game, with us as her pawns. I don't know why this is happening, but something is. I know you feel it too.'

'I do, Claudia, but . . .'

Claudia pushed on, needing to say what she'd wanted to say for weeks.

'I care about you, Sean, deeply. It's something I can't explain or even give a name to, but it's real, and I can't fight it anymore. And if we can give something of ourselves to each other, no matter how little, then perhaps that will be enough. I think I want you forever, but I know I need you for now. Do you understand what I'm saying? Am I making sense?'

'Yes, you are,' said Sean, looking like a deer caught in the headlights of an oncoming car, 'but I can't give you anything, Claudia, not even a little piece of me. It's not that I don't feel something for you, I do. More than I thought I'd ever feel for anyone again. But I can't. Don't ask me to explain. I just can't.'

'But you felt it, Sean. Just now. What there is between us.'

'I'm not sure what I felt, Claudia.'

His answer angered her and her frustration morphed into words.

'Not sure, Sean? Is that really what you're telling me? Lie to me, if that's what you need to do to get through this, whatever *this* is, but stop lying to yourself. It was a kiss, that's all. Or would have been if you'd just relaxed and let it happen. For the love of Christ, look around you. Do you see where we are? Could it *be* any more romantic?

'No,' said Sean, hesitantly, 'I suppose not.'

'So then what harm would a bloody kiss have done? We might both have enjoyed it. I know I would have. It might be what we both need in our lives right now. Instead, you took what could have been a beautiful moment and destroyed it'

'I know, Claudia, trust me, I do. But I couldn't let her down again.'

'Let *who* down?'

'Linz!'

Sean looked around him, as if the very mention of her name would somehow see her appear.

'Linz!' Claudia shook her head in disbelief. 'Seriously, Sean, I doubt she would have minded us having a bloody kiss. She turned and called out into the open glade. 'Would you, Linz?'

'Linz's name echoed back at them. Sean looked even more anguished than before.

'Don't say her name.'

'Excuse me?'

'Just . . . don't say her name.'

Claudia shook her head, unable to fathom what she had to do to get through to him.

'Seriously, Sean, you're worse than I thought. It was only going to be a kiss. We didn't have to fuck in the grass, although it might have been nice if we had.'

Sean backed off a pace as Claudia's anger manifested.

Claudia knew her anger was threatening to spill over. She didn't want it to reach a point where return would be impossible. She took a deep breath and tried to control her emotions. Sean hadn't really done anything other than be utterly insensitive. Sure, he'd maybe led her on a bit, but she'd pushed it more. She knew he was still in love with his dead wife. What had she expected?

'I'm sorry, Claudia, I don't know what else to say.'

Seeing the look on his face and recognising the shame he seemed to feel at what had happened, or *almost* happened, her anger evaporated. This wasn't how she'd wanted this to go. Not that she'd planned or expected it to happen at all. She tried to take them back to the place they'd been in a few minutes earlier.

'Look, let's just forget it. It's still a beautiful spot to chill out in. What say we sit down and dip our feet in the stream. We're friends. Sometimes friends mess up.'

'I don't think that's a good idea, Claudia. I think I need to go.'

'There's no need to be so dramatic, Sean. Come and sit down. We can talk about something lighter, like balloons.'

She threw him a reassuring smile, but Sean's face remained blank and his eyes were distant.

'No, I think it's best I go. I'm sorry.'

He turned and walked away, heading back the way they'd come.

'Go then,' Claudia shouted after him, 'but that's the last time you ever walk away from me, Sean bloody Jameson. The very last time. Don't come near me again.'

Her heart broke as she said the words. She didn't want it to end this way. She didn't want it to end at all. She fought the urge to go after him and let him go, waiting until he was out of sight before she sank to her knees and wept on the grass, alone among the daisies and snowflowers.

62

They saw each other again, by gates of the chapel of Santa Iruna, on the penultimate day of their journey. Robyn had wanted to visit the chapel to see the unique collection of religious statues housed there. She, Claudia and Babette were talking to two of the chapel nuns, who had set up a table by the gates and were stamping the passing pilgrims passports, when Sean walked by. Claudia looked up and their eyes met, briefly, before he walked on. She almost called after him. It was a monumental effort not to. She watched him go then turned back to the table to see Robyn and Babette looking at her.

'What?' Claudia asked, forcing a smile onto her face and wiping away a tear that had come despite her trying to stop it.

'Nothing,' they said, then busied themselves doing nothing.

'Good,' said Claudia, feeling anything but.

'I miss him, too,' said Babette. 'I was getting kind of used to him being around.'

'And you?'

Claudia looked at Robyn, expecting the same response.

'I always thought he was a wanker.'

All three of them burst out laughing.

Robyn, suddenly remembering where she was, put her hand to her mouth and looked down at the nuns. One of them was looking up at her with a look of disapproval on her face, leaving Robyn red-faced and flustered, much to the amusement of Babette and Claudia, who were struggling to stifle their laughter.

'I don't know what that word means, my child, but I will assume it is not a kindly way to speak of another of God's children. However, you are a pilgrim, as well as a sinner, so I must forgive you.'

Robyn hung her head, feeling suitably ashamed. The nun smiled and went back to stamping the passports of a group of excited young teenagers, all carrying French flags fixed to their packs, switching to perfect French as they chatted to her.

'Right, well that's you marked for Hell,' said Claudia, 'and it serves you right. Come on, let's get moving, it's our second last day and I'm going to enjoy every minute of it. I'm not going to think about anything that upsets me. Especially not him.'

'Good idea,' said Babette, smiling mischievously, 'but, just so I know, for how long are you planning not to think about him?'

Bugger off,' said Claudia, drawing another disapproving glance from the Sister, then headed off along the pathway Sean had just been on, thinking about him almost immediately. Babette and Robyn followed, giving her distance and time to reset.

After a quiet evening in the village of Opino, they walked out onto the final section of the Camino, meandering along country roads that were busy but not crowded. They stopped to wash their feet in the final river they would cross before reaching Santiago, a tradition that went back over a thousand years.

'I can't believe we'll be there, today,' said Robyn, drying her feet with her travel towel and pulling on her socks. 'I'm looking forward to getting into Santiago and completing what we set out to do. But I'm a bit sad that it's all going to be over.'

'Me too,' replied Claudia. 'I can't believe we've walked across northern Spain. There were times I thought we weren't going to make it.'

'I know what you mean,' Babette added, 'my hangover after Portomarin was hellish. I thought I was going to die.'

They laughed at, and with her.

'We've met so many nice people along the way,' said Claudia, 'and seen some wonderful sights.'

'Like Mark, falling on his ass in Pamplona,' said Robyn.

'And Major Tom surprising Claudia in Leon.'

'Yes, very funny, Babette,' said Claudia. 'I thought I was going to die of embarrassment when he strolled out beside you. I'm sure he heard me call him a *Klootzak*.'

Robyn snorted.

'You should have been more embarrassed about flirting with that young Irish guy. It was so see through, what you were up to. What was his name again?'

'Brendan. Yes, I was. I still am.'

Claudia blushed at the memory. Sean had seen it, too. She remembered him telling her as much on the Bridge of the Three Hundred Jousts.

'I wonder how he is?' Robyn asked.

'Brendan?'

Robyn shook her head at Claudia.

'No! I'm talking about Sean! I hope he's happy. He became part of our little Camino family. It's not the same now the family's broken up.'

'I hope he's happy,' said Claudia, 'with all my heart.'

She pictured Sean's face and tried not to be sad, but it was too late. She missed him. She hadn't thought she would, not as much, but she did. She stood up, needing to escape his shadow. Babette and Robyn continued to let her walk ahead of them, but they were all thinking about the same person.

A procession of tall eucalyptus trees lining both sides of the pathway seemed to welcome them home as they made their way onto Monte del Gozo, the "Mount of Joy", and up to its high point, giving them their first view of Santiago and the twin towers of the cathedral. The sight spurred them on and they descended quickly, entering the city from the east, passing through ever-narrowing streets filled with ancient sandstone buildings that looked down on them like a guard of Spanish knights. The distant sound of Galician bagpipes greeted them as they neared the centre of the old town, passing the Palacio de Gelmírez.

'What an incredible building' said Claudia, gazing up at the golden sandstone structure.

'It's named after Santiago's first Archbishop,' said Robyn, her nose still stuck in her guide book. 'He was responsible for the construction of the cathedral, sometime in the late twelfth century. According to this, it's considered one of the most outstanding examples of Romanesque architecture in all of Spain.'

'Put the bloody book away,' said Babette, 'and let's just enjoy the walk in without the history lessons.'

'You're right,' said Robyn, smiling at her friend, 'for once.'

Just ahead of them, down a final set of steps, was the single central arch of the Arco de Palacio, the tunnel gate that led out onto Obradoiro Square, where their Camino would finally come to an end. The haunting sound of the pipes created the perfect ambiance for their one hundred final steps, as they passed through the tunnel and out into the sunlit square.

The massive plaza that greeted them was formed from granite flagstones and bordered on all sides by incredible architecture. On their right, stood the magnificent *Palace de Rajoy*, the current town hall and seat of the Galician Parliament, to their left, the Cathedral of Santiago de Compostela, although from the acute angle they had entered the square, they could not yet properly see it.

It was mid-afternoon and there were hundreds of pilgrims gathered, hugging and kissing each other, crying and laughing at the same time, experiencing deep and unexpected emotions they could not vocalise at that precise moment.

'Let's walk out with each other,' said Babette, already looking a little teary. 'We should see it, together, for the first time.'

Robyn and Claudia nodded, not trusting their voices. They headed into the centre of the square, holding hands, avoiding looking over to the cathedral, then, as one, turned and looked up.

Claudia was immediately overwhelmed and could do little to hold back her tears. Not that any of them could. The sun was shining directly onto the face of the cathedral, as if it were being lit up by the light of God. It was one of the most amazing sights she had ever seen.

'It's . . . beautiful.'

It was a poor description, she knew, but she was totally overwhelmed by how she was feeling.

'My God,' said Robyn, 'it's so much more than I had hoped it would be.'

She dabbed her eyes with a tissue and handed one each to Claudia and Babette.

'We made it,' whispered Babette. 'We've walked five hundred miles in thirty-seven days. A million steps! I don't know why, but I feel sad. Like I don't want it to end. So many times, when we were headed here, I wanted it to be over. But now that it is, I want to be back at the start.'

Claudia, too, felt emotional, staring at the prize they had finally won.

'I think a lot of people here will feel the same, Babette. I know I do. It really has changed my life and how I think of it.'

They stood in silence for the next few minutes, gazing up at the ancient, holy building, reflecting on the journey they had made together.

Basking in their glory, the cathedral rose above them, framing the entire square on the eastern side. It's three tall towers were surrounded by an array of intricate carvings, the dominant images and representations of Christian faith. Claudia looked up at the central tower and smiled at the statue of St James. He was dressed as a pilgrim and seemed to be looking directly at them, understanding the journey and the journey's end.

You started all this. Thank you.

She followed the detailed façade down, revelling at the images of angels and demons, picking out every detail of the ancient carvings. The grand staircase into the cathedral, a diamond shaped, Renaissance-style entryway, the "Portico da Gloria", caught her eye. It formed the visual summation of Christian faith and was encrusted with carved, sacred images; Christ, sitting in majesty, surrounded by angels, his apostles and Old Testament prophets in attendance, with Heaven, Purgatory and Hell, their respective angels and demons making up the background.

Claudia was lost in the sheer beauty of the carvings when her attention was broken by hearing their names being called. She turned and saw Mark, accompanied by Bonnie and Clyde, heading towards them. Everyone hugged and kissed one another, all talking at once, recounting their tales of the past few weeks and the final walk into Santiago.

'Good to see you, Boston,' said Mark, giving Claudia a bearhug that left her laughing.

'And you, *Texas*. I take it you got here yesterday?'

'Day before, actually. You know me. It's the end of the journey that matters. Although, now I'm here, I think perhaps it's the other way around.'

'I know exactly what you mean, Mark. It's wonderful to be here, but bittersweet.

'Have you heard from Wendy?

'I spoke to her last night,' said Claudia. 'She's only a day or so behind. Her feet still aren't perfect, but they're good enough to make it. We'll see her soon enough. Her boyfriend and father are flying in to meet her. They want to say thanks to Sean, too, for what he did for her.'

'Where is he?' Mark asked, looking around as if expecting to see him. 'I thought you two were getting pretty darned tight.'

He gave Claudia a knowing smile.

Claudia shook her head.

'We were only ever just friends. He walked on ahead of us. He'll probably have been and gone by now.'

As she said it, a sense of loss and melancholy washed over her. She wished she'd been able to walk in with him.

'Hey! Claudia! Mark!'

They turned to see two familiar faces heading towards them.

'Romano! Helena! How lovely to see you,' said Claudia. How's the feet, Helena? We were just talking about Wendy's problems.'

'Fine, just fine. Have you had a lie down yet?' Helena asked, beginning the round of hugs.

'No,' said Claudia, 'kissing Romano on both cheeks. We've just arrived.'

Helena took hold of Claudia's hand and began to drag her away.

'I didn't mean it like that. Come on, all of you.'

'Trust her,' said Romano, ushering Babette and Robyn after them, 'it's seriously cool.'

Helena led them all back a few paces from the centre of the square, where a few other pilgrims were lying on their backs, on the warm flagstones, gazing up at the cathedral.

'Lie down,' Romano instructed, leading the way by lying down himself, 'and look up at the cathedral. Focus on the very top of the middle tower.'

Everyone followed his lead.

'That's so cool,' said Babette.

'Freaky,' agreed Claudia.

'I feel like I'm on acid,' Mark drawled.

'Well, you were around in the sixties,' said Robyn.

'You have a point, little lady,' replied Mark, and laughed along with everyone else.

'It's the height of the cathedral that does it,' explained Romano, 'and the towers on either side of the centre one. When you look right at it, like this, it's as if the whole thing's falling down on you.'

They lay in the sunshine, in silence, looking up and enjoying the strange sensation.

'Hello. Have you all expired? Or is this some sort of mass fainting at finally getting here?'

'Sean!' Mark jumped up and pumped Sean's hand, clapping him on the shoulder with his free hand. 'It's good to see you, boy.'

Babette scrambled up and threw her arms around his neck, smothering his cheeks in kisses.

'We thought we'd never see you again.'

Sean, Claudia noticed, didn't pull away from her. *Well that's progress, I guess. Maybe the ghost of Linz allows him to do that!* She immediately felt bad for having had such a petty thought. *Be nice. At least he said hello. He could have just as easily walked past.*

After hugging everyone else, Sean turned to her. He hesitated, looking unsure.

'Don't I get one?' Claudia asked, opening her arms. She was aware that everyone was staring at them.

'Of course,' said Sean, and moved towards her. 'Well done, Claudia. It's an amazing achievement.'

They hugged each other with only a little awkwardness. Everyone started chatting again, although Claudia noticed they had all moved a pace or two away from her and Sean. Robyn gave her a wry smile, which she ignored. She decided to play things cool, despite wanting to put her arms around him and tell him she was sorry for what had happened at the fairy glade.

'Have you been here long?'

'Just a few hours,' said Sean. 'It was pretty amazing, coming in to this.'

'And how do you feel, now it's over?'

'I'm really not sure, Claudia. Like I don't know how to feel, if that makes any sense?'

Claudia had the distinct impression he wanted to say something else. She waited, willing him to speak, but the moment passed. She broke momentary silence.

'Are you staying here, tonight, in Santiago?'

'Yes, but I'm leaving early in the morning.'

'Back to Scotland, I suppose?'

'No! I'm on a flight to Ibiza. Staying on a friend's boat while he's away in Hong Kong. I'm going to rest up for a while before I move on.'

'Sounds like fun.'

'It won't be,' said Sean.

Claudia realised they were making small talk. It made her sad they had come to that. She didn't know how to change it. Sean, although she was sure he felt the same way, didn't either.

'So, where are you staying tonight, Mr Jameson? Not in a shared albergue dorm, I take it?'

Sean turned and looked at a building behind them, on the opposite side of the square to the cathedral.

'I'm in the hotel.'.

'That's a *hotel*?' Claudia asked, surprised. It doesn't look like one. It's very grand, isn't it? I thought it was some sort of museum.'

'It's called the *Hostal de Los Reyes Catolicos*,' said Sean, in his best Spanish pronunciation. 'It's meant to be one of the most beautiful hotels in Europe. It *is* a bit fancy, I suppose. But I've just walked five hundred miles, so it seemed just reward.'

'Five star?'

'I think so. I didn't check.'

'Of course you didn't. You're a millionaire, Sean. Or is it a billionaire?'

'Just a plain old millionaire, Claudia. Same as you. You're in lighthouses and private beaches, aren't you?'

Claudia gave him a thin smile and looked suitably abashed.

'Sorry. That was a cheap shot. Money doesn't really count for much in the end, does it?'

'It's fine, Claudia. I think, perhaps, I deserved that. And you're right, it doesn't. It can't bring you the things that really matter.'

Claudia remembered the day they'd shared the sadness they were each carrying, telling each other their most intimate and personal reasons for walking the Camino. A day of sunflowers, caterpillars and frogs.

'I guess we both found that out on this crazy journey, Sean, didn't we? We said we'd hopefully get some answers at the end of it. If that's all we got, then I think it was worth it.'

Sean shifted his feet and looked uncomfortable.

'Look, I'm going to head over to shower and get some laundry done. Then I'm going to have an early night in a big soft bed. I saw you all and just wanted to come over and say goodbye. I also wanted to say thank you, to you, for caring. For taking the time to care about me, even when I was a pain. All the way along the Camino.'

The memory of first seeing Sean, in Saint Jean, leaning against the wall, and the other times they'd met, along the way, flashed through Claudia's mind. The café in Pamplona, the museum in Burgos, the night they had danced in Leon, and the day they'd found the fairy glade and been sprinkled in snowflowers. The pictures of her journey were many, but the indelible ones always seemed to have included him. She found it hard to believe there would be no more pictures to add.

'It was easy to do, Sean,' whispered Claudia.

Sean could see she was emotional, and felt the deeper connection between them that had always seemed to be there, return. It appeared they had been pushed together for one final moment time.

'Well, thank you anyway, Claudia. I'll not forget your kindness. Or you.'

The awkwardness between them slipped away as they each remembered the moments they had shared, and what might have been, and could still be, if they would only seize the moment. The air around them was heady and still, as if the Universe was waiting for them to understand why they were both in the same space at the same time. It would only take one of them to tilt and the other would turn.

'So, no more Major Tom, I hope?'

'I'm not sure about that. You know me, Claudia, I like my own space, pardon the pun.'

Sean smiled and laughed, attempting to lift the smothering mood. Claudia struggled to speak, but a voice in her head begged her to tell him how she felt, despite it might do no good.

They stood in silence, looking into one another. The square around them was filled with people, but neither of them could hear a sound. It seemed the world had stopped spinning, awaiting them both to come to their senses, the invisible stars, a hundred million miles above their heads, screaming to them to fight for each other. Their eyes spoke to each other, but their hearts looked away, saying nothing.

'I'll miss him,' said Claudia, finally, her voice breathy and trembling, 'Major Tom. I'll be thinking about him, wherever he floats off to.'

She was struggling to hide the sense of emptiness and loss she was feeling.

Sean, too, seemed to realise that this was the end of their journey together. He reached out and took hold of Claudia's hands, their fingers entwining, as if they knew not to let go.

'Goodbye, Claudia Montgomery. Say it to the others for me. I'm not so good with things like that.'

With that, he turned and walked off across the square.

'Nor am I, Sean Jameson,' said Claudia, quietly, 'not with you.'

She watched him until he entered his hotel, then turned and headed over to join the others. Robyn saw her coming and walked towards her.

'Where's he gone?'

'To his hotel.'

She put a hand on Claudia's arm.

'Are you okay?'

'No. But I'll be fine.'

Robyn could tell Claudia was as far from fine as it was possible to get. She tried to cheer her up.

'Everyone's meeting up at some restaurant behind the square, later tonight. It serves amazing octopus, apparently. It'll be fun.'

'Sure. Can't wait.'

Robyn could hear the sadness in Claudia's voice.

'I guess nothing worked out?'

'Nothing could, Robyn, and that's fine by me. Really, it is. Come on, let's find our hotel and grab a shower. I'm getting drunk, tonight, and I'm wearing a party frock.'

'Did you bring one?'

'Nope,' replied Claudia, trying to gee herself up, 'but I saw a Gucci shop when we were walking in. I'm going to spend an obscene amount of money and buy one that looks as sexy as hell, then we're going out to have fun.'

'Perfect,' said Robyn, 'count me in.'

Claudia looked across at the hotel, opposite, wondering if she should go after Sean, but knew it would be pointless. He, like the hotel doors, were closed.

63

There were sixteen of them seated together outside Casa Marcelo, on the Rua des Hortes. Everyone was in high spirits and the atmosphere was party-like and loud. Claudia, true to her word, had purchased a black, silk dress from the Gucci shop. It was short and tight and sexy as hell. More importantly, after over a month on the Camino, dressed in trekking clothes and hiking boots, it made her feel great. Robyn and Babette had gone for the same style of dress, in orange and white, respectively. The three of them had drawn more than one or two admiring glances as they made their way through Santiago old town.

Claudia chose the signature dish of beef tartare, followed by taster plates of tiramisu and lemon pie, ending the meal with a cup of velvety *cortado*. The wine was red and Galician, and being drunk in much larger quantities than it would normally have been, but everyone knew they did not have to walk the following day. By the end of the night, Mark was dancing on the table with Bonnie and Clyde, doing their best to recreate the flamenco dance they'd seen in Leon. Babette, having broken her vow to drink sensibly, was currently snuggling up to one of the Spanish waiters.

'I'm exhausted,' said Robyn, yawning for the umpteenth time. 'I'm going back to the hotel. Are you staying?'

'No way,' said Claudia, 'I'll head back with you. I've got to drive to Finisterre, tomorrow, although not till late afternoon, thank goodness, so we'll have plenty of time to get our Camino completion certificates from the Santiago Pilgrims office. I'll say goodbye to everyone then.'

'You must be looking forward to reuniting Hannah with Jonathon?'

'I am. I've come so far, Robyn, in so many ways, and it's all thanks to her. If I hadn't met her, I wouldn't be here. I wouldn't have met you and Babette.'

'Or Sean,' said Robyn.

Claudia looked sad for the first time that night.

'Yes. Even Sean.'

'So, you really *have* given up on him?'

'There's nothing to give up on, Robyn. I don't know what he needs to make him live again, but it sure as hell isn't me.'

Robyn didn't say what she wanted to say. It was Claudia's decision to make.

'What are you going to do about you and Paul? Are you still in love with him?'

Claudia thought about the question before answering.

'You know, if you'd asked me that at the start of this journey I'd have said, without doubt, yes.'

'And now?'

Claudia shrugged.

'Now, I'm confused. I still love him, but am I still *in love* with him? I don't know. We've barely spoken in the past two months. I guess I'll go home and see if we can work it out. But one thing's for sure, *I'm* going to live at the lighthouse. I'm going to make the place my home. And what I *do* know, more than anything else, is that I want a child. Even if it means I need to foster or adopt. It's what I truly *need* in my life to make it worthwhile and meaningful. I've learned to love myself again, on the Camino, now I want to give all the love I have to someone else.'

Robyn gave her a hug.

'It'll all work out, Claudia. I'm sure of it.'

They said goodnight to everyone and walked back to the hotel.

'Will Babette be all right by herself?' Claudia asked. 'That Spanish waiter was all over her.'

Robyn gave a sarcastic laugh.

'She's more than capable of dealing with him, trust me. And I think it's her that's all over him. She's a tart with a heart. I love her to bits.'

'And me,' said Claudia. 'She goes after what she wants and to hell with the consequences.'

'We could all learn something from that, I think. Not letting things we want to get away from us.' The tone and inference in Robyn's voice was crystal clear. 'Oh! We're here.'

'That was quick,' said Claudia.

She had barely noticed the walk to the hotel, lost in conversation.

'Goodnight, Claudia, my lovely friend. It's been wonderful to have had you with us on this incredible journey of ours. I'll see you for breakfast. Just don't make it too early.'

'I won't. Sleep well, Robyn. And thanks for allowing me to join you and Babette, it's been more fun than I ever expected it to be.'

They headed off to their respective rooms, Robyn taking the stairs to the first floor, leaving Claudia to take the lift.

Not more than a few hundred meters away, from his top floor balcony, Sean gazed across Obradoiro Square to the cathedral, holding a crystal glass half filled with Glenmorangie. Initially, he'd been disappointed when the bartender had apologised for not having had his beloved Coal Isla whisky, but the twenty-one year old Glenmorangie wasn't exactly a hardship. It was lighter than the Islay malt he preferred, but still complex and delicious.

The cathedral was bathed in light and looked even more beautiful that it had done that afternoon. Even if he had no intention of visiting, it was one of the most stunning buildings he'd ever seen. He was feeling melancholy, though not entirely sure why, although had realised, earlier, that he'd not seen Linz for weeks. Perhaps it was that, as well as the anticlimax that always seems to follow the end of an incredible journey, making him feel that way.

'We did it, my love,' he said, as he turned and walked back into his suite. 'I thought of you, coming into Santiago, this morning, just like we always talked about doing. I'd hoped you'd be there. I miss you.' He sat down on the couch by the fireplace and gazed into the flames, scrunching his bare toes into the sheepskin rug at his feet. He thought, again, of Linz, wondering where she was. And then he pictured Claudia. 'Christ, my head's a mess.' He knew, then, why Linz wasn't with him. 'I'm sorry I spent time with her, Linz. I was just so lonely. I should have been stronger. Please, my love. I need you.'

His hands began to tremble and the lights of the flickering fire began to grow hazy. His chest tightened and he felt the panic attack coming. Trying to fight it, he gulped the remaining whisky down and tried to breathe normally.

A sudden knock at the door startled him. He crossed the floor and opened it.

'Hello, Sean.'

'Claudia.'

'I'm sorry to bother you. I know it's late, but . . .'

'No, it's fine, I was just . . .'

Claudia looked past him, into the room.

'I heard you talking. Is someone here? I'm sorry if I've interrupted you.'

She turned to go, but Sean stopped her.

'Don't go.'

He looked back into the room. It was still empty.

Claudia was still trying to decide whether or not to just walk away. She'd not meant to come to his hotel. Something had just compelled her to. But now she was here, she had to say what she'd come to say.

'Can I come in, Sean?'

'Of course. Sorry.'

Sean stood aside and waved her into the suite.

Claudia still had on her new black dress. She'd seen a lot of men staring at her over the course of the night, and thought Sean might have said something about how she looked, but he didn't seem to notice. She started repeating the speech she'd written, in her head, on her way from her hotel.

'I know we said goodbye, earlier, in the square, but I think it could have been a better goodbye. Don't you? I also wanted to say something to you. Nothing bad. Don't look so worried.'

Sean smiled a thin smile then remembered he was the host.

'Would you like a drink. I've got a bottle of your favourite whisky.'

'Glenmorangie?' Claudia said, surprised.

'Yes. Let me pour you one.'

He went to find her a glass from the suite's kitchen area.

'Well, it's after midnight,' Claudia called after him, 'and you are flying out early in the morning. I don't want to keep you up. But why not?'

She sat down on the couch and watched Sean pour her a healthy dram. He came back into the main suite and handed it to her, then went to stand by the fire.

'What was it you wanted to tell me?'

'Just, that I think you are a lovely man. I watched you with Wendy and everyone else. They all loved you. You think you're not worth being loved, but you're wrong. You're not a bad person, even if you insist on thinking you are. You deserve to live, Sean. And to love again, someday.'

'Thanks, Claudia. I don't know what I've done to deserve all of that, but I appreciate it, really.'

Claudia felt suddenly embarrassed. She stood up, setting her glass on the fireplace mantle.

'And now that I've said my piece, I'll leave you in peace.' She moved towards him with her arms outstretched. 'A final goodbye hug?'

'Of course.'

Sean allowed her to embrace him, but his eyes were scanning the room. He thought of Linz. But she wasn't there, and he was feeling sad and lonely, almost to the point he couldn't bear. Claudia was warm and soft and smelt of ice cream and whisky. It was a heady aroma. He felt his chest tighten at the feel of her body against his.

'Be happy, Sean Jameson,' Claudia whispered. 'I wish I'd met you in another lifetime. Perhaps, in another, we will. But for now, you stay alive, and keep on walking.'

She moved back a touch, releasing him from her embrace.

'Claudia.'

Sean pulled her back towards him. He was struggling with something, she could see that. She stood still, letting him hold her, unsure of what was happening.

'What is it, Sean? What's wrong?'

'Damn you, Claudia. I don't want this. Stop doing this to me.'

He pushed her away, gently, but enough to make her step back a pace.

'I didn't do anything,' said Claudia, angrily.

She stepped forward and pushed Sean, the flats of her hands thumping against his chest, hitting him harder than she meant to. She was angry with him and finding it hard to control her emotions. She saw the shock on his face and tried to explain.

'I love Linz! I can't let her down again.'

Claudia hit him for a second time, her frustration with him rising like storm floodwater. She couldn't do this dance again.

'Then go and kill yourself, if that's what you really want? Keep loving a dead woman rather than taking a chance on loving a real, live, breathing one. You know, Sean, I thought you were the bravest man I'd ever met, but I was wrong. You're a coward! Nothing but a stupid, stubborn, utterly annoying, bloody coward.'

'Claudia!'

She hit him again, her hands balled into fists, this time trying to hurt him. As he was hurting her.

'Go on. Kill yourself. See if I care. If you really want to join . . .'

'Don't!' Sean pleaded.

But Claudia was too far gone to stop.

'Don't what, Sean? Oh, I'm sorry. I forgot the rules. Perish the thought I should say her name, *Saint bloody Lindsey*, the ghost who wants you to die! Who wants you to join her in her cold, bloody grave! Seriously? She's not telling you that. She never has been. Can't you understand that? She's dead, Sean. Dead! And you're not seeing her. It's only your own sick, deluded mind telling you anything different. Let her go, damn you. Let her go! If you won't do it for me, then at least do it for yourself.'

Sean had paled and he looked in anguish at the force of Claudia's outburst.

'Claudia, please. I can't . . .'

'I know you bloody can't, Sean. That's the bloody problem. You can't and neither can I. Not any longer.' Claudia stamped a foot on the floor to stop herself from hitting him again. She came to a sudden realisation and stepped back from him. 'That's it. I'm done with this. Goodbye, Sean Jameson. Goodbye and good luck finding your dead wife and kids. You'll never see them again, you bloody fool. Never!'

Sean's shoulders slumped. The look of pain on his face was something Claudia knew she would never forget. Her words, born out of anger, had been needless and cruel, cutting him more deeply than she had meant them to. Her hand flew to her mouth, too late to stop them, wishing she could take them back.

'I know that, Claudia,' whispered Sean. 'It's just that . . . I miss them, so much.'

His voice was raw and filled with pain, as if he had fully understood what she'd said and finally realised he *would* never see his family again. Claudia tried to comfort him.

'Oh, Sean. I'm so sorry. I didn't mean that. I didn't mean to hurt you. I'd never hurt you, don't you understand that?' But the fact was, she had. The sight of him standing there, broken and alone, was too much for her to stand. Her heart was breaking in two, knowing she done that to him. She walked past him, towards the suite door, intending to leave, then turned, trying to say some final thing that might give him some solace. 'Please don't be sad anymore. I know you're in pain. If I could take it from you, I would. Goodbye, Sean. I'll never forget you.'

Sean stared down at the floor, too ashamed to let her see his weakness.

'Claudia. I'm so lost. I've made so many mistakes. I'm trying so hard to fix them. To be a better man. I just don't know how.'

'Oh, Sean. You *are* a good man. If only you could allow yourself to see that. I wish I could help you see that.'

'Then help me, Claudia. Please. Help me.'

He reeled, unsteady on his feet.

Claudia came to him like a lioness coming to protect one of her cubs, closing the small space between that, moments ago, had been a chasm that could not be bridged. She wrapped her arms around him, holding him tightly.

'Oh, Sean, my darling. You're so sad. I can't bear it.'

'Claudia.'

She kissed his face, feeling his warm tears and the gentle rasp of his stubble against her skin, saying his name, over and over, reassuring him and trying to make him feel safe. She could no longer hold back her love for him. It was no longer something she could fight. Nor did she want to. Her overwhelming desire to protect him frightened her.

'Sean, I love you.'

She realised it was true. She *did* love him. But it was more than that. Far more. She was *in love* with him. She knew it in that moment. She was not afraid of knowing it, only that she might ever lose him. She fussed over him like a mother would her child, stroking his hair and kissing his forehead. She cupped his chin, lifting his face up to allow him to see her and how she loved him.

'Claudia. What have you done to me?'

She pulled away from him, misunderstanding the intent behind his words, fearing she had made the same mistake she'd made on the day of the snowflowers.

'I'm sorry, Sean. I'm so sorry. I'll leave, if that's what you . . .'

Sean pulled her back to him, holding her tightly to him.

'No! Don't leave, Claudia. Don't you ever leave me again. I don't want you to go. Everyone always goes.'

Claudia clung to him, as if his words might take him from her.

'I won't leave you, my darling.'

'Never, Claudia. Promise me that. I don't want to be lonely anymore.'

Claudia knew he was afraid. She wanted to take that fear away from him. She leaned back and looked up into his eyes, so that he would see the truth in what she was about to say.

'I will *never* leave you, Sean. Not if you don't want me to go.'

The dam holding Sean's emotions in check finally broke. He pulled her to him as a drowning child might grab for a lifeguard. They held onto to one another, afraid something might tear them apart, knowing they could not bear the physical loss of it. He ran his fingers through her hair, lightly brushing the nape of her neck and sending delicate bursts of electricity though her body, then broke the embrace and lifted her face level with his. They gazed into each other's eyes, aware something was happening they had no control over.

Like blind lovers, they explored each other's face, with light, tracing fingertips, as if seeing the other clearly for the first time, whispering each other's name, as if the names themselves, spoken, carried a power that ran back through time, to when the first man and woman had fallen in love. Sean kissed her forehead and eyelids, her cheeks and the bridge of her nose, telling her how beautiful she was with each soft touch of his lips.

Finally, he kissed her on the mouth.

The butterflies in Claudia's stomach took flight, fluttering lower, then lower still. She pushed herself against him and felt his arousal, hard against her thigh, sending another surge of lightening to her groin.

'I'm in love with you, Sean Jameson,' she whispered, and her need for him engulfed her.

'Claudia, my love.'

Sean slid the tip of his tongue across the underside of Claudia's top lip then pushed it deeper, forcing it between her lips. Her mouth opened to allow him entry and she felt a rush of wet, animal desire as his tongue sought hers.

She raised her arms, allowing him to lift her dress over her head. He tossed it to the couch and stepped back, looking at her. She was wearing a black silk bra with matching panties and high, black shoes. She'd bought them when she'd bought the dress. She watched him study her, his eyes shining with the hunger of a predator, and felt suddenly vulnerable.

But then the vulnerability changed.

Suddenly, Claudia felt powerful and sensual, liberated in the sight of his desire for her. Understanding the power she had over him, her own desire ignited. She pulled him to her and bit his shoulder, leaving a mark, though he barely reacted. Sean's hands slid down her back and cupped the cheeks of her bottom. He pushed his groin against her and let out a growl, low and rumbling, like the sound of a male lion.

Claudia heard herself moan, the pent-up needs of her body awakened. She pulled at the belt around his trousers, trying to tear it free, while Sean fingered the clasp on her bra, attempting to unhook it. Locked together, like teenagers in that first newly-discovered moment of uncontrollable lust, they stopped, momentarily, to look at each other, and laughed, then kissed again, continuing to undress each other. Feeling their way. Loathe to break the physical connection for even a moment.

Sean guided Claudia back towards the sheepskin rug and pulled her down onto it. On her knees, still locked in the kiss, she pushed him onto his back and sat astride his thighs, pulling at the buttons on his black silk shirt. Free of it, she leaned down and licked his nipples, flicking her tongue over them like a snake tasting the air for prey. She heard him groan and the sound of it excited her further.

Lifting his hips, Sean helped her ease off his trousers and boxers. His groans turned to gasps as her mouth enveloped him. She worked on him slowly, enjoying her power over him, Sean, his hands in her hair, guiding her moments. When he could stand no more, while he still had command enough to stop her, he pulled her away from his groin and leaned down to kiss her. The salty taste of her mouth and the lust in her eyes sent his need for her to new heights.

Claudia rose to meet him, her eyes sparkling like wet emeralds, lit by the flames in the fireplace. Responding to her attack, Sean rolled her onto her back, pinning her down by the shoulders. She fought him, spitting like a cornered leopard, dragging her nails across his back and drawing blood. He growled at her, his cornflower blue eyes turned almost black, scaring her, slightly, then dropped his mouth to hers. They kissed, lost in a raging lust.

Lifting himself off her, Sean reached down and hooked the fingers of one hand into Claudia's panties, pulling them down over her feet. She kicked them away and fell back, legs apart, urging him onto her. He covered her, staying his thrust, looking down into her eyes as if challenging her to move. His body was hard and coated in a light sheen of sweat, and he was trembling. As was she. She ran her hands down the curve of his muscular back, wiping hot sweat over his firm, round buttocks, returning the challenge in his gaze.

'Sean. Please.' Claudia heard the need in her whisper, although it was as if the words were being spoken by another person. She needed him inside her. Nothing else existed for her in that moment in time. Nothing but him. She wrapped her legs around his back and looked deep into his eyes. 'Make love to me.'

She felt him respond, her words having the effect she had known they would, driving into her with a cry of unbridled desire.

'My love!'

Claudia gasped as he filled her, body and soul. She meshed her fingers together at the small of his back, pulling him into her with each thrust. Sean took one of her nipples in his mouth, biting her hard enough to take her breath away, but not hard enough for it to have truly hurt. It switched something on inside her. Her breathing quickened and her cheeks and neck flushed. She was being taken to a place she had never been. She knew it and was afraid of how she would be, afterwards, but had long since abandoned any notion of control.

Sean kissed her again and they gazed into each other's eyes, connecting, bodies moving together, attuned to the subtle nuances of touch and sound, finding the place where deep physical, mental and spiritual connection converges.

Claudia rode the waves as they began to build. Slow, shallow ripples, washing over her like silken threads being teased across her skin. She lay on a shore of warm sand, bathed in bright light. The waves began to grow higher, becoming stronger and closer together, pulling her away from the light, until a final, massive wave engulfed her, dragging her down into a bottomless ocean. She cried out, or thought she had, so far removed from reality she could not be sure it had been real. Her soul left her body and she floated free of care. She had come to the place of living death. And she stopped fighting.

Giving herself up to the ocean, Claudia floated alone in the calm blue, warm blue, deep blue water. She could see only darkness. Hear nothing but the slow rush of the waves far above her. An image of herself appeared, standing in the Colosseum de Verona, at the end of the opera, *Tosca*, looking up at the night sky, a sweep of stars looking back at her. Light from ages passed. She heard herself ask the Universe for love to find her then wondered why the stars were laughing.

And then she understood.

Suddenly, she heard a voice calling to her from somewhere inordinately primal. She came awake, floating alone in the darkness, conscious of the call. *His* call. He needed her. And she him. She fought against the waves, rising out of the deep blue depths, swimming back towards the light, desperate to find her mate.

And he was there! Waiting for her.

Sean surged towards her, diving down through the waves until he found her. Claudia reached out and pulled him to her, calling his name, as he called hers, until they were joined in the same explosive crescendo. Spent, they sank into the blue, holding on to each other as the darkness enveloped them and the sunlight faded and the laughter of the stars was silenced.

For some time, afterwards, they lay together, entwined like pieces of washed up driftwood on a deserted beach. Sean's cheek was pressed against Claudia's. She could feel the warm, rhythmic rush of his breath on her skin. They were both still trembling, emotionally and physically spent from their lovemaking. Afraid of what she was feeling, aware she would never be the same again, Claudia wrapped her legs and arms around him, clinging to him like a baby capuchin monkey holding onto its mother. She whispered to him that she loved him. That she would love him forevermore. Loathe to surrender the feeling of oneness she had never known existed.

64

The sea was flat and calm, stretching out in front of Claudia like blue oil, mirroring the cloudless sky and making the horizon seem endless. Close to the shore, hundreds of seagulls floated on the viscous sheen like fluffy dabs of cotton candy. They were quiet and still, as if waiting for something to happen. The almost reverent silence was unnerving, but then this was the Spain's Costa del Morte, the "Coast of the Dead", which was apt, she thought, given her reason for being there.

The last time she'd looked out over this ocean had been from the top of Plymouth Light, three-thousand miles and a lifetime away. Or so it felt. She turned and looked up at the peak of Cape Finisterre, to the unpainted, granite lighthouse seven hundred feet above. Two lighthouse towers linked the beginning and end points of a journey that had unfolded by chance. A journey that had altered the course of her life in a way she could never have imagined. She remembered something Hannah had once said to her, in the Glass Menagerie, shortly before she'd died.

You may dance, knowing the steps to take, but it is always the Universe that calls the tune.'

'Sorry, my love, did you say something?'

Claudia squeezed Sean's hand and leaned into him, resting her head against his shoulder.

'Nothing, my darling. I was miles away. Thinking about how much things have changed in such a short space of time. It's as if my old life is so far behind me I'm losing sight of it. No matter how hard I try to understand how I've got to where I am, right now, it all seems to have just happened. It's as if I'm a pawn on a chessboard being moved by some divine hand.'

'I know what you mean. It can change in a heartbeat.'

Claudia knew what Sean was referring to. They had talked at length about his family and the accident that had taken them from him. She didn't let the conversation fade. They *had* to share these things. The things that still hurt them.

'Hannah loved chess. She used to say she was a pawn masquerading as a queen. She was, you know, in so many ways.'

Claudia extracted her arm from Sean's and took off her leather shoulder bag, setting it down on the pebble beach and removing the wooden box she'd carried Hannah's ashes in over the past few months.

'Do you want to be alone for this?'

Claudia was glad Sean had offered. She wouldn't have asked him to leave, but the fact he cared enough to ask made her happy. She hadn't been someone's priority for a long time. Emerald necklaces were one thing, but noticing how she was feeling was more precious.

'Would you mind? I want to say a few things to her before I let her go.'

'Not at all. I understand. Just call me if you need me.'

Sean kissed her on the forehead and meandered up the beach.

Claudia opened the box and took a deep breath. She was unsure how she felt, or how she was *supposed* to feel. It had been almost three months since Hannah's death. She'd mourned her over those months, especially on the Camino. This is where Hannah had told her she needed to be, to be with Jonathon. Perhaps it was why she wasn't feeling as sad as she'd thought she might.

She was also deeply in love.

'Well, crazy lady, here we are. I can't quite believe it myself. I doubt you can either.'

She glanced at Hannah, standing beside her, looking exactly as she'd done the first time Claudia had seen her standing at the Point.

'I knew you'd come, my dear. So, did you. Right from the first time we started talking about it.'

'I guess I did.'

Hannah looked past Claudia, towards Sean. Claudia followed her gaze. Sean was looking back at her and waved.

'What are you going to do about him?'

'I don't know,' said Claudia, waving back.

'He's very handsome.'

'He is.'

'And he needs you. Just as I did, my dear. You were always meant to come to the lighthouse. Just as you were always meant to be here, with him. This is where you needed to be to find what you really need. Does that make sense?'

'I think so.'

'It will.'

'I need to let you go, Hannah.'

'I'm ready.'

Claudia felt the sadness come as she said it. And the tears she had thought would not.

'I just don't want to.'

'I know.'

'I love you, Hannah. I always will.'

'Me too.'

'Will I see you again?'

Hannah touched Claudia's hand.

'Perhaps.'

'Say hello to Jonathon for me when you see him.'

'He's already here,' whispered Hannah, and turned away.

A light breeze blew in over Claudia's shoulder, coming off the land, which was unusual. It carried the smell of Spain, earthy and sun-warmed. She tipped the box and let Hannah's ashes fall. The breeze carried them out over the slightly rippling water.

'Goodbye, crazy lady.'

She turned to see Hannah some way down the beach, hand in hand with a man Claudia recognised from his picture above the fireplace in the Beach Shack. She looked up the beach, at Sean, and her heart soared for what she felt for him. She looked back to Hannah and Jonathon but they were already gone. Their circle complete.

65

They spent the next week in Paris. Each day was a new adventure, for Claudia, as Sean showed her *his* Paris. He showed her Paris in the little things; like how to use the city buses, the best street-food vendors in the Latin Quarter and the coolest cafés in the Marais district, which the French liked to call their *own* arrondissement. He showed her how to navigate the Metro, the best way, he assured her, to reach the tourist spots she *had* to see, and took her to Montmartre to see the paintings being sold by young, aspiring artists. Simple, small, but priceless things that meant so much.

Mostly, he showed her how to love again. And she, him.

'QuantumCloud has an office here,' Sean explained, when Claudia asked him how he was so familiar with the city.

'Will you visit it while we're here?'

Sean gave a haughty laugh.

'Not a chance. I'm not ready to go back. I doubt I ever will be.'

'So, what *will* you do?'

'I really have no idea, my love. But, as long as we're together, I don't care that much.'

Claudia liked the answer, caring little for where she would wash up, if she was washed up by his side.

The Parisians, Claudia found, liked to speak French, even if who they were speaking with couldn't. Thankfully, Sean's was excellent, which, apart from being impressive, was also very convenient. She found it had the oddest effect on her when she heard him speak it. It made him even sexier than she already found him. She made him talk to her in it when they made love; every morning, some afternoons, and most evenings. When Sean had brought this to her attention she'd informed him that they'd both dieted for long enough, and that there was nothing wrong in them gorging themselves, on love, in the city of love.

In the Louvre, she wept at the sight of the *Mona Lisa*, an image so indelibly imprinted in her psyche she already felt she'd seen it. Although the museum was busy, she and Sean stood alone, one lunchtime, staring at the masterpiece.

'I thought it would be bigger.'

'Size isn't everything, haven't you heard?' Claudia laughed at the look Sean gave her. 'Not that you have anything to worry about in that department, my darling,' she added, in a voice laced with intent, drawing her nails across the front of his thighs.

Even through his jeans, her touch made Sean shiver.

'Hussy,' he said, looking round to see if anyone was watching them.

Claudia turned her attention back to the First Lady of portraiture.

'I studied this painting at university. It's got some amazing and interesting history.'

Sean had already seen enough of it. It was a great painting, he supposed, but not really his thing.

'Such as?'

'Let me give you the juiciest details,' replied Claudia, 'I can see your interest waning.'

Sean wondered how she could tell.

'Not at all. But we've been staring at it for over half an hour.'

'Okay, just another ten minutes. I'll try to keep you enthralled.'

'Deal.'

'Right,' said Claudia. 'Well, the *Mona Lisa,* as you have already no doubt noticed, has no visible eyelashes or eyebrows.'

Sean looked back at the painting and wondered how he hadn't noticed. It was obvious now that Claudia had pointed it out.

'I had,' he lied.

'But she used to,' continued Claudia, knowing he hadn't. 'High-resolution scans have shown she was originally painted with visible brows and lashes. They disappeared, over time, possibly because of over-cleaning.'

'Da Vinci would be pissed-off to hear that,' said Sean, warming a little more to the painting, now there was some background history to go with it.

'Perhaps. But it's his own fault.'

'How come?'

'Leonardo used more than thirty layers of paint on the *Mona Lisa*. Some were thinner than a human hair. Perhaps the eyebrows and eyelashes were so thinly painted they came off the first time the painting was restored.'

'No wonder she looks annoyed. Though maybe she's just bored of being a model. Who knows how long she had to sit there doing nothing except looking straight ahead.'

'Actually, as with all his life models,' Claudia explained, 'she could get up every so often. In fact, Da Vinci liked to keep his subjects relaxed and entertained. So much so that he had six musicians play for her and installed a musical fountain, invented by himself, may I add, to keep her entertained.'

'You certainly know your stuff, my love, but then I keep forgetting you're both an artist and a gallery owner.'

Claudia kissed him on the cheek.

'So, not just a pretty face?'

'A beautiful face,' said Sean,

He leaned over and kissed her on the mouth, cupping one of her bottom cheeks in his hand.

'Unhand me, sir, and show some sense of decency.'

Claudia lifted Sean's hand away. The mischievous look in her eyes, though, suggested she wanted him to do otherwise. Sean squeezed her bottom again.

'We're in Paris, Claudia. It's expected.'

'Well, it's a nice segway, I suppose,' said Claudia wriggling away from him.

'Into what?' Sean asked, leaving her be.

'Well, at one point in time, Napoleon had the *Mona Lisa* hung on his bedroom wall, so that he could make love to Josephine, below it.

'Great plan.' Sean looked around him. 'You keep watch and I'll grab it. We can nail it up on our headboard back at the hotel.'

Claudia twirled a strand of his hair around her finger, wondering if there was somewhere they could hide and be bad together.

'I don't think we'd make it out alive. It's worth almost a billion dollars.'

Sean suddenly had a newly found respect for Da Vinci's most famous work.

'A billion! For that?'

'That's why she was moved six times during World War Two,' said Claudia, feeling Sean's wandering hands work their way back around to her bottom. This time she let him linger. She wondered what was wrong with her. She'd gone from having had no sex-drive to being horny almost all the time. 'To keep it out of Hitler's hands. He was a frustrated artist, but not fit to lick the soles of Da Vinci's sandals.'

'Agreed. Even if she's not the prettiest woman I've ever seen.'

'Interesting you should say that,' said Claudia, detaching herself from him and refocussing her mind on what she was supposed to be doing. 'There's a train of thought that suggests that Mona Lisa is actually a self-portrait of Leonardo da Vinci himself.'

'That's fantastic,' said Sean, unable to hide his mirth. 'Poor Napoleon, the great general, a man's man in anyone's eyes, hung a picture of a transvestite over his bed to make love to his woman.'

Claudia laughed along with Sean at the image he'd presented.

'I suppose you could put it like that.'

'Best we just leave it where it is then. Come on, Claudia, let's go back to the hotel. I'm all cultured out. We've been sightseeing all day. I need to see you naked and posing for me.'

'And just what sort of pose did you have in mind?' Claudia asked, taking Sean by the hand and leading him towards the gallery exit door.

'I'll think of it on the way back in the taxi. Less than what Mona Lisa has on, for sure. Perhaps just a pair of white socks and a pair of high heels?'

'Pervert,' said Claudia, already enjoying the thought of an afternoon in bed.

'Perhaps, but you love it.'

'I do,' said Claudia. 'I'm starving, again, myself. You need to feed me.'

'Now who's the pervert,' whispered Sean, passing a security guard who gave them a wink and a knowing smile.

The sky was moody blue, turning mauve on the horizon, and the birds, nestled in the trees along the Champs-Elysees, were singing evening songs, a prelude to dusk settling over the area known as the Golden Triangle of Paris. From the private terrace of their luxury suite, at the legendary George Cinq hotel, Sean and Claudia gazed out towards the Eiffel tower. The luxurious hotel, an art-deco landmark had been an amazing base for them to explore the city from, and the perfect place to retreat to, to continue living in the bubble they had created for themselves since leaving Santiago two weeks before.

Claudia was curled up in one of the comfortable outdoor chairs, wrapped in a fluffy, white bathrobe and sipping a glass of champagne, her hunger satiated. Sean sat opposite her in his boxer-shorts and t-shirt, replenishing his now considerably lower blood-sugar levels by devouring a plate of black grapes, washing them down with a Stella-Artois lager.

'What a wonderful day, my darling. And this place! It's a long way from the albergues on the Camino.'

'Just a bit,' said Sean, 'but each has its attractions. Do you miss it?'

'I miss Babette and Robyn. They were the perfect people to travel with.'

'It was funny when we pitched up that last morning at your hotel. The looks on their faces when they saw us walk in together.'

'Me looking like the cat that got the cream.'

'Well, you did, in a way. More than once, if I remember correctly.'

'Sean! Don't be filthy.'

'I thought you liked it?'

'That's not the point,' said Claudia, playfully. 'Now, what are our plans for tonight? I fancy a stroll along the River Seine, at least as far as the Marias district. Perhaps we could go back to that little restaurant we went to last week, you remember, after visiting the Picasso museum?'

'*L'Orangerie*, on the Isle de Cité?'

'That's it,' said Claudia. 'The food was marvellous. And it's so romantic looking out over the river at night.'

She looked down at her phone, buzzing on the table and felt a sinking feeling in the pit of her stomach. Sean noticed the look on her face.

'What's wrong?'

'It's Paul.'

Sean hauled himself out of his chair.

'You need to take it. I'll get dressed and pop downstairs to ask concierge to make our reservations for dinner. I'll organise the hotel limousine to take us there. We can walk back, it'll be much more romantic in the dark.'

'Sounds perfect,' said Claudia, stalling answering her phone.

'Talk to him, Claudia. I'll see you shortly.'

Sean went into their room, pulling the glass balcony-doors closed behind him. He dressed in the bedroom, not wishing to hear any of the conversation, unsure of how he felt about it, then headed out of the room, taking the elevator down to the lobby, where he spoke with the concierge about dinner reservations. He sat and read a newspaper, giving it half an hour before heading back up to the suite, where he found Claudia, still on the balcony, with a worried look on her face.

'What's up?'

'Paul's wondering when I'm coming home.'

'Oh!'

Claudia had been expecting something more.

'He sounded odd. Distant even. We talked, but it's like he's become a stranger to me. It's like I don't know him anymore. He thinks I'm still just visiting Paris. I didn't mention us.'

'Do you want to go home, Claudia? I mean, I suppose you have to at some point. We can't stay here forever.'

'My life is over there, Sean. Everything I own. My gallery. The house in Lexington. The lighthouse. Everything, that is . . . '

'Then perhaps you *should* go.'

'I was about to say, everything, that is, except you.'

'Sorry.'

'Do you want me to go, Sean? It seems like you do.'

'Only if you want to.'

Claudia felt as if something had shifted in how they were with each other, even from half an hour before. He was acting strangely. Pulling away from her as he'd done before. She'd thought that part of him gone.

'That's not an answer. And you know it.'

'I don't know what you want me to say, Claudia.'

'What about *us*, Sean? What about all we've talked about doing together, in Scotland, in Italy, or Switzerland. Anywhere, in fact, where you can be near the mountains you love so much?'

Claudia was becoming upset. She wanted him to be normal with her. To be *her* Sean.

'I was just thinking about you, Claudia. And Paul. He's still your husband. Perhaps he deserves an explanation. Even a chance to win you back.'

'Is that what you want? For Paul to win me back?'

Her heart lurched. They'd talked at length about their future together. She thought they were on the same page. Sean turned to one she had not thought was even there.

'Look, all I'm saying is that maybe he deserves a chance to talk to you. We're only a few weeks into this thing. He's been your husband for sixteen years.'

'This *thing!* So we're a thing, now, are we?'

'Don't be stupid,' said Sean, harshly, 'that's not how I meant it.'

He could see she was getting angry and tried to halt the coming car crash.

Claudia stood to face him, the anger in her blood sending warning flares flashing in her eyes.

'Perhaps you're right, Sean! Perhaps we *did* rush into this thing. Perhaps it was just the heady emotions of finishing the Camino and what's happened since that made me think it was something more.'

'Perhaps we did!'

Sean snapped at her, becoming angry himself. She was acting irrationally, twisting what he'd said into something he hadn't meant. It prompted Claudia to dig a little deeper, opening a hole for Sean to jump into, or over.

'Do you even love me, Sean?'

'Of course I do. You know I do.'

Claudia felt neither answer carried much conviction.

'But are you *in love* with me? Because I'm in love with you. I know that for certain. I thought you felt the same, but now I'm not so sure. In fact, when I think about it, you've never said those words to me. I have, to you, many times. But not you.'

'Of course I have. For God's sake, Claudia, why are you being so . . .'

'So *what,* Sean?' Claudia followed him as he turned and walked back into the suite. 'So needy? Is that what you were going to say?'

'No, I wasn't. Not that you're listening.'

Again, Sean's answer only stoked Claudia's growing anger.

'I am listening Sean, that's the problem. You've called me *darling,* and *my love,* but you've never actually told me you're in love with me. I'm here, trying to work out how to move forward, with you, ready to leave everything in my life behind. But you're acting as if . . .'

'I never asked you to do that, Claudia.'

The response was churlish. Even Sean knew it. But he couldn't reel it back.

'I know you didn't, Sean, but I wanted to. So that I could be with you. You asked me to never leave you, remember? Or was that just something you said to get me into bed? Have I just been a convenient two week fuck for you?'

'Don't be ridiculous, Claudia. Don't say that.'

'Then tell me you're in love with me. It shouldn't be hard to say.' Sean hesitated, unable to understand her anger, which was the worst thing he could have done. Claudia answered for him. 'Clearly, Sean, you can't. So perhaps I *should* just go home? It seems to be what you actually want.'

Sean's anger bubbled over, so that he spoke in anger, the words out before he could stop them.

'Go home if you want, Claudia. It's not like we're bloody married.'

The fight went out of Claudia. Part of her couldn't really take in what had just happened. An hour ago they'd been making love, now they were at each other's throats. It might have been their first fight, as a couple, but it had all the signs of being their last.

'That's right, Sean. But I thought, one day, we might be.'

'I'm already . . .'

Sean stopped speaking. He didn't need to go on for Claudia to know what he'd intended to say.

'Already married, Sean. Is that what you were going to say?'

She whispered the words, but they were thunderstrikes in her soul.

'I didn't mean it like that.'

'Yes, Sean, you did. And you know it. We both do. She's still there, isn't she? In your head and your heart. She always will be.'

'No!'

Sean barely convinced himself.

'You're a liar, Sean. You can't say you're in love with me because you're not. You're still in love with Linz.'

The realisation of it washed over Claudia. She had allowed herself to be wrapped in a cocoon of fantasy. She could see that now. And the cocoon, like spider's web, had been too easily torn away. She looked at Sean, her eyes imploring him to tell her she was wrong. Begging him to tell her he was in love with her.

Instead, Sean grabbed his jacket.

'I'm not doing this, Claudia. I'm going for a walk until you calm down and start making sense. I'll see you later.'

He stormed out of the suite's front door, slamming it shut behind him.

'You've walked away from me again, Sean Jameson,' said Claudia, softly. 'I warned you not to do that.'

She picked up her phone and went into the suite, closing the doors behind her, saddened about what she knew she had to do.

After an hour meandering the cobbled streets around the hotel, Sean decided to return. He'd thought about what Claudia had said and come to a realisation. He *did* love her. But he was also still in love with Linz. But he hadn't seen her for weeks and was unsure what that meant. Perhaps she had given up on him? The thought of not seeing her and the children still cut him to the bone, but the unbearable pain and loneliness he had been living with had abated, because of Claudia. They had to talk things through, to find a way forward.

He was surprised that he wanted to. That was new.

'*Monsieur* Jameson!' One of the girls in the reception area called to him as he entered the lobby. He went over to see what she wanted. '*Monsieur*, I have a letter for you. From your partner, *Madame* Claudia.'

Sean took the sealed envelope from the girl's outstretched hand and opened it.

Sean,

There is, I fear, too much hurt in you to allow you to truly love another woman. I can fight almost anything for you, but I cannot fight a ghost. A ghost who will never age and will always be perfect.

I love you with all my heart. I always will. But we can never be happy together unless you are somehow healed. I have prayed to your God that he will grant you that. I know you are angry at him, but I hope you allow him back into your life. Mostly, I pray you will have peace.

Love is the answer, Sean, and my love for you is as your love for Linz - unconditional. Part of me wishes I could be her. But I am not. I am Claudia. I am in love with you, my beautiful, sad and lonely man. When you can tell me that and mean it, I will there, waiting for you.
Goodbye, my darling.
Claudia

Sean reached out and steadied himself on the reception counter, alarming the receptionist.

'*Monsieur* Jameson, are you all right?. It is bad news? May I get you some water?'

'Is the hotel limousine at my disposal,' Sean asked. 'Quickly, tell me.'

The receptionist picked up the phone on her desk, punched in a few numbers, and spoke to someone at the other end before replying.

'The car is at the front of the hotel. Our driver, Hugo, will take you wherever you want to go.'

Hugo, prompted by Sean's offer of five hundred euros to get to Charles de Gaulle airport as quickly as possible, wove the black Mercedes Maybach through the busy motorway as if he were carrying a world leader being chased by international terrorists.

'If you lose your driving license,' Sean called to him, 'I'll pay you a hundred thousand euros. Just get me to the damned airport as quickly as you can!'

Hugo put his foot to the floor, hoping for the first time in his life to get a ticket. Twenty minutes later, the Maybach screeched to a halt at the departures gate drop-off zone.

'We're are here, *monsieur*. Quickly, find your woman.'

'Wait for me,' said Sean, I'll meet you at the arrivals parking area as soon as I find her.'

Hugo, like any true Frenchman, understood the vagaries of love, nodded.

'I will be here when you find her. *Bon chance*.'

Sean took off, running at full pace towards the doors leading into the airport terminal building.

It took ten minutes for him to find the information desk. Thankfully, there was no-one ahead of him. He asked the man behind the desk when the next flight to Boston was departing.

'It takes off in under thirty minutes, sir. A Pan American Airlines flight. Their desk is behind you, if you need a ticket, but I fear you will not make it. It's already boarding.'

Sean rushed over to the desk and spoke to one of the girls dressed in a light-blue, Pan Am uniform.

'Listen, this might sound crazy, but, my partner, well, we had a fight. I think she's going to fly home to Boston on your next flight out. It's leaving soon.'

'It is, sir, but I'm afraid it's fully booked. The next flight is . . .'

'No, you're not getting it,' Sean's voice was louder than he meant it to be. 'I don't want to join her. I just don't want her to get on the flight.'

The girl looked at Sean as if he was trying to teach her calculus.

'I'm not sure I understand, sir.'

Sean's frustration began to simmered.

'Are you a bloody idiot? I just told you my partner was getting on your flight and I don't want her to go. What's not to understand? Honestly, do you fucking people act like morons intentionally?'

The girl still seemed confused.

'There's no need to swear, sir. I don't want to have to call airport security.'

'There you go, being a bitch for no reason whatsoever.'

'Sir, now you're being aggressive. I'm going to *have* to call the airport police if you don't calm down.'

Sean's frustration boiled over.

'Fuck you!'

He took off towards the security gate, leaving the Pan Am assistant open-mouthed.

Hoping Claudia hadn't already gone through, he scanned the queue at the security gate, but there was no sign of her. He was too late. He turned and walked away, knowing she was already gone

Standing outside the terminal, Sean re-read Claudia's letter. The sky, even in the short time he'd been in the airport terminal, had turned as dark as his mood. It began to rain, turning from drizzle to downpour in under a minute. Fat raindrops landed on the letter, turning the ink-blue words into an abstract watercolour. Dejected, he dropped it on the ground and turned his gaze skyward, watching a plane that had just taken off. It The banked right, disappearing into a smother of angry cloud. *It could be hers*, he thought, *but probably wasn't.*

He cried up at it anyway.

'You promised you'd never leave me, Claudia. No matter what.'

'She lied to you, didn't she, hun?'

Sean looked round and sighed. His anger and the sense of loss fading like the ink letters on the note at his feet.

'Linz!'

66

The taxi drove past *Sans Cera*. Claudia looked at her gallery, thinking it might give her some sense of being home, but the colourful paintings and sculptures in the windows did little to raise her mood. She had come back to Lexington, but there were no yellow ribbons. Not that she would have cared.

The flight had been long and tiring and she was emotionally empty. She'd missed Sean from the moment she'd boarded the plane and had thought of getting off a number of times, but the point where that had been an option had passed. The plane had taken off into storm that had centred over the airport and cloaked the bright lights of Paris, although not enough to stop her seeing the twinkling lights of the Eiffel Tower, where she and Sean had stood a week before sipping Champagne.

'It's up here,' said Claudia, 'just past the big oak and turn right.' The driver took the turn and continued along by the golf course. 'Okay, just here, the one with the sloping driveway and the black gates.'

Parked up, the driver helped her with her bags, which were on wheels, so easy enough to walk down the driveway. Claudia handed him a hundred-dollar bill and told him to keep the change.

'Thanks lady, have a good night.'

Paul's car was in the driveway, but the house was in darkness. He was still in Los Angeles, Claudia knew, from their conversation the previous day. She'd call him in the morning to let him know she was back. They'd talk more at the weekend, if and when he came home. There were things she needed to say. She needed to tell him about Paris.

And Sean!

Paris! It seemed a world away, now. As if it had not even been real. As if she and Sean were characters in a fictional love story that had always been doomed to end. But their story had been real. She knew that from the pain the thought of him brought her. The memory continued to hurt her. She allowed it to. She needed to feel the pain to keep her from going mad with grief. She mourned the loss of him and wanted nothing more than to just turn around and go back to him.

But he had to come to her.

After letting herself into the house, Claudia left her bags in the hallway. All she wanted was to sleep. She'd watched three movies on the plane, but could not remember one of them. She needed to take a Valium and to lose herself in the comfort of nothingness. The house was still and silent, save from the creaking of the timbers as she climbed the stairs. *No mice and no clogs.* Sean had taught her the ridiculous song. The thought of it tortured her, coming into her head for no good reason.

The door to the master bedroom swung open on well-oiled hinges and her king-sized bed was more than a welcome sight. At least, it would have been, if it had been empty. There were two people on it, lying on the sheet, the duvet cast aside, lying on the floor. She couldn't see either of their faces. The woman, straddling the man below her, had her back to Claudia. Her hands were pressed flat on his chest and she was grinding herself on him, moaning loudly, clearly enjoying her efforts.

Below her, her partner responded eagerly, thrusting his hips up to meet her each time she moved forward on him, his hands, either side of her hips, guiding her movements. She had a voluptuous mane of dark hair which swished from side-to-side as she moved, athletic shoulders, and a narrow waist with smooth, alabaster skin, lit by the glow of the moon shining in through the bedroom window. She was moaning loudly, as was he, both close to the place they were ultimately aiming for.

For a moment, Claudia almost turned and left the room. It seemed, no matter how crazy it felt, she was intruding on something private. She would never know if she would have done. Afterwards, more than anything else, she would remember the entire scene with no little degree of amusement. Especially the look on Paul's face when he'd finally seen her. Although, right now, she wasn't laughing.

Neither was he.

'Claudia! Oh, Christ! Claudia!'

Paul's skin, even in the half-light, paled. He pulled a pillow over his chest. *To hide what?* Claudia had no idea.

'Hello, Paul,' said Claudia, calmly, 'please don't tell me it's not what it looks like.'

The woman, Claudia would later think, should have reacted by shrieking loudly, disengaging herself from Paul, then pulled a sheet over herself in an attempt to hide her nakedness. But she didn't. Instead, she stayed exactly where she was. On top of Paul. Although she did at least have the decency to stop grinding herself against him.

'Claudia. Obviously, we didn't expect you.'

Claudia struggled to contain her anger. Only just stopping herself from grabbing something and lashing out. She forced herself to reply.

'So the gallery wasn't enough? You wanted my husband as well.'

'Well you don't. That's been obvious.'

Things began to fall into place, for Claudia. She'd thought Paul was having an affair. All the pointers had been there from the start.

'It was you with him, wasn't it, that night at the apartment in Boston?'

'Yes. But if it's any easier to take, that was the first time we were together. I was in Boston, as you know. We just happened to bump into each other.'

'I'll bet! And after all I've done for you at *Sans Cera*.'

'No more than I've done for you. You've hardly been there in the past three months.'

Claudia felt the rage threatening to come to the surface, but, as quickly as it had come, it passed. Instead, a voice in her head asked her a question. It was Hannah's voice, and the question she asked changed everything.

'You walked the Camino, my dear, and the Camino always provides. Didn't it, for you? Haven't you found the answer yet? What do you *need* to make you happy? What do you *really* need.'

Claudia knew the answer.

The valley of silence that had descended over the bedroom prompted Paul to speak.

'Honey, I'm so sorry. We'd not been together, you and I, for so long. I was lonely and frustrated. It just happened. I was at the apartment. I went to get some . . .'

Claudia held up a hand to silence him.

'It's fine, Paul. Please don't try to explain.'

She smiled, which was probably very disconcerting for him, she suddenly thought. She didn't laugh, despite she felt like laughing. That would really freak him out.

'But, Claudia . . .'

'Paul, seriously, we both knew it was over before I left for Europe. I'm not angry with you. I'm not even shocked. I knew you'd found someone. I just didn't realise it was someone young enough to be our daughter. She shifted her gaze. 'Charity, you really are a clever girl. You'll go far, believe me. You can keep your job at the gallery, if you still want it. You're good at what you do. I'm happy for you to keep making me money. I'll tell Isabella what's happened. She'll want to fire you, of course, but I'll try and smooth it over. It's her call. She's irreplaceable, you're not.'

'Thank you, Claudia,' said Charity, smiling back at her. 'I'm sure Isabella will want what's best for the gallery.'

Claudia let herself laugh.

'I would stake my life on that, Charity. Isabella understands loyalty, something you'll learn the value of, in time, if you're lucky. Oh, and in case you're wondering, scheming your little schemes, the gallery's mine, not Paul's. He won't try to take it from me, will you, Paul?'

'No,' said Paul, more than slightly perturbed that Claudia was acting so calmly.

'Not now your new career's taking off. You really don't want to rock that boat before it comes fully out of the slips.'

'Claudia, I'm so . . .'

Claudia held up a hand to silence him.

'Save it, Paul. We can talk in a week or so. I've got a lot to sort out. We had fun, though, didn't we? More sun than rain, more laughter than tears, and more smiles than frowns. Take care of you. I'm going to take care of me. You may not need me anymore, but there's someone who does.'

67

Claudia turned Sky off the Pilgrims Highway and drove down into Duxbury, stopping briefly at her sister's house to collect something important. She promised Margot she'd be back later that day to tell her everything that had happened in Europe. Back in the car, she crossed Powder Point Bridge and headed along the isthmus towards the lighthouse. She glanced up at the church on Duxbury Hill, where Hannah's service had taken place, not so long ago, and felt a sense of belonging she had not felt in forever. The sun was shining and the sky was a blue canvas streaked with ribbons of white cirrus clouds. It was, she thought, a perfect day, and the perfect place to be to enjoy it.

She'd driven down the coast from Isabella's house, just outside Lexington, that morning, the Volkswagen's hood down, letting the wind blow her hair out of shape and relishing the salty tang of the ocean. She'd stayed with her since the night she'd discovered Charity giving charity to Paul, almost a month ago, but was ready, now, to face her future. That future, she had decided, would be here.

The lighthouse rose out of the grassy dunes ahead of her. She took the track from the car park to right up beside the old wooden tower and parked up. The gulls shrieked a greeting, as if they had missed her and were excited to see her return.

'What do you think, Sylkie? Good to be home?'

Sylkie, standing in the passenger seat, front paws on the dashboard, gave an excited bark. The little dog had been overjoyed to see Claudia when she'd stopped to collect her. She'd leapt into her arms and licked her face, barking and crying with sheer joy. Her tail was still wagging furiously.

Claudia climbed helter-skelter steps, thinking of the people who had climbed them before her. She looked down and smiled at Jonathon, who was standing behind one of his workbenches, sanding a newly made chair. He looked up and smiled at her then went back to work. She nodded to him and climbed on as his ghost disappeared. Up in the Glass Menagerie, she gazed out towards the Point and saw Hannah, sitting on the bench by Betsy's stone. She'd known she would be there to welcome her home.

'I'll be there soon, old friend. I need to see something first.'

In the centre of the studio stood Hannah's easel, the muslin cloth still covering the canvas she had been working on up until the day she'd died. Claudia wondered if she'd finished it. Filled with equal measures of excitement and trepidation she lifted the cloth and stood back to view it, understanding, finally, what Hannah had told her about the painting the very first day they had met.

It's a matter of perspective, my dear.

'You finished it, Hannah. And it's beautiful. You told me that it was not what you were looking at but how you were looking at it.'

The image of the Cathedral de Santiago rose into an azure blue sky, its three tall towers framed by intricate, biblical carvings. The central tower had the statue of St James at its top, looking down. The perspective of the painting was odd, the angles sheer and dramatic. It looked, the way it had been painted, as if the Cathedral was falling down upon the observer. It could only, Claudia realised, have been captured in one way.

'You lay in the centre of the square, in Santiago, didn't you? On your back, looking up at it, just as I did.'

She remembered the day in her mind's eye, picturing the cathedral, her friends around her and Sean looking down at her, smiling at her and asking what she was doing. The image was brutal and haunting.

Melancholy, but not wanting to be, she turned and headed down the stairs back out into the sunlight. The painting had stirred a memory of the two people she loved with all her heart. That they were both now gone from her was almost too much to take.

'Come on Sylkie, let's go for a walk. My nieces have clearly fed you far too well. You're getting fat.'

Sylkie, ignoring the jibe, wagged her tail and shot off ahead of her.

Claudia passed the big house and noticed it had been repainted and the fence repaired. The fresh white paint brought the big house back to life, and the windows, fitted with new glass, glistened. The workmen she'd hired before she'd left had done their job well. She couldn't wait to get really stuck into it and make it how she wanted it to be.

Walking through the sand dunes, she looked down at the beach and saw Sylkie, bottom up, hunting the ever-elusive crabs. She wondered if the little dog had ever caught one or ever would. It didn't matter to Sylkie, she supposed. She was doing what she needed to do to make her happy.

Reaching the Point, Claudia followed the shingle track around the base of the cliff then climbed over the round bulge of granite and followed the hidden passageway to the hidden steps. At the top of the steps, she walked out onto the grass and up to the bench. The ocean was as flat as sheet steel, blue silver rather than silver blue. In the distance she could see skiether, the sea and sky becoming one. She looked down at Betsy's stone and smiled.

'Hello, Betsy.'

'She's sleeping,' said Hannah, stepping up beside Claudia. Her wild red hair streamed out behind her, blowing in the wind coming in from across the ocean.

'I'll watch over her for you.'

'I know you will, my dear.'

'I've come home, Hannah.'

'We both have.'

Claudia knew she was saying goodbye.

'I won't see you again, will I?'

'No! Not now. But I'll always be here to talk to.'

'You better be, crazy lady.'

Hannah laughed and Claudia remembered a thousand other times they'd laughed together. And the day she had first stood there, listening to her speak of Betsy. It made so much sense, now the Universe had played its game with them. The chess pieces had moved into place, and the reason for them meeting was finally clear.

Hannah asked the question Claudia knew she wanted to ask.

'Did you find what you needed?'

'I found Sean.'

'And?'

'He *gave* me what I needed.'

'So,' whispered Hannah, 'you're no longer alone and adrift?'

'No,' said Claudia, quietly. She ran her hand, tenderly, over her stomach. 'I won't ever be alone again.'

68

Isabella was fussing over Claudia like an old mother hen. Helping her to get her luggage out of Sky's back seats.

'Are you sure you want to do this? I really don't think it's one of your better ideas.'

'I'm two months pregnant, Isabella. The baby's the size of a peanut. Seriously, I'm not helpless. I'm certainly perfectly capable of flying to Europe.'

'Are you sure I can't come with you?'

'No, you bloody-well can't,' said Claudia, grabbing a trolley and letting Isabella manhandle the two large suitcases and brown-paper-wrapped parcel onto it. 'You need to stay here and look after the gallery. Besides, if I'm going to convince Sean to come back with me, I need the situation to remain calm. I think you'd scare him half to death.'

'I'll wring his bloody neck if he doesn't. I mean it, Claudia, I don't care how attractive and wonderful he is.'

'And . . . relax,' said Claudia, 'remember, it was me who left him in Paris, not the other way around. He was having a hard time when I met him. He didn't hide anything. Besides, I made most of the running. It was my fault more than his that we parted.'

'Isabella clearly thought otherwise, but let it go.

'Where is he now, exactly? Do you even know?'

'In a hotel, in a mountain village in the south of France. Somewhere called Chamonix. It's on the border of Switzerland and Italy, according to his texts. We spoke, last week, but it was a bit awkward. He's still angry with me. I know he's going to climb that damned mountain of his in a few days from now.'

'Mont Blanc!'

Claudia nodded.

'Well remembered. It's been closed for the past month, due to freak snowstorms, but the weather's set to change for the better. He's going to climb it. I need to see him before he does.'

'And he's no idea you're coming?'

'If he knew, he'd probably tell me not to. But I'm going. He might tell me to bugger-off as soon as he sees me, but I'll take that chance. We can't work it out while we're thousands of miles apart.'

'And he still doesn't know about the baby?'

'Not yet,' said Claudia, shaking her head. 'I don't want it to seem as if I'm using that as some sort of trap. I was never going to tell him over the phone, but I'll tell him when the time is right. Now, this is happening, like it or not, so give me a hug and wish me luck.'

They hugged and kissed one another.

'Go get him, honey. I'm dying to see the man that made you fall so hard.'

'I didn't just fall, Isabella. I absolutely plummeted.'

'At least you got high enough to fall. I haven't even started to climb.' They both laughed. 'Oh, before you go, I think I've found a new assistant.'

Claudia shrugged, looking like she couldn't care less.

'Your call, Isabella, now you're a fully-fledged partner in the business. Personally, I wouldn't have minded Charity staying on. I cheated on Paul, to be fair.'

Isabella looked affronted at the suggestion.

'It was never happening. Not after what that ungrateful slut did to you. I couldn't bring myself to look at her, let alone work with her. And let's not forget that Paul cheated on you first, after coming home for your anniversary. And that he should have gone to Europe with you, just as he promised he would.'

Claudia laughed at Isabella's anger and the slur on Charity's character.

'That,' said Claudia, 'more than anything else, was the final nail in the coffin of our marriage. If he'd have come with me I'd probably never have met Sean, and probably wouldn't be pregnant. Maybe this is how it was all meant to be. Ironically, it was Paul who said I should get pregnant naturally, through making love. And that's what happened. It just wasn't with him.'

'Well I'm still furious with Charity, honey. She was just a scheming little minx.'

'It's done now, Isabella, so just hire who you want and I'll see you in a week or so. I'll stay in touch.'

'Make sure you do.'

'Look after Sky for me. And don't get too attached.'

'Can't promise that, honey. She's beautiful. I'm going to enjoy swanning around Lexington in her, hood down, looking all elegant and available'

Isabella smiled and waved her off, showing her softer side by letting a single tear spill down her perfectly made up face. Thankfully, a handsome stranger, coming out of the airport, stopped to ask if she was okay. A few minutes later, they were discussing where they were going to have dinner. Claudia, watching from the airport terminal doors, shook her head and laughed, hoped her best friend would never change.

Ten hours later, Claudia landed in Paris, where she took the connecting Air France flight to Geneva, arriving late afternoon. After checking into the Hotel Longmalle and eating a meal that seemed to consist of a lot of potatoes, cream and bacon, she slept until early the next morning. After a light breakfast, the hotel provided a private car to take her up to the mountain village of Chamonix.

The Citroen Aircorss SUV climbed into the foothills of the French Alps. The steep road wound through thick, alpine forest and crossed fast-flowing rivers fed by ice-cold, glacial meltwater flowing down from the far-off mountain range. Even from twenty miles away, Claudia could see the peak of Mont Blanc rising higher than the mountains around it, dominating the view. The early-morning sunshine turned the snow on its slopes a ruddy gold, making it look more like an active volcano with lava spewing down its sides.

'It is your first time here?' the driver asked, as Claudia marvelled at the awesome spectacle.

'Not in France. I've spent a little time in Paris, but it's my first time here in the Alps.'

'*Mais Oui*, it is among the most beautiful of places in the world. You are here to climb? Or to sightsee?'

'I'm meeting someone,' replied Claudia, 'at the Hotel Mont Blanc. At least, I hope I am,' she added, under her breath.

'A fine hotel, *Madame* Montgomery. You will enjoy your stay, I am sure. We will be there in fifteen minutes.'

Chamonix was a traditional little French mountain town filled with historic churches and charming wooden buildings, like something out of a movie set, or that you'd find on the lid of an old-fashioned biscuit tin, it seemed, to Claudia, on first seeing it. Only it was real. The driver turned into the Allée du Majestic and drove up to the parking area, where the concierge welcomed Claudia to the hotel and instructed the porters to take her luggage inside.

'Welcome to the Mont Blanc, *Madame* . . .'

'Montgomery.' said Claudia, following him into the hotel and admiring the opulent décor of the hotel foyer.

Large, black and white marble floor-tiles turned the foyer into a giant chessboard. Cream armchairs and luxurious sofas complemented the crisp, white interior, while dark, wood-framed mirrors reflected the sunshine at curious angles, making the place even more light and airy.

'It is to your liking, *Madame* Montgomery.'

'It's stunning,' said Claudia, 'really.'

'We are an old but fine hotel,' said the concierge, leading Claudia to a wall of windows overlooking the Mont Blanc mountain range, 'a true symbol of the valley at the heart of Chamonix. I never tire of the view, and I have been here all my life. Every morning, I waken to see the most beautiful peak in all of Europe, Mont Blanc. You are here to climb it, no doubt?'

He gave Claudia a smile that told her he was teasing.

'Perhaps another time,' said Claudia, returning his smile. 'I'm here to visit a friend. It's a surprise. One I hope he's pleased about.'

'If he is not, *Madame* Montgomery, then he is fool. Now, should you require my help, for anything at all, do not hesitate to ask. I am Henri Charpentier. Ask for me by name, day or night. I am at your assistance.'

'Thank you, Henri. That's very kind of you.'

Henri offered Claudia's his arm and led her to the reception desk

'Now, let us check you in and take you to your room. After lunch, you must take a walk around the gardens, or perhaps a visit to the village.'

'Do you have a booking reference, *Madame* Montgomery?' One of the well-groomed girls at reception asked.

'I'm so sorry. I don't actually have a reservation,' said Claudia, slightly embarrassed. 'Do you have a room available?'

The girl shook her head.

'I apologise, *Madame,* we have nothing. We are fully booked. It is the climbing season, you understand.'

'Of course,' replied Claudia, 'how stupid of me. I came to meet a friend of mine who is staying here. I just assumed you would have a room.'

'Do not worry,' said Henri, 'I am sure we can sort something out for you. What is the name of your friend?'

'It's Sean. Sean Jameson. He's here to . . .'

'Excuse me, *Madame,* please forgive my intrusion. I could not help but overhear. Did you say, Sean Jameson?'

Claudia turned to see who had spoken.

Standing behind her was a tall man with long hair and a full but short beard. His beard, like his hair, was dark, though streaked with the first growth of silver. His eyes were amber-grey with explosions of vibrant yellow flaring out around the pupils like a corona around a flaming sun. They reminded Claudia of a timber wolf she had once seen in a wildlife park in Montana. His eyes were the same colour and intensity.

'I did. Do you know him?'

'Indeed, *Madame.* He is in the mountains.'

'He's already climbing Mont Blanc?'

'No, *Madame,* he is . . .'

'My name is Claudia.'

She held out her hand and allowed the man to shake it.

'Claudia, please do not be concerned, he is only acclimatising. As he has been doing for the past few weeks. He is due to climb Mont Blanc, tomorrow. Allow me to introduce myself. My name is Pierre Ochanda. I am a friend of Sean's. We are both climbers, so, in a sense, we are brothers.'

'Oh, thank you, Pierre. Thank goodness he's still here.'

Claudia suddenly felt faint. It must have shown.

'Please,' said Pierre, taking her arm, 'do not be worried. Sean will soon return. Come and sit down. I was about to have some lunch. You will join me. At least until Sean arrives. We will sort everything out then. Isn't that right, Henri?'

'Of course,' said Henri, 'please don't be upset, *Madame* Montgomery. Allow me to take you through to the dining room. You *are* a little pale. I think, perhaps, *Monsieur* Ochanda is correct. Some food will help. Perhaps, even a small brandy?'

'Some lunch would be lovely,' said Claudia, allowing herself to be guided through to a dining room that looked out over the hotel gardens. 'I'd better pass on the brandy.' She turned to Pierre. 'Are you sure you don't mind me joining you?'

Pierre looked shocked at the suggestion.

'Since when has any Frenchman minded a beautiful woman joining him for lunch? Especially given where we find ourselves in a crucible of ice and snow.'

'Very romantically put,' said Claudia, glad of the invitation.

She was hungry, as well as a little flustered.

Pierre was forty-nine years of age and, like Sean, his business was in technology. He lived in Paris, where his company operated in the same markets as QuantumCloud, although was a much smaller concern. Claudia allowed him to order for them both. They chatted like old friends, rather than newly made ones, over creamy, potato soup sprinkled with finely chopped chives, served with fresh-baked soda-bread still warm from the hotel ovens.

'A glass of wine?' Pierre asked.

'Yes, that would be . . . On second thoughts, I'd best not.'

'Some mineral water, instead?'

'Perfect.'

'Now, tell me, Claudia Montgomery, from where have you arrived today?'

'I came up from Geneva this morning. I flew from Boston to Paris the day before.'

'A long journey. Possibly what made you feel a little faint. *Non?*'

'Probably.'

'And Sean. He is aware of your arrival?'

'No. He doesn't know, yet.'

'I see,' said Pierre. 'I wondered that he had not mentioned it. We had dinner, here, last night, as we have done for the past weeks, waiting for the conditions to change enough to allow us to climb our great mountain. There have been some terrible storms. I think, perhaps, now they are finally over.

'How high is it,' Claudia asked, taking a third piece of bread, loading it a rude amount of butter then dipping it into her soup. 'And is it dangerous?'

'Mont Blanc,' began Pierre, or *Monte Bianco*, as it is known by the Italians, is commonly known as the White Killer. It is the highest mountain in all of Europe, standing a little under eighteen thousand feet. Not as high as other such famous mountains, perhaps, but it has sharp teeth, and will bite, unless you know what you are doing.'

'*White Killer*?'

Claudia had paled, again, distressed at Pierre's description.

'*Zut Alors!* Please, Claudia, forgive me. Such a thing for me to say. It is dangerous, as all mountains are, but what is more dangerous is stupidity and lack of ability. Sean and I are experienced climbers. It is dangerous for amateurs, is what I meant to say. Inexperienced climbers and greedy tour operators who want to get their teams to the summit, no matter the risk. I am guilty of becoming over-dramatic.'

He smiled, trying to reassure her. Claudia, although still concerned, accept his explanation.

It's fine, Pierre, perhaps I am being a little oversensitive.'

Pierre moved the conversation and talked for the next half hour, regaling Claudia with tales of the mountains he had climbed around the world, his years trekking through South America, and of his passion for photography.

Claudia, in turn, told him of her lighthouse and the plans for her new gallery, as well as of her own recent trek across the Camino de Santiago. She relaxed and forgot about what he had said about Mont Blanc. *He has a way about him*, she thought, *that makes him easy to talk to.* There was a kindness within him that was at odds with his wolf-like exterior. She found him both charming and interesting.

'The Camino sounds like a wonderful adventure, Claudia. Sean did not talk much of it, other than to say it was where you and he first met.'

Claudia couldn't hide her surprise, given that she knew Sean normally played things close to his chest.

'So, he has at least mentioned me?'

Pierre smiled, understanding what she meant.

'He spoke a little of your time together in Paris. I think something must have happened between you, there, that was not so good.'

'Something *did* happen in there, Pierre. We both made mistakes. Mostly me. I hope to fix that. It is why we . . . I mean, it's why I'm here.'

Pierre stared at her like a barn owl looking at a mouse, tilting his head as if he were working something out.

'Of course! Now I understand. You refused the offer of wine, despite that I could see you wanted to say yes. And, just now, said, *we,* before correcting yourself. You went pale, earlier, and seemed a little faint, which I thought to be only that you were tired. Now I see there is but one explanation. You are with child.'

Claudia blushed. She knew it was pointless to lie.

'You should be a detective, Pierre.'

Pierre, his suspicions confirmed, leant across the table to take her hands in his.

'It is *magnifique*, Claudia. But, Sean, he knows of this?'

Claudia looked down at the table.

'No. I have not told him.'

'Then it will be a wonderful surprise for him. I am sure of it.'

'It may be, Pierre. I hope it is. But I'm not going to tell him. At least, not yet. Not until he has climbed this damned mountain of his. Nor must you.'

'*Mon Dieu*, why not?'

'I don't want him to climb at all, Pierre. I hope to convince him not to, but I will not have him climb it with the thought of our child in his head. I won't add to the weight of confusion he already carries. Not when it might be what causes him to have an accident. I cannot do that to him. I love him too much.'

'I understand your reasons, Claudia, but surely . . .'

'No! You must swear you won't tell him. Say it, Pierre, or I will leave and go back to America this very moment.'

'*D'accord!* All right, Claudia. I give you my word.'

'Thank you, Pierre, thank you,' said Claudia, and calmed. 'Now, tell me, how has he been?'

Pierre shrugged his shoulders.

'*Comme ci, comme ca!* He has many troubles, I think. This is not good for a climber. He takes risks, perhaps, that he should not. But with you here he will be less intense. I am certain of it.'

Claudia was about to ask Pierre to explain what he meant by Sean taking risks he should not, when Pierre stood up, looking at someone behind her.

'Sean, you are returned. How is it up there?'

Claudia had her back to Sean and his attention was obviously on Pierre.

'Good, Pierre, but bloody cold. Perfect for us both, tomorrow. Now, aren't you going to introduce me to your . . .'

Before he could finish, Claudia stood and turned to face him.

'Hello, Sean. Me Claudia.'

Sean was still dressed in his mountaineering gear. He'd let his beard grow out and his hair was longer than she remembered. It suited him. His face was tanned and he appeared fit and healthy, and his eyes were the same piercing, cornflower blue. He looked like a climber, she thought, rugged and strong. She felt her heart jump and had to stop herself reaching out for him.

Sean had played the moment over in his head any number of times since Claudia had left him in Paris. He'd imagined how he would hurt her, being cruel with his words, before sending her away. But that had been when his anger was sharp and fresh, the wounds raw and stinging, needing any salve, even hatred. But as the days had turned to weeks, that desire had faded. Now, seeing her in front of him, he realised how much he'd missed her.

'Hello, Claudia. I didn't realise you were coming.'

'Nor did I, to be honest.'

'It's good to see you. You look well.'

'It's good to see you too, Sean. So, do you.'

'*Merde*,' said Pierre, 'it is clear to see you both have no French blood in you.' He turned to Claudia, took her hand, and kissed it. 'I will leave you in the hands of this . . . *Scottish man*, who has no romance in his soul. If he does not want you, I shall be waiting to take his place.'

Claudia kissed him on both cheeks.

'Thank you, Pierre, for looking after me.'

'The pleasure was mine, trust me.' As he passed Sean, he whispered. '*Tres gentile*, my friend, she is how you say, fragile.'

Sean nodded and shook Pierre's hand.

'Thanks, Pierre. I owe you.'

'You own me nothing, my friend. I have spent only an hour with her and already know she is a special woman. Be happy she is here.'

Pierre left the room, heading into foyer.

Claudia retook her seat, unsure how to act. It felt odd being next to Sean. He was staring at her as if he had not quite taken in that she was here at all. She wondered if she'd made a mistake in coming. She wasn't quite sure what to say to him, so said the obvious.

'Was it good climbing, today?'

'Yes,' said Sean, not knowing if he should hug her, kiss her, or offer to shake her hand. In the end, he took Pierre's seat opposite her. 'I've been climbing a lot. Thinking about things. Wondering what the hell I'm doing. That sort of thing.'

He felt the awkwardness between them and didn't know what to do about it. He called the waiter over and ordered a large Glenmorangie.

'Probably the best place to think,' said Claudia. 'You love this place, don't you? You always said it was special.'

'I came here the year I met Linz. We did the Mont Blanc Circuit when we were still at university.'

'That must be a wonderful mem...'

Claudia stopped talking. They were making small talk. As they'd done in the square in Santiago. The same feeling must have occurred to Sean.

'What the hell are you doing here, Claudia?'

'I've asked myself the same thing, Sean. At the airport, in Boston, before the flight to Paris. Again, on the way to Geneva. Today, standing in the foyer, hoping I would see you. Afraid that I would.'

'And what was the answer?'

Sean took a slug of his whisky, enjoying the burn.

Claudia took a breath. It was honesty that would save them, nothing else. She remembered telling Sean the same thing, one sunny day, out on the Camino de Santiago.

'It was simple, Sean. I'm in love with you. I haven't changed how I feel. But things are very different now.'

She recounted the story of her disastrous homecoming; finding Paul in bed with Charity, her weeks staying with Isabella and her permanent move to the lighthouse.'

'That must have been hellish, finding him like that.'

Claudia nodded, but, Sean noticed, didn't seem upset. He was glad she wasn't hurting.

'It was and it wasn't. I'm glad it happened. It forced me to look at my life and make some decisions I'd been too afraid to make. I realised, in that moment, that our marriage had been over for some time. I felt guilty, I guess, about having fallen in love with you. I had to tell Paul that, face to face. I came back to do the same thing with you. To tell you that I want to spend the rest of my life with you.'

Sean gave her a look she could not decipher. *At least I told him.* She was glad she had. She would not press it. He changed the subject, so she felt her words had fallen on stony ground.

'So, you're staying here?'

Claudia shook her head.

'I don't have a room. They're full.'

'You really didn't plan this very well, Claudia. Did you?'

'I suppose not. Look, I know I've sprung this on you. But I had to come. I can find a hotel close by, if you don't mind me being in Chamonix. Perhaps we could find some time to talk. But if you don't want to do that, then maybe its best if . . .'

Sean reached across the table and took her hands in his.

'Stop talking, Claudia. I'm glad you're here. I've missed you. Really missed you. I love you too,'

Claudia thought she might expire, such was her relief.

'Oh, Sean, I thought . . .'

She felt tears forming in the corner of her eyes, this time, they were of joy, not sadness. Sean handed her a napkin.

'Don't cry. Everyone looking will think I'm a shit!'

'Let them,' said Claudia, laughing, 'I know different.'

Sean squeezed her hands and smiled.

'Good answer. And the right one. Now, you can stay here, with me, if you want. I have the penthouse suite.' He saw the smile on her face. 'And don't say, *of course you do.*'

'I wasn't going to,' said Claudia. 'I got kind of used to the way you like to travel.'

'And I got kind of used to you. Why did you leave me?'

'I was upset, Sean, at . . . well, you know.'

They were both silent for a moment, remembering what had happened in Paris.

'You promised you would never leave me, Claudia, that night in Santiago.'

'And you couldn't say you were in love with me, Sean. You still can't. But that's okay. I can wait for you to say that. Not forever, but for now.'

Sean looked down at the table, as if the memory of that night was being replayed on the white linen tablecloth.

'I came after you, you know. I chased you to the airport.'

Claudia was surprised.

'Did you? I thought you didn't care.'

'Well you were wrong,' said Sean. 'If you'd waited for me, at the hotel, you'd have found that out.'

Claudia could see the pain her leaving had cost him. She felt guilty, knowing he had tried to stop her.

'I'm sorry, Sean. I didn't mean to hurt you.'

'Well you did. You shouldn't have left that way. You should have given me the chance to fix things.'

'But what could you have fixed, Sean? I needed you to say you were in love with me. It would have given me the strength to change my life. As it happens, you already had, I just didn't know it at the time.'

Sean's brow furrowed.

'How did I do that?'

Claudia realised she'd said too much and struggled to form an adequate answer. Thankfully, one of the luggage attendants approached the table.

'I'm sorry to disturb you, Mr Jameson, but shall I take your wife's things up to your suite.'

Claudia looked up at the attendant.

'I'm not his . . .'

'Yes, thank you, that will be fine,' said Sean, not letting her finish, 'actually, just store them for now. I'll ring down for them later.'

'Of course, Mr Jameson.'

Sean let the attendant move away then held his hand out across the table.

'You must be tired after your journey. Do you want to come up and rest for a while?'

Claudia suddenly felt apprehensive and vulnerable.

'Do you want me to?'

Sean stood and offered his hand.

'You must know I do.'

They made love all afternoon. Not with the unbridled, sexual passion of their first night together in Santiago, or the heady excitement of the deepening romance they had discovered in Paris, but with the slow and deliberate tenderness of two people deeply in love. Afterwards, they sat together, cross-legged on the massive bed, sipping hot spiced-wine and eating cold apple-strudel, looking out through the double verandah windows towards the mountains.

'It's quite magnificent,' said Claudia. 'I thought Mont Blanc was just one mountain, but my driver told me it's actually the whole range.'

'He was right,' said Sean, dragging her over to him so that she was sitting, still cross-legged, between his legs, facing out to the view. He pointed to the highest of the peaks, washed light purple under the late afternoon sun.

'So, just to situate things a bit for you, Chamonix is the town at the base of the French side of the Massif du Mont Blanc, which is basically the whole set of mountains that host the highest mountain of the alps, Mont Blanc.'

'It looks amazing, my darling. No wonder you love it here.'

'It is! One side of the mountain lies in France, but the other side is in Italy. The summit is actually on the Italian side, but that's just a technical detail. If you look below the mountain you can see there's a massive glacier flowing down from it. It's called the *Mer de Glace*.'

'The Sea of Ice,' said Claudia, 'my French is just good enough to know that.'

'Exactly! It winds all the way down to Chamonix, through a valley called the Vallee Blanche.'

'Don't tell me,' said Claudia, wriggling in Sean's lap as his hands began to wander, the White Valley.'

She leaned over and picked up the last remaining piece of apple strudel and popped it into her mouth.

'Indeed, you greedy piglet. That's your third piece.'

Claudia pushed her bottom back into Sean's groin and snuffled her nose into Sean's neck.

'And we piglets always want more.'

'Be careful what you wish for, piglet' said Sean, and kissed her neck, making Claudia shiver.

She turned and climbed into his lap, allowing her dressing gown to fall open, revealing breasts Sean thought were ever fuller than he remembered them being.

'Then make it come true, my darling.'

Half an hour later, he capitulated.

'Okay, no more sex, Claudia. Not for at least half an hour. You're even more insatiable than I remember.'

'I've been on a diet, again, Mr Jameson, and I'm so terribly hungry.'

It was bliss, Claudia thought, leaning back against him, his arms wrapped around her. It felt that nothing could ever come between them. She wished she could capture the moment forever. It made her remember another such moment they'd shared.

'I did a painting for you. In the studio at my lighthouse. My first in the Glass Menagerie.'

'A painting! For me?'

'Yes,' said Claudia, 'of a moment in time. You'll understand when you see it. It's with my luggage.'

'You brought it all the way here?'

Claudia turned her head and looked up at him. She reached up and stroked his face, thinking he had never looked more handsome.

'I wanted you to have it, Sean. Whatever happened between us. I painted it for you. It's already yours. I just hope you like it.'

Sean leant down and kissed her on the mouth.

'I'm sure I will, my love. No one's ever painted a picture for me before. I'll need somewhere to hang it, though. I'm still kind of homeless.'

Claudia hesitated, afraid of what she was feeling and how what she wanted to say might scare him. But she'd travelled here to be honest about what she wanted for them both. She had to take a chance on letting him know *one* of those wants.

'We could hang it, together, if you come back with me to the lighthouse. We can make a life there for ourselves, Sean. One that would be wonderful.'

Sean didn't react as she had been afraid she might.

'Perhaps we could, my love. But, for now, let me get some sleep. I'm climbing, tomorrow, very early in the morning.'

Claudia looked shocked.

'But I thought, after today. This! I thought you might change your mind.'

'I came to climb Mont Blanc, Claudia. I have no choice.'

'You do have a choice, Sean. Why risk your life when you've got me and . . .'

She stopped herself just in time. Thankfully, Sean didn't seem to notice.

Sean stroked her cheek. She was sad, he could see that, but he couldn't change what he'd come to do.

'I made a promise to Linz. I need to finish what I started.'

'But what about us, Sean? What about you and me?'

'I never asked you to come here, Claudia. You left me. I thought it was for good. You just can't walk back into my life and expect me to start making different plans. I've been waiting to do this for months.'

'I don't, Sean. But things have changed.'

'Maybe for you, with Paul, but I'm not where you are. I'm not saying I won't be. Just not yet.'

Claudia felt betrayed and angry. She felt her temper rising.

'Damn you, Sean, I won't sit by and watch you die. I can't stay here with you if you're intent on doing that.'

'I'm climbing in the morning, Claudia. Nothing can change that.'

Claudia realised nothing she could say would change what Sean was going to do. She fought the angry in her. It had achieved nothing in Paris. It would achieve nothing here.

'Then tell me one thing, Sean. And make me one promise. If you love me.'

'What?'

'Just tell me you are not going up there to die. And promise me that when you come down this will end. Go up there for her, but come back down for me. Can you do that, my darling? If you can, then I can stand it. If not, I have to leave.

Sean looked out towards Mont Blanc, the mountain he would summit that next day, come what may. He looked back at Claudia. She seemed so frightened. He didn't want her to feel that way. Not over him. He needed to take away her fear.

'I'm not going up there to die, Claudia. Not on purpose. That' s never been what I intended to do. I called for Death to come for me, but I have to fight against her when and if she does. I will continue to do that. I will come back down if she spares me. That is as much as I can promise you. Is it enough?'

'It will have to be, Sean, won't it?'

'But I promise you that, when I do come down, I will end this. It will be the last challenge I do.'

'Sean! Do you mean it?'

'I promise, Claudia. The last.'

Claudia's relief was almost overwhelming. He *did* love her. His promise was enough to show him that.

'Thank you, my darling, that's all I needed to give me the strength to let you go up there.'

She kissed him, a lingering, sensuous kiss, wrapping her arms around him and holding him as if never wanting to let him go. He would climb and she would wait for him. She agonised over the decision to tell him about their child, but couldn't place that burden on him. *When he comes down, then I will tell him.*

'So, will you stay?' Sean asked.

'I will, my darling. But when you leave, in the morning, don't waken me. I'll be waiting for you, here, when you come back. I'll never leave you again after that. Not as long as I live. No matter what. Just make sure you come back to me.'

'I will, my love.'

Sean kissed her on the forehead.

'Call me the minute you're off the top of that damned mountain, Sean Jameson. You hear me! As soon as you can, you call. Promise me.'

'I promise.' Sean went to cross his heart then stayed his hand. Claudia noticed but said nothing. He was still wearing his crucifix. That, she felt, was a good sign. 'There's phone reception from the overnight hut I'm staying at after I've summited. I'll call you the moment I get there.'

'And then you pack your things and come home with me, or we'll never see each other again. I mean it, Sean. I'm in love with you, but I can't be in love for us both.'

'You know I love you, Claudia, don't you?'

'I know you do.' She stroked his beard, twisting bits of it in her fingers. A gentle, intimate touch. 'Make love to me,' she whispered, 'make love to me as if it's the last time you ever will.'

'It won't be the last time, Claudia. Have faith.'

'Have you found yours?'

Sean shook his head and pulled her to him.

'Why would I need it? It never worked before.'

They found a new connection and tenderness in their lovemaking. Claudia had her baby as well as the man she loved inside her. She prayed, silently, not knowing whom or what she was praying to, only that it was out there, echoing through the Universe. She hoped that whatever higher power might be listening it would answer her plea.

Bring him back to us.

69

Sean woke early. An almost full moon sent rays of white light lancing into the room through the balcony windows, allowing him to rise and dress without switching on his bedside lamp. Claudia was fast asleep. He had thought he might not climb, lying with her, shortly before they had finally gone to sleep. Their final lovemaking had felt very different. Despite having been apart for almost two months, it seemed they had become even closer. Although he could not understand how or why that might be.

He knew he loved her, but he wasn't *in love* with her. At least, not yet. Could he ever be? Could he allow himself to take that chance and open his heart? In the end, she would leave him, as everyone always did. He wanted her, but he didn't need her. Not as he had needed Linz. Not in the way that Linz still needed him. His loneliness and pain, although having lessened since the Camino, still remained, as did the ever present sense of guilt. His family had been taken from him and he had failed to go to them. How he felt was not as important as their need for him. Linz had explained it to him over the past weeks out in the mountains.

He left the bedroom, kissing Claudia lightly on the forehead, being careful not to waken her.

'Goodbye, Claudia,' he whispered, 'perhaps in another lifetime.'

Quietly closing the bedroom door, Sean went through the dining area into the suite's private entrance hallway. The porters had delivered Claudia's suitcases. Sitting next to them was a large, square package, wrapped in brown paper. It had his name written on it in bold black letters. He tore away the paper and stared at it, knowing immediately what Claudia had meant when she'd told him she'd painted a memory.

At the centre of the canvas was a dancer in a long, red dress. Her face was turned to one side and both arms held up above her head, reaching into the sky as she danced. A mane of jet-black hair flowed around her like the mane of an Andalusian stallion. Behind her, hinted at, almost abstract, were other dancers and guitarists, and the crowd, cheering and clapping under the orange streetlights. It was wild and dark and moody, but filled with vibrant colour, capturing the energy and joy of that heady night they'd danced together, in Leon, and found something in each other.

A note was taped to the side of the frame. Sean removed it and read it to himself. *Dancer in Leon. A gift to the man I fell in love with on that night.* Moved, he almost turned and walked back into the bedroom. But knew, if he did, he might not be able to leave. He had to keep his promise to Linz. She needed him. Instead, he opened the door into the hallway and left.

In the bedroom, Claudia stood at the windows until she saw Sean walk out into the carpark and climb into a waiting taxi. She waved after him as the car drove away, hoping he had seen her, knowing he probably hadn't.

'Come back to me, Sean. You promised you would. I hold you to that promise.' She ran a hand over her stomach. 'We need you.'

She turned and went back to bed, knowing she would not sleep, wondering if the prayer she had said, earlier, had been heard, and if it would be answered.

70

Sean arrived at the cable car station before sunrise, although daybreak heralded its coming by smearing the serrated edge of the mountains in the faintest brush of violet-blue. Over his full-body, merino-wool base-layer he wore a Berghaus climbing jacket and had donned a pair of fleece-lined, Montane, climbing trousers, a felt beanie, and his Scarpa Phantom mountaineering-boots. He had other clothing and climbing equipment in his rucksack and was well prepared for what lay ahead on a range famed for its volatile weather.

The cable car, even at such an early hour, was busy with climbers. Most were silent, focused on the climb ahead. It swung free of its guide rails, rocking slightly before settling into a silent glide, beginning the forty-five-minute journey up to where the climbers would begin their ascent, irrespective of the route they choose to take up Mont Blanc.

Chamonix grew smaller, the car ascending so quickly that it was soon a thousand feet above the Mer de Glace, an ice-field, in places, over six hundred feet deep and regarded as the largest in France. Broken into irregular ridges and deep chasms, it had been compared by the poet, William Coxe, to sea waves instantaneously frozen amid a violent storm. Under the light of a sinking moon, Sean considered it an entirely accurate description.

At the halfway-point transit station, most of the other climbers got out. They were, Sean knew, most likely practicing for a full ascent at a later date. Twenty minutes later, the car pulled into the world-famous Aiguille du Midi, the gateway to the Massif du Mont Blanc and location of the silver-coloured weather-station that doubled as the cable car terminal and offered unrestricted views over the French, Swiss and Italian Alps.

Sean walked out of the terminal and stopped at the viewing platform to gaze out over the French side of the mountain range. He was over twelve thousand feet up and the view was staggering. He turned back and looked up, marvelling at the sight of the mountain he had come to challenge.

At almost eighteen-thousand feet high, Mont Blanc was the undisputed heavyweight of the Alps and the highest peak in Western Europe. A huge, white dome surrounded by thundering glaciers, massive alpine faces and some of the world's most stunning alpine scenery. Sean knew, in his heart, that Linz was with him.

'Look my love, we're here. We said we'd come, didn't we? All those years ago.'

Hearing no answer, but knowing Linz would be waiting for him higher up, he put on his helmet and attached his crampons to his boots, tightened his rucksack straps and set off at a brisk pace. Despite it was still only six in the morning, he had to move quickly if he was to summit by midday and avoid the chance of avalanche on his descent.

Sean had decided to use a version of the Mont Blanc ascent known as the "Traverse of Les Trois Monts", because of the three peaks it crossed; Mont Blanc du Tacul, Mont Maudit and Mont Blanc. It was more technical and physically demanding than the "Goiuter Route", the most popular and easiest of the routes, but he would still summit in good time.

From the Aiguille du Midi, he descended the famous snow arête that made up the Midi East Ridge, the prominent ridge line in between the Pain de Sucre and the Dent du Crocidile, before turning back and heading towards the famous Cosmiques Hut, where he would spend the night, after summiting. As he passed under the beautiful south face of the Midi, he breakfasted on the hoof, eating three bananas and two high-protein cereal bars. Behind him, the sun broke free of the horizon, turning the ice-white landscape rose gold. The going was crisp and sure and he made better progress than he'd hoped. It was, he considered, the perfect day to climb.

Despite the appearance of the sun, the temperature had dropped below freezing, but there was little breeze, so the windchill was bearable without having to add extra layers. It was cold enough, however, for Sean to pull his Berghaus mitts on over his merino wool, liner gloves, to keep his hands warm. An hour later, he reached the Cosmiques Hut and stopped for a short break.

Looking back down the slope, he could see there were no other climbers behind him, though, in the distance, some five hundred feet above him, could make out a small group of climbers who had obviously started out from the hut at least an hour before.

After crossing the Col du Midi plateau, Sean climbed the northwest face of Mont Blanc du Tacul, reaching the high shoulder in just over an hour. There were several difficult crevasse crossings to negotiate, but they were all equipped with steel ladders, placed there by the local mountain guides. The sight of them made him think of Kamal, the Sherpa guide who had saved his life on Mount Everest. He sent him a greeting, one climber to another.

'Namaste, my friend. I hope you are well.'

From the top of the shoulder, he continued towards the north face of Mont Maduit, descending slightly before beginning to re-climb beneath some precarious looking *seracs*. One of the massive, overhanging ice-blocks could kill him instantly if it broke free and fell. He climbed higher, taking a diagonal line upwards, passing under them without incident. Just below the Col du Mont Maudit lay the infamous "Crux Step", forty or so metres of sharply-angled, frozen snow. It was a treacherous point which needed to be negotiated carefully. Having successfully climbed it, Sean traversed south to the Col de la Brenva.

Almost five hours had passed since he'd left the cable car terminal. The going had been tough, but no worse than expected. He looked over at Mont Blanc, resplendent in the sunshine, although, beyond it, noticed a bank of clouds massing like witches in a swirling, charcoal sky. The weather system was some way off, but, if it turned, summiting Mont Blanc might be in jeopardy.

'We'd better press on, my love.'

He looked around him but there was still no sign of Linz. He knew she would join him when the time was right.

It was still sunny, but the weather had begun to change for the worse. The temperature had dropped ten degrees in the last thousand feet, which, although severe, for Mont Blanc, was not unusual. It would get even colder up at higher altitude, but even more spectacular. The climb from Col de la Brenva to the top of Mont Blanc, Sean had been told by a mountain guide he'd spoken to, would be longer than it looked, but the scenery was the pay-off.

However, as the storm system from the north closed in, the mist began to descend, limiting his vision to under fifty meters.

Passing to the left of the Mur de la Cote rock step, Sean began to climb the seemingly never-ending, snow-covered slope above. The terrain was gentle and, in good weather, straightforward enough, but the cloud had thickened, bringing with it a new fall of snow that seemed to be getting heavier with each passing minute, and the wind was blowing so hard that he had to lean into it as he walked.

Above him, appeared the shadowy outline of four climbers, heading down, appearing out of the mist like ghosts. He thought he heard his name being called, though wasn't certain until the lead climber was almost directly in front of him.

'Sean! How are you going?'

'Pierre!' They hugged and clapped each other on the back. 'Where the hell did this weather come from?'

'It is the mountain, my friend. You know how she is. One minute we are in sunshine, the next, in this. The snow is getting heavier.'

'Did you summit?'

Pierre beamed a wide smile. His beard and moustache was frozen and bits of ice fell of it, making Sean smile.

'Yes. An hour ago. It was a good decision, it seems, to have spent last night at the Cosmiques Hut. The extra hour I had on you made the difference. I'm sorry you won't summit. At least, not today. Follow us down. You can try again, tomorrow.'

Sean shook his head.

'The storm will soon pass, Pierre. I need to get up there today.'

'Non! Sean, it is crazy to try. The fresh snow will increase the chance of avalanche.'

'It's not so bad, Pierre. I can make it.'

Pierre grabbed him by the jacket.

'Do not do this. You must come down. Think of your woman.'

'I am,' said Sean, pulling free of Pierre's hold. 'I truly am. Don't worry, I'll see you later.'

He walked on, head down, battling against the wind.

Pierre watched him leave then turned to follow his climbing companions who had just passed. He and Sean were experienced climbers and knew the risks, but risk was always mitigated, whenever possible. When the weather took over the mountain, the decision was not in doubt. You came down!

'Your friend is not following us?' Jean-Christophe, a climber with whom Pierre had partnered many times before, asked, as Pierre re-joined his own team.

'He is determined to summit.'

'But the weather, Pierre. It is madness to go on. We cannot allow him.'

'How can we stop him?' Pierre replied, shrugging his shoulders. 'It is his choice. We are climbers, Jean. We make our own decisions and live or die by them.'

Jean Christophe understood.

'Then if he cannot be stopped, Pierre, we have no choice. We must descend.'

Pierre looked up the slope towards Sean, now almost out of sight in the swirling snow and mist.

'*Mon deux!* And I have no choice either, Jean. Wait for me.'

'Five minutes, Pierre, and then we leave. With or without you.'

Pierre dropped his pack and rushed up the slope towards Sean.

'Sean!'

Above the howling wind, Sean didn't hear him, but without his pack, Pierre quickly caught him up.

'Pierre, what is it?' Sean turned to look at him, shrugging off the hand on his shoulder. 'Stop worrying about me. It's just a snow-storm. I'll be fine.'

Pierre hesitated before making his decision.

'I cannot let you go on without telling you.'

'Telling me what?'

'About Claudia,' cried Pierre, struggling to be heard above the howling wind.

Sean was confused.

'She's in Chamonix, Pierre. At the hotel.'

'Sean, listen to me. I must tell you something. Something Claudia told me, yesterday. She made me swear not to tell you.'

'Why would she do that?'

'Because it might interfere with your thoughts, Sean. Up here. She feared that the knowing of it might cause you to have an accident.'

'Is it that she's in love with me? Because I already know.'

'*Non*. It is not that.'

'Then what is it, man? Spit it out!'

'She is with child, Sean. Your child!'

Sean fell forward, grabbing onto Pierre for support, looking at him as if he could not fully comprehend what he was saying.

'Claudia's pregnant?'

'*Oui, mon ami*. You are to be a father.'

Sean knew instinctively it was true. There had been something different about her, not just in her lovemaking, but something in the gentle, almost serene manner of her being.

Pierre could see that what he had said had struck home. He hoped it would make Sean see sense.

'Come down, Sean. Come down for them both.'

'I will,' said Sean, shaking himself out of his stupor, 'but I must go on.' Seeing the confusion on Pierre's face, he tried to explain. 'I have Linz and the children's ashes in my pack. I will leave them on the summit. I don't expect you to understand, but I must finish this.'

He turned and walked on, leaving Pierre no choice but to let him go.

Not more than fifteen minutes later, the witches cloud hovered fully over Mont Blanc, obscuring the summit and pounding the upper slopes with heavy snow. The wind whipped at the hood on Sean's jacket like a poorly-set sail, lashing his face, and the snow was being driven almost horizontally, allowing him to see no more than a few paces ahead. His hands and feet had become so cold that he could barely feel them.

Some five hundred feet above him, a dark line appeared, spreading horizontally across the steep slope. The weight of the new snowfall had caused a fault in the older, compressed snow beneath it. The fault line spread, then ruptured, and a hundred-ton slab of densely packed snow broke free, rushing down the mountain towards Sean, coming onto him like a pack of snarling wolves.

Sean didn't hear or see the avalanche until it hit him, slamming into him at almost eighty miles per hour. It picked him up and carried him down the mountainside in a fraction of the time it had taken to climb it. He fought for breath as the snow wave took him, pulling him down into it, battering him with lumps of ice and snatching away his pack and ice-axe. He was slammed into a protruding rock, taking a savage blow to his head, then another, sending a spike of searing pain through his left leg. Somehow, through it all, he stayed conscious. After what seemed like an eternity, the rolling snow petered out to gently running sluff.

Sean gasped as he took in a lungful of icy air. Miraculously, he was lying on the surface, thrown under a rocky ledge. It would protect him, a little, from any further falls. More importantly, he was still alive! He began checking himself for injuries. He moved his right arm and screamed. It felt as if a shark had bitten into his torso. His ribcage had been pulverised, he could feel the bones grinding against each other and the pain, as he inhaled, was agonising. He could tell his left leg was badly broken just from looking at it, it was oddly twisted, below the knee, and his foot was pointing in the wrong direction. His realised his head was bleeding from a bloom of blood spreading into the snow next to his face.

'I don't think you'll be winning any dance competitions for a while, my boy.'

He laughed, but the lancing pain in his chest turned it to a cry.

Lying still, shallow breathing, he tried to figure out what to do next. He was battered and obviously broken, but the injuries might be survivable if he was rescued in time. The worst threat was that he was cold, and getting colder. The ice-wolves were gnawing at his hands and feet and the pain was becoming excruciating. He tried to ignore it, turning his thoughts to Claudia and the child she carried inside her. *His child.* As Alice and Toby had been his. He had loved them with all his heart. He realised he felt that same love for his unborn baby.

With his left hand, he reached up and took hold of his crucifix, somehow still in place around his neck, and prayed.

'Dear God. I've been angry at you for so long. I don't want to be angry anymore. I called on you, so many times, throughout my life, but you never came. I don't know why. I don't care any longer. I don't know why you let my father hurt me, or why you took my wife and children from me, only you can answer those questions. But hear me now. I ask not that you help me, only that, if I am to die, that you watch over Claudia and our child. I beg of you in the name of your own son, Jesus Christ, keep them safe.'

Sean stopped and listened to the mountain. It was quiet. Eerily so. The storm had passed as quickly as it had come. Far below him, he could see the faint lights of Chamonix, where Claudia was waiting for him. A sudden calm came over him and he felt his heartbeat slow. The light around him dimmed and the biting cold in his hands and feet stopped hurting. All his pain was gone. He knew, in that moment, that Death had come for him.

Below him, down the slope, he saw a dark shadow creeping up the mountain towards him. Reaching him, it hovered over his broken body, as silent as a shroud. The shadow stared down at him, into him, seeking his soul, and then it spoke. Its voice was not the wailing scream of the banshee, as Sean had expected it to be, but as the gentle rush of running water over stone.

'I heard you,' it whispered. 'I came.'

As the shadow began to smother him, drawing his life essence from him like a ghastly succubus, Sean pictured Claudia's face and realised why she had come to Chamonix. She had come so that his child might be with him. That he might know it, no matter it was not yet born. He pictured it lying in his arms, looking up at him, and he fought! He wanted to see his son or daughter being born. He wanted to love it and to be loved in return. And he wanted to live. For his baby *and* for Claudia.

He *could* love again.

'I've changed my mind,' he screamed into the dark face of Death. 'I don't want to die. I want to live. Do you hear me? I want to live. Please! Let me live!'

As he screamed, Sean felt his heart respond, pumping an injection of warm blood around his body, firing him with a draught of strengthening adrenaline.

'You lied!'

The shadow of Death hissed at him but pulled back, glaring at him, angered it had been cheated, and the snow wolves returned to feast, gnawing on his hands and feet with their icy fangs.

'That's it! Hurt me!' Sean screamed. He was in agony, the pain from his broken bones and the sub-zero cold almost unbearable, but if he could feel pain, it meant he was still alive. He could make it. He knew he could. Pierre was somewhere below him. He would have heard the avalanche and likely be on his way up to find him.

'Sean!'

He thought he heard a voice calling to him.

'Pierre! I'm here!' *I'm going to live! Thank you, God.* But he was cold. So very cold. The pain was beginning to ease again and his vision started to fade. Death, hovering only a short way away, moved back towards him. 'I'm here,' Sean called again, willing the shadow away once more. 'Over here.'

A figure moved up beside him. Standing over him, looking down.

'Hello, Dad.'

Sean looked up into the face of his son. He was confused as to how he was there, but didn't care. He smiled up at him, feeling the overwhelming love for him he had always felt.

'Toby, my little Caesar. I've missed you.'

'Me too, Dad. What have you done to yourself?'

'Just a stupid fall, son. Nothing to worry about.' Toby smiled at his father and knelt to hug him. As his son embraced him, Sean began to cry. 'I'm sorry, Toby. I'm so sorry.'

Toby kissed his father on the cheek.

'It's okay, Dad. Don't cry.'

Another voice took Sean's attention.

'Hello, Daddy. Have you fallen down?'

Alice was on the other side of him. She knelt and pressed her cheek against his, wrapping her arms around him, holding him as he had held her on the *Bealach na Ba*. Her skin was warm and soft. She smelt of chocolate cake and strawberry jam.

'I have, Princess.'

'You're awfully cold, Daddy.'

'I am, Princess, but your hugs are warming me up.'

Alice laughed and hugged him closer.

'You're just a big silly, aren't you, Daddy?'

'A big silly? Yes, Princess. I'm just a big silly.'

Alice kissed him and he felt his tears turn to ice on his cheeks.

'Don't cry, Daddy. Everything's going to be okay. Isn't it, Mummy?'

'Yes, my angel.' Linz put her arms around her children. 'Now why don't you two run along and play. I need to speak to Daddy.'

'Okay, Mummy,' they answered. 'Bye-bye, Daddy, we love you.'

They ran off across the slope, laughing happily.

Sean looked up at Linz. She knelt beside him and stroked his face, wiping away his frozen tears.

'Don't cry, hun.'

'Linz. I thought . . .'

'Ssshhh! It's going to be okay.'

'Are you angry with me, my love?'

Linz shook her head and smiled at him. Making him feel safe and loved. Like she'd always done.

'What for? You came. Just as you promised.'

'For wanting to stay with Claudia?'

'And the baby, hun. Don't forget the baby. You were always a wonderful father. You know that, don't you? Not like yours was. You were always so afraid you'd be like him, but you're not.' She turned her gaze towards Toby and Alice, playing in the snow. 'Look at them. They're happy. You made them happy. They love you so much.'

Sean broke down and wept as everything he had kept locked away finally escaped. Memories of his children came flooding back; Christmas days and birthdays, doggy walks on rainy days and summer picnics on Gullane Beach, winter snowmen built in Merrick's garden, with green faces and scarfs added when Toby and Alice had found a can of spray paint in his workshop, *Daddy Days* and spoon cakes. All the little moments of their lives. All the precious moments of his.

The bad things, too, came and went, pouring from the empty place like melted snow, disappearing like ballooning, winter breath. Meaningless, now, no longer to be feared or kept hidden away.

He was finally free and at peace.

Sean looked up at Linz. She was so beautiful. He loved her so much. And the children. But now he had to finally let them go.

'I'm sorry I failed you, my love. I've made so many mistakes.'

Linz knelt and kissed his forehead.

'Don't be. We all make mistakes, hun. We live our lives the best way we can. We don't get to choose how and where we end up. That's just the Universe playing its silly games.'

'I'll miss you, Linz. So much. And the kids.'

'We'll always be with you, hun. We'll always be together.'

'Will we, Linz? Promise?'

'I Promise.' She stood and held out a hand towards him. 'Would you like to dance with me? We never got to dance at . . .'

'Alice's birthday party.'

Linz smiled at him, remembering the day and forgiving him for all his failings.

'Dance with me now, hun. I love it when we dance.'

Linz stood up. She was surrounded by golden light and her antlers and wings were covered in sparkly, golden glitter. She was wearing her pale blue, summer dress and the sand at her feet looked soft and warm. Music began to play, although how, Sean could not understand. It didn't really matter.

'It's Shinedown, my love. Our song.'

Of course, it is'.

Linz began to sing.

'If I could find assurance to leave you behind, I know my better half would fade. But all my doubt is a staircase to you, up and out of this place.'

Sean took her outstretched hand and stood up, pulling her to him, holding her close as they began to dance. He sang with her, singing *their* song, as they had done so many times before.

'I'll follow you down to the eye of the storm, but don't worry I'll keep you warm. I'll follow you down, while we're passing through space, I don't care if we fall from grace, I'll follow you down.'

'I love you, Linz.'

'I've always known that, hun. Always!'

Sean knew she was telling him that she loved him and that he was safe, before she left.

'Linz? You know I won't be doing any more . . .'

'Ssshhh! Forget about the journal. It brought us to where we all needed to be. Let's just enjoy our dance. Look, the kids are watching.'

Sean waved to them. Alice and Toby waved back and then went running off into skiether.

Beyond them, no more than fifty metres on down the slope, Pierre and his climbing companions headed up the mountain. Pierre saw Sean waving at him and realised he was still alive. A wave of relief washed over him. He had heard the avalanche and feared the worst.

'Sean! Hold on! We are coming!'

Pierre reached him and knelt beside him. Sean smiled up at him and told him he loved him.

'I love you, too, you crazy fool. Now shut up and let me help you.'

He pulled out his satellite phone and punched in the number for mountain rescue. A helicopter from Chamonix would be with them in under twenty minutes.

Quickly, Pierre,' said Jean Christophe, trying to stem the bleeding on Sean's scalp, 'he is badly hurt.'

'Keep him alive, Jean. Just keep him alive until the helicopter reaches us. I will not allow him to die. He *will* see his child.'

Claudia was in the foyer of the hotel when Henri came over to speak to her. She'd already had dinner and was sitting alone, looking out over the Sea of Ice, wondering why climbers did what they did, finding no answer that made sense.

'*Madame* Montgomery, there is a call for you. Come. You may take it at reception.'

She stood and walked across the bright lit lobby.

'Hello, Claudia Montgomery.'

'Claudia. Can you hear me?'

The line was faint but she recognised the voice.

'Sean! Thank God! You kept your promise.'

71

The Pan Am stewardess cleared away Claudia's breakfast tray and smiled at the little girl sitting beside her, by the window. She had a pale-pink, teddy bear on her lap and was busy talking to it. The girl looked up and smiled back, melting the stewardess's heart.

'Your daughter?'

'Yes,' said Claudia, proudly. She reached over and stroked the child's face. 'Introduce yourself, sweetie, it's polite.'

'Hello. My name is Hannah Jameson. It's the same name as my momma's friend. She lives at a place called the Point. Right beside our lighthouse.'

'Your lighthouse?' The stewardess gave Hannah a wide smile and pointed at the name badge on her own jacket lapel. 'That sounds a wonderful place to live. My name is Debbie.'

'Hello, Debbie,' said Hannah, 'I'm very pleased to meet you.'

She held out her hand which Debbie took, looking equally as solemn as Hannah was. Hannah looked up at her mother, as if to say, *see, I am polite.* Claudia smiled at her and nodded, to Hannah's obvious pleasure.

'And what age are you, Hannah Jameson?' Debbie asked, enchanted by Hannah's angelic looks and impeccable manners.

Hannah looked up at her with a butter wouldn't melt expression.

'I'm five. My birthday was on the twenty-seventh of March. We had chocolate cake and Sylkie ate too much of it and got sick.' Seeing the look on Debbie's face, she added, for good measure. 'She's our dog.'

'Oh, that's terrible. Poor Sylkie. Is she alright now?'

'Yes. She likes to chase crabs.'

'I see.' Debbie looked back to Claudia who was shaking her head and trying not to laugh. 'She's a real honey, isn't she? Those beautiful blonde curls. And those eyes!'

'Cornflower blue,' said Claudia, 'like her father's.'

Debbie turned her attention back to Hannah.

'And what's your teddy bear called?'

Hannah lifted the little bear up in front of her, holding it across her mother's seat. Debbie reached out and shook its paw, introducing herself to is as she did. Hannah was more than pleased that she knew it was a real bear and not just a toy.

'Pookie. His name's Pookie Bear. My Daddy gave him to me.'

'Did he now?'

'Yes. We're going to meet him, today, in Embra.'

'Edinburgh, sweetie,' said Claudia, gently correcting her. She nodded to Debbie. "He's already there, actually, at his office in the city centre.'

'It's my office,' said Hannah, indignantly. 'Daddy told me it was.'

'Of course, it is, sweetie.' Claudia rolled her eyes and looked back at the stewardess. 'She's right, actually.'

'Lucky her. Bye-bye, Hannah, it was lovely to meet you. And Pookie.'

Debbie moved onto the next row of passengers.

'Now,' said Claudia, 'let's get your seatbelt on again, young lady, then we can look out of the window and see if we can find Edinburgh Castle. Your father's going to take us to visit it while we're on our holiday in Scotland.'

It was a little after midday when the QuantumCloud Mercedes that had collected them from the airport pulled up at Cramond Kirk gates.

'Where's Daddy?' Hannah asked, looking around for him.

'He's just texted, sweetie. He's on his way.'

A grey-haired, kindly-faced man walked up to Claudia, his hand outstretched. He was wearing a black cassock with a white clerical collar, which gave his identity away.

'Mrs Montgomery. I recognise your face from the photograph you sent with the email.'

'Father Mackenzie?'

Claudia took his hand and shook it. It was warm, despite the chilly spring day.

'My friends call me Mac. I'd be honoured if you would.'

'I'm so pleased to finally meet you, Mac. I've heard a lot about you. And you must call me Claudia.'

'From Sean, no doubt? Don't believe everything he's told you, Claudia.' Mac smiled and turned his attention to the Hannah, standing by Claudia's side looking up at him, clearly wondering who he was. She didn't look scared, which reminded him of another little girl he'd known who'd had the same green eyes and curly, blonde hair. 'And you must be Hannah?'

'My name is Hannah Jameson,' said Hannah, holding out her hand for Mac to shake. 'I'm five years old. I'm very pleased to meet you.'

'As I am, Hannah. And *you* must call me, Mac. If you like.'

Hannah thought about it, then nodded, making Mac smile. Pookie was in her left hand, hanging by her side. She lifted him up to allow him to see him properly.

'And this is Pookie Bear.'

'Hello, Pookie. You may also call me, Mac.' Hannah gave Mac her bestest smile, melting the second heart that morning. 'You know, Hannah, you remind me of a little girl I used to know. She looked a bit like you. She lives here, now, in our garden, right at the back of the church.'

Hannah screwed up her face, processing what he'd said.

'What a funny place to live.'

'It is, I suppose,' said Mac, but it's pretty. Would you like to see?'

'Yes please.'

Hannah skipped past him, under the whalebone archway and up the path towards Crammond Kirk. The cherry trees were in full blossom and smiled down at her as she passed beneath them.

Mac turned back to Claudia.

'Would you like to visit them, now, or wait for . . .'

'We'll go on through, Mac, if that's okay? It's been a long flight, although, thankfully, an overnight, so we both slept. Hannah's not quite sure what's going on, but she's excited. She knows she's here to meet some of her family. I don't want to keep her waiting around any longer.'

'Of course. I completely understand,' said Mac, and offered Claudia his arm.

They followed the pathway around the left of the church building, passing lines of lichen-covered gravestones spread out around the graveyard like wandering Celtic druids.

'They look positively ancient,' said Claudia, stopping at one that said, *Thomasina Moore, 1917-1994, much loved wife of Robert.*

Mac stopped beside the ancient stele.

'Some date back to the fifteenth century. Older, even, than America. The America discovered by Christopher Columbus, that is.'

Hannah, ahead of them, skipped past the druids, heading towards the wall at the back of the church, as if she knew where she was going. She stopped at the gate at its centre, painted black and topped with *Fleur de Lis* points, and peered in through the bars at a paved area, where four iron benches waited to be called into use. At each corner of the courtyard was a wooden planter filled with exploding blooms of purple lavender. Mac reached her and opened the gate, allowing Hannah and Claudia to step through.

'To your left,' said Mac, 'in the corner. Just by the . . .'

'By the apple tree,' said Claudia, letting go of his arm. 'Sean told me where to find them.'

'Look, sweetie.' Claudia pointed to the bronze plaque fixed to the wall. 'Can you read their names.'

Before Hannah could answer, they heard voices behind them and turned to see two figures heading towards the Remembrance Garden gate. Mac nodded a greeting to the nun.

'Sister Abagail.'

'Father.'

'Daddy!' Hannah cried. 'Where have you been?'

She launched herself into his arms as he stepped into the garden.

'Hello, my little angel. Sorry I'm late.'

'Hello, my darling,' said Claudia, 'I'm glad you're here in time to see Hannah meet them.'

'We'll give the three of you some time alone,' said Mac, 'but I'll see you before you leave.'

He and Sister Abagail walked across the square, taking the side door into the Kirk building.

'Who are they, Momma?' Hannah asked, as they stood looking at the plaque, 'and why have they got my name?'

'Remember I told you, sweetie, they're part of our family.'

Hannah ran her fingers over the names etched into the bronze plaque, then switched her attention to a robin that had just landed in the apple tree beside her. It seemed to be looking down at her. She moved under the drooping branches and stared at up it, leaving her mother and father standing alone.

Claudia looked down at the four names etched into the plaque.

'He did love you, Claudia.'

'I know he did, Pierre. But, in the end, I think he loved them more.'

'I could not save him, *ma chérie*. I tried. He was still alive when I found him, but his injuries, they were . . .'

Pierre stopped speaking, the memory of the day a scar still not healed. Claudia took hold of his hand and gave it a reassuring squeeze.

'Don't be sad, my darling. You did all you could. Everyone knows that. Sean is where he wanted to be. With his family. And you are with yours.'

'You were the last thing on his mind, Claudia. You and Hannah.'

Claudia smiled, ruefully, her heart aching a little at the memory of the awful day in Chamonix, when Pierre had called her from the hospital not long after the accident.

'I'm glad you told him I was pregnant, my darling. At least he knew he was to be a father again. Hannah has two fathers. She carries his name, while you carry her. She will understand, in time, that she has been loved by both.'

Pierre nodded, although he still carried the sadness at having not saved his friend, he realised he had been given a gift in being able to raise Sean's child as his own.

'I wish he could have seen her. He wanted so much to meet his child. It was the last thing he told me on the mountain.'

'He can, Pierre. I know he can.'

They spent some time beside the apple tree, Claudia telling Hannah all about her other family. After she had asked all the questions she wanted to ask, and seemed to understand what she was being told, they turned and walked out of the Remembrance Garden, passing the silent gravestones.

At the corner of the church, Claudia stopped and looked back. A gust of wind ruffled the apple tree, shaking the branches and sending a cloud of white blossoms into the air. They fell like flakes of snow, reminding her of a sunny June day, five years before. A day of sunshine and snowflowers, and of a lone sunflower standing in a field of a million others, close to a bridge where an ancient knight had once fought three hundred jousts for the woman he loved. She smiled at the memory. Pierre, seeing the look on her face, walked on ahead of her, allowing her a final, private moment.

Sean was watching her from beneath the apple tree. He looked just as he'd done when she'd last seen him, in Chamonix, climbing into the taxi to head to the cable car and up to Mont Blanc. He smiled at her and she felt his spirit touch hers. He turned and walked away, disappearing in only a few paces.

'Goodbye Sean Jameson. Thank you for Hannah. You gave me what I needed. I hope you are happy. I finally am. You were right, you know, that day out on the Camino. I didn't understand it. Not then. But I do now. Not all flowers face the sun.'

Printed in Great Britain
by Amazon

60953523R00388